JON ATHAN

DO NOT DISTURB

THE FIRST TRILOGY

For more information on this book or the author, please visit http://www.jon-athan.com/. General inquiries are welcome.
Facebook: https://www.facebook.com/AuthorJonAthan
Twitter: @Jonny_Athan
Email: info@jon-athan.com
Instagram: @AuthorJonnyAthan

Book cover by MiblArt: https://miblart.com/
Proofreading provided by Karen Bennett: kbennett4653@gmail.com

ISBN: 979-8-9902769-0-1
First Edition

ALSO BY JON ATHAN

Blender Babies (2023)

Shared by Two (2023)

The President's Son (2022)

When She Weeps (2022)

Do Not Disturb 2: The Platinum Palace (2022)

The Girl in the Attic (2021)

Am I Beautiful? (2021)

Do Not Disturb (2020)

The Groomer (2020)

Into the Wolves' Den (2019)

Lovesick (2019)

The Good, the Bad, and the Sadistic (2018)

Grandfather's House (2018)

The Law of Retaliation (2017)

The Abuse of Ashley Collins (2017)

A Family of Violence (2016)

WARNING

This omnibus contains scenes of intense violence and some disturbing themes. Some parts of this book may be considered violent, cruel, disturbing, or unusual. This book is not intended for those easily offended or appalled. Please enjoy at your own discretion.

CONTENTS

DO NOT DISTURB

DO NOT DISTURB 2

DO NOT DISTURB 3

JON ATHAN

DO NOT DISTURB

1

THE ARRIVAL

RAIN PATTERED AGAINST THE WINDOWS. THE DOOR rattled with each gust of wind. A flash of lightning beamed into the reception area, illuminating the racks of outdated newspapers and the stacks of old magazines around the tattered sofas. Then the thunder roared through the desolate desert surrounding the motel, echoing for miles.

Malik Simmons leaned over the reception desk, his hand on his shiny bald head. His iPad was hooked up to a tablet stand at the other end of the table. An episode of *American Horror Story: Hotel* played on the screen. A string of drool descended from his mouth. His eyelids twitched while his eyes rolled back. His hand slid across his smooth scalp, then his face hit the desk.

"Huh? Wha–What?" he mumbled as he awoke. He stepped back and glanced around. The room was empty. He muttered, "Shit, still here. Can't it be morning already?"

He looked over at the key rack behind him. Out of fifty, two keys—one for Room 101 and the other for Room 102—were missing. There were three guests at the motel: a young couple and a businessman. They were expected to check out in the morning. They weren't bothersome guests, they only needed shelter and a bed for the night, so they didn't call Malik for anything.

The clock struck three o'clock in the morning.

The witching hour.

Malik took a sip of his energy drink, then he leaned over the table and turned his attention to the iPad. He restarted the episode because he couldn't remember watching any of it. Another flash of lightning lit up the room, then the thunder screamed over the motel. The rain sounded louder—tap-tap, tap-tap, *tap-tap*.

Malik furrowed his brow. The pattern and the noise were inconsistent. It didn't sound like rain. Then there was another flash of lightning. The light cast the silhouette of a person and spherical object into the room.

The clerk glanced over at the door, then he gasped and staggered away from the desk. The thunder rumbled in the distance. A clown stood in front of the window to the left of the door. He wore a loose white jumpsuit with red pom-pom buttons down the middle and a matching ruff collar around his neck. His face and hands were painted white. His eyes were as dark as night and his fingernails as long as a bear's.

"Oh my God," Malik whispered.

He noticed the clown's nose was missing. It had been surgically removed. The remaining nub was painted red like his lips. The color was so vibrant, so familiar, that it looked like he was bleeding from his mouth. Rain dripped from the dark blue hair sticking out from the sides of his head. Injected with saline, his head—from his forehead to the back of his scalp— appeared inflated.

The clown held a red balloon in his hand, spinning and dancing with the wind. With his other hand, he tapped the window with his fingernails—tap-tap, tap-tap, *tap-tap*.

Malik felt like he was staring at a dangerous animal, a creature from his worst childhood night-mares. He pinched his forearm, hoping he fell asleep again and slipped into a dream, but he was already awake. He weaved and bobbed his head, trying to get a better look at his creepy visitor, but he couldn't identify him. He could see the sclerae of the clown's eyes were dyed black.

"Jayden, is that... is that you?" he asked. "Are you... What the fuck are you doing, bro?"

He stood on his tiptoes and looked over the clown. He saw a diner at the other end of the parking lot— *Gold Diner 80*. A man named Jayden Jenkins worked there as a cook. But the lights were off at the restaurant and the parking spaces in front of the diner were empty. The clock on Malik's iPad read: *3:17 AM*. Every day, the diner closed at two in the morning and opened four hours later.

"Not Jayden," Malik whispered, horrified.

He paused the video on his iPad, then he side-stepped past the reception desk. The clown didn't move, but the wind blew the balloon against the window. It *squeaked* and *howled*. Malik slunk forward, barely lifting his feet with each step. His knees hit the edge of the coffee table in front of a sofa. The clown remained motionless and emotionless. They gazed at each other, but Malik could barely see the shape of the clown's eyes.

Malik said, "You have to... You're, um... What do you want?" The clown stayed still. Malik guessed he couldn't hear him through the window. He leaned forward and shouted, "What do you want?!"

Once again, there was no response. The rain pattered and the balloon squeaked. An old pickup truck zoomed down the road, gone in seconds.

Malik yelled, "You have to leave! I'm going to–"

The clown smashed his head against the window, causing it to rattle while the balloon bounced on the glass like a ball. Malik gasped and hopped back. His lips trembled as he mumbled incoherently. Then the clown grinned at the clerk, showing him his sharp, filed teeth. He snickered, then he chuckled, and then he guffawed. He sounded like he was hiccupping.

Malik stumbled back behind the reception desk. He grabbed the landline phone beside the key rack. He held it up to his ear and looked back at the window.

The clown was gone.

Malik thought about calling the cops. He went through the conversation in his head, and it sounded absurd each time. *'I need the cops! There's a killer clown outside! Yes, a killer clown! Like a monster with black eyes, fangs, and claws! Really, it's true!'* He couldn't believe it himself, so he didn't expect anyone else to believe him.

He slunk around the desk, eyes stuck on the window. He approached the sofas and scanned the parking lot in front of the office. It was empty, flooded but *empty*. He looked out the window to his left. He saw the two-story motel—twenty-five rooms on each floor—and the other half of the parking lot. He had hoped one of the guests was playing a prank on him, but the lights were off and the rooms were calm.

He muttered, "Shit, what if..." He chuckled and ran his palm across his sweaty scalp. He said, "What if I *was* dreaming? No, what if I *am* dreaming right now? Or what if I'm hallucinating or something? Oh man, am I going crazy? I mean, I'm... I'm fucking talking to myself right now, aren't I? I'm just... Oh shit, maybe–"

He winced upon hearing a crashing sound behind him. He glanced over his shoulder. The door behind the desk—which led to the back office—was cracked open. The noise came from that room. He closed his eyes, took a deep breath, and turned towards the window in front of him. Heart pounding away at his sternum, he was expecting the clown to be standing in front of the window again.

A jump scare.

He had watched one too many horror movies.

He opened his eyes and let out a sigh of relief. There was no one in front of him. He headed back to the reception desk. He pushed the door open and peeked into the back office. There was a desk in one corner, a refrigerator in another, and a lunch table in the other. To the right, a tube television sat on an old, rickety entertainment center. There was a sofa to the left and behind that sofa there were three tall lockers.

Malik's eyes wandered to the long, rectangular window above the lockers. One of the panes was broken, rain blowing into the office through the gap. Shards of glass sprinkled on the lockers and floor. A steel juggling pin rolled on the floor between the sofa and the television. There was no one in sight.

"Anyone in here?" Malik asked as he stepped into the room. He could now hear the storm clearly thanks to the broken window. He grunted to clear his throat, then he said, "Well, we have an alarm system, you know? The cops are on their way already. And... And I'm armed. So, come out with your hands up."

'Come out with your hands up?' What am I? A kid? Why did I say that?—he thought as he gnawed on his bottom lip. He was bluffing, too. The motel didn't have an alarm system, the cops weren't on their way, and he

wasn't armed. He crept towards the lockers. He wrapped his arm over his forehead to block the rain, then he opened the lockers one by one.

Nothing.

Nothing.

And... *nothing.*

"Fucking kids," Malik muttered.

He went back to the reception desk, but he stopped in the doorway—frozen with fear. The clown stood in front of the desk. Rain dripped from his hair, face, and costume while shimmering on his balloon. Malik choked down the lump in his throat. He stepped forward and approached the desk, trying to act brave. His trembling was obvious, though.

He asked, "What the hell did you do to the window? You're going to have to pay for that, asshole, 'cause it's not coming out of my paycheck." The clown made an 'O' with his lips—a mocking *'oops.'* Malik huffed, then he said, "Real funny. Hilarious, huh? You won't be laughing when I call the police, though."

In a soft, eerie voice, the clown said, "I thought... the police... were already... 'on their way?' Hmm?"

The clown snickered. Malik sneered in annoyance.

He said, "So you *can* talk. Great, why don't you tell me what you want? What the hell is this? Some sort of prank? Are we on... Are we on TV? Who are you, man?"

The clerk reached for the clown's face, as if he were expecting to pull a mask off his head. He wanted to touch the remaining piece of his nose—the little nub. It didn't look like makeup. The clown leaned back and raised his index finger at Malik. He moved his finger from side to side—*ah, ah, ah!*

He said, "*Nooo...* touching."

Awe in his eyes, Malik asked, "Who the hell are you?"

"You don't know? Why, my name is... Pumpkin. *Pumpkin the Clown.*"

"Pumpkin? Like a... Like a freakin' pumpkin? Like on Halloween or–or Thanksgiving? You have to be kidding me."

Malik laughed nervously while shaking his head in disbelief. Pumpkin giggled again—*hiccup, hiccup, hiccup.* Then, in the blink of an eye, he stopped laughing. He glared at Malik with his pitch-black eyes. His lip curled, revealing some of his sharp teeth. Malik could see his teeth were real. Without taking his eyes off the clown, he reached for the landline.

"Behind you," Pumpkin hissed in a low, gravelly tone.

"Wha–What?"

"*Behind you.*"

Malik's legs shook uncontrollably, like a child holding his pee. His breathing intensified into desperate, terrified panting. He slowly turned his head. From the corner of his eye, he caught a glimpse of the person standing in the doorway to the back office. Malik fell against the reception desk, mouth and eyes wide open.

Gaggles the Clown stood in the doorway. At six-two, he stood two inches taller than Pumpkin. He wore a baggy white jumpsuit with stripes. His pom-pom buttons and ruff collar were dark green. His red hair was spiked up—a head of fire. His eyebrows were shaved off, replaced with curved nails. Vertical streaks of dark green were painted over his eyes from his cheekbones to his brow. With matching makeup, a wide grin was painted over his mouth.

But he wasn't smiling. He scowled at the clerk, his face knotted in disgust and anger. Like Pumpkin, his eyes were tattooed black, his teeth were filed down to fangs, and he traded his fingernails for claws.

Malik stammered, "Wha–Wha–What the–"

From the other side of the desk, Pumpkin wrapped the balloon's string around Malik's neck. It was a guitar string—*a garrote.* He giggled as he tightened it around Malik's neck and pulled him back. The small of Malik's back hit the edge of the desk. The iPad fell off the table, hitting the floor with a *clunk.* Malik's voice was stifled. He croaked and groaned as he scratched at his neck.

"He... He... Help," he whined.

His feet rose from the floor as Pumpkin tugged on the garrote. His face contorted in pain. He gritted his teeth until the enamel crackled and popped. It sounded like glass breaking in his mouth. Blood invaded the whites of his eyes while hot tears flowed down his rosy cheeks. More blood oozed out of his gums, too. It made him gag, as if it were poison.

The color faded from his cheeks and lips—pale, *paler*. Then blues and purples blossomed across his face. His eyelids narrowed to a squint and his head bobbed as he struggled to draw a satisfying breath.

In a deep voice, Gaggles said, "He's out."

"Grab his waist," Pumpkin said in his smooth, regular voice. "Get him back into the office. I don't want to make a mess out here."

"I hear ya."

"I mean it. We don't have time to clean."

"Yeah, yeah, sure."

Gaggles was a man of few words. He grabbed Malik's waist while Pumpkin unwrapped the garrote from around his neck. Limp but alive, Malik fell against Gaggles, face buried in his ruff collar. Gaggles dragged him into the back office. Pumpkin moseyed over to the window. He examined the parking lot, then the road to the right, searching for any lost souls. The place was deserted. He closed the blinds, then he locked the door.

Malik's eyes fluttered open. He was blinded by a bright light. He squeezed his eyes shut and coughed—a wet, phlegmy cough. He tried to reach for his chest, but he couldn't move his arms. He tried to kick, but he couldn't move his legs, either. His back ached and his head throbbed. He felt nauseous and dizzy. The light brightened, then separated into two and then three beams.

"Oh f–fuck," he muttered, his voice raspy from the strangulation.

After a few blinks, his vision focused and his mind cleared. He realized he was lying on the floor in the back office. Between the sofa and television, he was *taped* to the floor at the ankles and wrists. Each limb appeared to be taped thirty times over, forming small mounds of duct tape. He panted upon spotting the clowns. They sat on the sofa, staring down at Malik.

Pumpkin and Gaggles raised their right hands and waved at him, moving at the same pace. It was rehearsed. *They've done this before,* Malik thought. And that thought terrified him.

Breathing rapidly, Malik stuttered, "Pl–Please don–don't hurt me a–anymore. I–I'm begging you. I don't... Oh my God, I–I don't want to die!"

Pumpkin stood from his seat, causing Malik to panic. The clerk babbled incoherently, begging for his life.

Pumpkin crouched near Malik's shaking feet. In his clownish voice, he said, "Don't cry. If you cry... I'll cry."

"Oh fuck! *Fuck!*"

"Fuck! *Fuck!*" Pumpkin repeated mockingly before laughing.

"Oh man, please. The–There's money. There's a–a

lot of money, man! In the register, in the safe! We–We have credit cards, too! Ta–Take it all! Take everything!"

"Everything?"

"Everything! Anything!"

"Hmm... How about... your life?"

Malik stopped whining. He frowned at the clown and shook his head. He couldn't see it, but the garrote left a thin, red indentation around his neck. It was a symbol of survival for Malik, and a symbol of sadistic determination for Pumpkin. Murder was easy with the right tools—the squeeze of a gun's trigger, the thrust of a knife. But it took a *real* killer to strangle someone.

Malik knew the clown was serious. He knew he was going to die that night.

Pumpkin smiled and said, "Let's juggle."

He stood up and beckoned to Gaggles. His partner tossed three steel juggling pins at him. He caught them all. Then he pointed and winked at Gaggles. Gaggles took a handheld cassette player out of his pocket. He pressed the 'play' button. *Thunder and Blazes: Entry March of the Gladiators* played through the small speaker, loud and staticky.

Trying to replicate the music, Pumpkin sang: ♪ *Da da dadada da da dada da da.*

He hopped from side to side while juggling the pins. The pins *whooshed* through the air. One of the pins nearly hit the ceiling. They were heavy, at least ten pounds each. Eyes brimming with tears, Malik watched the clown with his mouth ajar. He was taped to the floor at his workplace, serenaded by a familiar tune, and surrounded by a juggling clown and a quiet clown.

A nightmare.

A night of tedious normality had turned into a surreal nightmare with Pumpkin's arrival.

Malik cried, "Why?"

Pumpkin kept singing: ♪*Da da dadada da da dada da da dadada da da.*

"Why? Oh God, why? Why are you doing–"

"*Oops.*"

Pumpkin tossed a pin forward. Malik watched it as it glided across the ceiling. Then his eyes bulged as it plummeted towards him.

"No! Pl–"

The pin struck Malik's face, then it landed on the floor with a *clank*. Malik's nose was broken and sliced. A wide gash stretched across the bridge of his nose. A slit of white cartilage was visible through the blood. His septum was crooked, jagged like the line on a heartbeat monitor. More blood bubbled out of his nostrils as he fought to exhale through his nose.

Three of his top incisor teeth were knocked out of their gums. He inadvertently swallowed them. Four of his other teeth were cracked. His upper lip was sliced open. His cheekbones broke, too. Upon impact, the back of his head hit the floor, leaving him dazed and lethargic. Pain rocketed back and forth—from his face to the back of his head, then back to his face and so on.

He felt like a woodpecker was trapped in his skull, pecking away at everything. The throbbing pain was debilitating, hitting him from every angle.

He let out a slow, ghoulish groan, like a zombie in a horror movie. But he stayed conscious. His mind wasn't ready to shut off the lights.

Pumpkin shouted, "Woah! Heads-up!"

He tossed another pin at him. It hit Malik's stomach. Malik raised his head from the floor and gasped. The air was knocked out of him. He felt a knot in his abdomen—inexplicable pressure. He felt like something was about to burst inside of him. *His intestines? His appendix? His liver? His stomach?* Blood frothed on his swollen, busted lips. Goops of the bubbly blood dripped across his cheeks and slid towards his ears.

"Please," he moaned.

"Whoops!"

The third pin hit Malik's genitals. A muffled *pop* came out of his pants before the pin hit the floor between his legs with another *clank*. Malik ground his teeth until the cracked enamel crumbled and trickled into his throat. He held his breath. It was his body's natural reaction to the pain. Then the back of his head hit the floor as he fell unconscious.

The song ended.

The crotch of Malik's pants turned black as he bled. His scrotum was cut open by the pin. One of his testicles was ruptured, the other was bruised. The glans of his penis was as red as a cherry. A stream of urine jetted out of his dick while he was unconscious, joining the blood in a warm pool of bodily fluids. His feet, hands, and head shook.

Pumpkin said, "Sleeping already... You're no fun."

Malik awoke four minutes later. He clenched his eyes shut and whimpered. A powerful headache attacked his brain. He lifted his head from the floor and looked down at himself. He felt a cold tingly sensation from his abdomen to his crotch. *Paralyzed*—it was the first possibility to hit his mind. Yet, he still felt burning, aching pain deep in his abdomen and crotch.

"N–No," he said weakly. "Please, no..."

Pumpkin stood over him with a fire axe in his hands. He smiled and said, "I like your hands. Can I have one?"

"Oh my God..."

"You said I could have *everything* and *anything*, didn't you?"

"God, help me..."

Pumpkin stopped smiling. In his regular voice, he said, "God can't help you. Satan can't help you, either. You're in our world now."

"No, God, no..."

Pumpkin raised the axe overhead. He waited for a moment, purposely trying to build the tension. He savored Malik's fear—*his desperation.* He swung the axe down at Malik's right hand. Malik clenched his fists, closed his eyes, and screamed at the top of his lungs.

His hand was severed just below his thumb's metacar-pophalangeal joint. After cutting through his hand, the blade bounced off the floor.

Ting!

Waves of dark blood flowed out of his hand. It was a sloppy, diagonal cut, so the remaining bases of his metacarpal bones stuck out of the flesh. Burning pain shot from his hand to his heart.

Ahh!—he screamed and he screamed. He yelled, "Oh my God! Help me! Oh God, no! *Oh God!*"

Pumpkin smiled devilishly and said, "That's more like it." He beckoned to Gaggles and said, "I'm ready to finish it. Give me a hand here."

Gaggles approached. He chuckled as he threw Malik's severed hand at Pumpkin. He gave him a hand —*literally.*

Pumpkin said, "Remember, just like we rehearsed. Don't let go. Pull *apart.* Okay?"

Gaggles responded, "I know what to do."

"Good."

Gaggles removed the tape from Malik's ankles. He grabbed his legs at the calves and pushed them up. Facing his partner, Pumpkin stood with one foot at each side of Malik's head. Blinded by his pain, Malik didn't notice the setup or Pumpkin's ridiculously large clown shoes. He swung his head in every direction and shrieked.

Pumpkin raised the axe overhead, then he swung it down at Malik's crotch. It sounded like he was chopping wood—*thud!* Then a wet *crunch* followed as he wiggled the blade inside of him. Under his pants and boxer briefs, Malik's penis was severed and his scrotum was cut in half vertically. The tubular insides of his ruptured testicle came out of his pants, like ground beef out of a meat grinder.

Malik stopped screaming. A thick vein stuck out of his head, slithering from his brow to his scalp.

Pumpkin chopped at his crotch again and again. He cut through his pelvis, breaking his bones and slicing through his organs—his rectum, his prostate, his bladder. Meanwhile, Gaggles pushed Malik's shaky legs apart. From above, he could see everything inside of the massive gash between Malik's legs. Through the blood, he saw yellow and white fluids as well as shades of blue and purple.

But he wasn't fazed by the gore. He caught a whiff of the metallic scent of Malik's blood. It made his taste buds prickle. He licked his teeth, then he smacked his lips.

Eyes wide with fear, Malik watched as his butchered intestines poured out of the wound and unfurled across his chest. His eyes rolled back in his head and his body shook violently. Blood splattered on the clowns, the furniture, the walls, and even the ceiling. He went into shock due to the traumatic loss of blood. He died shortly afterward.

The clowns bisected him, cutting him in half vertically from his crotch to the top of his head. His bisected organs were sprawled across the floor between him—his penis, his intestines, his pancreas, his liver, his heart, his brain. His eyes were still open to slits.

"I didn't get to hurt him," Gaggles complained.

Out of breath from all the chopping, Pumpkin said, "You get... first dibs... on the next one."

"Tonight?"

Pumpkin nodded and said, "Tonight."

2

ROAD TRIP

"Good evening, Nevada. I'm your host, Morgan Bailey, with Channel 5 News," a twentysomething blonde anchorwoman said with a smile. Her joyful expression turned grim and solemn in a second. She said, "First tonight, creepy clown sightings have been reported across the country—including dozens in our very own 'Battle Born State.' But is Nevada ready for a battle with these creepy clowns? Although many of these sightings appear to be part of an elaborate, coordinated prank, police tell us several schools across the state have been threatened through social media. And these threats appear to be–"

The video stopped to buffer.

Lacey Holloway sighed in disappointment as she watched the throbber on her cell phone—spinning, spinning, and spinning some more. The video didn't load.

She sat in the passenger seat with her bare feet hanging out the window, wind blowing against her sweaty, pedicured toes. Her curly brown hair undulated with the wind, flowing into the back seat of the sedan. Sunglasses shielded her chestnut brown eyes. She was a short, curvy woman. She wore a white tank top under a flannel shirt with the sleeves rolled up and light blue jeans.

She said, "Great. We've entered the dead zone."

"Dead zone?" Colton Curtis huffed, hands on the steering wheel and eyes on the road. "What is a 'dead zone,' Lacey? You're talking about, like... that old Stephen King book?"

"Stephen King? No, I'm talking about a *dead zone*."

"I heard you the first time. I just don't know what the hell you're talking about."

Lacey looked at the endless desert to her right—sand, cacti, tumbleweeds, and mountains. She looked past her boyfriend in the driver's seat. Then she glanced at the rearview mirror. She could see the heat haze rising from the sweltering pavement. There were no other drivers on the road. She didn't expect to find any hitchhikers out there, either—not alive, at least.

She explained, "A dead zone is a place where things go to die. First, the signal." She wagged her cell phone at Curtis. She said, "Then, the car. And, *finally,* the people."

"Oh really? And what about the animals?"

"They stick around to *eat* the dead people."

Curtis smiled and said, "*Oh*, okay, I get you. You're saying we're going to die out here, and then we're going to get eaten by vultures and coyotes, right?"

Lacey pursed her lips, raised her hands, and shrugged. She said, "I didn't say anything about vultures or coyotes..."

"You're crazy."

"*O*-kay, sure, whatever. But just remember what I said. Trust me, you won't be calling me crazy once this car stops working."

"I think I'm going to be calling you crazy for the rest of my life."

They shared a laugh. Lacey gently slapped her boyfriend's arm while Colton jabbed his index finger at her ribs to keep her at bay. Lacey gazed at Colton, eyes twinkling with love. *'For the rest of my life'*—his words kept playing in her head. They weren't married or engaged, but those words were important to her. They showed fearless commitment.

At twenty-nine years old, Colton was two years older than Lacey. He was a strong, healthy young man, standing an even six feet tall with firm muscles. Curly locks of sweaty hair stuck out from under his blue cap. Three days of stubble gave him a hardened look. He wore a blue short-sleeved button-up shirt with a white t-shirt underneath, jeans, and boots.

Colton said, "Speaking of crazy, don't get *too* crazy at the party. I don't wanna see pictures and videos of you shit-faced next week."

"*Hey,*" Lacey said, a smile of surprise on her face. "You're going to a party, too. And last time you partied, *you* ended up on Instagram passed out with dicks on your face."

"Well, let's be fair here. You can't just say something like that. They were *drawn* dicks on my face, not *actual* dicks."

"There's barely a difference," Lacey said, suppressing her laughter.

"There's a big difference, babe. Dicks on my face is... it's porn. *Drawn* dicks on my face... now that's art."

"Porn, art... what's the difference?" Lacey shrugged and snickered.

They shared another laugh.

Colton said, "But seriously, I know how crazy bachelorette parties can get."

"And I know how crazy bachelor parties can get."

"Yeah, yeah, you're right. Let's just promise we *won't* get shit-faced tomorrow night. Two drinks, maybe three, and that's it. And *no* strip clubs."

Lacey laughed. "What? Shouldn't *I* be telling *you* that?"

"Lacey, come on. I know all about the Dancing Bear, okay?"

"Oh my God, you're such a–"

Lacey gasped and Colton tightened his grip on the steering wheel as a *bang* reverberated through the interior of the car. Then they heard a loud hiss and a repetitive flopping sound. The hissing softened after twenty seconds, but the flopping continued. The car trembled and jerked to the side. They felt the vibrations.

"Shit," Colton muttered.

Lacey's mouth hung open in awe. Yet, she still smiled at Colton. Her face said something along the lines of: *I told you so.* The car rolled to a stop on the side of the road.

As he climbed out of the vehicle, Colton repeated, "*Shit.*"

Lacey sat there and watched as her boyfriend checked each tire. Part of her was scared, she didn't want to end up stranded in the desert, but the other part of her was proud. *I was totally right,* she thought. Colton crouched in front of the front right tire. Lacey opened the door and took one step out. She leaned forward and looked down at Colton from above the windowsill.

She asked, "What happened?"

Colton responded, "I'm not sure. It looks like... like..."

He leaned closer to the tire. A sharp bone protruded from the rubber. He couldn't identify it, but it looked like it had been whittled down to a sharp point.

With a furrowed brow, he said, "It's a... bone."

"A bone? What kind of bone?"

"I don't know, but this tire's done for."

"We have a spare in the trunk, right?"

Colton stood up and sighed. He shook his head.

With a hint of anger in her voice, Lacey asked, "*What?*"

"I lent it to David."

"Why?" Lacey's anger turned into annoyance.

"Because his girlfriend had a flat and he needed a spare. Why do you care anyway? It's my car, not yours."

"It's your car, but now I'm stuck out here with you."

Colton said, "We're not stuck."

He returned to the driver's seat and buckled his belt. He beckoned to Lacey—*close the door and fasten your seat belt.* Lacey was skeptical. As far as she knew, they couldn't go anywhere with a flat tire. But she trusted him. She closed the door and buckled her belt.

She puckered her lips, then she asked, "So, what's the plan, boss?"

"We drive. We drive very, very slowly."

"Can we... Can we do that?"

"It's going to be a little bumpy, but it shouldn't be a problem. If we see someone coming from either direction, we'll try to wave them down. If they don't stop, we'll get on the side of the road and let them pass us. I think we're close to a town anyway. Like a... a rest stop. I came through here a couple of times when I was a kid. You know, when my family used to go to Vegas in our old van. I'm sure there's something around here. There has to be, right?"

Lacey nodded and said, "Okay. But... I need you to do one thing for me before we go."

"What?"

"Admit that I was right. I'm *not* crazy and we *are* in a dead zone."

Colton rolled his eyes and sighed as he turned the key in the ignition. He muttered, "You shouldn't want to be right about something like that..."

"I think it's an RV," Lacey said as she stared out the windshield. As they rolled past the vehicle at five miles per hour, car trembling like a kid with a cold, she looked out the passenger window and said, "Yup, it's definitely an RV."

"What the hell kind of RV is that?" Colton muttered as if in awe.

He leaned forward in his seat, his chest a few inches away from the vibrating steering wheel. A Class B campervan was parked on the side of the road. The rusty exterior was splattered with paint—reds, greens, blues, purples, yellows. A large, dirty, faded decal of a Pierrot was stuck to the rear door. It looked like something from the 1940s or 50s. The campervan gave off psychedelic vibes.

He asked, "Should we check it out?"

"Are you joking?"

Colton pulled onto the side of the road. He parked about ten meters in front of the campervan. He turned in his seat and faced Lacey. They stared at each other for ten seconds, waiting for the other to say the first word. Lacey's concerned eyes said something along the lines of: *you're crazy.* Colton exuded a nonchalant, confident aura.

He asked, "What's wrong?"

"Colton, come on. That thing is straight out of a horror movie."

"So? Real life is a horror movie, Lacey. There are serial killers, mass shooters, deadly diseases, and... and there's just a lot of horror out there. I mean, your *mom* is straight out of a horror movie. You've heard that screechy voice and you've tasted her cooking."

"Oh God, shut up," Lacey said, trying to hold her laughter.

"That woman has no taste buds and you know it. Her steak tastes like our popped tire. Probably worse."

Lacey glared at him, but she could only maintain her façade for five seconds. She covered her mouth and chuckled. He was right: her mother's cooking was awful.

Colton said, "We'll knock on their window, we'll ask if they can give us a hand—a spare tire, directions, maybe a ride—then we'll leave. We'll be out of this hot desert and eating stale gas station hot dogs in no time. And if no one's there, we keep following the road to the nearest rest stop. It's that simple. What do you say?"

"Fine, fine," Lacey responded. "Just... Just don't be like those assholes in the movies. If I get a bad feeling about something—*anything* at all—we leave. Deal?"

"Deal."

They climbed out of the car. Colton approached the driver's side of the campervan while Lacey slunk over to the passenger side. The same groovy paint decorated the campervan's rolling door, but the rust was obvious. The rolling door's window was tinted black. All of the dusty, cracked windows were covered in hard water stains. They were opaque, invaded by thick clouds of browns and yellows. They couldn't see into the campervan, so they figured the occupants couldn't see out of it.

"It looks like this thing has been abandoned for years," Lacey said. "How could anyone drive something like this?"

As he examined the tires, Colton said, "I don't know, but the tires are still good and there are tire marks behind it, so someone's been driving it."

"You think someone's in there?"

"Where else can they be?"

Lacey put her hands on her hips and did a 360.

Sand, cacti, tumbleweeds, mountains.

Not a soul in sight.

She leaned over the hood of the vehicle. Through the grimy windshield, she spotted a tattered sunshade. She leaned closer to the rolling door's window, but she refused to touch it. It looked hazardous. Her nostrils flared as she caught a whiff of a strong metallic scent. But, once again, she couldn't see anything inside of the vehicle.

She said, "I think... Well... I know you hate my gut

feelings, but I think someone's in there. I think they're watching us."

"I was with you until the 'watching us' part," Colton responded. "But someone's definitely in there. I can feel it, too. Maybe they're sleeping."

Lacey made her way to the back of the campervan. Through a gap on the broken blinds over the rear window, she could see a torn blanket with black spots on a bed. It looked like dried blood. It was too dark to see anything else. Colton noticed the driver's seat window was rolled down about a centimeter. He leaned in with his ear over the opening—*silence.*

He knocked on the window and said, "Hello? Anyone in there? We could use some help." There wasn't a *peep* from the campervan. He knocked again and said, "We're sorry to bother you, we really are, but... We have a flat, you see? We could use some directions or a spare tire or a lift to the closest gas station. I mean, I... I could pay you."

Lacey approached and nudged his arm. She whispered, "Don't tell them you need help, you have a flat, *and* you have money. Are you trying to get robbed?"

"Oh, *please.* You really think someone's going to park this heap of junk out here just to try to rob people? Look around, Lacey. We're in a desert. A–A... A *deserted* desert."

"Deserted desert... That's just cheesy. Just call it a 'dead zone,' okay?"

They stared at each other with deadpan expressions, then they chuckled. The campervan was silent and still.

Lacey said, "So, um... I guess no one's home?"

Colton sighed, then he nodded. He said, "Guess so. They probably ran out of gas and started walking to the nearest rest stop."

"*Or*... They're just waiting for us to leave. You know, like when the Mormons come knocking and you pretend like you're not home. You hold your breath and watch 'em from your peephole."

"Normal people don't do that, Lacey. You just tell 'em to go away or... or tell 'em you worship Satan," Colton said as he leaned closer to the driver's window. He tried to peek through the gap, but he couldn't see anything but darkness. He said, "I feel like... like there's someone in there."

"I told you."

Colton said, "Maybe it's some horny teenagers or some college potheads." He shouted, "If you're smoking or banging in there, we don't care! We're not going to rat you out! Just say something! Anything! Don't leave us hanging out here! Come on..."

No one answered.

Colton muttered, "Shit."

Lacey patted his shoulder and said, "Think of it this way: at least we don't have to live with survivor's guilt."

"*What?*"

"Well, think about it. If there were some horny teenagers or potheads in there, they'd be unluckier than us. If we were in a horror movie, they'd die first, right?"

Colton looked at her with a dumbfounded expression. His face said something along the lines of: *did you really just say that?*

He huffed and snickered, then he said, "Come on, let's get out of here."

"What? What's so funny?" Lacey asked as she followed him.

"Nothing, nothing."

"Tell me."

"It's just that you're a... you're a geek, Lacey."

"A geek? How dare–"

They stopped laughing and glanced back at the campervan. A wry laugh emerged from the vehicle. Colton heard a clear snort. Lacey thought she heard a whistling or grinding sound.

Lacey said, "Holy shit, someone's actually in there. I was right. *Again.* I'm two for two."

Colton approached the campervan. He knocked on the window and tried to peek through the gap again, weaving and bobbing his head.

He said, "Hey, come on, don't be like this. We heard you. You don't have to help us out, you don't have to do anything for us, but don't be... Don't..." He groaned in frustration, then he said, "Don't be assholes. We're just looking for directions or a ride to the closest rest stop or... or some human contact. Hello?"

Lacey sucked her teeth. *That's not a good idea,* she

thought. She often joked about horror movies and books, she loved the genre, but at heart, she was a wimp—*a real fraidy-cat.* She was afraid of provoking people, especially mysterious people in creepy campervans in desolate areas. She grabbed Colton's hand and pulled him away from the vehicle.

Eyes on the campervan, Colton shouted, "Are you douchebags serious?!" He was ignored. He said, "Stupid stoners."

Lacey led him back to their car. She said, "Let's go. Forget about them."

"I'm sorry. I just... I lost my cool and I–"

She buckled her seat belt and said, "Don't worry about it, babe. Let's just go."

Colton saw the sincere fear in his girlfriend's eyes. He could see she just wanted to leave as soon as possible. He turned the key in the ignition, then they rolled away at about ten miles per hour.

The car coasted down the road, shaking while the popped tire *flapped* incessantly. Colton cycled between the windshield and the rearview mirror, hoping to spot a rest stop or another driver or even a hitchhiker—*anyone* or *anything* that could reignite his hope. Lacey held her cell phone out the window, searching for a signal. She tried to call 911, but there were no other service providers in the area. She was right: they were in a dead zone.

Colton said, "It's getting late. At this rate, we won't get to Vegas until tomorrow."

"Yup. We'd probably get there sooner by walking."

"We should call Matt or Susan or... or anyone. Let 'em know we're going to be late, you know?"

"I wish we could, but I've got no signal."

"Check my phone."

Colton whipped his hips to the right without taking his hands off the steering wheel. Lacey took his cell phone out of his pocket—*no data, no bars.* She held the phone up closer to the ceiling. A message at the top of the phone read: *no service.* She leaned on the windowsill and held the phone skyward.

No data.

No bars.

No service.

"Nope, nothing." Lacey said. "Shit. We're going to miss tonight's party."

"Yeah," Colton sighed. "At least we'll be around for the after-party. We'll call 'em as soon as we get to a motel or a pay phone."

"To be honest, I don't think it really matters. They'll probably be so shit-faced that they won't even know we're calling them if we do. I mean, they're probably going to have an orgy tonight. For all we know, we dodged a bullet... or a cumshot."

She laughed, but Colton remained quiet.

Lacey said, "What? Don't tell me you've always wanted to be part of an orgy? Colton? Hey, can you hear me?"

Colton didn't say a word. Lacey shook his shoulder, then she noticed he was squinting at the rearview mirror. She looked at it, too. She narrowed her eyes.

She said, "Is that... No, it's... Oh my God."

The speck in the rearview mirror grew larger by the second. The vibrant colors popped in the sun. Although she sat in the passenger seat of their car, the metallic scent returned to Lacey's nose. She felt like there was blood at the back of her mouth. Colton's brow was gnarled with surprise and concern. He placed more pressure on the gas pedal. They reached fifteen miles per hour.

Lacey said, "It's them. It's that cheap RV."

The campervan raced towards them at over fifty miles per hour. The driver blared his horn—one, two, *three times*. The horn echoed through the desert for miles.

Fear laced into her voice, Lacey said, "Colton, that's the same–"

"Put your seat belt on," Colton interrupted.

"Oh my God, I don't think they're going to stop. They're going to–"

"Put your seat belt on!"

Lacey hopped in her seat, startled by his shout. But she understood his panic. Her hands trembled as she buckled her seat belt. She squeezed her eyes shut and babbled incoherently—'*oh God, we're dead, we're going to die.*' She opened her eyes and looked at the rearview mirror. She squealed in fear. The campervan zoomed towards them. She felt like the large vehicle was going to spear through their car, ripping it in half, tearing them to pieces, and launching them through the road and desert.

She cried, "Oh God! They're going to hit us! Go faster! Oh God, *faster*, Colton!"

Colton sped up to thirty miles per hour. The car jerked to the side because of the flat tire. It emitted a *screeching* sound. He slowed to twenty-five miles per hour, afraid of losing control of the vehicle.

"What are you doing?!" Lacey yelled. "Don't stop!"

"I'm not!"

"Colton, please! They're going to hit us!"

"I can't go faster, damn it!"

"You can!"

"Lacey, shut the–"

The campervan's horn ripped through the air, louder than before.

Lacey looked over at the rear window and yelled, "Stop it! Leave us alone!"

She winced and turned in her seat as the campervan sped up. They could hear the other vehicle's rumbling engine now.

Eyes on the rearview mirror, watching as the campervan's reflection grew, Colton muttered, "Shit, no... Oh fuck... No, no, no, no, no!"

The campervan swerved to the left, grazing the car's rear bumper—wheels howling and horn blaring. It barreled past them in the oncoming lane, then it swerved left and right until it slowed to match Colton's speed. They drove beside each other at about twenty-five miles per hour, cruising down a long, desolate stretch of road.

Colton felt his heartbeat in his fingers. A lump crawled up Lacey's throat, silencing her. They stared out the driver's side window in shock. Through the dark, filmy passenger side window of the campervan, they saw the silhouette of the driver—a person with long hair. Over the loud engine and their flapping tire, they heard a childish giggle.

Colton whispered, "Who the hell is–"

The campervan veered towards them. In a knee-jerk reaction, Colton spun the wheel to the right. The campervan hit them. Colton's side-view mirror was snapped off. Webs of cracks spread across the rear passenger window and the windshield. The door was dented and the hood popped open. Colton stomped on the brakes and rolled onto the side of the road.

The campervan sped away, vanishing in the heat haze.

Colton and Lacey sat in silence for a minute. They stared at the road ahead of them, waiting for the campervan to return. *They have to finish the job,* Lacey figured as she thought about classic slasher horror movies. Colton clenched his jaw and focused on their options if the campervan returned—*drive into the desert? Fight back? Stay still?*

But the campervan didn't return.

As Colton climbed out of the car, Lacey rubbed her forehead and said, "Oh my God. Oh. My. God. Are you okay, Colt? They could have killed us. I mean, they... they *hit* you. They rammed *your* side. You could have died, baby." She leaned over the center console and asked, "Colton, are you okay? Honey?"

Colton checked the damage of the vehicle. The engine and the other tires were unscathed. He pushed the hood, then he placed his hand over his brow and searched for the missing side-view mirror. He couldn't see it. He sat down and buckled his belt, then he stared at the steering wheel. The same thought kept running through his mind: *I could have died, I could have died, I could have died.*

Lacey asked, "Are you okay?"

Colton snapped out of his contemplation. He shook his head, then he nodded, then he laughed nervously. Lacey chuckled with him. Relief had a way of making people laugh.

"I'm good," Colton responded. "You all right?"

"Yeah, yeah, I'm fine. I'm... I'm fucking scared, but I'm okay. What the hell was that?"

"A psycho. Or just some assholes."

"It looked like a girl."

"Or a douchebag with long hair."

Lacey huffed, then she looked out the windshield again. She asked, "So, what do we do now?"

Colton said, "It's going to sound crazy, but... I think we keep driving."

"Like... we follow them?"

"Yeah. We can't drive back or we'll run out of gas going nowhere. There has to be a rest stop coming up. There *has* to be."

"And what if they're waiting for us?"

"We just stop. We stop and we wait. But I don't think we have to worry about them. I think they were just assholes looking to scare us. It's over."

Colton turned the key in the ignition. The purr of the engine brought a smile to his face. He drove forward. Lacey was afraid. Her gut told her that it wasn't over. She didn't want to argue with her boyfriend, though. And she agreed with him—going back would have left them stranded if they didn't run into another driver.

She checked her cell phone for a signal again. She said, "As soon as I get some bars, I'm calling the cops." She wagged her finger at Colton and said, "And we're *not* stopping for anymore fucking RVs. Okay?"

"I'm with you on that one, babe."

"I knew it was a bad idea," Lacey muttered, arms crossed.

3

CHECKING IN

"Yup, it's a motel," Lacey said as she leaned forward and peered out the windshield. "It looks empty. But, I mean, like... *completely* empty. Abandoned, you know? Wow."

They rolled past a diner at the edge of the parking lot—*Gold Diner 80*. Two cars were parked in front of the restaurant. A few people moved about inside. They took a right into the parking lot. To the left, beyond the motel's front office, there was a gas station with a convenience store called '*Hassan's Market.*' There was an old wagon parked in front of the shop.

Colton parked near the front office. The couple leaned forward in their seats and looked up at the sign above the entrance. It read: *Motel Ace*. There was a large, rusty star beside the motel's name. Glowing blue in front of the broken, dusty blinds, a neon sign on the window read: *VACANCY*. There were only a few vehicles parked in front of the motel rooms to the right, including a semi-truck.

"Motel Ace," Lacey said. "You ever heard of this place before?"

"Nope."

"What do you think it's rated on Yelp?"

"Yelp? Really?" Colton responded. He smiled and said, "You're really crazy. You know that?"

Lacey pouted and cocked her head back. She asked, "What? Why?" Colton laughed as he exited the car. As she wrestled with her seat belt, Lacey asked, "Hey, what did you mean by that? Colton? I was being serious. You're always supposed to read the Yelp reviews before... Hey, wait for me!"

She slipped her feet into her sneakers, staggered out of the vehicle, and then raced to his side. She held his right hand with both of hers, like a girl following her father through a haunted house attraction. They entered the front office.

A young man stood behind the reception desk. His feathery black hair was combed over to the right, short and neat. His earlobes, stretched with gauges, dangled close to his shoulders. His septum was pierced, like a barn animal with a nose ring. His neck was tattooed to appear as if it had been slit and stitched together. His long-sleeved polo shirt hid the tattoos on his arms and chest.

A name tag on his chest read: *Todd Stone.* He looked drowsy and glum, his head down as he stared at the desk. He didn't welcome them with a smile. He barely acknowledged the couple.

Colton approached the desk and said, "Hey, sorry to bother you, but can we use your phone?"

"For what?" Todd responded.

"For wha..." Colton started to repeat him, then he shook his head. He said, "We got a flat down the road, then some maniac in an RV *rammed* us. The car's working, but we're not going to make it to Vegas like that."

Todd raised his eyes until he met Colton's. He nodded and said, "The pay phone's over there."

"Pay phone? You serious?"

Todd nodded.

Colton groaned in frustration. He looked at Lacey and asked, "You have a quarter and a dime?"

"It's fifty cents now," Todd chimed in.

Colton bit his lip as he grew angrier. He asked, "You have *fifty* cents?"

Lacey said, "No, I don't have any change. Well, maybe I have a dollar?" She took her wallet out of her bag. She muttered, "Shit, I only have a five."

Colton said, "Listen, um..." He squinted at the clerk's name tag. He said, "Listen, Todd, this is an emergency. Can you *please* let us use your phone or at least spare us fifty cents?"

"Can't. It's against our policy, sir. I can change that five for you if you want."

"To what? Twenty quarters? What the hell do we need twenty quarters for?"

Todd shrugged and said, "You need two for the pay phone. You can probably find a couple of coin slots in Vegas, too."

Colton glared at him. He wanted to jump over the desk, grab the chest of Todd's shirt, and slam the clerk's face on the table. Lacey sensed the tension in the room. She placed the five-dollar bill on the desk and slid it towards the clerk. Todd wasn't intimidated by them. He opened a drawer, then he placed five stacks of four quarters each on the desk—*twenty coins.*

With obvious sarcasm, Colton said, "Thanks a lot, pal."

"You're welcome," Todd said, monotone.

Colton and Lacey went to the grimy pay phones in the corner. They muttered amongst themselves. Lacey warned him about arguing with strangers in desolate places while Colton complained about the clerk's attitude. Colton put a quarter in the first pay phone. It was spat out into the change slot. He put a quarter into the second pay phone—the same result. He took a deep breath as he approached the third pay phone. He fed it a quarter and, like a picky baby at a dining table, the pay phone spat it out.

He marched back to the desk and said, "Hey, man, those pay phones don't work."

"Oh. Guess they're still out of order."

"You gotta be kidding me. Give us our cash back."

"I'm not a credit card, sir. I don't give 'cash back.'

We exchange bills for smaller bills or bills for coins, but we don't exchange coins for bills. It's our policy."

"You have a policy for that? Seriously?"

"Blame my boss."

Colton said, "Sure. Is he here? Can I speak to him?"

Todd said, "Nope. It's just me for the rest of the evening and night."

Colton took his cap off, shoved his fingers into his hair, and groaned. He was on the verge of snapping—and Lacey could see that.

Lacey said, "Look, we really need a phone. I'm going to be a bridesmaid soon. I'm missing my best friend's bachelorette party right now. Don't make me miss her wedding, too. Help us out here. Please."

Todd sighed, then he said, "Okay, the truth is: the landlines are out right now, so you can't use this phone. I thought the pay phones were wired differently. My boss told me to use those in emergencies, but... Whatever. I can't help you out on that part, *but* a mechanic—Jordan... somethin'-somethin'—will be here tomorrow morning. He's here every day at six o'clock. He fixes cars and some of our equipment. You just missed him, actually. He was fixing an ice machine. So, if you want my, uh... my recommendation: you should rent a room, spend the night here, meet Jordan tomorrow morning, and then get going."

Hands on his hips, Colton said, "Okay, okay. That's something, but... Say we wanted to leave and get out of here as soon as possible. Where's the closest town? Or the next rest stop?"

"Probably twenty-five or thirty minutes by car."

"That's not bad. No, that's–"

"That's at the speed limit," Todd interrupted. "I saw you two rolling in here. It'd take you a couple of hours to get there at that pace. At least two. And who knows? Maybe their phones are out, too."

"Right, right," Colton said. He glanced at Lacey and asked, "What do you want to do?"

The motel gave Lacey an uneasy feeling. She didn't trust Todd, either. But she was worried about getting stranded on their way to the next rest stop, especially with the sun descending beyond the horizon.

She said, "I guess we rent a room at this 'lovely' motel."

Colton looked at Todd and asked, "How much for a room?"

Todd said, "Um... Well... Forty-nine dollars a night?"

Colton and Lacey furrowed their brows. The clerk sounded like he was asking a question or trying to barter with them.

Colton said, "*O*-kay. So, forty-nine dollars? That's it?"

"Forty-nine times two—'cause there's two of ya—and some taxes. It's a hundred and twelve dollars. And change."

"A hundred and twelve and change… Okay, sure, whatever. You accept credit cards?"

"We do."

Colton handed him a Mastercard. Todd took the credit card to the back office. Colton tilted his head to the side and Lacey raised one hand up with her fingers pointing at the ceiling. Their gestures said: *what the hell?* They heard Todd fumbling about in the room. They heard a *squeaking* sound, too—like a sneaker sliding on a liquid.

After about three minutes, Todd returned from the room. He looked at the key rack. Only three keys were missing: Room 103, Room 202, and Room 204. He grabbed the key for Room 101.

Todd handed Colton the key and said, "There you go. Room 101. It'll be the first room on the first floor. Check-out is at eleven. We don't serve breakfast, but you can eat at Gold Diner 80—right there behind ya— anytime until two o'clock in the morning. They'll sell you as much coffee as you want for five bucks. Anything else, just ask."

Colton took the key and said, "So, um… My credit card?"

"Oh yeah," Todd said.

He took Colton's credit card out of his pocket and handed it back to him.

Colton said, "And, um… a receipt?"

"Printer's broken. I can get you one tomorrow if you'd like."

"Yeah, yeah. I'd like that."

"Great, then I'll see you tomorrow morning."

Colton and Lacey glanced at each other, discomfited by the awkwardness in the room. They stepped backwards, watching as Todd stared down at the desk again. They shared the same thought: *what the hell is he thinking about?*

As they exited the front office, Lacey said, "You know you're going to have to cancel that card, right?"

"I know," Colton responded.

They moved their car to the parking spot directly in front of Room 101. They unloaded their bags and entered the room. It was a dingy but welcoming room. In front of the window to the right, there was a table with one chair. There was a king-size bed with two nightstands on their right. To the left, there was a dresser with a flat-screen television on top. The green wallpaper was chipped and discolored while the rug was decorated with black spots.

The furniture was rickety, but it functioned. The bathroom wasn't anything special—a sink, a medicine cabinet, a toilet, and a bathtub/shower combo.

As she looked into the room from the doorway, Lacey said, "At least it's not infested with cockroaches."

"We haven't checked the pillowcases yet."

"*Ew,* don't say that."

"What? You can talk about 'dead zones' all day, but you can't handle some cockroach chat?"

"Cockroach chat? Oh God, shut up, Colton."

They bickered playfully as they unpacked their clothes for the night and examined the room. To their utter relief, there were no cockroaches in their pillowcases. There was a password for the motel's Wi-Fi on the dresser, but they couldn't find the network on their cell phones.

Lacey said, "No bars, no data, no Wi-Fi. We're still in the dead zone. We can't call or even message anyone. What do we do?"

"We ask that asshole 'Todd' about the Wi-Fi. Then we go get something to eat. I'm starving."

"And what if the Wi-Fi isn't working? How do we call our friends or the cops or... or anyone?"

"That's a discussion for *after* we know it's not working. Like, while we're eating something delicious from the diner. Preferably something that wasn't roadkill yesterday. Come on, let's go."

They walked over to the front office. Colton nodded at the door, communicating without saying a word—*'I'm not talking to that asshole. You talk to him.'*

Lacey opened the door and poked her head inside. She said, "Excuse me. Hey, *excuse me.*" Todd looked at her. Lacey said, "The Wi-Fi isn't working."

"Password's in the room."

"No, I mean it's not working. We can't even find it on our phones."

"Then I guess it's not working."

Lacey sneered and said, "Yeah, I know. That's what I said. Aren't you supposed to..." She shook her head.

As she closed the door, she rolled her eyes and said, "Never mind."

Colton said, "Still an asshole, huh?"

"A gaping one."

"That's, uh... That's disgusting, Lacey."

"I know," Lacey said. She smiled and said, "Dinner?"

"Yeah, dinner," Colton chuckled.

4

THE 'LOCALS'

THE DOOR CHIME RANG THROUGH THE DINER. IT WAS AN old-fashioned restaurant with wine-red walls, matching upholstery, and a checkered floor. Booths lined the walls under the storefront windows and tables cluttered the center of the diner. A jukebox in the corner played *(You're the) Devil in Disguise* by Elvis Presley.

Elena Gonzales grabbed two menus from the rack under the hostess podium near the front door. Her sandy hair was tied in a neat bun. Black bags hung under her eyes, but her brown irises glowed with life and optimism. She was a kind, pleasant young woman. She wore a red blouse, a matching skirt, and a checkered waist apron.

She said, "Welcome to Gold Diner 80. My name's Elena and I'll be serving you today. Are we sitting two this evening?"

"That's right," Colton said.

Elena snickered and said, "As you can see, we have *plenty* of seats. Would you like to sit at a booth, a table, or at the bar?"

Lacey responded, "A booth, please. They look comfy."

"They are. Right this way."

Elena led them to a booth to their right. Colton sat on one side, Lacey sat on the other. The sun cast a ray of dusk's red glow on them.

Elena placed the menus on the table and said, "I'll give you a couple of minutes to look at the menu. Holler if you need anything."

"Thank you," Colton and Lacey responded in perfect unison.

Elena went over to the other patrons. Gabe Webb, a middle-aged trucker, sat at the bar. His slick, grizzled hair stuck out from under his trucker cap, and salt-and-pepper stubble covered his strong, defined face. He ate a burger with bacon and barbecue sauce, a side of French fries, and a chocolate milkshake while flicking his thumb across his cell phone's screen.

The Marsh family sat at another booth. Jacob Marsh, another middle-aged man, was the patriarch. He looked meek, thin and fragile—emotionally and physically. He was dressed conservatively, like the rest of his family. Caroline Marsh was the matriarch. She sat next to her eleven-year-old son, Joey, watching him with eyes like a hawk. If she could, she would have chewed his food for him and spit it into his mouth.

The cook, Jayden Jenkins, could be seen through the kitchen pass-through window. He was young and fit—and bored out of his mind.

Colton ordered chicken and waffles with a strawberry milkshake while Lacey ordered a grilled chicken sandwich with a salad and a glass of orange juice. Elena brought them their drinks first.

She asked, "So, are you two staying here at Motel Ace?"

Colton responded, "Yup."

"Unfortunately," Lacey said.

Elena smirked and said, "It's not that bad, is it?"

"Have you stayed there?"

"*Nooo.* I'm out of here as soon as my shift ends."

Lacey said, "You're lucky. The room's a little old, the Wi-Fi doesn't work, their phone lines are down... It's a nightmare so far."

Elena puckered her lips and nodded. She said, "Yeah, I know what you mean. Our phones are down, too. I'd let you use my cell phone, but I only get reception *sometimes* while I'm out here." She frowned at the bar. She leaned closer to the table and whispered, "I think only that guy's phone is working. That trucker over there, you see? But I wouldn't talk to him if I were you. He's just... I wouldn't do it."

Colton and Lacey couldn't tell if she was afraid of

the trucker or if he was known for being an asshole. Gabe didn't hear them from the bar.

Elena asked, "Where were you headed anyway?"

"Vegas," Colton responded. "But one of our tires popped, then some asshole in an RV hit us. So, we're spending the night here until a mechanic meets us tomorrow morning."

"Wow. Are you... Are you guys okay?"

"Yeah, we're fine."

"We're lucky," Lacey said. "So, what do you think about, um... Okay, what's up with the motel's clerk? Todd? I mean, it's crazy. You are a *delight*. Like, I feel like I'm at a regular restaurant right now. He made me feel... uncomfortable. Don't tell him I said that, by the way. I don't want him to slit my throat while I sleep."

With disappointment in his voice, Colton said, "Lacey, come on."

He sounded like a strict father—*'for heaven's sake, not at the table, Lacey.'*

Elena said, "I haven't really seen him around before. I think they hired him last week, so maybe he's just getting into it, you know? I think Malik is working tomorrow morning. He usually works the night shift, but I didn't see him this morning, so maybe he changed his schedule. If he comes in tomorrow morn- ing, he'll help you much more than that other guy. Malik's a sweetheart, really."

Ding!—a bell rang. Jayden had finished preparing their food.

Elena said, "I'll be right back with your meals. Let me know if you need anything else."

Colton and Lacey ate their food while chatting about their day, their plans, and their meals. Lacey teased Colton about his meal, calling it 'junk food.' But she was happy to take a sip of his milkshake. They were disappointed by their road trip, rattled by their confrontation with the RV, but they found comfort and happiness in each other.

Their laughter was drowned out by a guffaw at the bar. They glanced over at Gabe, surprised by his booming voice. He held his cell phone up to his ear.

Gabe said, "Yeah... Yeah, brother, I'm here at Motel Ace again... Yeah, 'til tomorrow morning... No, brother, I need '*Spice*' this time. I miss that girl. She left a hole in my heart." He cackled again as he listened to the hoarse voice on the phone. He said, "I know! I know, brother! Left a hole in my pocket, too! But she's worth every dime. Oh yeah... yup... She knows how to handle my 'pole.' She knows what I like. She available or what? I need her at 103... Yeah, Room One-Zero-Three. You hearing me okay?"

He was requesting the company of an escort from an agency in a city nearby. Everyone could hear him, but he didn't care. He was shameless about it. Caroline placed her hands over Joey's ears to stop him from hearing Gabe. Like Colton and Lacey, Jacob fought to suppress his laughter. Jayden laughed aloud in the kitchen while Elena rolled her eyes.

Lacey said, "Well, I guess that's why she didn't want us to talk to him: he's a pig."

"I wonder if we can hear him 'oink' when he's fucking that hooker. He said Room 103, right? Sounds like he's staying pretty close to us."

"Shit. I'm going to need some earplugs, aren't I?"

Colton and Lacey walked down the aisles of Hassan's Market, looking through shelves full of food, tools, and knickknacks. They searched for earplugs, snacks, and alcohol.

Nagaoka Ayumi and Someya Risa, two Japanese college students traveling through the United States, wandered the store, too. The tourists took pictures of the snacks and selfies of themselves while speaking in Japanese. Their giggling was loud but sweet. They stayed at the motel for the experience. They wanted to catch a glimpse of every part of America.

Ayumi and Risa made their way to the cash register. They spoke to the clerk, Hassan Amari. The old man complimented them on their English and spoke about his struggles learning the language when he was young. He recommended some snacks and gave them some travel advice. Like Elena at the diner, he was an amiable person. Except for Todd, the 'locals' were welcoming.

"You see 'em?" Lacey asked as she scanned a set of shelves.

"See what?" Colton said, his eyes on a wall of alcohol.

"Earplugs."

"Ahh, you don't need earplugs, babe. He's going to be two rooms over."

"He sat at the other side of the diner, but I could hear him eating the entire time. It was so... so *moist*. I don't want to hear him moaning all night."

Colton grabbed a bottle of liquor. He wagged it at her and said, "Well, if he makes too much noise, we'll do the same. You know, we'll return the favor."

"Oh, yeah? And how are we going to do that?"

Colton shrugged and said, "I can oink just as loud as him."

Lacey said, "I don't want to hear you oink."

"Yes, you do."

"No, I *don't*."

"Umm. Yeah, you do."

Colton took a step towards her. Lacey's face tightened as she tried to stop herself from laughing. She stepped back and bumped into the shelves behind her. Just as she glanced back, Colton lunged at her. He rubbed his nose and lips on her neck while oinking. Laughter burst out of Lacey's mouth. The shelves rattled as she crashed into them again.

"Stop it!" she laughed. "S–Stop!"

Oink, oink, oink!

Lacey yelled, "Okay! O–Okay! You win! Just–"

"Excuse me," Hassan interrupted them from the end of the aisle. Colton and Lacey looked at them, cheeks flushed with embarrassment. Hassan said, "My wife is sleeping upstairs. She's feeling a little under the weather. Do you mind keeping it down a little? Please?"

"I'm sorry about that, sir," Colton said.

In a hushed voice, Lacey said, "We'll be quiet. Sorry."

"Thank you very much. I appreciate it," Hassan said before returning to the counter.

Colton looked up at the ceiling and said, "I guess there's an apartment upstairs. Oops."

"Yup," Lacey said. "Now you see why I need those earplugs."

They gathered some supplies for their night at Motel Ace: two Nestlé Drumsticks, a bag of Flamin' Hot Cheetos, a bag of Nacho Cheese Doritos, a Hersey bar, and a bottle of liquor, and earplugs for Lacey. They couldn't party with their friends, so they figured they'd party alone. They finally accepted the fact that they weren't going anywhere that night.

In their motel room, Colton and Lacey flicked through the channels on their television. They stopped on a rerun of an animated show—*American Dad*. On the rough mattress, lapping away at their ice cream, they reminisced about their relationship, talking about the movies and shows they had watched together. They didn't hear any of the other guests.

They were caught in a sense of comfort and normality. Their encounter with the RV was swept to the back of their minds.

5

ROOM 202

AYUMI LAY ON HER STOMACH, HER LAPTOP OPEN IN FRONT of her at the foot of the bed. Risa knelt on the floor near her best friend, her palms on the bed and her chin resting on her hands. They read their itinerary while looking at routes on Google Maps. The lamps on the nightstands and the bathroom light were turned on. An episode of a late-night talk show played on mute on the television. The curtains and blinds were closed, but some moonlight still seeped into the room.

With a slight accent and a tender voice, Ayumi said, "So, tomorrow, we'll wake up at six."

"Too early," Risa said, covering her mouth as she giggled.

"Okay, okay. Seven?"

"Better."

"Good. I'll put an alarm on. Then... Then we'll go to Vegas. We'll leave our luggage, then we'll go to the

Strip. The day after tomorrow... We have to drive almost six hours to go to Los Ang–”

Tap, tap, tap.

Someone knocked on their door.

Ayumi and Risa looked at the door with raised brows, then they looked at each other. It was late, and they weren't expecting any visitors.

Ayumi whispered, “Did you call the front desk?” Risa shook her head, her double Dutch braids swinging from side to side. Ayumi asked, “Then who's–”

Tap, tap, tap.

The visitor knocked again. Ayumi hopped off the bed. She slunk towards the door, eyes on the window as if she could see through the curtains. Risa stayed on her knees, but she leaned away from the bed. Her eyes glinted with anticipation—curiosity, *fear.*

Ayumi said, “Hello?”

Silence.

She shuddered as she stared at the door. She glanced back at Risa. Risa's face was twisted with dread. She tried to smile, but her lips wouldn't stop wavering. The silence stuck around for about a minute. They couldn't hear any people or cars outside. They didn't even hear a howl of the wind.

Ayumi turned to face Risa. She said, “Wrong room, maybe. Put some volume on the–”

They gasped as the door rattled. It sounded like

someone had punched it. They looked at the door with wide eyes, as if they were expecting it to come to life. Then they gazed into each other's eyes. Ayumi could see Risa was on the verge of breaking down. They were the same age, but she had always treated Risa like a younger sister. Maybe it was because of her shorter stature, maybe it was because of her childish demeanor. She felt an urge to protect her—to take charge.

She laughed, then she said, "Don't worry, it's nothing. We're at a motel with so many people. And the diner is still open. It's right across the parking lot. We've been watching too many scary movies."

Risa clenched her jaw and swallowed loudly. She could see through Ayumi's semblance of confidence. She stayed on her knees, arms wrapped over a pillow on her chest.

Ayumi said, "It's okay, it's okay." As she approached the door, she yelled, "One second."

She stood on her tiptoes and peeked through the peephole. She yelped and slapped her hands over her mouth as she staggered back. Gaggles the Clown stood on the other side of the door, illuminated by the exterior hallway's light. *A monster*, Ayumi thought. *An oni.* The clown's wild red hair, pierced brow, and sharp fingernails reminded her of an oni—an ogre from Japanese folklore.

"What? *Nani? Nani, Ayumi-chan?!*" Risa said as she jumped up to her feet.

'*Nani? Nani, Ayumi-chan?!*' translated to '*What? What, Ayumi?!*'

Ayumi lowered her hands to her chest. She felt her heart racing and her stomach turning. '*There's a monster outside!*' She didn't know how to explain that to her.

She said, "I think... We have to... We should call the cops."

"Why?"

"Risa, there's a..."

She stopped upon hearing a jingle. She turned her head and her eyes drifted towards the doorknob. She saw the lock turn and she heard it *click*. She rushed towards the door to fasten the deadbolt. The door swung open. The edge of the door hit her face, breaking her nose, cutting her lips vertically down the center, and chipping one of her upper incisors.

The floorboards rumbled as she collapsed. The room under theirs was vacant, so no one could hear her. She rolled onto her stomach, groaning and whimpering. Blood leaked out of her broken nose and sliced lips, trickling across her chin and neck. Splinters from the door protruded from the wide gash across her mouth.

Hands hovering under her jaw, she scrambled to the bathroom while screaming. Blood and tears dripped on her palms. She expected Risa to follow her, but Risa was frozen with fear. She covered her mouth and shrieked, unintentionally muffling her own shout for help. She sidestepped until she crashed into one of the nightstands as Gaggles marched past her.

Ayumi stumbled into the bathroom. She left the door open behind her for Risa. It was a dead end, but she refused to quit. She stopped in front of the toilet. She tried to open the window, but her hands slid across the glass each time. It squeaked and crackled as it moved up a centimeter. Their room was on the second floor.

I can jump, I can do it, we can jump, she told herself.

Risa crawled over the bed as Gaggles entered the bathroom. Crying hysterically, she ran towards the door.

"Help!" she yelled.

Before she could reach the finish line, Pumpkin the Clown emerged in the doorway. His scowl turned into a grin as she slid to a stop in front of him. His eyes feasted on her fear—*her panic.* She fell down on her ass, then she turned and crawled towards the bathroom. Pumpkin entered the room. He closed and locked the door behind him.

And he made sure to secure the deadbolt.

Pumpkin grabbed a fistful of Risa's hair and yanked her head back, lifting her from the floor while tearing a chunk of her scalp off. He pushed her onto the bed. Still screaming, Risa rolled onto her stomach and wiggled towards the headrest. She had her eyes on the cell phone on the nightstand. But Pumpkin sat on her before she could reach it. He grabbed another fistful of her hair and pushed her head down against the comforter.

In his soft, eerie voice, he said, "Baby, baby, *bae-beeee*. Where are you going? Don't you know? The circus is in town."

In the bathroom, Gaggles grabbed Ayumi's hair and pulled her back. He smashed her head against the cabinet mirror. The glass shattered, raining down into the sink along with drops of Ayumi's blood. A cut stretched across her brow—from her hairline to the edge of her eyebrow. He rammed her head against the cabinet again, pushing the door *into* the cabinet. More shards fell into the sink.

The cut on Ayumi's forehead widened. Glass fragments were sprinkled into the cuts on her plump, sensitive lips. An uncomfortable, frightening tingle accompanied the stinging pain throughout her face. Blood poured into her left eye, forcing her to close it. More blood covered the left side of her face and her jaw. She whimpered, legs wobbling under her.

Gaggles shoved her. Ayumi fell into the bathtub, bringing the shower curtain down with her. The back of her head hit the wall, knocking her unconscious. The clown grabbed the collar of her pajama shirt, then he tugged on it and tore it open down the middle. The buttons hit the walls and slid in the tub. He leered at her soft, perky breasts and licked his lips.

He pulled her pajama pants down, removing her panties at the same time. He rubbed the fuzz on her crotch with his thumb and chuckled. He threw a towel into the sink and soaked it.

In his deep, hoarse voice, Gaggles said, "Wake up, girl."

He squeezed her breast tightly, clawing at her skin each time—once, twice, *thrice*. He left eleven thin cuts on her breast. He sliced into her areola, too. Droplets of blood dripped from her erect nipple, one by one. He twisted her nipple—left and right, *left* and *right*. His sharpened, modified fingernails cut into it until he severed it. He held the little nub between his fingertips. Blood oozed out of the wound, rolling down to her ribs.

Ayumi awoke, whining in pain. She started to hyperventilate as soon as she saw the clown. She was pulled out of a void of darkness and dropped into a living nightmare. *Ow!*—she cried as jolts of pain shot through her chest from her sliced breast. She looked at her nipple, face scrunched up in horror, then she looked back at the evil clown.

Gaggles smirked and threw her severed nipple into his mouth. He chortled—a wet, throaty laugh—as he chewed on her nipple.

"No!" Ayumi cried. She tried to stand up, but she slid in the bathtub. Her blood didn't help. She yelled, "Help me!"

Gaggles grabbed the damp towel. He twisted it into a whip, then he flicked it at Ayumi. He slapped her face with it. Her long, silky black hair was flung over her face so she couldn't see a thing. But she felt the pain from the blow. A patch of red, bloody dots spread across her flushed cheek. He whipped her face again, aggravating her broken nose.

Ahh!—she screamed again.

Gaggles whipped her repeatedly. He snapped the towel at her head, her chest, and her arms. She tried grabbing it, but she was too weak and disoriented to get ahold of it. Her breasts turned red, then greenish and purplish bruises appeared. Her chest was dark red and swollen, contrasting against her pale abdomen and limbs.

"Stop! Please!" she cried. "Otousan! Otousan!"

'Otousan' meant 'dad' in Japanese. Fathers were supposed to protect their daughters, so she always felt safe with him. But he couldn't save her now.

Gaggles threw the bloody towel aside. He grabbed her by the hair and dragged her out of the bathtub. She slid across the floor, scratching at the clown's forearm while kicking at everything. Gaggles sat on her back, grabbed her cheeks, and lifted her head, forcing her to look at the bed.

He said, "Showtime."

Ayumi's vision was blurred by her tears and blood. She blinked rapidly to clear her eyes. She couldn't believe what she was seeing. She shook her head as Risa's pained shrieking drilled into her ears. Her heart sank and a lump jumped into her throat.

"No, no, n–no," Ayumi said weakly, her voice breaking. "Risa... Ri–Risa..."

Risa was already disrobed. Pumpkin sat on her back, penetrating her vagina with a large rubber chicken. It *squeaked* with each thrust. He forced it in until the toy's beak hit her cervix. The rubber chicken's body stretched her vaginal opening. She felt every rugged edge of the toy. The toy was dry and rough, and she wasn't producing any arousal fluid.

She felt nothing but pain—*burning pain*—as if her pelvis were set aflame. Her body was *invaded* by a foreign object. She was *ravaged* by a clown. This was rape, and it was horrifying. It was unnatural, it was unbelievable, and it wasn't supposed to be happening to her. She was traveling through the United States with her best friend, enjoying the trip of her dreams. She never hurt anyone.

Pumpkin said, "Oh, we have an audience. Watch me make this chicken disappear!"

As Pumpkin cackled and clucked, Ayumi cried, "Let her go! Let... her... go... please..."

Yet, the toy kept squeaking, Pumpkin kept clucking, and Risa kept weeping. She started bleeding from her vagina. The toy—from its beak to the base of its neck —was smeared with blood. The blood stained her vulva and the bedsheets, too. She felt a lump in her pelvis. She couldn't see it, but her vagina was prolapsing. It looked like an apple was coming out of her.

Ayumi's mouth was wide open. She finally closed

her eyes, realizing she didn't *have* to watch her friend's torture, but then she thought about Risa. She couldn't fathom the pain she was enduring. She couldn't abandon her. She cared about her too much to allow her to suffer alone. She opened her eyes again. Lips wrinkled like a tilde, she shrieked.

Pumpkin laughed as he swung the rubber chicken at the back of Risa's head—*squeak! Squeak! Squeak!* He pushed Risa's face against the bed, suffocating her with the bedsheets. Her muffled whimper was barely audible because of Pumpkin's laughter. She moved her head up and down and side to side, but she couldn't break free from the clown's grip.

She kicked the footboard with her bare feet. Her toes *popped* and one of her toenails cracked. Blood lined the broken toenail. She hit her ankle, too. But it was nothing compared to the pain emanating from her pelvis. Now she felt constipated. And she felt her bloody vagina sticking out of her. Questions flooded her mind: *what is that? What happened? What did he do?*

Pumpkin pulled her head up, allowing her to gasp for air, then he slammed her face against the mattress again. He held her down for twenty-five seconds, then he pulled her head up again. He leaned close to her face, grinning to show his teeth.

He said, "Ready for the grand finale?"

"Pl–Please, I–I'm a–"

Pumpkin pushed her face down against the bedsheets. He held her head down with both hands until her squirming abated. She barely clung to consciousness. The clown hit her with a barrage of hooks. He fractured her face, breaking her left cheekbone. Like her temples and cheeks, her ears turned red. A punch to the left side of her head left her ear ringing.

She remained conscious—dazed but awake. She groaned as her head spun. She didn't move a muscle, but she felt like the room was spinning. The bed was on the ceiling, and the ceiling was now the floor.

Pumpkin hopped off the bed, arms over his head and fingers wiggling with excitement. He said, "Ladies and gentlemen... well, *ladies*, we have a special show for you tonight. You've seen Houdini disappear, you've seen Hoffa disappear, you've even seen a rubber chicken disappear. But are you ready to see a *head* go *poof*?"

Risa didn't hear him and Ayumi didn't understand him. The clown's words were simple, but she couldn't decipher the message.

Risa whined, "Pa... pa... papa..."

Pumpkin crouched, vanishing from Ayumi's sight. He giggled as he fumbled about with something under the bed.

"Don't hurt her," Ayumi begged. "Don't... Don't kill us..."

Pumpkin poked his head out from behind the bed and peeked over at Ayumi. He snickered like a child playing a prank. He was tormenting her. Ayumi realized she had bumped heads with true evil for the first time in her life. How could anyone laugh during a time like that? *'Evil'* was the only answer she could find.

Pumpkin jumped up to his feet, a sledgehammer in hand. He stepped onto the bed, Risa's legs between his large shoes.

He swung the sledgehammer overhead and shouted, "Watch it disappear!"

"No!" Ayumi screamed.

As he swung it down, he yelled, *"Poof!"*

The ten-pound steel head hit Risa's head with a bone-crunching *thud*. The back of Risa's skull was pushed *into* her head. The shards of skull stabbed her brain. A piece of her brain popped out of a wound on her scalp. Her eyes bulged, then rolled back. Her legs trembled violently, shaking the entire bed.

"No, no... no... No! *No!*" Ayumi cried. "Risa! Risa-chan..."

Pumpkin wasn't satisfied with the results. He swung the sledgehammer overhead. Bits of Risa's mushy brain and strands of her hair clung to the sledgehammer's head.

"Poof!" he repeated as he struck her again.

The *crunch* of her skull shattering was accompanied by the *splat* of her brain bursting. Bits of her brain splattered on the bed and wall. A piece even hit the ceiling, stuck like a wet wad of toilet paper in a middle school bathroom. A column of blood shot out of the back of her head. It landed on Pumpkin's costume and face. He licked it off his lips.

Risa's legs stopped moving. She was dead after the first blow. But the show wasn't over until Pumpkin said it was over. He swung the sledgehammer at her head a third time, then a fourth time, and then a fifth time. He tenderized her brain and crushed her skull into dust. Blood soaked the bedsheets. Chunks of her detached scalp, an eyeball, and a severed ear floated in the blood.

He looked at Ayumi and yelled, *"Ta-da!"* He laughed and danced, holding the sledgehammer out in front of him horizontally like a cane. He said, "Thank you for watching our wonderful act: *The Disappearing Head!* But the show's not over yet. We have another trick up our sleeves. But first, I think my friend Gaggles the Clown wants to clean you up a bit."

"N–no," Ayumi repeated, tears flowing down her cheeks.

Gaggles said, "Don't move."

"Wh–Why? Why?"

Gaggles pushed her head down to launch himself up to his feet. He wasn't worried about her. He was confident in Pumpkin and himself. Ayumi knew she couldn't escape, too. She admitted defeat, gazing at her friend's brutalized body on the bed. She thought about Risa's family and friends. One person's death could lead to emotional agony for many people.

Then she thought about her own family. Images of

her father, her mother, and her little brother flashed in her eyes. She heard her father's last message: *Ki o tsukete!* 'Ki o tsukete!' meant 'be careful out there' in Japanese. She wasn't a religious person. Her idea of death was simple: *eternal loneliness in eternal darkness.* She wasn't ready for it.

She said, "Don't–"

Gaggles placed his foot on her back and yanked her head back. He scrubbed her eye with a toothbrush. Her eyelids snapped shut as a jolt of pain surged through her skull. Gaggles kept brushing away at her face. The bristle scratched her cheek, temple, and nose. She slapped his arms, but to no avail. The clown focused on her eye again. Her eyelashes were torn off and her eyelids were sliced.

He pried her eyelids open with the toothbrush. He scrubbed her eyeball with the bristle. She felt like there were dozens of splinters in her eye. The clown scrubbed the outer layer off her eye. He cut into the blood vessels in the vascular tunic underneath. He forced it *into* her eyeball. *Stabbed with a toothbrush—* Ayumi couldn't believe it. He left the toothbrush sticking out of her eye socket.

"Mom used to clean our eyes out like this when she caught us watching porn or peeping at the neighbor's little girl," Gaggles said. He laughed inwardly as he watched her squirm. In a deadpan voice, he said, "Then she cried like you when I cleaned *her* eyes. But you know the difference between you and her? Then and now? I used toothpaste last time."

From the bed, Pumpkin giggled and said, "The whitening kind. But her eyes were just as red as yours. Like little *crushed* cherry tomatoes."

Gelatinous blood dribbled out Ayumi's eye socket. It joined the blood on her cheek and nose. Half of her vision was gone. The other half was blurred by her tears. She gasped for air, overwhelmed by the pain. She scratched the carpet, trying to drag herself out from underneath the clown, but he was too powerful.

Pumpkin threw a machete at his partner. He said, "You were supposed to have first dibs. *Oopsies.*"

As he ogled the blade, speaking with his monotone voice, Gaggles said, "I don't care. I'm having fun... Too much fun..."

Ayumi croaked and groaned. She tried to call out for help in Japanese, but she couldn't say a word. Gaggles swung the machete at the nape of Ayumi's neck. The dull *thud* made it sound like he was tapping an overripe watermelon. Ayumi squeezed her eyes shut, gurgling sounds coming out of her gaping mouth. Gaggles wiggled the blade in her neck, then he yanked it out with one mighty tug.

He swung down at her neck again. He snapped her cervical spine. Blood squirted out as he wiggled the blade again.

Ayumi passed away.

Gaggles continued chopping at her neck. From above, in the massive wound, he could see tints of red, purple, blue, and white. He saw different textures and folds and ridges. Geysers of blood shot out of her neck as he severed one of her jugulars. The carpet was soaked. It took him five long, grueling minutes to behead her.

The tourists' blood was spread throughout the room—the bed, the walls, floor, and the ceiling. Some blood even landed on the curtains and television.

The clowns kicked Ayumi's head at each other, as if they were playing soccer in the room. No one heard them downstairs or next door. The tourists suffered alone in a foreign country, victims of a senseless crime.

6

WHAT IF...

"You hear that?" Lacey asked, mouth stuffed with chocolate. She heard a *thump* from a room upstairs. She said, "Sounds like the party's getting started."

Colton lay beside her on the bed, sipping on his liquor from a plastic cup and eating the Flamin' Hot Cheetos while watching television. He sucked the spicy red powder off his thumb and index fingers.

He said, "The trucker's next door, not upstairs."

"Yeah, so? Who's to say he didn't go upstairs to someone else's room to, you know, *fuck?* To expand his, um... his little party? I mean, it's *completely* possible that everyone in this motel is a sex-addicted prostitute."

"You think he's... he's *fucking* that family from the diner? You think that kid was a... a prostitute?"

Lacey puckered her lips and looked at the ceiling, acting as if she were actually considering the possibilities. A part of her wanted to continue the joke: *yes, he's a sex-addicted prostitute, too.*

She said, "Okay, okay. I forgot about them. If that kid wasn't there, though, maybe things would have been different. Or—*or!*—maybe his parents are prostitutes and they have him locked in the closet or the bathroom or something. I've read stories like that, you know?"

Colton glanced at her with a set of grim, unapproving eyes. He turned his attention to the television. Lacey's sense of humor was darker than most TV shows. And he loved it. It was part of her mystique— her charm. She appeared sweet and welcoming on the surface, but she wasn't afraid to talk about anything. He couldn't help but chuckle and shake his head as he took another sip of his liquor.

Smiling, he said, "I think those tourists are more likely to fuck that douchebag in the diner than that family."

"Probably. You think they're doing it right now?"

"The trucker and them?"

"No, those girls. I mean, it's *completely* possible that they're lesbians, right?"

"I mean, I guess so. When you look at it like that, *anything* is possible. It's 'completely' possible that the front desk clerk is gay and someone's fucked those massive holes in his ears. It's 'completely' possible that the trucker is an alien from outer space. It's 'completely' possible that this is a stupid conversation."

Lacey shrugged and said, "Okay, okay, I get your point."

They sat in silence and watched TV. Lacey put another piece of chocolate in her mouth. Like hard candy, she sucked on it and swished it around with her tongue. Colton sipped on his liquor and ate more chips. The episode of American Dad depicted Roger— a pear-shaped alien—becoming corrupt after working as a cop for a single day.

Another *thump* made its way into their room. It was followed by a muffled cry, although it sounded more like a moan to them. The thing about pain and pleasure was: it often looked and sounded the same.

Lacey said, "It sounds like a 'fuck' party to me."

"A *'fuck'* party?

"You know what I mean. An orgy, Colton. Like, what if that trucker and his hooker joined those tourists in their room and they're getting it on right now?"

"What if they're... Who cares?"

Ignoring him, Lacey looked at the ceiling and said, "It could be a foursome. I'd have to analyze each voice, each footstep, but it sounds like more than two people in that room." She glanced at her boyfriend with a smug smile. She asked, "You wanna join 'em and make it a sixsome?"

Colton said, "I believe that's called a 'sexlet,' babe."

"And how do you know that?"

"School," Colton chuckled.

"School? Bullshit, you perv."

She jabbed her fingers at Colton's ribcage. Colton held his cup up and tried to keep it steady so he wouldn't spill it. He tickled Lacey's stomach. Their laughter was louder than the groaning in Room 202. They were oblivious of the violence occurring upstairs. They called a truce and scooted away from each other, cautious but happy.

Teeth lined with chocolate, Lacey started eating the Flamin' Hot Cheetos. Colton sneered at her in disgust.

He said, "You joking?"

"What?"

"Chocolate and Cheetos? That's pretty fucking gross."

"What? Why?"

"I can see the chocolate in your mouth, Lacey. And you're eating Hot Cheetos. Chocolate and spicy chips? Are you trying to give yourself diarrhea?"

Lacey rolled her eyes, then she said, "Oh, please. You realize people around the world eat things like spicy chocolate, right?"

"Nope. Not true," Colton said adamantly.

"It *is* true. In Mexico, they have this dish called *'molé.'* I'm pretty sure you've eaten it before. What do you think the sauce is made out of? A lot of spices and *a lot* of chocolate," Lacey explained. "I had this idea once: chocolate-dipped Hot Cheetos. They're the perfect opposites. Like sweet and sour chicken or... or salt and vinegar chips."

"I think you're wrong. You're wrong about everything."

"If I had internet on my phone, I'd show you and you'd look so silly right now."

Colton saw the crusted chocolate on Lacey's teeth and lips. The chocolate was covered in the red Cheeto powder.

He said, "You should look in the mirror."

"Don't have to. I can see it in your eyes. You love me. Kiss me."

Colton leaned away from her and said, "Brush your teeth first."

"Kiss me," Lacey repeated as she leaned in closer.

"Brush first," Colton laughed.

"Kiss me."

"Later."

Lacey leaned back against the headboard, crossed her arms, and pouted. At heart, she wanted to laugh with Colton. She was just playing a role to tease him. Colton kept his eyes on the television, struggling to stop himself from grinning. They missed the party in Las Vegas, but they were having a wonderful time together at Motel Ace.

Without looking at him, Lacey asked, "You wanna watch porn and have sex?"

Colton turned towards her. Some chocolate clung to the left side of her mouth while some Cheeto dust powdered the other side. He wasn't a fan of her tastes —he really didn't like the idea of mixing chocolate with Cheetos—but he loved her and he couldn't resist her. He lunged for the remote and started flipping through the channels, searching for a glimpse of pornography.

Lacey was amused and bewitched by his behavior. She felt loved, appreciated, and understood. She was comfortable with Colton.

She said, "You see? I knew you loved me."

7

ROOM 204

"AND BE CAREFUL!" CAROLINE SHOUTED.

As he strolled out of the room, Joey yelled, "I will!"

"You know what, I'll go with you."

"Mom, it's right there."

"But you heard that noise. Let me put on my shoes and I'll–"

"Caroline," Jacob interrupted. He stood near the bathroom door, wearing a bathrobe and drying his hair with a towel. He said, "Let the boy go on his own. He'll be okay."

Caroline said, "You heard that noise, Jacob. It sounded like someone was screaming."

"It was probably just a movie. You know what horror movies are like these days."

Jacob winked and nodded at his son—*'Go on, sport. Get yourself a snack.'* Joey smiled at him and closed the door. His mother's yapping barely escaped the room.

Rain pattered on the roof and the handrail. The drizzle was intensifying. It was only a matter of time before it would transform into a violent downpour.

Two crumpled dollar bills in hand, he walked down the exterior hallway, staying close to the wall to avoid the rain. He looked at the number on the neighboring door: *203*. From the outside, the room looked vacant. He slowed down as he approached the next room. Although the blinds and curtains were closed, light from the room seeped out through the window.

The room number read: *202*.

His family had heard some muffled screams and groans coming from one of the neighboring rooms— and Room 202 appeared to be the only occupied room on the second floor. It was quiet now. He hurried past the door, believing someone would open it and snatch him away if he moved too slow. Room 201 was dark and quiet, too.

He turned the corner. A staircase led downstairs. Two vending machines and an ice machine hugged the wall. One of the vending machines sold snacks, the other sold drinks. The light above the vending machines was out. He squinted to scan the snacks. He couldn't decide between the chips or chocolate. Then he saw something from the periphery of his vision. His eyes widened and he staggered away.

A clown emerged slowly from behind the drink machine. He wore a baggy jumpsuit. The right side was a solid baby blue color. The left side had white and baby blue stripes. A well-worn blue bowler hat sat atop his head. His bald cap was obvious because it also covered his ears, so he looked like he was earless. A red smile was painted over his lips and blue paint was applied to his eyes.

The rest of his face and neck were painted white, like his gloves. His clothes were loose, one size too large, but he looked slim. He didn't appear menacing. He didn't modify his body like the other clowns. Inspired by John Wayne Gacy, he designed his costume to appear 'normal.'

"Hello, boy-o," the clown said in a soft, goofy voice.

"He–Hey," Joey stuttered, afraid but curious. He walked backwards until the rain hit his wispy brown hair and the nape of his neck. He stepped forward to dodge the rain. He stuttered, "Wh–Who are you?"

"Me?" the clown said. He took a step towards the boy. He said, "Why, I'm *Blue*. Blue the Clown. Do you know why they call me Blue?"

"Because... Because your costume is blue?"

"Oh! Good guess! Good guess!"

Blue clapped and giggled with excitement. Joey smiled, the anxious sort of smile introverts wore when meeting new people. His shoulders loosened. He was baffled by the clown's presence at the motel—he didn't see a circus in the area—but he wasn't terrified of him. Then Blue frowned and lowered his head, as if in shame.

He said, "But that's not the right answer. It's

because I'm blue, you see? Not like the color." He pointed at his frown and said, "Like this. I'm a sad, sad clown."

"Why? What's the matter?"

"Woe is me, woe is me. I have no friends. I'm a lonely, lonely clown."

"Oh... Um..."

Blue smiled and asked, "Will *you* be my friend?"

"I don't know. My mom said–"

"What's your name, boy-o?" Blue interrupted.

The boy rubbed the nape of his neck and said, "Joey..."

"Well, Joey, let me guess what you were going to say. Hmm... *Hmm...* 'My mom said I shouldn't talk to strangers.' Mommy doesn't want her 'baby' to get into any trouble. Is that right?"

Joey cracked another slight, anxious smile. He was embarrassed of his mother's overprotective personality. He didn't want to be seen as a baby. He nodded at the clown.

In a jolly tone, Blue said, "Well, let's go talk to her. I'm not a stranger if I meet your mom and dad, am I?"

"I don't think my mom would like that. She's... She's super strict."

"Don't worry. I'll tell her one of my favorite jokes."

"No, you can't–"

Blue turned the corner and headed down the exterior hallway. He said, "Now, which room was it? 202? 203? No, 204! Yes, yes! Two! Zero! Four!"

Joey furrowed his brow and whispered, "How did you... How did he know that?"

Awed, he unfurled his fists, dropping the dollars in a puddle near the railing. He followed the clown's lead, dragging his feet back to the room.

———

Tap, tap, tap.

Someone knocked on the door.

"That's him," Caroline said as she hopped off the bed.

Sitting at the foot of the bed, television remote in hand, Jacob said, "See? Told you he'd be fine. He's a big kid, Caroline. Gotta let them live."

As she opened the door, Caroline said, "What took you so–" She gasped and slapped her hand over her chest. Blue stood in front of her. Wide-eyed, Caroline asked, "Who are you?"

Blue said, "Why, I'm *Blue*. Blue the Clown. Do you want to hear a joke?"

"What are you... Where's..."

Caroline stopped as she spotted Joey behind the clown. She looked at Blue, then at her son. Her bulging eyes and gaping mouth said something along the lines of: *what the hell is going on?*

"Who's at the door, honey?" Jacob asked as he changed the channel to the local news.

The anchorwoman reported on a massacre at a

trailer park. The death toll was at twelve, but it continued rising throughout the night as more bodies were discovered and victims succumbed to their injuries at local hospitals.

Jacob whispered, "Jesus Christ."

Caroline beckoned to her son and said, "Joey, get in here. Right now, young man."

Blue said, "What has two legs, two arms..."

"Come here, Joey. *Now,*" Caroline said, ignoring the clown.

Joey said, "I can't, Mom. He's blocking me."

"Don't talk back to me."

"I know, but I really can't..."

Blue continued, "A fat stomach, two sagging breasts, a big *fucking* mouth, but no eyes?"

Caroline cocked her head to the side, narrowed her eyes, and placed her fingertips on her chest—*my God!* The storm worsened. The faint sound of rumbling thunder reached them from somewhere afar.

Blue leaned closer to Caroline and said, "*You.*"

He delivered a flat, unemotional laugh—*he-he-he, ha-ha-ha, ho-ho-ho.* They gazed into each other's eyes. Caroline was shocked, Blue was unemotional. A flash of lightning lit up the motel. The clown jabbed his index and middle fingers at Caroline's eyes. She covered her face with her hands and fell to the floor, screaming in pain. Blue mounted her waist. He took a spoon out of his pocket.

As the thunder rumbled, Blue shouted, "Let's scoop those eyes out!"

Jacob jumped up to his feet and yelled, "What the hell is going on?! Get off her! Get the hell–"

"Dad!" Joey cried.

In the exterior hallway, Gaggles grabbed Joey. He threw him over his shoulder and carried him into the room. The boy flailed on him, but he couldn't escape. Gaggles sidestepped around Blue, then threw Joey on the rough mattress. The wind was knocked out of the kid. He rolled around on the bed, wheezing and whining.

Jacob rushed towards Gaggles. He was unnerved by his wife's screaming, but their son was his priority. He hesitated upon catching a glimpse of the clown's face. The curved nails pierced over his eyebrows shocked him. Gaggles shoved him with so much force that he launched him off his feet. Jacob's lightweight figure helped. He landed on his ass and slid until he crashed into the dresser behind him.

He looked over at the entrance. Pumpkin had entered the room. He closed and locked the door behind him. Caroline thrashed about on the floor, slapping Blue and kicking Pumpkin's legs. Joey crossed his arms over his stomach and continued rolling from side to side while calling out to his mother. Jacob was a frail man—feeble, non-confrontational. He couldn't defeat three strangers. He needed help, and he knew that very well.

Jacob scrambled towards the bathroom. *Jump out the window, run to the front office, tell the clerk,* he thought. He threw himself against the bathroom window over the toilet, expecting it to shatter as if he were in an action movie. Instead, the glass rattled. He fell on the toilet, then he slipped into the bathtub. His bathrobe came undone, revealing his bush of pubic hair and his flaccid penis. Before he could get up, Gaggles kicked him back into the tub.

"No! No! Please don't hurt us!" Jacob pleaded. "Please! Take my wallet! Take everything!"

Gaggles tore the shower curtain off the rod above them. He threw the plastic curtain over Jacob's head and tightened the edge around his neck. Jacob slid in the bathtub, blinded by the curtain. Although it was difficult, he could still breathe under the plastic. But he panicked, causing him to pant, which led to a bout of lightheadedness.

"Pl–Pl–Pl…"

'Please!'—he couldn't croak out that one simple word.

Gaggles loosened his grip on the curtain, allowing Jacob to draw a deep breath. Then he tightened it around his face and neck again. The plastic fluttered as Jacob wheezed. His skin *squeaked* against the bathtub. He slapped his palm against the wall and pushed himself up, but he couldn't overpower the clown.

Gaggles smashed the side of Jacob's head against the wall. Jacob's arms fell limp. He was unconscious, but the plastic kept rustling as he snored. Gaggles slammed the other side of Jacob's head against the edge of the tub, then he swung his head back against the wall. *Thud! Thud! Thud!* The sound of the beating boomed over the other noise in the motel room—the sensationalized news, the crying, the laughter.

Pumpkin grabbed Caroline's arms and pinned them to the floor. Through her blurred vision, Caroline saw the two clowns above her. They laughed at her, their saliva spraying on her face. She thought: *a nightmare? Or hell?* She knew the stinging pain in her eyes was only a preview of what was to come. She could only think about her precious son.

She yelled, "Run! Joey, baby, *run!* Oh my God!"

From the bed, Joey cried, "Mommy!"

"Baby! Please!"

Blue thrust the spoon at her right eye. It slipped into her eye socket between her eyeball and the side of her nose. She shrieked until her vocal cords tore— until her voice was raspy and shaky. Blue wiggled the spoon in her eye socket. The muscles attached to her eye *crunched* as they ripped. The bottom of the spoon slid across the fat padding the walls of the eye socket.

A blot of blood spread across the sclera of her eye, like a drop of ink on a sheet of paper. Eyes wide, her pupils dilated in fear. Her gaze was vacant, as if she were gazing into the afterlife. She felt the spoon slide *under* her eyeball. Blood streamed out and rolled down the side of her face. She heard a *pop* in her right ear, then a loud, endless *buzz*. Her eyeball popped out of her socket.

Blue grabbed it with his fingers while shaking the spoon under it, like a key in an old lock. After a couple of tugs, the optic nerve was severed.

He held the eye up to his and said, "*I* see you. Get it? *'Eye'* see you?"

Caroline screamed through her gritted teeth. The clowns laughed as they threw the eyeball at each other, like kids playing a game of Hot Potato. Then Blue thrust the spoon at her other eye.

Gaggles smashed Jacob's head down against the floor of the bathtub. He pulled him back up, pressing his knee against his back. The shower curtain was drenched in blood and vomit. It barely moved with Jacob's slow, weak breathing. The clown removed the curtain. He smirked as he examined the extent of Jacob's injuries.

His face was swollen, bruised, lacerated, and broken—black and blue, bumpy and bloody. His skull was fractured all around. He suffered from a minor brain hemorrhage. It crippled him with nausea, dizziness, and lethargy, which led him to puke. There were cuts on his scalp, forehead, and nose. Chunky brown vomit was caked on his cheeks. Rivers of blood flowed around the puke.

Jacob was knocked out cold, beaten to the brink of death. Gaggles dragged him back into the other room. Blue had just removed Caroline's other eye. Part of the optic nerve still hung from the eyeball. Caroline convulsed on the floor, gasping for air. She could barely hear the clowns over the incessant buzzing in her ears.

As he turned his attention to the bed, Pumpkin said, "Looks like we still have one more guest to entertain." Hands on his knees, he leaned forward and, in a goofy voice, he asked, "Do you like *clowns,* little boy?"

Face twisted in pain, Joey scooted to the headboard. A pillow fell off the bed as he sat up. He couldn't recognize his father. He couldn't see his face through the blood, the puke, and the bumps. His mother's injuries terrified him, too. She was moaning in pain, gasping for life, but she looked and sounded like a monster to him.

Pumpkin asked, "Aww, what's the matter? You don't like our games?"

Sitting on Joey's mother, Blue pouted and said, "He doesn't like my jokes. That makes me *blue.* Boo-hoo."

"Why are you making my friend sad? Don't you like us, kiddo?" Pumpkin asked.

Shaking all over, tears and mucus cascading across his rosy face, a jet of urine ran down Joey's legs. His mesh shorts and tighty-whities were soaked. The yellow piss rolled off his knee and landed on the bedsheets. His sobbing grew louder. Caroline finally heard him over the incessant buzzing. Blind, she squirmed under Blue. She was debilitated by the pain, so she couldn't knock him off her.

Pumpkin clicked his tongue and shook his head. He said, "Bad boy. Bad, bad boy. You know what I have to do to you now, don't you?"

Joey kept crying.

"Sta... Stay... Stay..." Caroline croaked out.

She wanted to say: *stay away from him, you bastards!* Sprawled on the floor between the dresser and the foot of the bed, Jacob regained consciousness. He saw glimpses of light, but most of his vision was obscured by an unfamiliar darkness. He heard his family's suffering, though. A single tear rolled down his swollen cheek. He was helpless.

Pumpkin placed one knee on the bed. He said, "I have to..." He placed his other knee on the bed. He continued, "Bite. Your. Teensy. Bitsy. *Dick.* Off."

Joey had heard enough vulgar insults from his classmates to know about dicks and pussies. He wiggled to the edge of the bed. Pumpkin crawled over him, laughing maniacally. He grabbed the waistband on the boy's shorts and tugged on his clothing.

Caroline rolled over on her stomach and clawed at the floor, trying to drag herself out from under Blue. Her fingernails cracked from the pressure. Blood oozed out, turning her fingertips red as if she were finger-painting. She couldn't see where she was going, so she relied on her son's screaming.

"No!" Joey cried out. "No! Pl–Please! No, no, no!"

He grabbed his waistband and pulled his shorts up. Pumpkin pulled them down again—one inch, two inches. Joey pulled them up and nearly fell off the bed. Pumpkin tugged on the waistband once more—one inch, two inches, *three inches*. Joey felt a breeze on his crotch.

He yelled, "No! Help! Help me! Mommy, please!"

"Stay away from him! God, don't hurt him!" Caroline yelled.

She cried without producing any tears. She felt like she had abandoned her son because she couldn't see him. She couldn't protect him, couldn't coddle him, couldn't comfort him. *'Everything's going to be okay'*—she couldn't say those words to him because she didn't believe it herself. There was no hope in Room 204.

Pumpkin stopped pulling on Joey's shorts. He shouted, "Just kidding!"

As the clown laughed, Joey raised his shorts up to his belly button. He whimpered as he swiped at his face.

Sniveling, he stuttered, "Don–Don't kill me... Don't kill my–my mom a–and dad..."

"I'm not going to kill them, silly. I'm going to make them immortal. You too. You know what 'immortal' means, don't you?"

"Don't kill me... Please don't kill me..."

Ignoring his pleas, Pumpkin said, "It means to live forever. Forever and ever and *ever!* You know how I'm going to do that? I'm going to... cut your *heads* off. Then I'm going to make you into my little puppets. Puppet heads! You'll go on the road with me every year and make people smile every night!"

"No... No... Mommy..."

In his jolly voice, Pumpkin shouted, "Don't worry! Oh, please don't worry! Mommy's coming with us, too!" He stopped smiling and leaned closer to Joey's face. In a monotone voice, he said, "But I'm starting with you."

"Pl–Please don–"

Pumpkin bit Joey's neck. His sharpened teeth sank into the boy's soft flesh with the utmost ease, as if he had bitten down on a marshmallow. A stream of blood jetted out, spraying on the headboard. Joey's scream was cut short, replaced by groaning and gurgling. Teeth in his neck, Pumpkin shook his head to widen the wound.

Joey's skin made a *shredding* sound, like a thin shirt being torn. His jugular was ruptured. Blood jetted out of his neck, one squirt after another. A column of blood hit the back of Pumpkin's throat, causing him to gag and loosen his grip on Joey's neck. Joey's blood spumed out of Pumpkin's mouth. It frothed on Joey's lips, too.

Standing over Jacob, Gaggles joked, "It ain't cum, you fag. Don't choke on it."

Blue clapped and cheered, "Tear it off! Tear it off! Tear it off!"

"God, no!" Caroline cried. "No! My baby... My baby..."

Jacob sniffled and whispered, "I'm sorry…"

Pumpkin bit down on Joey's neck again. His upper teeth sank into the previous wounds while his lower teeth dug new holes into his neck. He growled as he shook his head again. Joey kicked the headboard. He flung his right arm in every direction, hitting the footboard and the mattress. His eyes were clenched shut while his mouth was wide open. He couldn't scream or whisper or even breathe.

He was scared to die. He had attended his grandmother's funeral, so he knew about death, but he never learned to accept that he would die someday. But, in that motel room, surrounded by killer clowns and depraved violence, he preferred death to pain. He just wanted the suffering to end. For the first time in his young life, with complete sincerity, he thought: *just kill me already.*

Mouth full of flesh, Pumpkin pulled his head back. Jacob's muscles stretched until they tore. His developing Adam's apple was severed, too. A large, gaping hole was left behind, blood as dark as crude oil. There were tints of white and blue in the wound. His hyoid bone was visible as well as cartilage from his Adam's apple.

His body shook, the headboard slamming against the wall. His eyes rolled to the back of his head. Blood bubbled on his mouth. A soft whistle accompanied the moist crackling sound escaping from his wound. He couldn't breathe. Pain flowed through his body. His heart pounded away at his ribcage, his brain throbbed in his skull. His senses were overloaded.

Pumpkin spat the flesh at Caroline's head before exiting the room. Caroline's face hit the floor. She couldn't see a thing, but she knew her son was fatally injured. Her son's pained croaking haunted her. Her physical pain was replaced by emotional agony. Jacob fell unconscious again. His brain was bleeding, and his heart couldn't take the sound of his son's struggle.

Pumpkin returned to the room, axe in hand. He tugged on Joey's hair, causing more blood to squirt out of his neck. Joey's head dangled over the edge of the mattress. The wound widened. Pumpkin held the axe overhead in both hands.

"Welcome to the circus, boy-o," he said.

Thump!

The blade hit Joey's neck, shredding his remaining muscles and breaking his cervical vertebrae. His head was barely attached to his body, dangling from his neck. His jaw locked up. He bit into his tongue.

Pumpkin raised the axe overhead, then he swung at him again. Joey was beheaded with the second swing. His head bounced on the floor, rolling towards the bathroom.

The clowns belly-laughed, overjoyed by their wicked actions. Pumpkin and Gaggles kicked Joey's head back and forth, like two kids with a ball in a schoolyard. Blue cheered for them, clapping and thrusting his fist into the air. The decapitated head hit

Jacob's face, but he didn't awaken. He was alive, but he had slipped into a coma. He was dying in his sleep.

"Joey... Joey... Joey..." Caroline repeated with a hoarse voice.

She was tormented by her son's silence and the clowns' laughter. She thought about her life as a loving wife and mother. Although she never hurt anyone, she blamed herself for the mayhem in that room. She had planned their family vacation. She felt like she forced Jacob and Joey to travel with her. She thought about death. Guilt made it easier for her.

I deserve this, she told herself. *We'll be together again soon. Even though I walk through the valley of the shadow of death...*

Pumpkin stomped on Joey's head to stop it from rolling. The other clowns stopped laughing. He threw the axe at Blue.

With a stern voice, Pumpkin said, "Take her fucking head."

8

LOVE IN THE AIR

"I CAN'T BELIEVE THEY DON'T HAVE ANY PORN," COLTON said as he flipped through the channels. Sitting in his underwear, he continued, "I mean, look at this dump. It looks *exactly* like the type of motel to have porn on TV. At least Cinemax or... or some DVDs or VHSes. Did you check the drawers? Maybe the closet? Actually, don't do that. I saw a movie once where there were snuff movies in some tapes in a shitty motel like this. I don't want to see that shit."

"VHS," Lacey repeated, amused. "This place looks more like... like the type of place where an amateur crew might set up shop to *shoot* porn. You know, the cameraman might stand in that corner there, there might be a guy and a chick here on the bed—maybe two or three guys—then there might be a pile of cocaine on the dresser. Oh, and another girl ODing in the bathtub. She's supposed to be an 'extra,' but she shot up too much smack. God, her parents are going to miss her."

Colton glanced at her with one eyebrow raised. Lacey took the remote from him and changed the channel, smiling with an air of undeserved pride.

Wind rushed through the empty parking lot, whooshing and howling. Gusts of wind and flurries of rain attacked the window, causing the glass to rattle. The rumble of thunder entered their room every few minutes. They heard the other guests in their rooms, but their voices were muffled. The storm masked the sounds of murder.

Colton said, "You... You take things to very, *very* dark places. You know that, right?"

Lacey laughed, then she said, "Oh please, Colton. You were just talking about snuff films."

"I was talking about a *movie* where someone finds 'snuff' films. A *movie*, Lacey. You're talking about dead hookers in bathtubs."

"*Hey,* I didn't say anything about a hooker, let alone multiple hooker-*sss*."

"Well, you made it sound like she was a hooker. I don't think amateur porn crews have groupies, you know? Why else would she be ODing in a bathtub?"

"Okay, okay," Lacey said. "It was *a little* too dark. I'm sorry. I'm just... I guess I'm just anxious, okay? I've been trying to act normal, but... that's it. I'm... I'm bothered."

Colton huffed, then he said, "Anxious? You? Now

that's hard to believe. I've never seen you anxious or nervous before. Bothered? Sure, you're always bothered, but anxious? No, never." Lacey didn't have a smart-aleck response for him. Colton said, "You're serious. Um... You okay?"

Lacey sighed, then she asked, "What do you think about Matt and Susan? About this whole... about... about their marriage?"

"Come on, Lacey. Don't change the subject. What's–"

"I'm not changing the subject."

Colton flung his head back, as if he were physically attacked by her words. He didn't understand her. He wanted to ask something along the lines of: *are you drunk?* But he didn't want to insult her. He didn't even want to tease her. He could see she was serious.

He said, "I'm happy for them."

"Me too. You ever... want to, like... You ever wish you were in their position?"

"You mean... getting married?"

Lacey grimaced and shook her head. She said, "I'm sorry. It's stupid. I drank too much, I got spooked by that stupid RV on the road, I'm tired, I haven't had–"

"Lacey," Colton interrupted.

They gazed into each other's eyes. The side of Lacey's mouth twitched as she tried to force a smile. Tears glazed her eyes. Colton caressed her cheek.

He said, "Listen, I'm... I'm not going to propose to

you here. I'll be honest: I'm not going to propose to you tomorrow night, either."

Lacey *gulped* and nodded. She looked at the ceiling and rubbed her eyes, trying to stop her tears from spilling out. She moved one of her legs off the bed. Before she could stand, Colton grabbed her arm with a gentle grip. They locked eyes again.

He said, "I know I'm not the most romantic guy. I'm not the most, uh... obvious guy out there. But, as cheesy as it sounds, I need you to know something: *I love you, Lacey.* I don't ever want you to feel like I don't love you or I don't care. You're the most important thing in my life. I just need time to... to get things right. I don't want to spoil anything, but I *will* prove my commitment to us. One way or another. I promise."

Tears of sadness turned into tears of joy. Lacey believed every word. She didn't fantasize about a lavish marriage ceremony with all of her friends and family, but she wanted *something* to seal the deal. She was satisfied with Colton's promise. She hugged him, pushing him to the edge of the bed. Colton had to grab the nightstand to stop themselves from falling.

Lacey said, "Thank you. Thank you so much."

Colton smiled and responded, "What? Were you really worried about that? Come on, Lacey, you know I can't get enough of you. I mean, I couldn't imagine going on a trip like this alone. If you weren't here, I'd... I'd miss you. And you know I don't want to miss a thing."

Lacey kissed his ear, then his cheek, then she stopped an inch away from his lips. She leaned back and tilted her head to the side.

She asked, "Did you just quote Aerosmith?"

"What?"

She hummed the chorus to Aerosmith's *I Don't Want to Miss a Thing*. She said, "It's that song from, uh... from Armageddon! Yeah, that's it!"

Colton snickered, then he said, "Shut up and kiss me."

"You totally just quoted a–"

Colton interrupted her with a kiss. He pushed her back onto the bed and rolled onto her. They continued kissing as they disrobed.

In Room 103, Gabe Webb lay in bed and watched TV while chewing on a stick of jerky. He wore a stiff bathrobe. It looked like it hadn't been washed in months, but he didn't mind. His hair was still wet, black locks glistening against the graying hairs. Boredom was written on his tanned, wrinkled face and dim eyes.

He heard the muffled screaming upstairs, too. He assumed the family from the diner—the Marsh family—was arguing up there.

He muttered, "Not so perfect after all, huh? I knew

it as soon as I saw you. You phony, two-faced, holier-than-thou motherfu–"

Someone knocked on his door. A broad smile blossomed on his face and his eyes lit up with excitement. He hurried to the door, like a child excited to see his father after work. He could have looked through the peephole or peeked out the window, but he wasn't worried about his safety. He had a naïve mindset: *nothing bad can happen to me, not here, not there, not anywhere.*

He opened the door and, grinning, he said, "You're late."

"I know, I know. I'm sorry, but... look at me," Monica Hudson responded, laughing.

Monica was a twenty-six-year-old woman. On the job, she was known as *'Spice.'* She wore a tight black dress and high-heeled boots, flaunting her curves and showing plenty of skin. Her curly black hair reached down to her shoulders, sopping wet from the rain. Beads of rain shimmered on her shoulders, collarbones, and thighs. She had only spent a couple of seconds in the rain, but her dress was already soaked.

The storm had intensified into a downpour. Her pimp—a man named 'Devon Haywood'—had dropped her off in the parking lot. Gabe was a trusted, repeat client, so a security check wasn't necessary.

"I'm soaked," Monica said.

"I can see that. Fucking sexy."

Monica rolled her eyes and asked, "Can I come in already? I'm freezing."

Gabe said, "Hold up a second. I'm liking this view." He leaned against the doorway. He pointed at her nipples and said, "You got cherries under that dress or are you just happy to see me?"

"Cherries? Really? Christ... I guess it's better than 'bullets.' Can I come in or not?"

"You didn't answer my question."

"The answer is: *I'm freezing, Gabe!*"

She laughed again as she pushed her way past her John. Gabe grabbed a fistful of her soft ass as she walked past him.

He said, "You're as beautiful as ever, Spice."

"We've been through this before," Monica said. She stopped at the bathroom doorway. She winked at Gabe and said, "Call me Monica."

"Monica... Yeah, I like that," Gabe whispered.

He was enamored with her. He slept with many prostitutes while on the road, a trucker's life was a lonely life, but he cared about Monica the most. By communicating on a first-name basis—no nicknames or fake names—he felt like their relationship was blooming.

In the bathroom, Monica found an unsealed envelope behind the sink faucet. It was filled with six hundred dollars. It was her rate for an overnight stay. Escorts called them 'donations.' She stashed the envelope in her purse, then she took a minute to adjust her makeup. As she applied her lip gloss, she saw some-thing move in the reflection of the cabinet mirror.

She glanced back at the window behind her. She caught a glimpse of a shadow. It looked like someone walking behind the building. She slunk towards the toilet, brow raised in curiosity.

"You know, I was just about to start jacking off," Gabe said, leaning against the bathroom doorway.

Monica hopped and gasped, startled by his voice. She said, "Oh my God, don't sneak up on me like that."

Gabe responded, "Sneaking? Who's sneaking?" He looked at the window, then back at Monica. He asked, "Everything okay?"

"I'm fine. I just... Why do you always stay at this creepy motel? I thought I heard someone screaming out there."

"Just the neighbor beating his wife," Gabe said in a casual, matter-of-fact tone.

Monica huffed and rolled her eyes again. She said, "Don't you ever want to, you know... take me some-where fancy? Why here? Why this dump?"

"It's convenient and cheap. But I'll tell you what: you convince Devon to give me a discount and, next time, I'll meet you in Vegas. How's that sound?"

"Sounds like you want to get blackballed for the rest of your life. You know Devon: *No. Discounts. Period.*"

"Well, then maybe... maybe next time we'll meet as 'friends.' After work, before work..."

Shh—Monica shushed him while placing her index finger on his lips. She liked Gabe and she appreciated his offer, but she couldn't see herself in an intimate relationship with anyone at the moment. She was married to her career. Love would only complicate things for her. She kissed him and untied his bathrobe.

She said, "Come on, let's shower. We have a wild night ahead of us."

"I already showered," Gabe responded.

"So, you *don't* want me to rub you down with my body? With my soapy *tits* and *ass?*"

Gabe sniffed his armpits, then he said, "You know what? I can use another shower."

He took off his bathrobe in one swift move. In his mid-forties, the man had a firm gut, a muscular chest, and thick arms. He was a strong guy.

Gabe grabbed Monica's ass and lifted her from the floor. He carried her to the bathtub. He turned the shower on.

Laughing, Monica yelled, "Wait! Wait! Wait! Let me take my clothes off first!"

9

———

MORE COMPANY?

Let's Get It On by Marvin Gaye played through a Bluetooth speaker on the dresser. Scented candles on the nightstands, the dresser, and the table in front of the window illuminated the room.

Gabe lay in bed, two pillows under his head. He moaned, stretched out, and curled his toes. Ecstasy flowed through him, pleasure in its purest form. Monica sat on her knees at the foot of the bed, bent forward. She caressed Gabe's testicles with one hand and stroked the shaft of his dick with the other. She bobbed her head while slurping on the glans of his dick. She circled it with her tongue while sucking. Pre-ejaculate and saliva dribbled down the shaft. She knew how to treat him.

Tap! Tap! Tap!

Someone knocked on the door. They couldn't hear

it over the music, the storm, and their moaning. *Purple Rain* by Prince started playing through the speaker.

Bang! Bang! Bang!

The door rattled in the frame. It sounded like a cop was trying to knock it down with a battering ram. Gabe's dick *plopped* out of Monica's mouth. They glanced at the door.

Monica smirked and asked, "More company?"

"I didn't call anyone else," Gabe said. "Devon knows I paid for an overnight session, right?"

"Yeah, yeah. We went over it in the car."

"You forget anything?"

"Nope."

Gabe sat up in bed. He held one hand over his upper lip and yelled, "No room service! We're okay! Skip us!"

They stared at the door, then their eyes drifted to the window. They heard the hard rain, but they didn't see anyone walk past their room. The unexpected visitor knocked three times again, but each knock was separated by five seconds of silence.

Tap...

Tap...

Tap...

Gabe hopped off the bed. He put on his jeans without underwear. His keys jingled in his pocket. Monica covered herself with the blanket. She grabbed her cell phone from the bag beside the bed. She tried to send a message to her pimp, but she couldn't get any reception at Motel Ace. The regular Wi-Fi password didn't work, either.

"A fucking dump," she muttered.

As he approached the door, Gabe shouted, "I said: no room service!" He opened the door. He narrowed his eyes and asked, "Who the hell are you?"

A young woman stood in front of him. She was more than a foot shorter than Gabe—four-ten, four-eleven on a good day. She wore a white-and-gray dress with a pink belt and matching pom-pom buttons down the middle, and striped stockings with tears across her thighs and shins. Her curly blonde hair was tied in two long pigtails. The ends of her hair were dip-dyed red, pink, green, and purple. Her bright, zany blue irises were surrounded by her jaundiced sclerae.

Her face was painted as white as a geisha's. The rest of her makeup was conservative—dark lipstick, matching eyeshadow. She wasn't wet.

With a spunky, confident tone, she said, "Let me introduce myself. My name's Puddin'. P-U-D-D-I-N-apostrophe."

"*Puddin'*?" Gabe said, voice laced with doubt. "Um... What do you want?"

"What's it look like, friend? I'm here for the party."

"Who's at the door?" Monica asked. She stretched her neck out while holding the blanket close to her chest. She couldn't see past Gabe. She asked, "Is everything okay?"

Without looking back at her, Gabe smiled amusedly and asked, "Monica, hun, is this a little surprise from Devon? A 'bonus' for a valuable customer?"

"Is *what* a surprise? Who's there?"

"A clown."

"Clown? Hey, Gabe, this isn't funny. Devon didn't send anyone. You know he doesn't do that. Just close the door."

"Can I come in?" Puddin' asked, twirling her foot and clasping her hands behind her back.

Monica yelled, "Gabe, close the door! Don't let her in! Just close it!"

Gabe dismissed Monica's panic. He was taller and stronger than their uninvited guest. He saw innocence in the clown's big blue eyes, too. He was equally aroused and interested in her. *I've never fucked a clown before, I wonder if her pussy honks,* he thought.

Puddin' said, "Okay, mister. How about we make a little bet? I'm a tough, smart girl. You're a tough, smart guy. Can we agree on that?"

"Sure," Gabe said as he crossed one arm over his chest and caressed the stubble on his jaw with his other hand.

"I bet you I can knock you out."

"You joking?"

Puddin' said, "Nope. I'm a clown, not a joker. If I can do it, I get to come inside. If I can't..." She leaned closer to him and, in a sultry voice, she said, "You can do whatever you want to me."

Gabe's mind ran wild with the possibilities. He

didn't pay Monica for a threesome, but he hoped he could convince her to participate. Monica kept yelling at him from the bed—'*Close the door! Gabe! Close the door!*' She wrapped the blanket around her body, like a towel at the beach, then she sat up in bed and reached for her thong on the floor.

She stopped with her fingertips on her underwear. She heard a muffled screech behind the bathroom door.

She said, "Gabe... Gabe, I think someone's trying to get inside."

Gabe didn't hear her. Eyes on Puddin', he said, "We got a deal. Show me what you got, shorty."

"Okie-dokie, big guy."

Puddin' raised her left arm and cocked it back while keeping her other hand hidden behind her. Gabe snorted and covered his mouth, trying to stop himself from laughing. He felt like he was about to fight a kid in elementary school. He considered pushing her down to win the bet, but he didn't want to ruin her costume.

He said, "Okay, let's just get–"

Puddin' swung her right arm forward. She held a stun gun in her hand. The laser sight circled Gabe's belly button because of her unsteady hand. Before Gabe could even see the weapon, she squeezed the trigger. The prongs penetrated his abdomen, sending jolts of electricity through him. The sharp pain left him feeling a lump in his stomach. He felt like his gut was pushed *into* his abdomen. He stiffened up and ground his teeth. Then he fell back and hit the floor.

"Gabe! Oh my God!" Monica yelled.

She stumbled towards the foot of the bed. She stopped upon spotting Puddin' in the doorway. She dashed towards the bathroom, but she slid to a stop as the bathroom door swung open. Gaggles blocked her other exit. He had entered the motel room through the bathroom window.

Monica shouted, "Help! Somebody help us! Oh my God, please!"

She crawled back onto the bed. She assumed she had a better chance fighting Puddin' than Gaggles. Gaggles grabbed her and pulled her back. He lifted her from the floor and swung her against the wall behind him. Her forehead punched a hole into the drywall. She was knocked unconscious. He raised her over his shoulder, then he slammed her against the bed—*an old-fashioned body slam.*

Puddin' strolled into the room, kicking the door shut behind her. She placed her hands on her knees and bent over beside Gabe.

She stuck her tongue out at him, then she said, "Ha-ha, I win."

Gabe shuddered on the floor, paralyzed by the shock. *Bitch*—his lips fluttered, but he couldn't say that word. Puddin' punted his face with her steel-toe boot, knocking him out while chipping two of his upper incisor teeth.

Gabe's eyes flickered open. *Between the Sheets* by the Isley Brothers played through the speaker. It sounded muffled and distorted in his ears. His vision was fuzzy, as if he were looking at life through a CRT TV. He saw the outlines of the bed and the dresser in front of him. The light from the bathroom glowed like a flare in the dark, amplifying the pain from his headache.

He shut his eyes and muttered, "What the fuck? Wha–What the hell? What... What the fuck happened?"

He leaned forward. He heard a chair groaning. He stared down at himself. He was duct-taped to the chair in front of the window. His arms were taped together at the wrist behind the chair while his legs were taped to the chair's legs at his ankles. He noticed his pants were soaked in urine. He pissed himself during the invasion.

"Fuck!" he barked.

"Oh, he's awake!" Puddin' yelled with excitement. "Couldn't hear him whining over this music. How do I turn this off?"

Gaggles responded, "Same way we turn everything off."

"Is that so?"

She approached the dresser. Gabe blinked rapidly to clear his vision. He couldn't believe it. An assortment of tools was spread neatly across the dresser beside the television: a claw hammer, a vise-grip, a slotted screwdriver, a retractable utility knife, a blow-torch, and a cordless power drill with a wide flat wood drill bit.

Gabe whispered, "God... G–God..."

Puddin' smashed the Bluetooth speaker with the hammer. The music stopped. The storm continued roaring outside.

"N–No... No, please, n–no."

Gabe heard a familiar voice. He glanced at the bed. He saw Monica handcuffed to the bedposts, limbs outstretched. Sweat glistened on her nude body. Blood seeped out of a cut on her scalp, dribbling over her brow and plopping on the pillows as she shook her head.

She cried, "Let me go. Please let me go."

"Monica," Gabe said. "Monica, hun, it–it's going to be okay. Hey, baby, look at me. Please look at me."

Monica kept her eyes on the clowns. She heard Gabe's voice, but she didn't listen to him. Back against the bed and arms restrained to the bedposts, she only cared about her own survival.

"Please don't hurt me," she begged. "The–There's money in my purse. Take it. Ta–Take it."

"It's going to be okay," Gabe said, bloodshot eyes filling with tears.

Hmm—the sound seeped past the female clown's lips as she tapped her chin with her index finger and bloated one cheek. She looked over the tools.

"What should I start with?" she asked.

Gaggles said, "The pliers."

"Oh, this thingy?" Puddin' asked as she wagged the vise-grip at him.

"Yeah, that 'thingy.' You know how to use it?"

"I do, I do."

Gabe asked, "What are you going to do? What the fuck is this?!" Puddin' ignored him. She crawled onto the foot of the bed. Gabe shouted, "Get away from her! Don't you fucking touch her!"

He hopped, moving the chair forward an inch. He wiggled his arms and shook his legs, but he couldn't break free from the tape.

Monica said, "No, please. What are you..."

Her eyes widened. Puddin' licked Monica's thigh, revealing her forked tongue—split vertically down the middle. She ran her tongue up to the prostitute's crotch. She gazed into her eyes with a look that said: *what are you going to do about it?* Then she flicked her tongue at her genitals. She licked both sides of her labia. She lapped at her over and over, licking her labia while barely teasing her clitoral hood.

Monica shivered—not out of excitement, but out of pure fear. A croak escaped her mouth. Fields of goosebumps appeared on her arms. The hairs at the back of her neck prickled. She had dealt with all types of sex in her life—every fetish and every position with every gender—but it was always consensual. She was now being molested by a clown.

And she was powerless.

"Get away from her!" Gabe yelled. "You bitch! You cunt!"

Gaggles approached him. He slapped him so hard that his jaw popped and his gums bled. Stunned by the blow, Gabe felt like he was hit with a brick. The clown stood behind him. He gripped Gabe's shoulder and pushed down on him to stop him from jumping.

He leaned close to his ear and said, "Enjoy the show."

"Don–Don't... Don't hurt her," Gabe mumbled.

Puddin' ran her tongue across Monica's shaved crotch and up her stomach. Her forked tongue unintentionally circled Monica's bellybutton. She licked the folds under her breasts as she straddled her waist. The handcuffs *clinked* and *clanked*.

"I think you're going to like this," Puddin' said.

She squeezed Monica's left breast and started licking her nipple. She felt every little bump on her areola. Then she sucked on her nipple.

"Oh my God," Monica whimpered as she looked up at the ceiling.

As she examined her erect nipple, Puddin' said, "Nice and hard. Attagirl."

"Why? God, why are you doing this to me?"

Puddin' closed the vise-grip over Monica's nipple. She twisted the adjustment knob and tightened the jaws over her nipple. *Ow!*—Monica whined. Jolts of pain surged through her chest. A drop of blood dripped out and flowed down her breast.

Monica yelled, "No! No! Please don't! *Please!*"

Puddin' twirled her wrist gently, tugging on Monica's nipple while twisting it every which way. Another drop of blood oozed out, like milk from a lactating mother.

"Ow! *Ow!* No, stop! Please!" the escort shouted.

Puddin' leaned back and pulled on the vise-grip using all of her weight. Monica's nipple tore, along with a piece of her areola. Monica shrieked and trembled under the clown. She only stopped to gasp for air. Puddin' tossed the severed nipple into her mouth. She chewed on it with her mouth wide open, like a llama eating grass. She swiped at her face, smearing Monica's blood on her chin.

With Gaggles snickering behind him, Gabe whispered, "Jesus Christ..."

Puddin' said, "Tastes just like pepperoni." She pouted and said, "Aww, that looks painful. Let Puddin' kiss it and make you feel better."

"S–Stop... Stop... Stop!" Monica screamed.

Puddin' sucked on her nipple again. She squeezed her breast and sucked—squeezed and sucked, *squeezed* and *sucked*—like a kid trying to get the last drop of juice from half an orange. Her taste buds tingled because of the metallic flavor of the blood. She was a nineteen-year-old cannibal. Unbeknownst to her, she had already contracted hepatitis C during one of her feasts.

She sighed with satisfaction after swallowing a

mouthful of Monica's blood. She licked her chest, then she lapped at her jugulars. She kissed Monica's chin, then her cheek, and then her lips. Monica sucked her lips into her mouth and whined. She swung her head to the right to dodge the clown's kiss. Puddin' kissed her cheek again. Monica swung her head to the left, so Puddin' licked the side of her mouth. Half of her tongue slid into her mouth.

Monica wanted to yell: *stop!* But she refused to open her mouth. Her words were muffled. It sounded like she was humming.

Puddin' grabbed her chin and turned her face towards hers. Monica saw the evil in the young woman's eyes. She loved violence, she danced to the beat of war drums, she bathed in her victims' blood. This wasn't about making a statement or robbing a rival pimp or getting revenge for something. This was *fun* for the clowns.

Puddin' kissed her again. Tears slid past Monica's sealed eyelids. *Let it end, let it end, let it end,* she told herself. Puddin' forced her tongue in Monica's mouth. Monica's bottom lip flapped out. Puddin' licked it, nibbled on it, then she chomped on it. Her teeth tore into her lip. Monica's eyes flung open as blood flooded her mouth. The burning pain caused her to scream.

The clown yanked her head back. Monica's lip tore with a moist *crinkling* sound. Rivers of blood streamed down Monica's cheeks and chin. Another *crinkling* sound came from her mouth. A droplet of blood went over her upper lip and flowed into her nostril. Although she knew it would only intensify the pain, Monica couldn't stop herself from shaking her head.

Puddin' felt her grip slipping. She opened her mouth, adjusted her aim, then bit down on her lip again. She shook her head and pulled it back, too. Monica's lips were plump and soft, but human flesh was durable. It took her three minutes of tugging and gnawing to rip it off her face. It wasn't as easy as it was in the movies.

Monica's bottom teeth and gums were exposed, each tooth coated with a layer of blood. The wound was mushy, bordered with jagged teeth marks. She groaned and hyperventilated.

Puddin' giggled as she chewed on the severed lip. She swallowed one mouthful of blood after another. She tried to tear it in half in her mouth so she wouldn't choke on it, but the flesh was too strong. She spat it out. It hit Monica's chest with a *splat,* like a wet slug.

Gabe yelled, "Monica! Fuck! Monica! Oh God!" He tried to jump again, but he couldn't overpower Gaggles. Through his gritted teeth, he said, "You fucking bastards. You sick, nasty cunts. Hurt me! Come on, bitch! Show me what you're made of!"

Puddin' winked at him and said, "Oh, don't worry, mister. You're next."

"Fuck you!"

"Fuck me? Hmm... No, I think we're going to fuck her."

"Fuck... What? No! Let her go! Hurt me! I'm right here!"

The chair moved forward another inch. The tape around his wrists started to tear, but no one noticed it.

Puddin' made her way to the dresser. She examined her collection of tools. Her eyes stopped on the cordless power drill. She crawled back onto the bed with the power tool.

In a panic, Gabe shouted, "No! Oh God! Get away from her! I'm begging you! Goddammit, what the hell do you want from us?!"

Puddin' sat between Monica's legs. She caressed her sweaty thighs with the drill bit. She aimed the cordless drill at Monica's crotch.

She said, "Which hole, which hole... Hmm..."

Gabe yelled at Monica, but she couldn't understand him. She couldn't feel the drill bit, either. The pain had sent her into a fatigued state. She stared at the ceiling and thought about the previous night. She had met one of her regulars at a hotel. They had sex twice, then her John went home to his family. She had never thought of it before, but at that moment, she wished she had a family of her own—a husband, a son, a daughter. She wished she had accepted Gabe's countless advances.

She turned her head and looked at him. She saw him screaming, jugulars bulging from his neck. She mouthed: *I love you.*

Puddin' forced the drill bit into Monica's anus.

Monica gasped and tilted her head back, jutting her chin up. The drill bit scraped her rectal walls. She felt an unusual sense of pressure in her rectum, as if she were about to defecate and her feces was crawling *up* her ass at the same time. She had had anal sex before, but it was never like that. The drill bit was wider, harder, *sharper.*

Puddin' forced it deeper into her ass—about four inches deep. She pulled it out an inch, then thrust it back in. She fucked her with a cordless power drill.

Tears and mucus covered Gabe's face. He was electrocuted, kicked, and slapped, but the physical pain was dwarfed by his emotional suffering. He was devastated.

Monica held her breath, clenched her fists, and curled her toes. Blood seeped past the drill bit and oozed out of her anus. She inadvertently clenched her anal sphincter. It made it harder for Puddin' to rape her with the tool, but it also worsened her pain. She felt like her pelvic cavity was flooded with acid. The burning pain was unbearable.

"Please... don't... kill... me," she croaked out between gasps.

Puddin' said, "Feels good, huh? Well, it's only going to get better. Should I squeeze this little trigger here? Huh? Should I do it?"

"Pl–Please... Pl–Please..."

"Please? Wow, you're really begging for it, aren't ya?"

Gabe said, "She's innocent. *We're* innocent. We–We didn't do a thing to you. Please listen to me. Come on, damn it!"

Ignoring him, Puddin' said, "Well, here goes nothing."

"No!"

Puddin' squeezed the trigger. The drill bit emitted a *buzzing* sound as it spun in Monica's rectum. Blood shot out of her anus in uncontrollable bursts, like explosive diarrhea. She felt something shoot up her large intestine, too. *Anxiety? Feces? Blood? Flesh?* Then she felt like her organs were twisting over themselves, tied into knots like shoelaces. The vibrations from the drill bit reverberated across her body.

Monica raised her head from the pillow and looked down at her crotch. The air was vacuumed from her lungs. Her eyes were wide with shock and awe.

Puddin' felt some resistance as she thrust the drill bit in and out of her. Blood splattered on her face. Some landed on the walls and curtains. A streak of Monica's blood hit Gabe's chest. He stared down at himself, then at his beloved escort. Like Monica, he couldn't scream anymore, either. *What else was there to say?*

Monica fell unconscious. A stream of urine jetted out of her urethra, spraying onto the female clown. The urine was dark, as if it were blended with blood. Her body continued to twitch.

Puddin' laughed and shouted, "Look, *look!* She's squirting! I told ya it felt good!"

She released the trigger and pulled the drill bit out of Monica's ass. The drill bit was drenched in blood. Strands of Monica's severed rectal wall were tangled around the drill bit. The rest of her mutilated rectum, as well as more blood and some feces, followed the drill out of Monica's anus—*a shitty, bloody prolapse.*

"Wow," Puddin' said. She looked at Gaggles with a devious twinkle in her eye. She asked, "Should I eat it?"

Gaggles was an awful person, he slaughtered people for fun, but even he had his limits. He didn't mind tasting blood to strike fear into his victims' hearts, but he wasn't a cannibal.

He said, "I have to get ready for the next room. Can you finish up on your own?"

"What's the matter, big guy? Can't handle a little raw meat?" Puddin' asked in a condescending tone.

"Can you finish up on your own or not?"

Puddin' rolled her eyes and said, "Yeah, yeah. I'll finish up with the blowtorch. Don't worry, I won't burn the place down." She shrugged and said, "Or maybe I will."

Gaggles looked down at Gabe. The man's face was ashen, whiter than the clowns' face paint. He smiled at him, amused by his shell-shocked state. He exited the room.

Gabe watched as Puddin' sucked Monica's pulpy

prolapsing rectum into her mouth. She suckled on it, like a baby with a pacifier. She moaned with pleasure, then she bit into it. Her mouth overflowed with blood. The metallic tang of the blood aroused her taste buds. It was followed by the bitter taste of her feces and bile.

Gabe slowly moved his arms up and down so as not to alarm the clown. He sliced into the tape around his wrists with splinters from the chair's backrest. He didn't think about saving himself or calling the cops. Thoughts of vengeance dominated his mind.

10

———

DO NOT DISTURB

COLTON AND LACEY FUCKED IN THE MISSIONARY position, fingers interlocked above their heads. Lacey's soaked pussy emitted a *squishy* sound with each thrust. The headboard slammed against the wall, following the rhythm of their sex. *Basic Instinct* played on the television. It was the sexiest thing they could find on short notice.

Colton said, "Call me daddy."

Deafened by pleasure, Lacey didn't hear him. She moaned, "What?"

"Call me daddy."

She heard him that time. She furrowed her brow and chuckled, then she moaned again as Colton kissed her neck and thrust into her.

She asked, "Are you joking?"

"No, babe. Call me–"

Someone knocked on the door. Colton slowed his thrusting while Lacey groaned in frustration. Colton held his index finger up to his lips—*shh.*

He whispered, "Maybe they'll go away if we're very, very quiet."

"Yeah, or maybe–"

Colton thrust into her as hard as possible, causing her to unleash another loud moan. He slapped his hand over her mouth and laughed. Lacey slapped his chest.

Muffled by his hand, she said, "You asshole."

The visitor knocked again—*tap, tap, tap.*

Colton smiled and said, "Now they know we're awake. Great job, Lacey."

"Oh, fuck you," Lacey responded.

Colton yelled, "Give us a minute."

There was no response. He hopped off the bed. He put on his underwear, then his jeans. Lacey stayed in bed, but she slipped into her panties and fastened her bra. She covered herself with the blanket.

She frowned and asked, "What's the point of a 'Do Not Disturb' sign if they're going to disturb you anyway?"

"Maybe it's an emergency."

"It's past midnight. We don't know anyone here. No one knows we're here. I mean, what kind of emergency could it be?"

"It better be a serious one," Colton said. As he

approached the door, he muttered, "Let's see who's tonight's cockblocker."

He peeked through the peephole. He leaned back, startled. Brow creased, he stared at the peephole for ten long, contemplative seconds. *I didn't see what I think I saw, did I?*—he thought. He looked through the peephole again.

Pumpkin stood outside of the door. He smiled at the peephole—a big, *toothy* grin. Colton could see his sharp teeth and the blood on his costume. He saw the bloody fire axe in the clown's hand, too.

"There's a clown outside," Colton said.

"Just because he stretched his ears that doesn't mean he's a clown," Lacey said, referencing the front desk clerk.

"No. Lacey, there's a clown outside. A real clown or... I don't know if he's really a clown, but... I mean, there's someone dressed as a clown outside."

"So, you... you're being serious? There's a clown out there?"

Colton nodded. Lacey gave him a deadpan look, then her cheeks inflated and her lips sputtered as she struggled to contain her laughter. But she stopped as soon as the visitor knocked again.

She huffed, then she said, "Come on. What are you doing? You're making me get up just to... what? See that asshole from the front desk? That pervert from the diner? Who is it?"

She approached the door. She stood on her tiptoes

and peeked through the peephole. She let out a short shriek before slapping her hands over her mouth. She looked at her boyfriend with a pair of wide, protruding eyes.

She whispered, "Who the hell is that?"

"Am I supposed to know?"

"No, but... but... who the *hell* is that, Colton?"

"I have no idea," Colton responded. He peeked through the peephole again. He said, "He's just standing out there. It's raining, but he doesn't look wet. Maybe... Maybe he came from another room. Maybe he *is* that trucker from the diner or the clerk from the front desk."

Lacey stumbled through the room, racing to dress herself. She said, "*Or* he's one of those clowns we heard about on the news. Those killer clowns, you know?"

"Killer clowns? *What?* Are you hearing yourself? There's nothing on the news about killer clowns."

"Okay, they didn't say they killed anyone, but they did say they were *trying* to hurt people and some of them were *armed*," Lacey said as she buttoned her jeans. She put on her tank top, then she said, "That clown has an axe. He looks evil. You're saying you want to open the door for him?"

"That's not what I'm saying."

"Then what *are* you saying?"

"I don't know, Lacey. We could be overreacting, right? This could be a–an elaborate prank. We could be on a hidden camera show or something. You could be panicking over nothing."

Lacey said, "There's a strange guy out there... dressed as a clown... covered in blood... and holding an axe. You think I'm panicking over nothing?"

Pumpkin knocked again. Lacey walked backward to the bathroom door. Like the other guests in the motel, she immediately considered the bathroom window as an alternate escape route. Colton put on his t-shirt, socks, and boots. He was scared, too, but he tried to stay calm and cool-headed.

He said, "I'm not going to open the door. I'm just going to talk to him. Okay?"

"Don't," Lacey said.

"We don't have a lot of options," Colton responded. He leaned closer to the door. He shouted, "Hey! Hey, man, what do you want?!"

Pumpkin didn't respond.

Colton yelled, "Whatever you're doing, we're not interested! We're not playing any games here! We don't want to be part of your YouTube video or anything like that! We just want to sleep and leave in the morning! So, um... Please, uh,... Just go away, okay?" No one answered. Colton said, "Hello? Are you still–"

Pumpkin slammed the axe-head against the door three times. The door shook in the doorframe, rattling and groaning. It looked as if it were about to explode off its hinges.

Colton stepped away from the door. Hands close to

her chest, Lacey shuddered and leaned forward against the bathroom doorway. Doubt clouded their minds and fear crippled their confidence. They were cornered.

The *hiss* and *crackle* of a blowtorch echoed through Room 103. Monica's prolapsing rectum was torn to shreds, decorated with teeth marks. Her hands and feet were burned to a crisp. Her pedicured toes—toenails as pink as peaches—melted and fused into her charred flesh. Her fingernails fused into her fingers, too, although some cracked and snapped off due to the intense heat. Lines of dark-red blood outlined the black, flaky skin.

Her left pinky finger—so thin and so short—was severed by the hot flame. Her right thumb had melted into her palm, bone reduced to ash.

Plumes of steam rose from her scorched, scaly face. Her eyeballs had liquified, eye sockets brimming with a gelatinous fluid. Parts of her scalp were burnt off, too, leaving patches of charred skin, boiled blood, and visible skull on her head. Her upper lip had melted, drooping into her cheek. Her teeth survived the attack, dusted with soot. Although it wasn't visible, the heat also boiled her brain.

Her burnt pieces emitted a sulfurous stench as well as an aroma resembling overcooked beef. The vile, unforgettable stench ingrained itself into everything in the room.

Monica survived the mutilation of her ass, the *consumption* of her rectum, and the burning of her extremities. But she passed away during the torching of her face. The burning pain and the brain damage sent her into irreversible shock. Goops of foamy saliva slid down the sides of her face. She welcomed her violent, tragic death with open arms. She had only hoped it would have arrived sooner.

Puddin' stood at the foot of the bed. Monica's blood was smeared on her cheeks and jaw. She held the blowtorch up to her face and flicked her tongue at the flame, acting as if she were about to lick it. She tormented Gabe. Yet, Gabe remained quiet. He rocked back and forth, eyes dim and sunken. The duct tape around his wrists was tearing, but he wasn't ready to make his move.

"I guess our little friend here couldn't handle the heat," Puddin' joked. She turned off the blowtorch as she approached Gabe. She bent forward with her hands on her knees. In a sultry voice, she said, "Hey, big fella. You think you can handle a gal like me?"

Gabe stared vacantly at Monica. He wanted to say: *give me a minute, you bitch, and I'll 'handle' you.* He kept a steady expression on his face.

Puddin' said, "Oh, look at you. Look. At. *You.* You're broken, aren't ya? But your body's fine. Mmm... I can play with you for a long time, can't I?

Much longer than that broken toy, huh? Let's play, big boy."

She sat on Gabe's lap, face-to-face. She hooked her arms around his neck, then she planted a sloppy kiss on his lips. Gabe sucked his quivering lips into his mouth. Everyone bled and everyone's blood tasted the same, but it was different in that room. The blood tasted like Monica's favorite perfume with a hint of iron because he *knew* it came from his lover.

Puddin' ran her forked tongue up and down his cheeks. She tried to slip her tongue into his mouth, but his lips were sealed tight. She sucked on his neck, then she lapped at his right nipple. She nibbled on it while rubbing his other nipple with her fingertips. She wasn't trying to pleasure him. She wanted to lower his defenses while making his nipples hard.

It was easier that way.

Gabe focused on sawing away at the tape around his wrists. *Kill this bitch, kill her friend, kill them all,* he told himself.

His face tightened as Puddin' chomped on his erect nipple. She tilted her head left and right, twisting his nipple in her mouth while looking up at him with smug eyes. Gabe moved his arms faster. *She won't notice what I'm doing because I'm in pain,* he thought. The sound of the tape shredding was faint compared to the clown's snickering and the storm.

Puddin' yanked her head back. She tore his nipple, along with half of his areola, off his chest. Gabe gasped, rosy-cheeked and teary-eyed. Drops of warm blood moved slowly down his gut.

Mmm-mmm-mmm—the sound seeped past the clown's sealed lips, along with some drops of Gabe's blood. As she chewed on his nipple, Puddin' said, "So yummy. You wanna try one?"

"I do," Gabe responded.

"*Oh!* You can talk again! And you want to play! How sweet! Okay, how about... I grab that box cutter over there and I... snip your other nipple off? *Snip, snip, snip.*"

As she giggled, Gabe said, "Why don't I beat the shit out of you instead?"

"Aww, are you still angry about your little girlfriend over there? I already drilled the shit out of her. Maybe I should–"

Gabe hit the side of her head with a powerful hook —*a haymaker*. Her head spun, her left ear buzzed, and her arms loosened around Gabe's neck. Gabe gripped her throat with his left hand to stop her from falling off him. He grunted as he jabbed away at her face. Her nose broke, bloody mucus bubbling out of her nostril. He chipped one of her teeth, launching it to the back of her mouth. It spun down her throat, like a ring down a drain. He hit her with another hook, fracturing her left eye socket.

Puddin' hit the floor between the table and bed. She squirmed while whining in pain. She was dazed, so she couldn't scream.

As he tugged on the tape around his ankles, Gabe muttered, "You stupid bitch... You think you're funny, huh? But you're not laughing now. No... No, you fucking cunt, you won't laugh again once I'm through with you. You bitch... Goddamn you, you bitch! I'm going to kill you! You hear me?! You're dead!" He looked at Monica's corpse. He said, "I'm sorry, baby. It–It's... It's all my fault. I'll get them for this. I promise, I'll make this... I'll make it..."

'I'll make it right.'

Gabe couldn't finish his sentence. Vengeance didn't make things 'right.' It never really fixed anything. It could conjure feelings of relief or success, but it couldn't change the past—couldn't resurrect the dead.

Puddin' struggled to her feet. She crashed into the table, then she fell onto the bed. She was dizzy from the blows to the head. Through her swollen eyelids, she saw double from her left eye. And pain shot through her skull every time she moved her left eye.

"You mo–motherfucker," she mumbled in her regular voice. "How... How dare you?"

She turned her attention to the tools on the dresser. She grabbed the power drill, the claw hammer, and the blowtorch. She heard the *tear* of the duct tape. Her legs were unsteady like a newborn fawn's. Even with a hammer, she knew she couldn't beat Gabe. She stumbled out of the room with some of the supplies.

She ran into the rain. She looked to her left, then to her right. She saw Pumpkin standing in front of the door to Room 101. Back against the wall, Gaggles stood beside the door.

Puddin' marched back to the exterior hallway. As she teetered towards the other clowns, she yelled, "He hit me! That motherfucker hit me! He cut the tape! Get him! *Kill him!*"

Gabe broke free from the chair. Hellbent on killing Puddin', he ran out of the room. He stopped in the exterior hallway. Part of him said: *fight them, kill them all, you can do it.* The other part of him said: *don't be stupid, get back in the room, you can't win.* He took three steps towards them, then he stopped as the clowns looked his way. He saw the bloody fire axe.

"Shit," he muttered.

He ran back into the room as Gaggles ran after him. Gabe secured the deadbolt and the door chain. Gaggles rammed the door with his shoulder. Gabe glanced around and searched for a weapon. *A lamp?* It couldn't hurt a man like Gaggles. *A chair?* He wasn't a lion tamer and, although ferocious, Gaggles wasn't a lion. He saw the remaining tools on the dresser: a screwdriver, a vise-grip, and a utility knife.

He slid the screwdriver into the back of his waistband. He couldn't use the vise-grip against the clowns in a brawl, so he left it behind. He grabbed the utility knife. A three-inch blade shot out of the handle.

The door shook again as Gaggles tackled it. The motel was old. The locks were weak. It was only a matter of time before the door would break down.

Gabe glanced back at the bathroom. He whispered, "Run... I can make a run for it... Yeah, I can, um..." He looked at Monica's corpse. He felt his throat closing. A tear in his eye, he said, "Monica... Baby... I don't know what to do. I'm sorry. I'm so sorry."

As he secured the door chain, Colton said, "Call the cops."

From the bathroom, Lacey asked, "What? Why? What's going on?"

"You were right. They're not playing games. They're going to kill us."

"*What?* Are you serious? Don't play games with me, Colton. Not like this. What are–"

"I heard a girl out there! She was yelling something like 'kill him' or 'kill them!' And there was another guy, another clown, waiting out there! He was... He was waiting for us to open the door. They're going to hurt us, Lacey. We need to call the cops."

"Okay, o–okay," Lacey stuttered. Hands shaking, she dialed 911 on her cell phone. The call couldn't connect. She said, "No signal. There's no signal."

Colton checked the landline on the nightstand. He dialed 911, but there was no dial tone. He punched the numbers in over and over—9-1-1, 9-1-1, 9-1-1.

He slammed the phone on the cradle and shouted, "Fuck!"

The doorknob jiggled. Hushed voices entered the room from the exterior hallway. They spotted a silhouette of a person with pigtails standing on the other side of the window—*Puddin'*. She knocked on the glass.

Colton said, "Find a weapon."

"A weapon?" Lacey repeated. "Oh my God, we can't go out there."

"We need weapons. They're going to–"

"We can't go out there! I'm not going!" Lacey cried.

Colton grabbed her shoulders and shook her gently. He said, "Lacey, we don't have to go out there. They can come in here. They have an axe for fuck's sake. They can smash through the window any second now. We need to defend ourselves when that happens. Find something. You're a... a... a horror junkie. You have to have some sort of idea in that head of yours."

Colton searched the room for a weapon. He grabbed the lamp, but it was too flimsy. He checked under the bed—*nothing*. He opened the closet. The clothes hangers could be used to strangle someone, but it would require a lot of wrestling. He grabbed the clothing iron instead. He held it from its cord. He planned on using it as a makeshift morning star.

Lacey thought about the hundreds of horror movies she had watched throughout her life. She couldn't think of a single way to defend herself. She drew a blank and froze up.

In Room 103, Gabe watched as the door shook. He

listened to the wood creaking and groaning, as if it were crying out in pain.

Gaggles barked, "Open the damn door, cocksucker!"

Gabe looked at his utility knife, then at the door. *What's this little thing going to do against a man with an axe or a blowtorch or a hammer?*—he thought.

As he walked backward, he said, "Monica, honey, I'll... I'll come back for you. I'll make sure your... your family can bury you. I'll take care of everything. I'll be back!"

He ran into the bathroom. He pulled the window up, but it came to a screeching stop after about five inches. He tugged on it, but it wouldn't budge. He thrust his elbow through the window. The broken glass sliced his elbow open from the joint to the center of his forearm. He hit the glass again, widening the wound on his arm.

Adrenaline protected him from the pain. Blood cascaded down the jagged, saw-like glass protruding from the windowsill. A loud *crack* tore through the room. He knew it came from the front door.

He yelled, "Fuck!"

"It's a joke, it's a joke, it's a joke," Lacey repeated. "It has to be."

She screamed as the axe hit the door. Splinters of wood flew towards her. The axe was pulled out. A slit of light from the exterior hallway entered the room through the hole. Pumpkin swung the axe at it again. More chips and splinters spiraled in every direction.

"Oh my God!" Lacey shouted. "Help! Help!"

With the third swing, a chunk of the door fell, crumbling like bread. The peephole was gone. Pumpkin laughed as he looked through the hole. The truth hit them: *killer clowns are actually attacking us.* The window rattled and the glass cracked. Puddin' had struck it with the hammer, but she was too weak to break it with one swing.

A steel trash can burst through the bathroom window, causing Lacey to shriek again. The trash can ricocheted off the sink, then bounced on the floor. Trash littered the bathroom: oyster pails, pizza boxes, a used condom, a dirty diaper, old newspapers, and outdated advertisement pamphlets.

"They're coming through the back!" Lacey cried.

Colton pulled her away from the door. He spun the clothes iron, ready to whip any intruders. He winced as Pumpkin chopped the door again. The window cracked with another *clink*.

"We're surrounded," he whispered with defeat in his voice.

"Through here!"

Colton and Lacey gazed into the bathroom. They recognized the booming voice. They just couldn't believe it.

Gabe poked his head into the bathroom through

the broken window. He beckoned to them and shouted, "Hurry! They're coming!"

They didn't have time to argue. He was bloody, and most of the blood belonged to him. He wasn't dressed like a clown, either, so they trusted him. They rushed into the bathroom, garbage crinkling and glass crackling under their shoes. Colton helped Lacey climb onto the toilet.

As Gabe helped her through the window, Lacey asked, "What the hell is happening?"

"I don't know," Gabe responded. "They... They killed my girl. They tried to kill me. These psychos are everywhere."

"Oh God. This can't be happening. No fucking way!"

"It's happening and you need to accept that. And you need to stop your screaming. Hunt or be hunted, girl."

Lacey dug her fingers into her hair and mumbled incoherently. Colton hissed as he climbed through the window. He had sliced his palm on the glass. He found himself behind the motel. A brick partition separated the motel from Hassan's Market and the desert. There were several steel trash cans and one dumpster in the alley.

"We have to hide," he said. "We can... We can split up. Each one of us in a different trash can."

As he jogged away, Gabe said, "No, no, no. Don't let them corner you. Run."

"Run? Where?"

"Just run, boy!"

Colton and Lacey watched as Gabe ran off in the rain. The door in their room broke open. They saw another clown climbing out the bathroom window in Room 103. They couldn't hide. Colton grabbed Lacey's hand and pulled her away. They followed Gabe's lead.

11

RUN

Bare feet splashing in the puddles, Gabe ran to the front office's back door. To his utter surprise, the door was open. He ran inside, but he stopped after a few steps. His face turned to stone. Colton inadvertently bumped into him, and Lacey crashed into Colton. Lacey gasped while Colton grimaced.

The center of the floor was stained with smears of dried blood—*Malik's blood*. A pungent metallic stench lingered in the room. Death stained the office with an aura of tragedy. They felt it in the air, as if Malik's tormented soul were still floating in the room. But the corpse was gone.

"What the hell happened here?" Lacey asked. "We were... Oh my God, we were just here. They killed..."

Her voice cracked and her lips shook. Fresh tears dripped from her eyes with each blink. She leaned against the wall and retched. Colton rubbed her back and whispered words of comfort into her ear—'Everything's going to be okay. Don't worry. We're safe.'

Gabe said, "Lock the door." They ignored him. Gabe yelled, "Lock the damn door! Now!"

Colton glared at him. He wanted to argue with him, but he knew he was right. He slammed the door and turned the lock. The door was stronger than the motel room doors.

He said, "Lacey, we're safe here. Look at the door. It's heavy. It–It's sturdy. And, look—*listen*—there are *three* of us now. It's fair, it's even. We just... We have to call the cops."

Standing near the desk in the corner, Gabe held the landline phone up to his ear and said, "It ain't happening. The line's out here, too."

"Yeah? Well, where's your phone? We heard you using it at the diner."

"My phone... I left it."

"You *left* it? Are you serious?"

Gabe jabbed his index finger at Colton and said, "Listen, buddy, you don't know what I just went through. I had to watch... They put a power drill in... That clown ate her..." He couldn't finish a single sentence regarding Monica's torture. He said, "Look at my chest. That *bitch* bit my nipple off. Another asshole was ramming my door. You think I had time to grab my phone? To even think about it?"

Colton hated the trucker's guts because of his phone call at the diner. But he now saw raw, unadulterated pain in the man's eyes. He saw human emotion. Something awful happened in Room 103, and he didn't want to know about it.

He asked, "What do we do now? Huh? Can we... Can we block the doors and wait until the cops come?"

"Why would the cops come if no one called 'em?"

"Someone must have called. There were other guests."

"Those other guests are probably dead already. I didn't see anyone out there. And I swear we heard screaming in our room. I thought they were arguing up there, but... it was those damn clowns. They killed 'em. I know it."

As she staggered towards them, Lacey said, "They... They killed the boy? The boy and his family?"

Colton hugged her and said, "Don't listen to him. They're probably locked in their room, waiting for the cops. We didn't hear anyone screaming."

"We didn't? But... maybe... maybe we did. Oh God, maybe we heard them die and we didn't even know it. We could have helped them. That boy... That poor boy. And those girls. What about those girls from the market? They were so young."

"Lacey, I need you to stay calm. Okay? Don't think about them. We need to think about ourselves."

Gabe said, "He's right. You need to keep your mouth shut and you need to start thinking like a fighter. Those people out there, they're going to kill us."

Lacey stuttered, "Wha–What if we talk–"

"*No.* No, you can't talk them out of this. They're dressed as clowns, but they ain't here to give us a show. They're here to kill. This is fun to them. If you give them the upper hand, if you fall for one of their tricks, they'll stab you in the back. Then they'll kill you one by one. And one of you will be the unlucky bastard who has to watch the other die."

Lacey lowered her head and whimpered. She clenched her fists and dug her fingernails into her palms, hoping the pain would wake her from this nightmare. But she wasn't sleeping. Killer clowns were hunting her and her boyfriend. Murder—*torture*—had occurred at the motel. Innocent people had died in the neighboring rooms. And she felt helpless.

The doorknob jiggled.

"They're in the office!" Gaggles barked from the other side of the door. "The office!"

Colton said, "Shit, shit, shit. What do we do?"

"We have to run," Gabe said.

"You have to be kidding."

"I'm not. We can't let them trap us. Not in here."

Gabe ran through the opposite doorway. He crashed into the front desk. Colton and Lacey followed him.

Lacey asked, "Where's the kid? The clerk? Is that... Oh my God, was that *his* blood back there?"

Colton said, "No, maybe... maybe he went to get help."

Gabe stumbled to the window to the left. He spotted Pumpkin and Puddin' exiting Room 101. Puddin' appeared to be carrying a large weapon. It looked like a rifle from afar. Gaggles' booming voice echoed through the parking lot again. Pumpkin and Puddin' glanced at the front office. They finally heard their accomplice.

"They know we're here," Gabe said. "They're coming. We have to run."

"Where?" Lacey asked.

As he ran out the front door, Gabe yelled, "Run!"

"Where?!" Lacey cried out. She ran to the door and yelled, "Where are you going?! Don't leave us! Please... Please don't leave us."

Colton saw Pumpkin and Puddin' jogging towards them. He grabbed Lacey's arm and dragged her out of the office. She slipped and slid behind him, struggling to keep up.

"The diner!" Colton yelled over the roaring rain.

Lacey remembered Todd's words—*'anytime until two o'clock in the morning.'* She couldn't remember the time. She could barely see the diner through the rain, too. But she figured it was their best bet. She heard the door in the office break open with a loud *snapping* sound. She regained her balance and sprinted beside Colton.

Gabe ran out in front of them, then he took a sharp left into the parking lot, like a wide receiver running a curl route. To Colton and Lacey, he looked like he was abandoning them. He took his keys out of his pocket and ran to his semi-truck, but he skidded to a stop before he could reach the driver's door, scraping his soles in the process. The tires were popped, punctured with knives and nails.

He jogged to the wagon nearby. It was owned by the Marsh family. The tires were flat. A kitchen knife stuck out of the left rear tire. The door was open, and the wagon was hot-wired to turn off the alarm. All of the vehicles in the parking lot were vandalized. There was no way out. They were trapped at Motel Ace.

Gabe's eyes widened as Puddin' walked towards him. He dashed to the diner. Puddin' aimed a crossbow at him. She shot a bolt at him. It whizzed past him and shattered the wagon's taillight. He ducked and nearly fell over, moving on his hands and feet—knuckle-walking, or perhaps knuckle-*running*, like a gorilla.

Puddin' yelled, "You can't get away from me." She balanced the crossbow on her knee and reloaded it. She still saw double from her left eye. She muttered, "You're lucky you fucked my eye earlier. I would have shot your balls off."

She ran after them. Pumpkin stood with the axe against his shoulder, laughing as he watched them. Their game of bait-and-switch—*trick*-and-*murder*—had turned into a real hunt. He enjoyed watching his prey scramble through the parking lot.

As they approached the diner, Lacey yelled, "Help! Help! Help us!" They could see Elena cleaning the tables, but the waitress didn't hear them. Lacey shouted, "Please! Help!"

Puddin' shot at them. The bolt hit the back of Colton's right leg, mutilating his hamstring. He fell to the pavement chest-first. He cracked a rib and scraped his palms. The puddles splashed as his leg shook. Blood soaked his pants leg and blended with the rainwater. Feathers of blood billowed out in the puddles, barely visible in the dark of the night.

"Fuck!" Colton shouted. "Goddammit! Ahh, *fuck!*"

"What happened?! What the hell happened?!" Lacey screamed. She became woozy after spotting the bolt in Colton's leg. She hooked her arms under his armpits and heaved. Holding her breath, she said, "You... have to... get up. Please, baby... we have to... move. Please... Oh my God... please move. I don't want to die... I don't... want to die."

Puddin' smirked and said, "At least I got one of 'em."

Gabe saw Lacey struggling to help her boyfriend. *Every man for himself,* he thought. An image of Monica's burnt face flashed in his mind. Then he saw Monica— nude, burnt to a crisp, prolapsing anus hanging between her legs—trying to help Colton. He blinked, then he saw Lacey and Colton again. He knew he would be haunted by guilt if he didn't help them.

"Goddammit," he muttered.

He ran back to them. He threw one of Colton's arms over his shoulder and grabbed his hip. Lacey hooked his other arm over her shoulders. They lifted him from the ground. Colton hopped on one foot, trying his best to keep up with them. A tingly, itchy sensation surrounded the deep wound. His foot felt heavier. Blood soaked his sock and flooded his boot.

Their hearts raced and their lungs burned. The rain was cold, but their bodies were hot. The sounds of splashing puddles, pattering rain, and wicked laughter surrounded them. They felt their hunters closing in, aiming at the targets on their backs, but they didn't look back. They focused on the finish line—*Gold Diner 80*.

12

REGROUP

THE DOOR CHIME RANG. *YOU SEND ME* BY SAM COOKE escaped the diner through the open door. Colton fell to the floor, pulling Lacey down with him. Blood and rainwater accumulated into a puddle underneath them. Gabe turned around and secured the door's floor latch lock. Rain cascaded across the glass, blurring everything. He could only see the blue glow from the vacancy sign at the motel's front office. The clowns had vanished.

"What's going on?" Elena asked as she approached the front desk, a small white towel in her left hand. She chuckled and asked, "And why are you shirtless? Are you..."

She noticed Gabe's missing nipple and the bolt in Colton's leg. The nights were slow at Gold Diner 80, easy and tranquil, especially near closing time. Insomniac guests from Motel Ace and truck drivers visited the diner for late-night meals and company. She once saw a man bleed from his nose because he had poked it too much, but she never saw *that* much blood before.

The employees at the diner hadn't heard a peep from the motel because of the storm. The music didn't help, either.

Lacey yelled, "I need to stop the bleeding! Give me that towel!" Elena hesitated. Lacey shouted, "Give it to me!"

Elena threw it at her. Lacey examined the injury. Through the hole in his jeans, she could see the bolt was buried deep in Colton's hamstring. She grabbed it, unintentionally wiggling it inside of him. He screamed and writhed in pain, then he held his breath and clenched his fists. Blood squirted out of his wound and landed on her arm and shirt.

She said, "I'm sorry. Oh God, I'm sorry." She wrapped the towel around the bolt, then she pressed down on it to slow the bleeding. She said, "Colton, I'm sorry. I don't know what to do. I didn't mean to hurt you. Please, baby, I'm sorry."

"It's... okay," Colton said, his face flushed and veiny.

From the kitchen, Jayden yelled, "Y'all all right over there?! Elena! Elena, you okay?!" He walked out from around the bar. Upon spotting the bloody, traumatized guests, he whispered, "Holy shit."

Gabe said, "We are under attack. You need to call the cops right now."

"And an ambulance," Lacey said. She caressed

Colton's hair and said, "You hear that, baby? We're going to get you an ambulance. You're going to be fine."

Elena asked, "What are you talking about? What's going on over there? Who attacked you?"

Gabe responded, "We don't have time for a goddamn interview. Call the cops. *Now.*"

Elena was skeptical. Their wounds were real, but she couldn't believe they were under attack. It sounded bizarre. She nodded at Jayden—*'call the cops.'* Jayden rushed to the other side of the bar and grabbed the landline phone from beside the cash register. It didn't work. He took his cell phone out of his pocket and started searching for reception.

"Holy shit," he muttered as he caught a glimpse of the guests' wounds. "What the hell did that to 'em?"

The cook wandered back into the kitchen, holding his phone up over his head. He found some signal in a corner beside a stove. He dialed 911. While Jayden called the cops, Gabe grabbed tables from the center of the diner and stools from the bar. He stacked the furniture in front of the entrance.

"Who attacked you?" Elena repeated.

Tears glistening in her eyes, Lacey said, "Clowns."

"Excuse me?"

"Killer. *Clowns.*"

Elena laughed nervously—*ha.* She didn't believe her. She believed they were attacked, it was obvious from their injuries, but she didn't believe they were attacked by clowns. It was absurd—the plot of a B movie. *I've seen this one before, haven't I?*—she thought. She waited for her to change her answer, but Lacey just focused on her boyfriend.

Elena said, "Hey, really, what happened? Did you... Was this some sort of accident?"

"What? You think *I* shot him with a fucking arrow?"

"I'm not saying you shot him on purpose. But, if you were doing something 'kinky' in your room, maybe... I mean..."

"She didn't... shoot me," Colton said, sprawled on the floor on his stomach. "It was... a clown. You don't believe us? Go... Go out there and see for yourself."

Elena watched as Gabe continued stacking the furniture in front of the door, like a kid playing with building blocks. A chair fell from the top and landed in one of the neighboring booths. He quickly replaced it with a stool. She could see that he was frightened. She looked out the window again. The rain made it appear as if the lights at the motel were pulsing and sashaying.

From the pass-through window, hand over the phone's microphone, Jayden yelled, "They want to know who attacked you! Hey, they want–"

"Clowns!" Lacey interrupted, frustrated. "Fucking clowns! Okay?!"

Jayden furrowed his brow and cocked his head back, as if to say: *what are you yelling at me for?* He looked at Elena. They shared the same skepticism.

Elena said, "Just tell 'em that it's a... a group of

young guys. Tell 'em…" She grimaced as she glanced at the bloody towel on Colton's leg. She continued, "Tell 'em that they're armed with a crossbow, they already shot someone in the leg, they, uh… they 'cut' someone's chest, and they're still out there. Somewhere in the motel or the parking lot."

Jayden paced in the kitchen as he relayed the information to the emergency dispatcher.

Lacey glared at the waitress and said, "I said clowns. *Clowns* attacked us. Now the police are going to come and they're not going to know who they're supposed to be looking for. They could… waste time stopping teenagers on their way here because of you. Why would you lie to them? Why won't you believe us?"

"It's not that I don't believe you," Elena responded.

"*You don't.*"

"I do. But even if I didn't believe you, this is for the best."

"What? Why?"

As he adjusted the table at the bottom of his pyramid of furniture, Gabe said, "You're right, girl. Clowns attacked and she doesn't believe you. But she's right, too. If she told 'em that a bunch of killer clowns were attacking us, the cops would have laughed their asses off and tossed us to the bottom of their list. Let's face it, they would have thought it was a prank and we would have been fucked."

Lacey looked down at Colton's trembling leg. The

blood had soaked through the towel, painting her palms red. She understood Elena's logic, but it didn't sit right with her. She wanted the clowns to pay for attacking them—for hurting her boyfriend, for attacking Gabe's escort, for slaughtering an innocent boy and his family.

She wanted vengeance.

From the pass-through window, Jayden said, "Hey. Hey! They said to put pressure on his wound. And, um... Yeah, they said *don't* take the bolt out. Do *not* take the bolt out."

"Thank you," Lacey said in a weak voice.

"Tha–Thanks," Colton stuttered.

I didn't want any of you to take it out anyway, he thought. Gabe stood in front of his barricade and watched the parking lot. Elena watched Lacey and Colton with sorrow in her eyes. *What really happened out there?*–she thought. Lacey tried to comfort Colton. She spoke to him about gambling at a Las Vegas hospital while he recovered.

"It's true. Slots are everywhere in Vegas," she said with an uncertain smile.

The jukebox played *What'd I Say* by Ray Charles.

After a couple of minutes, Jayden exited the kitchen and joined the others. Sopping wet and bloody, clothes torn or missing entirely, the guests looked like they survived an awful car accident.

"What'd they say?" Gabe asked.

Jayden said, "They said that they're on the way."

"Thank God," Lacey said.

Gabe said, "Good, that's good. I'm going–"

"*But,*" Jayden interrupted. He paused as everyone looked at him. He sucked his teeth, then he said, "But they're going to take another twenty or thirty minutes to get here."

"*What?*" Lacey asked in exasperation. "No way. No fucking way. Don't they have any, like, rangers around? You know, like... like highway patrol or something?"

"The, um... The lady... The dispatcher, she said that they're hands are full right now. I guess there are some 'unusual' fires in the city. They think it's arson or something like that. It's sounding a little crazy out there."

"Arson?" Lacey repeated. "What if... they did it?"

"Who?"

"The clowns. What if the clowns have other friends and those friends are starting fires in the city to distract the police?"

Jayden said, "You're talking about a... a clown invasion? You serious?"

He chuckled. He glanced at Elena, then at Gabe, and then down at Colton. They didn't laugh with him. His laughter slowed to a nervous snicker, then he stopped. He heard them talking about clowns, but like Elena, he didn't believe them.

He said, "I guess that could be a possibility, but I have no idea. That's all she told me."

Elena asked, "Can you try calling the front office of the motel? Maybe Malik is working already."

"I don't think anyone's there," Lacey said as she stared at the floor. "The office was... bloody. It looked like someone died in there. It was like a... a slaughterhouse."

"No..."

Gabe said, "It's true. We didn't see a body, but it was a bloodbath in there."

Elena nodded at Jayden and said, "Call Motel Ace."

Jayden ran back into the kitchen. He swung his cell phone around until he found some signal. He called Motel Ace's front office. The line was out of service. He dialed the number again, as if he didn't trust himself the first time. He heard the same tone: *wah, wah, wah.*

He yelled, "Their phone's out!"

"Shit," Elena muttered as she bit her fingernail. She said, "Call Hassan. Ask him if he's heard anything."

Jayden dialed the number for Hassan's Market. The market closed at ten o'clock. He heard the ringback tone. The line wasn't out, but Hassan didn't answer. Jayden called him again—*no answer.* He called him a third time. The ringing was deafening.

Ring!

Ring!

"It is two o'clock in the morning," Hassan answered angrily. "Who is this? And why are you calling me at *two o'clock in the morning?*"

Hassan was a caring, welcoming man, but everyone

had their limits. One call at night was enough to annoy him. Three calls in a row? It made his blood boil, especially because of his wife's failing health.

Jayden said, "Hassan, it's Jayden. I'm so sorry to call you like this, man, but it's an emergency. Look, there's some... Someone got... I'm going to put you on speaker, all right?"

"What are you talking about? Emergency? What's going on?"

Jayden put him on speaker. He said, "Listen, one of these guys is going to tell you about it."

"Tell me about what?"

Jayden held the phone up to the pass-through window. He mouthed: *you tell him about the clowns.* He knew Hassan could turn into one angry bastard, so he didn't want to tell him such an absurd story. Hassan would stop giving him free snacks and alcohol if he thought Jayden was pranking him. Lacey and Colton were too tired to continue telling their account of the events. *No one's going to believe us,* Lacey thought. Gabe searched for a weapon in the diner. He put a fork in his back pocket.

Elena said, "Hassan, it's Elena. Listen, there was a... an 'incident' at Motel Ace. Some of the guests were attacked. Three of them are here with us at Gold and... and they're injured."

"Oh my," Hassan said. "Is it serious? Do you need some supplies? A first aid kit? Bandages?"

"No!" Lacey yelled. "Don't leave the market! They're

still out there, okay? And they're dangerous. Please, stay inside."

"I can't believe this. Who's out there? Who attacked you?"

Killer clowns.

Elena gave Lacey the opportunity to answer honestly. Lacey lowered her head in disappointment. She agreed with them. Without proof, it was an unbelievable story—common in fiction, unheard of in reality.

Elena said, "We don't know. Some young guys with a crossbow and... and we don't know what else they're using, but they're armed. Listen, Hassan, we just wanted to know if you heard anything or saw anything strange tonight."

"I haven't, hun. It's been a normal night for us. Salma fell asleep in front of the TV again. She's looking like an angel..."

"That's good. You keep her safe, okay?"

"I will. Did you call the cops already? I heard your phones were a little 'off' over there."

"We did, but it'll probably help if you call them, too."

Hassan said, "I'll do that. Now, are you *sure* you don't need anything from me? It won't take me more than five minutes to book it over there, you know?"

"We're okay," Elena said. "It's serious, but... it looks like we'll survive. Cops should be here soon. You stay safe, okay?"

"You too. Call me if you need anything, hun."

"I'll talk to you soon. Good night, Hassan."

"Good night."

Jayden ended the call. *Roll Over Beethoven* by Chuck Berry played from the jukebox. The downpour subsided to a drizzle. The rain washed the windows. They could finally see outside. Pumpkin, Gaggles, Blue, and Puddin' were nowhere to be found. Lacey and Elena helped Colton crawl to the bar while Jayden checked on Gabe's barricade.

"Jesus. Guy's overreacting a little, ain't he?" Jayden muttered.

Gabe emerged from the kitchen with a frying pan in one hand and a Class K fire extinguisher in the other. There were three knives in the pan—two chef knives and a pairing knife. He placed the frying pan on the bar and the fire extinguisher on the floor beside Colton. He went over to the jukebox and turned it off. The music faded away.

"What are you doing?" Lacey asked.

Gabe grabbed one of the chef knives and explained, "We have to defend ourselves. To do that, we have to be able to hear 'em coming. We don't know how long it's really going to take the cops to get here. And we don't know if they'll even be prepared for them. Those clowns... They are vicious. I've..." His eyes filled with tears as he thought about Monica. He said, "The things they did to my girl... They're unspeakable. I'm not going to let that happen to me. No way, no how.

I'm going to kill 'em first. I swear, I'm going to tear them to bits..."

Gabe kept muttering about killing the clowns. The same question popped into the survivors' heads: *what happened in his room?*

Jayden said, "Hey man, if a cop sees me with a knife, they're going to shoot. I'm not getting shot for you or you or you or... I love you like a sister, Elena, but I'm not getting shot for you, either. Why don't we just make a run for a car? I mean, I'm parked right there. Like, literally ten steps away from the damn door."

Elena responded, "That's not a bad idea."

"It is," Lacey said. "How do you expect us to get to a car? Colton's leg has a bolt in it."

"Just leave me," Colton said.

"No. Shut up. Don't... Don't be a damn cliché, babe."

"God, Lacey, stop being so stubborn... so scared. The cops are on their way. I'll be fine. You just... just get out of here. Get as far away from here as possible."

"Colton, please stop talking like that. I can't hear this right now."

Speaking over them, Gabe said, "You can make a run for it, but your car isn't going to run very long. They sliced every tire out there. I checked my truck, a wagon, a sedan... These people are dressed like idiots, they talk like dumbasses, but they're smart. Chances are they already popped your tires and siphoned your gas. And they're probably surrounding us, too, waiting for us to make a wrong move. We're not going anywhere. Don't get comfortable, get ready."

Chef knife in hand, Gabe approached the booths and looked out the window. Although partially obscured by the cascading rain on the glass, he could see most of the parking lot now. Lacey reluctantly grabbed the paring knife, then she knelt beside her boyfriend. Jayden grabbed the other chef knife while muttering about his car, infuriated by the possible vandalization. Elena took the frying pan in her shaking hand. She wasn't a fighter, but her survival instincts told her to get ready for a fight for her life.

13

THE CAVALRY

THE *WHOOP* OF THE POLICE SIREN ECHOED THROUGH THE parking lot. A police cruiser stopped in front of Motel Ace. The windshield wipers moved back and forth, *clicking* and *swishing* rhythmically. The emergency lights on the vehicle's roof cycled between red and blue. Officer Hank Henley, a twenty-six-year-old rookie, sat in the driver's seat. He shone the vehicle's spotlight at the front office, then the motel rooms, and then the parking lot.

He said, "Dispatch, I'm 10-23. Motel Ace. Nothing out of the ordinary, but the front office looks vacant. Standby for a possible Code 8."

The female dispatcher responded, "10-4."

Gabe, Jayden, and Elena stood in front of the booths, squinting at the police cruiser. Lacey stayed with Colton at the bar, clasping his right hand between hers. She stretched her neck out, trying to look over the remaining tables and chairs between them and the windows. She was curious, but she didn't want to leave her boyfriend behind.

Elena said, "Jayden, you told them we were at the diner, right?"

"Yeah. I mean... Yeah, I did. I told them about the motel, too, but I said we were waiting here."

"What is he doing?"

Gabe sighed, then he said, "I told you we can't rely on them."

Hank aimed the spotlight at the motel rooms. He turned on his flashlight and put on his peaked cap. He climbed out of the car and walked to the front office, droplets of rain sliding down his navy windbreaker.

"Police!" he announced as he opened the door.

The light was off. Only the beam from his flashlight and the blue glow from the vacancy sign illuminated the room. He caught a whiff of the blood. He drew his firearm and slunk into the office.

He shouted, "Police! Come out with your hands up! *Now!*" He lunged forward and checked behind the reception desk—*empty*. As he approached the door to the back office, he yelled, "Police! Police! Put your hands up and keep 'em there!"

He hugged the wall, opened the door, and aimed his pistol and light into the room from behind cover. The light was now off in the back office, but his flashlight revealed the bloodstains. He saw the back door—the knob barely attached to it—

swinging with the wind. He had only spent two years on the force, but he already recognized the stench of death.

He scanned the room with his flashlight. The blood was old. The victim was missing. The suspect was gone.

He pressed the push-to-talk button on his radio and said, "Dispatch, I have a forced entry at Motel Ace and evidence of a traumatic injury. Possible 10-54. I need a backup unit and a wagon."

The dispatcher said, "10-4. Backup is on the way."

Hank yelled, "Police! Don't move! Police!"

He checked the room for any suspects or victims while trying not to contaminate the crime scene. He checked the lockers—*empty*. He checked under the desk—*nothing*. He approached the busted door. He opened it with his foot. He peeked out into the alley behind the motel. He spotted the broken window leading to Room 101.

He shouted, "Police! If you're–"

His car alarm went off. He turned and aimed his pistol into the office. He could see his flashing emergency lights through the other doorway. Finger on the trigger, he aimed his pistol at every corner as he made his way back to the reception desk. He knew how to use his handgun, he had completed his training like every other cop on the force, but he had never fired it at anyone before.

The strange call, the old blood, the broken window,

the missing clerk, the desolate motel—it all made him antsy.

He exited the building. His car alarm was ringing, but the parking lot was empty. The driver's door was dented, as if someone had struck it with a hammer. He approached his vehicle. He reached for the door handle, then he stopped. He walked to the other side of the vehicle while squinting at the diner. He saw Elena jumping and waving, as if she were doing jumping jacks. Gabe slapped the window. Jayden pointed at him, jabbing his index finger at him repeatedly.

He heard their faint shouts, but he couldn't understand any of their words. He assumed they were in trouble.

Hank pressed the push-to-talk button on his radio and said, "Dispatch, I've got a..."

As he updated his dispatcher, a clown's hand—claws tearing out of the white glove—emerged from under the police cruiser. The clown held a hatchet in his hand. He swung the hatchet up towards the front passenger tire, then he swung it at the officer's left ankle. The blade cut through his boot and severed his Achilles tendon. The clown giggled as he yanked the hatchet out of the cop's ankle.

Hank staggered and screamed. He felt his heel cord slither up his leg. The flashlight fell out of his hand. He turned and aimed his handgun at his vehicle, but he lost his footing. He tumbled to the ground and caught a glimpse of the clown's hand as it retreated under the car. He saw Pumpkin's wide, proud grin. He aimed the pistol at the clown, but he hesitated.

He was injured, but the clown appeared to be retreating. *'Police brutality,' 'excessive use of force,' 'trigger-happy cops'*—he had heard it all on the news before.

On his ass, he scooted back and shouted, "Drop the weapon and get out from under there! Now!" He gritted his teeth and groaned in pain. He called his dispatcher: "10-78. Dispatch, 10-78. Officer down. I have the suspect at gunpoint. He's armed with an axe... a–a... a hatchet. Dressed like a clown."

Pumpkin said, "Oh, howdy officer. Did I nick ya? I'm sorry. I was just trying to give you a hand... by taking a foot." He cackled, then he frowned upon noticing Hank's steady face. He said, "I'm sorry, mister. I was just trying to help. You have a flat, you see? I thought you could use a *toe* truck. Toe, tow... You get it?"

"Shut up! Don't move! Drop the weapon!"

"Aww, officer, your hand's shaking. Poor thing. It's your first time, ain't it? Your first time pointing that thing at a living person, right?"

"Drop the fucking weapon!" Hank ordered as he scooted back another foot.

Pumpkin crawled out from under the car. He said, "Shoot me. No, really, *shoot me*. I can show you my signature trick. I'll catch the bullet between my teeth."

Hank scooted back again and yelled, "I *will* shoot!

Drop the weapon and lace your fingers behind your head!"

"My fingers are 'laced' around this hatchet, officer. Why don't you–"

Hank shot his tire—*a warning shot*. The bullet ricocheted off the rim, then ricocheted off the pavement, spraying debris at them.

Pumpkin smiled and giggled, astonishment on his face. He placed the hatchet on the ground slowly, then he interlocked his fingers behind his head.

He asked, "Do you want to see a trick?"

"Stay quiet and don't move," Hank said. He pressed the push-to-talk button on his radio and said, "Dispatch, I need..."

"I'm going to take your voice."

"Don't move!" Hank barked as Pumpkin raised his interlocked hands an inch above his head.

"And I'm not even going to touch you. Are you ready?"

"Don't fucking move, asshole. You stay there and you wait."

"Count with me. Three... two..."

"Dispatch, get me a..."

"*One.*"

A bloodcurdling shriek reverberated from the diner. Elena's palms were planted on her cheeks, eyes and mouth wide open, frying pan at her feet. She couldn't stop screaming. Fiction became reality in the blink of an eye. Jayden's mouth hung ajar, shock written on his face. Gabe slapped the window while shouting the same word over and over: *fuck, fuck, fuck!* Lacey and Colton knew what had happened, although they didn't see it.

They had tried to warn the officer. They yelled and they pointed, but their efforts were in vain. They saw Pumpkin hiding under the police cruiser. Then they saw Puddin' aiming her crossbow at Hank from behind Colton's car.

Hank sat on the ground, the fletching of the bolt sticking out of the side of his neck. It tore through his muscles and ruptured his esophagus. Blood shot up into his mouth and ran down into his stomach. He closed his eyes and swayed from side to side, spitting out goops of blood. He felt it steaming in his stomach, too, as if he had swallowed a cup of boiling water.

He opened his eyes and tried to gasp for air, but he could only croak. He aimed the pistol at Colton's car and shot at Puddin'. The bullet hit the vehicle's rear bumper. Puddin' hopped away and giggled, amazed. Danger excited her.

"Shoot me again!" she yelled. "Come on, don't be a–"

Hank's arm swung as he shot at her again. The bullet struck the ground between her feet. If it had ricocheted, it would have hit her crotch.

She jumped with excitement and shouted, "Again! Again!"

From the periphery of his vision, Hank saw

Pumpkin jump to his feet, hatchet in hand. He swung his arm to the left and shot at him. The bullet shattered the rear passenger-side window. He shot at him again and hit the door. He squeezed the trigger a third time as his arm fell limp. He shot Pumpkin's oversized shoe, missing his foot by a centimeter.

Pumpkin looked down at the hole on his clown shoe, then he stared at the officer. He watched as the gun fell out of the cop's hand. Hank went down, his back flat against the ground. His hat fell off his head and bounced away, like a tumbleweed in a Western movie. His eyelids fluttered as he gazed into the night sky.

He thought: *I can't breathe. There's something in my throat. I'm dying. I'm dead. Mom. Dad. Mom... What happened? What's happening? What's going to happen?*

The rain washed the blood off his face. The bloody rainwater flowed out and surrounded him. He gently rubbed his neck with his fingertips. A crackling sound came out of his mouth. His nostrils flared as he drew short, panicked breaths. It was barely enough oxygen to keep him conscious. He felt like an astronaut barreling out of control in a science-fiction movie, spinning all over the place.

Pumpkin chuckled, then in his regular voice, he said, "The bastard almost shot me."

Puddin' approached him, crossbow against her shoulder. She said, "He almost shot me, too, ya know?"

"He missed you. He hit me. He almost shot my damn foot off."

"Ahh, stop complaining. Just go over there and take his foot," Puddin' said as she grabbed the officer's pistol. She said, "I'll get rid of this 'thingy.' Guns are no fun. Then I'll get our friend and the supplies. He's going to have fun in that car."

Pumpkin nodded and said, "Yeah, yeah. You do that." He threw the hatchet into the air, then he caught it. He said, "And I'll do this."

Hank's eyes moved down as Pumpkin entered his vision. More croaking and crackling came out of his mouth. He tried to say: *please don't kill me.*

Pumpkin swung the hatchet at Hank's mutilated ankle. The blade cut through his boot, severed shoelaces dangling to the left and right. It cracked his tibia. Blood leaked out of the other wound. Pumpkin chopped his ankle again. His tibia snapped. His foot was bent upward, toes pointing at his head at a 45-degree angle. It was barely attached to his leg by some ligaments.

With the third chop, his foot was cut off. His broken, splintered bone; mutilated ligaments and tendons; and ruptured veins protruded from the bottom of his torn pants.

Hank looked down at himself in shock. His face, red and wet, was covered in veins. He couldn't scream because of the bolt in his neck. He fell unconscious.

In his goofy clown voice, Pumpkin said, "Bravo!

Bravo! Let's give you a hand!" He grabbed Hank's severed foot. He said, "Or, let's give you a foot! Haha*ha!* You get it? *A foot!*"

He started juggling the hatchet and severed foot while skipping around Hank. Bloody rainwater splashed on the incapacitated cop.

Gaggles approached them, a coil of rope slung over his shoulder. He huffed upon spotting the cop's injuries. He dug into the cop's pockets until he found his car keys. He tied one end of the rope around Hank's right ankle. He tugged on the rope and dragged him to the police cruiser. He tied the other end of the rope to the vehicle's spoiler.

Elena cried hysterically as she ran around the diner. She had been working there for two years. She knew every nook and cranny, every entrance and exit, but she now drew a blank. As if it had transformed into a maze, she was lost in the small diner. Lacey stood beside Colton, watching the attack through the window.

"What are they doing to him?" she asked.

In awe, Jayden said. "I think they're going to lynch him."

"That's exactly what they're going to do," Gabe said. "Get your weapons ready. They're coming for us next."

"No! God, no!" Elena shouted. She looked at the ceiling, jumped, and yelled, "Help! Somebody help us! Please! Oh my God, please help!"

Gaggles entered the police cruiser. He made a U-turn, then the tires squealed as he stomped on the gas pedal and turned right. He sped towards the diner, dragging Hank's body behind him with his arms overhead. The skin on Hank's hands was peeled off by the wet pavement. Some of his fingernails snapped off, too.

"What the fuck?!" Jayden yelled as he fell to the floor. He scrambled away from the entrance and yelled, "He's going to crash into us!"

Gabe teetered back. His fight-or-flight response told him to run, but he felt compelled to stand his ground. Lacey crouched and grabbed Colton's arms. She tried to lift him from the floor, but he was too heavy.

Gaggles honked the horn and took a sharp left, drifting to avoid the building. Hank's body rose a foot from the pavement. He collided with the pole of a reserved handicap parking sign, shattering his rib cage. One of his broken ribs punctured a lung. Gaggles dragged him across the parking lot, slamming his body against parked cars, wheel stops, and poles.

Hank entered an endless cycle of pain and unconsciousness—awakening, fainting, awakening, fainting. His bones were crushed to powder inside of his beaten, bloody body. And the guests could only watch in horror.

14

ASSAULT ON GOLD DINER 80

"HE'S COMING," JAYDEN SAID AS HE PICKED HIMSELF UP. He grabbed his chef knife and yelled, "They're coming!"

Pumpkin and Blue approached the diner. Pumpkin wielded his handy fire axe while Blue held a sledge-hammer. Blue danced to the door, leaping and humming like a child at a park. He pulled on the handle. It didn't budge. He furrowed his brow and puckered his lips. He pushed on it—*locked*. He frowned as he stared at Jayden through the glass.

Blue pressed his forehead against the glass and asked, "Don't you want to be my friend? No one wants to be Blue's friend. That makes me... *blue*."

Pumpkin knocked on the window next to the entrance. He locked eyes with Gabe. Gabe didn't recognize them, they didn't hurt him or kill Monica, but he wanted to kill them anyway.

"Fucking clowns," Gabe muttered.

Pumpkin said, "Buddy, pal, friend-o. Please don't make my friend sad. We just want to play. We can show you a trick."

"Fuck off!" Jayden yelled. "Get out of here! The cops are on the way! You hear me?! The cops are coming!"

"The cops? Oh, yippee! You hear that, Blue? More cops, more friends! It's perfect, isn't it?"

Blue said, "But I wanted to play with them."

"Aww, you really like 'em, don't ya?"

Blue nodded, still pouting. The police cruiser drifted behind them. Hank's face hit the edge of a concrete wheel stop with an unnerving thud, causing the guests in the diner to wince. Hank's right cheekbone and his nose were pushed into his skull, forcing his right eyeball to pop out of its socket. He died upon impact.

The clowns looked unruffled, as if they didn't notice the sound. It was all part of their performance.

Pumpkin looked at Gabe with a blank expression and said, "You made my friend sad. Now we're going to make you sad."

He took five steps back while glaring at the trucker. He said nothing for thirty seconds. Lacey knelt beside Colton again, keeping him up to date with the attack. Elena mumbled incoherently behind the bar with her hands over her ears. Then Pumpkin's mouth moved.

"What did he say?" Jayden asked.

"I don't know," Gabe said. "It looks like–"

Blue swung the sledgehammer at the window. It shattered with a crashing sound, dozens of shards exploding into the diner. Fragments of glass dusted Gabe's hair, face, and shoulders. His left eye turned bloodshot while droplets of blood oozed out of his cheeks, like sweat from his pores. Jayden lurched away as a sliver of glass sliced his forearm.

Pumpkin broke the shards attached to the windowsill with a kick. He placed his foot on the windowsill and grabbed the edge of the window with his free hand. Through his blurred vision, Gabe saw an opportunity to fight back—an advantage. He ran towards the booth, glass cracking under his bare feet. Before the clown could step onto the table, he stabbed Pumpkin's left hand with the chef knife.

Pumpkin screamed as he fell off the windowsill, landing on his ass outside. The blade broke his third and fourth metacarpal bones, sending jolts of pain through his arm whenever he moved his middle and ring fingers. Blood flooded his glove. He struggled to his feet and growled at Gabe.

Jayden tumbled to the floor as Blue swung the sledgehammer at a window on the other side of the diner. He covered the back of his head with his hands to protect him from the shards of glass raining down on him.

"Play with me!" Blue yelled.

Jayden scrambled to his feet and shouted, "Elena! Elena, run!"

He lost his footing again and crashed into the juke-box. *Tutti Frutti* by Little Richard started playing. He threw chairs and stools at Blue to keep him out.

Jayden shouted, "The back door!"

Over her sobbing, Elena heard Jayden's voice. Despite the fear in his voice, it sounded like a message from God —a divine intervention. *The back door,* she thought. *This is how I survive.* Lacey heard him, too. She threw Colton's arm over her shoulder and tried to lift him. Colton cried, stools falling like trees next to him—*timber!*

"Go without me," he said.

Tears on her cheeks, Lacey said, "Shut up. Please shut up."

"Lacey, just run. Go to the back door. Don't let them corner you."

"Colton, I'm not going–"

Colton grabbed her chin, gazed into her eyes, and said, "I love you. Go. *Now.*"

Lacey shook her head and babbled. She was torn. Her mind told her to run: *'It's the only way you'll live.'* But her heart told her to stay with Colton: *'You'll never be able to live with yourself if you leave.'* Another window shattered behind her. The clowns' laughter wafted into the diner. She was surrounded by chaos.

Colton kissed her, then he said, "I'll be okay as long as *you're* okay. Run, Lacey."

Lacey said, "I love you, too."

She kissed him—a deep, passionate kiss. For Lacey, the sounds of madness were muted. The screaming, the crying, the laughing, the destruction—it was all gone. Colton was hit with contradicting emotions. He was relieved because he believed Lacey would survive if she left him behind. He was afraid because he didn't want to die alone.

Lacey said, "I'm not leaving you, you dope."

"Lacey, they're going to kill us."

"We die together or we live together. That's the deal, remember?"

"I–I don't... I don't remember signing a deal like that."

"You're an asshole."

They kissed again while laughing and crying.

Pumpkin climbed through the broken window. He swung the axe at Gabe, missing him by a foot but keeping him at bay. He jumped off the booth table and swung the axe downward. The axe head hit the marble floor, sending vibrations across the handle. Gabe thrust the knife at Pumpkin's arm, but Pumpkin dodged him.

The clown swung the axe at Gabe's legs. The blade cut through his jeans and sliced his shin. He fell forward and sliced his palms on the glass on the floor. The chef knife slipped away from him. Pumpkin swung the axe at Gabe's arms, as if he were swinging a putter at a golf course. Gabe pushed himself up to his feet, barely dodging the blade.

He grabbed the handle of the fire axe and pushed Pumpkin against the wall, sliding on his own blood in the process. He didn't feel the pain in his sliced soles, though. Rage assisted his adrenaline, protecting him from the pain.

Through his gritted teeth, he said, "You're all going to die here."

While trying to jerk the handle away from Gabe's grip, speaking in his normal voice, Pumpkin said, "That's supposed to be my line."

The song on the jukebox changed to *I Walk the Line* by Johnny Cash.

Elena slid to a stop in the kitchen, eyes wide in horror. She stuttered, "Ho–How did... did you get in here?"

Puddin' leaned against the wall beside the back door with her crossbow. She held up a keyring and shook it. The keys jingled. They belonged to Malik. The restaurant was operated by the owner of Motel Ace, so the keys opened every door in the lot.

She said, "I got the key, silly. Now stand still and let me show ya a trick."

"No! Please!"

Puddin' shot at Elena as she stumbled away. The bolt entered her upper back and exited through her chest, breaking her clavicle. Elena crashed into a sink.

Through the pass-through window, the others could see her scream.

As they stopped near the end of the bar, Colton said, "They're... They're back there. They're everywhere."

Lacey looked at the kitchen doorway, then at the front of the diner. Gabe had Pumpkin pinned against the wall, and Jayden and Blue wrestled over a stool. Blue was still stuck outside, but he was occupied. Gaggles drifted around the parking lot. The battle in the diner didn't concern him.

"We can leave... through the front," Lacey said as she struggled to carry Colton through the diner. "It's... safer. It... has to be."

She carried Colton back to the center of the bar. Colton tripped over a fallen chair, dragging Lacey down with him.

Upon hearing Elena's scream, Jayden pushed the stool's legs against Blue's chest with all of his might. Blue fell on the sidewalk with the stool on top of him. Jayden didn't care about the guests. He was only concerned about Elena. He jumped and slid over the bar. A bolt whizzed past Elena's head, shaving a lock of hair off her scalp. It entered the dining area through the pass-through window, barely missing Jayden.

Jayden rushed into the kitchen. Laughing, Puddin' shot him with the crossbow. The bolt hit his upper abdomen, puncturing his transverse colon and small bowel. Bile, digestive juices, and blood from his duodenum poured into his abdominal cavity. He fought through the pain and grabbed Elena's waist. He pulled her away from the pass-through window. She apologized to him again and again—*and again*. He collapsed as he pushed her towards the exit.

He said, "R–Run..."

"I'm sorry!" Elena cried out.

Hand on her bloody shoulder, she ran back into the dining area, but she slid to a stop behind the bar. She was caught off guard by the violence.

Pumpkin headbutted Gabe. His forehead was soft because he had injected it with saline, but he hit him with enough force to break his nose. Gabe pressed his body against Pumpkin's, trapping the axe's handle between them. He headbutted the clown. Pumpkin's bottom lip was cut by his sharpened teeth. Gabe headbutted him again before he could recover. He fractured Pumpkin's jaw. One of Pumpkin's teeth nicked Gabe's forehead.

They were equally dazed. Pumpkin spat at Gabe, then he headbutted him. They traded blows, smashing their skulls against each other in a fight for dominance.

Blue climbed through a broken window. He searched for his prey. He couldn't find Jayden in the dining area. He spotted Colton and Lacey at the center of the room.

He ran towards them and yelled, "Play with me!"

"Leave us alone!" Lacey screamed.

Colton pushed her away, then he rolled in the

opposite direction. Blue hit the floor between them with the sledgehammer. A web of cracks spread across the floor.

There Goes My Baby by The Drifters played from the jukebox.

Lacey stabbed Blue's chest with the pairing knife. She wiggled the blade inside of him, mutilating his pectoral muscle and scraping his ribs.

"You stupid bitch!" Blue shouted as he backhanded her.

Colton recognized his voice. He crawled to the bar. Lacey crashed into a table, then she tumbled to the floor. Blue swung the sledgehammer overhead. Before he could swing it down at Lacey, Colton sprayed the fire extinguisher at him. The mist burned Blue's eyes and irritated the stab wound on his chest. He released the sledgehammer and shrieked. The sledgehammer hit the floor and cracked it again.

He lurched to the soda fountain near the jukebox. He knew his way around the diner. He poured soda on his face until he found the lemonade. It stung his eyes. He pressed the small water button on the lemonade valve.

Elena ran to the door. She started dismantling Gabe's barricade. From the kitchen, Puddin' shot at Pumpkin and Gabe. The bolt zoomed past them and ricocheted off a window.

"Shit, almost had ya," she muttered.

Legs wobbling, Pumpkin and Gabe were barely

conscious. Their faces, swollen and lacerated, were covered in blood from their noses to their chins. Their heads pounded, jaws throbbed, teeth ached, gums bled. Gabe could hear Puddin' reloading the crossbow. She was a good shot with that weapon—great, even—so she wouldn't miss again. He had to change his strategy.

He mumbled, "You–You're going to–to pay."

Pumpkin spat a blob of blood at his face. He said, "You can't stop us. You're already dead, just like your whore."

As he took the fork out of his back pocket, Gabe said, "Go to hell."

He stabbed Pumpkin's left eye with the fork. Pumpkin unleashed a booming bellow. The fork's four tines penetrated his dyed eyeball horizontally. The left side of his vision darkened. Syrupy blood oozed out from between his crimson eyelids. The fire axe clanked on the floor. He screamed again as he touched the fork in his eye. Back against the wall, he slid down to his ass.

"Hey, get away from him, motherfucker!" Puddin' yelled.

She aimed the crossbow at Gabe as he sprinted away. Before she could shoot, Jayden hit her with a frying pan, striking the left side of her head from behind. She shot a bolt at the wall as she staggered. Jayden hit her again—*clang!* Her fractured eye socket shattered like glass. She saw double, then triple, then quadruple from her left eye. She knelt and bent over, dizzy and nauseous, then she lay down on her back.

"Whe–Where a–am I?" she said, words slurred together like a drunk's.

Gabe grabbed Lacey's arm and said, "Help the waitress. Get out through the windows. We'll be right behind you."

"Let go! I'm not leaving him!" Lacey lashed out.

"I'll carry him. Get out of here."

"I'm not going to–"

"We'll be right behind you, goddammit!" Gabe interrupted. "Help her and I'll help him! Okay?"

Lacey noticed a change in Gabe's demeanor. He was angry and authoritative, but he didn't sound selfish or crude anymore. She was worried about Elena, too. The waitress struggled to move the furniture away from the door. The windows beside the entrance were broken, but she couldn't think straight. Panic could turn the smartest person into the most irrational thinker.

Lacey said, "Don't you *dare* leave him behind. Take care of him. Okay? *Okay?*"

"I will. We'll be right behind you."

As Gabe helped him up to his good foot, Colton nodded at Lacey and said, "Go."

Lacey hesitated, but she was out of time. She expected the clowns to recover soon. She dashed towards the entrance. She pulled Elena away from the barricade while explaining their escape plan to her—

'Through the window, Elena! We get out through the broken window and we run like hell!'

Hunched over due to the pain emanating from his skewered stomach, Jayden towered over Puddin' with the frying pan overhead. Coated with tears and sweat, his face was twisted in pain and confusion. She shot him, she shot a cop, and she was accused of attacking the motel's guests, but she looked so innocent and young—*so babyish*. She couldn't have been over eighteen years old.

She cried, "Pumpkin! Pumpkin, baby, it hurts! Help me! Pumpkin, please!"

Pumpkin howled as he pulled the fork out of his eye. He thrashed around on the floor, hand over his mutilated eye. Lacey and Elena climbed out through the broken window over one of the booths. The police cruiser drifted at the other end of the parking lot. Gaggles was unaware of the clowns' failure to kill the guests.

From outside, Elena yelled, "Jayden! Jayden, you have to run! Oh my God, please run!"

"You can make it, you can make it," Lacey whispered as she watched Gabe and Colton hobble to the windows.

Staring down at the female clown, Jayden asked, "Why? Why did you... do this? You–You shot me. I–I never hurt you, but you... you shot me. What the hell is wrong with you people?"

Lower lip sticking out, Puddin' said, "Please don't kill me, mister. We were just having fun."

"Fun? This is fun to you?"

"No, not this. But watching you die is."

"Wha–"

Blue swung the sledgehammer at the back of Jayden's head. The back of his skull collapsed inward, pulverizing his brain, which prolapsed from slits behind his ears. His eyes bulged from their sockets. He died instantly. Yet, after hitting the ground, his body continued shaking.

"No!" Elena cried as she lunged forward.

Lacey grabbed her and stopped her from returning to the diner. She told herself that it was for the better. But the truth was: she didn't want the waitress to obstruct Colton's exit.

"Don't look, don't look," she whispered into Elena's ear. She covered her eyes with her hand just as Blue swung the sledgehammer at Jayden's head again. She looked away, too, and she whispered, "Please don't look."

Elena yelled, "Jayden! I'm sorry! I'm so sorry! I'm sorry, God!"

She blamed herself for Jayden's death. She froze in the kitchen when she was confronted by Puddin'. She ran after Jayden had saved her life. And she didn't look back until it was too late.

Colton and Gabe climbed out the window. They

joined the women on the sidewalk in front of the diner —bloodied, exhausted, traumatized.

"We have to go," Gabe said.

"Where?" Lacey asked. "They're everywhere. We can't hide."

"We just... If we can't hide, we have to keep running. We don't have time to argue. Just run! Now!"

They ran into the parking lot. Tears sprinkling from her eyes, Elena took one final glance at the diner. She could see Blue helping Puddin' to her feet, the wall behind them splattered with Jayden's brain. His head had exploded. Squishy nuggets of his brain, slivers of his skull, and pieces of his scalp floated in the blood pooling under him.

His legs continued shaking.

15

CATS AND MICE

THE POLICE CRUISER'S WHEELS SCREECHED AT THE OTHER end of the parking lot while *Surfin' U.S.A.* by The Beach Boys played in the diner. Lacey and Elena sprinted ahead of the men. Leaving a trail of bloody footprints behind him, Gabe helped Colton navigate the parking lot. Colton hopped on his only good foot, moving as quickly as possible to keep up.

"You won't get away!" Pumpkin barked as he crawled onto a booth, voice deep and gravelly.

The survivors heard the police cruiser behind them. Hank's dead body thudded and flapped behind the vehicle, contorted like a rag doll.

"He's coming!" Elena shouted.

Lacey yelled, "Don't look back! Keep running!"

The tires screeched behind them, then the police siren wailed. The red and blue emergency lights reflected on the puddles. The rainwater splashed and the engine purred as the car accelerated. The headlights hit them, casting their shadows on the pavement.

"We're not going to make it!" Colton yelled.

Gabe leaped to the right, taking Colton down with him. They landed in a parking spot. Lacey and Elena juked to the right, then cut to the left. The police cruiser zoomed past them. Gaggles growled as he stomped on the brake pedal. The car came to a screeching halt near the motel's front office. He slammed the bottom of his fist against the steering wheel, hitting the horn three times.

Honk!

Honk!

Honk!

He looked out the rear window and reversed towards the survivors. The car jounced as he ran over Hank's body. He swerved towards Lacey and Elena. They barely dodged the vehicle. The trunk hit Elena's hip. She dropped to her knees, she stood up, then she fell again. Her hip was fractured.

"Help me!" she pleaded.

Lacey grabbed her in a bear hug and helped her to her feet, walking unsteadily from parking space to parking space. Over the police cruiser, she saw Colton and Gabe lurching to the motel rooms. Over the sound of their heartbeats drumming in their ears, the men heard the police cruiser racing towards them. They screamed and jumped behind Gabe's semi-truck.

Frustrated, Gaggles put the pedal to the metal. He

imagined himself crashing into the massive truck, tipping it over, and flattening the survivors—*human pancakes*. But he knew a collision at that speed would have killed him, too. He swerved at the last second. He punched the steering wheel again as he took another U-turn.

He yelled, "You fucks! You fucking fucks!"

Lacey whispered, "They made it. They're okay." Elena whimpered and shivered in her arms. In a soft but panicky voice, Lacey said, "We're going to be okay. Just don't give up. Please, Elena, we have to go."

"Where?! Where the hell are we going? I just... I want to go home. Please just let me go home already..."

"Don't cry, hun, don't cry. Look, we'll go... to..."

Lacey looked at the motel. She wanted to regroup with the guys, but Gaggles stalked the parking lot in the police cruiser. She turned her attention to the front office. The back door was broken, so they couldn't lock themselves inside. Then she saw the light over the partition behind the motel. It came from Hassan's Market.

"The market," she said.

Eyes glowing with hope, Elena stuttered, "Ha–Hassan."

They limped towards the market while the men entered Room 103.

Gabe pushed Colton onto the bed. He closed the door, but the doorknob and the locks were broken. The softest breeze blew the door open.

As Gabe pushed the dresser to the door, Colton sat up and said, "We can't stay here. No, I... I have to get back to Lacey."

"We'll... find her... in a minute."

"I need to find her *now*," Colton said as he hopped off the bed.

"In a... minute."

"Fuck this shit, man. I'm not dying here with you. And I'm not letting *her* die out *there*."

The television wobbling on top of it, Gabe pressed the dresser against the door. He took the screwdriver out of his waistband. He stepped in front of Colton, stopping him before he could reach the bathroom door. He put the screwdriver in his hand. He took the utility knife out of his pocket. The blade *clicked* out of it with a push of the switch.

He said, "We stick together. We *fight* together. Don't go and start thinking with your dick on me. Okay?" Colton glared at him, breathing deeply through his nose. Gabe said, "Sorry. Let me rephrase that for you: don't... uh... don't start thinking irrationally. She's close. If they're in trouble, we'll hear them. But we can't help them if we're dead. We have to keep moving."

"We need to call the cops."

"They're already on their way. They'll be here any minute now. But we can't wait here for them. That dresser will only buy us a couple of minutes, maybe a couple of seconds if they're smart. They can break that window and rush in here. Four against two? With their axes and sledgehammers and crossbows? You think we stand a chance against all of them?"

Colton let out a long sigh of disappointment. He could barely feel his right leg because of the bolt in his hamstring. He was useless to Lacey in his current condition. The door cracked open an inch, but the dresser stopped it from swinging open.

Outside, Gaggles yelled, "Room 103!"

They heard footsteps in the exterior hallway.

Gabe threw Colton's arm over his shoulder and said, "We have to go."

They hobbled to the bathroom. Colton climbed out the broken window first. He crashed into the ground outside. Gabe sliced his sole open on one of the shards of glass protruding from the windowsill. He fell to the ground beside Colton, grunting and groaning. He clenched his jaw to stop himself from screaming. The cut was deep, exposing his yellow fat and stringy muscle.

Despite the grotesque injury, he rolled to his feet and lifted Colton from the ground. They limped down the alley behind the motel—past Rooms 104, 105, and 106. They stopped at Room 107. Gabe broke the window with a steel trash can. He helped Colton climb into the bathroom. Colton sliced his palms and forearms on the glass, but he didn't notice the cuts.

Gabe spotted Pumpkin at the other end of the alley. He yelled, "They're coming! Block the front door! Hurry!"

Colton stumbled through the motel room. He grabbed the chair next to the table and wedged it under the doorknob, then he secured the door chain. He doddered back to the bathroom, holding his screwdriver like a knife. He expected the worse. *That trucker's already dead, I have to fight them by myself, I have to save Lacey,* he thought.

Before Colton could enter the bathroom, Gabe emerged in the doorway. There were more cuts on his forearms and chest, shards of glass sparkling in the wounds, but he didn't notice the pain, either. He had suffered from far worse throughout the night already —true physical and emotional pain. He pushed Colton back into the room.

"The bedsheets," he said as he closed the bathroom door. He held the doorknob and leaned back. He repeated, "The bedsheets. The bedsheets."

"What?"

"Get me the bedsheets!"

Colton yanked the bedsheet off the mattress, like a magician pulling a tablecloth off a table. Gabe tied one corner of the bedsheet around the bathroom's doorknob and another around the neighboring closet's doorknob.

He said, "That should stop them from breaking in through the bathroom."

"But we're cornered now. We fucking cornered ourselves, man!"

"Calm down! We can... Listen, you keep that front door closed and I'll find a way out of here."

"How?"

They glanced over at the bathroom door upon hearing crackling glass and slow, cautious footsteps. Then they looked at the front door as the doorknob jiggled. They saw someone run past the window, hair swinging with each step—*Puddin'*. The door rattled as Gaggles rammed it with his shoulder.

Gabe grabbed the tall floor lamp from the corner of the room. He smashed the heavy steel base against the wall behind the bed.

He shouted, "Don't let them get inside!"

Colton couldn't believe what he was seeing. He counted three clowns around them. A cop was killed in the parking lot. He was separated from his girlfriend. Yet, Gabe's master plan appeared to be to break through the wall and enter another room. It was impractical.

It was desperate.

"Ahh, shit," Colton muttered.

He slammed his body against the front door just as Gaggles broke it open. Screws and splinters spiraled down from the broken doorknob. The flimsy chair tipped over. Back against the door, he slid down to his ass and used himself as a human doorstop.

Gaggles tackled the door repeatedly and yelled, "You can't stop us! You pussies! You cunts!"

He growled as he pushed the door with all of his weight. It opened an inch, two inches, then three inches. Realizing he was sliding with the door, Colton slapped his palms on the floor and pushed himself back against it. It slammed shut again.

Gaggles punched the door and shouted, "Fuck you!"

Colton felt like he was fighting a two-front war, but he noticed an unusual silence in the bathroom. Then Gaggles stopped tackling the door. Colton only heard the *thudding* and *clunking* as Gabe chipped away at the wall with the lamp.

Eyes wide with fear, he said, "They're planning something. They're coming back. They... They're coming back! Hurry up! Fuck, man, hurry up!"

Gabe shouted, "I'm going as fast as I can!"

He broke through the drywall, dented an air-conditioning duct, and cracked some wood. Above the dresser, the drywall in the neighboring room began to crumble. The buzz of a power drill interrupted him. It reminded him of Monica. He looked at Colton—and Colton looked back at him. Their shocked expression said: *oh shit.*

Gaggles knelt in the exterior hallway and drilled into the door. The flat wood drill bit spun through the wood, ripped Colton's shirt, and then tore into his shoulder. Blood sprayed onto the door, neighboring walls, and the floor while cascading down his back. He felt the door vibrating behind him. His bursa—the fluid-filled sac between his clavicle and humerus bones—burst. Then his bones crackled and popped.

The drill stopped spinning inside of Colton's shoulder, torn cloth and shredded muscle tangled around the drill bit.

Colton sobbed. He tried to jerk away from the door, but the drill bit was jammed *in* his shoulder. The slightest shudder wracked his body with pain—and he couldn't stop shuddering *because* of the pain. The cycle was endless. He gritted his teeth so hard that his jaw broke. Tears, sweat, and mucus glazed his rosy face. Moist *crunching* sounds came out of his shoulder. He gasped for air while his body tightened, stomach clenching and muscles contracting. He couldn't scream.

Gabe lurched towards him. Colton slid across the floor as Gaggles tackled the door again. The clown slid his hand through the crack and grabbed the edge of the door. Gabe rammed the door with his body, smashing Gaggles' fingers between the door and the doorframe. The clown screamed as his fingers cracked. Colton bellowed as the drill bit moved in his shoulder, then his head fell forward and he continued gasping.

Gabe sliced Gaggles' gloved fingers with the utility knife. The clown's index and middle fingers were severed with one swipe. His ring finger was sliced, too, barely attached to his hand. Gaggles slid his hand out from between the door and the door-frame. He held his bleeding hand to his crotch and screamed while walking in circles. The door slammed shut.

"We gotta go," the trucker said.

He hooked his arms under Colton's armpits. He lifted him an inch from the floor. Wide-eyed, pain surging from his shoulder, Colton shrieked and slapped Gabe's bare chest. He couldn't say it, but his message was obvious: *Stop! Stop! Stop!* Gabe lowered him back to the floor. He leaned forward and looked behind Colton. He saw the drill bit's bloody shank between him and the door.

To free him, he would have to go outside and use the power drill's reverse function. Even then, success wasn't guaranteed.

Gaggles threw his body against the door and yelled, "You fucker!"

Puddin' could be heard giggling in the parking lot.

The survivors stared at each other with awe in their eyes. A chainsaw roared in the bathroom. The door spat chips of wood as the chainsaw ate away at it.

From the bathroom, Pumpkin shouted, "I'm coming, boys!"

Gabe was in a quandary. Like most people, he valued his life more than anyone else's. He didn't know Colton, he didn't even know his name, but he saw a part of himself in him. He recognized Colton's love for Lacey. It was the same as his own love for Monica.

Colton saw the conflict in his eyes. He knew the odds were against him.

"Just... go," he croaked out.

Gabe said, "I'm sorry."

"G–Go..."

Gabe ran back to the bed. He attacked the wall with the lamp. He heard the bathroom door breaking behind him and the front door creaking open.

"Go!" Colton yelled.

Gabe punched the wall until his knuckles bled, splinters sticking out of the cuts. He squeezed through the hole, scraping his arms and torso. He hoisted himself on the dresser, then he jumped to the floor. He found himself in Room 108. It was the same as the others. He looked back into Room 107 through the hole on the wall.

Pumpkin charged into the room, wielding a running chainsaw. His stabbed eye was now bandaged. He saw Gabe through the hole. His scowl turned into a smirk.

Speaking over the chainsaw, he said, "Lookie, lookie. Your friend stayed behind to play with us. How sweet. You sure you wanna leave him here with us? We play a little rough, don't ya know? Come join us, why don't ya?" Gabe trembled with anger, blood boiling in his bulging veins. Pumpkin said, "No? Oh well. Don't go too far, friend-o. I'll be done with him in a minute."

Gabe stepped towards the hole in the wall as Pumpkin approached Colton. He had already watched

Monica die, but he felt compelled to watch Colton's death, too. Survivor's guilt festered within him, warping his mind. He felt like he was helping Colton by accompanying him in his death while punishing himself for abandoning him. *What have I done?*–he thought.

As he stood over Colton, Pumpkin asked, "Any last words?"

"Fu–Fu... Fuck... you."

"Ah, the classic. I'll make sure your little bitch cries like you when I fuck her with this chainsaw."

"You–You be–better not touch–"

Pumpkin swung the chainsaw down at Colton's head, cutting it vertically down the middle. Columns of blood burst out, streaking the curtains, the door, and the wall. The blood sprayed onto Pumpkin's face, too. He licked it off his lips, then he spat it out. He laughed wildly as the chainsaw vibrated in his hands. Colton's skull *cracked* and *popped* and *crunched*. His nose was torn off his face, stuck to the cutting chain. His left eye was crushed in its socket while his right eye was detached. Bits of his brain *splatted* on the wall and ceiling. He died while thinking about Lacey.

Gabe sighed shakily as he staggered away from the hole. He grabbed the floor lamp and started attacking the wall behind the bed.

The door chime rang through the market. Lacey and Elena, wet from the drizzle, slid across the linoleum floor. The market was supposed to be closed, but the lights were on. Lacey turned and closed the doors. She searched for a deadbolt or a latch lock, but she needed a key to lock the door.

One hand on her bloody shoulder and the other on her injured hip, Elena limped forward and yelled, "Hassan! Hass–"

Lacey slapped her hand over Elena's mouth and whispered, "Stop screaming." Elena's muffled cries seeped past her fingers. Lacey shook her gently and said, "Please stop. We're safe now. We're okay. But if they hear us, they'll find us. If they find us, they'll kill us. You can't scream, okay?"

Elena nodded, teary eyes as wide as golf balls. Lacey was skeptical, but she couldn't cover her mouth forever. She moved her hand away from Elena's face. Elena drew a deep, trembling breath, then she sighed. They looked over at the cash register at the other end of the market.

"Where is he?" Lacey asked.

"I–I don't know. Ma–Maybe... Maybe they got him already. Oh my God, do you think they killed him, too?"

"No, I don't think so. There's, um... There's four of them, right? We saw them all at the diner after they... after they killed the cop. And we called him right before, remember? He's okay."

"But what if there are *more* of them? What if they got in here and killed him after the call and before the cop got here? What if–"

"Keep your voice down," Lacey interrupted. "He's here. He has to be. He lives upstairs, right? Right?"

"*Yes,*" Elena snapped.

"Okay, so then we go upstairs. How do we lock this door?"

"I don't know. A key, I guess."

"Do you know where to..."

Lacey saw Blue running towards the market, rubbing the rain into his eyes. Elena spotted him, too. Before she could scream, Lacey covered her mouth again and pulled her down to a crouch. Elena whined because of the pain in her broken hip and pierced shoulder. They crouch-walked to the farthest aisle to their left. The refrigerators hummed, keeping the beer, soda, and energy drinks as cold as ice.

The door chime rang again.

"Come out and play, you swine!" Blue demanded. Hiding behind a rack of potato chips, the women responded with silence. Blue smiled and said, "Oh, okay. Alrighty. So, *this* is the game you want to play, huh? Hide-and-seek, cat-and-mouse... Sure. Why not? Let's play, little piggies."

He swung the sledgehammer at a freezer chest near the entrance. The sliding glass cover shattered, shards raining down on the ice cream products. He expected the women to scream or gasp with the loud noise, but they remained quiet.

In a hushed voice, softer than a whisper, Lacey said, "Don't... make... a sound."

They crouch-walked past an ATM, then into another aisle. Prepackaged salads, sandwiches, and beverages filled the refrigerated shelves to their left. Bread filled the parallel shelves to their right. They could see the cash register between those shelves.

Elena pointed at the door behind the cash register and mouthed: *there.*

They moved down the aisle. Unbeknownst to them, blood dripped from Elena's shoulder, leaving a trail behind them.

In his clownish voice, Blue said, "Please come out. I get *blue* when my friends hide. Don't make me blue." He grinned and yelled, "You don't want to see me when I'm blue!"

He swung the sledgehammer at a tall rack full of potato chips, chocolate, and other candy. It tipped over and hit the neighboring shelves. They fell over like dominos, products falling in the aisles. The last rack hit the refrigerators, breaking the glass doors. The shards of glass stabbed some of the cans and bottles. The beverages sprayed out and *hissed* loudly.

Elena gasped, flinched, and dropped to her knees, igniting the pain in her broken pelvis again. She drew a sharp breath and held it in, trying to stop herself from screaming. Lacey held her index finger up to her lips and placed her other hand over Elena's mouth. Her eyes, twitching and glimmering, pleaded for silence.

Blue squatted and looked under the fallen shelves. He said, "Not there, not there, not there, no... Oh!" He looked at the cash register. He said, "You were going for the phone, weren't you? No? No, that's not right. A phone can't save you. You were going to that door, right? I got bad news for you, ladies. That old man can't save you, either. And you'll have to get through me to get to him."

He laughed as he ran to the cash register, launching his knees up in the air with each stride. He jumped onto the counter and scanned the market from above. He couldn't see the survivors, but he saw enough of the market to safely assume their location. It wasn't a massive store after all. He spotted the trail of blood, too. He grinned at the bread aisle.

He said, "Oh well. I guess you're not here. I'm alone again, boo-*hoo.*" He jumped off the counter and started walking down the aisle in front of him. Sniffling, he repeated, "Boo-hoo, boo-hoo."

The women listened to his footsteps as they got quieter and quieter. Lacey weaved and bobbed her head, trying to peek through the shelves without exposing herself. Staying low, they sidestepped down the aisle. The door chime rang as the door swung open. They stopped again.

Silence.

Twenty seconds felt like twenty minutes.

Elena whispered, "Is he gone?"

Lacey shrugged and shook her head. They waited for another twenty seconds. *Plop, plop, plop*—Lacey finally heard the blood dripping from Elena's shoulder.

"You can't hide from me!" Blue yelled in a deep, hoarse voice.

Lacey grabbed Elena's hand and shouted, "Run!"

Blue's squeaky footsteps grew louder as he ran towards them. Elena staggered behind Lacey, unable to jog because of her broken hip. The rack of bread crashed into the floor behind her. Blue ran down the neighboring aisle. He swung the sledgehammer at the second rack of bread.

"Run!" Lacey repeated.

Elena's hand slipped out of Lacey's as the shelves hit her, launching her against the racks of alcohol on the wall to their left. Bottles of wine fell and exploded on the floor. Lacey stopped at the cash register and looked back. Elena limped towards her, but she slipped on the wine and landed face-first on the floor.

"No! No!" she cried. "Don't leave me! Please don't leave me!"

Blue stepped between them, smirking. He looked at Lacey, then at Elena, and then back at Lacey.

He asked, "Well, what's it going to be? Hero or zero?"

Lacey felt time slowing to a crawl. She saw Elena's gaping mouth, but she couldn't hear her scream. The sides of Blue's mouth rose as he snickered, but she didn't hear his laughter, either. Her eyes darted to the broom in the corner, then to the broken wine bottles on the floor, and then to the door behind the register. Her inner voice overlapped itself.

'Use the broom.'

'No, grab a bottle and stab him.'

'Just run.'

'She doesn't deserve to die.'

'He'll kill me.'

A *thud* upstairs interrupted her thoughts and brought her back to the real world. She heard the clown's laughter and Elena's begging.

"Help me!" the waitress shouted.

"I'm sorry," Lacey said.

She sobbed as she ran around the counter. She opened the door and found a staircase leading to the second floor.

As she scrambled up the stairs, she yelled, "Help! Help us!"

"Don't leave me!" Elena wailed.

She pushed herself off the floor, broken glass cutting into her palms. She elbowed Blue's chest, but he barely moved. It was as if a child had tried to push him down by blowing on him. As she stumbled past him, Blue hit the back of Elena's leg with the sledge-hammer, breaking her ankle and sweeping her leg out from under her. The back of her head hit the linoleum with a loud, unnerving *thump*. Blood trickled out of a cut on her scalp, blending with the wine underneath her. The bolt burrowed deeper into her shoulder. She lay there with her arms straight in the air, groaning through gritted teeth. She blacked out.

At the top of the stairs, Lacey knocked on a heavy door while shaking the doorknob. She cried for help, she heard hushed voices on the other side, but no one answered.

Elena awoke fifteen seconds later. She saw Blue— two Blues, maybe three—standing over her with a bottle of red wine in his right hand.

She mumbled, "Don't... Don't kill me. Please, I... I'm just a... a waitress."

Blue took a knee and caressed her hair. He said, "I'm not going to kill you. You're my friend, and Blue doesn't kill his friends. I make them happy. I'll put a smile on your face."

"N–No, please, I–I can't feel my legs. I can't feel–"

Blue struck her with the wine bottle. It shattered on her face, splitting her forehead open vertically down the middle. The gash stretched from her scalp to her glabella, exposing her skull underneath. Fragments of glass—covered in wine and blood—sparkled like rubies in the cut, stuck in her skin. Shards of glass were tangled in her bloody, sopping hair. She fell unconscious again, eyes rolling under her eyelids. She rocked back and forth on the floor.

The clown still held the broken bottle by its neck, its jagged edges like a shark's teeth. He lay the sledgehammer on the floor beside him. Elena was incapacitated. She was alive, but death loomed over her. He didn't expect Lacey to come down and fight him, either. He could hear her screaming and banging on the door upstairs, her desperate cries going ignored.

He grabbed a fistful of broken glass from the floor. He clenched his fist, crushing the shards in his gloved hand. Some of the glass cut through the glove and sliced his palm, but the pain didn't bother him. He loosened his grip, then he clenched his fist again. He broke the shards into smaller fragments. He forced two fingers past Elena's shaking lips and pulled her jaw down. Then he poured the bits of glass into her mouth.

Elena hacked as the glass went down her throat. Blue pushed her jaw up and forced her to close her mouth. The glass crunched between her teeth, scraping at her enamel. It pierced her gums and tongue. She inadvertently swallowed, sending the shards down her esophagus. The slivers lacerated her internal organs. Blood seeped past her sealed lips and ran down her cheeks. Her eyes opened to slits, sclerae bloodshot.

She felt an unusual warmth in her throat, chest, and stomach—*internal bleeding*. Her abdomen tensed up, and every movement led to excruciating pain. She wanted to run, but she was tired of suffering. She stayed still, accepting her fate.

Upstairs, the door swung open.

Hassan, dressed in his flannel pajamas, asked, "What is going on down there?"

Lacey pushed the door, shoved Hassan, and forced her way inside. She tumbled in the living room. She turned and crab-walked backwards until she crashed into a recliner. Behind her, Salma Amari, Hassan's wife, rested on the seat with a blanket draped over her. She wore flannel pajamas, too. A stroke had left her mute and chairbound. She was scared of their uninvited guest, scooting to the edge of the seat.

Lacey yelled, "Close it! Close the door!"

"Get away from my wife!" Hassan demanded

"Close it!"

"What is–"

"Oh my God, please!"

Although reluctant, Hassan did as he was told. He secured the locks while listening to the whimpers coming from downstairs.

Blue rubbed Elena's cheek and said, "You're not smiling. Let me show you a trick. I call it 'soda fountain.' You ever put Mentos in a bottle of Diet Coke?" Elena didn't respond. Blue leaned closer to her face and said, "It's kinda like that... but I don't have any Mentos... and the Diet Coke will be your blood."

He glassed her with the broken bottle, stabbing her neck at an angle. He severed her jugular, ruptured her windpipe, and cut into her thyroid cartilage. Blood erupted from the wound and sprayed out from the bottle's orifice. Blue leaned back and giggled as it hit his costume. Elena convulsed on the floor, face scrunched up in pain. Between her teeth, she ground the remaining glass in her mouth to dust. Crackling and croaking sounds came out of her mouth. She couldn't breathe. The back of her head hit the floor again. She passed away, but she continued twitching.

Another geyser of blood shot out of the bottle's orifice.

Mentos and Diet Coke.

16

CORNERED

"You have some explaining to do," Hassan said as he wagged his index finger at Lacey. "What is going on down there? What did you do to my market?"

Voice cracking, Lacey stammered, "You–You–You have to... Block the door. Please block the door. Use that sofa or that chair or the TV, just... just block the damn door!"

"I am not blocking a thing until I get some answers. You and your friends have been causing trouble *all* night. First with that crank call, now with all that ruckus downstairs."

"Me and my friends?" Lacey repeated, perplexed and terrified. "No, no, no. It wasn't us. It was the... the..."

The clowns—she couldn't say those words. She remembered their arguments in the diner. The situation was unbelievable. *Killer clowns?* It was absurd, a fever dream, a hallucination from an unwell mind, a drug-fueled delusion. She saw the genuine fear in Salma's eyes and the anger in Hassan's. She wanted them to believe her.

Hassan wanted to restrain her and call the cops on *her*. He believed she was responsible for the noise downstairs. *Drugs,* he thought. *She's drugged out of her mind.*

Lacey said, "I don't know what to say. We're... They're, um..."

"I called the cops," Hassan said. "Yes, *again*. They're on their way right now. You can explain it to them or me. I can help you—*maybe*—but... I don't know what the hell you did down there. It sounded like you broke a few windows and knocked over my shelves. Did you do that? Was it your boyfriend? Or was it Jayden? Oh, that little bastard."

"You called the cops?" Lacey asked. Her eyes lit up with hope. She stood from the floor and said, "I know this sounds crazy, but we're under attack. The motel, it's... it was attacked."

"Attacked? What do you mean by that?"

"We called you, remember? Elena, the waitress, she said we were attacked by someone with a crossbow. Now, downstairs, we... we were attacked again. He had a sledgehammer and he... he..."

"What? What did he do to my market?"

Lacey said, "Elena, she... she was..."

The anger in Hassan's eyes turned into concern. He

had friendly relationships with the employees of Motel Ace and Gold Diner 80. He didn't know Lacey, he thought she was a troublemaking tourist, but he trusted Elena. He bickered with Jayden every once in a while, but he cared about him, too. He looked at his wife.

Salma gazed into his eyes. Her eyes said something along the lines of: *help this girl.* They could communicate without saying a word.

Hassan asked, "Is she okay?" Lacey shook her head. Hassan sighed, then he said, "Damn. This can't be happening. I just spoke to her on the phone. I saw a cop car drive past my market."

"Didn't you hear the gunfire?"

"Gunfire? No, no. That was... It was thunder, wasn't it? No, don't tell me..."

Lacey said, "They killed him. They're trying to kill everyone here. They're psychopaths. And... Elena didn't want to tell you, but they're dressed as clowns. That's the truth."

Hassan stared at her with a steady, worried expression. He waited for the punchline, the end to her sick, twisted joke—*'just kidding!'* But it didn't come because she wasn't joking. Across from Salma, a recorded episode of *NCIS* played on a high-definition television on mute. He looked at his wife again. Salma's eyes said: *take it seriously.*

Hassan coughed to clear his throat, then he said, "It doesn't matter who attacked you. Something's wrong here and more cops are on the way. So, everything'll be fine."

"When?"

"Excuse me?"

"When did you call them? When will they get here?"

"I just got off the phone with them before I opened the door for you. I don't know when they'll be here, but they *will* be here."

"Oh God, no. They're not going to get here in time. We have to do something. Please block the door."

Hassan said, "Calm down, hun. You're safe here. He's not getting through that door."

"He has a sledgehammer!" Lacey shouted. "They're killing everyone! Haven't you been listening?"

Hassan raised his hands in a peaceful gesture. He walked backwards into a hall, then he turned and rushed into a bedroom.

Lacey asked, "What are you doing? Where are you going? Damn it, we don't have time for this."

She glanced around the living room. She thought about jumping out the window, but she didn't want to injure herself or abandon the elderly couple. She started pushing the heavy glass coffee table towards the door. It screeched on the floorboards.

Before she could push it more than a foot, Hassan returned to the living room. He held a compact .38 Special five-round revolver in his right hand.

Lacey smiled nervously and said, "You have a gun.

We have to... We have to find Colton. My boyfriend, he's still out there."

"No, no. We can't go outside."

"You have a gun! You have to do something!"

"I'm not leaving my wife and this gun's not leaving my hand, ma'am. We're safe here, so we *wait* here until the cops show up."

Lacey said, "No, no, no. They're going to kill–"

Someone knocked on the door three times, pausing for two seconds between each knock. Hassan, Salma, and Lacey turned their heads to look at the door. Ten seconds of deafening silenced passed. The visitor knocked again. Hassan aimed the revolver at the door, his hand trembling. He had purchased the revolver for self-defense, he had practiced with it at a shooting range, but he had never pointed it at a person before. Salma gripped the recliner's armrest, bulging eyes stuck on the door.

Lacey whispered, "It's him."

From the other side of the door, in a soft, eerie voice, Blue said, "I know you're there. You can't hide from me, little piggy."

The clown honked a horn, causing Lacey to gasp and teeter back. She sidestepped to the corner of the room, then she crouched between the entertainment center and a wall.

Hassan said, "You're trespassing. I already called the cops. They're on their way now."

"Oh, *are they?*"

"They are. The way I see it, you have three options: you walk away, you wait for the police, or you break in here and I stand my ground."

"Stand your ground? Hehehe, ha*haha*. Don't make me laugh too hard, old man, I might fall down these stairs."

Under her breath, Lacey said, "Old man? He... He knows you."

Hassan said, "I know my rights. I heard about what you did out there. I can shoot you. I'm... I'm allowed to defend myself!"

Tapping the door with his fingertip, Blue said, "Just because you *can* doesn't mean you *will*. I'm coming in. And I'm going to kill all of you."

"Don't do something stupid! Stay back!"

"Yes! Yes!"

"Stay out!"

Blue laughed as he hit the doorknob with the top of the sledgehammer's metal head. The doorknob snapped off. The door shook violently, groaning like a person in pain. He hit it again. The door blew open, splinters of wood, pieces of steel, and screws flying in every direction. Salma let out a dry croaking sound before slapping her hands over her mouth. Lacey dug her fingers into her hair and shrieked.

"Don't move!" Hassan demanded as he shook the gun at the clown. He stepped in front of his wife, using himself as a human shield. He said, "You move, I shoot. It's that simple. Now... Now drop the sledgehammer."

"Ah, ah, ah. You told me not to move, remember? I know how to play this game."

"Game? What are you... Don't get smart with me, okay? Put it on the floor."

"Hmm... And what if I don't?"

"*I shoot.* I said that already and I meant it. You got a hearing problem, kid?"

"Maybe I do, maybe I don't."

"Put it down!" Hassan barked.

Blue smirked and said, "Wow. You really think you're a cowboy, don't you? The sheriff of this little shithole, huh?" Talking like a cowboy, he said, "Well, listen here, partner. This room ain't big enough for the both of us."

The floorboard creaked as he took a step forward. Hassan stepped back. He extended his arm and aimed the gun at Blue's chest.

"Shoot him!" Lacey yelled from the corner of the room.

Blue took another step forward and said, "Shoot me."

Hassan stuttered, "I–I will. I–I'll shoot."

"Then do it."

"Wha–What are you... What's wrong with you, boy?"

Lacey shouted, "He'll kill us all! Shoot him!"

Blue stepped towards the shop owner and said, "Listen to the girl. Now's your chance—your *only* chance—to be a hero. I'm ready for it. Oh, I'm fucking ready! Do it!" The revolver's muzzle was a mere foot away from the clown's chest. Hassan couldn't pull the trigger. Blue huffed, then he said, "I knew you couldn't do it. Got me all excited for nothing. Now I'm blue... Boo-hoo, boo-*hoo*."

Hassan stammered incoherently. He lowered the revolver and aimed it at the clown's stomach. Although he was dressed as a clown, he could see Blue was a very young man—no older than twenty.

Hassan said, "You're right. I don't want to shoot you. But I know you don't want to do this, either. You have your whole life–"

Blue swung the sledgehammer down at Hassan's right foot with all of his strength, as if he were playing a high striker game at a carnival. He shattered every bone in Hassan's foot and flattened three of his toes— his little, ring, and middle toes. His toenails cracked and crumbled off. His first metatarsal—the bone behind his big toe—snapped and splintered *out* of his foot, soaking his slipper in blood.

Hassan staggered and screamed. He unintention- ally shot at the floor between Blue and himself. Salma gasped and grabbed the back of Hassan's shirt. Lacey dashed into the kitchen through an archway behind a sofa. *Run!*—it was the only thought in her mind.

Blue swung the sledgehammer up at Hassan's crotch. He hit his scrotum and perineum. His pelvis shattered like glass, causing him to wobble and drop the revolver. His scrotum burst open with an audible *popping* sound. His left testicle was crushed; the coiled, tubular insides squeezed out. It was barely attached to his body. His other testicle was dented. Blood drenched the crotch of his flannel pants. He pushed his knees together, then he collapsed with his hands over his crotch.

He gasped for air, then orange vomit came out of his mouth and landed on his face. Hand on his stomach, Blue chuckled and slapped his knee. On the recliner, Salma clasped her hands in front of her chest and begged for mercy without saying a word. Lacey slid towards the other kitchen archway. *Down the hall, into the master bedroom, block the door, climb out the window,* she told herself. But she stopped upon hearing Salma's whimpering. Although she was already dead, she heard Elena's cries for help in her head.

I can't keep running, she thought. *They're killing everyone. They're going to kill him, then her, then me. I have to do something.*

She was conflicted. Guilt told her to fight for the others, fear told her to fight for herself—selflessness versus self-preservation.

She ran to the kitchen counter. She took a dirty knife out of the sink. Then she rushed back to the living room.

Blue swung the sledgehammer at Hassan's chest, breaking five of his ribs and cracking his sternum. One of his ribs punctured his lung. Hassan coughed up bloody sputum. It drizzled back down to his face, joining the vomit. The slightest, weakest breath set his chest aflame. He started suffocating on his own blood and puke. Salma threw her arms over Hassan's body, as if that would shield him. She shook her head at Blue, as if to say: *no, no, please don't!*

The clown kept laughing, amused by the violence. He swung the sledgehammer up over his head. Before he could swing down at Hassan again, Lacey ran at him and thrust the knife into his side. The blade plunged into his ribcage, barely missing his axillary artery. The sledgehammer landed on the floor, snapping one of the floorboards. Lacey pushed him against the wall and stabbed him two more times while sobbing.

Blue winced and grimaced in pain, but he still laughed. He grabbed her neck and pushed her back. His grip was too weak to suffocate her. Lacey wiggled the knife inside of him, causing him to walk unsteadily. She took the knife out of him, then she stabbed his bicep, forcing him to release her neck. She grabbed his collar and pulled him away from the living room, then she pushed him through the doorway.

He rolled down the stairs, giggling as his bones cracked and crunched against the stairs' sharp edges. The laughter stopped with a loud *thud* at the bottom of the stairs.

"Oh my God," Lacey whispered.

She looked at Hassan and Salma. During the fight, Salma had thrown herself off the recliner. She lay on her elbows beside her now unconscious husband. Lacey wanted to help them, but she knew it was foolish. *In the movies, the killer always gets up,* she thought. Knife in hand, she made her way down to the market.

She found Blue squirming on the floor at the bottom of the stairs. His left ankle was twisted, foot pointing behind him at a 45-degree angle. Although it wasn't visible, his right shin was cracked. Blood leaked out from a cut on the back of his head, accumulating into a small pool in his bowler cap. He pressed his palm against the stab wounds on his torso, hissing and groaning.

There were three types of murder: premeditated, spontaneous, and accidental. Murder was never easy, but it was hardest for compassionate people when *thinking* was added to the equation. There was a difference between killing someone in a fight and *executing* someone. Like Hassan, Lacey wasn't a cold-blooded killer.

"I'm sorry. I'm so sorry," she said.

She raced to the refrigerators. She caught a glimpse of the broken bottle sticking out of Elena's neck. She closed her eyes and looked away, but the afterimage was already etched into her eyelids. She grabbed a water bottle from one of the refrigerators. The water sloshed as her hand shook.

She whispered, "Oh God, look what he did to her. That could have been me. He would have killed me if he had the chance. What am I doing?" Blue's groan was interrupted by his throaty cough, then he whined again. Lacey shook her head and said, "No. I have to... I have to do the right thing. I'm not a killer."

She walked back to the immobilized clown while avoiding Elena's dead body. She checked Blue's hands, then she crouched and patted his forearms. She made sure he was unarmed. She placed the knife on the floor behind her, far from Blue's reach.

She said, "Don't do anything stupid. I–I'm... I'm just trying to help you now. The cops... They'll arrest you."

Blue could only moan. Lacey poured water on his head to clean his wound. His bald cap slowly slid off. Her eyes widened.

"N–No," she stuttered. She pulled his collar down and poured water on his neck. As she rubbed the white makeup off his skin, she said, "You... You... It was you. You monster!"

The clown's ears were gauged, earlobes dangling away from his head. His neck was tattooed to appear as if it were slit and stitched. Todd Stone, the clerk who had checked them in, was Blue the Clown. Lacey connected the pieces: their tire was popped on purpose; Todd set them up in certain rooms so they wouldn't hear the other guests being slaughtered; murder was always their objective.

She slapped him, then she yelled, "You bastard! You... You killed so many people. You shot... my boyfriend. This was... It was all part of your sick plan, wasn't it? You wanted to kill us for fun? Is that it?"

Unrepentant, Todd smiled slightly and nodded.

Lacey cried, "I was going to help you. I thought you were just a stupid kid. The cops were going to arrest you. I wanted to... I was..." She closed her eyes and clenched her jaw. She said, "I was wrong. So fucking wrong. You don't deserve to live. Prison's too good for a monster like you. I–I'm... I'm going to kill you. Yeah, um... *Yes,* that's what I'm going to do."

Todd snickered, then he said, "You stupid bitch. You're just like... like everyone else. All talk... no action. You're not going to do–"

Lacey stabbed his neck. The blade severed his jugular, esophagus, and trachea. Todd squeezed his eyes shut. Lacey tried to drag the blade across his neck, but she couldn't cut through his muscles. She had to saw through them, pushing and tugging on the knife's handle. She leaned back and looked away as his blood squirted onto her shirt. She kept sawing. It wasn't a clean, straight cut, curving away from his tattoo at his Adam's apple. She cut his other jugular.

She felt him shaking from the handle of the knife. She let go of the knife and peeked over at him. She looked away in less than a second. She saw the shredded muscles, ligaments, tendons, and cartilage. She placed her hand over her eyes, unintentionally rubbing his blood on her face. She yelped and wiped her hand on her shirt. Her cheeks inflated, then she burped, and then she swallowed hard to stop herself from vomiting. Tears welled in her eyes and a frown twisted her face.

The violence was sickening.

She sat there and cried until Todd stopped shaking —nearly three minutes. And those were the longest three minutes of her life. She wiped the tears from her eyes and nodded in determination. *For Elena, for Hassan, for me, for Colton*, she told herself. She was afraid of being imprisoned for her violent actions— she executed an incapacitated person with excessive force after all—but she convinced herself that it was all necessary.

"We have to... to fight back," she mumbled as she crawled up the stairs.

Halfway up the steps, she struggled to her feet and walked the rest of the way up. She found Salma crying on top of Hassan. Hassan had passed away. She shuffled towards them. She grabbed Hassan's revolver. She had never held a revolver before, so she was surprised to see her steady hands. She had stopped shaking. *Point and shoot,* she thought.

Eyes on the gun, she said, "I'm going to try to stop this. I'm going to help as many people as possible. I won't... run anymore. I'm sorry about your husband... about everything. Please wait here. The police are coming. I'm... I'm sorry."

Lacey exited the apartment, haunted by the voiceless sounds of Salma's grieving. She stopped at the center of the market. She walked over to the shelves of alcohol while covering her view of Elena with her hand. She grabbed a bottle of liquor and poured it out. Then she took a lighter from the shelf under the cash register. Using her teeth and fingernails, she tore a strip off the hem of her shirt as she walked out of the market.

She approached the gas pumps and started filling the bottle with gasoline. A fire of vengeance roared in her eyes as she watched Motel Ace.

17

TURNING THE TABLES

"FUCK!" GABE YELLED AS HE SMASHED THE LAMP against the wall. He broke through the wall above the bed, but he barely scuffed the wall in Room 109. He hit the wall again and repeated, "*Fuck!*"

A chainsaw growled behind him. Pumpkin sawed the parallel wall, the air-conditioning duct, and a stud. Chips of wood and clouds of drywall dust and sawdust flew through the air. Gabe couldn't compete with a chainsaw. He stumbled towards the bathroom just as Pumpkin entered the room through the hole. The clown swung the chainsaw at him. Gabe leaned back and dodged it.

The trucker hit the side of Pumpkin's head with the lamp's hollow stand. It knocked him back, it would leave a bruise, but it wasn't enough to daze him. Pumpkin swung the chainsaw up, cutting the lamp in half. A spray of sparks and metal shavings shot out at them. Gabe staggered back, surprised. Pumpkin swung the chainsaw at his arm.

He cut Gabe's left hand in half. The diagonal cut stretched from the metacarpophalangeal joint of his index finger to the edge of his hand, following the center arch on his palm.

Gabe fell onto the bed, wailing in pain. He looked at his butchered hand, blood bubbling out and dripping onto his bare chest. Although they were already amputated, he felt a stinging pain in his *fingers*. The phenomenon was called 'phantom pain.' He raised his knees and slid back across the bed, barely dodging Pumpkin's chainsaw.

The chainsaw tore into the mattress between Gabe's legs, chunks of polyurethane foam and broken springs shooting out.

Gabe took the utility knife out of his pocket. He swung it twice at Pumpkin, quick like a trained swordsman. He cut Pumpkin's forearm, then he leaned forward and swiped it at the clown's face—a diagonal cut from his temple to the bridge of his nose. The blade nicked his eyelids, nearly cutting his only good eye.

"Shit!" Pumpkin yelled.

He pulled the chainsaw out and teetered back. His vision turned red as blood entered his eye socket and cascaded over the right side of his face. Gabe threw himself off the bed and reeled towards him. He sliced Pumpkin's neck, but the clown's thick ruff collar protected him. Blood trickled out of the wound, it stung, but it was superficial.

Gabe was afraid of the chainsaw. One bad step could lead to a severed foot. He didn't have the time or the strength to fight with the clown. He stabbed Pumpkin's leg, then he dragged the blade across his thigh in hopes of severing his femoral artery. He missed it by a millimeter, but the wound was deep. The blade had mutilated his quadriceps.

The chainsaw was thrust into the floor as Pumpkin hunched forward and pushed the trucker away. Gabe stumbled around the bed, utility knife in hand.

"Help," he yelled as he made his way to the exit.

The chainsaw chugged to a stop behind him. Pumpkin muttered indistinctly while trying to wipe the blood off his face with his gloved hand.

Gabe opened the door and stumbled out of the room. He stopped in the exterior hallway. Puddin' stood in the parking lot in front of him, a mere ten meters away. She rested her crossbow against her shoulder.

Staying in character, she asked, "Where do ya think you're going, bub? You didn't think we were just going to let you run out of here, did ya? Uh-uh. I still have to kill you. All twos of ya."

She was still seeing double because of her broken eye socket. Behind her, the police cruiser was parked in front of the diner at the other end of the parking lot. The headlights beamed through the wispy mist.

Gaggles sat in the driver's seat. A bandage from Hank's first aid kit was wrapped around his mangled hand. He was ready to race towards them and exact his revenge.

Hank, beaten and bloodied beyond recognition, was still tied to the police cruiser's spoiler.

Gabe took two steps back. He heard Pumpkin struggling to start the chainsaw in the motel room. He realized there was no escape. He thought about begging for mercy, but he couldn't forget Monica's burnt face and prolapsing rectum. *They killed her,* he thought. *How could I beg them to spare my life? They're going to kill me anyway.*

He looked down at his hands. His right hand shook out of fear and anxiety. His left hand—what was left of it—shook because of the pain.

Teeth chattering, he scowled at Puddin' and said, "Shoot me, bitch."

"With pleasure, doll."

She aimed the crossbow at him. Then they heard the police cruiser's horn—one honk, two honks, one *long* honk, three more honks.

Puddin' furrowed her brow and muttered, "What the hell is he–"

As she turned to look over her shoulder, she saw Lacey throwing a Molotov cocktail at her. Gaggles had been trying to warn her of Lacey's arrival. The Molotov cocktail exploded at the clown's feet. A ball of fire swallowed her while tall flames rose from the pavement.

She dropped the crossbow and shrieked. She ran towards Lacey.

Lacey aimed the revolver at her and yelled, "Stop!"

To her surprise, Puddin' ran past her. The clown stumbled through the parking lot. She patted her hair, then waved her arms above her as if she were whisking a swarm of flies away, then she tapped her shoulders, and then patted her hair again. *Severe, extreme, excruciating*—a single word couldn't accurately describe her suffering.

Her mind was sent into a frenzy. She had been taught to stop, drop, and roll, but she couldn't remember those instructions in the heat of the moment.

Run, stand, and scream?

Every inch of her body was burning. The layers of her skin peeled away so quickly, replaced by large gelatinous blisters. Her burning hair emitted a sharp sulfurous stench. She clawed at her dress, but she couldn't rip it open. Her polyester dress had already melted and fused to her skin. Her flesh blackened and charred.

She screeched as she collapsed in a parking space near Colton's car. She squirmed on the wet pavement, unable to muster the energy to roll and extinguish the flames. The flames eradicated her nerves. She stared up at the dark sky until her eyes boiled and her vision faded. Her eyeballs melted in their sockets, but she was still alive.

Gaggles was a violent killer—a disturbed sadist—but he cared about his crew. He punched the steering wheel and screamed. The tires howled as he stomped on the gas pedal. The police cruiser sped towards the motel—zero to sixty in seven seconds. Gabe lurched back into the room. Pumpkin had just started the chainsaw. The clown stepped towards the trucker, then he saw the headlights racing towards him.

"Aw shit," he said in his regular voice.

He dropped the chainsaw and turned to run. Gabe leapt onto the bed, slid across it, then fell off the other side. He put his hands on his head, closed his eyes, and screamed. The police cruiser barreled up the curb and bulldozed through the wall beside the door. The explosive crashing sound echoed through the desert. The car hit the bed, pushing the frame *over* Gabe. The vehicle was launched up, as if it had rolled over a ramp. The front bumper punched a massive hole into the ceiling, then it fell and broke through the wall. The rear wheels stayed on the bed and the others hovered about a foot above the floor, still spinning.

During the crash, a piece of debris had pushed the chainsaw. The chainsaw had severed Pumpkin's heel cord while breaking his tibia and fibula bones. His right foot was barely attached to his leg. It dangled behind him as he dragged his leg into the bathroom, leaving a trail of blood behind him. He threw himself into the bathtub. The crash sounded like a bomb—

deafening. He expected the building to collapse and crush them all.

Gabe stayed under the bed, listening to the creaking wood. He feared the bed would break and he would be crushed under it, but he couldn't move. Shock paralyzed him. He felt hot and cold. Blood from his mangled hand flowed across his scalp, joining the cold sweat oozing out of his pores. Slumped against an air bag with a bloody nose and an aching neck, Gaggles was unconscious in the driver's seat. The rope around the spoiler finally tore. Hank's bloody body lay on the pavement.

The drizzle extinguished the flames. Feathers of black smoke rose from the female clown's scorched body. Flakes of burnt skin and clothes floated through the air.

Lacey stared at the wrecked motel room with one hand over her mouth. The destruction was horrifying. She had seen fender benders in person and deadly car crashes on the internet, but she had never seen anything like that. She thought about Colton. He was supposed to be with Gabe. *This is my fault, this wouldn't have happened if I didn't throw that damn Molotov,* she thought. She wondered if she had accidentally killed the love of her life.

18

SURVIVAL

"Colton!" Lacey yelled as she sprinted to the motel room.

Puddin' whimpered and twitched on the pavement, her burnt, crispy arms crossed over her chest like an Egyptian mummy. In the motel room, Pumpkin cried in the bathtub. He tried to climb out, but he slipped on his blood and slid back in. Gabe walked out through the open door, leaving a bloody footprint behind him with each step. His skin was caked with plasterboard dust and riddled with splinters. He held his mangled hand against his stomach to try to slow the bleeding. It went numb during the crash.

As she approached him, Lacey asked, "Is he in there? Is he okay? Is he?!"

Gabe was dizzy and nauseous, lost and tired, cold and warm. For a moment, he thought Lacey was speaking Spanish. *¿Está ahí?* He shook his head and rubbed his eye with his good hand.

He asked, "Wha–What are you... What?"

"Colton! My boyfriend! You were with him. Is he okay? Hey, answer me. Tell me he's okay."

Gabe staggered and looked back into the motel room upon hearing the chainsaw roaring in his head. But there was no one there. *My imagination,* he thought. He remembered Colton's violent death. He glanced at the neighboring room. The power drill was still stuck in the door, which meant Colton was still sitting on the other side of it. He had been in Lacey's shoes before. He didn't want her to suffer like he did when he saw Monica's death.

"We have to go," he sighed.

"What? Wha–What do you mean? Where is he?"

"Come on, girl, let's–"

"*Where is he?*"

Gabe gazed into her eyes and shook his head. The gesture said it all. Lacey pushed past him and entered the wrecked motel room. She crouched and looked under the bed—*nothing.* She spotted the dormant chainsaw on the floor. Skin was tangled on the chain, blood smeared on the board. A piece of Colton's brain was stuck on the bumper spikes, but she couldn't have known it belonged to her boyfriend.

Beneath the surface, all humans were the same— fragile organs and sturdy bones.

She rushed to the bathroom and found Pumpkin in

the bathtub. He looked like he was bathing in his own blood.

Pumpkin barked, "You bitch! You fucking cunt! You —*ow!*—fucking bitch! This isn't over! I'm going to kill you!"

Lacey was unperturbed by his threat. She whispered, "Where is he? What happened?"

She exited the bathroom. Gabe stood in the doorway, afraid to go inside.

He beckoned to her and said, "Let's go. Please don't do this."

"What happened to my–"

She saw it from the periphery of her vision. She turned her head slowly until she faced the hole in the wall. Legs shaking, she approached it. Her eyes and mouth widened.

Colton's head was bisected, split open vertically. She could see the remaining chunks of his brain in each half of his skull. His left eye was crushed to mush. His right eye dangled out of its socket, hanging near his shoulder. His nose was gone, torn off his face. His mouth looked like it had imploded. The roof of his mouth had collapsed, his tongue was cut and crumpled like a student's homework at the end of a school year, and his teeth were ejected from his gums. The opening of his throat was visible from afar.

Lacey felt woozy. She didn't believe it at first, but she recognized her boyfriend's clothing and the bolt in his leg. Tears raced down her cheeks. She hiccupped, then she burped. She fought off the urge to vomit, but she couldn't stop herself from weeping. She released a bloodcurdling shriek. Gabe grabbed her and pulled her out of the room. She wrestled with him, she clawed at his arms, but she couldn't overpower him.

"Let me go! Let me go!" she demanded as they stumbled into the parking lot. Gabe wrapped his arms around her as she pushed him. They danced to the neighboring room. Lacey shouted, "You were supposed to watch him! You promised! You selfish bastard! You let him die! This is your fault!"

"I'm sorry," Gabe responded.

"I don't care! Just... Let me go! Let me see him! Please!"

"We have to go. You can't do anything for him now."

"I need to be with him!"

"He's gone. You shouldn't... see him like that. Not again."

Lacey grabbed his hands from behind her, unaware of his gruesome injury, then she pushed him away. Gabe yelped. His knees hit each other twice—*thud, thud!*—as his legs wobbled. Lacey gasped. She noticed his missing fingers. *He fought the clowns, too,* she thought. She couldn't blame him for Colton's demise. She grabbed his arms to stop him from falling.

"I'm sorry," she said weakly. She looked at the door to Room 107 as she hugged the trucker. She cried, "Colton, I'm so sorry."

"I'm so sorry," Gabe repeated, teary-eyed.

He felt like he was hugging Monica. Although he sought revenge and redemption, he felt forgiven. They cried in each other's arms, mourning the loss of their loved ones.

Gabe looked at Lacey's hand and said, "You... You have a gun. You have to go in there and... and kill them."

"Kill them?"

"Shoot them while they're down."

"I burned that bitch over there because she was about to shoot you. It's self-defense. I can't... I can't go around executing more people. The cops are coming. Hassan, the guy who owns the market, he called them again."

Gabe said, "I don't hear any sirens." He saw doubt written on Lacey's face. He said, "If they get up, they'll attack us again... and again... *and again.* Sooner or later, you'll have to pull the trigger. Self-defense and all that bullshit... it doesn't matter now."

"But what if... I already... I shot..."

Lacey killed Todd and burned Puddin' to a crisp. She wasn't proud of her actions. It was easy to say you'd kill for a loved one—hypotheticals were only words after all—but things changed when push came to shove. She glanced over at the wrecked motel room. She heard clunking steel and squeaky springs. *The police cruiser,* she thought.

Gabe said, "If you can't do it, I will."

The trucker looked anemic, pallid and feeble. He had lost a lot of blood throughout the night. Lacey was afraid he would shoot himself by mistake because he was so weak. She looked at the door to Room 107 and thought about Colton. She wasn't driven by revenge, but she felt a need to do something—*anything*.

She stuttered, "I–I can do it."

She walked back to Room 108. Gabe limped behind her, constantly glancing back at Puddin'. He found a sense of comfort in her suffering. Her punishment seemed appropriate—an eye for an eye, a burn for a burn. Yet, as if he were stuck in a horror movie, he expected her to get up and attack them again.

As she approached the door, Pumpkin lunged out of the room and swung a fire axe at her. He chopped her upper arm, breaking the shaft of her humerus bone and tearing her muscles apart. Lacey shot at the floor. The bullet ricocheted and hit the room's ceiling. She collapsed in the exterior hallway. Her eyes jutted forth as Pumpkin swung the axe up.

Colton.

Eyes on the blade, she could only think about her boyfriend—her lover, *her soulmate.*

As Pumpkin swung the axe down at Lacey, Gabe charged at him. The axe cut into his left shoulder, mutilating his trapezius muscle and breaking his clavicle. Yet, Gabe managed to push him back into the motel room. He slammed him against the dresser. Face buried in the clown's ruff collar, he jabbed his fingers at Pumpkin's bandaged eye.

Pumpkin screamed. A blot of blood spread across the bandage and harsh pulses of pain attacked his head. Hopping on one foot, he pushed Gabe against the bed's footboard. The trucker leaned back against the police cruiser's rear tire. Pumpkin grabbed the axe's handle and tugged on it. The blade slid out of Gabe's shoulder, followed by geysers of blood.

He swung the axe at Gabe's face. Gabe weaved, but the blade still severed the top half of his left ear. The axe punctured the rear tire. The tire's hiss was as loud as Gabe's screaming.

From the doorway, Lacey shot at Pumpkin. The bullet whizzed past them and struck the driver's door, which was now open. She hesitated. She couldn't remember how many cartridges were left in the revolver and she didn't want to shoot Gabe by mistake. Pumpkin winced, but he noticed Lacey's reluctance. He called her bluff.

He gripped Gabe's neck to stop him from moving his head. Gabe grabbed the clown's wrist with his good hand while Pumpkin swung the axe overhead. He saw his life flash before his eyes. Lacey shot at them again, but the bullet zipped past Pumpkin's head. Gabe kicked the clown's mutilated ankle, sending stabbing pain through Pumpkin's body. He pushed him back to the dresser.

Yowling in pain, blood squirting out of his ankle,

Pumpkin swung the axe down again. The blade shattered Gabe's kneecap. Gabe dropped to the floor with the axe sticking out of him.

Lacey hurried into the room. Both hands on the revolver, she shot Pumpkin in the head at point-blank range. She was shorter than him, so she shot up at him at an angle. The bullet entered the right side of his jaw, drilled through his gums and tongue, entered the roof of his mouth, and then exited through his left cheekbone near his earlobe. Flaps of skin and fragments of bone splattered on the green wallpaper.

The clown collapsed in front of the dresser. Flakes of burning gunpowder tattooed a ring around the small entrance wound. The exit wound was larger. Most of his cheekbone was missing. Cracked teeth rode waves of blood out of his mouth. Blood came out of his nostrils. His ears rang incessantly. The bullet missed his brain, but the excruciating pain made it feel like his brain had exploded in his skull.

Lacey stood over him, pressed the revolver's muzzle against his forehead, and pulled the trigger.

Click.

The revolver was empty. Blood frothing on his lips, Pumpkin grinned and chuckled.

"Why?" Lacey asked in disbelief. "Why are you laughing? Why?! *Why?!*"

The clown kept cackling. He only stopped to spit a blob of blood at the dresser, then he started laughing again.

Lacey said, "You fucking psycho. You killed every-one. And for what? Why did you..." She paused to choke down the lump in her throat. She asked, "Why did you have to kill him? Why'd you... do *that* to him? Why?"

Voice gurgly and husky, Pumpkin stuttered, "Fu–Fun..."

"Fun?"

Pumpkin snickered for a few seconds, then he coughed up some blood. He said, "Fun, bitch. You think... this is over? You... You think you won?" He laughed until he was interrupted by another cough. He said, "Thi–This isn't over. Everywhere... You–You'll see us e–everywhere. Every city in America is... is burning right now. When they put you on the news... your name... your face... The circus will come to your town and... and wipe out the rest of your family. Maybe tomorrow, maybe next month... maybe next year. But they'll come..."

He's bluffing, Lacey thought. Then she remembered the reports on the news about the clown sightings. They had been disconnected from the rest of the world since the previous afternoon. She remembered Jayden speaking about 'unusual' fires throughout the city after he called the police. A lot could happen in one night.

Not a distraction, she thought. *A siege.*

She squeezed the trigger three times, as if she had forgotten the cylinder was empty—*click, click, click!*

Pumpkin giggled. He groaned as he sat up slowly, propping himself up on his elbows.

Lacey stomped on his right foot. A *crunching* sound came out of his ankle as his remaining ligaments tore. He fell back against the floor and arched his back. More blood bubbled out of his mouth. The tip of her shoe pressed against his foot, she twirled her ankle as if she were crushing a cigarette under her sneaker. In a fit of rage, she lunged forward and kicked Pumpkin's chin.

The blood from his mouth rippled over his eyes and forehead. He gagged as two of his teeth went down his throat. She kept kicking him. She smashed his jaw to smithereens while breaking her own toes. His mutilated tongue was crushed between his mandible and palate. He started choking on his tongue and blood.

Lacey screamed as she stomped on Pumpkin's face, placing all of her weight and energy behind her. Her heel crushed his good eye. His modified forehead *popped* like a blister, saline and blood oozing out. His nasal bone collapsed over his nostrils. His skull was fractured. He had a brain hemorrhage. He convulsed on the floor.

Lacey tottered away, trying to keep her weight off her broken foot. She stared down at Pumpkin's bloody face. He didn't look human.

I did that, she thought. *He's dying. He's dead. I killed him. I'm a killer. Why couldn't I stop? What happened to me? What have I done?*

A hoarse cough interrupted her thoughts. She saw Gabe on the floor at the foot of the bed. She limped over to him.

As she reached for the axe's handle, Gabe said, "Don't. Please don't touch it." Lacey nodded reluctantly. Gabe said, "Get out of here. Run as fast as possible."

"I'm not leaving you."

"You said it yourself. The cops will be here soon. I can... I can wait for them."

"I've let too many people die already. I'm not letting you die here. It's time to leave this shithole."

19

ESCAPE FROM MOTEL ACE

THE SUN ROSE BEYOND THE HORIZON, PAINTING THE SKY with strokes of oranges, reds, and purples. The rain had stopped during the fight.

His arm over her shoulders, Lacey helped Gabe limp out of the room. They frowned upon spotting the dead cop in the exterior hallway. Lacey felt a sense of profound sadness as she stared at the power drill stuck in the door to Room 107. Hobbling past his room, Gabe was overcome with sorrow and guilt as he thought about Monica. They couldn't imagine what had transpired in the rooms upstairs. They contorted their faces in disgust upon catching a whiff of charred flesh. Puddin' had stopped whimpering and moving. They shared no sympathy for Puddin', they hated the clowns, but the violence still shocked them. They spotted Gold Diner 80's broken windows and the barricaded door from afar.

Overnight, Motel Ace had transformed from a cheap, outdated motel to a bloody battleground. The loss of life was a travesty.

And it was all for 'fun.'

The survivors made their way around the front office. They headed towards Hassan's Market. Through the windows, they saw the fallen shelves and blood on the floor. Lacey thought about heading up to the apartment to help Salma, but she knew she couldn't carry her down by herself and help Gabe at the same time. She figured Salma was safer up there anyway. She hoped so, at least. They planned on lumbering down the road.

"What is that?" Gabe asked.

"What?"

"Tha–That. Back there."

Lacey squinted at the partition between the motel and the market. She spotted a campervan parked behind the shop.

"No way," she said.

"What is it?"

"I've seen this RV before. Oh my God, we saw it on our way here."

They approached the campervan. Gabe leaned against the passenger door and pressed his sweaty, bloody face against the window. He couldn't see into the vehicle. Lacey walked around it, examining its unique paint job. She stopped behind the campervan and gazed at the decal of the Pierrot on the rear door. She couldn't forget it.

She said, "It's the same RV. They were watching us, *stalking* us, for so long. They planned it all out. Those sick bastards..."

"It's still open," Gabe said as he tugged on the handle.

He pulled the door open and peeked inside. There was a rusty stovetop, a sink full of dirty dishes, and a counter with a microwave on top and minifridge underneath. Across from the kitchen area, there was a small sofa next to the sliding door. At the back of the campervan, a dusty brown curtain separated the bed from the rest of the interior. Only the tattered, beige pillow—which looked like it had been soaked in urine—was visible from the passenger seat.

Gabe yelled, "And the key's still in the ignition!"

Lacey ran to the driver's door. She climbed into the vehicle and glanced over her shoulder. The odor of blood teased her nostrils. She turned the key in the ignition. The engine stalled. She turned it again and the engine started. She sighed in relief. She took the sunshade off the dashboard and threw it into the kitchen.

"Hop in," she said.

Gabe struggled to climb onto the passenger seat. The handle of the axe hit the glove compartment, aggravating his wound. Lacey gasped and covered her mouth as she watched his blood squirt out of his knee.

She said, "Oh God, are you–"

"Just drive," Gabe said, holding his breath.

He slammed the door and twirled his index finger at her—*come on, let's get going.* The vehicle rocked as it rolled over the uneven dirt. Each bounce aggravated Gabe's wound. He held his breath and gnashed his teeth. His face and chest were as red as blood. He panted as they reached the main road. Lightheaded, he rested his face against the dirty window.

"I'm sorry," Lacey said.

"Don't be. It ain't your fault."

Lacey glanced at Hassan's Market as they cruised past it. She said, "They killed the waitress. I left her to die, you know? Then they killed the owner of that market. I watched it happen. I tried to help, but... I was too scared, so I was too late. And now there's a woman up there, alone and afraid. I don't think she can move or speak... and I just left her. I think I'm just as bad as those clowns."

"Not even close," Gabe said, drowsy. "We're not all cops... or firefighters... Just because you didn't save someone... that doesn't make you as bad as a killer. Those clowns were monsters. Pure evil."

"Yeah."

"It might not mean much to you... maybe you hate my guts, but... thank you for saving me."

"Are you kidding me? *You* saved *my* life. Look at my arm. It's getting numb now, but it hurt like hell. And he would have done much more if it weren't for you."

Lacey laughed nervously while wiping the tears from her eyes. Gabe slipped in and out of consciousness. They sat in silence and drove for three quiet minutes.

"Hey," Lacey said, wide-eyed. "Hey! Look!"

Gabe's eyes fluttered open. He saw red and blue lights ahead. He rolled the window down an inch. He heard the emergency sirens.

"Thank God," he said, tears of joy flowing down his cheeks.

They couldn't help but laugh and cheer. Lacey placed more pressure on the gas pedal and honked the horn. They saw a fleet of police cruisers racing towards them.

Behind the survivors, the curtain slid open. Gaggles emerged from under a torn blanket with a chef knife in his hand. He stepped off the bed, arms away from his body to keep his balance. He ran forward and stabbed Lacey three times. He plunged the blade into her breast, then he stabbed her between the ribs twice. Blood drenched her tank top in seconds.

In a knee-jerk reaction, she stomped on the gas pedal. She swerved left and right as she shrieked. Gabe grabbed the clown's arm and stopped him from stabbing her a fourth time.

"Die!" Gaggles yelled.

The campervan crashed into the police cruiser at the front of the fleet head-on. Gaggles was ejected through the campervan's windshield. His head was split open, a jagged gash from the back of his scalp to his nose. Every bone in his neck was broken. He crashed through the police cruiser's windshield. His torso was inside the car while his legs remained on the crushed hood.

The cop suffered from whiplash, his jaw and nose were broken, but he survived the crash.

The campervan rolled down a slope on the side of the road. The sounds of steel clunking and crunching and glass shattering and crackling joined the sirens and screeching tires on the road. The campervan stopped upside down in the desert, wheels spinning. Clouds of dirt billowed out, surrounding the crash site.

Lacey awoke seconds after the crash, broken arms dangling down towards the vehicle's ceiling. She bled internally as well as from her nose, mouth, cheeks, and left eye. Shards of glass from the shattered windshield had torn her face open and pierced her eye. She hacked as she tasted the blood at the back of her mouth. Blood from her stab wounds flowed across her collarbones and neck. The seat belt had saved her life.

She dry-heaved upon spotting Gabe's body on the dirt in front of the campervan. He was ejected during the crash. He wasn't moving, wasn't crying, *wasn't breathing*. It was a quick death. Two decapitated heads had flown out of the vehicle during the crash, too—the heads of Caroline and Joey Marsh. Jacob's head was on the ceiling behind her. The clowns intended on keeping the heads as souvenirs—*hunting trophies*.

Lacey saw cops running to the campervan to rescue her. She looked at Joey's head, then at Caroline's, and then she stared at Gabe's body. The carnage was devastating. She sobbed as she thought about Colton and the other victims. Unable to withstand the physical and emotional pain, she fell unconscious again. Along with Salma, she was one of the last survivors of the massacre at Motel Ace.

JON ATHAN

DO NOT DISTURB 2

THE PLATINUM PALACE

1

NEW ARRIVAL

"WE'RE LATE," ROB FARRELL MUTTERED.

A duffel bag slung over his shoulder, he trailed behind Dustin Pearson in the multistory car park. In bold yellow paint, the number '1' was painted onto the columns around them. Other signs on the columns pointed them towards the exits, staircases, and elevators.

Without looking back, Dustin said, "I know, man, I know. Just follow my lead."

He forced a smile and waved at a group of employees loitering next to a set of elevators. They waved back at him, although they didn't feign happiness like he did. Above the elevators, a sign read: *Welcome to the Platinum Palace!*

Rob said, "Don't draw attention to yourself."

"I'm acting natural," Dustin responded quietly through his clenched teeth.

"Stop waving and keep walking, bozo."

"Yeah, yeah, whatever."

The men marched towards the exit. They wore matching uniforms: Dark navy shirts and pants. And on the back of their shirts, in all capital letters, a word read: *SECURITY*. Dustin's hair was buzz cut while Rob had a head of feathery blond hair. They were both burly, although it looked like Dustin was packing a few extra pounds on his abdomen.

As soon as they exited the parking garage, the ceaseless chatter and laughter on the Las Vegas Strip struck their ears. They heard every emotion in the human body—from drunken regret to starry-eyed excitement, destructive rage to total happiness. It was nighttime, but the Strip was always so bright that some drunks could have mistaken it for morning.

The men crossed the driveway and went up a short flight of stairs. Dustin scanned his badge—which functioned as an identification card and a key card—on the wall-mounted card reader next to the double doors. The doors unlocked with a satisfying *click*. They opened the doors and stepped into a hallway. There was a walk-through metal detector and a CT scanner in front of them.

Another security guard stood on the other side of the metal detector. An identification badge was clipped to his shirt. Next to a picture of himself, the name on the badge read: *Edwin Martin*.

Dustin nodded at him and said, "How's it going, Ed?"

"Not bad," Edwin replied. "You?"

"I'm not doing too bad myself. Busy night?"

"For me? Nah. York's got *another* stick up his ass, though, so steer clear from him. Swear to God, that guy's always getting fucked so he wants to fuck the rest of us."

Dustin emptied his pockets and took off his belt. He threw all his belongings in a plastic bin.

He asked, "What's up with him?"

"Same ol' bullshit. Procedure this, protocol that. I'm telling you, we need two or three managers per shift."

"We just opened. Management probably thinks nothing–"

Before he could step through the metal detector, Dustin felt Rob tugging on the back of his shirt. Sinking his teeth into his bottom lip, the expression on Dustin's face said something along the lines of: *Oh shit, my bad.* He took a step to the side and beckoned to Rob.

He said, "Almost forgot about our friend here. Edwin, this is Rob. He's new."

"New?" Edwin repeated. He looked at a monitor on his side of the metal detector. He asked, "Rob what?"

"Farrell," Rob said.

He put his duffel bag on the CT scanner's conveyor belt. Then, like Dustin, he emptied his pockets, took off his belt, and put all of his belongings in a plastic bin.

He approached the metal detector and asked, "Am I good to go through?"

"You're not on tonight's shift. Let me see your badge."

"I'm supposed to pick it up tonight."

Edwin checked the scanner's monitor. He saw what appeared to be rolls of duct tape and bundles of zip-tie handcuffs.

"What is this?" he asked. "What's in the bag?"

"Supplies for the equipment room. Order Number 3079. You're supposed to know all of this already."

Dustin asked, "What's with the third degree, Ed? I told you, he's new."

"Just give me a sec," Edwin said. He pressed the push-to-talk button on his radio and said, "Mike, I've got a 'Rob Farrell' at Security Gate 1. He doesn't have a badge and he's not on the team list. Please advise. Over."

There was no response.

After fifteen seconds of silence, he changed the channel on his walkie-talkie, pressed the push-to-talk button, and asked, "Anyone got a location on York? Over."

The radio buzzed, then a woman said, "Meeting at the command center. Over."

"Shit."

"Am I good to go?" Rob asked.

Edwin looked him up and down. Nothing about his appearance rang any alarms in his head. He was wearing their uniform after all. He trusted Dustin, too. They got acquainted during their training. The duffel bag concerned him, but Rob's explanation made sense. The hotel had recently opened, so they were still settling in.

He said, "Come on."

The metal detector *beeped* three times as Rob stepped through it. Edwin used a handheld metal detector to scan his body from his feet to his chest. It didn't beep.

"Anything in your pockets?" Edwin asked.

Rob pulled his pockets out and said, "No, sir."

"Let's try it again then."

"Sure."

Rob went through the metal detector, causing it to *beep* three times again. He spun around, waited five seconds, then walked through the metal detector again with his hands up. It *beeped* three more times. Edwin scanned him with the handheld metal detector and patted him down, but he didn't find anything.

Dustin said, "C'mon, Ed, hurry it up. I've got shit to do."

Edwin curled his index finger at him, as if to say: *Come here.* The metal detector went off as Dustin walked through it.

"Nothing in my pockets, either," Dustin said with a shrug.

Irritated, Edwin lowered his head and rubbed his eyes. He had very little training when it came to faulty equipment.

He sighed, then said, "Go ahead."

Dustin and Rob gathered their belongings. Rob held the duffel bag in his hand and walked ahead.

As they walked away from him, Edwin said, "Dustin. Hey, *Dustin.*" When Dustin glanced back, Edwin pointed at him and said, "Don't mess this up for me, man. You hear me?"

"Loud and clear, bud. I'll see you around."

"We're clear, but he slowed us down," Rob said in a hushed voice as they continued walking. "I'll meet you after I pick up the rest of our 'tools.' Get in that room and get the ball rolling."

"Hold up, hold up. What are you talking about? You're supposed to stick with me. What if they catch me? What if they call my–"

"Don't panic. You understand? Whatever happens, do *not* panic. I'll be there soon. Remember, he's counting on us."

Dustin stopped walking. He watched as Rob took a left down the hall and vanished around the corner. Other employees—mostly security guards—moved through the service corridors.

"Yeah, I can do this," Dustin murmured as he shuffled forward, barely lifting his feet with each step. "I just have to follow the plan. He's counting on us— *on me.*"

Through another set of double doors, Dustin found himself in the casino's command center. At the other end of the room, the wall was covered in monitors. As directed by Norman York, the security manager, the monitors showed live footage of different areas throughout the premises, including the casino floor, the lobby, the restaurants, the shops, the pool area, a parking garage, and some of the service corridors.

There were three columns and three rows of desks in the room, and there were two monitors and two phones on each desk. Two narrow walkways separated the columns. Supervisors—dressed in suits—stalked the walkways and crept behind the desks, monitoring the employees closely as if they were inmates working in a prison. Meanwhile, the employees at the desks kept their eyes on the gamblers while communicating with the security guards roaming the rest of the resort.

Dustin went to a desk on the left side of the room. He smiled at his neighbor, a thirtysomething woman named Felicia White, before taking his seat and logging into his computer. He spotted Norman chatting with a supervisor in front of the wall of monitors. Pushing fifty, he was a stern-faced man with graying hair and a thick mustache. He didn't notice Dustin's tardiness.

As a supervisor walked behind him, Dustin said, "Sorry I'm late. Some guy was holding up the–"

"Not now," the supervisor interrupted.

He kept moving and spoke into the radio in his hand, but his words were unintelligible. *He's talking about me,* Dustin thought. Trying to act natural, he checked a couple of surveillance cameras as he waited for another supervisor to walk past his desk. When the coast was clear, he pulled a USB thumb drive out of his back pocket and plugged it into his desktop.

He cycled through some more surveillance feeds and answered a call from a guard in the casino while a computer worm from the thumb drive infected the security network.

Meanwhile, Rob entered a locker room. Since there was another man in the room, he went to Dustin's locker—3215—and acted like it belonged to him. He took Dustin's windbreaker out and threw it on. Then he styled his hair in a mirror on the locker door. He swiped the hair away from his forehead, back over it, then away again—killing time.

The other man left five minutes later.

Like a crab on a beach, Rob walked sideways in front of the lockers. He read the numbers on each locker in his head. *Not that one, no, nope,* he thought. He walked around the corner and went down another aisle, running his eyes over each locker until his gaze settled on a number.

2125.

He pulled on the locker's handle. As expected, the door popped open. Inside, he found a folded uniform, a pair of shoes, a gym bag, and a pair of headphones. He dug his hands into the pants pockets, then checked under the uniform—*nothing*. He opened the gym bag and moved the musty clothes around—*nada*.

"Damn it," he whispered.

He lifted the large sneakers, but he stopped before he could check under them. They were unusually heavy. He found a five-round revolver hidden in each shoe.

A smile stretching across his face, he said, "Attaboy."

He tucked the revolvers in the back of his waistband and returned to Dustin's locker. He took a walkie-talkie out of his duffel bag.

After changing the frequency, he pressed the push-to-talk button and said, "Lena, be ready at the door. It's time."

In the command center, a man stood from his seat and said, "York, we've got some slow down over here."

At the front of the room, York turned to face the employees and said, "Be specific, Mr. Sinclair."

"It looks like the system is crashing, sir. We're having trouble swapping between surveillance feeds."

"What do you mean it's crashing?"

From another column of desks, a woman said, "Sir, we're experiencing the same slow down."

Norman walked to the row of desks in front of him and checked the computers. Some of the computers were lagging while others were completely frozen.

Dustin savored the dumbfounded expressions on his coworkers' faces, fighting to stop himself from grinning. The computer worm was working as planned.

"Should we reboot?" a man asked.

Norman said, "Get up and step away from your workstations. *Now*." He nodded at a supervisor and said, "Call our tech guys. We have to *assume* our network's infected."

And just like that, Dustin's urge to grin was gone. He wasn't expecting Norman to catch on to their plan so soon. His eyes and lips twitched as sweat dribbled down his face and tickled his skin. He glanced at the double doors. The thought of running grew in his mind to the point that it felt like a physical lump on his brain.

Norman said, "Inform the team leaders on the ground. We'll have to reorganize." He turned his attention to the other employees and said, "You heard me, didn't you? Leave your possessions and step away from your workstations. Don't touch anything until we get to the bottom of this. We'll–"

"Sir, our signal's being jammed," the supervisor interrupted.

From a desk, a man said, "The alarms aren't working, either."

Norman said, "Call the police. If you can't call them from in here, go outside and–"

Dustin jumped to his feet and shouted, "Nobody move!"

He pulled his cell phone out of his pocket and lifted his shirt, revealing the pipe bombs strapped to his abdomen—*a suicide vest*. The other employees responded with gasps and shrieks. In the neighboring workstation, the woman fell off her seat as she tried to roll away. Most of the employees cowered under their desks and ran into the corners, panic resetting their minds and wiping away their training. Derrick Banks, one of the supervisors, lurched towards the double doors.

"You open that door and I blow up this entire building!" Dustin yelled, the words rushing out of his mouth.

"*Stop,*" Norman said sternly while raising his hand at the supervisor.

Derrick froze with his fingers wrapped around the door handles. He tightened his grip on them as he seriously considered running out. Then he thought about his family, his coworkers' families, the families staying in that part of the hotel. He refused to jeopardize everyone's safety. He stepped away from the door with his hands up.

Some of the employees breathed a sigh of relief. Others continued to whimper and whine under their desks. They tried to call the police, but their cellular signal was disrupted as well.

With a sneer of disbelief, Norman asked, "Mr. Pearson, what are you doing?"

Dustin said, "Just stay calm and everything will be

fine. We don't want to hurt anyone, but we will if we have to."

"We?"

Duffel bag slung over his shoulder, Rob approached Security Gate 1. Upon hearing his footsteps, Edwin looked back at him.

"You get your badge yet?" he asked.

"Better," Rob said.

He drew the revolver from the back of his waistband and pointed it at Rob's face. The muzzle was about six inches away from his nose.

Edwin raised his trembling hands and stuttered, "Ta–Take it easy."

"Open the door."

"Wha–What?"

"Keep your hands up. Turn around. Go through the metal detector. Open the door. Easy-peasy, Eddie, easy-peasy."

"Ye–Yeah. Yeah, o–okay. I'm cool, man. You be cool, too, all right? Just relax."

Edwin did as he was told. Rob followed behind him with the revolver pressed against the back of his head. The metal detector went off again. Edwin opened the doors. He found a young woman, Lena McKee, waiting outside. A duffel bag on the floor next to her, she stood there with her hands clasped behind her back and twirling her foot. Her hair was tied in two long pigtails—a pink one and a blue one. She wore a white blouse, denim shorts, torn fishnet tights, and boots.

In a soft, childish voice, she said, "Well, mister, aren't ya gonna help me with my bag?"

Edwin looked at the bag, then at Lena, and then at Rob.

"Well?" Rob said.

"Yeah, sure," Edwin said. "Whatever you say."

While grabbing the bag, he peeked over at the car park next door. He didn't see or hear any other employees. He followed Lena back into the building. Rob handed her a revolver, then locked the doors behind them. The metal detector rang as they all walked through it—nine sharp *beeps*.

Rob said, "Into the command center."

"Don't move!" Dustin shouted as the doors swung open.

Edwin shambled into the room. Rob and Lena followed him inside. Again, Rob locked the doors behind them.

Lena said, "Relax, Dusty, it's only us."

"Don't call me that."

"Huh? I thought that's what you wanted us to call you."

Norman asked, "What do you people want?"

Ignoring him, Dustin said, "I'm Sharpy, okay? *Sharpy*, not Dusty."

Standing behind him, Rob placed the muzzle of the

revolver against Edwin's right temple and said, "Quiet down, everyone. No one will get hurt as long as you follow our instructions." Rattled, the employees whined and trembled. Rob said, "I want you all to come out in the open. We'll drag you out if we have to. We're only going to restrain you. If you let it happen, we'll leave you alone for the remainder of the night. If you fight, we're going to shoot you on the spot. It's that simple."

Norman said, "I'm the security manager, Norman York. If this is about money, you don't need thirty-some hostages to get it. Let them go and keep me. I'm all you–"

"Don't move, Mr. York. We'll get to talking soon. First, we have to take control of the situation. We don't want your employees to make the wrong move and get you all killed, do we?"

"I do," Lena said, smirking.

Dustin said, "Shut up."

"*You* shut up."

Rob asked, "Do we have an understanding, Mr. York?"

Norman didn't have many options. All of the employees in the command center were unarmed. Most of the guards in the rest of the resort were unarmed, too. Only some off-duty cops working security at the casino had guns on them, but they were unaware of the situation in the command center. Despite outnumbering the intruders, he knew they couldn't overpower them, outrun their bullets, or survive an explosion.

He said, "We have an understanding."

"Great," Rob responded. He kicked one of the duffel bags forward with his foot and said, "Let's get started."

Elbow-to-elbow, the employees sat on their asses under the wall of monitors. They were so close to each other that they could hardly move. Their arms were bound behind their backs with zip-tie handcuffs and, out in front of them, their legs were taped together at the ankles. Strips of duct tape sealed their mouths, too. They sang a chorus of muffled groans and grunts.

Norman stood between them and Rob. Dustin and Lena had rebooted the security system. They answered calls from the hotel staff and other security guards while keeping them away from the command center. Lena sat with her legs kicked up on a desk. She applied white makeup to her face with a brush while speaking into a headset.

Norman said, "You're not going to get away with this. Any second now, someone is going to try to open that door. When they notice it's locked, when they can't contact me—not your little lackey, but *me*—they're going to realize something's wrong and the police are going to get involved. And you know what? It won't take them long to get here because they're already on the casino floor."

"I know," Rob said. "We're already tracking them."

"Tracking... What exactly are you planning here? You're going to shoot it out with the cops? Going to blow up the hotel to make some bullshit social statement?"

"We're taking over the hotel. The *entire* thing."

Norman said, "You think it's as easy as saying it out loud? Look at yourself. Look at your 'partners' for crying out loud." He pointed at Lena and said, "She looks like a damn clown!"

Lena rolled her eyes and said, "Because I am one, bozo."

"Whatever this is, it isn't going to work. If you won't negotiate with me, you'll have to talk to the police. I'm a hard ass. Ask your buddy Pearson over there. But the LVMPD are harder. They won't play your games."

With a shaky smile, Dustin said, "Rob... it's time. They're already setting it off. At Motel Ace, in Reno, in NYC... all over the place. It's actually happening."

"Time for what?" Norman asked.

Lena said, "*Finally*. We don't have to do the whole 'Die Hard' terrorist thing anymore. Y'know, I'm surprised you guys didn't go for the Russian accents."

Dustin said, "They're German in Die Hard. Well, Hans Gruber is German. He was played by Alan Rickman, who was actually English. I–"

Rob raised a hand, calling for silence with the gesture. He kept his eyes stuck on Norman's.

Monotone, he said, "I'm a clown, too, Mr. York, and I like games."

"Excuse me?" Norman said.

"You wanna know what my brothers and sisters call me? They call me Spike—Spike the Clown. And you wanna know why?"

"Goddammit, don't tell me this is some sick joke for your damn social media garbage."

"It's because of my *spikes*."

Norman wagged his index finger at him and said, "I swear you're going to..."

His voice trailed off and his eyes grew as Rob tugged on his own hair. His blond wig rose from his head. Under the wig, a mohawk of sharp metal spikes stuck out of his scalp—from his forehead's hairline to the occipital bone at the back of his skull.

Rob looked down and thrust his head at Norman's face. The spikes cracked his chin, pierced his lips and stabbed his gums, and punctured his nostrils. The durable, pointed metal nicked his cheekbones, too. Dazed by the headbutt, Norman staggered back. But his lips were still skewered by the spikes. They stretched away from his face, as if he were puckering them up for an exaggerated kiss. The spikes slid out as the wounds opened up.

He crashed into the wall of monitors. Blood gushed out of his nose, dyeing the graying hairs on his mustache red. The blood cascaded over his teeth and filled his mouth, spilling out of the punctures on his cheeks and chin like water through bullet holes on a tank. The staff below him screamed and sobbed, unable to move away as his blood rained down on them.

Before Norman could find his bearings, Rob rushed forward and headbutted him again. The back of Norman's head bounced off the monitor behind him. The spikes cut into his nasal septum, lips, and right cheek. His head spun and his legs rocked. Rob grabbed Norman's jacket at the chest to stop him from collapsing. He swung his head back, then thrust it forward for another brutal headbutt.

With the third headbutt, Rob's mohawk tore up the left side of Norman's face. His upper lip was partially detached. His bloodied mustache dangled *over* his mouth. His upper gums, mutilated by the spikes, were visible in the grisly wound. A spike entered his left eye socket, cutting through his lower eyelid and grazing the eyeball as it slid underneath it.

Norman blacked out. Lena cheered at a desk while the hostages squirmed across the floor and cowered in the corners of the room.

Laughing, Rob unleashed a rapid barrage of head-butts, tearing Norman's face to shreds. His upper lip was severed. The bloody, hairy piece landed between their feet with a loud *splat*. His cheeks tore from the corners of his mouth to his ears—a long, squiggly

Glasgow smile. Broken teeth fell from his gums and rode a wave of blood out of his mouth. His nose was crushed, mushy like a squashed tomato. One of the headbutts dislocated his jaw and left a deep dent on his chin.

Rob stopped after the thirteenth headbutt. Blood coated his face like sweat on a runner after a marathon. His forehead glowed red. He had harmed himself during the beating, but he still grinned and chuckled. He released Norman's jacket, allowing his stiff body to fall to the floor. The other employees wailed. They couldn't recognize their boss. It looked like his face had been eaten by a wild animal.

Out of breath, Rob said, "Lena... Kill 'em... Kill 'em all."

"With pleasure!" Lena yelled as she sprung up to her feet.

The hostages screamed louder as the clown approached them. She stopped next to Felicia White, who had wormed her way to the walkway between the desks. Lena crouched next to the hostage and pulled a utility knife out of her pocket. The knife made a *clicking* noise as she slowly drew the blade.

Click...

Click...

Click.

Felicia rolled onto her back and shook her head at Lena. Although the tape reduced her voice to a garble of noise, her message was clear: '*No! Don't! Stop!*'

"What's that? I'm sorry, I don't understand a thing you're saying," Lena said, voice laced with faux concern. "Oh, I know! I'll help you by giving you another mouth! Genius, don't ya think?"

She straddled Felicia's chest, her knees close to her shoulders, then pushed her face down with her free hand to pin her head to the floor. She drove the blade into her neck, only a few inches below the hostage's right ear. It went in with little resistance. To the hostage, the stabbing felt like a strong pinch. She started to panic as a warm sensation spread across her neck.

Lena dragged the blade to her right. She started sawing as she closed in on the first set of jugular veins. She knew she had to cut deep into her victim to reach the internal jugular. And she succeeded. Blood spurted out of the right side of Felicia's neck, weakening after each squirt. She writhed under her attacker, unable to break free from the zip-tie handcuffs or the tape.

The blade slid across her neck and severed her larynx. Blood rose into her mouth and poured into her trachea.

Lena began sawing into her neck again, thrusting and pulling on the blade in an attempt to sever her other jugular veins. She missed the internal jugular. She didn't notice, though. It didn't matter anyway. Felicia had lost enough blood to guarantee her death. It puddled around her and splashed on the neighboring wall. The blade stopped under her left ear.

"Wait, I think I can hear something," Lena said.

Felicia's eyes rolled back as she spasmed under the clown. Gurgling sounds came out of the thin crevice on her neck.

Lena leaned down and tilted her head to the side. She put her ear close to Felicia's wound, as if the woman's neck were a seashell.

She said, "Yeah. Yeah, I do hear something. It sounds like... like..." She sat up, grinned, and exclaimed, "It sounds like the circus! I wonder if I can hear circuses in all of your necks, too. Guess there's only one way to find out."

The other hostages cried and wiggled away as Lena approached them with the bloody utility knife.

As he watched the chaos unfold, Rob held a radio up to his mouth and asked, "Twisted, can you hear me?"

A deep, raspy voice responded, "I hear ya. Go."

"We're ready. Tell the boss his palace is waiting for him."

2

WELCOME TO THE PLATINUM PALACE

A COMMERCIAL PLAYED ON THE TELEVISION'S WELCOME screen. The video cycled through views of the hotel's facilities while a male voiceover said: "Here at the Platinum Palace Resort & Casino, dine at seven diverse world-class restaurants, pamper yourself at our state-of-the-art spa, take a dip at our seven-acre pool complex, and experience outstanding entertainment at our specialty theater featuring live performances and films from around the globe. At the Plat–"

Andrew Castillo, laying on one of the queen beds in the hotel room, pressed a button on the remote and switched to the Video on Demand menu. He flicked through the genres until he stumbled upon a collection of superhero movies. His twelve-year-old mind was fascinated by superheroes and supervillains. His nine-year-old sister, Lily, bounced around on the other bed while prattling on and on about the pools, arcades, an aquarium, and M&M's World.

Their parents, Adrian and Laura, unpacked their suitcases between a bed and a coffee table. They were young parents, barely on the cusp of their mid-thirties. Laura couldn't help but sneak an occasional peek out the floor-to-ceiling windows while organizing the clothes. She was *obsessed* with Vegas. The colorful and vibrant lights filled her with childlike wonder and joy. She loved gambling, too.

From their room on the 30th floor, they had a view of the hotel's other tower, the pool complex below, and the city.

Laura squinted at the other tower and, with a hint of playful jealousy, she said, "I can't believe people are actually going to *live* there. Those condos must cost a fortune."

"They're not even finished building the place yet," Adrian responded.

"I want to live there!" Lily shouted as she hopped on the bed. "Can we live there, daddy? Can we? Can we?"

"You want to move to Vegas, hon?"

"Uh-huh!"

"What about your friends back home? You don't want to see them again?"

"They can come, too. It's so big here."

Staring at the condominium tower while folding

her son's jeans, Laura whispered, "I wouldn't mind living here, either."

Adrian laughed. Lily reminded him of his wife. *She's got the 'Vegas bug' too*, he thought. He took a white button-up shirt out of a suitcase. He removed his t-shirt, revealing the white tank top he wore underneath it, then put on the button-up shirt and rolled the sleeves up to his elbows. He was ready to go out and gamble.

He approached the beds and asked, "What about you, Andrew? You want to live here, too?"

Eyes glued to the television, Andrew said, "I want to watch Avengers."

"Well, that's a lot cheaper than moving."

Lily jumped up once more, then landed on her butt on a fluffy pillow. She crawled to the foot of the bed and looked up at her father with her big puppy eyes.

"I don't wanna watch that," she said. "I wanna watch the Minions."

"You already watched it a million times," Andrew said.

"Nuh-uh!"

"I watched it with you a million times, Lily."

"So what?"

"That means you *did* watch it a million times."

"*Nuh-uh!*" Lily repeated.

Laughing, Laura said, "All right, all right. You two settle down. If you can't agree on a movie, *I'll* have to pick one for you."

The siblings scoffed at each other. Andrew stayed on the bed and continued browsing the movies while Lily approached the windows and stared out at the bright city. *Like a Christmas tree,* she thought, eyes twinkling with fascination.

Adrian sat next to Andrew and asked, "You riding the roller coaster at New York-New York with me this time? I think you might finally be tall enough."

Andrew frowned and looked down at himself. He crossed an arm over his chest and rubbed his shoulder. Adrian recognized his anxiety. He used to be afraid of heights when he was a child as well. He wanted his son to have fun—to explore, *to live*—but he wasn't trying to pressure him into doing anything he didn't want to do.

"Or maybe we can give it a try next year," Adrian said as he patted his son's knee. "We can go to the arcade tomorrow instead. Y'know, I think there's still a House of the Dead game at Circus Circus. You going to help your old man beat it?"

"Yeah," Andrew said, a smile tugging at the corners of his mouth. "It'll be easy."

"That's what I like to hear."

Laura said, "Remember, your dad and I are going out tonight. We'll be right downstairs. If anything happens, anything at all, you give us a call. Our phones are going to be on and loud."

"Why can't we go with you?" Lily asked, still peering down at the city.

"Because kids aren't allowed in the casino while the

adults play. You guys are going to stay here and watch a movie. And you're not going to open the door for anyone, right? *Right?*"

"Right," the siblings replied in unison.

"Perfect. And I want you in bed by the time we get back. Now let's go over all of the rules again and pick a movie together."

Adrian stood from the bed and said, "I'll go buy some fresh water and snacks for the kids. What do you guys want?"

"Caramel popcorn and Buncha Crunch," Andrew said.

"Cheerios and gummy bears!" Lily blurted out, her face against the window.

As he walked away, Adrian said, "You kids ever hear of these things called 'fruits'? Y'know, bananas and apples?"

Lily said, "I want cheerios and gummy bears and bananas and apples!"

She was now jumping, her nose sliding against the smooth glass. Her parents laughed, tickled by her innocent response.

"All right, I'll bring *something* back," Adrian said as he exited the room.

"Hey, don't start playing without me!" Laura hollered.

Lily stopped bouncing and said, "Mommy, I see police lights."

Adrian took the elevator down to the first floor. He walked through the wide, twisting, mazelike hallways, weaving through the foot traffic on his way to the casino. The corridors were wide with high concave ceilings, dark walls, and crimson carpeting with a psychedelic pattern. It was all brightly lit to keep the gamblers awake.

During his walk, he found the glass doors leading to the pool area. The pools had closed a few hours earlier, but the spa was still open. A group of young college students loitered out there, tempted to break the rules and take a dip. Some tourists took selfies around the pools and snapped pictures of the resort, too.

The hairs at the nape of Adrian's neck stood at attention as he heard the noise in the casino. It was simultaneously awful and pleasant—harsh but fun, chaotic but familiar. It was music to his ears. And, as he got closer, he could identify every instrument and every vocalist: The clunking of levers and clacking of buttons, the whirring and ringing and beeping of slot machines, the gamblers cursing at themselves and their dealers, and the tourists chatting excitedly.

A shit-eating grin appeared on his face as he reached the casino. His eyes widened and brightened as he scanned the slot machines. He wasn't tall enough to look over them, but between them, he caught some glimpses of the card tables. He felt like every blackjack dealer in the building was calling his name. While heading to the lobby, which was seamlessly connected to the casino, he even caught himself occasionally standing on his tiptoes to get a better view of the games.

Soon, Adrian, soon, he told himself.

He followed the signs to the lobby at the front of the hotel. Between some clusters of slot machines, staircases led down to the buffet and an arcade. Other pathways around the casino branched out to the theater, an eSports lounge, and some restaurants and stores. The entrance to the condominium tower was built but sealed due to the ongoing renovations.

Adrian entered a small convenience store—*Like Royalty 24/7*—next to the lobby. He stopped in front of the refrigerator and browsed the drinks. He puffed out a short breath and swung his head back, as if he were hit with a sucker punch.

"Six dollars for a bottle of water?" he muttered.

Adrian wasn't the wealthiest man on his block, but he had money. The problem was, he didn't have six-dollars-for-a-bottle-of-water money. He figured he was better off going to a convenience store on the Strip or checking out the vending machines. But since he knew Laura was waiting for him, he chose the vending machines.

He wobbled forward and nearly fell into the refrigerator as someone bumped into him. While regaining his balance, he saw a couple behind him—Owen Campbell and Nora Grant, a couple from Canada. They were hugging and laughing while walking, somewhat buzzed and totally in love.

"Oh shit, sorry about that," Owen said. "Are you okay?"

Adrian said, "It's fine."

Rosy-cheeked, Nora said, "We're really sorry about that. We should really watch where we're going."

"Seriously, don't worry about it."

Owen said, "Yeah, okay. Thanks."

As they walked away, Adrian heard Nora snicker and ask, "Why'd you say 'thanks'? You almost knocked him over."

He didn't catch Owen's response, but he could see him blushing. He watched as the couple walked around the store, giggling, flirting, and taking pictures of everything. He admired their young love. Outside of the convenience store, he ran into the opposite—*old anger*. He saw an elderly couple scolding a bellhop for his handling of their luggage.

The argument caught Adrian's attention because the bellhop, a young man named Jordan Carter, had helped his family with their bags earlier in the evening.

He shrugged at Jordan, as if to say: *What can you do?*

Jordan puckered his lips and nodded. All he could do was wait for his manager to arrive. Adrian retraced his steps and headed back to his room.

3

THE CALL

"You're not out here trying to turn a trick again, are you?" Franco Ferraro asked.

With one hand on his steering wheel, he shone his flashlight through the open driver's window and pointed it at the sidewalk. The beam of light followed Rosa Jiménez, a 21-year-old woman, like a spotlight on a stage. His patrol car rolled down the street next to her at about five miles per hour.

Rosa raised a hand at him to block the light from hitting her eyes. Her skintight yellow dress was riding up, exposing the fold of her ass.

"Why're you askin'? You lookin' for some company?" she asked.

"You know that's enough for me to book you, right?"

"Oh, c'mon, you know I'm just playin' with you. You think I'm gonna actually 'solicit' you while you're in uniform, Officer Ferraro? You know I'd wait until you were off duty. I ain't stupid."

"Stop," Franco said as he pulled over next to her.

Rosa groaned and rolled her eyes. She stopped and turned to face the patrol car with her arms crossed over her chest. There was a two-story apartment building behind her.

Franco said, "I saw you on Fremont, Rosa. Saw you chatting it up with some guys. Were you working again?"

Rosa responded, "I don't do that anymore." She bent over with her elbows on the driver's door windowsill. Smirking, she said, "I'm lookin' for a *real* relationship these days with a *real* man. Someone like you, Ferraro."

She was half-joking, half-serious. She was attracted to men like Franco, but she knew it would never work out between them.

At 33 years old, the beat cop had bushy black hair, soft brown eyes, and stubble across his jaw. He had two notable scars that made him hard to forget. The curved scar on his face stretched from his left cheekbone to the nasolabial fold directly above the corner of his mouth. The other scar was on his neck, a horizontal mark between his Adam's apple and his jugular. Years earlier, he had been slashed by a doped-up pimp while trying to arrest a prostitute.

"You're not smiling," Rosa said. "That mean you gonna arrest me or what?"

There was a moment of silence between them.

Franco said, "No. But I will if I see you on Fremont again. Don't walk that track, Rosa. It's not worth it."

"I wish I didn't have to, officer, but some of us don't have a lot of options. You either walk the track or life walks on you. We're getting fucked either way, huh?"

"You've got options, kid. You have to fight harder to find them, but they're out there."

"Yeah? So, what do you think I should do?"

Over the radio in the patrol car, a female dispatcher said, "Any available unit in the downtown area. We have a possible breaking and entering at Jack's Jackpot Motel on South Bruce Street."

Rosa huffed and leaned away from the vehicle. She asked, "You gonna take that?"

Franco had known her since she was sixteen years old. He had visited her home several times on domestic disturbance calls to stop her father from killing her mother during their arguments. He knew all about her troubled upbringing. And, after she turned eighteen, he found out that she had turned to prostitution to get away from her family. He had been trying to bust her pimp for years in an attempt to rescue her, but to no avail. He didn't want to abandon her out there like everyone else did, but she was right.

Life didn't give them many options.

And in one way or another, everyone got fucked in Las Vegas.

He said, "They're turning up the heat this weekend.

Stay off Fremont if you want to stay out of jail." He grabbed his radio and said, "Dispatch, this is Unit 33. I'm close to that B&E. Over."

As the officer drove away, Rosa waved and shouted, "Thanks for the tip! You're one of the good ones, Ferraro! Can't believe you're not taken yet!"

"Dispatch, I've got a crowd in the parking lot here at Jack's Jackpot Motel," Franco said, holding the radio up to his mouth. "Send another unit. I'll keep you posted. Over."

"Copy," the dispatcher responded.

Franco cruised into the motel's parking lot. He parked next to the front office and took a quick glance around. It was a two-story motel with an L-shaped layout. The exterior hallways leading to the rooms faced the parking lot. The balconies on the second floor overlooked the pool behind the motel.

The guests in the parking lot converged on the patrol car, waving him down as if he didn't already see them. They looked shaken up. Their overlapping voices entered the vehicle as he opened the door.

Melissa Lovell, a young blonde, yelled, "He was going to kill us!"

"It was a clown!" Brandi Jackson, Melissa's room-mate, said.

Franco stepped out of the vehicle and said, "All right, all right. Is anyone hurt?"

An elderly woman pushed forward, shook her index finger at the officer's face, and said, "I saw him, too."

From the other side of the patrol car, a man said, "The asshole broke my window and busted the door."

Raising his voice but not quite yelling, Franco said, "I need you all to quiet down and step away from the vehicle." The guests stepped back, their voices dropping to whispers. Franco asked, "Is anyone hurt?"

The guests looked each other over.

"I don't think so," Melissa said.

"When and where did the breaking and entering occur?"

"It was our hotel room, like, twenty minutes ago. My name's Melissa Lovell."

"I'm Brandi," Brandi said. "We're staying together."

Franco asked, "Which room?"

The man on the other side of the patrol car answered, "115. It's right across the parking lot. The one with the broken window. Can't miss it."

Franco's gaze shifted across the motel until he spotted the broken window, then he glanced back at the man.

He asked, "And you are?"

"Jeremy Snyder. I'm the manager."

Franco said, "Wait there. All of you, wait here. More officers are on the way to take your statements."

As he walked ahead, he beckoned to Melissa and said, "Come with me."

Melissa and Brandi had been holding hands so tightly that their fingers went numb. Melissa nodded at Brandi, as if to say: '*I'll be okay.*' Brandi exhaled loudly, returned the nod, and released her hand. Melissa followed Franco through the parking lot.

Franco said, "Are you two staying in this room alone? Anyone else I should know about?"

"It's just me and Brandi."

"Are you from around here?"

"No. We're from California. Berkeley."

"College students?"

"Yes, sir."

They stopped in front of Room 115. An upside down 5 was the only number on the door. The metal 1's had been knocked off, replaced with deep, splintering cracks. The door looked like it had been attacked with a fire axe, but it was too sturdy and thick to break down. The window next to it was broken, though, shards of glass shimmering on the floor and windowsill. The curtains swayed and rustled with the breeze.

Franco shone his flashlight through the broken window. He saw two beds and two suitcases. The back door, which led to the pool area, appeared intact.

He asked, "Did you get a look at him?"

"It was a clown."

"A clown?" Franco repeated.

"A clown with an axe."

Franco gave her a deadpan. Melissa expected him to laugh. It sounded absurd to her, too—and *she* was the victim. She was surprised to see the cop nod at her. Working as a beat cop in Las Vegas, he had seen it all. This wasn't the first clown he had to arrest. He took a steno pad out of his pocket, flipped it open, and then took a pen out of his utility belt.

"What was he wearing?" he asked.

"Um... A clown costume, I guess."

"You're going to have to be a little more specific."

Melissa said, "Well, um... He was... Like... Um..." She dug her fingers into her hair and said, "I don't know, sir. I've never done this before."

"I understand. Start with the basics. Gender, ethnicity, size."

"The basics. Yeah, okay. He was a big guy. A fat guy. Like, he was as wide as that door. He was light skinned. Probably a foot taller than me. Maybe a little more than that."

While jotting the information down, Franco asked, "And how tall are you?"

"Five-three."

"Do you remember what he was wearing? A wig? Makeup? Anything like that?"

Melissa stared down at the ground and nibbled on her thumb's fingernail. Then she looked at the motel's front office.

She said, "We saw him earlier when we were going

out to dinner. He was in front of the motel, dancing and telling jokes and making balloon animals for the kids. He was wearing a white shirt with black polka dots on it and... and white pants with black stripes. He had white makeup all over his face with a red smile painted over his mouth and black around his eyes. And his nose was red, too. It's kinda hard to explain, sorry."

"You're doing fine," Franco said. "Please continue."

"He had a red wig, but the strangest part was... his forehead looked huge. It looked like it was swollen. I mean, *very* swollen. I thought his head was going to explode or something. When we got back from dinner, he was gone. We were getting ready to go out again when someone knocked on our door. We looked through the peephole and out the window... and we saw him. He wasn't wearing the shirt anymore, but we *knew* it was the same clown from earlier."

Franco evaluated his notes. *A tall, wide, heavy, shirtless man with a red wig and clown makeup wearing white pants with black stripes*, he thought. *And a 'swollen' forehead. Sounds like something from a horror movie.* He wondered if it was all part of an elaborate prank. He had heard about the mysterious clown sightings reported across the country. But the genuine fear on Melissa's face convinced him that she was telling the truth.

In an understanding tone, he asked, "What happened after he knocked?"

Staring at the battered door, Melissa said, "He kept

knocking, but we didn't answer. We called the front desk instead. And I think he noticed because he just... he went berserk. He started hitting the door with an axe. We panicked, so we started screaming. Then he broke the window. I froze up. So, Brandi pulled me away and took me out through the back door. That was when we heard the manager yelling at him. It was the manager and a custodian, I think. They chased him away."

"Did you see which way he went?"

Melissa pointed at the gate next to the motel and said, "When we heard them, we went over there and watched from the other side." She turned around and pointed across the street. She said, "We saw him running that way. A couple of cars almost hit him. He kept going, though. I think he was going to the Strip."

"I think so, too."

Another police cruiser rolled into the parking lot. The chatter from the guests got louder as they waved the car down. Two police officers exited the vehicle.

Franco said, "Thank you for your assistance, Ms. Lovell. You can join the others now, but please don't leave the motel. We may have to interview you again."

After Melissa walked away, Franco got on his walkie-talkie and said, "Dispatch, the suspect at the Jack's Jackpot Motel B&E has fled the scene. Suspect is a white male with a heavy build, 300 pounds, six-four with a red wig and clown makeup. Shirtless but wearing white pants with black stripes. Last seen running towards the Strip about 30 minutes ago."

"Copy," the dispatcher said. "Any injuries?"

"None. I'm going to try to catch up to the suspect. He may be heading to the STRAT Hotel or Circus Circus."

"Copy."

Franco informed the other officers at the crime scene and left them to interview the other witnesses. Then he climbed into his patrol car and headed to the Strip. On his way there, he used the spotlight mounted on the driver's side door frame to illuminate every alleyway, the bright light crawling over the grimy brick partitions and overflowing dumpsters.

Over the radio, his dispatcher said, "We have multiple reports of a disturbance at the Platinum Palace. Guests and staff are reporting screaming in the hotel tower. There was also a report of a man dressed as a clown on the property."

"Unit 33, I think that's my guy, dispatch," Franco said. "I'm southbound on Las Vegas Boulevard. ETA at the Platinum Palace is seven minutes."

"Copy."

Franco turned on his emergency lights and sirens. The chatter on the radio continued. Bumper-to-bumper traffic clogged the street while pedestrians swamped the sidewalks. In clusters, tourists took pictures of the STRAT observation tower, the tallest tower in Las Vegas. Promoters roamed the streets, pestering everyone about clubs and buffets. Cops on foot patrol had to stop the drunks from beating each other.

Yet, despite all of the inconveniences, the atmosphere on the Strip was jubilant.

Then another call came through the radio.

The dispatcher said, "We have a trespassing complaint at the STRAT Hotel. A woman dressed as a clown is refusing to leave the lobby."

"Another clown?" Franco whispered.

A third call came in, then a fourth, and then *a fifth*. And every call dealt with clowns causing disturbances. The dispatcher directed the available units to several hotels across the Las Vegas Strip.

Franco didn't need it to be spelled out for him. He knew all of the sightings were connected. He believed it was a coordinated effort, but he didn't know if it was a prank or terroristic in nature. He didn't receive any reports of serious injuries or threats.

He put the pedal to the metal and sped to the Platinum Palace.

$$4$$

THE BOY

ADRIAN STOOD IN THE VENDING MACHINE ROOM ON THE thirtieth floor. Three vending machines hugged the wall in front of him—two for drinks, one for snacks. To his left, there was an ice machine. The room had no doors, so the opening to his right led directly to the hallway. The elevators were located around the corner.

He had already purchased two water bottles for his kids. He couldn't find any of the snacks they had asked for, so he opted for the closest alternatives: A plain old Crunch bar, gummy worms, and Cheetos.

"Why didn't I just order them a pizza?" he muttered as he collected the snacks.

In his peripheral vision, he saw a person standing outside of the room. He could only see his big red shoes and yellow pants.

Adrian stood up straight, balancing the snacks in

his folded arms. He was about to step out and excuse himself when a bout of confusion stopped him. His eyes shrank to slits and the corner of his mouth rose in an uncertain smile.

A boy—no older than twelve years old—stood before him. He wore yellow overalls with red pom-pom buttons down the middle and a red-and-purple plaid shirt underneath. His face was caked with clown makeup and on his head was a multicolored afro wig.

"Hell–*o?*" Adrian said. The boy stared up at him, attentive but silent. Adrian said, "Think you might be in the wrong hotel, kiddo. You sure you're not supposed to be at Circus Circus? I hear there are a lot of clowns over there."

Adrian chuckled, but the boy stayed quiet. The humming from the ice machine saved them from an awkward silence. He squeezed past him and checked down the hall, looking both ways as if he were about to cross a busy street. There was no one else in sight.

"Are you lost?" he asked.

The boy kept staring at him, eyes unblinking and lips sealed. He didn't look frightened or concerned. His face was devoid of emotion, as blank as a mannequin's.

Adrian said, "Wait here. I'll call the front desk and see if they can find your parents."

While walking to his room, he heard the boy's footsteps behind him. The kid followed him around like a frightened stray dog looking for a new home.

"All right, I guess you can just stick with me," Adrian said. "That works, too."

He stopped at the door labeled *30214*. He tapped his key card on the card reader above the door handle. It unlocked with a loud *click*.

"Don't move," he said. He propped the door open with his foot and said, "Laura, give me a hand over here. Laura, honey, come here."

Laura was sitting on a bed with Andrew and Lily. She was flipping through the menus in search of an appropriate movie for the kids.

She handed the remote to Andrew and said, "Remember, if you two can't agree on a movie, I'll be picking one for you. Let me go see what Daddy brought you."

Lily said, "I hope it's apples and peanut butter."

From the doorway, Adrian said, "Lily, you did *not* ask for apples and peanut butter."

"Yes, I did."

Laura said, "Did you at least get any..." Her voice tapered off as she turned the corner and spotted the little clown in the hallway. She smiled and asked, "And who is this little gentleman?"

Adrian said, "No idea. He just showed up while I was at the vending machines down the hall. He won't talk to me, but it looks like he doesn't mind following strangers to their rooms. Mind watching him while I call the front desk?"

"Sure, why not?"

Adrian entered the room while his wife took his place at the door. He set the snacks and water down on the workspace next to the entertainment center, then went to the phone on the nightstand between the beds.

"Is someone else here?" Andrew asked.

Lily crawled to the foot of the bed and peeked over at the door. Her eyes lit up as she spotted their visitor.

Smiling from ear to ear, she looked back at Andrew and exclaimed, "It's a clown!"

Laura crouched in front of the boy and said, "Hello, sweetheart. I like your little costume. What's your name?"

The boy didn't respond—not a peep from his mouth or twitch on his face. His odd behavior made goosebumps rash out on Laura's arms. She was afraid the boy was a victim of abuse, rendered mute by the horrors of the world. Even though they weren't related, she felt a motherly responsibility to protect him.

Lily said, "I like clowns. Can I go play with him, Daddy?"

"Not now, honey," Adrian said.

He had called the front desk, but the line was busy. He called the concierge desk and heard the busy signal again.

Dah-dah-dah!

Laura touched the boy's shoulder and asked, "Are you okay? Are you lost?" A man and a woman walked past the room. Laura stood up and said, "Excuse me. Do you know this child?"

"No, sorry," the woman said. She stopped and cracked a smile upon noticing the boy's costume. She said, "The kid probably wandered off from Circus Circus."

"That's what I was thinking, but I don't know how he'd end up on the thirtieth floo–"

"We don't know that kid and it ain't none of our business," the man interrupted. He grabbed the woman's hand and said, "Let's go. We don't got time for this shit."

As she was pulled away, the woman said, "Sorry."

Watching them from the doorway, Laura whispered, "What a prick." She heard a *ding* from the elevator bank. She squatted in front of the boy again, clapped, and said, "Okay, we need to think about how we're going to find your family."

The boy lowered his head and asked, "You wanna see my special magic trick?"

Laura was startled by his voice. She wasn't expecting him to say anything and he sounded as if he were speaking with something in his mouth. He seemed to have trouble articulating his S's.

"A special magic trick, you say?" Laura asked. "What is it?"

"Look, I can make my tongue disappear."

The boy pulled a flexible piece of pink rubber—a toy tongue—out of his mouth. He looked up at Laura with a gaping smile. His canine teeth had been filed into fangs. A chunk of his tongue was missing. It appeared to have been cut clean off. The *new* tip of his tongue was straight instead of curved.

"Oh my God," Laura said as she stood up, eyes wide with horror.

A female clown jumped out behind the boy and yelled, "*Hiya!*"

"Oh my God," Laura repeated as she winced.

"I see you found our little boy. We call him 'Bud' because he's our buddy. You get it?"

Laura nodded, then shook her head. She understood her, but she didn't know how to respond.

The female clown said, "So, you mind if we come in so we can all be buddies?"

Holding the phone up to his ear, Adrian glanced over at the foyer of the room and asked, "Everything okay, hon?"

Speechless, Laura ran her eyes over the female clown. Like Bud, her face was painted white. She wore a white dress decorated with colorful polka dots, red stockings, and matching shoes. One of her pigtails was pink and the other was blue. She had undergone plastic surgery to make her ears pointy, like an elf's.

"Well?" the female clown said.

"Who are you?" Laura asked in an unusually high-pitched voice.

"Room service," a man's deep, guttural voice came from the hall.

Lugging around a large duffel bag, another clown walked into her vision from around the corner. The large, nightmarish man wore a jumpsuit with a white ruff collar, white gloves, and big red shoes. The left side of the jumpsuit was red and the right side was yellow. He was bald, but two subdermal implants made it look like horns were growing on his forehead.

The man's eyes, however, captured Laura's undivided attention. The whites of his eyes were pitch black —dark voids of cruel apathy. They stood out against his painted face. At first glance, it looked like his eye sockets had been hollowed out, leaving two endless craters on his skull. She had never seen anything like it before.

Dah-dah-dah!

Adrian muttered unintelligibly as he heard the busy signal again. Every customer service line at the hotel was busy. He slammed the phone on its cradle.

"Daddy, there's more clowns," Lily said as she stared curiously at the entrance from the foot of the bed.

"*What?*" Adrian responded with a touch of annoyance. As he walked over to the foyer, he said, "Laura, what's Lily talking..."

His voice faded out but his lips kept moving as he spotted the clowns outside of their room. The first thought to pop into his mind was: *Robbers.*

The male clown grabbed Laura's neck and rushed forward, pushing her into the room. Laura stumbled backwards. She would have fallen if it weren't for the clown's firm grip on her neck. Her neck was thin and

his hand was huge, so his fingertips were just *millime-*
ters away from her spine. She felt like he could have
crushed her throat with a little more pressure.

The small of her back was slammed against the
workspace next to the entertainment center. Her
tongue stuck out of her mouth and grunts escaped her
throat as she dug her fingernails into the clown's wrist.
The physical pain from the assault couldn't compare to
the emotional suffering caused by her children's
shrieks of terror. She cared about them more than she
cared about herself.

"Let her go!" Adrian shouted.

He swung at the clown, landing a hook square on
his chin. The clown crashed into the wall next to
him. Adrian struck the side of the clown's head—a
jab to the ear. The intruder released his grip on
Laura's neck. She rolled off the desk, crashed into a
rolling chair, then fell to the floor. The rolling chair
spun between the beds. Sobbing, Andrew and Lily
scrambled to the head of the bed and huddled
together.

The other clowns watched from the doorway,
unconcerned by the noise.

The male clown ducked, forcing Adrian to hit the
wall above him. Before he could swing at him again,
Adrian gasped and bent over. The wind was knocked
out of him. He teetered back, then forward, and then
back again. He raised his fist, ready to swing at the
clown again, but then he felt something hot *in* his

abdomen. And it quickly got hotter. It took him a moment to recognize it as pain—*searing pain.*

He looked down at himself, his vision cycling between hazy and clear. Blood soaked through his white shirt. All at once, he was stabbed three times to the right of his belly button. The blades ripped into the ileum of his small intestine. Blood now traveled through his intestines like water through pipes in a building. Through the holes on his glove, he could see the three long blades that had been surgically inserted into the clown's left hand, sticking out from between his knuckles.

He slowly brought his gaze back up to the clown's eyes, utter astonishment written on his face. His expression said something along the lines of: '*This can't be real.*'

Putting his shoulder into it, the clown punched him with his free hand and knocked Adrian out cold with one blow. The blades slid out of Adrian's stomach as he spilled onto the bench at the foot of the bed. Laura was on her hands and knees, gasping for air as she rubbed her red neck. The kids continued crying and calling out to their parents.

As the female clown stepped into the room, Bud said, "That girl likes clowns."

"Is that so?"

The boy nodded.

The female clown said, "Thanks for the tip, Bud. You know our circus is always looking for new members. Now get outta here and help the others. Time's a-wastin."

"Okay," Bud said.

The boy skipped away. The female clown watched him with a smile until he vanished around the corner, then she shut the door and secured all of the locks.

5

ROOM 30214

ADRIAN'S EYES FLUTTERED OPEN. DAZED, HIS HEAD swung from side to side. His vision was blurred by the light, but he recognized the hotel room's light gray walls and dark gray carpeting. The room spun around, walls spinning and ceiling seesawing. He felt like he was strapped down to a moving merry-go-round. Muffled voices surrounded him from every angle. Some of them sounded like they were coming from different rooms and different floors.

"Daddy's awake!"

The screechy, feminine voice aggravated Adrian's headache. He was afraid to glance over at the end of the room. He wanted to believe the voice belonged to one of his kids or his wife, but he couldn't convince himself. He hadn't blacked out after drinking and gambling all night, his kids weren't trying to wake him up for a day on the Las Vegas Strip, and the violent intrusion wasn't a nightmare.

It was all real.

He leaned forward as the pain in his abdomen returned. But he couldn't sit up. He lay spread eagle on the bed. With torn pillowcases, his wrists were tied to the headboard and his ankles were bound to the bench's legs at the foot of the bed. He couldn't scream, either. A piece of clothing was stuffed into his mouth and a strip of duct tape was slapped over his lips. His nostrils flared as his breathing intensified.

The female clown walked to the foot of his bed. She grabbed his bare feet, then ran her fingertips down his soles. The entire bed moved with Adrian's frantic shaking.

The clown said, "I'm sorry, 'Daddy.' We didn't get to introduce ourselves before we rudely let ourselves in. Where are our manners? The name's *Binks*. You wanna know why they call me that?" Adrian answered with a loud groan. Binks said, "Well, if you're nice, I might show ya."

The clown ducked her head, held her hands over her mouth, and giggled, as if bashful. Upon hearing their stifled cries, Adrian looked over at the end of the room and saw his family around the coffee table. Laura sat on a chair with Lily on her lap, her hand over the little girl's eyes, while Andrew sat on the other seat. They were unrestrained with tape over their mouths.

"Oh, don't you worry about them," Binks said. "I'll be taking *special* care of them."

Adrian thrust his head off the mattress and shouted at her. He wanted to say: '*Stay away from them!*' But it came out as another long groan.

Binks said, "Aww, don't flatter me now. You can thank me later, okay?"

Adrian yelled at her again but stopped once he heard the toilet flushing. The male clown entered the room.

Binks said, "Let me introduce you to my friend here. You can call him *Twisted*. Twisted the Clown. I think you already know why we call him that." She leaned forward, cupped a hand around her mouth, and whispered, "It's because he's a real twisted guy and he's also a clown if ya didn't notice."

Twisted said, "Watch the family. I play first this time."

"Yeah, yeah, just don't kill him before it's my turn," Binks said. She went to the coffee table and sat on the armrest next to Andrew. She nudged the kid with her elbow and said, "Watch this."

Andrew whined and leaned away from her. He plugged his ears with his index fingers and stared down at the floor.

Twisted stabbed the mattress under Adrian with his claws, then walked between the beds. Without any resistance, the mattress tore with a crinkling sound. He stopped near the headboard and stared down at

Adrian. Adrian had managed to scoot to the opposite side of the bed, but his left arm remained outstretched.

"Binks and the others love to perform," Twisted said. He pulled his claws out of the mattress and said, "Me? I'm just here for the slaughter."

Although it was difficult to understand, Adrian pleaded for mercy. In one swift move, Twisted swung his claws up at Adrian's head, as if he were trying to uppercut him. Adrian squeezed his eyes shut and stiffened up, expecting the blades to impale his head. He heard a loud whoosh instead. *Did he miss?* he thought, too scared to open his eyes.

His family's cries grew louder, then the hearing in his left ear faded. He felt like he had hot water stuck in his ear. He cracked his eyes open. He saw Twisted chuckling next to him with fresh blood on one of his claws. As he turned to look to his left, Adrian felt the hot blood pouring out of his ear canal and he saw his severed ear on the pillow next to him.

In a sudden barrage, stabs of pain attacked the left side of his head. It was accompanied by a feeling of pins and needles and a throbbing headache. Only his earlobe and some craggy cartilage remained attached to his head. His temporary loss of hearing and his excessive bleeding unnerved him.

There can't be THAT much blood in my ear, he thought. *He must have slit my throat. Oh God, he slit my throat! I'm dying!*

"Don't pass out. Don't spoil the fun," Twisted said. "Breathe through your nose or I'll rip it off your face."

Adrian didn't realize he had been holding his breath until he let out a whistling exhale through his nose. He glanced over at his terrified family. He told himself that it was only a matter of time before security or the police showed up, and he only had to stay strong and conscious until then to protect his family. So, he took a deep breath through his nose.

"Good boy, good boy!" Binks cheered as she clapped.

Twisted grabbed Adrian's left hand and squeezed it before he could curl his fingers into a fist. He said, "Just like bananas for your kids' cereal."

Adrian tried to say: '*What? No, wait!*'

Twisted pressed the cutting edge of one of his claws against Adrian's ring finger—right on the joint closest to the tip. The blade nicked him. The pain was minor, especially compared to the amputation of his ear, but it still sent him into a panic. He screamed while twisting and turning hopelessly.

Pausing between each word, Twisted repeated, "Just. Like. Bananas."

The clown thrust his claws up, driving the blade through Adrian's fingers. It severed his ring and index fingers along the creases at his joints. Meanwhile, his middle finger was split in two closer to the center of the digit. Two of the severed fingertips landed on the pillow and the other fell onto the nightstand between the tables. Blood dripped from the stumps at the ends of his fingers. It was drizzled in zigzagging, dotted lines on the headboard, the nightstand, and pillow.

Adrian held his breath again, big veins standing out on his neck and forehead. It was his body's natural reaction to the terrible pain in his hand. Since he couldn't cry, his family wept for him.

"Can't forget the little one, right?" Twisted said. "We *never* forget the little ones."

With the same claw, he amputated the tip of Adrian's pinky. It bounced off the pillow, then rolled between the mattress and headboard. Blood flowed down to his wrist, soaking the torn pillowcase and the cuff of his sleeve. Adrian arched his neck and slammed the back of his head on the mattress. His eyes swiveled in their sockets. The headboard groaned and the bench moved a little as his limbs flopped.

During his panicked reaction, the restraint around his left wrist slid up to the ball of his thumb. His blood was working like a lubricant.

Barely intelligible, he shouted, "Bastard!"

Twisted laughed at him as he walked to the foot of the bed. He slid his claws across the bottom of Adrian's left foot. The blades nicked and tickled him.

Binks looked at the family and asked, "How're y'all liking the show?"

Laura shook her head at her. Like her husband, she was hoping to comply long enough for security or the police to show up. She was beginning to realize that rescue wasn't on the way and her husband was going to die—they were *all* going to die—if they didn't stop the clowns.

She ripped the tape off her mouth and said, "Stop it. Please, God, stop this! Leave him alone!"

"Hey, what do ya think you're doing?" Binks asked with a shrug. "I told ya, you're not supposed to take that tape off."

"I'm sorry. I'm so sorry. But please—*please*—don't do this. I'm begging you. We'll give you anything you want. Just stop hurting him. Please!"

"I want you to put that tape back on your mouth. You're ruining the show for everyone."

"What is wrong with you people?! Take our money and leave!"

Shaking in his seat, Andrew stuttered, "Ma–Mom, I–I'm scared."

"Don't lose control, Binks," Twisted said. "I'm not ready for you to lose control yet."

"Why don't you mind your own business, bub? I can handle this," Binks responded. She pointed at Laura and said, "And *you*. You better start behavin' yourself or I might take one of your kids and intro- duce 'em to my friends. My friends love 'playing' with kids."

Eyes wet with tears, Laura yelled, "God, no! Leave my children alone, you monster! Don't touch them!" She wrapped an arm around Lily and pulled her closer to her chest. She reached out to Andrew with her free hand and said, "Come here, Andrew. Baby, please, come here."

Binks said, "Don't move, kid."

"Leave him alone!"

"You leave 'em alone!"

"I–I'm scared," Andrew repeated, paralyzed by his fear.

Laura said, "I'm here, honey. I'm right here. I won't let–"

Adrian bawled, interrupting her. Twisted had punctured his sole below his middle toe with one of his claws. Moving the blade down steadily, he cut between the thick, gray calluses at the ball of his foot. Then the claw slid down the center of his arch. The sharp tip *wiggled* inside his foot as Adrian's body shook. The blade came to a stop at his heel.

"Stop. Please stop," Laura whimpered.

Twisted grabbed Adrian's mutilated foot with both hands. He dug his thumbs into his sole, one on each side of the grisly gash. It was a thin, wavy cut, like a long curly hair. The clown moved his thumbs in opposite directions. A squirt of blood came out of Adrian's foot as the wound widened. A jolt of pain shot up his leg.

In the gash, Twisted saw the butchered muscle and white ligaments. He saw some tints of purple and blue amidst the blood, too. More blood gushed out. Some drops hit the clown's chin.

As he convulsed, the pillowcase tied around Adrian's left ankle ripped. Twisted fell back and landed on his ass between the bench and the entertainment center.

"Don't lose control, Twisted," Binks said mockingly.

As Twisted got to his feet, Adrian's left hand slid out of the improvised restraint. Twisted thrust his claws down at his abdomen just as Adrian scooted to the opposite edge of the bed. The blades ripped his shirt and grazed the right side of his abdomen before plunging into the mattress. He grabbed the phone—base and all—from the nightstand and swung it up, smashing it against the clown's jaw.

Rocked by the blow, Twisted lurched away. He crashed headfirst into the television, cracking the screen with his forehead and horns. He fell to his knees in front of it, pulled himself up to his feet, then dropped to his knees again. Adrian reached for the restraint around his other wrist. He stopped for a second upon noticing his severed fingers. Although traces of pain lingered, most of his fingers had gone numb. He used his thumb to pull on the pillowcase.

Binks said, "Gee, guess you really weren't ready to lose control." She grinned at Laura and asked, "But can we ever actually be ready to lose control? It wouldn't make sense, would it? You can't really lose control if you're ready for it, right?"

Laura stared at her with her mouth hanging open. She couldn't believe Binks was still trying to crack jokes despite the shifting circumstances. A voice in her head told her to run while another voice told her to fight. She needed a push—a nudge, *a sign*—to help her decide.

"You're crazy," Laura said.

"You say that like it's a bad thing," Binks replied.

Adrian freed his right arm. He ripped the tape off his lips, then pulled the clothing out of his mouth. He recognized the garment—his daughter's underwear. It hadn't been worn since its last washing, but it disgusted him all the same.

He grabbed the last restraint around his ankle and shouted, "Run!"

And that was the sign Laura needed.

"Run!" Laura yelled.

She lunged forward and grabbed Andrew's hand. She pulled on his arm, but Andrew froze up. A dark stain appeared on his crotch and quickly spread to his legs. The clowns scared the piss out of him—literally. Lily jumped off her mother and took the tape off her mouth. She took a few steps towards the exit, but she stopped as Twisted struggled to his feet and blocked her path. She turned around to run back, but Binks had already pounced on her mother, slapping her and pulling on her hair. And her father's injuries terrified her. He didn't look like the kind-hearted man who kissed her every morning and tucked her into bed every night. Although her father was a victim, in Lily's young, panic-stricken mind, he was no different from the killer clowns.

She dropped to her elbows and knees and crawled under the bed. She mistook the groaning and squealing from the bed frame for snarling from the killer clowns. She felt like she was surrounded by monsters.

Binks tugged on Laura's hair and slapped her face repeatedly. The *whack* of each slap reached the hallway, louder than the family's synchronized crying. Laura didn't know how to defend herself. The closest she had ever been to fighting someone was an argument with customer service about cancelling a gym membership. With her eyes shut, she swung at Binks' arms and kicked the clown's thighs.

Between the slaps, she said, "Run... And... Andrew... Lily... Run!"

The heavy chair fell back. Binks released Laura's hair before she could be pulled down with it. Laura flew off the seat and crashed into the window.

As if speaking to a dog, Binks shouted, "Stay, girl! Stay!" She smiled at Andrew, who hadn't moved an inch during the fight, and said, "Good boy."

She got on all fours and peeked under Adrian's bed. She found Lily laying on her stomach under there, whining with her thumb in her mouth.

"Come to Binks, my lil' honey bunny," the clown said.

Laura stood up while leaning against the window. She saw Binks reaching for Lily under the bed and Twisted trying to get his head straight in front of the entertainment center. *Weapons*, she thought. She opened the cabinet next to her and grabbed the clothing iron. Her protective instincts took over. She jumped over the fallen chair, then swung the clothing iron down at Binks' head. The blow left a small cut on her scalp, adding some red to her colorful hair.

"*Ouch!*" Binks yelped as she slapped her hand over the cut.

Laura wrapped the clothing iron's cord around Binks' neck, then pulled on it, strangling the clown while forcing her to stand on her knees.

"Stay away from my baby!" she hissed.

Adrian broke free from the last restraint. As if passed through to him telepathically, he shared the same thought with his wife: *Weapons*. But as soon as he stood from the bed, he bellowed in agony. The pain in his sliced foot was reignited. He knew he had to push through it, though. Their survival was on the line. He hopped over to the corner of the room behind Andrew's chair and grabbed the floor lamp.

He looked at his son and, between breaths, he rasped, "Go... Andrew. Get your... sister... and run."

But no matter how hard he tried, Andrew couldn't

get off the chair. He could only move his head to watch his parents fight to protect him.

Adrian swung the lamp at the window three times. He wasn't trying to shatter the window, though. He only wanted to break the lamp's shade and its bulb— and it worked. The flimsy shade fell to the floor and the bulb broke, leaving sharp shards sticking out of its metal cap. The long lamp became a heavy spear. He limped past his wife, who continued to strangle Binks, and thrust the lamp at Twisted. He missed the clown's neck by a foot.

Twisted leaned to his left and swung his claws at the lamp. The blades *clanged* upon hitting the metal tube.

Adrian pulled it back, then thrust it at him again. The shards of glass tore through the clown's costume and stabbed his chest. Small bloody spots bloomed on the yellow fabric, like petechiae on a bruise. Twisted grabbed the lamp's tube and pushed it away. Adrian tried to thrust it at him again, but he was overwhelmed by the clown's strength. He stumbled back, crying with each painful step. He crashed into the window at the same time as the lamp's heavy base.

Some thin cracks appeared on the reinforced glass.

The men started playing a game of tug-of-war for the makeshift spear. Binks was able to get to her feet and squeeze her index fingers under the cord around her neck. She ran backwards and slammed Laura against the window. Laura's grip on the cord wavered.

Binks took four wobbly steps forward, then quickly moved back again. The clowns took turns ramming the window with the lamp's base and Laura's body. The lamp *banged* against the window while Laura's spine *thudded* on it.

Bang! Thud! Bang! Thud! Bang! Thud!

Unbeknownst to them, the web of cracks was rapidly growing.

And, after the eighteenth hard hit, the window shattered.

Laura screamed. She released the cord and dropped to her knees. Wheezing, Binks fell forward and landed next to the chair. Lily kept crying under the bed while Andrew brought his feet up onto his seat and wrapped his arms around his head. Caught off guard by the destruction, Twisted let go of the lamp and stepped back.

Adrian seized the opportunity and thrust the lamp at his stomach. The shards cut through his costume and cut his abdomen above his belly button. The shards weren't long or strong enough to pierce his abdominal muscles, but Adrian mustered enough energy to push the clown back with the homemade spear. They moved closer to the foyer.

A cool breeze blew into the room through the broken window. Emergency sirens blared in the distance. Echoes of screams and faint voices reached the hotel room, too.

Laura saw one way out of the room—*the broken*

window. The ledge was narrow, wide enough for one person to sidestep across it at a time. She convinced herself that it was a viable escape route. But she couldn't reach Lily without having to fight Binks and she knew Adrian wasn't going to be able to walk on the ledge because of his mangled foot.

She didn't want to abandon anyone, but she was afraid she would lose *everyone* if she wasted anymore time. She broke down—sweating, trembling, panting, sobbing—at the mere thought of leaving her husband and their daughter. Her heartbeat accelerated and her throat tightened as Binks stood up.

"I'm so sorry, Lily!" she cried. "Adrian, save her!"

Laura grabbed Andrew in a bear hug and lifted him from the chair. Hysterical strength made it easier than ever before.

"Mommy," Andrew said in a trembling voice.

Laura lunged over the large shards of glass sticking out from the windowsill, jagged like a shark's teeth. A gust of wind hit her. Her upper body tilted in a circular motion as she fought to keep her balance.

"Mommy!" Andrew screeched.

"Shh, shh, shh," Laura shushed the boy while caressing the back of his head. "It's going to be fine. Everything's going to be okay, I promise. I just need you to walk next to me."

"I can't! I can't! I–"

"Andrew, please!"

"–can't! I'm scared! I can't do it!"

"You have to, baby! Please, you have to do this!"

From the foyer, fingers wrapped around the lamp's pole, Twisted shouted, "Binks! The woman!"

Binks waved at him and said, "Yeah, yeah. I got 'em."

Adrian's eyes bugged out and his heart jumped up to his throat as he looked back at the broken window. Laura had set Andrew down on the ledge. They were holding hands and sidestepping to the right. Andrew disappeared around the corner first, then Laura.

"Laura, no!" he yelled.

Binks kicked the glass sticking out of the windowsill, then leaned forward and watched the shards fall to the pool area.

"Like sharp raindrops," she whispered, eyes glittering with joy.

The clown stepped onto the ledge and looked to her right. Laura and Andrew had reached the neighboring room. With her back to the glass, Laura banged on the window and called for help. The curtains were closed, so they couldn't see into the room. Andrew sidestepped with his eyes closed while firmly gripping his mother's hand. He was so scared now that liquids were pouring out of his eyes and ass—tears and diarrhea, respectively.

Binks brushed the shards away with her shoe, then she sat down on the ledge with her feet dangling over the side. She looked down and, between her shoes, she saw the guests in the pool area. They were all looking up at the hotel tower. Some held cell phones up to their ears and called the police while others pointed their phones at the room to record the scene for their social media accounts.

Tragedy had a way of attracting large audiences.

Binks said, "There's no point in running, y'know? I mean, where will ya go? It's not like someone's gonna open a window and let ya into their room. The windows don't open, you goofs. Besides, look around. Even if you get away from this room, from this hotel, you won't get away from *us*. Vegas is our carnival now."

Laura inspected the city. Red and blue lights flashed in the streets. Columns of black smoke curled up into the sky from burning cars and buildings. Screams reverberated from every direction. Then three quick bursts of gunshots rang out on the Strip. Two of the bursts were weak, like knuckles popping in rapid succession, and the other was alarmingly close and loud.

The city was under siege.

"Mom, I'm scared," Andrew whimpered.

"It's okay, baby, it's okay," Laura said. "Just don't look down. Keep going. Please, honey, you can't stop."

"Aww, is he afraid of heights? Bud used to be scared of heights, too," Binks said. "It was so cute. You wanna know how he got over it?"

Laura banged on the window behind her and yelled, "Help! Somebody help us!"

"We held him over a ledge just like this one—

maybe not so high—and we 'pretended' to drop him," Binks continued. "I mean, technically, we did drop him. *But*, we caught him, too."

"Help!"

"After that, the little devil wanted to do it again! Amazing, right? So, boy-o, if you want my advice, look down."

"Shut up!" Laura snapped as she glared at the clown.

"Look down! Look down!"

"Stop it, you bitch!"

Giggling, Binks shouted, "Boo!"

Andrew's eyes flew wide open as his foot slipped off the ledge. Standing on one foot, his weight shifted forward and his arms flailed wildly. He felt a painful knot in his stomach, a tight sensation in his chest, and throbbing in his skull. The lights in the city spun around him, blinking and jiggling in his vision. His gasp blended with the gasps in the pool area.

"Andrew!" Laura yelled.

She tightened her grip on his hand and tried to pull him back onto the ledge. With her other hand, she grasped at the smooth glass behind her, trying to find something—*anything*—to anchor her down. But it was too late. A powerful gust of wind flung Andrew off the ledge and Laura, refusing to let him go, fell with him.

Five seconds.

It only took them *five seconds* to fall 130 meters. They crashed at 110 miles per hour, putting an abrupt end to their screaming. Andrew landed in the jacuzzi about half a second before Laura hit the pavement next to the pool.

For Andrew, the water didn't change a thing. The drop was too high, so it was like he had landed on concrete. Nearly every bone in his torso was fractured upon impact—his sternum, his ribs, his clavicles, his spine. His head hit the jacuzzi's ledge face-first, instantly decapitating him. His head landed in a bush next to the spa. A wave of bloody water hit the guests standing around the pool.

Laura hit the pavement with a thunderous *bang*. Her face was flattened, pushed *into* her skull. A hole was punched into her chest, propelling her crushed breasts towards her armpits. Her spinal cord was snapped at her neck and lower back. For a brief moment, she was folded in half with her feet over the back of her head. She bounced off the pavement, then landed in the pool. A cloud of blood surrounded her body.

The guests shrieked and scattered. With a hand over his mouth in disgust, a young man ran up closer to the jacuzzi to record Andrew's dead body. He wasn't going to miss his chance at capturing a viral moment.

Teary eyes on the broken window, Adrian stopped fighting Twisted. He didn't have to see the fall to know what had happened. The bloodcurdling shrieks and the *bang* told him everything. Their deaths opened the door for grief, and grief quickly got to work breaking his heart and blackening his mind. He was conscious but unable to move or speak. His eyes were vibrating in their sockets and his cheeks were twitching.

Binks stood up on the ledge and said, "Well, that takes care of that." She stepped back into the room and asked, "You think you can handle this guy or what?"

Twisted hit Adrian's chest with the lamp's heavy base. The blow knocked the wind out of him and pushed him back against the communicating doors— the doors connecting their room to the neighbor's— next to the entertainment center. Twisted roared as he continued ramming the lamp against his chest. It cracked one of Adrian's ribs and bruised his chest. He was too weak to fight back.

"Lily," he said weakly as he caught a glimpse of his daughter.

Twisted thrust the lamp at him for the umpteenth time. Adrian was knocked unconscious. The first communicating door was blown off its hinges and the other door flew open. Adrian fell into the neighboring hotel room. Twisted was about to follow him into the room to execute him when he saw three young men in there. They all stared at the clown with bewildered, concerned eyes.

One of the guests, a college student named Blake Lowery, raised a hand at Twisted and said, "Take it easy. Don't do anything stupid."

The clowns used manipulation and the element of surprise to get into their victims' rooms and get the better of them. They also picked their victims wisely, targeting small families and couples to lower their chances of being overwhelmed.

Twisted was ready to kill, but he decided to play it safe. He didn't want to risk losing a fight to the college students and put a premature end to his night. He pointed the lamp at them and retreated from the doorway.

He said, "Binks, it's time to go. Let the Hellfire take care of him."

"What's the matter, big guy?" Binks asked as she waltzed over to him. She smiled broadly upon spotting the other men. She waved at them and said, "Hey there, neighbors!"

Baffled, Blake returned the wave. The violence and destruction looked real, but he was starting to believe it was all part of an act.

"He–Hey," he stuttered.

"You wanna play with us, too?"

"Goddammit, girl," Twisted said sternly. "Get going or I'm leaving you behind. We'll see if you can 'play' on your own."

Binks said, "Oh, I can take care of myself. *But...* I'd rather bring Deadface a little present."

"What are you talking about?"

Blake asked, "Is... Is everything okay?"

Ignoring him, Binks skipped to the beds, then tiptoed between them. She heard Lily whining under the bed. Her cheeks inflated as she tried to suppress her laughter, but she couldn't hold it. Spittle sprinkled from her mouth as she giggled. She got down to her knees, then dropped to a prone position between the beds.

"Hiya," she said.

"Mommy!" Lily cried, her thumb still in her mouth.

"I'm your mommy now. Welcome to the circus, babe."

"Mom–"

Binks grabbed the girl's arm and dragged her out from under the bed. She carried her close to her body, Lily's face pressed up against her bosom.

As she ran to the exit, she yelled, "Bye, neighbors!"

Twisted said, "You got lucky. Stay out of our way and I might forget about you."

Before any of the college students could respond, the clown ran out of the room with the lamp. He followed Binks down the hall.

"Daddy!" Lily's cry echoed through the thirtieth floor.

6

CHAOS

"THIS IS UNIT 33. I'M 10-23 AT THE PLATINUM PALACE," Franco said, holding his radio up to his mouth.

There was no response. Guests crowded the hotel's entrance, making plans for the night and waiting for their Ubers. He noticed some of them were swinging their phones up in the air, as if searching for cellular signal. Their chatter sounded like gossip, and gossip was never a good sign.

Making his way up a short flight of stairs, Franco held down the push-to-talk button on his radio and said, "Unit 33. Ten twenty-three at the Platinum Palace. Responding to a disturbance. Dispatch, how do you copy?"

He stopped at the top of the stairs and squinted at his radio. Yet again, there was no response. His attention wandered to the commotion at the lobby to his right. A mob of angry guests gathered in front of the check-in counter. Like politicians, the front desk clerks answered their questions without actually *answering* their questions.

'*One moment please.*'

'*I'll check on that.*'

'*Let me ask my manager.*'

As he approached the front desk, Franco overheard the guests' complaints: The employees weren't checking them in to their rooms and the guests couldn't access the hotel's website or app to do it themselves. Despite all of the noise in the lobby, guests continued gambling in the casino. They couldn't hear most of the ruckus over the slot machines anyway.

Franco put one hand on his holster and raised the other. He said, "Las Vegas Police. We got a call of a disturbance."

His announcement went unheard by most of the staff and guests. A small family and an elderly couple got out of his way. The front desk clerks kept the rowdy guests at bay while the hotel's security guards tried to pry a door open behind them. The sign on the door read: *EMPLOYEES ONLY.*

Franco moved up to the front desk and, raising his voice, said, "*Police.*"

As if rehearsed, the receptionists released a simultaneous sigh of relief. A receptionist with red hair came closer to him. In cursive handwriting, the name tag clinging to her chest read: *Pamela V.* The grumbling from the angry guests continued behind the cop.

"There was screaming in the hotel tower," Pamela said in a low but clear voice, so as not to alarm the guests.

"Which room?" Franco asked.

"A few."

"On which floor?"

"A... A few," Pamela repeated, her voice faltering.

Franco's mind immediately hunted for the most rational explanation: *A fire. Some sort of gas leak. A shooting.*

"Any gunfire? Any alarms?" he asked.

"We don't know, sir."

"What do you mean you don't know?"

Pamela said, "The phones are down and the–the... the 'system' is down. We can't even check anyone in right now."

Talking to his radio, Franco said, "Unit 33. Dispatch, I need additional information on that disturbance at the Platinum Palace. A name, a room number, anything."

He was met with total radio silence.

"Where are the rest of you?" a man asked.

Franco looked to his left and saw a middle-aged man in a navy blue uniform jogging behind the front desk, his jacket *swishing* with each step. Short of breath, the man stopped next to the other security guards and said something to them. '*SECURITY*' was printed on the back of his jacket in white capital letters.

He turned around to face the cop and asked, "Where are the paramedics? The fire department? The other cops?"

Franco said, "I'm Officer Franco Ferraro. I'll get more units out here as soon as I can, but first I need to know what's going on. Are you the security manager?"

"No, no. My name's Lee Miller. I'm just a security guard. I'm... Shit, I don't have time for this. Two people just fell in the pool complex. A woman and a kid. I don't know what to do."

"Take me there."

"Yeah, follow me."

Separated by the front desk, they hurried alongside each other, pushing past the guests and employees. Past the desk, Lee took the lead.

Franco asked, "How bad was the fall?"

"Are you squeamish, officer?"

"Squeamish? How bad is it? Did anyone perform CPR yet?"

Lee looked back at him as they ran past the path to the eSports lounge. Franco noticed the sickly pallor on his face. The security guard's silence spoke volumes about the severity of the situation.

Speaking loudly as if it would change a thing, Franco held his radio to his mouth and said, "Dispatch, 10-52 at the Platinum Palace." There was no reply. He yelled, "Damn it, I need an ambulance at the Platinum Palace!"

"It's no use," Lee said. "The phones and radio

signals were disrupted a couple of minutes ago. A guest was barely able to call you about the fall before they were disconnected."

They went down another wide corridor. After a few turns, they found a horde of nosy guests blocking the doors to the pool area. Like drivers rubbernecking at the scene of a fatal car accident, they all wanted to catch a glimpse of the tragedy. People were fascinated by death and gore. The human mind craved violence as much as the body craved food.

"Police!" Franco shouted. "Move! Get out of the way!"

The men pushed through the crowd. There was another security guard and a bellhop, Jordan Carter, on the other side of the glass doors. Like Lee's, their faces were discolored and sweaty. They were shaking all over. They had locked the doors to cordon off the scene, although some guests and spa employees still lingered in the pool area.

Lee tapped the window and mouthed: '*Open up.*'

Keys jingling in his trembling hands, the other security guard unlocked the doors. Franco marched out to the pool area. Walking backwards, Lee followed him.

Hands outstretched before him, he said, "I need everyone to remain calm and return to your rooms."

"Is that blood?" a man asked.

A woman asked, "My God, is that a child? Is that a boy in the jacuzzi?"

"I think it is," another woman said.

Lee nodded at the other security guard and said, "Lock it."

Franco stood between the jacuzzi and the pool, motionless like a statue. He now understood why most of the staff looked like they worked at a haunted hotel.

Broad streaks of blood—almost black in the moonlight—stained the concrete under his shoes. Behind him, a young woman sat on a lawn and cradled an unconscious woman's head in her arms. She called out for help, but to no avail. To the left, a couple of employees, all in white uniforms, wept outside of a small, detached building. The bright neon sign above the building's entrance read: *The Royal Spa.*

Although Laura's face was crushed and Andrew's body was headless, they floated 'face' down in the water. The water in the jacuzzi was completely red. Laura's corpse drifted towards the center of the pool, blood continuing to billow out of the massive hole in her chest. At first glance, it looked like debris or trash was floating around her.

Upon closer inspection, Franco realized it was just more human remains: Threads of skin, bits of broken bone, her shattered teeth, her detached nose, and her severed heart.

Lee approached him, but he kept his back to the crime scene. He didn't have the stomach to look at the bodies again.

He said, "Look up at the tower to my left. You see

the broken window? Witnesses say they saw them fall from there."

Franco remained quiet. He heard the security guard, but he didn't even think about responding. Staring at the decapitated boy, he thought: *What could have led to something like this?*

Lee shook his arm and asked, "Are you listening?"

Franco opened his mouth to respond, but he belched instead. The gore made him sick and light-headed. He turned away from the bodies and took a moment to compose himself.

"Where... Where are these witnesses now?" he asked.

"They left."

"You just let them leave?"

"You think anyone would want to stay out here with... with this 'mess'? I've had to move two security guards and a bellhop into the spa after they blacked out from seeing *them*. I couldn't force those guests to stick around. I don't even want to be here."

Franco asked, "Why didn't you move the witnesses to the spa or have security take them into the employee area? What the hell were you–"

"Hold on," Lee interrupted. "They didn't tell you at the front desk?"

"Tell me what?"

"We lost contact with the command center and access to the employee area over an hour ago. The telephone lines, the internet, our radios, cell phone signals, it's all been cutting in and out since then. We can barely communicate with each other."

The puzzled expression on Franco's face said: 'You have to be kidding me.' He looked over at the casino. His hand went straight to his holster as he considered the possibility of an elaborate heist occurring at the resort. Then his gaze traveled to the broken window far above them. The pieces didn't fit. *Why would robbers enter a hotel room and throw a woman and a child out the window?* he wondered.

"Did they jump?" he asked.

"Huh?"

"Did the witnesses mention if they saw them jump? Was it a murder-suicide?"

"They saw them fall. One of them said they saw someone else sitting on the ledge up there, too. They didn't mention anything about pushing or jumping, but they saw someone."

Franco looked at the women on the lawn and asked, "And what happened to them?"

"My aunt needs help!" the young woman cried. "Why aren't you helping us?!"

Lee said, "They were heading to the spa when the victims fell. The older one was so shocked that she fainted."

"You call an ambulance for her?"

"I did. A couple of guests called them, too. We got through to them before the signal went out again. But you're the first one to show up. Where is everyone?"

Franco looked up at the night sky. He saw the smoke, smelled the fires, and heard the sirens. The men's eyes met as a distant burst of rapid gunfire reached the resort. At that moment, they knew they weren't alone. The entire city was crying out for help. All emergency services were occupied.

Franco pointed at the other security guard and said, "I need you to carry this woman's aunt to the spa. Get *everyone* out here into that spa and lock the doors. Wait for medical assistance or additional police. Don't open that door for anyone else."

"Yes, sir."

The guard went to the women on the lawn. Jordan ran forward to help him, but Franco stopped him.

The cop said, "Not you."

"What? What do you mean?" Jordan asked, his voice tight.

"I have reason to believe that there are armed suspects in the resort. I'm going to find them and try to corner them until backup arrives. In the meantime, we have to ensure the safety of the guests and staff. But we can't evacuate the entire resort in an *orderly* fashion if we can't communicate with each other."

"A–Armed suspects? Evacuate? What am I supposed to do about all that?"

Franco pointed at the audience beyond the glass doors and said, "First, get all of these people away from here. Send them back to their rooms and tell them to shelter in place. If they ask why, tell them that the police are searching for an armed suspect who's holed up in one of the rooms. I need you to tell all of your coworkers to do the same thing. Once the ground floor is cleared out, all of you need to find somewhere to shelter in place as well. Lee and I will take care of the hotel tower." He looked at Lee, pointed up at the broken window, and said, "We're going to work our way up to that room while checking on the rest of the guests."

"Got it," Lee said.

Jordan said, "Wait up, man. Just... Just wait a second. I'm not a security guard. I'm a bellhop, man! I get paid to carry bags for people, not risk my life for 'em!"

On the verge of tears, he put his hands on the back of his head and paced in front of them. He was young and hopeful. He had a lot to live for. Franco understood his fear. He was asking him to risk his safety for people who hardly ever acknowledged his existence. He gripped his shoulder to stop him from pacing and read the name tag on his shirt.

He said, "Jordan, I wouldn't be asking you to do this if it wasn't an emergency. And I wouldn't be giving you this task if I didn't trust you. I know you might be tempted to run, but we need you to do this. You *can* do this. The sooner you get it done, the sooner you can shelter in place, too."

Franco was right. Jordan thought about running. He even considered accepting the job and running anyway just to get the cop off his back. Then he saw the victims in the water. His stomach twisted with revulsion while his heart ached from the tragedy. *Will another kid die if I don't help them?* he thought.

He said, "I'll do whatever I can. But if I–"

He was interrupted by another rapid rattle of gunfire—louder, *closer*. It sounded like it was coming from an automatic rifle in quick bursts. The men recoiled as an explosion roared through the area. They felt the floor vibrating under their feet. Then they heard screaming on the Strip.

"Holy shit," Jordan said, wide-eyed. "Was that a bomb?"

Franco said, "Unlock those doors and get these people to their rooms. Move it."

Jordan stared up at the condominium tower to his left. A pillar of fresh smoke rose behind it. The explosion had occurred nearby. He thought about his friends working at the Platinum Palace and the other casinos on the Strip. They were all in danger.

"Move it!" Franco demanded.

Jordan sprang into action. As soon as he unlocked the glass doors, Franco and Lee barreled into the crowd. They elbowed their way through the guests. They had to check on the blast, so they retraced their steps and ran back to the resort's entrance.

The guests in the lobby couldn't hear the gunfire, but they had heard the explosion. They dispersed, running to the exits, retreating to their rooms, and hiding with employees in the shops and restaurants. Most of them abandoned their luggage, leaving suitcases and bags unattended in the lobby. Behind the front desk, security guards and receptionists kept trying to break the door to the employee area down.

The gamblers and dealers, deafened by the slot machines, stayed in the casino. Only a few of them ran out, but they had no idea what was going on. They were only following the herd.

Outside, Franco and Lee ran across the designated ride-sharing driveway. They sprinted across a lawn, then came to a stop in the parking lot in front of the resort. The street was almost empty, only a few tourists and vehicles straggling behind. A van, surrounded by abandoned cars with broken windows, burned on the road in front of the neighboring hotel. They heard more bursts of gunfire. It sounded like it was coming from a hotel room down the street.

Lee said, "The city's burning. I've never seen anything like this."

"Neither have I," Franco said.

Over the radio on the cop's chest, cutting in and out, a dispatcher said, "All available units. Shots fired... officer down... Boulevard and Park Avenue... All avail..."

"Ten-one, dispatch. Say again," Franco replied. He heard a muffled voice under the crackle of static. He said, "Dispatch, my signal is weak. I need additional units and an ambulance at the Platinum Palace. How do you copy?"

The static was harsher and the voice shriller.

An alarm rang in the Platinum Palace, making a pulsing *whoop* sound. The men heard a loud *clunk* at the entrance, then a *rattling* noise. A gate descended behind the doors.

"Someone overrode the security," Lee said.

"One of your people?" Franco asked.

"No, I don't think so. They wouldn't lock the building down. Not with all those people in there and not with two dead bodies in the pool complex. They'd wait for... you."

Franco glanced back at the burning van, then at the resort's entrance. He was torn between assisting his fellow officers and aiding the staff at the Platinum Palace. The soundtrack of chaos—composed with emergency sirens, rifles, bombs, and injured victims—played around him. He saw people stumbling over each other at the foyer as they hurried out of the building. He figured the defenseless staff and guests at the resort needed him more than his fellow officers.

He gestured to Lee and said, "Follow me."

The men ran back to the entrance and crouched under the descending gate, then they made their way back to the lobby. Despite the alarm, some gamblers continued playing at the slot machines. It was like they were glued to their seats.

In the lobby, an old woman tugged on the cop's sleeve and asked, "What is going on with that darn alarm?"

Arms linked, two young women walked up to him with worry on their faces.

"What's happening?" one of them asked.

Franco shouted, "There's an armed intruder in the building! I need you all to go to your rooms and lock your doors! If you're not staying here, take shelter in one of the shops! Don't answer your doors for anyone except the police!" He hurried to the front desk and beckoned to the employees huddled around the locked door. He said, "Forget about the door for now. Get all of the guests to their rooms, then find somewhere to shelter in place."

Pamela said, "It wasn't us. We didn't set off the alarms."

"I know."

"Officer, wait!" Pamela hollered as Franco took a step away from the desk. He stopped and looked back at her. The receptionist said, "We heard people laughing on the other side of the door."

"Laughing?"

"Yeah. And it was loud and creepy. I don't know how else to describe it. It just wasn't normal."

Franco remembered the disturbance at Jack's Jackpot Motel. The suspect was dressed as a clown, and clowns were associated with exaggerated laughter. He wondered if the clown sightings were connected to the violent disturbances across the city. *'Killer clowns are on the loose!'* Although the evidence supported his theory, he couldn't announce it because he didn't entirely believe it himself.

As he walked away from the front desk, he said, "Remember, once you're in your rooms, don't open the door for anyone except the police. If you see anyone in a costume or mask, *hide*. Don't be a hero."

"Costumes? What in heaven's name are you talking about?" the elderly woman asked.

Franco and Lee ran off. Some of the guests heeded the cop's advice and outran them, racing to the elevators. The rest stayed behind in the lobby and casino, baffled by the situation. By the time they reached the elevator bank, the waiting lines extended into the hallways leading to the rooms on the first floor.

"You got a baton?" Lee asked, standing on his tiptoes to peek over the crowd.

"We're not just going to beat our way to the front of the line."

"Then what *are* we going to do?"

"We'll squeeze past them. We have to check on the guests on this floor anyway. Once we're done here, we take the stairs up to the second floor and we keep working our way up to that room with the broken window. There are stairs in this place, aren't there?"

"Yeah, but that room is probably on the 25th or 30th floor. Who knows how long it'll take us to get up there?"

"Then we better work fast."

7

GRIEF

"They're not answering, dude."

Masculine but soft, a disembodied voice swirled around in Adrian's head. Yet, he saw nothing but darkness, trapped in the void between consciousness and unconsciousness.

"He needs a doctor," another male voice said. "I can't do anything else like this."

A third voice, more nasally than the others, said, "Just drag him back to his room and wait for the police, man. I'm seriously going to throw up."

Adrian's eyes flickered open. His vision was blurred and shaky. The two figures towering over him looked like they were merging into one person, although they were actually moving away from each other. He inhaled deeply, but a sharp pain in his chest interrupted it. He jutted his chin forward and exhaled through his clenched teeth, sending big drops of foamy spittle up into the air. The saliva landed on his forehead and in his hair.

"He's awake," one of the men said as he crouched next to the victim. He pressed his palm against Adrian's chest to stop him from sitting up. He said, "You shouldn't move right now."

Adrian propped himself up on his elbows and glared at each man in the hotel room. Blake Lowery was crouching next to him. Benjamin Penn was leaning back against the wall next to the busted communicating door. And Peter Rodger stood between the beds, holding a cell phone up to his ear. They were college students, barely old enough to drink, gamble, and make life-changing mistakes.

Blake said, "I think you're going to be okay. I tried my best to patch you up with Peter's first aid kit, but I... I've never seen anything like this in any of my classes."

Squirming and hissing, Adrian looked down at himself. His torn shirt was soaked in sweat and blood. Like a tsunami, pain blasted through the left side of his body—one agonizing wave after another. He felt a fire burning in his chest, the heat growing stronger with the slightest breath. A gauze roll was wrapped around his foot. The stumps at the ends of his butchered fingers were covered with Band-Aids. There were large Band-Aids over the cuts on his abdomen, too.

The sleeve of his shirt was torn. Like a sweatband, it was wrapped around his head to stop the bleeding from his severed ear.

Still holding the phone up to his ear, Peter said, "My mom, uh... She doesn't let me travel without a first aid kit in my luggage."

"No one asked," Benjamin said.

"But you guys always clown me when you see it."

"What do you want me to say? Sorry? You're a real hero?"

"I don't know, dude. I'm just saying. I've never been in a situation like this before."

Adrian stopped listening to their argument. He saw Blake's mouth moving, but he didn't hear a word from him, either. Peter's voice echoed through his head: *'You guys always clown me... Always clown me... Clown me... CLOWN.'* Images of the violent attack in his room flooded his mind. Laura and Andrew's shrieks drowned out Peter's voice. He pushed Blake's arm away and struggled to his feet.

Blake said, "Whoa, man, what are you–"

Adrian screamed as soon as he placed some pressure on his left foot. Fresh blood streamed out of his sliced sole and soaked through the gauze roll. He fell into Benjamin's arms.

Blake wrapped an arm around him from behind and said, "Your foot is cut. It's bad, man. You shouldn't walk on it."

"Get off me!" Adrian barked.

"Dude, your foot," Peter said.

Blake said, "You're just making it worse for yourself. You need to–"

"I need to help my family!" Adrian interrupted. "They need me! Let me go!"

He broke free from Blake's clutches and reeled into his hotel room. He landed on his knees between the entertainment center and a bed. The sight of blood brought a big lump into his throat and sent his mind into a frenzy. He couldn't tell if the splatter stains on the wall, headboard, pillows, bedsheet, and carpet came from him, his family, or the clowns. The thing about blood was: It all looked the same.

His eyes went to the shattered window. He tried to stand, but his left leg buckled from the pain in his foot and he spilled to the floor. Adrenaline helped him fight through the agony and push forward. He crawled over to the window on his hands and knees. Moving cautiously, Blake followed him into the room. They had all heard the screaming and saw Twisted at the end of the brawl, but they hadn't entered the room to investigate the damage.

It had all the telltale signs of tragedy.

Adrian stopped in front of the window, glass crunching under his knees. He put his hand on the wall, leaned forward, and peeked over the ledge. He couldn't identify them all the way down in the pool complex, but he could see the corpses floating in the bloody water. He knew it was Laura and Andrew. He felt it in his bones, grief spreading through his skeleton like metastasis. He screamed at the top of his lungs.

He screamed and screamed and screamed some

more, sharing his suffering with the Las Vegas Strip. The screaming aggravated his broken rib, but the physical pain couldn't compare to his emotional agony. He felt like *he* had fallen with them, like *he* had hit the pavement at over 100 miles per hour, like *he* had been decapitated and snapped in half. They were dead and gone, but their pain lingered in him.

He stopped screaming only after he ran out of breath. Woozy, he nearly toppled off the ledge and joined his dead family members.

Blake caught him before he could fall out of the hotel room. He pulled him back into the room and sat him down against the wall next to the window.

"Shit, man, be careful," he said.

"My family," Adrian cried. "My family... Laura... Andrew... God, Andrew... No, no... It can't be..."

His words slurred into an indecipherable babble. Blake stood up and looked out the window. He saw people running around the pool area, skittering wildly like ants trying to dodge the hot beam from a kid's magnifying glass. He saw the corpses in the bloody water, too. If Adrian hadn't been crying about his family, he would have mistaken them for children's pool toys. But he was smart, so he could piece it together.

His family fell, he thought. *No, they were attacked. They were thrown out the window.*

He looked at the communicating doorway. He remembered seeing the clowns in the room. He knew they had attacked Adrian, that much was obvious, but he wasn't aware of the murders they had committed.

The college students didn't even know they were staying next to a small family. When staying in hotels, most people didn't go around introducing themselves to their temporary neighbors. They had heard the ruckus, though. At the time, they had assumed a deal had gone wrong between a prostitute, a pimp, and a John or a drug dealer and a drug addict. They had tried to call the front desk and the police to report the disturbance, but the lines were busy.

Blake said, "Peter. *Peter!*"

"What?!" Peter yelled from the other room.

"Call the police!"

"What do you think I've been trying to do?!"

"Call them again! Use my phone, Benny's phone, the landline... Keep calling until they answer!"

Peter and Benjamin sensed the desperation in Blake's voice. They grabbed all of their phones and dialed 911. Blake looked out the broken window again, awed. Red and blue lights flashed through the blanket of smoke over the streets. People wailed as loud as the emergency sirens. Struggling with denial, Adrian wagged his head frantically. Tears flew from his face, hitting the wall and carpet. He stopped shaking his head as he caught sight of the bed in front of him.

"Li–Lily," he stuttered as he crawled forward.

Blake squatted next to him and said, "Hey, you have to stop moving. You're going to hurt yourself."

"Lily. My daughter... My baby..."

Adrian pushed Blake away and scrambled over to the bed. He checked under it. He could see under the other bed, too. Lily was gone. He crawled back to the window. He only saw two corpses in the pool complex. His daughter could have landed in a bush or her body could have been carried away already, but he refused to believe the worst-case scenarios. A spark of hope, dim and weak, flickered in his chest.

"She's alive," he said.

Blake put one hand on Adrian's chest and grabbed the back of his shirt with the other, holding him back as if he were a ferocious dog.

He said, "Careful, man."

Words shooting out of his mouth, Adrian said, "Lily, my daughter, she–she's still alive. The clowns, they must have taken her."

"We're calling the cops right now. They'll help–"

"The fucking clowns!"

"–you and your daughter."

"That bastard! That bitch!"

"Calm down! You're going to hurt yourself!"

Adrian grabbed Blake's arms and pulled himself up to his feet. His left leg wobbled as pain surged up from the gash on his sole. But he stayed on his feet. Hope filled him with determination. He heard Laura's apprehensive voice in his head: *'Adrian, save her!'* This was his only chance at redeeming himself—at fulfilling his wife's last wish.

"I have to save my daughter," he said. "She needs me."

"You have to wait for an ambulance. The cops will find your daughter."

From the communicating doorway, Benjamin said, "Blake, we're not getting any signal."

They all looked at the foyer of the room. The door was cracked open. They saw a man in a neon mesh tank top and denim shorts hurtling down the hall. Then, in the opposite direction, a pair of guests ran past the door. They were sniveling and panicking.

Adrian knew they weren't running away from the accident at the pool complex. They were running to their rooms because there was an active threat in the resort.

"The cops aren't coming," he said. As he limped to the bed, he pointed at the broken window behind him and said, "Look around you. The city is burning. And those clowns are responsible. I won't let them hurt Lily. I... I let this happen, but I *won't* let them hurt my baby."

He sat on the bed and ripped his other sleeve off. It looked like he was wearing a vest now. He tied it around his left foot as tightly as possible, hoping it would help him walk.

He searched for a weapon. He thought about using the clothing iron, but he remembered seeing Laura use it against Binks. It wasn't very effective. He looked at the small lamp on the nightstand between the beds. The broken bulb hurt Twisted and kept him at bay, but he wasn't looking to just ward off the clowns.

He wanted to *slaughter* them.

The light bulb gave him an idea. He took off his button-up shirt—what remained of it—and hobbled over to the bathroom.

Watching him, Blake asked, "What are you going to do? You going to run around the hotel hunting clowns? Looking like *that?*"

Adrian entered the bathroom. He bundled the shirt over his fist, as if it were a boxing glove, then he punched the mirror. Shards rained down into the sink. He picked up the largest, sturdiest, sharpest piece and wrapped the shirt around the bottom half of it—just tight enough to firmly hug the glass but not tight enough to break it.

From the foyer, Blake stared at the makeshift shank in Adrian's hand and said, "You can't be serious."

"Leave me alone, kid," Adrian replied.

"If the cops see you with that, they'll shoot you. Seriously, look at yourself. You're covered in blood."

"He's right," Benjamin said. "At least take a shower first."

"Shut up, Benny."

"What? I was agreeing with you."

"I'm not telling him to take a shower before he leaves. I'm telling him not to go out there."

As he limped out of the bathroom, Adrian said, "You don't get it because you don't have families of your own. You don't have wives and kids. You *are* kids. Lily's depending on me, and *no one* is going to stop me from protecting her."

Blake saw the icy resolve in Adrian's eyes. He realized that he didn't truly understand a parent's love for their children.

He said, "I won't help you hurt anyone, but I'll help you get around this place."

"No," Adrian said sternly.

"What's up with you? I'm trying to help you, man."

Adrian pointed the shank at him. Blake raised his hands and stepped back until he crashed into a wall.

"Oh shit," Benjamin murmured.

Adrian said, "You're barely old enough to be here. You're a kid. A good kid, but still a kid. Whatever's happening out there, it's serious. You need to stay here and lock the doors. Get back to your parents. Don't..." His voice broke. He grunted, then said, "Don't let them suffer like me. Stay alive."

Blake kept his mouth shut and his hands up. He nodded in agreement.

Adrian lowered the shank and said, "If you get through to the police, tell them that two clowns attacked my family. A woman with pink and... and blue hair, and a bald man with horns on his head. I don't know how else to describe them, but they... they were clowns. That's what they were."

"I saw them," Blake said. "I'll tell them everything."

"Thank you."

Adrian shambled to the doorway. He looked down the hall to his left, then to his right. He saw droplets of blood on the carpet and smears on the walls to his right. He assumed it was Twisted's blood. He followed the trail, leaning against the wall to keep the pressure off his injured foot.

Blake closed the door and secured the swing bar lock. He sighed, then said, "Keep calling the cops and the front desk."

The trail of blood led Adrian to the elevator bank. There were three elevators to his left and three to his right. He pressed the elevator call button and checked the numbers above all of the sliding doors. The elevators appeared to be stopping at every floor. The closest elevator was on the 27th floor, but it was already going down.

He hobbled over to the fire escape door across the hall. He opened it and slipped through the doorway, catching himself on the guardrail. It only took him a couple of seconds to catch his breath at the top of the stairs. His cut foot was starting to go numb. He didn't want to worsen the wound or waste his energy, so he sat on the guardrail and slid down to the landing below.

8

ROOM 15212

"ALMOST READY," OWEN CAMPBELL ANNOUNCED AS HE adjusted the collar of his button-up shirt in the bathroom mirror.

In the hotel room, Nora Grant sat on a wingback chair and stared at the curtains covering the floor-to-ceiling windows. Her eyes were narrowed with a mix of curiosity and concern. She wore a black dress and matching pantyhose. Her wavy black hair barely reached her shoulders and her bangs touched her eyebrows.

She asked, "What about that noise we heard earlier?"

"What noise?" Owen asked.

"That... That bang, that boom. That... That *kaboom*."

"Kaboom? Really?"

"You know what I'm talking about, Owen."

"There's always a party in Vegas, sweetheart. Or maybe it was just a car crash. Or, you know what, maybe it was an accident at one of those construction sites. I heard they're building another new resort."

Nora pushed one of the curtains aside and looked out the window. They had a view of the Las Vegas Strip from their room on the 15th floor. She couldn't see over the neighboring buildings, but she saw the street in front of the Platinum Palace. Her eyes widened as she spotted the van burning in front of the hotel next door.

"Owen!" she yelled. "Owen, come here! You have to see this!"

"Are you just going to point at the 'Eiffel Tower' and pretend like it's the real thing again?"

"Owen, seriously!"

Owen noticed the shift in her tone—from puckish to horrified in a matter of seconds. He stepped out of the bathroom and found Nora beckoning to him. He went to her and looked out the window from over her head. He saw the burning van, the flashing police lights, and the pall of black smoke hanging over the city. Then gunfire erupted outside.

They cowered away from the window and stared at it for a moment, then they looked at each other. The sound of gunfire reached their room again. They moved farther away from the window.

"That was a gun, wasn't it?" Nora asked. "Oh my God, Owen, was that a gun? Like a machine gun?"

"I... I don't know. It could have been an old car engine."

"I didn't see anyone driving on the street. All the cars looked abandoned out there. And one of them is on fire. Is there a shooting going on? Like a–a mass shooting?"

"It's possible, I guess."

Nora pressed her palm against her forehead, walked in circles, and said, "I knew it. I knew this was going to happen sooner or later. We should have just stayed in Canada and gone to Niagara Falls."

Owen grabbed the phone from the nightstand and pressed a button to call the front desk. He heard the busy signal before he could raise the handset to his ear. He pressed a button to call the concierge and heard the same tone. He checked his cell phone—no bars, no data, no Wi-Fi.

"What's wrong?" Nora asked in a quick, nervous tone. "Why do you look like that? Like you just lost all your money on one stupid bet? Like someone just told you we're going to die? Oh jeez, tell me you lost a big bet, Owen. I don't want to die in Vegas."

Ignoring her, Owen sat on the bench at the foot of the bed and turned on the television. He was relieved to see the hotel's advertisement on the television's welcome screen. He changed the channel. An episode of *Family Guy* was playing on Adult Swim. He flipped through the channels until he landed on a news broadcast.

"Oh my God," Nora said as she sat down next to her boyfriend.

From behind a news van at Park Avenue, a cameraman captured footage of a shooting taking place. The gunmen fired down at the streets from several broken windows at a nearby hotel. Cops on the street moved from cover to cover, hiding behind abandoned cars and ballistic shields as they made their way across the street.

Under a red BREAKING NEWS banner, the main headline read: *LVMPD issue emergency shelter-in-place order.* Under that, the subheadline read: *Las Vegas under siege, hundreds dead in simultaneous shootings and bombings.*

"No effing way," Owen said.

Nora asked, "What are we supposed to do now?"

"Um... Well... I guess we do what the news is telling us to do: Shelter in place."

"But it says that there were shootings *and* bombings. What if someone bombs this hotel? We could end up trapped up here. A fire could block all of the exits or the whole building could collapse. Isn't there some sort of safe room we're supposed to go to? Or what about an evacuation plan? Should we leave?"

"And go where? We took an Uber from the airport, remember? You think there are going to be any Ubers out there right now? Or are you suggesting we run through the streets while these psychos are shooting from their windows?"

"I don't know what to do, what to think. I know I'm talking too much and I don't mean to put so much pressure on you, but I'm just so–"

"Nora," Owen interrupted. She looked him in the eye. He said, "We're going to be okay. I'm not going to let anything bad happen to us. Let's just watch the news and stay inside until this is over."

Nora smiled thinly and said, "Yeah. You're totally right. Can you just, um... Can you check the locks on the door? Then check them again?" She laughed and asked, "Can you triple-check?"

"Of course."

Owen went to the door and looked through the peephole. The corridor was empty. He fastened the swing bar lock, then secured the deadbolt, and then checked the locks two more times. He flashed an OK sign at Nora as he returned to the bench.

They flipped through the channels, watching different news reports concerning the terror attacks. Mass shootings were occurring across the Strip. Some of the cameramen captured footage of dead bodies on the streets and sidewalks.

The couple huddled together and stared at the door as a stifled scream seeped into their room. They heard a rush of footsteps in the hallway. A door slammed somewhere out there. Then a second scream, clearer than the first, entered their room.

"Was that a woman?" Nora whispered.

"Sounded like it. Or it could have been a kid."

"We should do something, right? I mean, if it's a kid, we *have* to do something, don't we?"

"I don't think there's anything we can do, Nora. We don't even know if it came from this floor. Maybe we should just turn off the TV and the lights and–"

Tap, tap, tap.

Someone knocked on their door.

They gazed into each other's eyes, lips sucked into their mouths and lungs filled with air. Nora muted the television. Twenty seconds of dead silence passed.

Tap, tap... tap.

Their unexpected visitor knocked again. Owen held his index finger up to his lips as he slowly stood up.

Nora pulled on his arm and mouthed: '*Don't go.*'

"I'm just going to look through the peephole," Owen whispered.

"Don't," Nora said, barely audible. "Please."

Owen touched her hand and nodded at her, as if to say: '*Everything's going to be okay.*' Nora strengthened her grip, then she let go of him. She knew she couldn't stop him. She was curious, too. Owen slunk over to the door and peeked through the peephole. A laundry cart was parked in front of the door. He didn't see or hear anyone in the hallway. He eyed the locks, then snuck back over to the bench.

"Who is it?" Nora asked.

Matching her hushed tone, Owen replied, "I didn't see anyone. There was just a cart out there."

"A cart?"

"Like a... a room service cart. The ones for laundry, y'know?"

"Was it there before?"

Owen shrugged and said, "No, I don't think so."

Nora said, "But someone definitely knocked. So, what do we do now?"

"Whoever it was, they're gone now. Maybe—*hopefully*—they thought our room was vacant and they moved on. So, let's just stay quiet for now. We'll keep trying to call the police and the front desk. We'll be fine as long as we stay here."

Nora thought about the screaming and the laundry cart. Her wild imagination told her someone was hiding in the cart, waiting for them to open the door so he could jump out and shoot them. She agreed with Owen, though. If someone was in the cart, he couldn't get in as long as they kept the door shut.

"Yeah, okay," she said reluctantly.

Owen and Nora stayed on the bench, watching the television on mute while checking their cell phones for any signal. They sent text messages to their families, but they went undelivered. Footage of SWAT personnel gathering outside of Circus Circus played on the TV. Considering the resort's circus theme, the police assumed it was the killer clowns' base of operations.

Behind the couple, unbeknownst to them, the deadbolt on the communicating door turned slowly. A dull *clicking* sound came from the door as it unlocked. Although the room was quiet, Owen and Nora didn't hear the noise. They were focused on the news and their cell phones. The doorknob rotated at a snail's pace. Then the door inched open.

Nora's pupils dilated with fear as she saw the door opening on the television's reflection. Terror muted her voice and seized her body. She couldn't scream or move. Owen didn't notice the intrusion until he heard the hinges *squeak* behind him. It made the hair on his arms prickle. He jumped up and looked back at the communicating door.

"No," he said.

Tears dripped from Nora's puffy eyes with each blink. She stayed seated, but she saw their visitor on the television's reflection.

Spike the Clown stood in the communicating doorway, his arm outstretched in front of him with a revolver in his hand. He pointed the gun at Owen. His entire head was now covered in white makeup. Vertical streaks of black paint stretched from his forehead to his cheekbones and a broad red smile was painted over his mouth. His nose was as red as a cherry, too. Shirtless, he wore red overalls with white polka dots and big matching shoes.

A wide, heavy man stood behind him, rolls of fat rippling over his waistband. His face was decorated like Spike's. He was shirtless, too. He wore a red wig and white pants with black stripes. The clown's forehead was inflated, jutting out like a cliché brainiac with an oversized head in a cartoon.

Owen threw his hands up, as if he were surrendering to the police. His focus cycled between the revolver, the mohawk of sharp prongs sticking out of Spike's head, and the fat clown's inflated forehead. It all terrified him equally.

Spike smirked and said, "Look at you. Didn't even have to tell ya to put your hands up. Good boy. Now, turn around and put your hands on the wall."

"Don't hurt us," Owen said. "If–If you want our money or our room, you can have it. We're good people. We–We're Canadian."

"Is that so? Well then, you be a good Canadian and do as I say before we decide to skin the both of ya and turn ya into Canadian bacon. We clear?"

Spike entered the room without taking the revolver off Owen's chest. The fat clown followed him. A duffel bag was slung over his shoulder and he held a fire axe in his hands.

Speaking quickly, Owen said, "Holy guacamole, yes. Yes, yes, yes, we're clear." He turned around and put his palms against the wall. He said, "Nora, come here. Do what they–"

"*Hey,*" Spike interrupted. "I didn't tell her to move. I

said you two better follow *my* orders. Are you forgetting who's in charge here?"

"I'm sorry. I was just... I'm trying to... Please don't hurt her. If you want money or you need a–a hostage, then... then I'm your guy. I'll give you whatever you want and do anything you say."

"I want you to stay quiet. I don't want to hear you speak unless you're answering a question of ours. Now, get down on your knees and don't take your damn hands off that wall."

"Ye–Yes, sir," Owen replied.

He followed his instructions, one knee at a time. Nora kept her eyes on the television, watching the clowns while panting and trembling.

Spike said, "Now put your hands behind your back. My friend here is going to cuff you. If you make any sudden movements, I'm going to blow your girl's head off. Make her brains fly like confetti. Can you imagine that, buddy?"

The fat clown threw the axe and the duffel bag on the bed. Nora gasped and flinched as she felt the bed frame shaking. Her nose wrinkled as she caught a whiff of his stench. He smelled like old, stale sweat and fresh urine. The clown snickered, amused by her fear and disgust. He opened the duffel bag and pulled out a bundle of zip-tie handcuffs. He used a pair to cuff his wrists and another pair to bind his ankles.

Owen shuddered as the clown's moist breath caressed the back of his neck, then he hissed as the zip-tie handcuffs were secured. They cut off the circulation to his hands and feet.

The fat clown patted Owen's back and asked, "What's your name?"

"Oh... Owen."

"Owen what?"

"Owen Campbell, sir."

The clown said, "It's nice to meet ya, Owen. My friends call me *Tubs*. I guess 'Fat Ass' wasn't clownish enough for 'em, huh?" He looked at Nora and asked, "What about you? What's your name, sugar tits?"

Nora didn't acknowledge him. She was watching Spike through the reflection on the television, as if hypnotized by his revolver. On the news broadcast, the police were escorting the reporters away from Circus Circus while asking them to stop recording due to security reasons. The news crews continued recording anyway.

Owen said, "Her name is–"

"No talking!" Tubs shouted.

He grabbed the back of Owen's head and thrust his face at the wall. The loud *thud* of the blow reverberated. Owen's nose was broken, blood erupting from his nostrils.

Nora pressed her palms against her cheeks and shrieked.

Tubs pulled Owen's head back, then thrust it at the wall once more—twice more, *thrice more*. The television wobbled with each hit, nearly falling from its wall mount. There was a gash on the bridge of Owen's nose. His cheekbones and the bony ridge over his left eye cracked. His left eyebrow tore open, like a hairy caterpillar bisected longways. Blood cascaded over his eye and splashed on his cheek.

Nora's scream intensified as she spotted the blood on the wall. She jumped up to her feet and ran. She didn't think about it; she just did it. Her survival instincts took complete control, overpowering her love for Owen. She set her sights on the foyer, but as soon as she passed the bed, Tubs made a grab at her. She juked right, slipping past his grasps, and went for the communicating door.

Owen's limp body fell to the side next to the entertainment center.

She slid to a stop in front of Spike, the revolver a mere yard away from her face. Her eyes darted to her right. The fire axe called to her.

Spike said, "Don't even think about it."

Just as she lunged for the axe, Tubs grabbed Nora in a bear hug from behind and pulled her back.

"No!" she yelled.

Spike took one step forward and said, "I warned you."

"No! Don't kill me! Please don't–"

"Sayonara."

"–kill me! No!"

Spike squeezed the revolver's trigger. *Clack!* Nora shut her eyes, lowered her head, and gasped. Starting at her forehead, a terrifying warmth spread through her skull. *Blood*, she thought with confidence. *There's a bullet in my head. I'm dead.* She felt a warm liquid trickling down her forehead and cheeks. Then she noticed her racing heartbeat.

While keeping her eyes closed, she furrowed her brow and cocked her head to the side. She began to question herself: *Am I really dead? Is this what death's supposed to feel like? Why can I still move? Why can I still feel? Why can I still smell him?* She heard the clowns laughing around her. Her eyes cracked open to a squint, then widened to the size of golf balls.

She was simultaneously relieved and disappointed to be alive.

A small white flag hung from the revolver's barrel. Over a comic book-like explosion effect, in all capital letters, the flag read: *BANG!*

"You're going to wish this was the real thing," Spike said, grinning.

Nora said, "Please, I don't wanna die. Don't–"

Tubs pushed her towards Spike, then threw a haymaker at her, putting all of his weight into it. The punch landed on the back of her skull, leaving her head bouncing around like a speed bag. It was like being hit with a cinder block. Knocked unconscious, she fell to the floor between the clowns.

Spike looked at Tubs and asked, "Was that so hard?"

"I took her down, didn't I?" Tubs said. "I could've done all this by myself."

"No, you couldn't."

"C'mon, Rob, these Canadians–"

Spike ran up to him and said, "Don't *ever* say my name while we're performing."

Tubs shrugged and said, "They're knocked out. What's the big deal?"

"It's all part of the big boss' plan. You want me to tell him you ain't following his rules?"

"All I'm saying is, I could have taken care of this room on my own. It was a piece of cake."

Spike pointed at Tubs' face and said, "Don't be too confident in yourself, tubby. If you hadn't fucked up at that motel earlier, I wouldn't have to be here supervising you. I hope you learned something 'cause you're on your own now. Think before you act. Outsmart them before they outsmart you. Got it?"

Sneering, Tubs said, "Got it."

They glared at each other. Annoyed by his failures, Spike was ready to headbutt him. Tubs, on the other hand, was tired of the ridicule.

"Spike!" a woman called out from the hallways. "Spikey! *Spyyy-keyyy!* You around here?"

The clowns looked at the foyer of the room, then at the communicating doorway.

Tubs asked, "Is that Binks?"

"Yeah," Spike responded.

They heard her knocking on a door across the hall.

Despite no one answering, she asked, "Hey, are my friends in there?"

"We're in here!" Spike shouted.

"Spike? Is that you? Where are you?"

"Room 15212! Come in through the room next door. It's open."

"Spike! I can hear ya, but I can't see ya! Are you dead? You in heaven, Spikey?"

"Heaven?" Spike repeated, astonished. "Drop the act, girl! I just said we're in Room 15212!"

"Oh," Binks responded.

She entered Room 15213, which was vacant, and approached the communicating doorway leading to the Canadian couple's room. She was holding a fire extinguisher.

She said, "I heard you say Room 15212, but that could have been a room in heaven, y'know? Or hell. Or *'Thugz Mansion.'* I mean, who knows where you'll end up when you die."

"What do you want?" Spike asked.

"Deadface is looking for ya. Needs you to help him finish setting up the main event."

"Anything's better than babysitting this bastard."

"Fuck off," Tubs muttered.

Spike said, "Do me a favor, will ya, Binks? Help him restrain these two and make sure he doesn't fuck anything up."

"Sure. Sounds like fun to me."

Spike exited the room through the communicating

doorway, then slammed the door on his way out of Room 15213. Binks and Tubs stared at each other while listening to the snoring from the unconscious couple. Tubs was nervous around Binks, crossing an arm over his flabby chest as if trying to hide his body, while the female clown seemed indifferent. She didn't care about his appearance or the violence.

She said, "Well, what are we waiting for? Let's start tying."

***

Nora awoke with a gasp and a jerk. Her vision was blurry and dark. It took her a moment to realize there was a pillowcase over her head. She whined as she felt the throbbing pain at the back of her skull. She went to sit upright, but she couldn't lift her head from the pillow. She gagged instead, her whole body moving with her quick breathing. Her neck was taped to the mattress underneath her. It was just tight enough to squeeze her throat but not quite tight enough to suffocate her.

Although she could barely see through the pillowcase, she looked to her left, then to her right, then back to her left. She could only see the light from the lamps and the outlines of the furniture around her. She was sprawled across the bed, arms and legs pulled away from her body. Her wrists and ankles were tied to the bedposts with the torn bedsheets. She couldn't see herself, but she knew she was naked. She felt the cool breeze from the air conditioner on her sweaty skin.

"Ha... Help," she croaked out.

"Look, she's awake," Binks said. She stood behind the recliner next to the floor-to-ceiling windows. She said, "Listen to that baby cry. Gets me all hot and bothered. How about you guys? You hot and bothered?"

Owen sat on the recliner, arms bound behind his back and torso taped to the backrest ten times over. There was a strip of bloodstained duct tape over his mouth. The bleeding from his nose and torn eyebrow had slowed. His legs were unrestrained, so he was free to kick wildly, but he couldn't muster the energy to stand and break free from the tape. He sobbed and mumbled incoherently.

Tubs approached the foot of the bed with the fire axe. He said, "Oh, I'm definitely hot and bothered. I'm ready to start playing."

Binks leaned over the recliner's backrest, rested her hands on Owen's chest, and said, "Don't let us stop ya. Start playing, big guy. Show us what you're working with."

"Don't mind if I do."

"Plee... Please," Nora said, her voice softer than the sound of Tubs' breathing.

Owen screamed and kicked at the bed, missing it by a foot. *Don't do it,* he wanted to say. *Kill me instead!*

Tubs raised the axe over the footboard. He tapped

Nora's left ankle with the axe's sharp edge—once, *twice* —then he raised it overhead.

"Hold on a sec, buster!" Binks yelled.

"Huh?" Tubs grunted as he lowered his weapon.

"I know you're not going to start by chopping her foot off, right?"

"What's the problem?"

"It's too early for traumatic injuries. She could go into shock. Her heart could explode! Plus, it's way too boring, man. Get creative."

Tubs nodded as he examined Nora's nude body. He had planned on chopping her into as many pieces as possible. Dismemberment was his favorite pastime. His gaze stopped on Nora's crotch. He looked at the slit between her labia, then at the axe's edge. Like a toddler figuring out a shape sorter, it clicked in his mind.

He said, "I got it. I'll *fuck* her with this axe. Just ram it up in there."

"N–No," Nora whimpered.

Owen shouted something inaudible, veins sticking out of his neck and tears clinging to his blood-crusted eyelids.

Binks put her index finger on her puckered lips and hummed, deep in thought. Then she squinted an eye and shook her head at Tubs.

She said, "I like the idea, but I agree with them. You have to slow it down a little. You ever hear of foreplay?"

"You want me to cut her clitoris off with my axe?" Tubs asked.

"Not exactly, but you're getting close. Let me show ya something, big fella."

Binks strutted over to the bed. Nora squealed as the clown crawled onto the mattress. Binks mounted her captive's waist, moving her hips back and forth jokingly as if she were riding a man's cock. Owen lunged forward and yelled at her, but *'get off her'* sounded more like *'mother!'* Tubs was aroused, rubbing his crotch with his free hand while smacking his lips.

Binks leaned forward and groped Nora's breasts. She massaged them for a minute—squeezing them, pushing them together, pulling them apart—then circled her areolas with her index fingers. Nora cried and fidgeted under her. Although she knew her limbs were tied to the bedposts, she kept trying to cross her arms over her chest to stop the molestation.

As she flicked and pinched Nora's nipples, Binks looked back at Owen and asked, "You wanna know why they call me Binks?" Owen responded with a blurt of incomprehensible noise. Binks said, "I'll show ya."

While Owen screamed endlessly in the corner of the room, Binks sucked Nora's right nipple into her mouth. She made loud *slurping* noises.

"S–S–Stop," Nora stuttered, voice raspy because of the tape over her neck. "Why? God, why?"

Binks stopped, opened her mouth as wide as possible, then slurped up a mouthful of Nora's breast. She had so much tit in her mouth that Nora's nipple was close to tickling her uvula. Then she bit down on it.

Nora shouted, "No! Please! Ouch! Ow! Ow!"

Binks' teeth penetrated Nora's breast. Blood dribbled across her torso—to her collarbone, to her sternum, to her armpit, to her stomach. Nora writhed in pain, unintentionally helping Binks tear into her breast with each quick, frantic movement. Binks bit down harder and shook her head while giggling.

"Stop! Stop!" Nora cried. "Plee–"

She yelped again as Binks started pulling at her breast with her teeth. They could hear the loud *crinkle* of her flesh tearing over all the hoarse breathing and sobbing and screaming in the room. Head spinning, Nora began holding her breath while her stomach knotted up. Saliva foamed through her clenched teeth, wetting the pillowcase over her head.

Owen kept pushing forward in his seat. The tape around his torso started to tear. He could see the stringy, bloody tubes *in* his girlfriend's breast.

With one final tug, Binks tore off a big chunk of her breast. Blood splattered on the pillowcase over Nora's head, the headboard, and the wall. The pillowcase fluttered as Nora released a long exhale. Her stiff muscles slackened and her head rolled limply on the pillow. The powerful jolt of pain from the partial amputation caused her to black out.

Nora's nipple was replaced with a jagged crater. Binks spotted slits of yellow fat in the breast before blood filled the wound. She looked over at Owen.

Owen was shocked into silence. A clown—the

lower half of her face drenched in blood—sat on his unconscious girlfriend with her severed nipple in her mouth. She sucked on it like a binky.

Without taking it out of her mouth, she said, "And that's why they call me Binks." She jumped off the bed and slurped up the string of bloody drool hanging from her lower lip. She said, "Foreplay, Tubs. Tease 'em before you start sticking your axe in their holes."

Tubs said, "I've got an idea."

While he rummaged through his duffel bag, Binks walked to the recliner. She stood behind it and bent over, sucking on the severed nipple next to Owen's ear to torment him. But Owen focused on his girlfriend. He tried to say *'wake up'* a couple of times, but it sounded like *'makeup.'* He felt the tape weakening around him. He only hoped the clowns wouldn't notice before he could break free.

Tubs emerged from the bag with a revolver in each hand. He stood at the foot of the bed and aimed the guns at the ceiling, smiling proudly.

Binks took the nipple out of her mouth and asked, "What are ya gonna do with those? Shoot her? That ain't foreplay, pal." She glanced at Owen, winked, and said, "That's what we call gunplay."

"No, no," Owen moaned.

Tubs said, "It's foreplay. All part of the show. Check this out." He turned to face the bed and tapped Nora's leg with the revolver's barrel. He said, "Wake up, cunt. I've got a little trick to show ya."

The fat clown started juggling the revolvers, throwing the guns through the air and passing them swiftly from hand to hand. Nora regained consciousness during the performance. Through the thin pillowcase, she saw the clown standing at the foot of the bed and two objects spinning around him. Blood overflowed from the crater on her breast as she shuddered. The pain burning in her chest was unbearable.

"Now I know why Spike had to take care of him," Binks whispered to herself as she cowered behind the recliner. She said, "Hey, big guy, you sure that's a good idea?"

Tubs caught the revolvers by their grips. He raised the one in his left hand and squeezed the trigger. *Clack!* A white flag shot out of the barrel.

He said, "They're just props, girl. Don't worry, I know what I'm doing."

"If you say so," Binks said.

"Watch this. I'm gonna make her cum with this thing."

Owen leaned forward and screamed. Despite the duct tape, his first word was clear: '*No!*' The rest of it consisted of slurred obscenities. It took Tubs quite a bit of effort to get onto the bed due to his weight. First, he climbed onto the bench at the foot of the bed one knee at a time. Then he crawled over the footboard. He was already wheezing.

"Please, God, don't let me die," Nora said weakly. "Please protect me. Ta–Take care of me. Please, God..."

Tubs thrust the muzzle of the revolver at Nora's crotch. He moved it around to spread her labia open.

Nora screeched, fingers and toes curling. She looked down at the clown, then closed her eyes and looked away. She didn't know what he was forcing into her vagina and it didn't matter. The penetration was painful and unwelcomed. Although he wasn't using his penis, this was an act of rape.

Binks said, "You're supposed to spit on it. C'mon, you never fingerbang a lady before or something?"

Tubs pulled the revolver out of Nora, then he drooled onto her vagina. The saliva was mucusy, thick and bubbly. He spread it around her labia, then thrust the barrel back into her vagina.

"Ow! God, save me!" Nora shouted.

Tubs pushed all three inches of the barrel into her. He wiggled it around, pulled it out, pushed it back in, and then repeated the process. He fucked her with the revolver.

Binks sniggered, then said, "God? Silly girl. You're in Sin City. Vegas is for the godless, baby."

The recliner slid forward as Owen hopped and roared. The clowns paid him no mind, though. They were captivated by the torture.

Binks said, "I hear ya fucking her with that toy, but I'm not hearing any dirty talk from ya. C'mon, Tubs, have some fun. I thought you were into this. Thought you were one of us."

"I am," Tubs replied. "Just... I, um... I've never done this in front of anyone before. I usually work alone."

"Oh. Then just pretend like I'm not even here. I won't make a sound. Or imagine us in our underwear. I used to do that at the old folks' home I used to work at. Lots of tighty-whities and diapers in that place. Some thongs, too, believe it or not."

Tubs sped up his thrusting. He pounded the space between her anus and vagina with the trigger guard. Scraped by the revolver's hard edges, she began to bleed. A big drop of blood crawled down to her asshole. Nora continued sobbing while begging for mercy. She jerked violently with each thrust.

Trying to talk dirty, Tubs said, "You're getting close, huh? You dirty girl, you..."

"Bitch," Binks whispered from behind the recliner.

"Huh?" the fat clown responded, still thrusting.

"Call her a dirty bitch."

"That's what I meant."

"But it's not what you said."

"I thought you were going to shut your–"

A slightly suppressed gunshot interrupted him. The room went dead silent. Awestruck, they all stared at the revolver in Nora's vagina. Thin feathers of smoke curled out of her pussy. Blood oozed out around the barrel, lining her labia like lipstick. It flowed down to her anus, then dripped onto the mattress. After ten seconds, Nora started gasping and convulsing.

Goggle-eyed and stony-faced, Owen stopped

wrestling with the tape around his body. He stared at his girlfriend and, although his voice was unclear, he said her name repeatedly.

"Aww, you idiot, that's a real gun!" Binks yelled. "You could have tortured her for hours, made a real statement, but you killed her!"

Tubs said, "How was I supposed to know? They all look the same."

"The real ones are heavier, bozo!"

"I'm a strong guy, okay? They felt the same to me."

"You're such a liar."

Nora grunted, gasped, then entered a long, violent coughing fit. And with each cough, blood was sprinkled on the pillowcase over her head. The bullet had traveled through her vagina, pierced her uterus, penetrated her intestines at multiple locations, and stopped in her stomach. Bullet fragments rode the rivers of blood flowing through her abdominal cavity.

She hadn't even realized that she was shot through her vagina. It wasn't a common way to die—not in real life, not in horror movies, *not anywhere*—so the thought didn't cross her mind. She knew something had happened, though. The tremendous pain and intense heat in her pelvis and abdomen were debilitating.

She knew she was dying and there was nothing anyone could do to stop it. She tried to pray one last time, but she couldn't stop coughing.

Tubs took the revolver out of her and got to his feet

at the foot of the bed. A torrent of blood spilled out of Nora's vagina. The red stain grew larger under her pelvis, nearly touching the edges of the mattress. Binks put the severed nipple on Owen's head, as if it were a party hat. Owen remained still.

"I'm outta here," Binks said as she approached the bed. "The other guys were right. You have no idea what you're doing. You're a killer, but you're not like us. And that's why Deadface won't let you be part of the show. To be honest with ya, I have no idea why he keeps you around. Might be a self-esteem thing. You got a bigger gut than he does."

Tubs scowled at her and said, "I'm a better killer than you, Spike, and all the other clowns out there."

"I think you mean 'bigger' killer. Y'know, 'cause you're so fa–"

Tubs grabbed her throat and lifted her up a little, forcing her to stand on her tiptoes. She gagged, then gasped, and then giggled.

In a small, strangled voice, Binks said, "I... wouldn't do... that. I'm his... favorite. Deadface... He'll fuck ya... worse than you fucked her... if you hurt me."

There was murder in Tubs' eyes but hesitation in his shaky grip. He was tired of the clowns' bullying, but he also agreed with Binks. He knew their boss, a man known as *Deadface*, would torture him in the most unimaginable ways if he broke any of their rules. And Deadface had a strict 'no-infighting' policy in his carnival of death.

Tubs released her neck and stepped aside, half his face scrunched in annoyance. Binks coughed in an exaggerated manner, rubbing her neck and sticking her tongue out.

Upon regaining her breath, she said, "Jeez, pal, didn't know you had anger issues, too. What's your problem?"

"I want to be in the show. I want Deadface and the rest of you to respect *me*. I'm tired of you people treating me like a fuck up."

Binks looked daggers at him and asked, "First of all, what do you mean *'you people'*?" They had a tense stare down, like fighters before a title bout. Only Nora's weak whining and Owen's slow, loud breathing surrounded them. After a few seconds, Binks cracked a smile, leaned in closer to Tubs, and asked, "People say that in movies, right? 'You people?' Did it sound cool?"

Tubs said, "I'm serious. I'm not playing this game, this damn character, unless I get some respect. Tell Deadface to put me in the show. I'm ready."

Binks said, "All right, all right. I hear ya. But you've gotta prove yourself first, bub. You just screwed everything up right now, didn't ya? So, I can't vouch for ya if you're just going to go up on stage and mess up in front of everyone. That would make *me* look bad, and I *never* look bad. So, I'll tell you what..."

Head on a swivel, she examined the room. Her eyes stopped on the fire extinguisher next to the recliner.

She had forgotten about it. She grabbed it and handed it to Tubs.

"Kill that guy with this," she said. "But do it right. Get creative. Have fun. If you impress me, I'll forgive you for messing up my fun and I'll talk to Deadface for you. Deal?"

"Deal," Tubs said. "I'll show you how it's really done."

"That's the spirit. I'll be back to check up on ya later. Good luck."

"Don't need any luck. I can do this. I *can* do it!"

Binks frolicked out through the communicating doorway without saying another word. Fire extinguisher in hand, Tubs turned his attention to Owen. The guy was shellshocked. In his eyes, the world around him was swallowed by an impenetrable darkness. He didn't see or hear the clowns anymore. It was only him and his recliner and Nora and the bed in that hotel room.

Tubs raised the fire extinguisher over his shoulder, then thrust it at Owen. He stopped before he could make contact with the side of his head, though. *Too easy*, he thought. He aimed the bottom of the fire extinguisher at Owen's crotch and considered bashing his genitals into a pile of bloody mush. He shook his head. It was brutal but not very creative.

Like authors struggling with writer's block, Tubs had a bad case of *killer's block*.

He stomped and shouted, "Goddammit!"

9

CAN'T BE STOPPED

THEIR BACKS TO THE WALL, FRANCO AND LEE stood next to a door. Sweat shimmered on their brows and soaked through their shirts. They were breathless, tired from climbing the stairs and leading the guests to safety. Pointing it down at the floor, Franco held his pistol in his hand. Lee was unarmed. Above the door, a sign read: *15TH FLOOR.* From above and below, the sounds of pounding footsteps and terrified voices echoed through the stairwell.

A middle-aged Asian woman stopped on the landing at the top of the staircase in front of the men.

Franco pointed at her and said, "Get back to your room."

The woman said, "The news said there was a shooting. Shootings and bombings and–"

"Go back to your hotel room and lock the door. Don't answer the door for anyone except the police."

"My husband was in the casino. He's not answering his phone."

"Ma'am, please go–"

"Something's wrong! He always answers his phone! We need to find him! I have to–"

"Ma'am, please!" Franco interrupted.

Exhaustion and irritation added some extra *bass* to his voice. It was enough to startle the woman and Lee. Someone gasped above them, then a door slammed below them.

Franco sighed, then said, "We don't have time for this. We need everyone in their rooms so we can secure the area. I haven't heard any gunshots or any explosions in this resort. When we return to the casino, I'll personally escort him back to your room if I find him. What's his name?"

The woman stuttered, "Her–Herbert Ramsey. I'm Monica. He's thirteen years older than me and he wears glasses. He–He's always wearing them. Doesn't even like taking them off in the shower. His hair is white, but he's balding, okay? He's going bald and he's trying to stop it, but it's not–"

"I think that's enough information for us to find him. What's your room number?"

"It's... 17225."

"Go back. Please."

The woman leaned forward and looked down over the guardrail. She thought about running to find Herbert anyway. All hell was breaking loose, so time was of the essence. But she trusted Franco. He was tired and frustrated, but she saw sincere compassion in him. She nodded at him, then reluctantly ran back up the stairs.

The men listened to her footsteps soften as she moved farther away from them. Her footsteps ended with the slam of another door.

Lee asked, "Want me to go back down and find him? We haven't found jack shit so far anyway. I doubt anyone is shooting from any of the floors above. We would have heard it by now."

Franco said, "Let's clear out this last floor together. If we don't find anything, I think it'll be safe for you to check on the rest of the tower by yourself and I can go down and secure the rest of the resort."

"I think it would be best if we found a way into the command center ASAP. Then, we can take control of the security system and see *everything*. It would be a whole lot faster than checking each floor."

"We can talk about that *after* we make sure the guests on this floor are safe. Okay?"

"You're the boss."

Franco grabbed the door handle and nodded at Lee, as if to say: '*Ready?*' Lee returned the nod. After a deep breath, the cop opened the door and stepped into the hallway. Lee waited a few seconds before following his lead. Being unarmed, he had to keep his distance so as not to interfere if they were attacked.

The corridor was quiet and empty. They made

their way down. Franco knocked on each door and announced himself as law enforcement. While the cop informed the guests who opened their doors to him about the ongoing crisis, Lee watched Franco's back and listened for any suspicious activity. Although some of the guests were overwrought, they all agreed to stay in their rooms.

The men took a left at the end of the hall. It was another corridor with more hotel rooms on each side.

At the other end of the hall, they saw a barefooted man in a bloody tank top and jeans limping away from them—*Adrian Castillo*. They could see the bandages wrapped around his head and foot. Although he was clearly injured, Franco was concerned by the shank in his hand. He couldn't allow him to freely roam the resort.

"Freeze!" he shouted as he pointed his handgun down the corridor. "Drop the weapon! Drop the weapon!"

Adrian glanced back while continuing to hobble away. He had stopped on the floor to check on the elevators. They were still busy, so he was going back to the emergency stairwell to continue heading down. He had no plans on stopping for anyone. Considering he was attacked by people in clown costumes, he didn't trust anyone in uniform—including the police.

He opened the door to the emergency stairwell and slipped away. He slid down the guardrail to the landing below.

"Shit," Franco muttered. "We have to catch up to him."

He hurried forward while keeping his handgun up. He took cover behind a laundry cart in front of a door, checked his surroundings, then pushed forward.

Following him, Lee said, "I think that was a guest. He looked injured."

"Guest or not, we can't let him run around this place like that."

"That's why I'm saying we should get into the..."

His voice faltered and he stopped in his tracks. He looked at the door to his right. It was cracked open. The number next to the door read: 15213. He heard a soft voice and a gurgling noise.

"*Hey,*" he hissed at Franco.

The cop was already two doors down. He glared at Lee and shrugged, angered by his lollygagging.

Lee pointed at the door next to him and, just above a whisper, he said, "It's open. I hear someone."

Franco looked back at the emergency exit. He noticed a trail of blood leading to the door. Although he was eager to catch him, he hoped the bloodstains would help him track down Adrian later. He returned to Lee's side. He heard the noise, too. It sounded like someone trying to speak and gargle at the same time.

Franco pushed the door open and crept into the room. He checked the bathroom first—*clear.* Then he examined the bedroom—*clear.* It looked like no one had checked into the room. His gaze was pulled to the communicating doorway. The noise, now clearer than before, was coming from the neighboring room.

Room 15212.

A man in the other room said, "Deepthroat it, you bastard. Stop... fighting me."

Brow furrowed, Franco slunk over to the communicating doorway with his pistol raised. Lee entered the bedroom, an uneasy feeling twisting his stomach up.

"That's... it," the other man said. "This'll show 'em."

Franco stopped in the doorway. His eyes grew large while the color on his cheeks faded. Catching a glimpse of the room from over the cop's shoulder, Lee put one hand on his stomach and the other over his mouth. The uneasiness he had felt earlier turned into pure fear and debilitating revulsion.

They saw Nora tied to the bed, wearing only a bloodstained pillowcase over her head. Her arms had gone limp. Blood from her severed nipple had reached the blood smeared on her crotch and thighs. It was all bright red on her pasty skin. The genital mutilation was obvious. Meanwhile, the giant bloodstain on the mattress underneath her was as dark as night. She wasn't moving, wasn't breathing.

Yet, despite her horrific death, they glossed over her and focused on the terrible scene in the corner of the room.

Owen was still restrained to the recliner, but the tape was removed from his lips. His head was tilted back and his face had crumpled like plastic, an ugly mass of lines and ridges. Tubs stood next to him. He had forced the fire extinguisher's nozzle into Owen's mouth and down his throat. It had entered his trachea, causing his windpipe to rupture while a large lump protruded from his neck like an enlarged Adam's apple.

Tears ran down the sides of Owen's head. It was enough to slick thick locks of his hair back. The intense pain in his throat and fear in his heart caused him to piss his pants.

"Dah... Don't move," Franco croaked out.

He had seen plenty of acts of inhumane violence throughout his career—prostitutes beaten to a bloody, swollen pulp; abused children locked in cramped closets; drug addicts stabbing each other to death with used syringes—but he had never seen anything like *that*.

Fingers firmly wrapped around the fire extinguisher's handles, Tubs glanced at the doorway. He looked momentarily taken aback.

"You a cop?" he asked.

"Don't move!" Franco yelled. "Don't fucking move!"

"Like, a *real* cop? I thought we killed all of you already. No, wait a second."

"Keep your hands where I can see them!"

"You're one of us, aren't you? Did Binks put you up to this? Is this a test?"

"Shut your mouth! Get that out of his mouth and step away! Now, damn it!"

Laughing, Tubs said, "You just told me not to move, didn't you? Can't have it both ways, can you?"

Owen twitched and groaned sluggishly. Blood from his torn trachea frothed on the corners of his mouth. His eyes rolled back, leaving only his bloodshot sclerae visible through the slits between his eyelids.

Franco shouted, "Get it out of him!"

Tubs said, "Sure, sure. Let me just help 'extinguish' his heartburn if you get what I'm saying."

"Get it out–"

Tubs squeezed the handles. The hose slithered outside of Owen's mouth, then straightened out seconds later. A muffled *whooshing* sound came from the fire extinguisher. Monoammonium phosphate—a dry chemical powder—rapidly filled his trachea and lungs. The lump on his throat grew to the size of a melon, bulging veins curving around it. White powder came out of his busted nose.

"Drop it! Drop it!" Franco demanded.

Sidestepping, he hurried into the room in search of a clear shot. He didn't want to shoot Owen or the fire extinguisher. From the foot of the bed, he shot at Tubs four times.

Two of the bullets struck the left side of his chest, breaking his ribs. One of those rounds pierced his lung and stayed lodged in there while the other exited through his back. The through-and-through shot ricocheted off the window and hit the ceiling. A third bullet hit his upper abdomen, grazing his stomach and large intestine. Slightly below it, the fourth round entered his descending colon.

Tubs tottered back and crashed into the window behind him. He stopped laughing and started coughing. Yet, despite the shooting, he kept squeezing the fire extinguisher's handles.

There was an unusual feeling of pressure in Owen's ears and, as the pressure got stronger, a hot, stinging pain emerged. He felt like his head was about to explode. Although he had given up on life after Nora's death, his body impulsively fought to survive. He tried to reach up to pull the hose out of his throat or scratch at his neck, but he couldn't break through the tape around his body. Instead, he clawed at his pants and convulsed.

His chest expanded as his lungs ballooned. Then a faint *cracking* noise came from somewhere in his body. Franco mistook it as a rib snapping, but one of Owen's lungs had actually burst. The other one popped a few seconds later. Blood leaked from his ear canals, nostrils, and the corners of his eyes. It glazed his eyeballs, turning them completely red. He coughed up clouds of bloodied powder.

"Drop the weapon!" Franco barked as he fired his gun again.

The bullet went through Tubs' left shoulder. The window behind him shattered. Tubs finally released the fire extinguisher. It hit the recliner's armrest, then landed on Owen's lap. The clown took a step forward, then lost his balance and went reeling to the right. He fell in the corner of the room between a nightstand and the window.

The curtains rustled as a cool breeze blew into the hotel room.

Pointing the gun at Tubs, Franco sidestepped to the recliner and said, "Lee, check her."

Keeping his hand over his mouth, Lee crept up to the communicating doorway. He saw the cloud of bloody powder floating around the recliner, like tiny red snowflakes. He looked at Nora's lifeless body and shook his head. His legs trembled; he wasn't paralyzed, but he couldn't muster the courage to move forward. He was stuck there, aghast.

Franco checked on Tubs. The clown was sitting on the floor with his back to the wall, an elbow on the nightstand, and a hand over the holes on his chest. He was still breathing. Although his training had taught him to secure the suspect immediately, Franco felt compelled to help the victims first. He holstered his weapon and darted to Owen's side.

"Jesus Christ," he muttered.

Owen twitched erratically, but it looked like he had already stopped breathing. Franco pulled on the fire extinguisher's hose. With each tug, a crackling sound came out of Owen's mouth.

Realizing Lee hadn't moved, Franco yelled, "Lee! Help her!"

Lee said, "She... She's... dead."

"Goddammit, man, move it!"

The nozzle slid out of Owen's windpipe. It stopped at the back of his throat. Goops of foamy blood fell from his lips as his head swung forward. Franco grabbed the hose with both hands and leaned back. He plucked the nozzle out of his mouth. Gurgling sounds came out of Owen's throat. Franco put his fingers on his neck to check his pulse—*nothing.* He began chest compressions.

Tubs said, "He's... gone. This whole city... is gone. It's... ours now. And it ain't the only one, either. We... We can't be stopped."

He chuckled, then coughed and cried softly. Failing to resuscitate Owen, Franco attempted to contact his dispatcher through his walkie-talkie. There was no answer.

Panting hoarsely with each pause, Tubs said, "You ain't... listening. They can't... hear you... 'cause we won't... let 'em. We control the Platinum Palace. We control it all. Deadface is..." He coughed again, then laughed deliriously. Tears running down his painted face, he said, "He's going to kill you all and... and burn the world in one day. You can't stop... the Hellfire."

Franco pointed at him and shouted, "Shut the fuck up! You just killed these people, you damn psychopath!"

"And we're going to... to–"

"Quiet!"

"–kill a lot more."

Tubs moaned as he reached for the back of his waistband. Franco drew his handgun and aimed it at him. Before he could say a word, he saw a revolver in the clown's hand. They shot their guns at the same time. A bullet entered Tubs' skull through his forehead and exited through the back of his head. A streak of blood and wormlike bits of brains splattered on the wall behind him. The revolver dropped from his hand and his head slumped forward, blood pouring out of the hole on his brow in a steady stream.

Franco approached him. He narrowed his eyes at the clown's inflated forehead. The liquid trickling out of his head was blood mixed with saline. Upon further examination of his red wig, face paint, pants, and physique, he recognized the clown. *Jack's Jackpot Motel,* he thought. *You're the one who tried to break into those girls' room.*

He was about to kick the revolver away when he spotted the flag sticking out of its barrel. It read: *BANG!* For a moment, the fact that he had killed an unarmed person troubled him. He looked at Nora, then at Owen. And just like that, the shooting didn't bother him very much anymore. He pulled Tubs away from the wall, rolled him onto his stomach, and although he was obviously dead, he handcuffed him.

Franco and Lee were speechless. They only heard the distant sirens outside and blood plopping in the hotel room.

Staring at the ceiling so he couldn't see the carnage, Lee asked, "Did you hear what he said?"

"Yes," Franco said, sounding defeated.

"There are more of them and... and they're killing people. That means someone probably pushed that woman and her kid from that room upstairs. God, we have to evacuate the hotel and get the hell out of here."

"We're going to need help, but I can't call it in until we regain control of this damn resort. We need to get back down to the first floor and get you into the security center before we do anything else."

"Or we can find a way out of here, find some phone signal or get to a police station, and send help."

"I might be the last cop in this place, so I'm not going anywhere. And you're the only person I can fully trust right now, so you have to do this. Thousands of lives are at stake."

"I'm not a... a..."

Lee's throat dried out the instant he caught a glimpse of Nora's corpse. He covered his mouth, dry-heaved, and staggered into the room next door.

"Hey," Franco called out. "Hey!"

He followed him into the neighboring room. Lee sat on the bed and stared down at the floor. The violence took a heavy toll on him. He was haunted by the dead bodies in the pool complex and Room 15212. Unlike Franco, he had never seen more than a *slightly* bloody scuffle during his career as a security guard.

Franco put his hands on Lee's shoulders and said,

"I need you to keep your head on straight. I can't do this without you."

"I–I'm not a hero."

"I'm not asking you to run into a hail of bullets or dive headfirst into a raging fire, Lee. I'm asking you to do your job."

"We don't even know how many of them are out there or what they're armed with or what they want. Didn't you hear him? He said something about a–a... a fire. Hellfire or something like that. They could be planning on blowing this place up. Shit, we even heard an explosion outside earlier!"

Franco said, "I hear you. That's why we need to get you into the security room. Someone has to override the security system to get those gates up and get a distress signal out. I don't know how to do that. You do. If you leave or if you lock yourself in here and give up, you could be helping these damn clowns kill thousands of people. We've already got a dead kid in the jacuzzi, Lee. I don't even want to think about how many children are in danger here."

Dozens of young faces flashed in Lee's mind. He had seen those children around the resort with their families earlier in the day. They didn't do or say anything memorable, they were just kids being kids, but now he couldn't get them out of his head. He couldn't abandon them. He wiped the tears from his eyes, then swiped at his nose with the back of his hand.

He said, "I'll do whatever I can to help. But... I'm

really not a hero. I won't go into any other hotel rooms. I can't see anything like that again."

Franco said, "I'll take care of the guests and the clowns. You just get into that security room and help us take back control of this place before it's too late."

Lee nodded and said, "Let's do it."

Franco turned to exit the room, then he looked at the communicating doorway. He couldn't leave the victims like that. He went in there and grabbed two pajama robes from the closet in the foyer of the room. He placed one over Nora's body and the other over Owen's. They deserved better, but that was the best he could do. He didn't show any pity for Tubs, leaving him exposed in the corner of the room.

He exited the room with Lee, closing the door behind him. Pistol drawn, he led Lee back to the emergency stairwell and they started making their way down to the first floor.

10

SPLITTING UP

FRANCO PEEKED THROUGH THE NARROW CRACK BETWEEN the door and the jamb. The elevator bank and hallway were clear. The floor indicators above the elevators kept changing, so he knew people were still moving around in the guest tower. He closed the door quietly, then leaned forward and looked up the stairwell. He didn't see any movement, but he heard a pair of footsteps drifting away from them.

Leaning back against the wall next to him, Lee held his walkie-talkie out in front of him and whispered, "No one's answering. I think something bad went down while we were clearing the rooms. It got worse down here. I know it."

"I know," Franco replied. "Looks like the hallways have been cleared out. I doubt the guests organized themselves and got up to their rooms in an orderly fashion. There must have been another clown down here that scared everyone away. Possibly multiple armed suspects. We can't be too sure."

"Multiple armed suspects? I don't know if you noticed, but I don't have a gun. I told you already, I can't go out there and play hero, especially not without a weapon. There are some tasers and batons in the storeroom, but those bastards already barricaded all of the doors to the employee area."

"Then we kick a door down."

"They'll hear us before we even make a dent. Then what? I get shot? I get a fire extinguisher shoved down my throat? No way, man. I'm not–"

"*Shh.*"

Franco cracked the door open and peeked out into the hallway. It was empty, but he heard some slow footsteps out there. They gradually faded away.

He closed the door again, then said, "Change of plans. I'll stay out here. I'll help as many guests as possible. If I see a clown, I'll try to arrest or incapacitate them. In the meantime, you get into the employee area. If you can't take control, at least try to take down their signal jammers and send out a distress signal."

"But the doors are barricaded."

"There has to be another way in. Think, Lee."

Lee looked around, as if he were searching for a hidden entrance in the stairwell. He thought about breaking a window in one of the rooms on the second floor, climbing down to the street, then trying to sneak in through one of the employee-only entrances. *It won't work,* he told himself. *They've probably barricaded every door by now.* His gaze landed on a ventilation shaft under the stairs in front of him.

"The machine room," he said. "The room behind the elevators. I can open it with my keys. There's a ventilation shaft in there that leads to the employee area. I think it was a locker room or a storeroom. But I'm sure one of the maintenance guys mentioned it."

"Can you fit?"

"It'll be tight, but I think I can manage."

"Good. Think you can manage to contact me once you're in there, too?"

Lee held his walkie-talkie out and said, "Take it. It's useless now and I won't need it in there anyway. I'll call you if I can, but if that place is overrun... I can't fight an army of clowns with my bare hands."

Franco took the walkie-talkie and said, "I don't expect you to. I only want you to remember this: Whatever happens, don't forget about these people. Get help, Lee."

"I'll... I'll do my best."

"Which way is the... What did you call it?"

"The machine room. It should be the only door to our right out there."

Franco said, "I'll watch your back until you get that door open. From there, you're on your own."

"And where are you going?" Lee asked. "Worst-case scenario, I can tell the cops where they might find you if I have to sneak out of here. Best-case scenario, I can help you through the surveillance system if those damn clowns aren't around."

"I'll be around the casino looking for any guests that got left behind. Now, you ready to get moving?"

"As ready as I'll ever be."

Franco opened the door a little and looked out. There was no one in sight. Pistol up, he crossed the hall and investigated the elevator bank—*clear*. Then he checked the hallway again. He saw the door at the end of the hall. A placard on the door read:

EMPLOYEES ONLY
Machine Room

With his back to the machine room, he crouched behind a trash can outside of the emergency stairwell and aimed his handgun down the hallway.

Without looking back, he said, "You're clear."

Lee dashed to the locked door. A keychain with over a dozen keys jingled in his hand, but he already had the correct key pinched between his thumb and index finger. Due to his jitters, he momentarily struggled with the lock. As soon as he heard it unlock—*click!*—he took one final look at the police officer.

Although he envied his bravery, he couldn't help but feel like he was staring at a dead man. He entered the machine room and locked the door behind him.

The loud mechanical noises made his head hurt, but he was pleased to see the room was empty. He removed his jacket, then took a multi-tool out of his pocket and approached a ventilation shaft at the end of the room.

Since he didn't hear any screams behind him, Franco assumed Lee had made it into the room safely. Staying close to the wall and keeping his finger on his handgun's trigger, he jogged forward. He stopped at the end of every hallway and checked his surroundings, maintaining his situational awareness.

In the hallway leading to the pool area, he found a child's light-up sneaker, a woman's pair of high heels, a trampled sweatshirt, and two suitcases. He noticed the dark stains spattered all over the crimson carpet, too. He tried to tell himself that someone had spilled a drink, but he knew it was blood—*a lot* of blood.

A stampede had taken place in the hallway as well as a couple of brutal beatings. The signs of a violent struggle and the lack of bodies told him a few kidnappings had also occurred.

Where did they take you? he wondered.

As he made his way down the hall, he looked out at the pool area. There was no one out there and the lights were now off at the spa. He wondered if Jordan and the other security guards had succeeded in evacuating the first floor of the resort.

Franco followed the hallway to the casino. He ducked behind a slot machine and canvassed the area. Most of the racket from the machines continued—the music, the beeping, the whirring—but the gamblers were gone so no one was around to pull on the levers or mash the buttons. The card dealers abandoned their posts, too.

He crept down an aisle with nickel slots at each side. He stopped at the end, checked his surroundings, then crossed over to a curved aisle with quarter slots. He heard heavy footsteps and faint voices around him. He lowered himself to a crouch between two stools and waited. About thirty seconds later, he couldn't hear them anymore.

Staying low, he hurried to the end of the aisle. He inspected his surroundings again. At first glance, he didn't see any clowns or guests. He took two steps forward, then came to a sudden halt. An expression of confusion dawned on his face as he stared at the card tables to his right. A set of lumbering footsteps beyond the slot machines in front of him broke his concentration.

Franco crawled back behind cover. He waited a few seconds until the footsteps faded away, then he looked out at the card tables again. He could see Adrian under one of the tables. He recognized him from their brief encounter on the fifteenth floor.

He's not one of them, Franco thought. *But why would he leave the hotel tower and hide down here? What the hell is he thinking?*

Then he remembered Monica Ramsey, the Asian woman from the emergency stairwell. She was willing to risk her safety to find her husband. Love—*true love*—made people do dangerous things. He believed Adrian was risking his life for someone else.

Franco crouched his way down the aisle between the rows of slot machines, trying to catch up to him. Just as the cop reached the card games section, Adrian scrambled to another table. He moved quickly despite his injuries.

"No!" a woman screamed, stopping the men in their tracks.

A skinny clown dressed as Elvis Presley dragged a young blonde woman out from behind a roulette table. He went by '*Hound the Clown*' on account of his favorite Elvis song being 'Hound Dog.' On a strap, a semi-automatic rifle was slung across his back. He wrestled with her flailing legs, swaying this way and that way. Franco moved to the closest card table to get a better angle. He aimed his pistol at the clown, but he hesitated. He couldn't get a clear shot because of the woman's floundering. Collateral damage was a good cop's worst nightmare.

Holding onto her legs, Hound shouted, "I got another one!"

A clown in a white jumpsuit with purple pom-pom buttons and matching ruff collar approached them. Frizzy purple hair surrounded the inflated bald spot at the center of his head. He wielded a battery-powered chainsaw, versatile and powerful. A pump-action shotgun was slung across his back.

Hound said, "She's a pretty one. Look at that body. But, hey, I ain't selfish. How about you and I take her to a room and have some fun? Our little secret, eh?"

"No!" the woman yelled. "Help! Help me!"

While she screamed helplessly, the clown in the jumpsuit said, "Not her. Deadface needs a girl like her for the show. Get her to the green room. I'll let 'em know you're on the way."

Hound asked, "Can't I have a lil' fun before I gotta take her over there? It's not like I'm gonna kill her. I'll just fuck her before I dump her, all right?"

"No! Don't! Please don't!" the woman cried. "Help me! Please, someone help me! Someone help... m–m–me."

Her voice broke on the last word. Feeling her abject terror, Franco tensed up. Murder was physical while rape was physical, psychological, *and* emotional. Rape was like being killed from within and being left alive on the outside—death of the soul. And being raped and murdered was like dying twice.

But Franco couldn't pull the trigger. He saw other clowns patrolling the casino floor beyond the card tables. He was outnumbered and outgunned. He couldn't tell if the clowns were wearing suicide vests under their costumes, either. It was too risky for him to shoot. Stealth was his best option, so he holstered his handgun and drew his baton.

The clown in the jumpsuit said, "The boss doesn't want any 'tarnished goods.' If they're going to be in the show, they have to be fresh. So, keep your rotten dick out of her and get her to the green room. Don't make me tell you again."

"Fine, I'll go check out the rooms and find a 'tarnished' piece of ass for myself later," Hound said. As he dragged the blonde woman away, he muttered, "And my dick ain't rotten, asshole. They're just pimples..."

After a few seconds, the woman's cries were drowned out by the noisy slot machines. The clown in the jumpsuit continued his patrol.

Franco noticed Adrian had moved farther away from him. He seemed unconcerned about the other guests—unconcerned about *himself*. Franco decided to follow him. *Maybe he knows where he's going*, he thought. *Maybe he's looking for this 'Deadface' guy, too.* He crawled from table to table until he reached the end of the card games section.

By then, Adrian was already traversing another maze of slot machines.

Franco caught glimpses of him between the bright displays. He followed his trail, only stopping and hiding to let the patrolling clowns walk past him. He reached a Wheel of Fortune game next to one of the main walkways. He saw Adrian go down an escalator from afar. Above him, a sign with an arrow pointing in that direction read: *The Royal Buffet.*

He looked both ways, as if he were crossing a busy street, then he ran across the walkway. Before he could reach the escalators to the Royal Buffet, a childish whimper stopped him. It came from another set of escalators to his right. With an arrow pointing down, the sign above the escalators read: *Your Majesty's Game Room.*

Franco looked at the arcade, then at the buffet, then back at the arcade. He didn't want to lose Adrian, but he couldn't abandon a kid in need, either. He heard another feeble cry. He was a good cop and a better person, so he couldn't resist it. Running backwards, he took one final glance at the buffet, then turned and headed down to Your Majesty's Game Room.

11

YOUR MAJESTY'S GAME ROOM

THE TODDLER'S SEVERED HEAD WAS PURPLE AND bloated, his eyes swollen shut and his lips inflated into a permanent pucker. The boy's ears were squashed under locks of disheveled brown hair, like bubble gum under a sneaker. Veins, muscle fibers, and flaps of shredded skin dangled from his neck like wet noodles. The head was on its side at the bottom of an indoor basketball arcade game's ramp. The game was splashed with the boy's blood—on the backboard, the rim, the net, the ramp.

Wearing a jumpsuit with a black ruff collar, a lanky man stood in front of the arcade game. The left side of his jumpsuit was white and the right side was black. Similarly, he wore a white glove and white shoe on his left hand and foot, and a black glove and black shoe on his right hand and foot. Painted white, he had the perfect egg-shaped head—no hair, no nose, no ears.

Like some of the other clowns, there were vertical black streaks of paint over his eyes. A black smile was painted over his mouth as well. The sclerae of his eyes were dyed black and his incisor teeth were filed to sharp points.

He called himself Demon.

Demon, the Jester from Hell.

He picked up the toddler's severed head and studied it, unbothered by the barbaric violence. He threw it down at the ramp, as if he were dribbling a basketball, but it didn't bounce.

He picked it up again and, in a loud but calm voice, he said, "We saw the girl before she went *poof*. If you don't want to end up like this poor boy, I suggest you tell me where she's hiding."

He jumped and threw the severed head. It went straight through the net, then rolled back down the ramp.

"*Swish!*" Demon exclaimed.

He turned around and surveyed the arcade. It was designed like a square doughnut with escalators in the middle. Although no one was playing any of the games, upbeat music and sound effects came from the arcade cabinets. It wasn't nearly as loud as the casino, though. Next to the basketball arcade games, there were three Skee-Ball machines.

A scrawny 13-year-old boy, Trent Reid, was taped to one of the Skee-Ball machines' slanted backboards. His face was decorated with clown makeup, smeared by his tears and sweat. His legs, which were unrestrained and mostly bare because of his shorts, were covered in welts and bruises. Stifled cries seeped out from behind the piece of tape over his mouth.

Demon grabbed one of the hard balls. Behind him, a man and a woman screamed. It was all incomprehensible but emotional. He ignored them.

He said, "This boy is too old for our circus. If you won't tell me where the girl is hiding, I'll rip his balls off and juggle 'em for you. And if you *still* won't talk, I'll take the man's balls and toss 'em into the mix. Then, *woman,* I'll shove them all down your throat and watch you choke on their testicles. Might even get you to swallow one or two."

He chuckled as he rolled the ball up the lane. The boy cried out as it hit his knee with a loud *thud.* Demon grabbed another ball and rolled it up—faster, *harder.* It hit the kid's thigh. Trent struggled against the backboard, wiggling around and swinging his legs out of pain and desperation. The tape around his torso was beginning to loosen.

"Ah, shit," Demon said. "So close to a bull's-eye. Should I try again?"

The man and woman responded with a synchronized scream. Their response was easy to understand that time: '*No!*'

Demon said, "Fine, fine, fine. I won't steal his family jewels—*yet.* Let's see what you have to say for yourselves first."

He strolled away from the Skee-Ball machines. He walked past some table hockey games, then past a wall of light gun games. The arcade was filled with different versions of *The House of the Dead*, *Silent Scope*, *Time Crisis*, and other classic rail shooters.

Men, women, and children were slumped up against each arcade cabinet. Some of them lay on their sides next to the games. They had been executed, shot in the backs of their heads. Their blood and brains were splattered on the arcade cabinets' displays and plastic guns. Some of the arcade cabinets were damaged by the through-and-through gunshots.

An old, balding man was on his knees with his head down on the floor and his pants around his ankles. One of the plastic guns from a rail shooter—a big toy rifle—was rammed into his ass. Blood from his torn rectum dribbled out and turned the white pubic hair on his sagging scrotum red. It was hard to tell if he had been sodomized before or after his execution.

Demon stopped in front of a coin pusher game. The machine's glass panes were broken and, inside of the game, the beheaded toddler's body was sprawled across piles of bloody medals and shards of sparkling glass.

A middled-aged man, Terrance Reid, sat on the floor under the game. His outstretched arms were pulled up and bound to the machine with zip ties. Like his son, there was a strip of tape over his mouth. A wide stripe of blood extended from a deep gash on his left temple to his neck.

Demon crouched in front of him and said, "I don't want you to waste my time. If I don't get my hands on that girl in the next ten minutes, I'm going to hurt you and your family." Terrance shook his head and mumbled something unintelligible. Demon curled his lip and asked, "Are you laughing at me? Do you think this is funny?"

Bug-eyed, Terrance shook his head faster.

Demon said, "Maybe... Maybe it was the juggling. Can't take me seriously if I'm talking about juggling your testicles, right? So, let's try something else. What about, um... Let's see, how about... How about... Ah, I got it. If you don't tell me where the girl is hiding, I'm going to cut your son's dick off and then I'm going to mash it into your wife's pussy."

Terrance wagged his head in every direction, jerked around, and screamed as loud as possible, crying out for help while wrestling with his restraints.

Demon smirked and said, "Oh, you don't like that one, do you? What's the matter? You the jealous type? Don't want to watch your son fuck your wife? Or does it go against your precious 'beliefs'? I'll make it easier for you. Think of it this way: It ain't incest if his dick isn't attached to his body. Really, his dick would be more like a dildo. A puny, fleshy, bloody dildo."

The clown snickered. Terrance went into a craze of panic, thrashing about against the coin pusher. The arcade machine slid a mere *millimeter* despite his strenuous efforts. The clown burst into an obnoxious guffaw. Behind him, Trent whimpered and flopped around on the Skee-Ball machine's backboard. He understood every word out of the clown's mouth. And around the corner in front of him, Demon heard a woman wailing.

He closed his eyes and moved his hand as if he were holding a conductor's baton, orchestrating the music of suffering. To Demon, murder was like sex. His victims' cries sounded like a romantic song in his ears. Instilling fear was an act of foreplay. The torture was the penetration and the actual murder was the orgasm. And he topped it all off with desecration of the human remains as if it were a post-orgasm blowjob.

After a few seconds, he stopped waving his imaginary baton upon noticing Terrance's sudden silence. He opened his eyes. Terrance was grumbling while leaning to his right and looking over the clown's shoulder.

Demon quickly turned to look back. He saw Trent taped to the Skee-Ball machine and the dead bodies in front of the light gun games. The boy was quieter now, too.

The clown smiled and asked, "Was that our missing girl? It was, wasn't it?"

He made his way back to the Skee-Ball machines, checking behind every arcade cabinet in his path. He didn't find the girl. Her name was Mikayla Reid. She was nine years old. The clowns had spotted her with her family during the initial attack in the arcade. They had lost track of her during the massacre, though.

Demon sighed in disappointment, then walked back. He pointed at Terrance and said, "I know someone else is here. I can feel it. You're only making this worse for yourselves, you know? The longer you hide her, the more time you give me to think about how I'm going to hurt you. And I'm so very *fuckin'* good at hurting people."

He walked around the corner, moving past the prize counter and some fighting games. He stopped in the racing games section. Kellie Reid sat in the driver's seat of a *Crazy Taxi* arcade machine. She was taped to the chair at her chest and thighs while her arms were cuffed to the steering wheel with zip ties.

Demon bent over next to her and grabbed the steering wheel. Like Terrance, she sobbed deliriously under the bloodied tape on her mouth. She was traumatized by the violence and terrified for her family. The zip ties around her wrists were so tight that her hands were turning purple. The nylon cut into her wrists, too. Yet, she kept fighting with the restraints.

"Just tell me where she's hiding," the clown said. "Trust me, she's better off with us. We're not going to kill her. Not even going to touch a hair on her little head. We're going to adopt her. We have a prince in our circus. And you know what they say: Every prince needs a princess. If she stays here, if she stays anywhere in this hotel, she's going to die in the Hell-fire. Is that what you want? You want that girl to burn..."

His voice petered out. Despite the music from the surrounding games, he noticed Terrance and Trent had gone silent again. A feeling of heavy tension hung over him. He felt someone lurking behind him. Shock crossed his face as he turned around. He found Franco standing behind him, swinging his baton at the clown.

Demon staggered to his right. The baton missed his head and hit his left shoulder instead. The clown landed on the seat of a *Mario Kart Arcade GP* cabinet. He snarled in anger and pain while gripping his busted shoulder.

Franco stood over him with the baton cocked back over his shoulder. He hesitated to attack him again. He didn't want to hit the clown's head in the first place. He understood the potentially lethal consequences of such a blow. But he had hoped to knock him out with one hit so he could handcuff him without incident. And, even if he didn't care about lethal force, he couldn't shoot Demon without alarming the clowns upstairs, either.

He said, "Don't move, you–"

"Cop!" Demon yelled. He kicked Franco's stomach, although he was aiming for his crotch. On his back, he squirmed over the neighboring Mario Kart cabinets' seats and shouted, "Cop! We got a cop down here! Cop!"

The Reid family cried harder than ever before, reinvigorated by the police officer's presence. The clowns patrolling the casino couldn't hear them over the slot machines, though.

Do something, the little voice in Franco's head said. *They're counting on you.*

He leapt onto the racing seats and swung the baton in quick succession. He cracked Demon's left kneecap with a swing. He heard the bone *crunch*. Then he hit his left thigh twice before banging on his hip once. Desperate to stop him from screaming for help, he swung the baton at his crotch, too. He hit his pubic region.

Although the baton missed his genitals, Demon instinctively hunched over and cupped his hands over his groin. He kicked Franco's chest, simultaneously knocking the cop back and pushing himself off the racing seats. He landed on the other side of the connected *Mario Kart Arcade GP* cabinets.

Franco jumped off the racing seat and ran towards the downed clown. He holstered his baton and was about to draw his stun gun when Demon got to his feet. The clown lurched towards the cop. He tackled him and chomped at his face. Franco stepped back and dodged his sharpened teeth. He couldn't break away from the clown, though.

While pushing forward, Demon tried to bite the cop's neck. His teeth *clacked* as he missed again. Franco was slammed against a crane game. The baton fell from his belt and landed on the floor. One of the game's glass windows shattered, shards slicing the back of his head and neck. His upper body slid into the game, blood from his cuts drizzling onto the collection of *Minions* plushies below.

Unable to reach his face and neck, Demon bit into Franco's right arm. His teeth easily tore through the cop's sleeve and sank into his bicep. Franco felt the hot blood racing down his arm. Although he wanted to push the clown away, he was more concerned about losing his handgun. So, despite the pain pulsing through his pierced bicep, he grasped the clown's elbows to keep control of his limbs while searching for an advantage.

Franco's blood gushed out from the corners of Demon's mouth. Teeth buried in his muscle, Demon tried to lean away from the cop and ease himself out of the crane game. He couldn't breathe in the narrow space with a mouthful of blood. The thought of stealing Franco's handgun didn't cross his mind. He was thinking about biting his nose off or ripping his Adam's apple out of his neck. He couldn't break free, though.

Franco felt like his muscle was rising away from his bone. There was a feeling of pressure in his elbow and shoulder as the tendons stretched.

"Stop it!" Trent shouted as he swung the baton at Demon's lower back.

The boy had broken free from his restraints. He

had tried to free his parents, but he couldn't break their zip ties. He took the strips of tape off their mouths, though. They yelled at him from their arcade machines, trying to stop his reckless behavior to no avail.

"No, baby! No!" Kellie cried.

Terrance shouted, "Run, Trent!"

Trent swung the baton at the clown again. Demon barely reacted to the blow. It frustrated him more than it hurt him. The boy was too weak to do any damage with the baton, but he kept trying. He swung it at the clown's left leg. The blow reignited the pain in his broken kneecap. Close to buckling, his leg wobbled violently.

Demon opened his mouth and released the cop's bicep. The pain in Franco's arm began to subside. Before he could fully recover, the killer clown jumped up and headbutted him square in the chin. Franco was dazed by the blow. Demon pushed him into the machine, forcing him to sit on the bloodstained plushies and broken glass.

"Stop it, asshole!" Trent yelled as he swung the baton once more.

Demon turned around to face the boy and grabbed the baton mid-swing. Trent froze up, spooked by the clown's strength and the parallel streams of blood on his chin.

"Run!" Terrance shouted. "Go, Trent! Get out of here!"

"You little fuck," Demon snarled. "I'm going to play Skee-Ball with *your* balls."

Kellie yelled, "No!"

His vision hazy, Franco heard the family's anguished cries and saw the clown lunge at the boy. In a knee-jerk reaction, Trent thrust the baton forward. The tip of the baton tapped Demon's scrotum. Although the pain wasn't debilitating, Demon felt like someone had pinched his testicle. He jumped back.

Franco lost control of himself. He had to protect Trent by any means necessary. He grabbed the crane game's claw above him and gave it a good tug, pulling it down to his chest. His bicep stung as it contracted, blood squirting out of the holes on the muscle. He wrapped his legs around Demon's waist from behind and pulled him back into the arcade machine.

While swinging his elbows back at him, the clown yelled, "Motherfucker!"

Kellie shouted, "Kill him!"

"Get out of there, Trent!" Terrance demanded.

Franco grabbed Demon in a rear naked choke, then thrust one of the claw's stainless-steel fingers at his face. The claw pierced his right eye, curving into it. The clown let out a guttural bellow. A gelatinous fluid oozed out of his ruptured eye and lined his eyelid. It looked dark due to his dyed sclera. His eyelids twitched, sending a drop of the liquid down his cheek. It was a tear mixed with blood and vitreous fluid.

Franco drove the claw in deeper and jiggled it

around like a key in an old lock, stirring the inside of his eye. The other two steel fingers were wrapped around Demon's head. Franco released the claw. It started to rise automatically, as if it were carrying a prize up to the ceiling. Demon howled in pain as his dyed eye extended out of its socket, stretching out of his face like black goo. The muscles attached to his eyeball ripped one by one.

Demon's eye was gouged out. He fainted for a few seconds, regained consciousness, then fainted again. The claw slid off his head, closed, and then rose to the game's ceiling. A piece of the severed optic nerve hung from the mutilated eyeball. The crane moved to the front of the machine, then the claw opened again. The eyeball fell from the steel finger and rolled down the prize chute.

Franco pushed the clown away. Demon face-planted in front of the kid. Trent's parents called out to him, but the boy couldn't move. He was stunned by the horrific violence. He remembered playing that very same crane game with his dad minutes before the raid. *Keep your eye on the prize*, his father had said. And now there was a human eyeball waiting to be retrieved from the prize chute.

"Don't... move," Franco said, out of breath.

He took a set of handcuffs out of his utility belt. Demon rolled onto his back and unleashed a ghastly moan. He shoved his hand into his pocket and wormed towards Trent.

"Stop!" Franco yelled. "Show me your hands!"

From the coin pusher machine, Terrance shouted, "Trent!"

Franco and Trent saw the outline of a rectangular object in Demon's pocket. They both assumed it was a weapon—a pocketknife, a gun, *a bomb*. Franco reached for his pistol. *No*, he thought. *I can't lead all of those clowns down here.* He considered using his stun gun, but those weren't always effective. If it didn't neutralize him, he feared Demon would still be able to injure Trent.

In what felt like slow motion, he ran forward, grabbed the crane game next to them, and tipped it over. A sharp edge at the top of the heavy machine hit Demon's forehead. The arcade cabinet's windows shattered and, with a loud, hair-raising *crack*, the top half of the clown's head burst open. Bits of crushed brain and bone fragments surfed out of his skull on a wave of blood. His left eye bulged out due to its collapsed socket.

In his death throes, Demon's limbs continued to shake. He had a walkie-talkie in his hand. Eyes wide and mouth agape, Trent stared down at the dead clown. His parents watched in stunned silence. A cold sweat glistened on Franco's pale face. The violence disoriented him. He had killed two people in less than an hour—and he had a feeling he was going to have to kill a lot more before the night was over.

"Get us out of here," Terrance said.

His voice snapped Franco out of his shock. The cop pulled Trent away from the dead clown and brought him to his father. He cut Terrance's zip ties and tape with one of his multi-tool's blades. Terrance hugged his son as soon as he was freed. He pushed the boy's face up against his chest to block his view of the carnage.

"Thank God," he whispered.

While cutting one of Kellie's zip ties, Franco said, "He was looking for someone."

"My daughter," Kellie replied quickly. "I need to get my daughter."

"Is she alive?"

He cut the other zip tie.

"Yes, yes, yes," Kellie said as she tugged on the tape around her chest.

Franco sawed into the tape with his blade and asked, "Where is she?"

"She's here. She's hiding. Please hurry. I need to get my daughter. Get me off this damn seat."

"We'll find her, ma'am. Are you injured?"

"Aren't you listening? My daughter needs me! Get me out of here!"

"I understand that, ma'am, but I need you to–"

Although he wasn't finished sawing through the tape around her thighs, Kellie managed to break free from the chair. She pushed past the cop and ran to the prize counter. Franco drew his handgun and followed her while keeping an eye on the escalators. The last thing he wanted was for the clowns in the casino to come down into the arcade and ambush them.

"Mikayla," Kellie said as she opened a long, wide chest behind the prize counter. It was full of plushy toys, big and small. Pushing the toys aside, she said, "Mikayla, baby, it's mommy."

"Ma... Mom?" a girl whimpered from behind a giant stuffed lion.

Kellie pushed the toy aside. A smile blossomed on her face. She found her daughter sitting on top of a stuffed whale in the corner of the toy chest. The girl was trembling, her cheeks wet with tears. When the clowns started rounding up the guests in the arcade, Kellie had instructed her daughter to hide in the toy chest. Mikayla didn't witness the massacre, but she had heard everything. The sound of violence was stuck in her eardrums, like sonic scars.

Kellie lifted her from the chest and held her in her arms while whispering words of reassurance into her ear. Terrance and Trent joined them at the prize counter, their backs to the bloodbath.

Terrance said, "You have to get us out of here."

"There's no way out," Franco said. "You have to hide and wait."

"Hide and wait?" Kellie repeated. "My Lord, these animals are killing people. We heard gunshots and explosions all over the place. This is a–a–a *terrorist* attack. Where are the rest of you? Where's your SWAT team? Where's the military? Where were *you?*"

"If you want the truth, I know about as much as you do. I don't know if backup is coming. Don't know if the National Guard is on its way. All I know is: The hotel's been seized by those maniacs, the building is on lockdown, and every exit is blocked. I need you to cooperate."

"You can't expect us to stay down here. Look at what they did to these poor people. They... They killed children. For heaven's sake, they killed babies, officer."

Face against her mother's bosom, Mikayla cried, "No! I don't wanna die!"

Trent was shuddering and sniffling, struggling to keep himself from dissolving into tears. He was only just entering his teenage years, but he wanted to act like his father—strong, confident, brave. Unbeknownst to him, Terrance was worried and unnerved, too. He was better at hiding his fear, though. Kellie bounced Mikayla in her arms and kissed her forehead repeatedly, trying to keep the situation under control.

Franco said, "I know you're all scared and you want to get out of here, but you have to listen to me. It's not safe up there."

"It's not safe down here, either," Terrance said. "They could come down here at any moment and we'd be sitting ducks."

Franco looked at the double doors behind the prize counter. The identical signs on each door read: *EMPLOYEES ONLY*. He turned one of the door handles. It was unlocked.

"Did you see any of those clowns go through here?" the cop asked.

Terrance said, "No. They went upstairs after... after the killings. Only that clown stayed behind to look for Mikayla."

Kellie said, "I saw some employees leave through there when this all started. They didn't bother to help anyone. Those selfish bas..."

'Bastards.'

She stopped before she could finish that word. Despite all of the violence, she was still reluctant to curse in front of her children.

She said, "Those selfish *people* are probably long gone by now. They could have done something."

Franco said, "Stay close to me and stay quiet."

The Reid family followed him into the service corridor. Franco checked the first door to his left— *locked.* Aiming his pistol down the hall, he moved to the door to his right. It was unlocked. He cracked the door open and peeked through the slit. It was a storage room. Lockers filled with different types of prizes and supplies and replacement parts lined the walls to his left and right. Old arcade cabinets stood in the corners of the room under black tarps. Cardboard boxes and plastic bins were stacked in the middle of the room. There was no one in there.

Franco beckoned to the family and said, "Get in there and barricade the door. Don't let anyone in except for the police."

"Are you sure that's a good idea?" Terrance asked. "What if they come down here?"

"They won't."

"But what if they *do*?"

"Then they'll see that dead clown in the arcade. They're not going to be looking for a family or a kid. They're going to be looking for me. And if you haven't noticed, I'm bleeding pretty badly. If they're smart, they'll follow my blood. I'll make sure to lead them away from you. Stay quiet and you'll be fine."

Terrance and Kellie saw the blood on the cop's right hand. His bicep bled profusely. They noticed some drops of blood crawling down his forehead like sweat. Although the wounds weren't visible, the cuts on his scalp were deep. Some bloodied glass fragments glittered in his bushy hair like tiny rubies. They could see he was sincere about helping them.

The Reid family entered the storage room. With some help from Trent, Terrance started dragging one of the broken arcade cabinets to the door.

Before closing the door, Kellie said, "Don't forget about us."

"I won't," Franco replied.

"Good luck, officer... and thank you."

She closed the door before Franco could respond. His face instantly contorted into a grimace of agony. He had been bottling his pain since his adrenaline wore off shortly after the brawl with Demon. His bicep burned unceasingly while bolts of pain shot through his scalp with the slightest movement of his head.

He holstered his firearm and took out his multi-tool. He used its blade to cut the lower half of his right sleeve off. Then he tied the fabric around his bitten bicep. After hearing the arcade cabinet slam up against the door, he drew his handgun and hurried down the hall. He wiped his blood on the walls as he traveled through the service corridors.

12

THE ROYAL BUFFET

"You fucked with the wrong man! I'm going to kill you all! I'll rip you bastards to pieces! *To pieces!*" George Moreno growled, face shiny with tears and sweat.

He was a short, round 66-year-old man with white hair and a matching mustache. His adult son, Victor, sat next to him, snuffling and babbling incoherently. Pamela, Victor's wife, sat beside him with her eyes closed and head down. Tears shimmered on her pink cheeks as well. Shoulder to shoulder, they were seated in a half-circle booth at the Royal Buffet with a table in front of them. They were tied together at their chests and thighs, and handcuffed behind their backs with zip ties. They couldn't move without working together.

George shouted, "Connie! Connie, sweetheart, it's going to be okay! We're going to get you to a hospital! An ambulance is coming! It's coming, Connie! I know it!"

"Ma–Mom," Victor whined. "Mom, I don't know what to do."

In front of their booth, four rectangular dining tables were pushed together to make one big table. Nude, Constance 'Connie' Moreno—George's 60-year-old wife—lay on her stomach at the center of the makeshift table. Her limbs were taped to the surface at her wrists and ankles. She was conscious but unmoving, taking only two breaths every minute. She was afraid to move. Every inch of her body hurt, pain circulating through her like blood.

The back of her thighs had been flayed. Most of her quadricep muscles had been stripped from her femur bones, leaving massive craters on the backs of her legs. Blood pooled in those fleshy cavities. Most of her blood ended up on the tablecloth, though. Only some chunks of mutilated, stubborn muscle remained. Despite all the blood, slits of her bones surrounded by blue and green veins were visible in the grisly wounds.

George shouted, "You evil bastards! Let her go! You wanna fuck with someone?! Fuck with me! I'm right here! I'm–" He retched upon catching a whiff of the beefy, metallic stench hanging over them. In a tight voice, he said, "Good God, what have you done to her? How could you... do this? God, how?"

Across from the Moreno family, Twisted sat at the other end of the makeshift table with a fork in his right hand. There was a strip of grayish-brown meat on the plate in front of him. Blood was drizzled on top of the meat and on the plate like red wine steak sauce. It had been seasoned with onion, garlic, pepper, and salt. He stabbed the meat with his fork, then used one of the claws sticking out of his knuckles to saw it off. The blade *screeched* on the plate.

The noise echoed through the quiet buffet. The room was dimly lit. Some booths were lit up by the orange glow from table lamps and sconces while most were completely swallowed by shadows. A majority of the lights were either turned off or broken by the clowns. In one corner of the buffet, there was a 20-foot salad bar next to a fresh juice station. In another corner, there was a dessert table and a pizza bar. At the center of the buffet, there was a small rotunda, which served as an omelet station in the morning and carving station in the afternoon.

Expressionless, Twisted shoved the meat into his mouth and chewed it loudly. Blood dripped out of it with each bite, like juice from an orange. The meat was tough and the tang of blood was strong, but he managed to tear through it without a struggle. It wasn't his first time consuming human flesh. He swallowed it with a loud gulp, then he smirked. He wanted the Moreno family to hear him swallow Constance's flesh.

His voice wavering, George said, "I... I was a cop. I know people. Strong people. People that owe me favors. They can... They can help you if you let us go. Or they can hunt you like animals if you don't stop this."

Twisted said, "I want to eat her ass."

"You bastard!"

George jumped in his seat and leaned to his right, but he couldn't move much because of Victor and Pamela. They were timid—too weak to fight, too scared to run.

"Victor, move!" George cried with raw desperation in his voice.

"I don't know what to do," Victor repeated.

"Goddammit, boy, man up! Help me help her!"

George and Victor had a complicated relationship. They loved each other, but Victor had always felt a sense of disapproval and disappointment from his father. He was supposed to follow in George's footsteps and become a cop. Instead, he earned a Liberal Arts degree and became a self-employed painter. Pamela worked as a nurse, so she was the breadwinner in their relationship. It didn't bother her at all. As a matter of fact, their living situation upset George more than anyone else. He had learned to accept their choices, although he still disagreed with them. He was only lashing out in the buffet because he was afraid of losing his wife.

Constance smiled thinly at them and, in a weak voice, she said, "It's... okay. I'm... okay. It's not... his fault. Don't... scream... at... at... him."

George stammered, "I–I–I know, sweetheart. I–I'm just... I'm angry. Don't talk now. Save your energy, okay?" Shifting moods in an instant, he glared at Twisted and yelled, "Let her go!"

"Serve me her ass, Mr. Cuckoo," Twisted said.

"No! No! No!"

On Twisted's right, another clown emerged from the shadows, clasping his hands behind his back. He wore a white toque blanche, a matching double-breasted short-sleeved jacket, loose black-and-white striped pants, and a pair of big red clown shoes. His clothes were speckled with blood from dozens of victims. His face was decorated like the other clowns' and he wore a big red rubber nose.

In a calm tone, he said, "It's *Chef* Cuckoo."

"Well, *chef*, stop talking and start cooking," Twisted replied.

Chef Cuckoo stared deadpan at him for ten seconds, then he cracked a smile and said, "Gladly."

He walked backwards into the shadows.

At the booth, Victor said, "Pamela... Pam... Pam, what do I do?"

Keeping her eyes and mouth shut, Pamela responded with a whimper.

George said, "Move with me. Victor, move your ass!"

"I can't do it," Victor responded. "I don't know why, but I can't."

"Victor, your mother needs you."

"It's... okay," Constance murmured.

Chef Cuckoo returned to the makeshift table with a

carving knife. It had an 8-inch blade with a sharp point.

Standing next to Constance with his eyes glued to her flabby behind, he said, "One plate of the finest ass coming right up."

Adrian watched the torture from under a table in the dark. He could see Chef Cuckoo using the carving knife to flay Constance's ass. The clown threw the severed strips of skin aside. They slithered through the air like vegetable peels before landing on the floor with *splat* sounds. The woman cycled between soft whimpers and sharp yelps.

Adrian was furious. He wanted to help the Moreno family, wanted to avenge his wife and son, wanted to rescue his daughter. But he knew he had to play it smart. He had already lost a fight against Twisted and he could see Chef Cuckoo had an affinity for extreme violence. He couldn't handle both of them at one time.

Find Lily first, deal with the clowns later, he told himself.

Sticking to the shadows, he crawled from table to table and investigated every dead body in his path. Most of the adult patrons had been executed, shot twice in the head and twice in the chest. It appeared to be overkill for the sake of it. Nearly every corpse in the buffet was shirtless and a few had their pants removed.

Chunks of flesh had been carved off their backs and thighs.

They're cooking and eating people, Adrian thought. *It's a buffet of human remains.*

Slumped over in another half-circle booth, he found a man with a head like a block of Swiss cheese —riddled with holes of varying sizes. Adrian put his hands over his mouth while fighting to suppress a retch.

Parts of the man's scalp sagged down to his face as well as the nape of his neck. His ears had been shot off his head and his nose had been shot *into* his skull. His left eye looked like it had sunk to his cheekbone while his other eye somehow rose to his brow. Gelatinized brains seeped out of the gunshot wounds. The bullets had crushed his skull and reorganized the broken bones.

His head reminded Adrian of the creatures in John Carpenter's *The Thing*. It was hard for him to believe someone could do something like that to a person. He decided to focus on the children. He was only looking for Lily after all.

At the makeshift table, Chef Cuckoo cut into Constance's exposed gluteus medius and gluteus maximus. A splash of blood leapt out of her ass as he severed her superior gluteal artery. The blood flew a meter into the air before landing on the tablecloth and clowns. More blood squirted out of the artery as Chef Cuckoo moved the blade. The second wave washed over the Moreno family, as if they were sitting in the splash zone of an attraction at a water park.

Constance fell unconscious due to the enormous pain and severe loss of blood. Her bleeding slowed to a trickle after ten seconds.

Frowning, George said, "Connie, no. Connie, honey, open your eyes. Don't sleep, sweetheart. Don't do this right now."

Chef Cuckoo cut an oval-shaped piece of muscle off Constance's ass. He put it on a white ceramic plate next to her body.

Twisted said, "Take the other cheek, too. I want my 'friends' to join me for this special meal."

As he skinned her other ass cheek, Chef Cuckoo looked at the Moreno family and asked, "How do you like your ass? Rare? Medium-rare?"

"I'm going to kill you!" George shouted as he lunged forward. Bouncing in his seat, he repeated that same sentence over and over: "I'm going to kill you! I'm going to kill you!"

His son and daughter-in-law could only shed tears and babble.

Adrian scrambled to another booth. He found two dead kids lying face down under the table. He flipped one of them over. He felt mixed feelings of sadness and relief. It was a boy who had been shot in the back of the head. He could see into his skull through the large exit wound on his forehead. He laid him on the floor gently.

His vision finally adjusting to the darkness, he could see the other dead child was a dark-haired girl. There was a gunshot wound at the back of her head, too. His heart dropped and his mouth dried up entirely. He subconsciously held his breath as he stared at the corpse. He didn't hear the crying from the Moreno family or the laughing from the clowns.

Only one thought—one name—remained in his head: *Lily*.

Moving slowly, as if he were afraid the corpse would disintegrate into dust if he moved any faster, he rolled the girl over. He squinted at her, confused. Her face was skinless and her eye sockets were hollowed out. He felt a cry building up in his throat. Then he looked down at her torso. He didn't recognize her clothing. The girl was taller than Lily, too.

He bit his bottom lip and let out a long, quiet exhale through his nose. The concoction of sadness and relief returned to his body.

She's not here, he thought.

Adrian crawled under the table and glanced over at the entrance of the buffet upon hearing the approaching footsteps. Chef Cuckoo finished slicing another piece of flesh from Constance's ass. He threw it on the plate—*splat!*—then looked over at the entrance. Twisted and George did too. In a state of shock, Victor and Pamela didn't notice the footsteps.

"Look who it is," Twisted said.

George said, "No, it's... This isn't right. You people are evil."

Bud stood in the entrance. George hadn't seen him commit any acts of torture, but it was clear to him that Bud was part of the killer clowns' crew. Bud's lack of revulsion around the gore gave it away. Throughout his career as a cop, George had dealt with children as both victims and suspects. He knew kids were capable of heinous crimes, but he never thought he'd see a child participate in a massacre like the one occurring in the Platinum Palace.

As the boy approached the makeshift table, Twisted asked, "What do you need, Bud?"

"You hungry?" Chef Cuckoo asked.

Bud nodded.

Twisted laughed and said, "We've got plenty of food around here. You wanna eat some ass, boy?"

"Don't," George said. "He's just a kid. How could you turn this boy into a monster like you? How could you do this to a child?"

Chef Cuckoo stroked Bud's forehead and said, "The boy's missing his tongue. Let's start slow. How does some ice cream sound?"

Bud smiled and nodded excitedly.

Twisted said, "Fine. The ice cream will be his appetizer. When you're done cooking that ass, I want you to make the boy some spaghetti with that special 'ground beef' I like so much."

"Your wish is my command," Chef Cuckoo replied.

He grabbed the plate of butchered ass, patted Bud's back, and said, "Follow me, child."

The clown chef led Bud to the dessert table. Bud grabbed a sugar cone, then eyed the ice cream dispenser. Meanwhile, Chef Cuckoo went into the kitchen and started grilling the pieces of muscle.

Twisted said, "I'm tired of eating alone, so you're going to join me."

"*Never*," George hissed.

"If you refuse, we'll–"

"I refuse, motherfucker."

"–start cooking the other woman."

"No! No, please!" Pamela blurted out, spittle flying from her mouth.

Victor said, "Don't hurt her. Don't you *dare* hurt her!"

Twisted said, "We'll eat every piece of her. We have a lot of hungry clowns in this place."

George shouted, "Keep your hands off my family!" Bud approached the table with a cone of vanilla soft serve. George looked at him and said, "Help us, kid. Get help. Call someone. Do something. Please, son, don't be like them. My wife is dying. Don't you understand what's going on?"

Bud looked at him, then at Constance, then at Twisted, and then at his ice cream cone. He shrugged and took the rubber tongue out of his mouth. Since his real tongue was nothing more than a nub, he slurped up the ice cream with his puckered lips.

"Jesus Christ, help us," George said.

I'm not going to find Lily like this, Adrian thought as he stared at the clowns. *Only they know where she is.*

He searched for a weapon. The silverware on the tables caught his attention. Spoons, forks, and table knives couldn't compete with Twisted's claws or Chef Cuckoo's sharp blades. Over the makeshift table near the center of the room, bright light poured out through the passthrough window behind the pizza bar.

Go to the kitchen and find a real weapon, he told himself.

While Twisted continued tormenting the Moreno family, Adrian crept his way around the buffet. He moved past the carving station, took a break near the salad bar, then stopped at a booth between the juice bar and the dessert table. Chef Cuckoo came out of the kitchen with two plates of cooked human meat. He brought the food to the long table, placing one plate in front of Twisted and the other in front of Victor.

Adrian snuck behind the pizza bar, then scrambled into the kitchen. It was a wide, bright room, counters and cabinets and large appliances hugging every wall. A long kitchen island took up the middle of the room. A beefy, rotten stench lingered. He went to the counters to his left and rummaged through a drawer.

Teary-eyed, Victor gazed at the meat in front of him. It was barely cooked, more red than brown. He was quiet now, shocked into a state of total disbelief. The same thought kept repeating in his mind: *That's my mom.*

"Help them eat it," Twisted said as he sawed into the piece of meat on his plate with his claws.

George said, "We won't." He looked at Victor and Pamela and said, "Don't you do it. That's your mother. She... She needs us to be strong for her. Is–Isn't that right, Connie?"

Connie was still unconscious.

With a fork and knife, Chef Cuckoo cut the meat in front of the Moreno family. He stabbed the severed piece with the fork and lifted it up to George's face.

"Stay away from me," George snarled. "I'll bite your fingers off if you get any closer."

Chef Cuckoo snickered and said, "He's feisty."

"Give it to the younger one," Twisted instructed, mouth full of Constance's cooked ass.

Chef Cuckoo held the fork over Victor's mouth. The young guy nearly went cross-eyed trying to look at the meat without moving his head. His mouth cracked open and a gurgling sound came out of his throat. George jumped in his seat in an attempt to pull Victor away. He could see his son was folding under the pressure already.

"Don't," George said. "Vic, please. The police are coming. Don't do it. Think about your mother."

Twisted swallowed the meat in his mouth, then

said, "Think about that pretty lady next to ya. You want her to end up like your mama?"

"Shut up! Don't talk to him! Talk to me, 'big shot.' You think you're tough? You think I haven't dealt with punks like you before? Show *me* how tough you really are. Come on! Untie me, you cowards!"

Twisted stood from his seat and said, "Guess we're doing this the 'hard' way. It's no biggie to me. In fact, I should be thanking you. I prefer young meat." Whining, Pamela mouthed a silent prayer as the horned clown approached her. Twisted swiped her black hair off her shoulder with his claws and said, "The young meat is juicier."

"I'll do it," Victor squeaked out.

"What?!" George shouted. "Don't you dare, Vic!"

"I–I'll do it. Just don't hurt her."

"It's your mother! It's your... your mother."

George's anger withered away as he caught a glimpse of Constance's motionless body. She didn't appear to be breathing anymore.

Twisted pressed one of his claws against Pamela's neck, causing her to gasp and wince. The blade nicked her. A drop of blood ran down to the indentation between her collarbones.

"Please don't do this," Pamela cried softly.

"Start eating, little man, or I'll start slicing," Twisted said.

Victor's teeth chattered and his lower lip quivered as he opened his mouth. Tears and mucus and saliva raced down his pale face. He felt like he was being forced to choose who he loved more—his mother or his wife. And the truth was, he had unconditional love for both of them. His family meant everything to him.

His quivering lips touched the meat first. It was still warm. Then he scraped it with his teeth, trying to take the smallest bite possible.

Twisted shouted, "Stop playing with me! Eat it all or I'll rip her throat open!"

Pamela squealed as the clown's claw sank deeper into her neck. The blade rested against her external jugular vein.

George said, "Victor. Victor, listen to me. I don't want to say this, but it's the truth. They're going to kill us anyway. They're toying with you. Look around you. Everyone's dead. You can buy time, but you can't... you just can't 'negotiate' with people like this. They've already made their choice. You don't have to–"

Victor bit the meat off the fork. A jet of blood surged out of it and hit the back of his throat, activating his gag reflex. The cooked flesh rolled to the tip of his tongue. He moved it over to his cheek to stop it from falling out. Mouth wide open, he chewed on it. More blood squirted out of it with each chomp.

George cringed as he listened to the moist chewing and the blood swishing in his son's mouth. His face drooped in disappointment.

Despite biting down hard and grinding it between his teeth, Victor couldn't tear through the meat. He felt like it had grown in his mouth. At the same time, he felt like his throat had shrunk. He wasn't thinking about his mother anymore. Now, he was afraid he was going to choke on the meat, like a child afraid of swallowing a pill.

Watching keenly, Chef Cuckoo said, "Go on. You can do it."

Victor chewed on it for a few more seconds, took some deep breaths through his nose, then threw his head back and swallowed. They could see the tough meat travel down his throat in the form of a bulky lump on his neck. Then he gasped for air and bawled. Blood and drool cascaded down his chin.

"Get him some water," George said. "Show some humanity."

Twisted pulled his claw away from Pamela's neck. He said, "Good job, good job. I'm not easy to impress, but you–"

Victor puked a maroon sludge—his mother's chewed ass. He retched, then burped, and then puked again. The second column of vomit was orange, watery and frothy.

"Poor thing couldn't keep it down," Chef Cuckoo said. "Want me to put it back in?"

Twisted chuckled, then said, "Leave it. He did good. And he can do better. He's a survivor. Besides, he's going to need some extra space in his belly for your 'special' spaghetti."

"Oh. Is it time for the main dish already?"

"It is," Twisted answered as he walked to Constance's body. He turned around to face the Moreno family and said, "Same rules as before: If you don't eat Mr. Cuckoo's 'special' spaghetti–"

"*Chef* Cuckoo," the cook corrected.

"–I'll start cutting your girl into little pieces," Twisted continued. "Then you'll have to eat *her*. And if you keep refusing, I'll keep chopping you up until there's only one of you left. And that last man standing, that unlucky fella, I'm going to cut him up and feed him to himself."

"Just kill us already," George said. "Get it over with."

"My neck hurts," Pamela whispered. "Am I dying? Am I dead?"

Twisted raised his left hand over his head, then swung his claws down at the back of Constance's head. One of the blades entered her skull with a cracking *thud*. It was jammed in her broken bone and sliced brain. The blade at the center of his hand partially scalped her from behind. Blood drenched her hair and flowed down to her cheeks and forehead.

"No!" George shouted. "Christ, she... she's already gone, you monster. Why won't you let her rest?"

Twisted wiggled his trapped claws while pulling on Constance's hair. A *squelching* sound came out of her skull as the blade mutilated her brain. Then he pushed the claws down with all of his might. There was a loud *cracking* noise, then the blade went straight through her head. The top half of her skull was severed at an angle. It rolled around like a plastic bowl falling in a sink.

George gasped. A part of him had wanted to believe that Constance could still be rescued—that the police could swoop in, kill the clowns, and revive his wife. With half of her head detached, he knew resuscitation was no longer possible. This terrible truth silenced him. He stared vacantly at his wife's corpse.

Chef Cuckoo dug his gloved hand into Constance's skull. He grabbed a fistful of her brain and tugged on it. It didn't budge. So, he used the carving knife to cut a fist-sized lump of her brain off.

"That should be enough for two plates," the cook said. "Or would you like three?"

"Two will do," Twisted responded. "One for Bud, one for them."

"And what'll you be having?"

"If our guests of honor don't cooperate, I'll have her breasts."

"As you wish. I'll be back in a jiffy."

Chef Cuckoo headed to the kitchen. Bud went to the dessert table and filled his cone with more vanilla ice cream. He had finished his treat during the show. Twisted ran his fingers across Constance's brain just to torment the survivors. The Moreno family sniveled, mourning the death of their matriarch.

In the kitchen, Chef Cuckoo put the lump of brain on a hot skillet. Vegetable oil crackled around it. Then blood from the organ started to ooze out and sizzle. Water simmered in a pasta pot next to the skillet. He took a wooden spoon out of a drawer and prodded the brain with it, trying to break it down into smaller pieces. While letting the crushed organ brown, he added a dash of salt to the water.

He hummed the melody of *Thunder and Blazes: Entry March of the Gladiators* as he headed to the pantry to get the pasta: ♪ *Hmm hmm hmm-mmm-mmm hmm hmm hmm-hmm hmm hmm.* He stopped humming as he reached the center of the aisle. An oven to his left caught his attention. It was a standard oven used for basic cooking and baking. It was on, heat emanating from it. He couldn't recall using it for any of his cooking, though.

He glanced over his shoulder at the double doors to his right beyond the kitchen island. The signs on the closed doors read: *EMPLOYEES ONLY.* He looked at the pass-through window and the doorless doorway to his left.

He asked, "Is there a little mouse in my kitchen?" There was no response. He asked, "Did you leave me a surprise in the oven? Perhaps some oven-roasted *ratatouille*? Hmm?"

He could only hear the Moreno family's faint cries. He laughed in amusement. He enjoyed playing games with his friends and victims. He opened the oven and peered inside. The red glow from the oven's bake element lit up his excited face. But his smile slowly folded into a frown. The oven was empty.

While the clown gazed into the oven, a cabinet door on the kitchen island inched open. Holding his breath, Adrian crawled out with a chef's knife in his right hand. He stood up, swayed for a short time, then steadied. Just as Chef Cuckoo was about to stand, Adrian swung the knife at the cook, like a boxer throwing a hook at his opponent.

The blade pierced the side of the clown's neck, coming to a stop in his esophagus and trachea. Blood spurted out of his severed jugular. It rained down on the ceramic tile flooring, flowed across the blade, and streamed down to his white jacket.

Chef Cuckoo noticed he couldn't draw a decent breath before he realized he was stabbed. He felt uncomfortable at first—a tickle in the throat—then he felt a pinch and his neck started to heat up. Within seconds, the uncomfortable warmth turned into a raging fire of anguish. His face cramped in a grimace of horror and pain.

He reached for the knife sticking out of his neck. He flinched as soon as he touched the handle. Blood joined the gurgling and crackling sounds coming out of his mouth. On wobbly legs, he turned around to face his attacker. Barely moving his head, he looked Adrian up and down, as if to say: '*Do I know you from somewhere?*'

Adrian was expecting an instantaneous death. At the very least, he was hoping the stabbing would have debilitated the killer cook. He didn't account for the adrenaline flooding Chef Cuckoo's body. Chef Cuckoo smiled and raised his finger at him. He opened his mouth as if he were about to speak, but more blood came spewing out.

Expecting the clown to attack him, Adrian glanced around for a weapon. His eyes stopped on the skillet on the stove. Plumes of smoke rose from the burnt brains. Before he could run to it, the clown staggered away from him. He teetered towards the stove, bouncing off the parallel counters to his left and right.

Chef Cuckoo knew he was already dead. His mortality didn't bother him, though. Death was part of the deal. He only wanted to warn Twisted and Bud so the clowns could continue killing in his name.

For a moment, Adrian was bewildered by the clown's behavior. His eyes followed the clown's course, then they grew as he spotted the pass-through window. Chef Cuckoo's plan finally *clicked* in his head.

He's getting backup, he thought.

He lurched towards him. The pain in his left foot was reignited with each step, but he fought through it. He grabbed the clown and pulled him back before he could reach the pass-through window.

Dizzy from the loss of blood and lack of oxygen, Chef Cuckoo spun and dropped to his knees. Adrian grabbed the knife's handle and pushed on it, driving the blade deeper into his throat. It split his esophagus and windpipe in two. With his head tilted back, the clown started hacking up a mist of blood.

Adrian gripped the back of the clown's head with his other hand. The pain returned to his sliced fingers, too. He thrust the clown's face at the stainless-steel countertop. Chef Cuckoo's rubber nose *honked*. The wound on his neck stretched as the blade's cutting edge moved towards his Adam's apple.

Adrian pulled the clown's head back, then thrust it at the edge of the countertop again. *Honk!* Blood spilled out of his crushed nostrils. *Honk!* Adrian smashed his face on the countertop a third time. Some of his upper incisor teeth were dislodged and fell from his mouth, bouncing on the floor around his knees like Mexican jumping beans on a hot pan.

In the buffet, Twisted glared at the pass-through window behind the pizza bar. He had heard the honking and could see the smoke from the burnt brains.

"Cuckoo!" he hollered. "What the hell are you doing in there?"

He heard a fourth *honk*, then two loud *clanks*. He rotated his neck left and right, watching the kitchen and checking on the Moreno family. The Morenos continued mourning Constance's violent death.

"Cuckoo!" Twisted yelled. Again, his partner didn't answer. He heard some more *clanking* sounds. Using the chef's real name, he yelled, "Preston! Quit playing and get your ass out here!"

In the kitchen, Adrian was now ramming Chef Cuckoo's forehead against the hard edge of the countertop. Deep gashes stretched over his eyebrows. The rubber nose had fallen off his face. His legs shook as his skull cracked and his brain hemorrhaged. His shoes squeaked on the tiles.

Adrian had lost control of himself. There were only two things on his mind: Self-preservation and his daughter.

After slamming the cook's face against the counter for the twelfth time, Adrian wrapped his arms around Chef Cuckoo's body from behind. He leaned back against the kitchen island to take the pressure off his injured foot, then he dragged the clown back to the oven. With his own adrenaline wearing off, he felt queasy as he caught a glimpse of Chef Cuckoo's face. It had been reduced to a bloody pulp.

I did that, I'm a murderer, he thought, disgusted with himself. *And I can't stop now. Lily needs me.*

He shoved the clown into the hot oven, then closed it. Although the chef was already at death's door, Adrian looked for something to use to block the oven. His search was interrupted by the sound of approaching footsteps in the buffet. He dashed towards the doorless doorway and took the skillet off the stove on his way there. The boiling oil popped explosively, drops landing on his arms and knees. Chef

Cuckoo's blood and the blood from his injured foot helped him glide across the tiles.

As he entered the kitchen, Twisted said, "Preston, what is–"

Adrian swung the skillet at him. He missed him by a meter, but the hot oil and cooked brains hit the clown's face.

Twisted stumbled back, slapped his hands over his face, and howled. In his head, the sound of his skin *sizzling* sounded louder than his screaming. The oil washed away some of his face paint. His skin reddened, then turned pink and puffy. His black eyes burned and his eyelids swelled up. He crashed into the wall behind him, his legs rocking below him. His discolored face began to peel, and blood dribbled out from his second-degree burns.

Adrian pounced on him and swung the skillet again. It hit the clown's hands, damaging his claws. One of the blades snapped in half. The base of the blade moved in his hand, cutting through the muscles between his metacarpal bones. Adrian hit his claws with the skillet again. Another blade broke in two and the other was bent forward. The bent claw curved into the clown's forehead. He didn't feel it, though. The pain from the cooking oil burns was much greater.

Adrian hit the side of his head with the skillet. Twisted's legs gave out and he dropped to the floor. Adrian mounted his chest with his knees against his shoulders to stop him from fighting back. He grabbed his ruff collar and raised the skillet overhead, ready to continue the beating.

"Ow!" he cried out as a drop of hot cooking oil hit his scalp.

From the corner of his eye, he saw another clown standing in the doorway behind him. He was about to hurl the heavy skillet at him, but he stopped mid-swing. It was Bud. He recognized him from earlier in the night. The boy's lips were smeared with ice cream. He held a half-eaten sugar cone in his hand. He seemed interested but unbothered.

"You," Adrian said. "You tricked me. You led them to my family. This is all your fault. You little... You deserve to... to..."

'*Die.*' That word was stuck in his throat. He wanted to insult him—blame him, *kill him*. But his desire for vengeance clashed with his own fatherhood. His love for his kids had spawned his appreciation for all children. He couldn't hurt a child. It wasn't in his blood. And Bud reminded him of his son, Andrew.

"Get out of here," Adrian said through his gritted teeth. "Don't let me see you again."

Bud stared at him for a few more seconds, then he stuffed the rest of the cone into his mouth and walked away. He grabbed another sugar cone at the dessert table and filled it with chocolate soft serve.

As the boy walked past the combined tables, George asked, "What's going on in there, son? Hey, talk to me. Help us. Hey!"

The boy strolled out of the buffet while eating his ice cream.

In the kitchen, Twisted moaned and squirmed under Adrian as he awoke. He noticed the ringing in his ear first, then his inability to move his arms. Then he felt the throbbing pain across his swollen face. His groaning grew into a monstrous roar.

Adrian grabbed his neck and said, "Stop crying, motherfucker. Where's my daughter? Where did you take her?" The clown kept moaning and writhing under him. Adrian shouted, "Where is she?! Answer me!"

He swung the skillet down at Twisted's face, but he stopped before he could make contact. Twisted was his last lead. Without him, he had no way of finding Lily without having to search the entire resort. A blow to the head could have caused a traumatic brain injury, and he couldn't afford to kill him.

Not yet.

Adrian opened the cabinet next to them. He couldn't see inside of it, so he grabbed the first thing that came to hand: *A stainless-steel cheese grater.*

He slapped Twisted and said, "If you don't talk to me, I'll start grating your face off. I swear I'll do it. Where's my daughter?"

Swinging his head in every direction, Twisted said, "I don't... know."

"My daughter! Where is she?!"

"Shit, man! I don't know! I can't even... see you. I

can't see shit. It burns. Burns like hell. What did you... Ah, fuck me, what did you do?"

Twisted's vision was blurry due to the hot cooking oil in his eyes. He knew who Adrian was talking about —he had only abducted one child with Binks after all —but he couldn't think straight, so he couldn't give him a straight answer.

Adrian said, "Room 30214. You psychopaths broke into our room and you... you..." He choked up while trying to talk about his wife and son. He said, "You and that boy and that woman. You broke into our room and attacked us. You took my daughter and I want her back. Where is she?"

"I... don't... know."

"Yeah? Fine. You want me to be like you, then I'll... I'll be like you."

Adrian pressed the cheese grater against Twisted's forehead, pushing his head back against the floor. *For Lily,* he told himself, struggling to overcome his hesitation. *Fight fire with fire, evil with evil.* He wasn't an expert in torture. He only knew what he saw in movies and read in books. Most parents would say they would kill for their children, but it was different when push came to shove. Most regular people weren't ready to torture or kill someone at a moment's notice.

"You're dead," Twisted said. He groaned again, then yelled, "Help! Get down here! Demon! Binks!"

Adrian closed his eyes and dragged the cheese grater downward. The right side of Twisted's forehead was scraped off. The skin over his horn was cut open, revealing his bloodied silicone implant. The tail of his eyebrow was detached from his skull. It dangled over his upper eyelid. Blood shot out of the thick, squiggly vein on his temple. It hit the floor and flooded his eye socket.

"Help!" Twisted screamed as he thrashed about.

Adrian pulled on the cheese grater, but he met some resistance. He opened his eyes and frowned. He had to fight the urge to vomit.

For Lily, he told himself again.

Strands of the clown's skin were tangled in the cheese grater's large holes. So, he jerked the cheese grater around until the skin ripped off with an unnerving *shredding* sound. The strands of skin hung from the holes like strings of cheese. Twisted's skull was visible in the glistening, skinless patch of flesh on his forehead.

Adrian turned the grater to its prickly side and pushed it up against the clown's exposed skull. That alone was enough to aggravate the wound and hurt the clown.

"Where'd you put my daughter?" Adrian asked. "Is she still alive? Tell me something."

"Help! He... Hell... Help!"

"Tell me!"

Adrian grated Twisted's forehead again. The spiky edges tore the rest of the flesh off the right side of his brow. It made a weak screeching sound as it scraped his skull. The grater detached more of his eyebrow and cut his cheek, too.

"Deadface!" Twisted shouted. "She–She's... Ahhh, shit! She's with Deadface!"

"Deadface?" Adrian repeated. He stopped mincing the clown's forehead, but he didn't remove the cheese grater. He asked, "Is that a person?"

"Yes! Yes, damn it! Get off me! Kill me or get off me, you cunt!"

"Where can I find him? Does he have Lily?"

Twisted responded with a cry of pain. Adrian shook the cheese grater, peeling more of the muscle tissue off his forehead.

"Where is she?!" he barked.

"The show... She's getting a–adopted at the show. Your girl... She–She's joining the circus."

"Where?"

Hysterical, Twisted sniggered and said, "The greatest show in the world..."

"*Where?!*"

Twisted lost consciousness again. To protect him from the pain, his body shut down completely. He was alive but unresponsive.

"Wake up," Adrian said. "Talk to me, damn it. Where's Deadface? Where's the 'show'?"

He moved the cheese grater, hoping to jolt him awake with some pain. He heard the clown grinding his teeth—nothing more. He looked over his shoulder at the doorless doorway. He heard the Moreno family calling out for help. He was afraid they were going to attract the other clowns. He assumed Bud was leading them to the buffet already anyway. He was out of time.

I can't get caught here, he thought.

He grabbed the edge of the neighboring countertop and pulled himself up to his feet. He hobbled over to the stove, took a carving knife off a counter—the same knife Chef Cuckoo had used to mutilate Constance's body—then returned to Twisted. He bent over, inhaled deeply, then stabbed Twisted's neck five times in rapid succession. He wasn't going to give him the chance to recover.

Knife in hand, he walked away from Twisted's body and headed to the double doors behind the kitchen island. On his way, he smelled the vile scent of Chef Cuckoo's roasting corpse in the oven. It was so sweet yet so rotten. He heard the Morenos calling out to him again, too. He didn't want to leave them behind, but he felt like he had no choice.

"I'm sorry," he said as he hurried to the double doors to escape the stench and the cries.

He found himself in the service corridors. He didn't know where he was going, but he knew he had to find Deadface in order to save his daughter. He leaned against a wall and kept moving forward, dragging his injured foot behind him.

13

THE COMMAND CENTER

"What the hell... was I thinking?" Lee muttered between his ragged breathing. "It's like a... damn maze... in here."

As if he were John McClane, he wiggled his way through a narrow ventilation shaft with a lighter in his hand. The lighter's flickering flame barely illuminated his path. The sheet metal rattled and groaned around him as his elbows and knees banged on it, the noise echoing through the shaft. It sounded like the entire ventilation system was about to collapse.

He was doused in sweat from head to toe. His polo shirt and pants made a sloshing sound, like a wet mop being dragged across a kitchen floor.

"Ah, shit!" he groaned.

A sharp edge in the shaft had torn through his sleeve and cut into his shoulder. He craned his neck to the right to try to catch a glimpse of the culprit, but he couldn't see much behind him. His blood darkened his shirt's blue sleeve. The gash stung, but he didn't feel the blood. It blended with his hot sweat.

Mocking himself, he scrunched his face up and said, "The machine room. The ventilation shaft. It'll be tight, but I can manage." He huffed, then said, "I've been crawling through here for, what? Thirty? Forty minutes? A damn hour? I'm going to... to suffocate. I'm going to die in here if I don't... don't..."

Stop talking, he told himself, realizing he was wasting his breath by speaking out loud.

He continued dragging himself through the shaft. A sharp edge nicked his forearm, then another cut a hole into his pants, exposing his sweaty boxer briefs. Upon reaching a fork in the road, his lighter went out. He reignited it, then evaluated his options. Straight ahead, only darkness waited for him. He saw light at the end of the shaft to his right.

An exit, he thought.

Lee was smart, although the heat and lack of oxygen left his mind foggy. He knew he was going to have to kick the vent's grille out in order to escape. So, he crawled forward, then feet first slid into the shaft to his right. Unable to look behind him, he wiggled his way to the exit. After a few minutes, the grille rattled as his boots touched it.

He moved down as far as possible, pushing on the grille with his feet. It creaked and groaned, but it didn't budge. He didn't want to kick it because he didn't want to alarm any clowns with the noise. He scooted down another inch, his pelvis rising from the sheet metal, then pushed on the grille again—but to no avail.

No choice, he thought.

He took the multi-tool out of his pocket and, with a flick of his thumb, he accessed its three-inch blade. It was his only defense. He started stomping away at the grille. The banging sounds reverberated through the ventilation system. He was sure everyone in the employee area could hear him. It took him a minute to kick the grille off the vent. It clattered as it hit the floor.

He was expecting someone to grab his ankles and drag him into a horde of killer clowns. He held the multi-tool tight in his damp hand, his heart racing and head swimming.

But he didn't hear or feel anyone behind him.

He crawled out of the vent. As he let himself drop slowly, his feet dangled and banged on the wall below the shaft. His head came out of the vent before he could touch the floor. Holding onto the edge, he took in a big gulp of air and looked behind him. He was in a locker room. He dropped to the floor and quickly turned around while swinging his knife at the air.

Whoosh!

Keyed up, his shoulders hitched up to his ears and his knuckles turned white as he tightened his grip on the multi-tool. Although his lungs were screaming for oxygen, he held his breath. The aisles around him were empty, he could see that clearly, but he was still expecting a killer clown to pounce on him.

They're waiting for me to move, he thought. *Maybe they're hiding in the lockers. Maybe they're going to jump out at me.*

A minute passed, quiet and uneventful.

He slunk forward and checked the door to his left. It was unlocked, so he opened it a crack and looked out into the hallway. Streaks of blood were smeared on the floor and walls. Bits of flesh clung to the bloodstains like flecks of peeling paint. Again, he didn't see or hear anyone. He opened the door a little more and stuck his head out to look down the other side of the hall.

More blood was smeared on the floors and walls. He saw a black high heel shoe. And next to the shoe, a thick bundle of long black hairs floated in a puddle of blood.

Lee closed the door and stepped away. He didn't see any dead bodies out there, but he knew the awful truth. He felt it in his gut.

It was a massacre, he thought.

He began to tear up thinking about his coworkers. He wasn't the best of friends with any of them, they had only known each other for a few weeks, but nevertheless, he cared about them. Some of them were half his age. He thought about their goals and dreams. Others had families of their own. He knew a coworker who had recently welcomed a newborn girl to her life.

The true frailty and unpredictability of life never

really hit him until that very moment. He took a minute to calm himself, wiping his face and taking big, noisy breaths.

"Gotta keep my head in the game," he said. "Gotta stay one step ahead of 'em."

He decided to secure the locker room first so he wouldn't be attacked from behind. Holding the knife out in front of him, he walked down the aisles and peered into every locker through the tiny vents on the doors. The lockers labeled 3215 and 2125 were left open. He didn't find anything suspicious inside them.

Lee opened the door and peeked into the hallway again. With no one in sight, he tiptoed out of the locker room and quietly shut the door behind him. Although the hallway was painted red with blood, he recognized the area. Crouching and staying close to the wall, he made his way to the command center.

Standing outside of the double doors, a sense of foreboding filled him. He didn't know what was waiting for him on the other side of those doors.

Clowns? Bloodshed? His boss? His boss dressed as a clown surrounded by bloodshed?

There was no other way into the room, though, so he had no choice. He raised the blade overhead and barged in.

Lee stopped, gasped, and dropped the multi-tool. He was struck with a sudden bout of lightheadedness. His abdomen tightened up, intestines twisting into a knot of disgust. A severed head was planted on each desk in the room. There were dozens of them. Despite being beheaded, his coworkers were still restrained and slumped up against each other on the floor under the wall of monitors. The clowns were gone.

He closed his eyes and wobbled over to the wall behind him as a throbbing pain attacked his temples. He slid down to a knee, then picked himself up. He was close to fainting from emotional shock.

"Thi–This can–can't be real," he said in a quivering voice.

This time, it took him three minutes to go from trembling violently to a gentle shudder. There was nothing he could do about the dead bodies or severed heads. He wasn't going to collect the heads in a basket like apples or spend an hour dragging the corpses out. He focused on his objective: *Get help*. Eyes open to a squint, he moved to the front of the room. He looked up at the monitors with his arm over his chin to block his view of the dead bodies lined up below him.

"It's a... bloodbath," he said as he watched the live surveillance footage.

In the food court, the camera at a fried chicken restaurant recorded a pudgy clown gouging a woman's eye out with a drumstick. As soon as he tore it out, he shoved the eyeball in his mouth and thrust the drumstick at her other eye. The cameras at the pool complex showed a group of clowns trying to break into the Royal Spa while some guests and employees cowered inside. A female clown was in the pool, attempting to use Laura's body as a floatie. Andrew's head was in the pool now, too. The clowns had used it earlier for a game of water polo.

He saw guests running in the hotel tower's hallways and emergency stairwells, searching for their loved ones as well as escape routes. Two clowns rummaged through the condominium tower's first floor. It was under construction, so they were gathering power tools to use on their victims. Some cameras caught footage of the area in front of the Platinum Palace. A limousine raced down the street. A clown with a rifle stood through the open sunroof and shot at the surrounding buildings while laughing. No patrol cars followed it. The police were overwhelmed by the siege.

"I have to do something," Lee said.

He turned to run to a computer but stopped and shut his eyes right away. His headache returned as he caught a glimpse of the severed heads on the desks. The extreme violence was jarring. He had seen gore in horror movies and read about atrocities occurring in war-torn countries, but it didn't prepare him for the real thing. Eyes narrowed, he moved to a desk in the front row.

"I'm sorry," he wheezed as he reached for the head on the desk while looking up at the ceiling.

He moaned as his palms touched the head's sopping wet hair. He heard a *squishy* noise come from its neck—what was left of it—as he lifted the head from the desk. He was on the verge of puking, fighting off the vomit with mouthfuls of saliva. He placed the head on the neighboring desk right next to the other severed head, then turned away, bent over with his hands on his knees, and dry-heaved.

As he stood up straight and wiped the drool off his lip, he noticed the bloodstains on his knees. His eyes flew open as he looked at his hands. There was blood on his palms. He realized the severed head's hair had been soaked in blood.

Where did it come from? Did they scalp it or something? Was it leaking from its ears? Did I touch its brain? Was it someone else's blood? The questions zapped through his mind.

Sobbing, he rubbed his palms on his shirt and pants. Despite wiping the blood off, his palms remained pink.

"Get a grip," he said in a panicky voice. "Get a damn grip, Lee!"

He concentrated on the computer in front of him. It was functioning properly. It appeared to be one of the computers the intruders had used to access the security system after infecting the rest of the network with the computer worm. He considered raising the security gates and activating the emergency alarms. Hands hovering over the keyboard, he looked back at the double doors.

They don't know I'm here, he thought. *If I turn on the alarms and open this place up, I'd be calling them all to me. I can't do that. Not now.*

As he turned to look back at the monitor, he caught another glimpse of the severed heads next to him. One belonged to a blonde woman and the other belonged to a bald man. He tucked his head, chin on his chest, and raised his hand over the side of his face to block his view of the gore. He was racked with survivor's guilt, face reddening with a flush of shame and disappointment.

"Do something, Lee," he whispered. "They're all dead, but you can still save... someone."

He sat on the rolling chair in front of the desk and looked up at the monitors on the wall in front of him. He wanted to save everyone, but he didn't know how to help a single person. His eyes were drawn to a monitor in the upper right corner of the wall. He saw Franco traveling through a service corridor with his handgun drawn. Two monitors to the right, surveillance footage showed Adrian limping through another service corridor.

Lee didn't recognize Adrian, but since he wasn't dressed as a clown and he appeared to be sneaking around like the other survivors, he trusted him. His eyes brightened with a newfound sense of determination.

"If I help Franco, we can help everyone else," he said.

He examined the desk. There was a bulky walkie-talkie next to one of the monitors. He turned it on and cycled through the different channels. He only heard static.

Reciting his plan aloud as if he were afraid he'd forget it if he didn't, Lee said, "Find the signal jammer. Turn it off. Contact the police. Then help Franco. I can do this."

14

THE GOOD GUYS

"SHOW ME YOUR HANDS!" FRANCO DEMANDED, AIMING his pistol at Adrian.

They stood about five meters away from each other in a service corridor. Sidestepping with his back to the wall, Adrian had just turned the corner. He held a carving knife in his right hand. Twisted's blood—fresh and hot—was still dripping from the 8-inch blade. His other hand wasn't visible from Franco's position. The pistol in the cop's hand swayed gently from side to side, like tall grass in the wind. He gripped it firmly in both hands, but due to the stinging bite on his bicep, he couldn't stop his right arm from trembling. He groaned as he reluctantly dropped his right arm to his side.

Keeping the pistol on Adrian, he said, "Drop the weapon and put your hands up slowly."

Adrian stared at him with blatant skepticism in his eyes. He had only stopped walking because he recognized Franco's police uniform. But upon closer examination, he started to notice the tears on his clothes as well as the blood on his arms and neck. Doubt infiltrated his mind and filled his head with frightening possibilities: *He could be one of them. He could have stolen that uniform. That could be someone else's blood. He could be a real cop and a real idiot. He could handcuff me and stop me from finding Lily.*

Likewise, Franco didn't trust Adrian. The guy had more blood on him than he did, and he was holding a large, bloodstained knife. His distant, unfriendly demeanor didn't help, either.

"Drop the damn knife," the cop snapped, growing frustrated.

Adrian said, "I can't. *I won't.*"

"Put it down. Please, man, I don't want to do this to you."

"My daughter needs me. She's in danger. Get out of my way."

"Your daughter?"

Franco took a quick glance over his shoulder to ensure no one was sneaking up on him. From the periphery of his vision, he saw Adrian take a step forward.

"Don't move," Franco said while taking two steps back.

"I don't have time for this, damn it!"

The cop said "Neither do I! But I can't have you walking around this place with a weapon. I know you've seen what's going on in here. That much is obvi-ous. Drop the knife and let me help you. C'mon, man, tell me... tell me about your daughter. I can find her." As Adrian lifted the knife to point it at himself, Franco put his finger on the trigger, took another step back, and ordered, "Don't move!"

Unafraid, Adrian said, "You think you can help me? You're the only cop I've seen in this place all night. And you're down here hiding!"

"Calm down. Don't make–"

"You coward!"

"–any sudden movements."

Adrian walked to the center of the corridor and turned his body to face the cop, revealing his empty left hand. Franco took another step back, preparing to redeploy if the distraught man charged at him.

"You don't know what's going on here," Adrian said with a sneer. "You have no fucking clue. You lost all control, didn't you? No, no. You never had it in the first place, did you, you useless prick?! Where were you when we needed you? Huh? Where the hell were you when those clowns broke into our room and... and threw my family out the window?! My wife! My boy! Andrew, my–my... my son! Where were you?!"

His bellow echoed through the corridors. He paced from wall to wall while weeping and rambling about his family. Franco looked behind him. *He's going to lead them to us,* he thought. *I've gotta get this guy...* Mid-thought, his face turned to stone. He looked back at

Adrian with big, surprised eyes, as if he had run into a long-lost relative. He remembered the dead boy and woman in the pool area. He realized Adrian's family were some of the first victims of the attack.

He lowered his pistol and said, "I'm sorry."

"*Sorry?!*" Adrian yelled as he stopped pacing. "I don't need your apologies. I need you to get out of my damn way."

"My name is Franco Ferraro. I'm with the LVMPD. I can help you. What's your daughter's name?"

"If you're not going to shoot me or arrest me, get out of my way. I'm running out of time here."

"Exactly. So, let me help you. I've cleared several parts of this hotel already. I can tell you if I've seen her and we can cross off where we've been. We can find her faster if we work together. And I promise you, we *will* find her."

Although some reluctance lingered in the back of his mind, Adrian felt the sincerity in the cop's voice. His shoulders slackened and his breathing slowed.

He said, "My name is Adrian Castillo. My daughter's name is Lily. She's nine years old. She has, uh... curly black hair. Her eyes are like caramel. When they were younger, her older brother A–Andrew used to tease her about it. He used to pretend like he was going to eat her eyes because he loved caramel popcorn." He massaged his neck as he felt his throat shrinking. He grunted, then said, "She was wearing a–a long-sleeved shirt. It was white with little, uh... little dog heads on it. Like polka dots but black dog heads instead. Silhouettes, you know? Shit, I don't know how to explain it."

"I get the picture. I searched about half of the hotel tower with a security guard. I've gone through the casino and the arcade, too. Where was she last seen?"

"We were staying on the 30th floor. Two clowns took her from my room. A man and a woman. I killed..."

He stopped during his confession of murder, but it wasn't because he felt guilty or ashamed. He replayed Twisted's final words in his head: '*The greatest show in the world.*'

"One of the clowns who took her. A mean son of a bitch with fake horns on his head. I killed him," he said matter-of-factly.

Franco's face stiffened. He knew Adrian had hurt someone—the bloody blade told tales of violence—but he wasn't expecting him to be so cold about it. He understood him, though. Parents were instinctively protective. And when they failed to protect their children, they sought justice—and justice was often confused with vengeance.

Adrian continued, "That clown said something about 'the greatest show in the world.' He said Lily was being 'adopted' by someone who calls himself Deadface."

"Deadface?" Franco repeated. "I've heard that name before."

"Franco," a quiet voice said from his radio. "Franco, do you copy?"

Franco took the radio out of a pocket on his utility belt. He held it up to his mouth and said, "Lee? Lee, is that you?"

Lee was sitting at the desk in the command center, hunched forward in his seat with his head down to avoid the carnage around him. He was watching Franco and Adrian through the surveillance footage playing on one of the monitors in front of him. He was watching another surveillance feed in another window on the screen. It showed clowns gathering in the buffet. Bud had led them to Chef Cuckoo and Twisted. Demon's death in the arcade had gone unnoticed.

"Yeah, it's Lee," he said. "I'm in the command center. I've got eyes on you through the surveillance system."

Franco and Lee both looked up at the ceiling. They found the security camera on the wall behind Adrian, right in the middle of a three-way junction in the corridors.

Lee said, "I got the signal jammers down. I've tried contacting the police, but I think these guys have other jammers around the Strip. I'm not getting anyone. I raised a silent alarm, but... Listen, if I turn on any of the other alarms or raise the gates, they'll know I'm here. Now, I *can* do that and slip out through the back, that's not a problem for me, but you're going to need my help if you're going to take these clowns on. I can see everything from here and I know this hotel like the back of my hand. The choice is yours. What do you want me to do?"

A little smile played around Franco's lips, but he fought it off. He didn't want to look like he wasn't taking Adrian's suffering seriously. He was impressed by Lee's sudden selflessness. A part of him was expecting him to abandon them after they had split ways.

Speaking at the walkie-talkie, he asked, "Are you injured?"

Lee said, "I'm fine, but..." He sighed shakily, then on the brink of bawling, he said, "They killed every-one, Franco. They slaughtered everyone, then they abandoned this place like it was nothing. I... I can't even tell how many dead bodies are in here."

Franco's face stiffened again. His eyes met Adrian's. Adrian was disturbed by the news, too, but he was jumpy instead of rigid. He was ready to move.

The cop said, "If you can stay, we'd really appre-ciate your help, Lee."

Lee sniffled while wiping his nose and eyes. Like a car engine struggling to start, he made a grinding noise with his throat to clear his voice.

He pressed the push-to-talk button on his radio and said, "I can stay. What's the plan? Where do you need to go?"

"Lee, I want to kill two birds with one stone," Franco said. Gazing into Adrian's eyes, he said, "I guess it's more like save one bird and kill the other. I'm looking for a nine-year-old girl and a clown who goes by Deadface."

"That'll be a whole lot easier if you gave me an idea of where to start looking."

"I think this 'Deadface' person is their leader. This hotel is supposed to be some sort of palace, right? You guys got a throne anywhere around here?"

Cycling through the surveillance feeds with a click of the computer mouse, Lee said, "I can check the penthouse suites, but I'd only be able to see the hallways on that floor."

"The show," Adrian said, taking a few steps towards the cop while dragging his injured foot behind him. "Tell him about the show."

Franco asked, "How about a theater, Lee? You got one of those around here?"

"Give me a sec," Lee replied.

He combed through the surveillance feeds. He saw the clowns patrolling the casino floor and stalking the hotel tower's halls. He stopped on footage showing a large group of survivors holed up in the eSports lounge. He didn't spot any small children or clowns, though. In a gift shop, he found a young couple hiding behind some shelves. He stopped again as he stumbled upon a surveillance camera recording the Grand Platinum Theater.

The massive 3,000-seat venue was used to host

musical performances, magic shows, extravagant circus acts, plays, and stand-up comedy shows.

Now, hundreds of guests were strapped to the chairs in the auditorium. The killer clowns patrolled the aisles between the banks of seats, armed with rifles and blades and power tools. More victims were being dragged into the auditorium—some kicking and screaming, some limp and unconscious. There were some kids in the audience as well.

Speaking to his walkie-talkie, Lee said, "There's a gathering at the Grand Platinum Theater. I'm seeing hundreds of hostages tied to the seats and dozens of clowns patrolling the area." He switched to a different angle and said, "See some kids, too, but hard to make any of them out."

"Lily has to be there," Adrian said.

Franco asked, "Lee, can you get us to the theater?"

Lee said, "Might be a little tricky. I don't know which doors are open and which are barricaded, but, um... Yeah. Yeah, I can get you to that theater. Give me a sec to plan your course. Just a second, fellas, just a second..."

Franco pointed the walkie-talkie at Adrian and said, "If we're going to do this, we're doing it my way. We can't go in guns blazing. I don't have enough ammunition to shoot through all of these clowns. Stealth is our best option." He looked down at Adrian's foot. There was a trail of bloody footprints behind him. He asked, "Can you walk on that?"

"Even if they cut my feet off, I wouldn't stop looking for my daughter," Adrian said.

"That's not what I asked you."

"Don't worry about me. Whatever happens to me, you only concern yourself with saving Lily. Curly hair. Caramel eyes. White shirt with dog heads on it."

Before Franco could respond, they heard the echo of a door hitting a wall. It came from behind Adrian.

Over Franco's radio, Lee shouted, "Move! They're in the corridors!"

"Tell us where to go," Franco said, speaking rapidly.

"Straight forward, then take a right! Hurry!"

Franco ran forward. Adrian turned around and followed him. He gasped and slipped after taking five steps. On his way to the floor, a geyser of blood spurted out from under the soaked cloth around his lacerated foot. He landed on his elbows. His injured foot couldn't handle the pressure anymore. He felt another twinge of pain from his cracked rib, too.

"Shit," Franco said as he holstered his pistol and sprinted back to him. He grabbed Adrian's right arm, threw it over his shoulder, and heaved him off the floor. He said, "You gotta jump on your good foot and jump fast. Work with me."

He walked forward at a brisk pace with Adrian hopping on his right foot next to him. The problem was, with each hop, a twinge of pain rocketed from his cracked rib and more blood dripped from the gash on his sole. They took a right and hurried down the hall.

They heard footsteps, disgruntled voices, and doors slamming behind them.

From the radio in the cop's utility belt, Lee said, "Take the next left."

As they moved into the next corridor, Adrian lost his balance and crashed into the wall to his left. Yet, sandwiched between the cop and the wall, he kept hopping forward. Franco looked back as the noise behind him grew louder. His free hand went straight to his holster as he spotted Adrian's trail of blood.

"Come out and play, little man," a man said in a singsongy voice.

Another man yelled. "He's in here somewhere! I can smell him!"

The guy started snorting like a pig.

"Hurry to the end of the hall and take another left," Lee said through the radio. "They're getting close."

Adrian was afraid he was slowing Franco down. He knew that if they were captured together, their chances of saving Lily would be reduced significantly. He would have to leave it up to luck, and average Joes like him rarely won big in Vegas. At heart, he was also hoping the clowns would spare him and take him to the theater so he could be closer to his daughter. He pushed Franco away.

"Go," he said. "Find Lily and get her out of this hellhole."

"Stop wasting time," Franco responded, pulling on Adrian's arm.

Adrian jerked away from his grip and said, "I can't keep up with you. It's impossible. And they'll catch us both if you don't move now."

"I'm not–"

"Stealth is *your* best option. You said it yourself. So, you go through the back and I'll try to go through the front. I'll distract them for you. Just remember what I said: Whatever happens, *save Lily.*"

The burden on Franco's shoulders got heavier. He had promised Monica Ramsey—the woman in the stairwell—that he would bring her husband back to her. He told the Reid family at the arcade that he was going to go back for them. And now he was being asked to go into the clowns' circus—into their stronghold—and rescue a girl.

"Damn it, guys, they're coming up on you," Lee said. "Move it."

There was no time to argue. Unable to make another verbal promise, Franco gave Adrian a nod. As he turned to leave, Adrian grabbed his shoulder and pulled him back.

He whispered, "Tell her I love her."

Again, the cop could only nod. He sprinted down the hall and took the first left. He started running with long strides to try to soften his footsteps. Lee led him towards the theater.

Adrian leaned back against the wall and pointed his knife down the hall behind him. The clowns were right around the corner. He felt something tickle his cheeks. He thought it was blood from his severed ear or sweat, but it was tears. He hadn't cried since he discovered his family's fate earlier in the night. He started to chuckle. And he didn't know why he was crying or laughing.

It's over, isn't it? he thought.

Hound the Clown stepped into the hallway. He was holding a machete in his hand. A pudgy clown—wearing a tattered tank top, baggy yellow pants, and big red shoes—stopped behind him. Armed with a heavy fire axe, the guy was out of breath.

Hound said, "Looky here, looky here. We found our killer." Tilting his head to the side without taking his eyes off Adrian, he yelled, "We've got him!"

"Yeah, you caught me," Adrian said, still laughing.

As they approached, Hound banged his machete on the wall and the other clown dragged his axe across the floor. The blade made a screeching noise.

"You think you're tough? Think you're nasty?" Hound asked. "You don't know what nasty is, but we can show you."

Between gasps, the pudgy clown said, "You killed... Cuckoo. I'll starve... without him."

Adrian said, "I killed that bastard with the fake horns, too. I'll kill all of you."

Hound cackled, then said, "Our dicks are already so far up your ass but you don't even know it yet. You're *fucked*. There's more of us around than you think. And some of us don't wear makeup."

"You clowns really love talking, don't you?"

"Talking and killing."

I'm sorry, Lily, Adrian said in his mind, as if he could communicate telepathically with his daughter. *I love you, darling.*

"This the guy?" Binks asked as she approached the clowns from behind.

She had another severed nipple in her mouth. This one belonged to Constance Moreno, the butchered woman left behind in the buffet. She stopped between the clowns, suckling on her fleshy pacifier.

Running her eyes over Adrian, she said, "You did a great job on our guys back there. Cuckoo was a little overdone, but some of us like it crispy. We could use a guy like you. You ever thought about joining the circus?"

"You," Adrian said in awe.

"*Moi?* Have we met before, bub?"

"You... You killed... killed..."

Binks took the nipple out of her mouth, then with exaggerated, faux curiosity, she asked, "Who? Who'd I kill? JFK? Harambe? Your family?"

"*My family,*" Adrian said, his head shaking with rage.

"Yeah, I thought so," Binks said with a shrug. "I wasn't born when JFK got capped and I never worked at no zoo. I don't know why people keep accusing me of killing people and animals I never been around. You kill dozens of people and suddenly everyone thinks you're responsible for all the world's atrocities. It's unfair, don't ya think? I only kill–"

"Shut up! You fucking clowns talk too damn much! Where'd you take my daughter?!"

Binks looked at Hound, then at the other clown, and then at Adrian. The clowns stayed quiet.

"Where's my daughter?!" Adrian cried.

Binks groaned in frustration and rolled her eyes, then said, "You just told me to shut up. How am I supposed to know when I can talk and when I can't?"

"You psycho bitch, where is she? Where's Deadface?"

Binks' eyes shone with excitement and a mischievous smile bloomed on her face. Unperturbed by Adrian's knife, she moved closer to him. Adrian stood his ground.

"You know Deadface?" Binks asked.

"I know you took my daughter to him. And if he touched a hair on her head, I'm going to kill him and the rest of you."

"I remember you now. Your daughter's that cute girl who loves clowns, right? Yeah, she's fine. Eating cotton candy and gummy bears while she waits for the show. And you're right. She is with Deadface. And you wanna know something else? I think he'd *love* to have you in the audience for the big show. It's the greatest show in the world, y'know?"

"Take me to him."

"Sure. I can get you a ticket to the show. You'll be my guest of honor. Just drop the knife."

Adrian didn't trust her. Her eerie smile made his skin crawl. Yet, he knew he didn't have much of a choice anyway. He wasn't strong enough to overpower three clowns at once. *If they want to kill me, they're going to do it either way,* he thought. He had already bought Franco enough time to get away, too. The blade *clanged* as it hit the floor.

Binks' smile broadened. The other clowns chuckled behind her. Adrian blew out a long exhale of defeat through his nose, fully expecting them to pounce on him.

"Get him a wheelchair and roll him up to the theater. And do it quick. I don't want him to miss the show. Deadface has a lot to say," Binks said. As she strutted away, she hollered, "And don't touch a hair on his head, either, or I'll kill the both of ya!"

15

THE GREATEST SHOW IN THE WORLD

"Where is she?" Adrian asked, agitated. "Where's my daughter, you pricks?!"

A duffel bag slung over his shoulder, the pudgy clown pushed him down an aisle on a wheelchair. Hound walked in front of them. An audience of battered, traumatized survivors surrounded them. They were taped to their seats with some empty chairs between them. The duct tape over their mouths muffled their cries, but all together, they sang a deafening song of misery. It was even louder than the racket in the casino.

The wheelchair came to a stop five rows away from the stage. The big clown hooked his arms under Adrian's armpits from behind while Hound grabbed his legs.

"Lily!" Adrian shouted.

The clowns put him in the neighboring aisle seat.

The pudgy clown pulled two rolls of duct tape out of his bag. He gave one to Hound and they started to tape Adrian to the seat. The big clown taped his torso to the backrest while Hound taped his arms to the armrests.

While looking around frantically and wrestling with the clowns, Adrian shouted, "Lily! Honey! I'm here! Daddy's here! Lily! Lily, say something, baby! Lily!"

Lily was nowhere in sight. He couldn't hear her, either. He stopped screaming, realizing his voice was being drowned out by the ceaseless sobbing around him. He had to conserve his energy. He scanned the room again in search of his daughter. Towards the middle of the row in front of him, he found the surviving Moreno family members—George, Victor, and Pamela—restrained to some seats.

"I'm sorry!" he cried out to them.

They couldn't hear him over all of the weeping in the room. Victor and Pamela hung their heads in shame and whined while George continued to fight with his restraints and, despite the tape over his mouth, vow to avenge his slain wife.

Adrian saw more clowns patrolling the aisles, too. He also noticed the bulky cameras set up throughout the auditorium. Some were aimed at the audience while most appeared to be recording the stage.

"What are you people doing?" he asked.

The clowns ignored him. Hound began taping his

thighs to the seat. Binks walked up to the group from the stage. She sat on the wheelchair, reversed, then turned to face Adrian. She kicked her legs up on his left arm, using his limb as a footrest. The weight of her legs aggravated his mutilated fingertips. He glared at her.

She said, "You're right on time, big guy. Gotta admit, I was a little worried you might miss the opening act. But here you are! And I got you one of the best seats in the house. Close enough to see all the blood and guts but not quite in the splash zone. Wait. Did you wanna get wet during the show? I think we still got time to move ya."

"Where's Lily? You said you were taking me to my daughter," Adrian said.

"Now don't go putting words in my pretty little mouth. I said I was bringing you to the show to see Deadface. And he'll be on soon. He's got a lot to say. I think you'll really dig it. Your precious little girl... Lily, right? She'll come out *later*. Like, at the *end* of the show. She's part of the grand finale."

"Let her go. You want a show? Put me on stage and I'll give you one. Do whatever you want to me but let her go."

"C'mon, you act like we want to hurt her. Well, we don't. She's precious to us, too, y'know? She's going to be part of our family now. I haven't decided if I'm going to be her big sister or her mother, though. What do you think? Am I ready to be a mom? Deadface thinks so. I'd probably do a better job protecting her than your old lady did, huh?"

"Fuck you!"

Startled, Binks jumped in her seat. The wheelchair rolled back and her legs fell from his arm.

She giggled, then said, "Jeez. I guess you don't think I'm ready to be a mother. A simple 'no' would have been enough."

Adrian said, "You sick, evil bitch."

Binks beckoned to Hound and said, "Hand me the tape."

"My family did nothing to you. Laura was an amazing mother."

Binks ripped a strip of tape off the roll.

Adrian continued, "Andrew was a good boy. An innocent boy! We didn't deserve this! You deserve to–"

Binks slapped the tape over his mouth. She shushed him, then leaned close to his ear and whispered, "Enjoy the show."

She walked down to the stage while the other clowns went back up the aisle. Left behind and restrained to his chair, Adrian stirred about in his seat and called out to Lily repeatedly. But his smothered voice now sounded like everyone else's. The lights dimmed in the auditorium. The clowns stopped patrolling and turned their attention to the stage, which remained illuminated by the spotlights.

Adrian stopped screaming and stared at the stage. Some of the other audience members did the same.

The auditorium was thick with dread. Someone was coming.

———

A man entered stage right. He was a tall guy in oversized white pants with red suspenders and big red shoes. He was shirtless, revealing his muscular arms and chest as well as his firm paunch. There were spatters of red spots on his pants. Pale red smears stained his arms, chest, and belly. His black hair was slicked back and tinted red with blood.

Although he had never met or seen him before, Adrian identified him before the man reached the microphone stand at center stage. His 'face' gave his identity away—because it wasn't *his* face. Tied to his head with durable string, he wore another man's skinned face over his own like a mask. The mask of human flesh was painted like the other clowns' faces, but the corners were bloodied.

Deadface, Adrian thought, horrified.

The other survivors saw a monster. Some were scared silent while others cried louder. The clowns in the auditorium looked up at him in total admiration and awe. He was more than their leader.

He was their god.

On stage, speaking into the microphone in front of him, the man said, "I'll start with an apology."

His voice was deep and hoarse. It sounded natural,

though, unlike some of the other clowns' exaggerated voices. He was dressed for the part, but he wasn't playing a character.

He continued, "Forgive me if I bore you or if I happen to go off on a tangent. I'm no public speaker, no politician, no preacher, no snake oil salesman. Hell, I worked as a carny most my life. My government name was Lance Spencer. I was born on September 11, 1969, in Uvalde, Texas, out of wedlock to a Bernard Spencer—a handyman—and a Dolores Becker—a schoolteacher. Spent years living with pa, years living with ma, then back with pa, then back with ma. I've lived everywhere and nowhere. I've spent my life moving in and out of prison, physically and mentally. Spent more time looking for my purpose than I have *living for* my purpose. More time asking questions than finding the answers. But I'm a different man now. Lance Spencer died when he found his purpose. And he gave his body, his flesh, to me."

He went quiet and studied his audience. The mask over his face hid his facial expression. He looked calm and confident, though. He grabbed the microphone with both hands and pivoted to face a camera to his left.

He said, "You may address me as... *Deadface*. I am the ringmaster of this grand circus. I am the mastermind of this great cleansing. I am the *catalyst of chaos*. To the authorities around the globe watching me now: *Hello there*. You are welcome to visit us at any moment.

The doors may be locked, but that's never stopped you before. A word of warning, though. If you interrupt my show, the *thousands* of guests at the Platinum Palace—this wonderful landmark of greed—will be killed. Explosives will detonate across the first floor and every exit will be set ablaze. As soon as you pull the trigger... we'll pull ours."

With the revelation, the audience's weeping reached a horrifying crescendo. The sounds of their seats squeaking and rattling increased along with their panic, too. Wide-eyed, Adrian glanced around and searched for anything that remotely resembled an explosive. *He's bluffing,* he told himself. *He has to be.* Chuckling, Deadface turned to face forward. He waited for them to settle down. Their cries started to fade after a minute, then weakened to whimpers after two.

Running his eyes over the bank of seats directly in front of him, Deadface said, "Welcome to our carnival of chaos. We're operating in the smallest towns and biggest cities around the world. Los Angeles. New York City. Toronto, Canada. Tokyo, Japan. Paris, France. Bangkok, Thailand. Even the remote city of Supai, Arizona, and your little neighbors outside of Vegas at Motel Ace." His gaze fell on Adrian. He said, "We are broadcasting live to millions of people, but *you* have front row seats to the show. You get to watch it in person while the rest of the world watches their back-yards burn from the safety of their homes. Just like people have been doing for decades."

From afar, Adrian could see the malevolence in his eyes. The man meant business. He had been looking for Deadface for hours, but now he only wanted to find his daughter and get her out of the hotel before it was too late.

Deadface said, "You, the audience, probably want a reason. 'Why are they doing this? Why is this happening to me?' And you, the authorities, probably want a list of demands. I'll tell you, first and foremost, we're here to give you the greatest show in the world. We are entertainers after all. Secondly, we're here to spark a revolution. We were outcasted by society because of our deformities—mental and physical. But we were never different. We had the same three guarantees in life that every human has had since the beginning of mankind: Birth, suffering, and death. I want to inspire people like us to join the circus and free themselves from the shackles *you* put us in."

He paused to let his message sink in. While glancing around, Adrian thrust his arms up to try to break free from his restraints. The tape around his forearms tore little by little. Most of the audience was sobbing or trying to break free from their restraints. A couple of elderly hostages had fainted. The clowns listened attentively. One of the cameramen on the stage was wiping tears off his face.

Deadface continued, "If we fail tonight, ten, twenty, thirty, forty, *fifty years* from now, 'experts' will still be searching for explanations. '*How* did clowns take over the world for a night? *Why* did they do it?' And if we succeed... the world will be a better place. Earth will be a utopia. Either way, our message will be delivered to the masses. And with that, let's start the show."

"Try the doors in front of you," Lee said.

Franco had lowered the volume on his radio, so Lee's voice sounded softer than a whisper. He could hardly hear him, but he didn't have much of a choice. He was still navigating the service corridors and he didn't want any lurking clowns to hear the noise from his radio. Pistol in hand, he dashed to the doors.

He stopped, took a second to inhale deeply, then opened the door and aimed his handgun through the crack. He saw the side of a slot machine, then he spotted a clown gambling at an adjacent game. The cop closed the door just as the clown turned his head to look in his direction.

Franco redeployed, jogging backwards while pointing his pistol at the double doors. His finger rested on the trigger. He was expecting the clown to rush into the service corridor. He stood there for almost a full minute. His heartbeat slowed as he finally released the air in his lungs. He walked backwards, then sidestepped into a hallway to his right while pulling the radio out of his belt.

"Damn it, Lee, are you trying to get me killed?" he hissed, holding the walkie-talkie to his mouth.

Lee said, "I'm sorry, I'm sorry. I don't have a map with me. I'm trying to piece this place together through the surveillance feeds while leading you through it. It's not an easy task."

"You work here, don't you?"

"I'm a security guard on the floor, not a surveillance officer. I know this place's layout, but every service corridor looks the same from here. And hey, it's not like I've been working here for years. We just opened 10 days ago for crying out loud."

"All right, all right. I get it. Let's just focus on getting me to the theater *alive*. Before sending me through any other doors, try checking if the coast is clear first."

"That's what I've been trying to do," Lee said.

He was still seated at the desk in the command center. There were two monitors in front of him with two windows open on each. On the monitor to his left, he watched the surveillance feeds recording the service corridors. He kept his eye on the cop and watched the hallways around him. On the monitor to his right, he viewed the different areas in the hotel. He had a hard time mapping the place out. Acute stress addled his brain and warped his memories, throwing most of his training out the window.

"Do you have eyes on Adrian?" Franco asked.

"Last time I saw him, he was being taken away on a wheelchair by a couple of clowns. I lost track of them in the casino, but it looked like they were heading to the theater," Lee said. He switched to a live feed of the Grand Platinum Theater and said, "I can't see him in there, but it looks like something's about to go down."

"Then we have to speed it up. Where am I going?"

"Um... Go... Go straight down that hall you're in. Take a left and you'll see another set of double doors. Those should open up to another service corridor."

Franco put the radio in his utility belt, jogged down the hall, and murmured, "I hope you're right..."

16

———————

ACT ONE

TANDING STAGE LEFT WITH THE MICROPHONE IN HIS hand, Deadface said, "Please welcome our first performers to the stage. They've traveled a great distance to be here tonight, abandoning their studies for the vices of Sin City. And assisting them tonight, we have Spike the Clown! Give 'em a round of applause! And if you can't clap, snap your fingers!"

The audience continued to scream and weep. Adrian was surprised to hear some people snapping their fingers in the rows behind him, though. He assumed they were complying with the clown's demands in hopes of receiving preferential treatment. Although they were frightened by the threats of bombs and fires, they preferred their seats in the auditorium to the stage.

Blake Lowery entered stage right, hands bound behind his back with zip ties. Behind him, Spike rolled two metal tables on wheels onto the stage. The tables were latched onto each other. There was a large rectangular box on each table. The boxes were pushed together, and Peter Rodger lay inside of them. His head, hands, and feet stuck out through holes on the sides of the box. The young men were sniffling.

There was a handsaw with a massive 27-inch blade on top of the boxes. It had a handle on each end and blood was smeared on its teeth.

Adrian recognized the hostages on the stage. They were the college students staying in the room next to his. They had helped him recover after the violent attack on his family. He saw them as good people—*good kids*. He noticed one of them was missing, though. *Benny,* he thought. *They called him Benny.* He searched for him in the audience, but he could barely see through the darkness.

Deadface pointed at Blake and said, "This gentleman's name is Blake Lowery. The young man in the box is Peter Rodger. Am I correct?"

The clown held the microphone out in front of him. Blake couldn't speak with the excess saliva in his mouth. He nodded and mumbled something at him.

"Plee–Please don't do this," Peter whined. Although the microphone was far from his face, the entire audience could hear his shaky voice. He said, "I–I want to see my family again. I want my–my mom. I wanna see my dad."

Adrian's face tightened and his heart broke as he

listened to Peter's cries. He clenched his fists and rocked back and forth in his seat, loosening the tape around his arms and chest. He didn't know much about Blake or Peter, but his paternal instincts told him to protect them like they were his own kids.

Deadface brought the microphone back to his mouth and said, "We caught these men while they were attempting to flee from our special carnival."

The clowns in the auditorium erupted in a chorus of booing and jeering. The leader gave them a few seconds to get it out of their systems.

"Settle down now, settle down. I need you to listen to the rest of their story before we proceed," Deadface said. The clowns became quiet while the hostages continued crying. Deadface said, "They had another friend with them. His name was Benjamin Penn. These three gentlemen—Blake, Peter, and Benjamin—snuck into a bar and tried to break a window overlooking a garden. I'm sure this is obvious to most of ya, but... *they failed.*"

The clowns in the auditorium cheered. Only one question surfaced in Adrian's head: *What is wrong with these people?*

As the cheering tapered off, Deadface said, "One of ours, Milo the Clown, caught them in the bar. Outnumbered, he shot at them. That was when Benjamin used himself as a human shield to protect his friends. To protect *them*." He jabbed his index finger at the college students on the stage. While the clowns booed them, Deadface said, "I commend Benjamin for his bravery and sacrifice. *Benjamin* was one of the good ones. *Benjamin* deserved to be part of our utopia. *Benjamin* deserves a round of applause!"

And, as if they were a studio audience following an APPLAUSE sign, the clowns cheered on cue.

Deadface said, "At the very least, Benjamin was rewarded for his selfless act with a quick, painless death. I was told he died from a bullet to the head. I doubt he felt a thing. Now, what happened afterward is why we're here now. Peter ran. He ran into the kitchen and tried to knock another door down. He had *no* problem abandoning his friends. Blake, on the other hand, he stayed with Benjamin. This poor young man even tried to resuscitate him. Picture that for me, will ya? His friend has a hole on his forehead and a bigger one in the back of his head, brains are splattered all over the place, and Blake still sits there and tries to revive him. Isn't that an incredible act of humanity?"

The clowns clapped and nodded in agreement.

Right on cue.

Deadface continued, "Let me tell you something. Society is black and white. It's *this...* or *that*. You're either the rich or the poor, the exploiter or the worker, the punisher or the punished, the fucker or the fucked. Kill or be killed. Eat or be eaten. Live or die. There is no in between in today's world. Even when you may feel like you're in the middle, it's only because the people above you *want* you to feel that way, because they *let* you feel that way." He looked at Blake and said, "Mr. Blake Lowery, today—in front of an audience of *millions*—you will entertain the masses with a special 'trick.' You will saw your friend in half, then you'll put him back together."

Peter yelled, "Blake, don't! I'm sorry, man! I–I wasn't trying to leave you!"

"Don't make me do this," Blake said.

Teardrops, goops of mucus, strings of slobber, and beads of sweat sprayed from his face as he shook his head in a frenzy. He knew there was no illusion involved. He was being instructed to kill his friend in front of the world. He took a step towards Deadface, but Spike grabbed his arm and pulled him back. The clown used a pair of pliers to cut Blake's zip ties. He let him go, stepped back, then pulled a six-round revolver out of his waistband and pointed it at Blake.

Blake clasped his hands in front of his chest, turned to face Spike, and said, "I'm begging you, bro. I'll do anything."

Spike said, "You're pathetic. Your family's probably watching you, you know? You want them to see you grovel, you pansy?"

He hocked a loogie at his face. Blake wiped it off his nose and cheek as he teetered back to center stage. He clasped his hands in front of his chest again and got down to his knees in front of Deadface. He looked up at him, then dropped his head. The rotting mask made him queasy.

He said, "Don't make me do this, s–s–sir. Anything but this. Please, sir, I'm begging you. I'm... I'm fucking begging you!"

Deadface clicked his tongue, then said, "Blake, now's your chance to prove yourself. Show the world that you're a survivor. If you don't, we'll take Peter out of the box and put *you* in. Then *he* will have the opportunity to perform for us. And you know him well. He was ready to abandon you earlier. I think he'd be willing to kill you to survive."

"Blake!" Peter shouted. "I'm sorry! I–I didn't want to run but–but–but I was scared! I was scared, dude! I'd never hurt you, man, I swear. Please... Please don't kill me."

Deadface said, "And if—by some miracle—Peter refuses to perform as well, Spike will *happily* step in and saw the both of you in half." He patted Blake's head and asked, "Are you the punisher or the punished? Will you kill or be killed? The choice is yours, son, but before you decide, think about your family. Think about your future. Think about Benjamin's sacrifice. Now go. Make us proud."

He helped Blake up to his feet and directed him towards Peter. Blake shambled to center stage. He stood in front of the boxes with his back to the auditorium. The edge of one of the boxes blocked his view of Peter's head, but he could still see his flailing hand and hear his cries. He thought about his own family. He wondered if they would be proud of him if he decided to spare Peter or if he would only be hurting them by sacrificing himself.

He thought about Peter's family, too, and the rest of the audience around the globe. *The whole world will see me do it,* he thought. His legs wobbled as he saw the blood on his shirt. It was Benjamin's. He remembered the hollow look in his dead friend's eyes after the shooting in the bar. The afterimage of Benjamin's ghostly face was burned onto his retinas. It magnified his fear of death.

From his seat, Adrian screamed. He was trying to say: *'Don't do it, kid! They're just going to end up killing you anyway!'* It was incomprehensible due to the tape on his mouth.

Palm pressed against his brow, Blake said, "I don't wanna die, man."

"Blake, no! Don't!" Peter shouted.

"I'm sorry, Peter."

"Don't! I don't wanna–"

Blake picked up the handsaw and moaned. The clowns burst into applause, masking Peter's voice. There was a twinkle of pride in Deadface's eyes. The handsaw vibrated as it hit the boxes. Overwhelmed by the noise and the adrenaline pumping through him, Blake couldn't steady his hands. He kept missing the slit between the boxes. When it finally slid into the narrow gap, the saw dropped down onto Peter's body. It was situated on his abdomen just below his belly button.

"I'm sorry," Blake repeated.

He thrust the handsaw forward. It made a whistling sound as it moved through the slit. The blade's teeth ripped through Peter's shirt and nicked his lower abdomen. The rattling in the boxes grew louder as Peter writhed. Leaning back to leverage his weight, Blake tugged on the handsaw. The sound of Peter's skin tearing open was louder than the sound of his shirt ripping. Fresh blood dripped from the blade's teeth.

In a total panic, Peter was now reduced to saying the same thing over and over while occasionally yelping between words: "No! No! No! *Ow!* No! No! No! *Ahh!*"

Blake pushed the handsaw forward. The blade's teeth ate away at a thin layer of fat. His clammy hands slipped off the handle as he yanked the handsaw back. He fell on his ass. The clowns in the auditorium cackled like it was the funniest thing they had ever seen, holding their bellies and slapping their knees.

"Don't stop," Deadface said. "Black and white. No in between. You either get the job done or the job'll do you in."

"Stop it!" Peter cried. "Blake, stop, man! It fucking hurts!"

Blake ran back to the boxes. He crashed into the handsaw's handle, propelling it forward. The blade cut into Peter's abdominal muscles next. Peter ground his teeth and held his breath. His hands and feet flapped about, fingers and toes curling and unfurling again and again. He felt his abdominal muscles *separating* and heard the fibers *crackling* as Blake pulled on the handsaw once more. His head whirling, he unleashed the air in his lungs as a bellow of agony.

Blake closed his eyes, bent over, and placed his hand over his chest. His friend's pain made his heart ache.

He said, "Don't... Stop, Peter... Peter, stop. I–I can't do this if... if... you..."

He dry-heaved before he could finish his sentence. He grabbed onto the handsaw to stop himself from falling, unintentionally driving the blade's teeth deeper into Peter's abdomen.

"I don't want to see you fail, Blake," Deadface said. "I can see you're a fighter. You deserve better than this. So, we'll help you out. Spike, give him a hand."

The clown with the spiky metal mohawk shoved his revolver into his waistband, then said, "Sure thing, boss." The clown moved to the other side of the boxes and grabbed the other handle. He gestured to Blake and said, "Grab onto this thing. If I have to do this on my own, I'm going to headbutt your balls. If you even got any, you pussy..."

Blake grabbed the handle with a feeble grip. He lurched forward as Spike pulled on the handsaw. His forehead hit the box with a *clang*. The clowns in the auditorium guffawed. Blake's suffering was nothing more than an act of slapstick comedy to them—and they *loved* themselves some slapstick comedy.

After recomposing himself, Blake leaned back and pulled on the handle. As if he were playing a game of tug-of-war, Spike gave the handsaw another mighty tug. The blade's teeth cut through Peter's intestines. The muscular tubes were split into several pieces—some straight like rigatoni, others curved like macaroni.

The blood on the metal table began to run off its edges in red waterfalls. It pooled under the table.

Peter's bellows transformed into harsh gurgling noises. His head went limp and his eyes rolled. Blood foamed out of his mouth. The red, frothy goops crawled over his face and went into his hair. The blade came to a stop on his spinal cord and thoracolumbar fascia—the diamond-shaped connective tissue at his lower back.

Looking over the box, Spike said, "Work with me so we can get this over with. Push when I pull and pull when I push. Fast and strong cuts. Got it?"

Blake just wanted it to be over. Whimpering, he rammed the handsaw's handle with his chest. They went back and forth for two minutes. They knew they had fully bisected Peter's body after hearing his spine *snap* and the saw's teeth *screech* against the metal table. Once finished, they couldn't tell if the gurgling noises were coming from Peter's mouth or abdomen.

Blake stepped back and said, "I'm sorry... Peter... Peter, I'm sorry."

Peter was unresponsive.

Deadface asked, "Is it finished?" Spike gave him a nod. The leader said, "Then it's time for the next step. Show the audience that this isn't a mere illusion. Show them why this is the greatest show in the world!"

While the clowns cheered in the auditorium, Spike unlatched the tables and then rolled them away from each other. Small coils of severed intestines *splatted* on the floor. Still attached to him, longer intestines rolled out and dangled from his upper body.

A cameraman entered center stage. He got a closeup of Blake's thousand-yard stare, then he recorded Peter's bisected body. The event was now being live streamed to tens of millions of people around the world.

"Now, Blake, finish the trick. Put him back together," Deadface instructed.

Blake said, "He..." His voice immediately cracked. He tried to swallow, but his mouth was completely dry. He said, "He's already... dead. I... I killed him."

"Blake, finish the trick or Spike will finish you. You know the rules. We didn't make them, but we will enforce them."

Spike walked up to Blake. He drew the revolver from his waistband and pressed the muzzle against the side of the college student's head.

He said, "You want your family to watch you die

after what you just did? All you have to do is push those tables together. It ain't hard."

"I killed him," Blake repeated in a guilt-induced trance.

"And we'll kill you if you don't finish the job. We'll blow your brains out, then we'll skull-fuck you *live*. And I'm talking a *real* skull-fucking. You want your 'mommy' and 'daddy' to see that? You want your friends to see that? You want the *world* to see it? Hmm?"

Humiliation didn't cross Blake's mind. He didn't care if his body was defiled after death. *It's not like I would feel it or even know about it,* he rationalized. He only cared about his survival and his family.

Wanting to avoid Peter's head, he approached the table with his friend's lower half on top of it. He pushed the table towards the other one. Peter's hanging intestines made a *squishy* noise as the tables collided. Despite the guts caught between them, Blake managed to latch the tables together.

"Attaboy," Deadface said. "Now, let's see if you're a magician... or a killer. Drumroll, please."

The clowns in the auditorium—some seated, most standing—stomped their feet. Spike returned the revolver to his waistband and opened the boxes. He grappled with Peter's torso, pushing his hands and head through the holes. The makeshift drumroll stopped. The clowns waited with bated breath.

Spike lifted Peter's upper body out of the box and said, "Didn't work."

The clowns groaned and booed.

Deadface said, "As expected. But we did see something special tonight. We saw the birth of a star. Blake Lowery fought to survive... and he won. I think we'd all like to see just how far he can go." He looked into the dark auditorium and asked, "What do you think?"

"Hell yeah!" a woman yelled.

Surprised, Adrian flinched upon hearing the feminine voice in the aisle next to him. He stopped rocking in his seat and peeked over his shoulder.

"Encore! Encore! Encore!" Binks shouted with her hands cupped around her mouth.

The other clowns chanted with her. "Encore! Encore!"

Binks stopped next to Adrian's seat. She looked at him and said, "I really know how to fire up a crowd, huh?"

Deadface said, "You heard them. Spike, escort Blake back to the Green Room and prepare him for the next act. And get the cleaning crew out here." As Spike dragged Blake off the stage, Deadface turned to face the audience and said, "Let's give him another round of applause."

The clowns clapped and laughed and whistled. Instead of cheering, the hostages wailed. Clowns dressed in janitor uniforms walked onto the stage and started mopping up Peter's blood and guts.

Binks crouched next to Adrian and asked, "How're you liking the show so far?" Unable to speak through his gag, Adrian glared at her. The clown giggled, then said, "Oh yeah. Kinda hard to talk with that tape over your mouth, ain't it? If you play nice, I might take it off for ya. The show's just getting started, and it's only going to get better and better."

Adrian tried to say 'Lily,' but it sounded more like he was humming in agreement.

'Mm-hmm.'

"Your daughter, right?" Binks said. "Nah, I ain't a mind reader if that's what you're thinking, but people like you are *so* predictable. Don't worry about her. Seriously, I know I kid around a lot, but that girl is going to be A-OK. She reminds me of... well, *me*. Y'know, I joined the circus when I was a kid, too. Deadface and his friends found me at a park. Lots of his friends are dead now, though. I don't really remember what I was doing there. Matter of fact, don't really remember anything about my life before the circus. I think your daughter will be the same. She'll forget all about you in no time, bub."

The tape around Adrian's right forearm was loose enough for him to slip free. An urge to attack Binks came over him. His fingers curled into a fist. He leaned closer to her while she stared up at the stage. Then he thought about Franco and the plan. He leaned back in his seat and inspected the theater. There were no signs of his daughter or the cop. Surrounded by the killer clowns, he only had one chance to distract them. He figured he was better off waiting until he felt like Franco was ready to save Lily.

He opened his hand and breathed out through his nose.

17

THE GREEN ROOM

"Those double doors will either take you to the pool complex or another hallway," Lee said.

Slinking down a service corridor, Franco held the radio up to his ear like a cell phone. Since he was closing in on the theater, he lowered the volume to an almost imperceptible level. Mixed with some static, the security guard's voice sounded like a fly buzzing around his ear. His right hand rested on his holster. He couldn't hold his pistol at all times due to the deep bite on his bicep, but he was ready to draw at a moment's notice.

Lee continued, "Either way, you're clear. There shouldn't be any clowns around there."

Franco nudged the door open. A cool breeze struck his hot face and the sound of distant gunfire reached his ears. He caught a glimpse of some artificial grass and a whiff of chlorine. He closed the door.

He moved the walkie-talkie to his mouth and whispered, "I've got pools."

Then he returned the device to his ear and headed back down the corridor. He stopped at a three-way junction. He came from the hall to his left, so he continued moving forward. Except for the pitter-patter of his quick footsteps, the employee area was quiet. He felt like he was the last survivor on the loose.

Lee said, "Take the next right. That set of doors will take you to the other service corridors on the west side of the building. Should be clear, but I'll start scouting ahead."

Franco took the next right and found another set of double doors. He drew his pistol and pushed one of the doors open slowly with his shoulder. The hallway was clear. There were more doors to his left and right.

He held the walkie-talkie over his mouth and asked, "Got eyes on me?"

"I do. Go straight down that hallway and go left. I'll check the rooms around you for any clowns."

"Got it."

Franco holstered his weapon again to ease the pressure on his wounded bicep, but he kept his hand on the pistol's grip. Holding the radio up to his ear, he snuck down the hallway. He moved past a door to his left, then a door to his right, and then stopped at the second door to his left. Dried blood was smeared on the door handle and frame as well as the wall and floor. The blood-trail led down the hall in front of him, ending just a few meters away in a massive red stain.

His curiosity got the best of him. He put the radio in his utility belt, took his pistol out, and opened the door. His eyes widened a little, then his face twisted into a grimace of fear and anger. He was looking into the kitchen of one of the resort's restaurants—a place called *The Palace Steakhouse*. The ceramic tile flooring looked like it had been mopped with blood. Blood-stains decorated the walls, too.

Like a flower in a vase, a severed arm stuck out of a stock pot on the stove. A small, limp hand hung over its rim. An elderly man lay on the long kitchen island in the middle of the room. Like a frog in a high school science class, his body was split open vertically down the middle. Small candles were strewn across his exposed organs. Melted wax hardened on his intestines. The clowns had turned him into a human cake for nothing more than their sick pleasure.

Franco shut the door and holstered his weapon. He brought the walkie-talkie back up to his ear.

"You hearing me?" Lee asked. "Don't go through there. Some clowns are standing next to the slot machines outside of that restaurant. Go straight down the hall and take a left. It's clear."

The cop followed his instructions. He walked next to the trail of blood. His eyes stayed fixed on the enormous human-sized stain at the end even after he passed it. *How many people have died under my watch?*

he asked himself. *A dozen? Dozens? A hundred?* He had already lost count of how many dead guests and clowns he had encountered. The body count rose with each area he visited. He took a left at the end of the hall.

Lee said, "You're close. It's either the next right or the one after that. You should see some stairs going down. If not, you'll be in the lobby of the condominium tower. The condominium tower is still under construction. They're just finishing up the first floor's renovations. I don't have a good view of the area, so be careful."

Franco opened the door cautiously. He stared into the condominium tower's poorly lit lobby. The floor was covered in plastic and littered with hammers, screwdrivers, sledgehammers, and cordless drills. Step stools and ladders stood near the walls. Black and yellow cords snaked across the floor and wires curled out of holes on the walls and ceiling. The air was fresh in there. He heard a growling engine on the street, too.

"The way out," he said.

He closed the door, then stepped back and took a mental note of the entrance. As per Lee's instructions, he went around the corner and took the next right. The next set of double doors opened up to a short passageway leading to a shorter flight of stairs. He went down the stairs and ended up in another hallway. And at the end of that passageway, there was another staircase leading up. He was moving *under* the condominium tower's entrance. He went up the stairs and found another set of double doors.

Lee said, "You're close to the theater. Go through those doors, then go left. You'll be 'backstage' in no time. But I can't guide you anymore. The clowns have obstructed most of the cameras in that area, so I'm blind over here. You're going to be on your own. I'll still be around, but I'm going to try to open some of the gates that these clowns aren't guarding. I'm going to try to get as many people as possible out of here."

Speaking into the walkie-talkie, Franco said, "Thank you, Lee. You did great tonight. You get out of here safely, too, okay? Take care of yourself."

"I will, brother, I will. Good luck in there."

The cop put the radio in his utility belt. He held his pistol in his good hand and opened one of the doors. The service corridor, which resembled all the others, was empty. He crossed the threshold and quietly closed the door behind him, then he went left.

Bloody footprints and shoe prints zigzagged across the floor. The stench of gasoline stained the air. A booming voice penetrated the thick walls, reaching the corridor as a loud hum. Smaller voices—some ecstatic, others pained—came from down the hall along with *thuds* and *clunks* and *clacks*.

Both hands on his pistol, Franco followed the deep

voice. In a half-crouch, he stayed close to the wall to his left. He could feel it vibrating as the voice got louder. He stopped between two parallel doors. There was a green emergency exit sign above each door. The voice sounded clearer to his left, so he assumed it was coming from beyond that door.

He touched the door's push bar and whispered, "No alarm. Please, no alarm."

After releasing a shuddery breath, he pushed the door open. A ray of light from the hallway sliced into the darkness in the auditorium. He couldn't make anyone out in the audience, though. He spotted a clown standing in an aisle between two banks of seats, but he had his back to the emergency exit. All of the clowns' eyes were glued to the stage where Deadface was delivering another speech.

"Life is a game of chance," Deadface was saying. "For ninety-nine percent of the population, it's more unfair than fair, more unjust than just, more painful than it is painless. You could do everything right, be the best person you could be, then get killed by a drunk driver while crossing the street or overdose on medicine your doctor shouldn't have prescribed to you or be blown to bits in an explosion caused by a gas leak. We're always playing a game of chance... and most people don't even know it."

Simply by listening to his voice and observing his mannerisms, Franco could tell he was watching the clowns' leader in action. He considered assassinating him there and then. Even with an injured arm, he was confident in his marksmanship. But he knew Dead-face's death wouldn't stop the clowns. It would only enrage them. He also noticed some gasoline tanks in the aisles. *They're going to burn the place down,* he thought. *I'm running out of time.*

He shut the door before any of the clowns could see him. Staying low, he moved down the hall with quick, quiet lunges. He took a left, then a right. Just a few steps into the hallway, he heard a door open in front of him. He stopped walking, but he couldn't stop himself from sliding on the floor. His shoes *squeaked* as his feet weaved under him. He heard some voices and footsteps in front of him. He leaned back and fell on his ass, then he scrambled behind a janitor's cart to his left.

"Boss says it's time, so it's time," a man with a raspy voice said.

Another guy said, "I'm just saying. Ain't he going to let us have any fun? I wanna get on stage, too, y'know? I wanna be a star, man."

Franco peeked out from behind the large yellow garbage bag attached to the cart. He saw two clowns standing in front of a door halfway down the hall.

"Watch your mouth, boy. This ain't about getting famous," the man with the raspy voice said.

"I know what it's all about. When it all goes down, I just don't want to be forgotten. That's all I'm–"

The other man knocked on the door and hollered,

"Deadface wants two more! That Blake kid and someone else! Said the other one's your choice!" He looked at the other clown and said, "Shut your trap. If the boss hears you talking like that, he'll make an example out of ya. Then you'll be wishing you were forgotten."

The door opened.

"No!" A man's scream echoed through the employee area.

Jordan Carter lurched into the hallway. The clowns grabbed him before he could slip away. They grappled with him, punching him and slamming him against the walls. Franco recognized the hostage. *The bellhop from the pool area*, he thought. *Goddammit, I should have let him leave when he had the chance. He's here because of me.* Then Blake was pushed into the hallway. Spike followed him out of the room.

"And don't kill her!" Spike yelled into the room before shutting the door.

"Puh–Puh–Please don't make me do this," Blake sobbed. "I–I don't want to do this anymore. I wanna go home. Le–Let me go home. Please..."

Spike pointed at the bellhop with his thumb and said, "Be careful with that one. He's feisty."

"Let me go!" Jordan shouted.

The clown with the raspy voice said, "Don't worry. We'll tie him up when we get out there. He..." He dodged an elbow from Jordan, then punched the bellhop in the back of the head. He said, "He's only going to need one hand anyway."

Spike said, "Then let's get this show on the road."

Franco watched as the clowns dragged the hostages down the curved hall next to the door. He heard another door open again.

Deadface's voice entered the service corridors: "Ladies and gentlemen, it's almost time. In a moment, you'll witness Act 2 of the greatest show in the world!"

The door slammed, cutting the clowns' applause short. The cop waited for fifteen seconds, then moved to the middle of the corridor. He pointed his pistol at the door to his right. The sign next to it read:

GREEN ROOM
 E01

He followed the curved hall until he stumbled upon a door to his left. He could hear some applause beyond it. His gut told him the clowns and hostages had just gone through it. He pointed his handgun at it, expecting one of the clowns to return. The sign next to the door read:

BACKSTAGE
 Left Wing

Realizing the coast was clear, Franco returned to the green room and planted his ear on the door. He heard some suppressed cries and retching in the room. *More hostages,* he thought. He grabbed the door handle in his free hand and squatted down next to it. He put his finger on the trigger and steadied his arm. He knew he was going to have to shoot to kill if he was caught by one of the clowns. He turned the handle—it was unlocked—then eased the door open a little and looked through the gap.

Five makeup tables with vanity mirrors lined the wall to the right. There was a locker in the corner beyond the tables. A three-seat sofa and an end table hugged the parallel wall. At the center of the room, there was a recliner and a coffee table. The recliner faced a large flat-screen television mounted on the wall. A water cooler, a minifridge, and a snack table stood next to the door.

A man with grizzled hair was tied to the recliner. Blood trickled from a gash on his temple as well as his busted nose. The liquid appeared black on the duct tape over his mouth. Furious, he screamed and jumped in his seat. Two women and one man were seated on the floor under the television, their hands bound behind their backs with zip ties. Their mouths were taped, too.

Bud sat on the sofa and played *The Binding of Isaac* on a PlayStation Vita. A little girl in clown makeup sat next to him. She stared at the sledgehammer on the coffee table in front of her. There was blood on its fiberglass handle.

A man sat on a makeup table. He was dressed like a magician with clown makeup caked on his face. He wore a top hat, a white button-up shirt, and black pants. His black coat was draped over a chair in front of the neighboring makeup table. His fly was open, exposing his erect penis and saggy scrotum. He called himself Chinko the Magic Clown.

A young raven-haired woman knelt in front of him, hands bound behind her back. Forced to fellate him, she was gagging and retching. There were traces of vomit on her chin and blouse. Chinko gripped the sides of her head firmly so she wouldn't break free. He forced his entire dick into her mouth, the glans hitting her uvula with each thrust.

"I told you I could make my cock disappear," he said, snickering.

Franco watched in shock from the narrow gap between the door and the jamb. He was conflicted by his oath to serve and protect and his promise to Adrian. *Find Lily,* he told himself. *Save the girl, make things right, then save everyone else.* He was about to close the door when he saw the young clowns on the couch again.

The boy's indifference unsettled him. He could see

that he was part of the crew of killer clowns. The girl was different, though. She was shaking and sniveling. Tears smeared the white makeup on her face. And she wasn't dressed in a costume like the other clowns. The pattern on her long-sleeved shirt caught the cop's attention.

'*Like polka dots but black dog heads instead.*' Adrian's voice replayed in Franco's mind. He was looking at Lily Castillo.

Tensing up, Franco closed the door and took a moment to collect himself. He glanced over at the backstage entrance, fearing an attack from behind. He holstered his pistol, then touched the canister of pepper spray in his utility belt. *No,* he thought, shaking his head. *The room's too small. It would hit everyone.* He drew his stun gun instead.

He cracked the door open again. Bud was engrossed in the video game while Chinko was captivated by the oral rape.

Franco pulled the door open. As soon as the gap was wide enough, he slipped into the room and shut the door behind him. The clowns didn't hear him over the music from the game and the woman's gagging. Chinko didn't notice his intrusion until the stun gun's laser sight—a thin, bright red beam—flashed in his vision.

"What the fuck?" he muttered.

Franco was hesitant to tase him with his dick in the victim's mouth.

He said, "Get away from–"

"Cop!" Chinko yelled as he lunged at him.

"Freeze!"

Chinko tackled Franco, slamming him against the door and pushing the stun gun down. Franco heard the victim's clear cries over the other hostages' stifled whimpers. Knowing she was out of the way, he aimed the stun gun up and squeezed the trigger. Chinko groaned ghoulishly while his teeth clattered. As stiff as his penis, he leaned against the cop.

"Show me... your hands," Franco said as he pushed him off him.

Limbs shaking, Chinko crashed into a makeup table. Franco's eyes bulged from his sockets. The stun gun's probes had struck the clown's scrotum and pierced his right testicle. The veins on Chinko's erect dick appeared to be slithering while his loose scrotum rippled like a wave. Some blood dribbled across his ball sac.

Chinko fainted. He fell on top of the makeup tables, then plummeted to the floor, bringing a chair down with him. His hat flew off his head and landed in front of the hostages under the TV. He was wearing a curly red wig underneath it.

As Franco holstered his stun gun and reached for his handcuffs, Bud ran up to him and stabbed his thigh with a pocketknife. Without looking, the cop swung his elbow at him. He hit the kid's left temple. The rubber tongue flew out of the boy's mouth. He bumped into the minifridge, causing the door to pop open, then he dropped to the floor.

Franco's heart picked up the pace as he gaped at the rubber tongue. He thought it was real, thought he had caused him to bite his tongue off. He didn't intend on hitting the kid *that* hard. He got down on his knees next to him and took a flashlight out of his utility belt. Aiming the beam of light into his mouth, he saw the boy's trimmed tongue but no blood.

"He's getting up!" the female victim shrieked. "Look out!"

Gasping and whining, Chinko grabbed the edge of a makeup table and pulled himself up to his feet. Pain blazing across his genitals, he instinctively grabbed onto the wires hanging from the probes and tugged on them. He heard something *crunch* in his scrotum. He screamed and spun around. His eyes met with Franco's, who was now standing over Bud's unconscious body.

Chinko went for the sledgehammer on the coffee table. Franco rammed him with his shoulder before he could reach the weapon. The clown was hurled back against a vanity mirror. The hostages screamed as it shattered. Large pieces of broken glass rained down on the makeup table, breaking into smaller shards.

Dazed and breathless, Chinko grabbed the first shard that came to hand and swung it at the cop. He sliced the left side of Franco's face, right above his jawline. Some of his stubble was shaved off, bloody hair spiraling through the air. With the second swing, he cut the right side of the cop's lower neck.

Franco ducked to dodge Chinko's third swing. He grabbed a shard from the table and, in a desperate act of self-defense, he swung it at the clown's semi-erect penis. The glass cut through half of Chinko's shaft before crumbling in Franco's hand. The clown ejaculated blood through the side of his dick in quick spurts.

Chinko dropped his shard, slapped his hands over his crotch, and screamed. He felt his dick spinning between his legs like a chandelier during an earthquake. He hit the floor face first and howled in pain.

Franco looked at the door, then at the boy. Bud squirmed and moaned as he regained consciousness. An expression of dismay dawned on Franco's face as he brought his gaze back to Chinko. He realized that, although he was already neutralized, he couldn't stop the clown from screaming or fighting back without killing him. And if he didn't stop him from screaming or fighting, he'd be putting himself and the hostages at risk.

He reached for his handgun, then yanked his hand back. *No*, he told himself. *Too loud.* He was taught to shoot to kill, he was capable of killing people, but he wasn't equipped or trained to *execute* a person. He thought about pistol-whipping him to death, but he didn't want to damage his weapon. The sledgehammer caught his attention. He didn't want to scar Lily by bursting the clown's skull, though.

He took a pair of handcuffs out of his utility belt. He grabbed the back of Chinko's shirt and dragged him to the locker in the corner of the room, then knelt on his upper back. He poked the clown's neck with the handcuff's single strand. It made him gag, but it didn't penetrate his skin.

Harder, Franco said to himself. *I need to end this now. I need to hit him harder!*

He clenched the single strand between his middle and ring fingers. He grasped Chinko's forehead, pulled his head up, then punched his neck, driving the curved steel into his throat. The clown's screaming was replaced with coughs and grunts.

Franco continued sawing through his neck, moving the single strand in and out of him. He felt the clown vibrating under him. He saw the drops of bloody spittle spurting out through his clenched teeth. It blended with the blood puddling under them. It took him three minutes to reach the center of his neck. The deep gash looked like a black hole. Chinko's body kept trembling, but he had already stopped breathing.

"Behind you!" the female victim yelled.

Before he could react, Franco felt a blade plunge into his shoulder. He turned around and cocked his fist back, ready to stab his attacker with the handcuffs, but he stopped as he saw Bud standing behind him. Despite the threat, he couldn't muster the nerve to hurt the child, let alone kill him. That level of cruelty wasn't in his blood.

He grabbed the boy, slammed him against the wall face first, then handcuffed him. From the handcuffs, Chinko's blood ran down Bud's hands. Then the cop threw him into the locker and sealed him inside. Bud screamed and banged on the door.

Exhausted, Franco took the knife out of his shoulder and staggered over to a makeup table. On a vanity mirror, he checked on his injuries. The cut on his throat worried him the most. *Flesh wounds*, he thought. *I'll live.* Through the mirror, he saw the survivors behind him. Except for the man on the recliner, who was still yelling, they all looked at him in awe and horror. His brutality caught them off guard.

The female victim wiped her mouth with her blouse, then started helping the hostages under the TV. She kept a wary eye on Chinko's body, as if she were afraid he was going to reanimate.

"What's your name?" Franco asked as he hobbled over to Lily.

The girl flinched and scooted away from him. She sat with her feet up on the sofa and her knees up to her face.

Franco knelt in front of her and said, "I'm a cop. A police officer, okay? 911, you know? You're safe now. Talk to me, kid. What's your name?"

"She's not like the boy," the female victim said. "They brought her in here earlier and... and they put that makeup on her face."

Franco gazed into the girl's eyes and asked, "Are

you Lily? You were staying on the thirtieth floor? Your room was very, very high up, right? You came with your... your mom and dad and brother. And your dad, his hair's a little curly like yours, isn't it? His name is Adrian, right?" He gave a joyless laugh, then said, "If I'm right, then your dad's been looking for you."

Lily lowered her legs. Her lips were pulled down in a big frown and her whole face was twitching.

"Ye–Yes," she squeaked out. "My... My name is... is Lily Castillo. I want my mommy and daddy. Where's my mommy and daddy?"

Franco said, "Your dad, um... He's close. He's in the theater next door. I'm going to get you out of here and back to him. I'm getting *all* of you out of here. I just need you all to stay calm and follow my lead. Give me a minute to think this through. That's all I need." Staring at the door with uncertainty in his eyes, he whispered, "Just a minute."

18

ACT TWO

"Let me go!" Jordan shouted. "You can't do this!"

Center stage, the bellhop sat at the short end of a dining table, which was taken from one of the resort's restaurants. His body was tied tightly to a chair with durable rope—around his chest, his midsection, his thighs, his shins, his ankles. His right hand was handcuffed to one of the table's legs while his other arm was left unrestrained.

He used his free hand to push himself away from the table and claw at the rope around his body. No matter how hard he tried, he couldn't break free.

Blake sat across from him, blubbering and yammering on about his friend's death. Unlike Jordan, he was left unrestrained. The clowns didn't see him as a threat.

Standing in front of their table, Deadface raised the microphone to his mouth and said, "Life is a game of

Russian roulette. You risk dying every second of your life. You might be able to delay it, but sooner or later, death comes for everyone. Hell, in today's world, even those that have been immortalized through their achievements can be erased from history—can be *killed* again. I'm here to tell you that death is not something to *fear*. It's something to *anticipate*. It's not something to run *from*. It's something to run *towards*. Everything that we experience in life leads to this point. What you are about to witness is the ultimate game of chance."

The leader stepped to stage right. Revolver in hand, Spike entered from stage left and approached the table. The hostages screamed for mercy. The clown thumbed the gun's cylinder release latch, then rolled the cylinder out. He removed five of its cartridges, then he spun the cylinder before pushing it back in.

He stepped behind Blake and said, "You point this revolver at anything but your head and we'll play target practice with your nutsack."

Holding it by its barrel, he held the revolver out in front of Blake. The young man looked at the revolver, then at Spike's grim face.

"Why are you doing this to me?" he asked in a high, whiny voice.

Deadface said, "Take the gun, Mr. Blake Lowery. Put it up to your temple. And pull the trigger. Easy as one-two-three."

"Why are you doing this to me?!" Blake repeated as he swung his head to look over his other shoulder.

"We do this to ourselves every second that we live. Awake. Asleep. It doesn't matter. We're always playing this game of chance."

"Why me?! Why?! I don't want to do this anymore!"

From the other side of the table, Jordan yelled, "Let us go!"

Deadface said, "You're here because you're a survivor, Blake. I have a good feeling about you. Everything will be fine. Keep fighting. Keep surviving. Take the gun."

"Don't do it!" Jordan shouted. "Don't play their game!"

His mouth an inch away from Blake's ear, Spike whispered, "You know the rules, kid. You don't play, you don't live. You want my advice? Don't think about anything. Just put it up to your head and pull the trigger. If you're lucky, you live. If you're not, it'll all go black in a flash and you'll hardly feel a thing."

Blake stared at the revolver. He had never shot a gun before. The closest he ever got to holding one was when he played light gun shooters at arcades. The concept was the same, though, so easy a toddler could do it—*point* and *shoot*.

Deadface faced the audience and asked, "Can we give him some motivation?"

The clowns in the auditorium clapped and chanted: "Take! The! Gun! Take! The! Gun!"

Blake was afraid of accidentally killing himself, but he found himself agreeing with Spike. A bullet to the head sounded a whole lot better than getting bisected by clowns or being shot in the genitals. Death was the easy way out. And if he survived, he could at least buy himself some time.

He followed Spike's advice. He took the revolver out of the clown's hand. It was lighter than he had imagined. He closed his eyes, then put the muzzle against his temple. As the clapping and chanting came to an abrupt stop, he squeezed the trigger.

Click!

The audience exploded in applause.

Blake gasped, then cried. Tears oozed out from between his sealed eyelids. Despite surviving, he looked defeated as he lowered the weapon. Spike took the revolver out of his hand. He opened it up, spun the cylinder, then closed it again. Standing behind Jordan, he put the revolver in the bellhop's free hand and then grabbed his wrist to stop him from moving.

The clown drew a hunting knife from a sheath attached to his waistband. He held its sharp, sturdy four-and-a-half-inch blade against Jordan's neck.

"Same rules apply, chump," he said as he released the bellhop's wrist. "You point that gun at anything but your head and I'll cut your head off. And I'll do it real slow."

Jordan turned his head to glare at him, but he stopped halfway through the motion as the blade nicked his neck. He felt it caressing his thick jugular and the side of his Adam's apple.

"Why are you just sitting there?" he cried out to the audience. "Do something! Help us! *Fight!*"

With his eyes on the bellhop, Deadface said, "Like your buddy here, you've been playing this game every day of your life. You're in control this time. Your fate is in your hand—*literally*. Are you one of the 'special' ones, Jordan? Are you a survivor?"

"Shit, shit, shit," Jordan muttered.

He had no choice. He raised the revolver and put the muzzle to his temple. His mouth turned into a perfect 'O' with each loud exhale, then he shut his eyes and started screaming. After five seconds, he squeezed the trigger.

Click!

The hostages flinched, then bawled. Spike took the gun out of his hand, then pulled the knife away from his neck. He repeated the process—opened the revolver, spun the cylinder, and then closed it—and walked back to Blake.

Deadface said, "We have millions of people watching now. Millions of people opening their eyes to the *truth* about life. Who'll win? Who'll lose? Nobody truly knows. A 50-50 chance is not a sure thing. All we know is that it's time for *one* of these young men to die. That's life. Unfair and unpredictable."

As he handed the gun to Blake, Spike said, "Do it again."

Tapping his feet on the floor nervously, Blake accepted the revolver. In one quick motion, he raised the revolver to his temple and squeezed the trigger.

Click!

"Oh fuck," he moaned.

Deadface laughed inwardly, then said, "See? I knew I had a good feeling about you for a reason. You've got balls, Blake. You're scared of death—hell, we all are—but you've got what it takes to face it head-on. You believe in yourself. You control your fate. I can see a little of myself in you, son. You're special."

The audience went wild for Blake. Spike spun the cylinder again and walked to the other side of the table. He put his hunting knife up against the bellhop's throat, slicing him again, and put the revolver in the young man's free hand.

In a low voice so Deadface wouldn't hear him, Spike asked, "Are you special, too? Do you 'believe' in yourself? Show us what you got, tough guy."

"Fuck you," Jordan said weakly. "I–I won't die here."

He put the gun to his head and stared at his forced opponent. Unlike Blake, his mind was filled with memories and thoughts. He remembered the last time he visited his family for a barbecue and thought about what would happen if he shot himself in the head. He pictured death as a void—darkness, *nothingness.*

He closed his eyes and yelled, "I won't die–"

The gun went off as he squeezed the trigger. The gunfire echoed through the auditorium, silencing everyone. The bullet entered his skull through his left temple and became lodged in his brain. Geysers of blood spewed from the small hole on the side of his head. It landed on Spike's hand and streaked the floor. Jordan's mouth hung open and his eyes rolled back. He uttered a deep, long groan while his head undulated like a snake.

After a short period of awed silence, Deadface said, "Looks like we have ourselves a winner. Mr. Blake Lowery!"

From his seat, Adrian watched as the clowns around him celebrated Jordan's death. The tear on the mass of tape around his right arm had stretched, but it was hidden by the shadows. He could now easily free his arm, but he continued waiting for the perfect moment to strike.

"Now that really *blew* my mind," Binks said as she approached Adrian's seat from behind.

She crouched next to him with her hands and chin on his left arm. She looked up at his face with a pair of innocent, playful eyes.

"Blew his mind, too, huh?" she said with a devilish smile. "So, how're you likin' the show so far?"

Adrian wanted to kick and scream, but he bottled his anger to gain her trust. Calm and cool, he said something to her. It was only two words, but his response was distorted by his gag anyway.

"Oh, *duh!*" Binks said as she smacked the side of her head. "Keep forgetting about that darn tape on your mouth. Well, I'm sure you're just as excited as the rest of us. And it's going to get better than that. I think your girl might be up next. I hope she can see you from up there. Don't worry, she won't be playing with guns."

Although he knew she couldn't understand him, Adrian responded to her again. This time, he spoke for ten seconds. He hoped his behavior would pique her curiosity—and it did.

Binks said, "You're in a chatty mood, aren't ya?" She got up in a half-crouch, put her lips against the makeshift bandage over his severed ear, and in a sultry voice, she whispered, "Me too."

She giggled as she peeled the tape off his mouth, then she squatted down again with her chin on his restrained arm.

"Got something on your mind?" she asked. "Going to try to pull a fast one on lil' ol' me? Got a trick up your sleeve? Hmm? *Hmm?*"

Keeping his cool, Adrian asked, "What's going to happen to Lily up there?"

"Nope, no spoilers. Sorry, bub."

"You won't hurt her, will you?"

"We don't hurt family... unless they betray us... or they annoy us... or they spoil stuff! People who spoil movies deserve to be tortured. Seriously, I learned that lesson the hard way and I haven't spoiled anything in forever."

"Listen, I appreciate your, um... your dedication to your performance, but I'm talking to you... person-to-person. I know there's a decent human being in you. I can see it in your eyes. Can you tell me about my daughter?"

"Sorry, guy, but sweet talk won't get you anywhere with me," Binks replied. "I like it dirty, y'know? And this ain't no 'performance.' Performances are for actors. Does that blood look fake up there? This is the real thing. *We're* the real thing."

As two clowns carried Jordan's corpse—along with his chair—off stage, Deadface grinned and said, "Blake, Blake, Blake. I believe you might be the luckiest man in the world. I think it's about time we set you free. Men like you and me should never be in shackles. Spike, escort this young champion to the green room. I'd like to have one final word with him before we cut him loose."

With a hint of jealousy, Spike said, "If I didn't spin it for him, this kid would have gotten himself killed up here."

"What are you trying to say?"

"He got lucky 'cause of me. If you're thinking he's one of us 'cause he survived, I suggest you think again."

"Well, you know me, Spike. When people give me advice, I like to get into their heads, walk in their shoes, and *wear their faces*. Want to lend me yours?"

Deadface glared at his right-hand man while Spike avoided eye contact and retreated from the confrontation. The other clowns laughed, oohed, and aahed.

Staring into the auditorium, the leader said, "You can help a man, but you can't pause this game of chance. Slam on the brakes to stop yourself from running over a man trying to cross a busy highway... and that man might just get pulverized by a semi-truck in the next lane. Operate on a patient to save his life... and that patient might just die from 'complications' overnight. Blake won this game fair and square. He's earned a break. Now, before Spike spoils the mood further, I'd like to celebrate Blake's victory by officially welcoming the newest members of our troupe. You see, there are other ways to win at this game of chance. You can take matters into your own hands and kill yourself in the traditional sense. Or you can kill your *mental* self and allow yourself to be reborn. Like myself. Like the clowns you see around here tonight. Like the youth you'll soon see on this stage."

Adrian stopped listening to him. *He's talking about Lily,* he thought, his heart sinking. He had to buy her some time. Every second mattered.

"Why don't you put your money where your mouth is?!" he blurted out, interrupting Deadface's speech.

The clowns peered in his direction. They weren't sure if the voice came from one of them or one of the hostages.

Noticing the confusion, Binks stood up, pointed

down at Adrian with both of her index fingers, and hollered, "It was this guy!"

A spotlight moved across the auditorium. It stopped in the bank of seats in front of the stage. Adrian was still in the dark.

"Little more to your right," Binks yelled.

The spotlight crawled over them.

Deadface asked, "And who might you be, sir?"

"It doesn't matter," Adrian responded. "This is supposed to be the greatest show, right? You're supposed to be entertainers, *right?* So far, all we've seen are regular people playing dangerous games. Why don't you have your buddy up there... What did you call him? Spike? Why don't you have Spike put his money where his mouth is? Let him play some Russian roulette."

Spike said, "This is the guy who killed Twisted and Cuckoo."

"He's also the little girl's daddy," Binks announced.

"Sounds like he should be the one up here testing his luck. Maybe he can play a game of Russian roulette with his daughter."

"You're a coward," Adrian said. "All talk, no action."

"Fuck off. Cover that fucker's mouth before I make him deepthroat this revolver."

Binks said, "I don't know. I kinda agree with him. This is *our* show after all."

"Then you come up here and play, you stupid bitch," Spike hissed.

"Hey, you were the one saying you were lucky."

Deadface looked at Spike and said, "She's right. You want to take credit for Blake's victory, want to tell me my gut feeling is wrong about our winner, want to talk like you're running the show, then put your money where your mouth is."

Spike scowled at Adrian. The clowns in the auditorium goaded him on with insults: *'You pussy! Coward! Bitch! Punk! Poser!'*

As Spike returned to the table, Blake cried, "No! No! I was finished! I won! I–I lived!" He looked at Adrian and yelled, "We helped you, man! It's your fault if I die! This is all your fault! You selfish bastard! You sick–"

Spike slapped the back of his head and said, "Quiet down, boy."

The clown sat on the table in front of him. He placed his foot between Blake's legs, the tip of his shoe caressing his crotch. He opened the revolver, loaded a cartridge, then spun the cylinder.

Blake's cries ignited a pang of guilt in Adrian. He felt like there was no other way, though. He had to risk Blake's life in order to protect his daughter.

Spike closed the revolver, then held it out in front of Blake and said, "You first."

"But I already won."

Deadface said, "Believe in yourself, Blake. Kill the doubt in your head. Kill your mental self. Be born again. You are me and I am you."

Blake took the revolver from Deadface. He held it near his lap and stared dejectedly at it, as if looking at an heirloom left behind by a loved one. His tears plopped on its grip. He raised the gun to his temple. The audience fell silent. Adrian held his breath while Binks playfully nibbled on her fingernails.

Blake squeezed the trigger.

Click!

Blake sighed, a smile tugging at his lips. There was a collective gasp in the auditorium, then another round of applause.

With pride in his eyes, like a parent watching his child achieve his dreams, Deadface said, "I knew you had it in you."

Spike snatched the revolver out of his hand. He opened it, gave the cylinder a long spin, then slammed it shut. Without any hesitation, he put the muzzle against his temple and squeezed the trigger. A thunderous *bang* silenced the audience. A bullet went straight through Spike's skull—in through one temple and out the other—and hit a chair in the auditorium. The clown's eyes turned blood-red in an instant. One of the spikes on his scalp was detached, flipping through the air like a coin. Blood squirted out of the sides of his head in a pattern, one after the other—first the left, then the right, then the left again, and then the right again.

He fell off the table and hit the floor face first. He was already dead, but his body kept convulsing. His sharp mohawk scratched the floorboards as his head shook.

The audience was stunned by their peer's quick death. Only a female hostage, fed up with the violence, shrieked from behind her gag.

Deadface said, "And our winner is... Blake Lowery!"

He started clapping. The other clowns in the auditorium remained quiet. Then Binks clapped along with him. Within seconds, the rest of the clowns joined them.

Deadface said, "You are one of us now, Blake. You are me and I am you, and *we*... are *one*. From this day forward, you will be known as Lucky. Lucky the Clown!" He paused so the audience could cheer for him some more, then he said, "Get him back to the green room. Make him feel like part of the family. And get this mess cleaned up. We've got a show to finish."

Hound walked onto the stage. He patted the survivor's shoulder. Blake kept sitting there, motionless and speechless. He couldn't believe he was still alive. Hound grabbed his arm and pulled him off the seat. They exited stage left while two other clowns dragged Spike's body to the opposite exit.

Binks said, "Lucky? That's a dog's name, ain't it?"

Adrian ignored her. He searched the room for any signs of Franco or his daughter. Then he looked at Binks' neck. He was ready to attack.

19

THE GRAND FINALE

"You're one lucky bastard," Hound said as he pushed Blake forward in the curved hallway. "It ain't easy joining our circus, y'know? You gotta pass some tests. Trials and tribulations and all that good stuff. It's a lot harder than pointing a gun at your head and pulling the trigger. But, hey, I ain't gonna argue with the big boss. I'm just saying, you should be grateful, Lucky."

Blake groaned upon hearing his new nickname. *Don't call me that,* he wanted to yell. He had earned the nickname—and his survival—by killing his close friend and winning a game of Russian roulette. Survivor's guilt told him that he didn't deserve to live. He teetered from side to side, holding his clasped hands up to his mouth as he cried.

Hound shoved him again, forcing him to continue walking. They could hear the echoes of footsteps and banging from a locker. It sounded normal amidst the chaos.

The clown said, "We're kinda like brothers if you think about it. We're family. Now, don't go and tell anyone about this—seriously, they won't believe you anyway—but what do you say you and I test your luck later? Let's go over to the hotel rooms and see if we can find us a nice piece of ass we can double-team. What do you think? Can we get *lucky*, Lucky?"

Blake stopped in his tracks.

Hound walked around him and said, "C'mon, man, I'm just tryin' to..."

His voice trailed off and his eyes jutted out. Franco stood outside of the green room and held the door open. The last hostage stepped out. The young woman looked confused, as if she had just stepped into a labyrinth of hallways. Franco pointed her to the other hostages, who were already following his directions and sneaking down the hall. Lily stood next to the cop, her fingers wrapped around his utility belt.

"What the hell is going on here?!" Hound yelled.

There was startled silence. The hostages stopped sneaking and glanced back at the clown. Franco stepped in front of Lily and put his hand on his holstered pistol. An air of tension filled the hallway. Hound's hand inched towards his pocket. The cop and clown stood there like dueling cowboys in a Western movie.

"Don't move," Franco said. "You can still get out of this alive."

He didn't want to shoot him because they were so close to the auditorium. He was willing to let him walk away, although his cop's intuition told him to arrest him. Hound's hand stalled, then continued drifting towards his pocket.

Franco said, "Keep your hands where I can–"

Blake rammed Hound with his shoulder, sending him reeling towards the wall to their left. Hound's head bounced off the wall with an unnerving *thud*. Dazed, he fell to his hands and knees. Blake sprinted past the surprised survivors.

"Go!" Franco yelled. "Straight down, left, then right! Just like I said!"

The hostages ran. Franco grabbed Lily's hand and pulled her away from the green room, unintentionally hurting her elbow and shoulder. She couldn't run as fast as him, either. So, he picked her up and ran with her in his arms.

Hound pushed himself up to his feet and ran after them. He crashed into the wall, then dropped to his knees at the center of the hall, then picked himself up again. He took a pocketknife out of his pocket and gave chase.

Looking back over Franco's shoulder, Lily yelled, "He's coming!"

Franco drew his handgun and turned around. Walking backwards, he pointed his gun at the clown.

Hound slowed his run to a stroll, matching the cop's pace. They heard Deadface's deep voice through the walls and doors slamming down the hall.

"I'll shoot," Franco said. "I don't want to do it, but I will."

"Gimme the girl," Hound growled.

"You can't win here."

"Give her to me!"

Lily flinched in Franco's arms and hid her face in his shoulder.

Franco said, "I only need one shot to put you down. There's a show going on in there. Chances are they won't even hear the gunshot or your cries—*if* you survive. I'm telling you: You can't win. I'm giving you a chance to walk away with your life. Take it."

While the cop continued walking backwards, Hound stopped. An expression of doubt dawned on his face, as if he had just realized he had brought a knife to a gunfight. He knew he couldn't outrun a speeding bullet. He loved killing, but he wasn't completely sold on the idea of dying. He started walking backwards as well, then he sprinted to the closest backstage entrance.

With his pistol raised, Franco kept his eyes on him until he vanished around the corner. He turned and jogged to catch up to the others.

"My daddy," Lily whined as she pulled on Franco's collar. "I want my mommy and daddy."

Franco stopped next to the emergency exits. The

one to his right led to the auditorium. And Adrian's last known location was the theater. The cop wanted to get Lily out of the building, but he also felt compelled to rescue her only surviving parent.

He put Lily down on the floor, crouched in front of her, and said, "Listen to me. Your dad is somewhere in the theater behind this door. He asked me to get you out of here. He said he'd find you later and–"

"I don't wanna leave by myself! I want my family!"

"Shh, shh," Franco said.

"I–I want my family."

"I know, I know. But if we're going to find your dad, you have to listen to me. These clowns are dangerous people. You know that, right? *Right?*"

"Uh-huh," Lily responded, nodding and sniffling with fresh tears running down her painted cheeks.

"So, when we go through that door, you have to stay close to me and you have to be quiet. No matter what you see or hear, you can't make a sound. And if I tell you to run or hide, you do it. You understand me?"

"Uh-huh."

Franco said, "Hold onto my belt."

He got up to a half-crouch and faced the door. His heartbeat accelerated at the thought of taking Lily directly into the clowns' circus. *It's suicide,* he thought. But he couldn't leave her unsupervised in the service corridors with Hound and the other clowns patrolling the area. He was convinced that she was better off with him.

He pushed the door open and crept into the auditorium. Holding onto his belt, Lily followed him.

Standing center stage, Deadface said, "Tonight, we welcome a new generation to our circus. The newest members of our family are young and impressionable. They have yet to be tainted by the *evil* of the world. We've all seen this evil before, haven't we? I'm talking about the politics, the corporations, the social media, *the bullshit.* Under our care, these children may not have to kill their mental selves. We'll teach them to be free before society can teach them to be slaves. They'll join our collective–"

"Pig!" Hound hollered as he ran onto the stage. "We've got a cop!"

"What the hell do you think you're doing?" Deadface asked as he lowered the microphone. "Stop interrupting the show and go handle him. He isn't the first cop we've killed in this dump."

"I saw Chinko's body in the green room. He's dead."

"Go. Handle. Him."

As Deadface turned to face the audience, Hound said, "The girl... He took the girl. And he's got a gun."

"He took our little flower Ms. Lily Castillo? The youngest one?"

"Yeah, her."

Deadface looked at the audience and said, "Now that spoils everything, doesn't it?"

The clowns in the auditorium glanced around and chatted amongst themselves about the escape. While looking around, Binks' eyes landed on a man at the opposite end of the row of seats to her right. It was Dustin Pearson. In whiteface, he was now dressed as a clown with a baggy, colorful jumpsuit and a pointy hat on his head.

"Hey you!" Binks shouted. Dustin looked in her direction but not at her. Binks said, "Dusty! What are you doing here, bozo?!"

Dustin could hardly make her out in the darkness, but he saw her figure and recognized her voice.

He yelled, "Sharpy, bitch! My name is Sharpy!"

"Whatever! You're supposed to be in the security room, dumbass! Why are you even here?"

"I got bored!"

"You goof, the show's ruined 'cause of you!"

Dustin pointed at himself and said, "This isn't my fault. You guys were supposed to be watching 'em, not me."

Speaking over the chitter-chatter, Deadface said, "Looks like there'll be a change in our schedule, ladies and gentlemen. Due to a pesky intrusion, we must end the show early. I would have loved to welcome some new members to our family, but I can't afford to delay the grand finale with a cop on the loose. I could be assassinated any second now. That's not my ending. No, siree, not mine."

In the dark auditorium, Franco and Lily hid between two rows of seats. The cop put his hand over the girl's mouth as a clown ran up the aisle next to them.

Deadface continued, "I won't—*can't*—die from a bullet. I can't die a regular death because I am not a regular person. I can only... *ascend*. I am... *unerasable*. I am... *permanent*. Do you know why I wear this mask?" He paused, as if waiting for a response. He said, "I wear this mask and many just like it because I am everyone. And tonight, my message will be *in* everyone. My image will be seared in your retinas. I am the true embodiment of humanity... and humanity is destined to self-destruct. It is time for the Hellfire to begin."

Franco and Lily crouched their way down the row of seats, squeezing past the hostages. The hostages called out to them but went ignored. The patrolling clowns didn't notice them, either. Franco and Lily emerged in an aisle, then juked into another row of seats. Franco peeked over a chair and searched for Adrian. He couldn't find him amongst all of the weeping survivors.

But Adrian could see them. A Molotov cocktail of emotions exploded within him. He was relieved and delighted to see his daughter. He barely recognized her with the paint on her face, but he was positive it was her. At the same time, he was scared for her wellbeing and furious at Franco for bringing her into the theater. He shook his head as Binks poured gasoline on him.

"Sorry, buddy, but you heard the man," she said, shaking the gasoline container. "It's time to start cooking. Don't worry, I'll make sure you get extra crispy."

The other clowns started soaking the seats in gasoline. Some of the clowns ran down the rows and dumped gasoline on the hostages.

Deadface said, "To my family around the world: Kill until you die. We will be reunited soon. To the world, remember this: I am all, and we are one."

He threw his microphone aside. Hound brought him a red gasoline container. Deadface raised it overhead and took a gasoline shower, dousing himself from head to toe in the flammable liquid. Afterward, Hound handed him a candle lighter. Pointing it away from himself, Deadface squeezed the lighter's trigger. It ignited with the third *click*.

In a strong, unafraid voice, he said, "I am immortal."

He held the flame up to his waistband and ignited the gasoline. A ball of fire burst from his crotch. The flames quickly crawled up his torso and barreled down his legs. His body was engulfed in a matter of seconds. Yet, he remained calm and steady. Center stage, he got down in a meditative lotus position.

The audience—in the auditorium and through the live stream—watched in awe. His self-immolation evoked imagery of Thích Quảng Đức, a Buddhist monk who had burned himself to death in an act of political protest. But Deadface's actions were part of a gruesome horror show. He turned himself into a symbol of anarchy and violence.

"My God," Franco said.

"What's happening?" Lily asked. "Is it my daddy?"

"Keep your eyes down, hold on tight, and only listen to my voice."

"O–Okay..."

Franco led her between the rows of seats. The cries from the trapped hostages grew louder as they realized they were going to be burned alive soon.

"I'm sorry," the cop whispered, his words lost in the noise.

Standing next to Adrian and staring up at the stage, Binks said, "Beautiful, ain't it? When I catch our girl, I'll make sure she burns just like that." She looked down at Adrian and asked, "Or should I throw her out a window like her mama and brother? What do you think?"

Adrian said something and beckoned to her, but Binks couldn't hear him over the surrounding noise. The bank of seats behind her was set ablaze. The screeching from the trapped hostages grew louder as the roaring fire swallowed them whole.

On stage, Deadface's human mask, now burned to a crisp, began to crumble. The mask's chin disintegrated first, revealing the leader's jutting jaw. A piece of the mask's forehead fell off. Then the strings burned and the rest of the charred mask plummeted to his lap. Flames lapped at his hard, angular face.

Binks leaned in close to Adrian's face and asked, "What was that? Did you say you want me to light her on fire, *then* throw her out a window?"

"I said we'll burn here together," Adrian responded.

He slid his right hand out of the torn tape and grabbed the back of Binks' neck. He pulled her closer to him and then chomped at her face. His upper teeth sank into her left cheek next to her nose while his lower teeth cut *into* her right nostril.

Binks shrieked. She slapped his shoulders and face while trying to pull away from him. His teeth were buried deep in her face, though, jaw locked like a vise. The more she fought, the more she suffered. And the more she suffered, the more she fought. She stopped screaming as blood flooded her nasal cavity. She coughed up drizzles of blood instead.

With the banks of seats burning around them, Franco carried Lily in his arms and hurried to the end of another row. The orange glow from the flames illuminated the auditorium while a blanket of smoke covered the ceiling.

"Daddy!" Lily yelled and pointed in front of her.

Franco crouched behind a seat and shushed her. To his utter relief, the patrolling clowns paid them no mind. They were busy laughing as they set the hostages on fire. The cop craned his neck to look over the seat. He spotted Adrian and Binks. He looked at Lily and held his index finger up to his lips. Although she was antsy, Lily nodded with understanding.

Franco carried her across the aisle.

Meanwhile, Deadface tipped over on stage. Without making a peep, he had passed away from shock. His upper body was cooked—pink, red, and black, and blistered, pulpy, and charred. His polyester pants melted, fusing with his blackened, toasty legs. His corpse continued to burn.

In the auditorium, Binks grabbed onto Adrian's shoulders, pushed him away, and whipped her head back. Her nose, as well as part of her cheek, was torn off. Screeching, she collapsed in the aisle with her hands over her face. She rolled from side to side as if she were on fire. Adrian spat the severed nose at her. His face, chin, and neck were covered in her blood.

Franco stopped a few seats away from Adrian, awed by his bloodied appearance. Lily was simultaneously afraid of her dad and grateful to see him. Although he was injured and bloody, she recognized the fatherly kindness in his eyes. Franco set her down behind him, then rushed to Adrian's side.

"I'm going to get you out of here," he said, tugging on the tape around his other arm.

Adrian looked at his daughter and said, "Lily, I'm... I'm so sorry, hon."

"Dad..." Lily said with a wavering voice.

"I love you so much, darling. But you... you have to run. Leave me."

"Daddy, no..."

Franco looked up at him, then over at the bank of seats to his right. A wall of fire was closing in on them. They were out of time. He stared into Adrian's eyes with admiration and regret.

"I'm sorry," he said.

Adrian said, "Don't be. Just make sure she gets out alive."

Franco nodded.

"Daddy, no!" Lily cried as she leapt onto him. Arms hooked over the nape of his neck, she nuzzled his chest and yelled, "I don't wanna go! I don't wanna go! I love you, daddy! Don't make me go!"

With a half-smile and tears welling in his eyes, Adrian kissed the top of her head, then said, "I love you, too." He gave Franco a nod and said, "Save her."

As he pried Lily's arms off Adrian, Franco repeated, "I'm sorry."

"Daddy, please! No!" Lily sobbed as she was carried away.

Holding Lily tightly in his arms, Franco retraced their steps. Dodging the remaining clowns and raging fires, they made their way back to the emergency exit.

Binks rose unsteadily to her feet. She wept hysterically, bloody snot bubbles popping where her nose used to be. She took a few wobbly steps up the aisle before Adrian grabbed her arm and pulled her back.

He said, "We'll burn together."

Binks screamed for help, but no one heard her over the crackling flames, cackling clowns, and crying hostages. The fire from the neighboring bank of seats spilled into the aisle, setting her ablaze. The fire spread onto Adrian, too. He screamed along with her as his skin peeled away, layer by layer.

Yet, he never let her go.

20

THE GREAT ESCAPE

"Da–Daddy," Lily cried, her voice breaking.

Carrying her in his arms, Franco sprinted down the service corridor. He tried to recall Lee's directions but drew a blank. Then a blast echoed through the building. He felt the floor shaking under his feet. Five seconds later, there was another explosion. The ceiling-mounted fire sprinklers activated with a synchronized *hissing* sound while fire alarms *whooped* at regular intervals.

Sliding on the wet floor, Franco rammed the doors at the end of the hall with his shoulder. The doors swung open and they stumbled into the casino. The pathway to the theater was to their right and the sealed entrance to the condominium tower was to their left. An alarm wailed in the casino, too, but the sprinklers didn't activate in the massive room.

"We're almost out," Franco said to Lily. While the

girl continued crying for her family, Franco held his radio up to his mouth and said, "Lee. Lee, can you hear me?"

He felt Lily shaking in his arms. The casino was cold and, like him, she was soaked because of the sprinklers.

Over the radio, Lee said, "Franco, Jesus Christ, there was an explosion in the theater. Where are you?"

"In the casino," Franco answered. "I've got her. I'm going to bring her to you. Get a door open for us, then get her out of here."

"I don't wanna go," Lily said. "I want my mommy and daddy and Andrew."

As Franco jogged towards the lobby, Lee said, "The doors are either barricaded or the locks have been sabotaged over here. It would take too long to get her out through here."

"There has to be a way out," Franco said.

"There is, there is. I started opening the gates and evacuating the building while you were looking for the girl. You're better off slipping out through the front entrance. The gate got stuck about a quarter of the way up, but there's enough room for you to squeeze through."

"What about you? How are you getting out?"

The radio went silent for a couple of seconds.

Lee said, "I'll get out through the back once I finish evacuating the building."

Franco knew he was lying. Just like Adrian, he

could tell Lee was planning on sticking around until the very end. He respected his decision, so he didn't bother trying to change his mind. It wasn't the best time to argue anyway. They ran past another cluster of slot machines and found a horde of guests crowding the resort's entrance.

Plagued by panic and selfishness, the evacuation effort was in a state of disarray. The survivors shoved and clawed and yelled at each other.

"Children first!" Franco shouted over them. "Let the children through first!"

The arguing turned into screaming as gunshots rang out from behind them. Another burst of gunfire echoed through the building—and then another. It sounded like it was coming from high-powered rifles in different sections of the casino.

Two male guests collapsed near the entrance. One bled from his chest and the other was missing part of his skull. Some of the survivors kept pushing forward, trying to escape through the gap under the security gate, while others hit the ground and scrambled away in search of cover.

Franco yelled, "Lily, cover your ears!"

Lily plugged her ears with her fingers and buried her face in his chest. Franco drew his pistol and ran into the casino. Bloodcurdling screams and gunshots came from every direction. Bullets struck the slot machines next to him. Some rounds were lodged in the machine's polycarbonate surfaces while others ricocheted.

Franco kept moving but started stepping sideways to face his attacker. He saw the gunman—a chubby clown armed with a modified rifle—standing behind a blackjack table. With a clear shot, he emptied the rest of his magazine. Out of the nine shots, four hit the clown's torso and one pierced his throat.

Franco sprinted through the maze of slot machines. He felt like he was going in circles. The games were different, but they all looked the same to him. He heard running footsteps all around him. Lee's voice buzzed through the radio on his belt, but he didn't have time to talk. He emerged at the opposite end of the casino from the entrance.

"Damn it," he muttered.

To his left, he spotted two clowns at the condominium tower's entrance—Dustin and Hound. Dustin pointed his way, then they chased after him.

Franco ran into a nearby restaurant. He turned off his radio when it buzzed again. He ran past some tables and made his way to a set of doors with circular windows at the end of the room. He slid to a stop in a kitchen, the doors swinging back and forth behind him. He gasped and pushed Lily's face closer to his chest to shield her from the carnage he had discovered.

Then a look of recognition came over his face. He had seen this kitchen before. He remembered the severed arm in the stock pot and the dissected man on the kitchen island. He was back in the Palace Steakhouse. His horrified gaze wandered to the door beyond the kitchen island. He thought back to his brief visit to the condominium tower's lobby—the fresh air, the car engines, *the way out.*

Straight down the hall, take a left, then the first door on the right, he told himself.

"In here!" Dustin called out from outside of the restaurant.

Franco couldn't outrun or overpower them with Lily around, so he had to outsmart them. He took the canister of pepper spray out of his utility belt. He turned on a stove burner with a bloodstained skillet on top. He placed the canister of pepper spray on the skillet. Then, with Lily in his arms, he squeezed into a cupboard under a sink a few feet away. He closed the cupboard door just as the clowns entered the restaurant.

"You have to stay quiet," Franco whispered rapidly. "Cover your face and close your eyes. Hold your breath when I tell you to."

Lily snorted, then pulled the collar of her shirt up to her nose and shielded her eyes with her hand. Franco was a bundle of nerves, unsure if his plan was going to work. But like a gambler, he bet it all and let luck decide his fate.

Dustin and Hound barged into the kitchen. The sound of a door crashing into a wall made Lily flinch. Franco held her tighter.

Dustin said, "They came through here. I saw 'em."

"I'm going to skin that pig and his little bitch," Hound said.

"Find 'em!"

They rushed down each side of the kitchen island while banging their machetes against the countertops. Dustin ran straight past the stove, missing the canister on the skillet.

As he reached the door to the service corridor, Hound said, "They're not in here. Let's go before we lose 'em."

"Wait up," Dustin said. "Let me check the pantry."

"What? You getting hungry?"

"They could be hiding."

Hound opened the door to the service corridor, poked his head out, and scanned the hallway. He asked, "What if they're running?"

"You heard the saying: They can run, but they can't hide."

As he reached for the door leading to the pantry, another explosion rocked the building. The kitchen doors flapped violently, the pans hanging over the kitchen island clattered against each other, and some cupboard doors popped open. Frightened by the noise, a squeal escaped Lily's mouth.

The clowns stopped. They looked back into the kitchen, then grinned at each other. They couldn't locate the origin of the cry with pinpoint accuracy due to the noise in the room, but they knew it came from somewhere in the kitchen.

"Told ya," Dustin said.

Hound opened the large cabinets in the room while Dustin searched the smaller cupboards lining the walls. Sitting under the sink, Franco and Lily listened as the clowns closed in on them. Hound opened a refrigerator, then checked the freezer. As he reached the sink, the canister of pepper spray caught Dustin's eye.

"What's that?" he said.

"You got 'em?" Hound asked from the other side of the kitchen island.

"No, man, there's a–"

The canister exploded with a loud *bang*. A cloud of pepper spray swept through the kitchen.

"Hold your breath!" Franco yelled as he kicked the cupboard open.

He pressed the girl's face against his chest with so much pressure that he was close to suffocating her. Lily did as she was told. Elbow over his face, Franco charged through the mist of pepper spray. It still stung his eyes and throat, blurring his vision, impeding his breathing, and leaving him disoriented.

Dustin dropped to his knees with his hands over his face, alternating between a piercing scream and a wet cough. The pepper spray coated most of his body. He looked like he had received an orange spray tan with his clothes on. The loud detonation left his ears ringing. He started gagging, then vomiting. It came out yellow and runny, like egg yolk, then it was clear and foamy.

Hound tottered around and rubbed his eyes. Thick strings of mucus hung from his face. Like Dustin, his eyes were as red as blood.

Franco carried Lily into the service corridor. He lurched forward to put some distance between them and the clowns. He felt like he was running on a moving walkway in an airport while the walls tilted left and right around him.

At the end of the hall, he pulled Lily's head away from his chest and stammered, "A–A–Are you okay?"

"My eyes... hurt... so much," Lily said, wheezing with each pause. "I... I... I can't breathe. I... I'm scared. I'm... *Ow!* It hurts!"

"I know it hurts. But you... you have to be strong, Lily. We're almost out. It's almost over."

Franco took a left, then opened the first door to his right. In the condominium tower's lobby, a fresh breeze caressed their hot skin and cooled their stinging lungs. They heard hushed, panicked voices around the corner in front of them.

"If anything happens to me, find a way out," Franco whispered as he set Lily down. "Stay behind me."

"O–Okay..."

Franco crept across the lobby. Around a corner to his right, he found an elevator bank. And beyond the elevators, an emergency exit was propped open with a brick. The voices, although still quiet, got a little louder. He heard a fence rattling, too. Through the doorway, they saw a large group of guests huddled on a lawn. They were helping each other climb an 8-foot-tall chain-link fence.

The temporary fence, outfitted with white privacy slats, surrounded the condominium tower. It was supposed to be replaced with a taller, more luxurious fence after the final renovations were completed.

Franco gave Lily a gentle shove from behind and said, "This is our way out, kid."

Lily was afraid to step out. She knew about death, but she never had any firsthand experience with it. She understood people and animals died, she knew death was irreversible, but she never fully accepted the fact that her family would pass on someday—that *every-thing* died. She didn't want to leave the hotel because she didn't want to leave her family. Although she knew the truth in her heart, a part of her believed they were still alive.

"Go on," Franco said. "This is what your dad wanted, sweetheart. You can't stop now."

You have to run. Lily heard her father's voice in her head. *Leave me.* She closed her eyes and nodded, sending tears down her rosy cheeks. She walked out through the emergency exit.

"Hey, we've got a kid over here," a man in the group said. "Get her over the fence. Hurry it up."

Franco took one step out, then he heard footsteps

behind him. Before he could turn around, he was chopped with a machete. The blade cut his trapezius muscle at the base of his neck. It slid out of him as he ducked and turned to face his attacker. Hound swung the machete at him again. Franco jumped back to dodge him, but he wasn't fast enough. The blade hit the left side of his head, slashing him from his cheek to the back of his skull—and splitting his ear in half.

"They're here!" a woman screamed.

"No!" Lily cried as she grabbed the back of Franco's shirt. "Don't hurt him!"

Without looking back, Franco yelled, "Get her out of here!"

As Hound wound up the machete for another swing, the cop ran forward and tackled him. Lily lost her grip on him. She ran after them, but a woman from the group pulled her back.

"Get the children out first!" the woman shouted over the panicking survivors.

Franco and Hound ended up in the elevator bank. Franco held onto Hound's wrists to stop him from swinging the machete again. Hound pushed Franco back against a set of elevator doors. He launched his knee up at him but hit one of the doors instead. Franco drove him back towards the parallel elevator. Due to his butchered trapezius muscle and bicep, he was much weaker than the clown, so he was quickly over-whelmed.

Hound pushed him back. They teetered into the

lobby where their feet got tangled in a mess of cords and they spilled to the floor. The machete flew out of Hound's hand on the way down. They rolled away from each other and grabbed anything they could use as weapons. The men got to their feet. Franco had armed himself with a cordless drill while Hound held a long Phillips-head screwdriver in his hand.

Franco squeezed the drill's trigger and lunged at him. Hound stabbed the cop's side three times—starting from his lower ribs and making his way down to his waist. Franco groaned as he thrust the drill at Hound's chest again. He was expecting gallons of blood to spray it. He only managed to push Hound back a little, though. In the glow from a work light on the other side of the lobby, he saw his tool was missing its drill bit.

Hound thrust the screwdriver at him a fourth time. It cut a hole on his shirt but didn't penetrate his skin. Since he couldn't stab him with it, Franco swung the drill at Hound's head, smashing it against his temple. Then, as the clown staggered back, he swept his legs out from under him. Hound landed hard on the floor and had the wind knocked out of him. Fighting through the pain, Franco scrambled behind him.

The cop grabbed a sheet of plastic from the floor. He wrapped it around the clown's head three times over, then grabbed him in a rear naked choke and lay back on the floor under him. The plastic crinkled and rustled as Hound writhed. He raked his fingernails across Franco's arms but failed to hurt him. He clawed at the plastic, too, but he only tore through a single layer of it. With each attempt to breathe, the plastic fluttered into the clown's gaping mouth.

Hound's writhing weakened to some feeble twitching after about two minutes. Franco understood suffocation wasn't *that* easy, though. He had met victims who had been beaten until they pissed themselves, strangled into unconsciousness, and left for dead in ditches—only to get up moments later without any immediate medical assistance. Brain death required persistent pressure and time. And only death could stop Hound from pursuing Lily.

Franco eyed a hammer on top of a step stool to his right. He sat up with Hound's body on top of him. Keeping one arm around Hound's neck, he leaned to his right and made a grab for the hammer. He missed it, his arm slamming against the floor. Hound coughed and squirmed. Franco tightened his chokehold. The clown clawed at his face, leaving four thin cuts on his forehead and slicing his eyeball.

His eye throbbing with intense pain, Franco's chokehold slackened. He tightened it again as Hound pulled away from him. Unable to reach the hammer or the cordless drill at their feet, Franco pulled the heavy-duty flashlight out of his utility belt. Although thin, it was hard and heavy. He bashed Hound's head with it over and over—*and over again*. The flashlight turned on and off with each hit.

With the fourth blow, a smattering of blood drizzled onto the plastic. The splatter stain grew larger with the fifth, sixth, seventh, eighth, and ninth blows. A bloody, messy outline of his face stained the plastic.

Franco took the plastic off Hound's head and quickly mounted his chest. The clown's nose was busted, his nasal septum broken into a greater-than sign. There was a cut over his right eyebrow and his right eye was swollen shut. Mouth ajar, his lips were sliced and some of his teeth were chipped. He was breathing in fast, gurgly inhalations.

In a fit of rage, Franco forced the flashlight into Hound's mouth bezel first. Hound gagged once before the flashlight slid past his uvula. He tilted his head back and tried to wiggle out from under Franco. He only made it easier for the cop to force the flashlight farther down his throat. It entered his esophagus and appeared as a large lump on his neck.

Franco punched the lump as if it were a speed bag in a gym. He threw jabs at Hound's neck until the flashlight broke in his gullet. The lump and his Adam's apple were pushed *into* his throat. The bright beam from the flashlight shone through the translucent skin on his cratered neck as a red glow. The clown stopped moving during the beating.

Still and silent, Franco stared at the dead clown for a minute. He reminded him of the brutalized victims in the casino. He had resorted to using their tactics to murder—and it made him feel like a monster. He held his breath and ground his teeth to stop himself from screaming. He didn't want to attract the other clowns to him. He spent another minute crying.

After regaining his composure, he put his hand over his mutilated side and staggered out of the lobby. Outside, the group of survivors had shrank. Most of them had made it over the fence or moved to other parts of it to avoid the clown. He didn't see Lily out there. Gritting his teeth through the pain, he started climbing over the fence.

21

WHAT HAPPENS IN VEGAS

THE RISING SUN AND BURNING BUILDINGS PAINTED THE sky orange. Gusts of wind blew blankets of black and white smoke over the city. The stench of burnt bodies and smoke wafted through the streets. People wept and screamed on every block. Dead bodies—tourists, hotel employees, police officers and SWAT members, and even some clowns—littered every street and side-walk. They had either been shot, maimed, dismembered, ran over, or set aflame—or all of the above.

Next to the Platinum Palace, Franco limped down a sidewalk and searched for Lily. He saw some of the survivors from the hotel running away from the property. He raised the volume on his radio and held it up to his mouth.

"Lee," he said. "It's Franco. How do you copy?"

There was no answer.

Franco said, "Lee, we made it out, but I lost track of

the girl. If you're still in the surveillance room, I need you to check the exterior cameras. Do you copy?"

Again, no answer.

Franco muttered indistinctly. He put the radio in his utility belt, then took out his police radio from another pocket.

Speaking into it, he said, "Dispatch, this is Unit 33. I need immediate assistance at the Platinum Palace. I repeat: Ten-thirty-three at the Platinum Palace." As he waited for a response, he glanced around the street and shouted, "Lily! Lily, it's the police! I'm here! It's okay now!"

He didn't hear a peep from Lily or the radio. He got down on his hands and knees to check under a van parked next to the building—*nothing*. He crawled forward and checked under the other abandoned cars on the street. He saw a dead woman under a truck. One of the vehicle's front wheels had flattened her abdomen. There was a severed arm on the lane marking as well as some shoes.

As he stood, Franco's radio buzzed. Then his dispatcher said, "Officer Ferraro, do you copy?"

"I hear you!" Franco exclaimed, shedding tears of relief.

"What is your location?"

"I'm outside of the Platinum Palace. Making my way to the Boulevard."

"Are you injured?"

"Yes, but I can move."

The dispatcher said, "Officer Ferraro, the National Guard has arrived. There is a coordinated effort to rescue hostages and neutralize the terrorists. I need you to get to your police cruiser. Turn your sirens on and head to the nearest precinct or community center. Can you do that?"

Franco stopped and checked on a crashed sedan. It had hit a streetlamp. The passengers—a man in the driver's seat, a woman in the passenger's—had been shot in the head. He noticed most of the vehicles on the street were either inoperable or filled with dead bodies. He figured his patrol car had suffered a similar fate.

He continued walking, making his way past the condominium tower. He saw smoke rising from the Grand Platinum Theater.

He said, "I'm not sure. I don't have eyes on my vehicle."

"Understood. Get to the closest precinct. And be careful. There have been reports of... *children* dressed as clowns on the Boulevard. Some of them are wearing... suicide vests. They've downed multiple officers and troopers since last night. I'm sorry to say this, but... If you see one, don't take any chances. Officer Ferraro... Kill on sight."

Traumatized by the reports, the dispatcher sounded like she was saying things she didn't want to say. The young clowns were like child soldiers, trained to bait and kill cops and troopers. Franco's heart fluttered in his chest like a hummingbird trapped in a cage. An image of Lily's painted face flashed in his mind.

She looks like a clown, he thought. *They'll shoot her if they find her first.*

"Lily!" he yelled as he ran forward.

He checked under, inside, and behind every car on the street. He sprinted around the theater and hurried to the resort's entrance. The gate was still jammed but no one was trying to escape anymore.

"Don't tell me you went back in," he muttered.

His fingers shook so badly that he couldn't get his other radio out of his utility belt. While struggling to get it out, he inspected the abandoned cars—taxis and vehicles with Uber decals plastered on their windows —in front of the entrance.

Then he saw her.

Lily stood on the center divider on the street in front of the Platinum Palace. Eyes closed and stomping her feet, she cried out for her family.

"Lily!" Franco yelled as he barreled towards her.

She didn't hear him over her sobbing and the sound of crackling flames all around her. She called out to her mother.

As he ran through the parking lot, Franco noticed a squad of troopers moving towards Lily. The troopers aimed their weapons at her. They could see she wasn't holding any firearms, but they couldn't be sure she didn't have any explosives strapped onto her. They surrounded her while positioning themselves to avoid crossfire. Despite his injuries, Franco ran faster than he ever had before.

As he reached the sidewalk, a trooper yelled, "Don't move!"

Franco kept going. Just as he grabbed Lily in a bear hug, using his body to shield hers, he heard gunshots. He shut his eyes and winced. He didn't feel like he was riddled with bullets, but he had never been shot before so he didn't know what it was supposed to feel like. He wondered if adrenaline was protecting him from the pain or if he had failed to reach her in time. *Is she dying in my arms?* he thought. *Or am I dying in hers?*

"Show me your hands!" the trooper demanded.

"A–Are you o–okay, mister?" Lily asked.

Franco opened his eyes. He leaned away and looked at Lily, then he examined himself. They were fine. The gunfire had come from somewhere behind them.

"Show me your hands!" the trooper repeated.

Franco put his hands up and turned around slowly. He said, "I'm a police officer with the LVMPD. My name's Franco Ferraro, Unit 33. Check my badge. Call my captain or the chief. The girl's with me. She's a victim."

The troopers were skeptical. They frisked him thoroughly and made sure Lily wasn't armed with any hidden explosives. After verifying the cop's identity, Franco and Lily were placed in the back of a military truck with a group of survivors and injured police offi-cers. The truck was heading to a hospital.

As they drove off, Franco looked out the back of the truck. He watched a group of troopers and non-disabled cops prepare to breach the Platinum Palace through the front entrance. A fire truck and an ambulance sped past the military truck. They headed towards the resort as well. He wondered if they could save anyone—if there was even anyone left to save.

Sitting next to him, Lily hugged him and cried softly into his chest. She aggravated his injuries, but Franco didn't stop her.

He patted her shoulder and said, "It's okay. It's okay."

"It's not," a man chimed in.

He was sitting across from them, eyes red and watery. His t-shirt was torn into a toga, revealing the cuts on his chest and shoulder. His black hair was messy and he had a trimmed goatee. He spoke with an accent, but Franco couldn't identify it.

He said, "It's the end of the world."

"Be quiet," Franco responded.

"But it's true. My family... My family in Thailand, they said Bangkok and Phuket are burning. They said the world was on fire. *The world.* There is no peace anywhere. No peace..."

"Are we... going to be okay?" Lily sobbed.

"It's over, Lily. The clowns won't win," Franco said. "We're safe now."

Lily sensed a hint of doubt in his calm voice. He reminded her of her father, strong even in the face of adversity. She hugged him tighter. Franco stared out at the street, watching as the truck swerved around cars and sped past dead bodies and severed limbs. He pictured the world burning just like Las Vegas.

With even more uncertainty in his voice, Franco repeated, "It's over."

JON ATHAN

DO NOT DISTURB 3

GOLDBRUSH

1

THE TRAVELING CIRCUS

"HOW MANY HORROR MOVIES START LIKE THIS?" TERRI Herrera asked.

She sounded like she didn't want an answer, though. She was leaning back against the front passenger door of a red hatchback, staring off into the unending desert. The sun descended behind a range of mountains, turning the sky purple, pink, and orange. The car's hood was propped up. Her boyfriend, Simon Lee, muttered indistinctly to himself as he investigated the engine for the umpteenth time.

"I don't know a lot of movies that *start* with a car breaking down," he said without taking his eyes off the engine. "I think 'The Hills Have Eyes' has a scene like that. 'Wolf Creek,' too, right? What else? What else? Um... Oh, what about 'House of Wax?' The remake, remember? A lot of people gave it shit because it had

Paris Hilton in it, but it's actually pretty good. We should have a movie–"

"*Simon,*" Terri snapped, just under a shout.

Simon leaned away from the car, then craned his neck to his left to get a better view of his girlfriend. She stood there with her head down, fingertips pressed against her forehead. Her hair hung between her fingers, covering most of her face.

"What's wrong?" he asked as he approached her.

"You're not seriously asking me that."

"What? You have something against Paris Hilton?"

Terri glared at him. Simon stared deadpan at her. They only heard the rustle of the wind blowing through the dry shrubs in the area. The side of Simon's mouth rose in a sly smile and one of his shoulders jumped up in a half-shrug. Terri held her death stare for a moment longer, then gave a one-syllable laugh—'*Ha*'—and shook her head. She was frustrated, she blamed him for their current predicament, but she couldn't stay angry at him.

"We don't have time to talk about horror movies or Paris Hilton," she said.

"Well, technically, you started this conver–"

"Simon, seriously, I need you to listen to me," Terri interrupted. Simon pulled his lips into his mouth and nodded. His girlfriend continued, "We've been stranded in the middle of nowhere for hours. We have no cell phone signal. The last time we saw a car was fifteen, maybe twenty minutes ago, and they didn't even slow down. The sun is setting, so it's going to be pitch-black and freezing out here soon. What are we going to do?"

"I... I don't know what to tell you. I offered to walk to the closest rest stop, but you don't want to stay alone and you don't want to leave the car."

"If I stay alone, what am I supposed to do if some psychopath stops and abducts me? And we can't just leave our car unattended. It has practically *all* of our belongings."

"Hey, I'm not saying I don't agree with your reasoning, I'm just saying you're not leaving me with a lot of options."

"So, you're saying this is my fault?"

"What? No. No, that's not–"

"I told you the car was making some weird noise before our last stop," Terri said, wagging her finger at him. "The mechanic at the garage heard it, too. He offered to take a look and you said no."

Walking back to the front of the car, Simon ran his fingers through his wavy black hair and said, "I thought it was a scam. I was taught to always get second opinions from doctors and mechanics. But, either way, I offered to walk back there and get help earlier, remember?"

"And there you go, blaming me again."

"God, Terri, I'm not blaming you. I just think you're

overreacting. Sooner or later, someone is going to find us. They have to. Besides, isn't this what we wanted? Adventure? It wouldn't be a real road trip without some bumps on the road, right?"

"I don't think it counts as a 'road trip' if we spend more time on the side of the road instead of on it."

Simon started mumbling to himself about the problem. Terri blew back her wispy brown bangs and brought her attention back to the desert. She started to count the cacti in the area to kill time.

One cactus. Two cacti. Three cacti. Four cacti...

The sky darkened and the temperature dropped with each passing minute. Only the hatchback's headlights and hazard lights kept the darkness from swallowing up the stranded travelers.

Terri said, "We should get in the car. There could be some snakes or coyotes out here."

"I think I've almost found the problem."

"Simon, you've been staring at that thing for hours. Let's get in..."

Her voice died out as she turned to face the car. Down the road, far off in the distance, she spied a speck of light. It grew brighter as it moved towards them.

"Simon," she said.

"I heard you. Can you just let me—I don't know—*try* to fix this?"

"I think that's a car. I think someone's coming."

Simon stretched his neck to the right. He saw the approaching light, too. He walked out onto the road. A smile of relief blossomed on his face.

"What are you doing?" Terri called out to him from behind the hatchback.

"I'm getting their attention."

"You're going to get yourself killed. Get off the road."

"They can ignore me if I'm just waving at them from the side of the road. We're out of options and we're desperate. We need them to stop or we're going to be stuck here all night."

"Oh God, you're crazy. If they don't slow down, you *better* get out of the way or you're dead. You listening to me?"

Simon waved a hand at her, as if to say: '*Yeah, yeah, whatever.*' He was confident the vehicle was either going to stop or drive around him. He didn't believe a random driver would intentionally plow through him. But as he watched the vehicle racing towards him, he noticed it was speeding up. He narrowed an eye and touched his chin. Second thoughts crept into his mind. *This is a bad idea,* he told himself.

But he couldn't move—couldn't even breathe. Only his heart was pounding in his chest. His legs felt heavier. His shoulders hitched up to his ears. The smile was wiped off his face.

The couple could see the vehicle was a compact

RV. They heard the rattling and roaring of its engine. The noise softened as the RV slowed down. Simon's shoulders sank as he let out a long breath. Having regained control of his body, he stepped to the side of the road, stopping next to the driver's door. The RV, old and filthy, rolled past them. It was hauling a light-weight travel trailer. It pulled onto the side of the road, parking in front of the hatchback.

"You looked like you were about to shit your pants," Terri said.

"I almost did," Simon responded.

"Well, did you see the driver?"

"N... No. Why?"

"Was he alone?"

"I didn't see anyone, Terri. Why're you asking so many questions?"

As Simon walked over to the front of the hatch-back, Terri followed close behind him and said, "Because that's a creepy-ass RV. If there are a bunch of creeps in there, I don't want to talk to them. Just ask them if they have a working cell phone we can borrow for a few minutes. If they invite you in, do *not* go inside."

"Why?"

Terri grabbed his arm to stop him. They stood next to the trailer. It was dirtier than the RV, covered in streaks of mud, dark splatter stains, and scrapes and dents. The tinted windows appeared to be blocked from inside.

"I know you're not stupid," Terri said. "I also know that you like to 'go with the flow.' Your gut is telling you to catch a ride with them. 'Hitchhiking is part of the adventure. Go for it, dude.' That's what your gut is telling you, right?"

"My gut doesn't call me 'dude,' but yeah, sure, that's *kinda* what I'm thinking."

"Your gut is going to get us into some serious trouble. You've seen 'The Texas Chainsaw Massacre' and 'The Hitcher' and–and like a million other horror movies with hitchhiking and they all end with death."

Simon said, "First of all, those are just movies. Secondly, in those movies, the hitchhikers are the bad guys. And *we're* the hitchhikers in this situation. You got a secret I should know about?" Terri laughed sarcastically and rolled her eyes. Simon put his hands on her shoulders and said, "Let's just see what they're all about before we start making any decisions. C'mon."

He walked over to the RV's camper door. Terri followed him, staying close behind him. They didn't see anyone sitting in the front passenger seat. They could hear *Sing, Sing, Sing* by Benny Goodman playing from somewhere inside of the vehicle. The music was scratchy and crackly, as if playing from a busted speaker.

Simon knocked on the camper door and said, "Hello?"

They heard a commotion in the RV—thuds, creaks, muffled voices. Then the camper door rattled.

"This dang thing is stuck again," a woman said. "Pips! Hey, Pipsqueak! Stop playing with yourself and give a girl a hand over here, will ya?"

Simon and Terri looked at each other, confusion written on their faces, then looked back at the RV. There were more thuds, more creaks, more muffled voices. The door swung open.

A young woman with short blonde hair—permed and stylishly tousled—stood in the doorway. She had a cleft lip and bright blue eyes. Her white dress had vertical red stripes and red pom-pom buttons down the middle. It had two large pockets on the front. Thick white gloves covered her hands.

A large, round, bald black man stood behind her. He was wearing a jumpsuit. The left side of it was black with white polka dots. The right side was white with thin black stripes. Matching his ruff collar, black pom-pom buttons ran down the middle of his costume. He wore white gloves, too. His right ear suffered from permanent perichondrial hematoma—cauliflower ear. From the back of his head to his cheek, jagged scars surrounded his deformed ear.

"Well, hey there," the woman said in a bubbly tone. "Having some car troubles?"

The black man walked to the cockpit. He sat down in the driver's seat, breathing noisily and mumbling unintelligibly.

"Um... yeah?" Simon said with a hint of doubt in his voice, as if he were asking a question.

"What seems to be the problem?"

"Actually, we, uh... we have no idea."

"Dang. Well, we don't have a mechanic on board, so I'm afraid we won't be much help. We can't tow you around, either. We got plenty of room in here, though. How about a ride to the closest rest stop?"

Simon opened his mouth to speak, but before he could get a word out, Terri poked his ribs with her finger and side-eyed him.

He coughed to clear his throat, then said, "We appreciate the offer, but we don't really want to leave our car behind. Do you have a cell phone we could borrow? We can pay you to let us use it."

"Sorry, but we don't own any cell phones. And even if we did, you won't find any signal out here. This is what they call a dead zone."

"Shit," Simon muttered. He looked at Terri and asked, "What do you wanna do?"

Standing on her tiptoes, Terri leaned close to Simon's ear and whispered, "I don't trust these people."

"We don't have a lot of options here."

"Let's just go back to–"

The blonde woman clapped to get the couple's attention, then said, "We gotta go soon. We'd be happy to take you to the closest rest stop or drive you around until you find some signal for your phones, but I'm going to have to take that offer off the table in a minute. Clock's ticking."

Simon said, "Yeah, I'm sorry to keep you waiting. I know you've got places to be, so... I'll go with you." He glanced back at Terri and said, "You can stay in the car. I'll be back as soon as possible, I promise."

"Great!" the blonde woman exclaimed. She took a few steps backwards into the RV, beckoned to him, and said, "C'mon in."

"Wait," Terri said. Simon stopped after taking his first step into the RV and looked back at her. Terri sighed, then said, "I can't stay out here alone. I'm going, too."

"The more, the merrier," the blonde woman responded, simpering.

The RV sped down the empty road. *Take the 'A' Train* by Duke Ellington played through the stereo. The whirring air conditioner circulated the stench of days-old sweat, sulfur, and beef through the vehicle.

"The name's Kelsey," the blonde woman said. "Kelsey Vaughn. But my friends call me Boo-Boo."

She was sitting sideways on a chair in the RV's dinette—a small booth for two. Across from her, Simon and Terri sat next to each other on a tattered two-seat sofa. Limbs stiff and eyes wide, Terri stared unblinkingly at the back of the RV. She had heard something—a few *clacks* and *thuds*—but she hadn't seen anyone. Simon couldn't help but smile. He was amused by the situation.

Boo-Boo pointed at the cockpit and said, "That's our friend, Lloyd. Lloyd..." She puckered her lips and tilted her head, then hollered, "Hey, Lloyd! What's your last name again?"

"Uhhh," the driver groaned in deep thought. "It's, uh... It's Wallace."

"Oh yeah! Thanks!" the blonde woman shouted. Returning to her inside voice, she said, "Sorry about that. He's a little slow. Something about a childhood accident. He's got trouble paying attention 'cause he's always listening to a little song in his head. *Anyway*, we call him Pips. Like Pipsqueak, y'know? It's ironic 'cause he's so big and strong. You can call him that, too, but you gotta win his friendship first. And we can't be friends if we don't know your names, right?"

"That makes sense, I guess," Simon said. "My name is Simon. This is my girlfriend, Terri. It's nice to meet you. We really appreciate what you're doing for us."

"You're very, very welcome, Simon, and it's a plea-sure to make your acquaintance. So, how did the two of you end up in the middle of nowhere?"

The RV bounced and shook with a bump on the road.

Boo-Boo said, "Slow down, Pips. And turn that music down, we have guests."

Muttering to himself, Pipsqueak did as he was told.

Simon started talking about their cross-country trip, which they were documenting for their YouTube channel. Terri's heart sank as she watched a door at the back of the RV swing open slowly. A man—wearing a threadbare tank top and dirty white pants—stood in the bathroom with his back to the door. She could see his slicked-back hair and the side of his face. He appeared to be shaving.

"Who is that?" Terri asked, her voice shaking.

Noticing the unadulterated fear in her eyes, Simon stopped talking. He turned his head, following her gaze to the back of the RV. He narrowed his eyes upon seeing the man in the bathroom.

"Who? Him?" Boo-Boo asked, pointing at the rear of the RV with her thumb. "That's the big boss. Well, the big boss of *our* little crew. I can't tell you his real name, though. Even if we all become besties, I'm afraid I can't tell you that. It's confidential. Just call him Captain Gashes, okay?"

"Captain... Gashes?" Simon repeated, wonderingly.

"Hey, Cap!" Boo-Boo yelled. "You gonna come out and say hi? We've got company, y'know?"

In a deep, raspy, uninterested voice, Captain Gashes responded, "Get 'em some drinks and keep 'em comfortable. I'll be out in a minute."

"Boo-Boo, Captain Gashes, Pipsqueak... What kind of names are those?" Simon asked.

"They're clown names, *duh!*" Boo-Boo said as she sprung to her feet.

She strutted over to the refrigerator in the kitchen next to the dinette. She took two water bottles out, turned around, then kicked the door shut behind her. She threw a bottle at Simon. He caught it. She tossed the other bottle at Terri. Eyes locked on the bathroom, Terri didn't react, so Simon caught it before it could hit her chest.

He put her bottle down on her lap and said, "You okay?"

Boo-Boo returned to her seat and asked, "Haven't you ever heard of a traveling circus?"

"No, not really," Simon answered. "I didn't even know circuses still existed."

"*Ha!* You hear that, Patty? He thought clowns were extinct!"

She spoke to the empty chair across from her in the booth, then she cackled and slammed the table with the bottom of her fist a few times. Eyes on the road, Pipsqueak's shoulders bounced as he snickered. The guests furrowed their brows at the empty seat. Terri's breathing intensified. The grave expression on Simon's face broke as he chuckled. *They're clowns,* he thought. *This is part of their act.*

"So, what's Patty's clown name?" he asked.

Boo-Boo stopped laughing in an instant, sneered at him, and said, "Does she *look* like a clown?"

"Um... I'm not sure."

"What? You need glasses? Or are you trying to make fun of her outfit?"

"N–No, I just... I'm sorry, I'm not sure what's going on or what to say. I've never been to a circus before."

Boo-Boo let out a pent-up breath, then said, "I suppose I can forgive you. It's true after all. Not a lot of people know circuses still exist. We haven't been very popular recently, so I guess I can't blame you for not knowing how to act in our presence. At least you don't hate us, right? *Right?*"

"No, no, of course not."

Simon's voice cracked with the last two words. A nervous wreck, his mouth and throat had dried up. He opened his water bottle and took a swig of his drink. In total disbelief, Terri gaped at him. She was taught to never accept drinks from strangers.

"Good," Boo-Boo said. She glanced at the bathroom upon hearing the running water in the sink, then said, "You wanna know something funny? Captain Gashes doesn't like being a clown. Oh no, he hates it. Our leader *hates* being a clown. Crazy, huh? But you wanna know why he does it?"

"Why?" Simon asked.

"He thinks of our costumes as disguises."

"Disguises? Why would he–"

"What're you telling them?" Captain Gashes interrupted.

He was standing in the bathroom doorway, now facing the RV's occupants. He was clean-shaved. The left side of his face was gnarled with acid-burn scars.

Only half of his left eyebrow grew out. Crow's feet surrounded his eyes. He looked much older than Boo-Boo and a little older than Pipsqueak, but he was stronger than both of them.

Boo-Boo's smile shrank, but she kept a mischievous smirk on her face. The atmosphere in the RV shifted from bizarre to grim.

Captain Gashes entered the cramped kitchen space and, in a monotone voice, he said, "Don't listen to her. I love being a clown. I *want* to love it, I mean. I just haven't found my talent yet. I ain't good at face painting. Can't juggle. Don't have the balance for tightroping. Can't ride a bike, so I can't ride a unicycle either. I don't even know how to make a damn balloon animal."

The couple were at a loss for words. But they shared the same thought: *What the hell is going on?* Captain Gashes sat sideways on the chair across from Boo-Boo.

"Careful, you're sitting on Patty," Simon joked, followed by an awkward laugh.

Giving him a dirty look, Boo-Boo said, "What are you talking about? Patty's in the bathroom. She *just* said she was going."

"Oh, right, um... I was just... I'm sorry, I don't know what I'm saying."

He took another swig of his water. Terri grabbed his forearm with a tight grip. Her eyes said: *Stop it.*

"Is it me or is it getting kinda hot in here?" Simon asked.

"It's you," Captain Gashes and Boo-Boo answered in perfect unison.

"Oh, ye–yeah, I guess you're–"

"Can you let us go?" Terri blurted out.

The clowns in the booth eyeballed her for a quiet moment. Pips drummed his fingers on the steering wheel, his vacant stare fixed to the road.

Captain Gashes huffed, then said, "The door's right there, girl. You can jump out anytime. We're not going to stop you."

"Just make sure you start rolling *before* you land," Boo-Boo said.

"Can you stop the car and let us go?" Terri asked, sounding like she was on the verge of weeping.

Captain Gashes said, "We can do that. No problem, toots, no problem at all. But are you sure you want to be out there all alone at this hour?"

"I–I don't... feel so good," Simon mumbled.

His face, knotted in a pained grimace, turned pale. Cold sweat shimmered on his brow and glistened on his neck. His upper body swung from side to side while his head whirled.

"Ahh, shit, looks like the boy's going to puke," Captain Gashes said before standing up and making his way to the cockpit. "Pull this piece of crap over, Pips."

Terri tugged on Simon's arm and asked, "What's wrong? Hey, what's wrong?" Along with strings of drool, Simon unleashed a stream of incomprehensible chatter from his mouth. Terri looked daggers in Boo-Boo's direction and shouted, "What did you give him?! What did you do to him?!"

"Calm down, calm down," the female clown said, giggling. "He's probably just carsick. Give him some more water."

"No! Fuck no! You... You put something in his drink, didn't you?"

The RV jerked to a stop on the side of the road. Captain Gashes grabbed Simon's arms and lifted him from the sofa.

"What are you doing?!" Terri screeched. "Where are you taking him?!"

"We live here, girl," Captain Gashes said. "He ain't puking in our home. It smells bad enough already."

He kicked the camper door open, then dragged Simon out of the RV. Terri followed them outside, and Boo-Boo followed Terri.

"Stop!" Terri yelled. "Stop it! Let him go!"

"Would you shut your goddamn piehole?!" Captain Gashes brayed as he turned to face her.

Simon slipped out of his arms. He crashed into the side of the RV. It stopped him from falling to the ground. He was still conscious, but his legs looked like they were close to buckling, wobbling wildly. Terri staggered back. She looked over her shoulder at Boo-Boo, then back at the crew's leader. She was sand-wiched between the clowns. There were no other vehi-cles on the road and no people or animals out in the desert—not a soul in sight.

Captain Gashes said, "I'm only taking your pansy excuse for a boyfriend to our trailer. We got a bed in there and a first aid kit. We're going to take care of him. Is that okay with you?"

"I don't think she trusts us very much, Cap," Boo-Boo said.

"Is that so?"

It was absolutely true. Terri didn't trust any of them. She had seen too many horror movies and true crime series to have any faith in complete strangers. The crew's dirty RV and trailer didn't help. Despite appearing black in the moonlight, the dark splatter stains on the trailer started to remind her of streaks of blood. She had never been around a decomposing body, but she was now convinced she had been smelling the awful stench of death inside of the RV.

Captain Gashes said, "If that's the case, you're welcome to join us back there. You're free to supervise us while we take care of your boy. What else can you do? You going to wait out here in the cold—the *freezing* cold—hoping someone else will pass by and offer you a ride? That ain't happen-ing. We're the only 'Good Samaritans' out here. And as Good Samaritans, I'm afraid we can't leave your boyfriend out here with you in this condition."

"That's right," Boo-Boo chimed in. "He deserves so much more than death by hypothermia."

"So, what're you gonna do, buttercup? You coming with us? Or are you gonna abandon your boyfriend?"

Although the clowns hadn't threatened her directly, Terri felt like their lives were in danger. She looked at Simon. She didn't know what was wrong with him, but she knew she couldn't help him out there in the cold, desolate desert. He couldn't run away with her, either. She hated to admit it, but he was a lost cause in his current state—a burden, *a liability*. She told herself that her boyfriend was better off in the trailer with the clowns while she ran to find help.

"Yes," she squeaked out, voice filled with fear and shame.

Captain Gashes chuckled and said, "You're one cold bitch. I like that. I really do." He stopped laughing instantaneously and said, "But we can make you colder. Get her, Boo-Boo."

"With pleasure, Cap," Boo-Boo responded. "I need to put on my makeup first, though. Pips!"

Running backwards into the desert, Terri took a picture of the RV and the trailer with her cell phone. Although blurry due to her shaky hands, it showed Captain Gashes and Boo-Boo standing outside with Simon. Visible through the open camper door, Pipsqueak was caught on camera standing in the RV.

Terri's thought process was simple: If she could show the police the picture, the cops could track the RV down and save Simon.

And if things took a turn for the worse, at the very least, she was hoping it would help identify her captors if she were abducted. She didn't want to believe she was going to die.

She turned and sprinted into the desert. She immediately lost her footing on the rugged terrain, causing her to lurch into the darkest darkness she had ever seen.

Hurling it like a frisbee, Pipsqueak threw a mask out of the RV. Boo-Boo caught it, pulled its strap over the back of her head, then adjusted the mask over her face. It was the perfect fit, as if it were molded from her face. Black makeup was painted around the eyeholes. It dripped down to the mask's cheekbones, like mascara tears. There was no mouth hole, but red lipstick covered its lips. The lipstick spread to the center of her cheeks in a wide, kittenish grin.

She drew a straight razor from a pocket at the back of her dress. With a flick of her wrist, the blade—sharper than a scalpel—swung out of the handle. While Captain Gashes carried Simon into the trailer, the female clown chased after Terri. Holding the straight razor overhead, ready to swing it down at a moment's notice, she giggled and ran with long, confident strides. It wasn't her first time running through a desert.

It wasn't her first time hunting a person, either.

Slipping and sliding, Terri fought to stay on her feet. As her vision adjusted to the darkness, she could make out the mountain skyline off in the distance. She hoped to lose them in the hills. But despite all of her running and scrambling, she felt like she wasn't getting any closer to the mountains. She glanced over her shoulder upon hearing a set of quick footsteps and some maniacal laughter.

She could see Boo-Boo was catching up to her—closer, closer, *closer*. She also spotted another set of headlights on the road. A car cruised down the oncoming lane, heading towards the RV. She went left, hoping to make her way back to the road in a wide arc. She charged through a patch of dried shrubs. She tripped over a stone and fell to her knees but quickly scrambled to her feet and kept running.

"Help!" she screamed, her voice echoing through the desert. "Stop! Don't go! Oh God, please stop! Help us! Help!"

'Help!' Her vocabulary was reduced to that one word, and she kept screaming it over and over while jumping and flailing her arms. She felt a breeze behind her. She couldn't tell if it was the wind or Boo-Boo breathing down her neck. She refused to look back, though, afraid it would only slow her down. With adrenaline and fear coursing through her, her heart was beating fast, her lungs were burning, and her legs were shaking.

She yelped and stumbled as a stinging pain rippled across her upper back. With her handy straight razor, Boo-Boo had slashed her diagonally from right to left. She was running right behind her victim, matching her pace. The clown swung the straight razor at her again, slicing the middle of her back horizontally from left to right. The sharp blade scraped her spine as it tore through her flesh with the utmost ease.

Terri yelped again. She fell forward but continued running on all fours. The cold wind blew through the gaping holes on her shirt, caressing the deep, blazing gashes across her back. Boo-Boo sliced her lower back three more times. Blood flew off the blade in crimson whips with each slash. Although her voice was softened by her mask, she was laughing throughout the attack. They were getting close to the road.

Terri could make out the oncoming vehicle—a station wagon. She stood straight, slowed down, and took a deep breath, preparing to produce the loudest shriek of her life. But before she could make a peep, Boo-Boo rammed her with her shoulder. After side-stepping a few times, Terri lost her balance, her ankle twisting with an audible *pop*. As she plummeted, she caught a brief glimpse of the station wagon rolling past the RV without slowing down. She fell three feet into a ditch full of cacti.

She landed on her right side. The cacti spines—reaching about three-fourths of an inch long—penetrated her arm, her lower abdomen, her hip, and her thigh. The stiff spines came to a stop after hitting bone and cartilage. Some stopped *in* her firm muscles, others skewered her softer muscles entirely. Droplets of blood oozed out of the wounds, like sweat dripping from a pore. Some of the smaller cacti had hairlike spines. They were caught under her skin like splinters of wood—dozens and dozens of splinters.

The slightest movement ignited a flare of unbearable pain across the right side of her body. She felt the spines sink deeper into her flesh and new spines pierce her skin as she sobbed.

Standing at the top of the ditch, Boo-Boo cackled into her hand despite the mask covering her face. She laughed so hard that her upper body swung around like an inflatable tube man at a car dealership. Tears of glee made her eyes glitter in the moonlight. She had to put her hands on her knees to stop herself from falling over. It took her a minute to recompose herself and catch her breath.

She stood up straight, waggled the straight razor at her crying victim, and said, "You gotta have the worst luck in history, lady. You got this *whole* dang desert but you land in a hole full of cacti."

She slapped her knee with her free hand as she laughed some more. She shook her head and waved her hand in front of her masked face, as if to say: '*I'm too much!*' As she calmed herself, she slid down into the ditch. She lunged cautiously over and around the cacti, making her way to Terri. She stood over her victim, one foot at each side of her thighs.

"*Ouchies,*" she whined as a cactus' spine pricked her bare shin. "These things really do hurt, huh? And I thought you were just overreacting."

"Gah... God... Plee–Please don't," Terri cried, trying her best to stay still.

"God? I'm not God, silly. I told ya, my name's Boo-Boo. You wanna know why they call me that?"

"Don't hurt... me. I–I don't wanna die."

Lowering herself to a half-crouch, the clown said, "It's because I see ghosts and ghosts see me. I scare people, too." She glanced at the top of the ditch to her left and said, "Isn't that right, Mick?"

Terri followed Boo-Boo's gaze, weeping in hoarse bellows. There was no one there. She tried to crawl out from under the clown, but she only worsened her pain as the cacti spines wiggled around inside of her.

Speaking to her invisible friend, Boo-Boo said, "That's right. So, what should we do with her? Wanna take her back to the trailer?"

"Simon!" Terri cried. "Help me! Please!"

"No? You think *I* should have some fun?"

"Simon... I–I'm sorry... God, I'm so sorry."

"That *does* sound like a great idea, buddy," Boo-Boo said before turning her attention back to Terri. "Hey, listen up, Mick has a great idea. He's chock-full of 'em. I killed him last year and he's been watching me work ever since then, so he knows all about pain and suffering. Watch this."

"N–No, no, please, no."

Boo-Boo bent over, grabbed the collar of Terri's shirt, then rolled her onto her back. More of the cacti spines spiked her torso. She felt like she was laying on a bed of nails. The wide gashes on her back, opened up by the clown's straight razor, started to tingle. The sensation frightened her.

Numbness was never a good sign.

Boo-Boo pulled on the collar of Terri's shirt again. As the clown swung the straight razor at her, Terri recoiled, looked away, and screamed. Instead of cutting her, however, Boo-Boo tore her shirt open vertically down the middle. Then she cut Terri's bra right down the center, grazing her sternum. The clown pushed her torn bra and shirt aside, revealing her bare torso.

"So far so good," Boo-Boo said.

Although she was in pain and it hurt to move, Terri impulsively crossed an arm over her chest to cover her breasts. She writhed on the cacti, trying to worm away from the killer clown. Seminude and injured, she felt exposed—*violated*—and she knew it was only going to get worse.

She raised a hand at the clown, palm out, and cried, "Please stop! Don't do this! Don't! Stop!"

"Don't stop?" Boo-Boo repeated.

"No! Please–"

"Whatever you say, lady," the clown said with a shrug.

"–stop! Stop it! It hurts! Please, it hurts so much!"

Disregarding her pleas, Boo-Boo used her straight razor to lop off the arm of a cactus. She held the arm in her free hand. The spines cut through her thick glove and stabbed her palm and fingers. Blood dripped out from under the glove, lining her wrist before dribbling down her forearm.

"It's not so bad once you get used to it," she said. "Here, let me give you a hand. Or maybe I should say 'let me give you an *arm*.' You get it? Because it's a cactus arm! Ha!"

"Help me! Help–"

Boo-Boo swung the cactus arm at Terri's chest. Four spines penetrated the top of her right breast. Terri shrieked and slapped it away. The spines were left in her tit. Boo-Boo swung the cactus arm at her again. She struck her victim's forearm, leaving a spine sticking out of her muscle. Again, Terri swatted the plant away. She started punching and kicking the clown.

"What are you doing?!" Boo-Boo yelled in frustration. "You're ruining my act, dang it!"

She swung the straight razor at her. The blade tore the outer side of Terri's left forearm open horizontally —from her wrist to her elbow. Her pulsing muscles, purple veins, and pieces of her bone were visible in the gaping gash. Blood sprayed out of the wound as she swung her limp arm around frantically, huge drops splashing on her chest and face as well as the cacti and soil.

The clown jumped forward and stepped on Terri's left elbow, pinning her arm to the ground. She swung the cactus arm at her victim's other breast. Three spines entered her tit. One of them went straight through the center of her erect nipple. A drop of blood seeped out of it. Two more spines penetrated her left breast with Boo-Boo's next swing.

Once all of the spines were detached from one side of the cactus arm, Boo-Boo rotated it a little, then continued beating her. And when Terri used her arm or hand to cover one breast or the other—or both— she swung around her defenses. Clearly having a blast, she acted like she was playing a game of Whac-A-Mole.

Whac-A-Tit.

Terri felt like she was being pummeled with a branch. Dozens of spines were buried deep amongst the thin layers of fat and lobules in her breasts. Blood leaked out of some of the puncture wounds, rolling out like red teardrops. Her tits were covered in red welts and patches of petechiae—tiny, bloody dots.

Heavy breathing and a barrage of footsteps interrupted the beating.

Boo-Boo tossed the cactus arm aside and looked to her left. Vision blurred by her tears, Terri stared at the night sky. The stars appeared to jitter. Her eyes moved to her right as the footsteps came to a stop. Her face twisted with anguish. The tears spilled out of her eyes, crawling over the bridge of her nose and down the side of her face.

Pipsqueak stood at the top of the ditch, hunched over as he fought for air. He was holding a fire axe.

"What's up?" Boo-Boo asked.

Panting with each pause, Pipsqueak said, "We... gotta... go. Mar... Mars... Marshall says–"

"Captain Gashes, you doofus. Don't forget his rules. He doesn't want you saying his real name."

"Oh, yeah... yeah... Captain Gashes... He says we can't stay here no more. Can't stay... in the open. Gotta keep moving."

"Dang, I was just getting started. Oh well, I guess he's right. Can't get caught before the big night. Dead-face wouldn't like that."

"Nope."

Boo-Boo beckoned to him and said, "Get down here and give me a hand. We need to finish the job."

Pipsqueak slid down into the ditch. He nearly lost his footing but Boo-Boo pushed him back with her elbow to stop him from falling on top of Terri.

Pips asked, "Can I do it now?"

"Do what you do best, big guy," Boo-Boo replied.

Staring up at the clowns, Terri said, "Simon... Ma–Mom, Dad... I–I'm sorry."

Holding it with both hands, Pipsqueak raised the fire axe overhead. He waited three seconds—three seconds that felt like three minutes—then he swung the axe down. The blade hit her neck with a loud, wet *thump*. Her head tilted back, hanging over a barrel cactus, and she squeezed her eyes shut tightly.

She unintentionally bit down on the tip of her tongue as she ground her teeth, severing it. Blood spumed out of her mouth and came out of her nose.

Pipsqueak stepped on her upper chest, just above her spiked breasts, and yanked the axe out. Her neck was open in a big, meaty fissure. More blood geysered out of the large wound while her head swung limply to and fro. Her cervical vertebrae had shattered. Only some muscles kept her head attached to her neck.

Yet, her eyes appeared to be moving under her sealed eyelids. Gurgling and hissing noises came out of the wide wound on her neck.

As Pipsqueak raised the fire axe overhead, preparing for a second swing, Boo-Boo said, "Hold on a sec. Look. She's still alive." Pips looked uninterested, keeping the axe up and ready. The female clown asked, "What do you think she's thinking about?"

She figured she was thinking about something deep, like her life, the frailty of humans, or her next destination. The truth was, Terri wasn't thinking about anything at all. Although she was still alive, it had all gone black. She had already reached the point of no return.

"Want me to stop?" Pipsqueak asked.

Boo-Boo watched their victim for another ten

seconds. The gurgling sounds continued but her eyes stopped moving.

"She's gone," she said. "Go for it, you lug."

Pipsqueak swung the fire axe down. Terri was decapitated. Her head bounced on the ground a few times before settling next to a bloodstained barrel cactus. Pipsqueak grabbed it by the hair, then waddled out of the ditch.

"Wait," Boo-Boo said.

"Huh?" Pipsqueak answered, stopping at the top of the ditch.

"We should bring one more souvenir. Y'know, something for her boyfriend. I've got the perfect idea."

She plucked one of the cactus spines from Terri's left breast, then she unbuckled the victim's pants and pulled them down.

***

Although heavy with sleep, Simon's eyes flickered open to a blur. His nostrils flared as he drew some snorting breaths. He caught a whiff of the stench of decay. The corners of his mouth were wet with drool. A cold sweat coated the rest of his body. His concern grew as he noticed his fast heartbeat.

He mumbled, "Wha–What... Where... What's..."

He couldn't think straight, so he couldn't finish a sentence. He began to find his bearings as his vision came into focus. A cracked mirror—covered in dark brown spatter stains—was installed on the ceiling. He could see he was naked and lying down on an examination table, which resembled a gynecological bed.

It was mounted to the floor, but it jiggled and creaked with every movement. His legs were strapped to the elevated footrests with his feet locked into a set of stirrups. His arms were tied to the armrests at the biceps, crooks of his elbows, and wrists. Belts strapped his body to the bed at the waist and chest.

"What the fuck?" he muttered.

He glanced to his left, then to his right. The room was small. Mirrors—dirtier than the one on the ceiling—were installed on the walls with shelves fixed underneath them. The shelves were filled with tools—hammers, screwdrivers, hatchets, pliers—as well as an unusual assortment of personal belongings—wallets, cell phones, hats, Polaroids, a magic wand, a magician's hat.

A cage sat on one of the shelves. A white rabbit rested inside of it, surrounded by his droppings. He nibbled on strands of Timothy Hay.

Simon finally looked straight ahead. His pupils dilated with fear. Captain Gashes sat on an unsteady stool in front of the bed. His face was now smeared with white makeup. He had applied it sloppily, leaving some parts of his forehead and jaw exposed. Black makeup surrounded his eyes.

He dipped his index and middle fingers into a red liquid in a bucket at his feet. Then he used the liquid to paint a smile over his neutral lips—from the center of one cheek to the other.

It didn't take Simon much longer to connect the pieces. He was in the clowns' trailer. And when that realization set in, he saw the bigger picture. He remembered the things he spoke about with his parents and friends in high school, rumors he read on social media, pictures he saw on the news. He recognized the clown sitting before him.

As Captain Gashes wiped his hands with a dirty rag, Simon asked, "Are you going to kill me?"

"I'm guessing you know who I am now," Captain Gashes answered as he tossed the rag over his shoulder at the corner of the trailer. "What gave it away? I know it wasn't this stupid fucking clown makeup. It wasn't my face or my voice, either. You would have been shitting bricks as soon as you saw me if it was. No, let me guess... It's this room, right?"

After a short moment of silence between the men, Simon gave a slight nod.

Captain Gashes said, "I haven't used this trailer since I went into hiding... Ten years ago? Maybe eleven? It hasn't changed much since then. I have a roommate now." He pointed at the rabbit, then said, "Boo-Boo calls him Marshmallow. Says it goes with my name—my real name. Don't mind him, though. We're saving him for a special trick. Now you... You got one hell of a memory, boy. Or maybe I got myself one hell of a reputation. Shit was getting too hot for me back then, though. I had to change my MO. Had to go into hiding for a while. Let me tell you, there ain't no better place to hide than the circus."

Captain Gashes' real name was Marshall Mann. He was a 49-year-old serial killer with a body count of 29. He enjoyed torturing victims in his trailer, which he previously kept parked in an abandoned junkyard. But his thirtieth victim escaped before he could finish the job, leading to a nationwide manhunt for him. He vanished with his trailer before he could get caught.

Captain Gashes continued, "I'm not the biggest fan of these clowns' methods, though. They like to perform in front of an audience. They like public spectacles. I like a more... private, personal, *intimate* experience myself. Guess that's why they only gave me a taste of blood every now and then. Maybe that's why they didn't put me on the Vegas crew." He cast his eyes down at the floor and muttered, "They said I was too well known. Said I couldn't blend in 'cause of my past. Said I wasn't 'inconspicuous' enough. So they lumped me in with 'The Rejects.' That's some bullshit. They got motherfuckers with dyed eyes and fake horns and spiked mohawks heading out there. They call that 'inconspicuous?' Fucking amateurs. They just didn't want me there because they don't think I'm as good as them."

Simon wasn't sure what he was rambling about. Only one name was swirling around in his head.

"Did you... kill Terri?" Simon asked in a weepy voice.

"Terri?" Captain Gashes repeated as he brought his gaze back to his captive. "You're talking about your lady?"

"Yes."

"You want the truth?"

"Yes," Simon said, now holding his breath with anticipation.

"I didn't lay a finger on that girl," Captain Gashes said before pausing for dramatic effect and adding, "but Boo-Boo and Pips sure had a good time with her."

Simon shut his eyes, sending tears cascading down his cheeks. He didn't need it spelled out for him. Before he even asked the question, he knew the answer in his gut. He blamed himself for Terri's murder. *Why didn't I listen to her?* he asked himself repeatedly.

Captain Gashes said, "At least they brought you a souvenir. Look. Hey, lookie here, boy."

Simon's eyes cracked open. Captain Gashes snatched a glass off a shelf to his right. It had about two ounces of blood in it. Inside of it, there was a cactus spine. And impaled at the end of it, there was a pea-sized piece of human flesh, like an olive on a skewer in a martini.

He took the cactus spine out, held it out in front of his prisoner, and said, "This is your lady's clitoris."

A sob escaped Simon's tight, dry throat. Then he retched and looked to his right. But he could still see the clown and the glans of his girlfriend's clitoris speared on the cactus spine through the mirror. He looked to his left, then up, but he couldn't escape the sight. He had to close his eyes.

With a smile tugging at his lips, Captain Gashes said, "Don't be like that. Hey, if it's any consolation, they didn't snip it off until *after* they beat her tits with a cactus and chopped her fucking head off."

"Fuck," Simon whimpered.

"Look at me. Open your eyes, boy. Open 'em or I'll skull-fuck you."

Simon opened his eyes to slits. Captain Gashes put Terri's severed clitoris on his lip, then slurped it into his mouth. Unable to keep them open, Simon closed his eyes again and turned his head.

"Now you fucked up," Captain Gashes said as he gnawed on the clitoris, blood squirting out from between his teeth.

He threw his head back and swallowed the flesh in a loud gulp, then pounced on him and grabbed his captive's flaccid penis. Simon's eyes flew open. He wiggled his hips and screamed. The clown held the cactus spine up to his penis. He was aiming for his urethra, but due to Simon's frenzied movements, he pricked the guy's glans. The hot pain in his cock made him panic, and panic made him twist and turn. The cactus spine pierced the head of his penis four more times.

Captain Gashes tightened his grip on the shaft of

his penis, jerked it towards him to limit Simon's movement, then adjusted his aim and slid the cactus spine into the urethra.

One fourth of an inch.

Half an inch.

Three fourths of an inch.

Only a microscopic piece of the cactus spine stuck out of his rosy urethra. The other end came out of the shaft of his penis, right under the glans. A droplet of blood oozed out of his urethra, joining the other drops on his glans.

As Simon howled in pain, Captain Gashes said, "You best start listening to me, boy. I'd love to tear you apart piece by piece, but you ain't my target. We don't have to do this the hard way. No, siree. You see, we're looking for something bigger than two dumbass backpackers. Now I may have my disagreements with the man and his following, but Deadface has sent us—and others like us—out into the word to make a statement. And it's one I agree with: The world deserves chaos. So, I need someplace to stir up some shit. I need a motel, a hotel, a villa, a fucking small town. I need somewhere with pussies like you that I can fuck until they tear and bleed. So, tell me: Where were you staying?"

Simon had dissolved into a blubbering mess, squirming and weeping and babbling incoherently. Only some of his words were intelligible. Piecing them together, it sounded like he was saying: *'Take... it... out!'*

"You act like I cut your cock off, you pussy," the clown said. "You wanna feel pain? You wanna feel *real* suffering? I'll give you a taste."

He snatched a pair of vise-grip pliers off a shelf. He leaned over Simon and held the vise-grip close to his chest. Before he could make his move, the RV took a turn, causing the clown to stagger. A screwdriver, a wallet, and a flip phone fell from a shelf. Something rolled behind the examination table. After steadying himself, the clown brought the vise-grip back to his victim's chest. Simon's eyes were closed, so he didn't see it coming.

Captain Gashes closed the vise-grip over his captive's left nipple. Simon's eyes bulged as a sharp, tingly pain shot through his chest. Captain Gashes tightened the vise-grip's jaws by turning the adjustment knob, then he rotated his wrist to twist Simon's nipple. With the same motion, he contorted the fat on his pectoral muscle, amplifying his pain tenfold. The clown squeezed the vise-grip until he heard a *click*, then he yanked the tool back towards him.

Simon's nipple, areola, and a chunk of skin were torn off with a *shredding* noise, leaving a crater of bloody, mushy flesh on his chest. Blood ran down his soft stomach in two squiggly lines. As his victim cried louder, Captain Gashes loosened his grip on the tool and sucked the nipple into his mouth. Savoring each bite, he chewed it unhurriedly—*casually*—like a big piece of flavorful gum.

"Let's try this again," he said.

He opened the vise-grip, then closed it over the shaft of Simon's penis. The blades nicked it. The pain was mild compared to his other injuries, but *any* pain around his groin was enough to send his mind into a frenzy. He gasped, putting an end to his hysterical sobbing, then he started sniveling and shuddering and swinging his head.

"No, no, no, no, no," he whined.

"Where were you staying?"

"N–No, no–"

"Where were you staying?!"

"No–Nowhere... We–Were... wandering. It was a... our road trip before graduation. We slept in cheap hotels and–and in the car. We couch-surfed. We stayed... at a friend's house in Victorville before coming here. Victorville, California. Tha–That was the... the last place."

"Wandering? You got millions of miles of road in this whole damn country and you 'wander' right into our RV. Ain't that a bitch?"

"You're going to kill me," Simon said in a surprisingly matter-of-fact tone.

Ignoring him, Captain Gashes said, "All right. I ain't turning this piece of shit around and going back to California. I need to be close to the action. So, where were you headed?"

"Goldbrush."

"Goldbrush? Where the hell is that?"

"It's a... Shit, it hurts... It's a small town. In the desert. South of Vegas. Southeast, I think."

"How small?"

"I–I don't know. I've never been there. They say only, like... like forty or fifty people live there. Hikers go there... during the day. We... Me and Terri... We were going to go out there to hike the trails. We were going to make a new video."

"Goldbrush," Captain Gashes said as he nodded, taking a mental note.

Simon stuttered, "If–If you're going to... to kill me... can you... let me call my mom? Please?"

The clown chuckled, then asked, "You serious?"

"Please?"

"Why would I let you do that? So, you can tell her a wanted serial killer is on the loose? So, you can tell her a killer clown is about to kill ya? Huh? You think I'm stupid?"

"I... I text her every night before I sleep. I promised her I–I would do it before I left home. I just... I want to tell her that I can't message her anymore. Tha–That I can't see her anymore. That I'm okay but... I have to go away."

Captain Gashes stared deadpan at him in a period of uncomfortable silence. The trailer jounced as it rolled over a pothole. Again, something bounced behind the examination table, thudding and clunking.

"I'll tell you what," the clown said. "I've got your ID. I know where you live. After we're done with this whole shindig—I'm talking about the whole shebang —I'll go over to your place and send your mom to hell so she can visit you. I'll send your whole damn family."

"No, please, I'm–"

Captain Gashes squeezed the vise-grip's handles. The jaws pierced the shaft of Simon's penis at the base. Blood bubbled out of the cuts, soaking his trimmed pubic hair and flowing across the grooves of his scrotum. As his victim convulsed and screamed, the clown turned and wiggled the vise-grip, widening the wound. Blood spurted out of his irritated urethra like semen during an explosive orgasm.

Head tilted back and eyes rolling up, Simon's cries turned to weak croaks. He passed out and went silent.

While squeezing the vise-grip with all of his might, Captain Gashes pulled on Simon's cock. It stretched, then tore off. Simon awoke to a ball of electrifying pain bouncing around his pelvis, back and forth between his hips. One of his testicles retracted into his lower abdomen. Both of them ached. He watched as blood squirted out from the small, fleshy stump protruding from his crotch. He tried to scream but only a guttural groan came out of his mouth.

The RV slowed down, then sped up. Terri's severed head came rolling out from behind the examination table, stopping at the clown's feet.

Grinning, Captain Gashes said, "Look who it is."

Grabbing it by the hair, he lifted the head from the floor, then held it out in front of Simon. Simon kept trying to cry and scream, but he could only draw some hiccupping gasps while twisting and turning in agony.

The clown said, "She didn't want to miss the grand finale. Guess she wanted to see you get a taste of your own medicine."

He lunged forward and forced the amputated penis into Simon's mouth. He jammed his fingers in there, too, making sure to push the cock deep into his throat —bloody, deep-throating autofellatio. Simon swung his head around as he suffocated on his own penis. He looked like he was trying to puke it out, but it was lodged in there.

Captain Gashes dropped Terri's head. It rolled under the examination table. He watched Simon with satisfaction, waiting patiently for the life to leave his body. Simon stopped moving after two minutes of struggling. There was only the sound of blood *plopping* inside of the trailer.

Captain Gashes took a walkie-talkie out of his pocket, pressed the push-to-talk button, and said, "Boo-Boo, you still got that map up there?"

After about fifteen seconds of silence, Boo-Boo responded, "Yup. You got a plan, Cap?"

"Look for a place called Goldbrush. Should be south or southeast of Vegas. Tell Pips to get us there before the big night."

"Got it. You all done back there? Wanna make a quick stop?"

"Not yet. I'll let you know when I'm ready."

"All righty then."

Captain Gashes put the walkie-talkie back in his pocket, then grabbed a bloodstained cleaver from a shelf to his right. He swung it at Simon's neck, starting the decapitation process.

The rabbit in the corner continued nibbling on its hay as he watched the beheading with an empty stare.

2

WELCOME TO GOLDBRUSH

Every Breath You Take by The Police ended abruptly mid-verse. Angelina Navarro stopped in her tracks and sighed in annoyance, her hiking boots rooted in the dirt. She plucked the Bluetooth earbuds out of her ears and took her cell phone out of her pocket. Since her earbuds were no longer connected to her phone, she knew the batteries had been drained.

"Shit," she muttered.

She popped the earbuds into a charging case, then shoved it into her pocket. She turned her attention back to her phone. On the status bar, a message read: *No Service*. The clock showed: *10:15 AM*. She had been walking for over an hour and a half after a two-hour bus ride to the trailhead parking lot.

She lowered her phone and surveyed the area. Through the heat haze rising from the ground, she saw nothing but dirt, dry shrubs, cacti, a handful of trees, and mountains far in the distance. Ahead of her, she saw two rippling humanoid figures on the same trail. It was an older couple, hiking side by side.

If she hadn't seen them earlier in her journey, she would have assumed they were wild animals or a mirage.

Although there were no paved roads out there, tire tracks lined the hiking trail. There were more tire tracks out in the desert, too. Only the locals knew how to safely navigate the desert in vehicles. She hadn't seen a car since she left the trailhead parking lot, though. She put her phone back in her pocket, slipped her fingers under the straps of her backpack, then continued marching forward.

She knew the area well. It wasn't her first time there, but she was hoping it would be her last.

Angelina was a twenty-year-old woman. She was wearing a long-sleeved gray shirt—pits dark with sweat—and khaki hiking pants. Her sun hat protected her face and neck. A few locks of her short black hair stuck out from under the hat. Thin bangs covered her forehead. Her septum was pierced with a horseshoe ring.

After walking for about fifteen minutes, she started to make out the shapes of small buildings in the heat haze. A deep pang of anxiety slowed her legs down and sped her heartbeat up. She hadn't been to the town since she left her home to attend boarding school at the age of thirteen. Although she was supposed to return home after graduating, she decided to stay in the city.

She chatted with her younger brother, Gilbert, through social media often and occasionally exchanged a few emails with her father, Kurt. She hadn't communicated with her mother, Heather, at all in over two years, though.

She walked past a sign on the side of the trail. In all capital letters, a message read: *WELCOME TO GOLD-BRUSH*. Under it, an arrow pointed straight into town.

As she approached, a white pickup truck rolled out from the other side of a building. It turned, then cruised her way. The truck came to a stop next to her. She didn't recognize it. If she were in the city, she would have kept walking and prepared her pepper spray—just in case. But she trusted the people of Gold-brush. The community had always been close-knit and welcoming.

The truck's passenger window rolled down.

"No way," the guy in the driver's seat said, smiling. He took his sunglasses off, leaned over the center console, and said, "Angie?"

Returning the smile, Angelina squinted at him and angled her head to the side. She studied the guy's face —well-defined, clean-shaved, bronzed, young—for a short while. She pointed a finger gun at him as her eyes and mouth widened.

"Danny?" she said with a hint of uncertainty. "Danny Paddock?"

"The one and only. Holy shit, I haven't seen you since... since middle school, right?"

"Yeah. You were one year below me, but we still had the same teacher."

In perfect unison, they said, "Mrs. Padilla."

They shared a laugh of comfort. Angelina's shoulders slackened as her anxiety waned. Danny's eyes went to the straps of her backpack, then to her sun hat.

He said, "Don't tell me you hiked all the way out here?"

"I did," Angelina responded with a shrug.

"Seriously? I could have picked you up. I'm in and out of here almost every day."

"I don't have your number, smart guy," Angelina said playfully.

"You could have called your dad and he could have let me know."

Angelina pulled her lips into her mouth and cast her eyes at the ground. Her anxiety returned with a grip on her neck, turning her throat into a pinhole. She glanced over at the town and wondered if her family had already spotted her. She could see the back of the local convenience store—*Goldbrush Essentials*. There was a shed across from it. A few hikers walked down the paths.

"They don't know I'm back," she said.

Danny sucked his teeth, then said, "Family business. I get it. Say no more. So, are you planning on staying overnight?"

"I'm not sure yet."

"I think the teacher is renting one of the rooms at the Bunkers' lodge this week. It's some new guy. There should be a vacant room, though. The tourists don't really stay overnight. They're just here for some pictures, you know, so you might have some luck there if you don't want to stay at your parents' place. And if you don't have anywhere else to go, I'll be back later in the afternoon, so let me know and I can ask my mom to let you bunk over at her place or I can give you a ride to a motel out of town. I know some decent places."

"Oh Danny, I can't ask you to do something like that. Wasting hours going back and forth just for me, that's crazy. I can take care–"

"Hey, it's no big deal, all right?" Danny interrupted. "I come in and out of here all the time to make sure my mom gets her glaucoma meds. And I know you can take care of yourself. You can make your own choice later and I'll respect it. I mean, I don't know if I can just let you walk out there in the desert alone at night—I don't know *anyone* who would take that hike—but... Just let me leave that offer on the table for you, okay? For old times' sake."

Angelina had some great memories with Danny. Although she was a year older than him, they played together when they were kids, they finished their homework together, and they chatted with each other all the time from each other's homes using walkie-talkies. Their families were close, too. She could tell he was still a nice, honest person.

She nodded at him and said, "Thanks."

"No problem," Danny said. "I'll give you my number when I get back, so don't leave without saying goodbye, all right?"

"I won't. I promise."

"I'll see you later then. Good luck, Ange."

Angelina waved at him and watched as he drove away. She took a deep breath before marching on. Upon entering the town, she felt an unusual mix of nostalgia and dread.

Goldbrush mostly consisted of houses separated by swathes of desert and short stone partitions. There were a few outhouses along the outskirts of town. The convenience store provided the residents with processed foods and other household essentials. It was connected to an out-of-business firework shop called 'Goldbrush Sparks.' There was a school for students from kindergarten to eighth grade. There was a police field office, a restaurant and a café, a community garden, and a lodge with four rooms.

As part of a plan to expand thanks to investments from the town's wealthy Bunker family, a historical village was under construction and another lodge was in development—although the latter hadn't broken ground yet.

Angelina knew her way to her parents' house. The town hadn't changed much over the years after all. But she wasn't ready to face them. Wanting to waste some time, she waltzed into Goldbrush Essentials, the door chime ringing as she pushed the door open. Right away, she recognized the man standing behind the counter to her left—Ben Jones, the owner. He was skimming through some sheets of paper on a clipboard.

He was a fifty-five-year-old man with a thick peppered goatee. His long black hair—streaked with gray—stretched below his shoulders. He had an approachable demeanor.

"Welcome," he said.

He glanced her way, then did a double take. He put the clipboard down on the counter next to the cash register. There was a twinkle of happiness in his eye.

Angelina smiled and waved at him, then went down the aisle to her right, walking past a freezer chest loaded with ice cream, shelves filled with household goods and snacks, and racks stacked with magazines. She stopped at the end of the aisle. The *House of the Dead* 2 light-gun arcade cabinet in the corner was off. She remembered playing the game with her dad, her younger brother, and Danny when she was a kid.

She took a water bottle out of the fridge in front of her, then made her way around the store. She walked next to the wall of refrigerators. At the back of the shop, the wall was lined with old but functioning slot machines. She made her way back to the cash register. The wall behind the checkout counter was covered by a rack filled with cigarette packs. Above the rack, she spotted a double-barreled shotgun hanging on a wall mount. The mere sight of the gun made her skin crawl.

I hope you never have to use that thing, she thought.

Ben was smiling now. Angelina shook off her jitters. She put the bottle down between them, then put her elbows on the counter and leaned forward. Her mannerisms hadn't changed.

"Yeah, it's me," she said.

"Well, I'll be damned," Ben said. "I didn't think I'd ever see you again, little one."

"I'm not so little anymore."

"You'll always be a 'little one' to me, kid. Where've you been?"

He scanned her water bottle, then slid it closer to her.

Angelina took her wallet out of her pocket and said, "I, um... decided to stay in the city after graduation. I took some classes at the community college. I didn't get a degree or anything, but... I'm still working on it—on me."

She put two one-dollar bills on the counter and slid them towards him. Ben took her money, then handed her a receipt before putting her change in her hand.

He said, "That's really good to hear."

"Really?" Angelina responded, her brow furrowed. "You're not going to give me some speech about abandoning the town and my family and the people?"

"Of course not. If you ask me—and don't tell your

mother because she's made it clear that she's *not* asking me—I think you made the right choice."

Angelina was speechless, but from the befuddled expression warping her face, Ben could tell she wanted to ask something along the lines of: '*Are you serious?*'

"Goldbrush is a nice place to grow into an adult and shrink into an elder," the clerk said. "But it's not the best place for young adults like yourself. You spent, what? Thirteen years here before you left?"

Angelina nodded.

Ben said, "You've seen enough of these deserts. You deserve to see the rest of the world and explore every opportunity that comes your way. *You* are the future after all. You know we love you like family and we can always use another helping hand around here, but we can't keep you for ourselves. Why limit yourself to benefiting 40 people when you have the potential to touch—to help—40 million? Or more?"

Angelina had been beating herself up for days prior to heading out to Goldbrush. She had prepared herself for an onslaught of hate and disappointment from the residents. She wasn't very surprised by Danny's kindness because they were the same age. She figured he would understand her decision more than anyone else. Ben's support caught her off guard because he was an elder. His belief in her helped her believe in herself.

She felt a burst of confidence surge through her.

She looked up at the ceiling, hoping the laws of gravity would stop her tears of joy from spilling out.

"Thank you," she said.

The door chime rang. Two hikers, drenched in sweat and breathing harshly, entered the convenience store.

Angelina wagged the water bottle at Ben and said, "I'll swing by again before I leave. Have a good one, okay?"

"You too, Angie," Ben said. "Let me know if you need anything. You know where to find me."

As she walked away, the hikers approached the counter. They exchanged pleasantries, then the tourists asked for directions to some sightseeing spots in the area. With her newfound sense of determination, Angelina exited the store and set out on the dirt paths leading to her parents' house on the other side of town.

3

———————

THE REUNION

Angelina stood before the front gate and examined her parents' house. With a creamy yellow exterior, it stood two stories tall with an attached garage. The front lawn was light green with some shades of yellow. A gray pickup truck with a camper cap was parked in the driveway. The home hadn't been renovated since she left the town. It looked a little smaller than what she remembered, though.

She pushed the front gate open. The hinges squealed. The noise sparked memories of her childhood.

'*Mom, I'm back!*' she heard an echo of a young version of her voice at the back of her head.

She strolled over to the front porch. She put her finger on the doorbell, stalled for a few seconds, then pressed it.

DING-DONG.

And then the waiting game began. Behind her, the chatter from the hikers on the dirt paths faded away. The wind stopped blowing, too. She only heard her heartbeat and it was so loud—so clear—that it sounded like it was coming from somewhere outside of her body. She felt every bead of sweat crawling down her forehead and neck. She stared at the peephole, wondering if someone was watching her.

"Mom, I'm back," she whispered, voice barely audible.

The front door swung open. Her thirteen-year-old brother, Gilbert, stood there. He looked like he had just woken up, wearing a wrinkled white t-shirt and a pair of flannel pajama pants. His eyes grew large as he recognized his sister.

"Angie!" he exclaimed.

He grabbed her in a tight hug. Angelina laughed as she tottered back, close to falling off the porch. His thick curly black hair, which grew out like a bicorne hat, tickled her jaw. She wrapped her arms around him and guided him back to the doorway.

"It's good to see you, too," she said.

As they leaned away from each other, Gilbert asked, "Why didn't you tell me you were coming?"

"I wanted to keep a low profile and I know you can't keep a secret, remember?"

"What? I never told anyone that you were the one that clogged the toilet at Danny's house."

Angelina's eyes sharpened and she said, "Shut. *Up.*"

Gilbert cackled while his sister pretended to punch him. Then she started laughing with him. She felt embarrassed, Gilbert knew exactly how to humiliate her, but she didn't mind. It was part of being a family. Although they had stayed in contact, it felt good to *see* and *hug* her brother for the first time in over half a decade.

"I can't believe you still remember that," she said as they settled down. "So, uh... Mom and Dad... They home?"

"Dad's here. Mom's at the garden."

"The backyard?"

Gilbert said, "No, I mean, the community garden in town. The one they started when you were gone. She's, I don't know, 'gardening' with Mrs. Holt, I guess." He glanced over his shoulder and shouted, "Dad! Angie's here!"

"Hey, what're you doing? I need a minute to... to get ready."

"Get ready? For what? It's just dad."

"Yeah, but I need to think about what I'm going to..."

Her voice drifted off as she heard the footsteps behind her brother. Her father, Kurt, emerged from an archway to the right. He was a tall, burly man with long, wavy hair and bronzed skin. The second he saw his daughter, a big smile spread across his face—the type of smile that looked painful to hold.

Just as she opened her mouth to speak, he seized

her in a bear hug, lifting her from her feet and spinning her around. She tittered with childlike joy and she couldn't hold back her tears anymore.

"I missed you so much," Kurt said as he set her back down on the porch.

He kissed her forehead, then pulled her in for another hug.

"I missed you, too," Angelina said, sniffling as she unintentionally wiped her wet face on her father's flannel shirt. "I'm sorry. I'm sorry for–"

"No, no, no," Kurt interrupted. "We're not going to start with that. C'mon, let's go inside. I'll get you a drink and we can sit and talk. You must be exhausted from the trip."

"Need help with your bag?" Gilbert asked.

"No, um... thanks," Angelina responded, fighting off an urge to bawl her eyes out. "I've got it. I've got this."

Angelina sat at the round kitchen table across from her father. She had removed her sun hat and backpack. Her fingers were curled around a glass of water. Kurt couldn't stop smiling, eyes bright with amazement. Gilbert was leaning against the archway behind them, hands in his pajama pockets. Every now and then, a drop from the leaky sink faucet interrupted the awkward silence in the room.

"I like the ring," Kurt said, pointing at his daughter.

Angelina touched her nose piercing, as if she had forgotten it was there, then said, "Thank you."

"It makes you look like a bull," Gilbert commented. Angelina and Kurt looked his way. The boy shrugged and said, "What? I didn't say it was a bad thing. It's cool."

"Anyway," Kurt said before turning his attention back to his daughter and continuing, "how've you been, Ange?"

"I'm... doing well," Angelina responded.

"You have to tell me more than that. What are you up to these days? How's life in the city?"

"I, um... I've been taking classes at a community college. Mostly math and history and science and... the basics, y'know? I took some business classes, too, but I don't really know what I'm going to focus on yet. I never really thought about the future—my future— until after I went to boarding school, so I don't really know what I want to be."

Gilbert squinted an eye at his sister. He had goals— pass his classes, stay close to his best friend, beat a couple of video games—but he hadn't thought about his future much. He loved creating things, though. He had always wanted to develop his own video game, but he never saw it as a potential career.

Kurt said, "You're still young, honey. You might feel like you're running out of time, but you've got your whole life ahead of you. Remember, life isn't a race. You don't have to compete with anyone."

"I know," Angelina said with a trace of doubt in her voice.

"How about outside of your school life? You got a job? Maybe a special someone I should meet?"

"Didn't you used to like that guy, Justin?" Gilbert asked.

Angelina made a *tsk* noise with her mouth, then rolled her eyes and said, "Oh, shut up."

"What? Mom used to say she thought you two were going to get married whenever you guys came back from studying. He's back in town now, too. He's a cop. He's got a gun but he never lets me hold it."

Kurt said, "Didn't I tell you to stop asking him?"

"I'm not gonna do anything bad with it. I just wanna blast some birds."

"You're not going to 'blast' anything. Guns aren't toys and birds aren't–"

"Dad," Angelina interrupted, eyes glued to the table. "I'm sorry, but I didn't come here to talk about school or work or my nonexistent love life."

The kitchen fell silent again with only a *plop* in the sink from the leaky faucet every few seconds.

"I reckoned you weren't here for a reunion," Kurt said. "You would have called beforehand if you were. So, what's on your mind, darling? You in any trouble?"

No matter how hard she tried, Angelina couldn't speak. The ever-growing lump in her throat blocked her voice. She lifted her glass to take a sip of her water, but it almost slipped out of her hand. She wasn't sure if it was because of sweat from her palm or the beads of condensation clinging to the glass. She tightened her grip and took a swig.

She said, "Can we talk in private before…"

Her voice fell away as she heard the front door open. Taking her sweet time, she turned her head to look through the archway. The door closed, then a lock *clicked*. She followed the sound of approaching footsteps to the archway. Her heart dropped as her mother, Heather, stepped into her line of sight. She was the same height as her daughter, just a few inches taller than Gilbert. Unlike the rest of her family, she was a brunette with pale skin and freckles.

"Finally awake?" she asked as she put a hand on her son's shoulder. "You didn't eat junk food for breakfast again, did you?"

A tote bag was slung over her shoulder. It was filled with her personal belongings. She kept medical supplies—adhesive bandages, super glue, antibiotic ointment, aspirin, a bottle of saline solution—in the smaller pockets. Although she was a housewife, she acted as a local gardener and an amateur medic, treating minor injuries and ailments. She knew her limits, though. During medical emergencies in town, she was always the first to call for an evacuation helicopter.

Gilbert stared at his mother with an uncomfortable grimace, baring his clenched teeth. Kurt grunted to get Heather's attention.

Heather's smile melted away and her eyes darkened when she recognized her daughter. Gilbert looked at his mom's hands. She was shuddering. Kurt couldn't tell if he was seeing excitement or rage in her eyes. Angelina knew the answer. An air of tension filled the kitchen, smothering all of them. The leaky faucet stopped dripping for a long moment.

"Get out," Heather said.

Angelina had been expecting to hear something like that from her mother. But a part of her—a tiny, naïve part of her—had been hoping her mother would welcome her with open arms. It hurt her to know that she was right about her.

Kurt beckoned to his wife and said, "Honey, come sit and–"

"We need to talk," Angelina interrupted.

"Get out," Heather said, raising her voice but not quite yelling.

"Mom, I'm trying to–"

"Don't call me that," Heather hissed with a finger raised at her daughter. As she walked towards the table, she said, "Don't '*Mom*' me. Don't tell me we '*need*' to talk. Don't talk to me like you have *any* say in this house. You don't. You abandoned us. You pushed us out of your life. You don't belong here. Get out before I call the cops and have them arrest you for trespassing."

Angelina gave a fake laugh, then said, "You're crazy if you think the cops are going to arrest me for sitting here. Dad invited me inside."

"*You're* crazy if you think I'm going to let you talk back to me!"

"Hey!" Kurt hollered as he rose to his feet. He stepped between his wife and daughter, a palm pointed at each of them, and he said, "What the hell's gotten into you?"

Angelina said, "I only came here to talk."

"You came here to tear us apart," Heather said. "You think I haven't seen the emails you sent to our little Gilbert?"

Gilbert raised his brow and murmured, "You read my emails?"

Ignoring him, Heather continued, "You've been planting *fantasies* about the city in his head while slandering our town and disrespecting our neighbors for the past year. You think I can't see what you're trying to do? Hmm? You're trying to poison your brother. You're trying to get him to run away just like you did. You want to destroy our town, our home, *our family!*"

Attempting to calm her down, Kurt went in for a hug. Heather pushed him away and continued arguing with him. Angelina didn't hear a word from them. She focused on her brother. Looking like a little boy witnessing his parents fight for the first time, confused and concerned, he was watching their parents argue while gripping the archway with one hand.

Heather was right about Angelina, though. She visited her family to try to convince Gilbert to explore his options after boarding school. But the matriarch was wrong about her daughter's intentions. She didn't want to get Gilbert out of Goldbrush to hurt her family. She wanted to free him to help him grow.

Speaking over her parents, Angelina said, "I came here to reconnect with my brother because I love him. If he decides he wants to go to boarding school and never come back to this fucking town, that's *his* decision, not yours or mine. He deserves the right to make his own choices. He doesn't deserve to rot here because his mom is an overprotective bitch."

"Angelina, stop," Kurt scolded.

"You see? You see?" Heather said to her husband. She looked at Angelina and asked, "What did I ever do to you to make you hate me?"

"I could ask you the same thing," Angelina responded.

"You pushed us away first. *You* hurt *me* first. You betrayed us, abandoned us, for no reason. We never abused you. We gave you everything you needed."

"Except my freedom."

"Your freedom? You're talking like we treated you like a slave. Why? Because I wanted you to come back from boarding school?"

Misty-eyed, Angelina said, "You never gave me the opportunity to even *think* about my future. You had it all planned out for me to come back here and stay here for the rest of my life. You never asked me what *I* wanted for myself. Not once. You gave me food and water and shelter and... and love. I know that. But as soon as I started thinking for myself, you turned your back on me. *You* abandoned me before I even graduated. And... God, I don't even know why I'm telling you this. You never listen and you never cared. Fuck it, I'm out of here."

"Good," Heather said, crossing her arms and looking away.

"Angie," Gilbert said as his sister stormed out of the kitchen.

Angelina kept walking. She heard her parents squabbling in the kitchen. Her father was trying to defuse the situation but her mother wasn't having any of it. At the foyer, she grabbed her backpack and sun hat, then stomped off out of the house, leaving the front door swinging behind her. She made it past the front gate. She looked left and right, as if preparing to cross a busy street. There were only a few hikers on the dirt road, though.

"Angelina!" Kurt called out as he hustled towards her.

She looked back at him. She took one step to her right, ready to continue walking, but then she noticed the sadness and regret on her father's face. He stopped on the other side of the gate.

"I can't be here right now," Angelina said. "I'm sick of her. I'm tired of this place. I should have never come back."

Kurt said, "I'll talk to her."

"For what? She never listens."

"So we can have a civil conversation. You have a lot to say. She has a lot to say. Let's try to talk about this instead of... doing whatever happened back there. Let's give this another shot."

Angelina rubbed her temple and glanced around, weighing her options. She was worried she wasn't ready to talk to her mother in a civilized manner because she had trouble controlling her tongue. She didn't mean to call her mom an 'overprotective bitch,' but in the heat of the moment, she couldn't stop herself from blurting it out. She needed time to calm herself. She couldn't allow her emotions to ruin her mission. She was genuinely looking out for Gilbert's best interests.

She said, "I'll leave tomorrow night. If she's willing to talk... we'll talk then. I'm not going to argue with her, though. If she starts looking for a fight, I'm leaving."

"I get it. Come back inside. You can stay in your room until–"

"No. I mean... Thank you but no. I'll stay at the lodge. If there are no rooms, Danny said he can take me to a hotel outside of town."

"Are you sure? We have plenty of space."

"I'm sure. I think it'll be better this way. I'll come see you tomorrow, okay?"

Kurt gave a reluctant nod and said, "Sure, I'll see you tomorrow. Come get me if you need anything, okay? I love you."

Walking away backwards, Angelina said, "I love you, too."

She turned around and marched down the dirt road. Doubt clouded her mind, leaving her vulnerable to cowardice. A little voice in her head told her to keep walking forward and leave town. *And don't look back*, it said. Another voice told her she had to see it through to the end, no matter the outcome. *For Gilbert,* she told herself. *For me.* She took a left at a crossroads and headed towards the village square.

4

GOOD NIGHT

GOLDBRUSH'S VILLAGE SQUARE—LOCATED IN THE center of town—featured a lodge, a restaurant, a souvenir shop, and a small grocery store with fresh produce. Across the plaza, there was a post office and an empty helipad. The helipad was reserved for emergencies. Although the residents knew their way in and out of town without any paved roads, the mail was sent and delivered by mule and horse to be cautious. ATVs were used only during harsh weather conditions. The community garden and historical village—the latter being under construction and covered in blue tarps— were located beyond the plaza.

The village square was bustling with activity. The souvenir shop was closed since the owners, Herbert and Monica Ramsey—a couple who lived next to the Navarros—were out of town. The Ramseys were staying in a resort in Las Vegas called *The Platinum*

Palace for a few days. Tourists still snapped pictures of themselves in front of the shop. Although they also took pictures of the wood-frame building next door, most of the tourists didn't seem interested in the lodge. Goldbrush was a great place for hikers, nature lovers, and photography enthusiasts, but there wasn't much else to do, especially at night. A day in town was enough for most people.

Angelina observed the two-story lodge. It looked like a large house. It had two guest rooms on the first floor and another two on the second floor. The free-standing sign next to the lodge read:

The Gold Star
Lodge & Breakfast

A white banner with red handwriting hung under the first line. In all capital letters, the banner read: *DELUXE*.

"The Gold Star... Deluxe?" Angelina said questioningly.

The lodge was open for as long as she could remember. The banner was new, though. She couldn't recall anything 'deluxe' about the hotel. She took a gander at her surroundings and thought about her past. Not much had changed at the village square. Even the tourists looked the same. She remembered seeing more disposable cameras than smartphones back in the day, though. Her eyes stopped on the police field office down the trail to her right.

It was a compact booth with windows all around it for 360-degree viewing. The window at the front of the booth had a speak-thru intercom and a pass-through slot.

Angelina's curiosity got the best of her, so she moseyed over to the booth. She walked past the souvenir store, the local restaurant—a joint called *Goldbrush Eats*—then crossed an intersection and strolled past a house. As she got closer to the booth, she saw Sergeant Justin McKinney inside of it. He was a 23-year-old man. His hair was cut high and tight, and his face was clean shaved. Perfectly average, he wasn't too tall or too short, too muscular or too flabby.

"Justin," Angelina said as she approached the booth's window.

"Yeah?" the cop answered. "May I help you?"

Angelina pointed at herself and asked, "Remember me?"

From behind a counter, Justin looked her up and down. He gave her a half-smile and shook his head.

"I feel like I know you, but if I'm wrong, I don't want to call you by someone else's name," he said.

"Angelina Navarro. Our families used to have cook-outs. You used to help me with my homework before you left for boarding school."

"*Angelina*," the cop said, nodding. "I thought I

recognized you. The nose ring threw me off a little. I like it, though. You're all, you know, grown up."

"You too. I almost didn't recognize you in your uniform. Looks good on you."

"You're too kind," the cop said with a touch of sarcasm.

Angelina caught sight of his wedding ring. Although she was three years younger than him, she had a crush on him when she was a young girl. She thought about her life in Goldbrush, her years away from home, and what could have been. But she didn't regret any of her choices. She was happy for him as long as he was happy for himself.

"So, have I met the lucky lady?" she asked, smiling while looking at his ring.

Justin glanced at his hand, then back at his old friend and said, "Oh. No. Well, I don't think so. I met her in Oro City while I was in the police academy."

"Oro City? That's close to Vegas, isn't it? What're you doing all the way out here? Don't tell me you downgraded and moved her back here with you."

"No, no," the cop responded, laughing. "I don't live in Goldbrush anymore. We have an apartment in Oro. I'm assigned to this field office because I know the area better than the rest of the rookies. I only work the day shift, though. Soon as I finish my probationary period, I should be back on a beat in the city."

"How's the 'beat' here? It has to be the most boring job in the world, no? Nothing ever happens in Goldbrush. You remember the cop that used to work here when we were kids? The really, y'know, hefty guy?"

"Officer Renner."

"*Yes!* Frickin' Renner, man. I don't think I ever saw him leave this booth except when he had to use the toilet or when he was going home. Do you remember when we got caught pocketing a pack of Reese's and some M&M's at Ben's shop?"

"The good ol' five-finger discount," the cop said with a smirk.

"Ben threatened to call the police on us but he never did. I know he said it was because he believed we were good kids and we learned our lesson after he scolded us, but thinking back, it was probably because he knew Renner wasn't going to do shit about it anyway."

"I shouldn't be saying this, but... he probably would have confiscated those M&M's as 'evidence' and ate 'em while no one was looking."

"He probably would have eaten them with *all* of us looking."

They laughed. Justin's chuckle was suppressed by the window.

As they settled down, the cop said, "I'm glad you're back, Angie. People really missed you around here."

"People?"

"I visited a few times while I was in the academy and I've been working this beat for a few months now. People talk. They said you never came back after you went off to boarding school. Don't get me wrong, though. I get it. Seriously, your choice is your choice. It's just, um... Your mom talked to me a lot, you know?"

"Oh jeez..."

"She was heartbroken when you left the nest. I'm not going to sit here and pretend like I'm a doctor, but she's been really... depressed. I'm talking the... the *deep* type of depression. Even when she was smiling and laughing when we spoke, I could see it in her eyes and hear it in her voice. It got worse when my parents and sister left town a few years ago."

"Don't tell me about *her* struggles, Justin," Angelina said. "Don't try to guilt me into forgiving her."

"I'm sorry, I'm not trying to guilt you into anything. I don't know what you two are going through. I'm just saying... Dealing with loneliness is harder when you're in the middle of nowhere. I know it's not easy being alone in a big city, either, like you were. I just hope you two can reconcile. I can't see anything bad or negative or whatever coming from that."

"I, um... Yeah, I hear you," Angelina said meekly, bowing her head in deep thought.

"I'm sorry if I said too much," the cop said with a nervous smile. "I don't really get a lot of time to socialize these days. I need to work on my conversation skills, huh?"

"You're good, you're good. I appreciate you being real with me. Look, I have to go get a room at the lodge before they're all booked out. I'll come talk to you later if you're not busy."

"Sure thing. I'll be here if you need anything."

As she walked away, Angelina made a peace sign with her hand and winked at the cop.

Angelina strolled into the lodge's front office. Lindsay Bunker, a thirtysomething dark-haired woman, was standing behind the reception desk. Squinting behind her eyeglasses, she skimmed through a negative review of *The Golden Lodge* posted on a travel site. Angelina didn't recognize her, but she had heard about her from her correspondences with her brother.

Lindsay, along with her husband Brett, had moved into Goldbrush shortly after Angelina was sent to boarding school. The couple had purchased *The Golden Lodge* from the previous owner. They had also invested money in the town's historical village development. Some residents, including Angelina's mother, accused the Bunkers of attempting to gentrify the town.

In a whisper, Lindsay read a sentence of the review aloud: "The owner gave me an 'evil' eye whenever I saw her." She cocked her head back, sneered, and muttered, "I did no such thing."

Angelina approached the reception desk and said, "Hello. Do you have any rooms available?"

"How many nights?" Lindsay asked without taking her eyes off the monitor.

"Just one."

"Lucky for you, we have 'just one' room left. It's $175 a night. Includes breakfast. I need to see a valid ID and a credit card."

"One hundred... seventy-five... dollars? Seriously? It used to be $50 a night when I was a kid. Maybe $70 on a holiday."

Lindsay finally wrenched her gaze off the monitor to look at her guest. Then she pivoted her body to face her, one hand on her hip and the other on the desk.

"You from around here?" she asked.

"I grew up here."

"You got a name?"

"Angelina Navarro."

"Navarro? You wouldn't happen to be related to Kurt and Heather Navarro, would you?"

Angelina said, "They're my parents."

"I see. Well, Angelina, I hope you're not as hard-headed as your mother and you can respect our right to price our rooms as we see fit. Things have changed since you were a child. Since taking over, we've spent over $100,000 on renovations to turn this place into a *deluxe* lodge. Forty-inch flat-screen TVs in every room with satellite television, custom-made draperies, new bathrooms, new king-sized beds, and we've upgraded our air conditioning and heating units. Some of your neighbors even come to stay with us when they need a vacation."

"O–kay," Angelina said, baffled by the speech. "Fine, I'll take the room."

She took out her driver's license and credit card.

Lindsay said, "We may be able to work something out, though. Maybe get you a little discount."

Angelina raised her brow at her. She saw a glimmer in the clerk's eye. She couldn't tell whether it was a spark of evil or a dollar sign.

Lindsay said, "We're looking to expand the lodge with a few more rooms and maybe open a few more businesses in the area. We can get a tour guide agency up and running in no time. Maybe even start using that helipad for a heli-taxi service. That's a whole lot of business—a whole lot of *money*—for this little town. The problem is, Goldbrush actually votes on these types of things. And your mother is always voting against us. And when she votes against us, she gets everyone else to follow her. Can you talk to her for us?"

"I'd appreciate a discount, but you're asking the wrong person. There's no way my mom would listen to me about anything. She's been talking to me with her hands over her ears for years."

Annoyed, Lindsay groaned and wagged her head. She charged Angelina for the room, then grabbed a key from the key rack behind her.

"Room 202," she said. "Stairs are down the hall to your right. You can grab breakfast down here until 10

AM. We serve fresh bread, cereals, and fruit. We've got a vending machine, too."

Angelina accepted the key and said, "Thanks."

She headed up to her room. It was small but clean. The bathroom near the foyer provided the essentials— a sink, a medicine cabinet, a toilet, a shower, and towels. At the other side of the room, the door next to the window opened up to the balcony, which overlooked the community garden and historical village.

In front of the window, there was a table with two chairs. Two nightstands surrounded the king-sized bed to her left. Across from the bed, a flat-screen television sat atop a dresser, which also contained the minibar in its cabinet. The dark red wallpaper and brown carpet were spotless. Yet, nothing about the room screamed 'deluxe.'

"What a rip-off," Angelina muttered.

She settled in. After unpacking, she checked her cell phone for signal—*no bars*. Exhausted from the long journey, she lay in bed and relaxed while channel surfing. When she got bored, she took a nap for a few hours. And when she awoke, she went out to the balcony to appreciate the view.

Although the unfinished historical village was an eyesore, the view of the sun starting to set behind the mountains in the distance was beautiful.

Her nose twitched as she caught a whiff of cigarette smoke. She leaned over the balcony guardrail and looked down at the ground below. Then she heard someone blowing out a cloud of smoke. She looked to her right—around the wall separating the rooms' balconies—and spotted a guy with buzz cut hair on the neighboring balcony.

He was smoking a cigarette while admiring the view and listening to music through his Bluetooth earbuds. He looked tired, black bags hanging under his eyes.

Upon noticing Angelina staring at him from the corner of his eye, the man set his cigarette down on an ashtray, took an earbud out of his ear, and said, "The lady down there said it was okay to smoke. I'm not bothering you, am I?"

"It's fine."

"You sure? You're kind of staring."

"Am I?" Angelina responded, blushing. "Sorry about that. I just haven't seen you in town before. Do you have family around here? Friends? I'd ask if you were here on vacation, but you don't look like you're dressed for a hike."

The guy looked down at himself, as if he didn't remember his own outfit. He was wearing a button-up shirt with the sleeves rolled up, slacks, and dress shoes.

"Yeah, I guess I don't really blend in with the tourists," he said. "I work at the local school, the Goldbrush Education Center."

"Oh, you're a teacher?"

"That's right. My name's Alexander. The kids call me Mr. Guzman, but you can call me Alex."

"It's nice to meet you, Alex. I'm Angelina."

"It's a pleasure to meet you. So, what's your story? Tourist? Resident?"

Angelina said, "Today, I guess you can call me a tourist. I used to live here, though. I went to the Gold-brush Education Center, actually. If I remember correctly, the teachers usually went home after school. What's up with you? Miss the last camel out of here?"

Scratching the side of his head, Alex said, "Long story short, I had to stay late the past few days to finish some work, so I decided to stay here. The week's almost over anyway, so I figured I can stay tonight and tomorrow, then head back home for the weekend."

"I get ya. So, you have any plans tonight?"

"Plans? Like..."

Alex noticed her kittenish ways. She was smiling at him while nibbling her lower lip. He started to blush as well.

"I guess I'm not really doing anything tonight," he said.

"Wanna hang out?"

Alex tilted his head to the side and looked her over, searching for a trace of deceit. He never had much trouble meeting women, but it usually took some effort on his part. He had to initiate every conversation, he had to win over their trust. It all seemed too good to be true.

He said, "If you're okay with answering... How old are you?"

"Twenty. You?"

Alex chuckled nervously while looking around and rubbing the nape of his neck.

Angelina said, "You know, the longer you think about it, the less likely I'm going to believe you."

"I'm... thirty-two."

"Thirty-two, huh? You look younger than that. But, hey, I like older guys."

"Sorry, let's just slow it down a little. Listen, I don't think we should be 'hanging out.' You're a former student at the school I *currently* work at, you used to live here so the other residents probably know you—I probably even know your parents—and you're twelve years younger than me. It just wouldn't look good if we were seen in public."

"Who said anything about being seen in public?" Angelina responded.

Alex's cheeks turned redder as he gave another anxious laugh. Although she was trying to keep her seductive image afloat, Angelina couldn't stop herself from laughing.

She said, "Look, I just don't want to be alone tonight, okay? If you want the truth, this is my home but it doesn't *feel* like home anymore. I'm only here to... to take care of some family business. I have a 'big' day tomorrow and I don't want to think about it now. I like your vibe, you know, and I like that you're not from here. I wanna talk a little more without this wall between us. Help me get my mind off things, yeah?"

Alex looked her straight in the eye. He sensed her sincerity.

"You're not a serial killer, are you?" he asked.

"Statistically, most serial killers are men, so I should be asking you that same question."

"I guess there's only one way to find out. You wanna 'hang out' in my room or yours?"

"Mine," Angelina said without hesitation. "C'mon, let's have a drink."

5

THE HIGH STRIKER

"What's this?" Danny whispered, leaning forward in the driver's seat of his truck.

He took his foot off the gas pedal. The truck kept bouncing and jerking as it rolled through the desert. In his high beams, he saw an RV with a trailer parked a few meters away from a tree with a crooked trunk. As his truck crept closer, he spotted a woman in a white-and-red dress next to the RV's camper door—*Boo-Boo*. She wasn't wearing her mask. She was jumping and waving at him.

Danny stopped his truck near the trailer but left his high beams on. The bright lights illuminated the area next to the RV—the footprints and tire marks on the soil, the dried vegetation, the tree with the large stone next to it. There were no other people in the area. There were no animals out there, either. The desert felt more desolate at night.

"What the hell?" he muttered.

Boo-Boo continued jumping and swinging her arms over her head, as if trying to wave down another vehicle. Danny opened the driver's door and stepped out. Over her labored breathing, he heard faint music playing in the RV—*The Lady is a Tramp* by Frank Sinatra.

Danny walked to the front of his truck and asked, "Are you lost?"

The woman finally stopped jumping. She put her hands on her knees, bent over, and wheezed.

Danny said, "Are you okay? Do you need–"

Without looking in his direction, Boo-Boo raised a finger at him, as if to say: '*Be quiet for one second.*' She panted for a few more seconds, then she stood up straight and put her hands on her hips.

Still out of breath, she said, "Sorry about that, handsome. I was just finishing up my jumping jacks. How can I help ya?"

Danny stared at her with a dumbfounded face. He snuck a look at the RV, then swept his gaze around the surrounding area, and then looked back at her.

He said, "It's not safe to be out here alone at night."

"Is that a threat or a pick-up line?"

"What? It's a... Ma'am, it's going to get colder and darker soon. It'll be easy for you to get turned around if you're not familiar with the area. You can end up driving into a ditch or crashing into a stone or a tree.

There's some dangerous wildlife in the desert, too. You don't want to be out here right now."

"Is that so?"

Hands clasped behind her back, Boo-Boo approached Danny with big, exaggerated steps, as if she were wearing a pair of floppy, oversized shoes. Danny peeked over his shoulder upon hearing a bush rustle behind him. He looked forward as the clown's footsteps stopped. She was standing about three meters away from him.

She said, "You sure seem to know this area well."

"I'm from here."

"From where? The desert?"

"No. I mean, yeah, I guess. I'm from Goldbrush."

'*Goldbrush.*' Boo-Boo's eyes lit up upon hearing the town's name. She folded her hands in front of her crotch and started twirling her foot.

She said, "What a coinkydink. I've been looking all over the place for Goldbrush. You mind taking me there? We can follow you in our RV."

"I can't take you there right now. Even if you were to follow right behind me, it's too dangerous. Especially with that trailer. You're better off heading back to the trailhead parking lot and waiting for sunlight. And did you say 'we?' Are you with other people?"

"Of course I am. You think I'm out here partying all by myself? My buddy Pipsqueak is in the RV trying to read the map. Captain Gashes is somewhere around here. I think he had to take a leak. And Bob... Bob's standing right behind you."

Danny felt the hair at the nape of his neck prickle. He shot a glance over his shoulder and reeled away from the truck. There was no one behind him. He didn't see anyone inside of his vehicle, either. He looked back at the clown with a half-smile and furious eyes. It was the type of expression that said: *'What the fuck is wrong with you?'*

"What?" Boo-Boo said with a set of puppy eyes. "You act like I said he's going to hurt you. Bob's good people, okay?"

"I don't know what kind of game you're trying to play, but you and your 'friends' shouldn't be out here. You said one of your friends was going to go piss, right? *Right?*"

"Yup."

"If he's real, you need–"

"What's that supposed to mean?"

"–to get him back here before he gets lost or hurt or both."

"*If* he's real?" Boo-Boo repeated, her voice shifting from playful to angry. "What are you trying to say? Hmm? All of my friends are real, pal."

"Fine, okay, whatever," Danny said, growing flustered. "Goddammit, what are you people even doing out here?"

"I told you already, we're looking for Goldbrush. We heard there were a few people there. Like forty or fifty. That's what Simon told Captain Gashes before he kicked the bucket. We're going to go there and we're going to kill *everyone*. It's going to be raining blood."

"Wha–What?"

Her eyes grew wider and brighter, and a zany smile stretched across her face. She took a step towards him. He sidestepped to his left, preparing to retreat back into his truck.

Boo-Boo said, "You haven't heard the forecast, mister? It's going to rain so much blood that it's going to turn this desert into a red sea. Human organs and limbs will fall from the sky like hail. Arms, legs, eyeballs, hearts, livers, fucking gallbladders and medulla oblongatas!"

She bent over, crossed her arms over her abdomen, and laughed deliriously. Danny took another step to his left, blocking one of the headlights with his body. The alarms in his head told him to run like hell. But fright turned his feet to anchors.

Boo-Boo suddenly stopped laughing and shouted, "Now, Bob! Get him now!"

Refusing to humor her, Danny shook his head and said, "You need help. I–I'm going to get help, okay? Get in your RV and wait there. Please."

"Dang it, Bob! How did you miss him? He's standing right there! Ahh, jeez, I guess it is kinda my fault. I should've let you keep your thumbs. Well, it's a good thing we have a backup plan."

"A backup plan?"

Danny heard some hurried footsteps behind him. He looked back and caught a glimpse of Captain Gashes, his arm outstretched in front of him with a handgun in his hand. The clown pistol-whipped him, smashing the butt of the handgun against Danny's right temple. Danny blacked out, hitting the ground in front of the truck. Dark blood trickled out of a gash on his forehead. He started snoring and twitching.

Captain Gashes glared at Boo-Boo and asked, "What did I tell you about running your mouth?"

Boo-Boo looked skyward, tapped her chin with her index finger, and hummed in contemplation. She brought her gaze back to her boss and shrugged.

"Can I get a hint?" she asked.

"You're either gonna end up running it into my fist or your mouth's going to leave us running from the law."

"Oh yeah, you did say that. But that's not a hint, Cap. You just gave me the answer. That's no fun."

"Yeah, yeah, smart-ass. You wanna have some fun? Go get Pipsqueak and some rope."

Boo-Boo asked, "We bringing this guy to the trailer?"

"No time for that," Captain Gashes said as he rolled Danny onto his back.

He pried the guy's eyelids open, checking to see if he was still unconscious or just faking it. Danny was out cold.

Captain Gashes said, "We need to find this place by

tomorrow night or we'll miss our cue. No point in driving if we don't know where we're going, and no point in putting him in the trailer if we're not driving." He looked at the nearby tree and said, "I've got a better idea."

Danny regained consciousness but kept his eyes closed. He saw a dark red color as light from the high beams passed through his eyelids. He heard footsteps and hushed voices in front of him. He could hear *It Don't Mean a Thing (If It Ain't Got That Swing)* by Duke Ellington and Louis Armstrong playing from somewhere to his right. The blood from his gashed temple had reached his neck in a wide, warm stripe. Struck with a terrible bout of vertigo, he felt like he was rocking from side to side endlessly.

His eyes opened to slits. Although the world was spinning around him, he could tell he was looking down at himself. As his vision adjusted, he realized he was tied to the tree's crooked trunk with his hands bound behind his back. He felt his heart plummet into his stomach. His pants and underwear had been pulled down to his ankles. His genitals were resting on the stone in front of him. Panting feverishly, he lifted his head and looked around. He saw three shadowy figures in front of him. After a couple of blinks, his vision focused a little more.

Boo-Boo was doing jumping jacks in front of the pickup truck. She was now wearing her clown mask. Pipsqueak watched her. Although he wore clown makeup, his face was expressionless. He was using a sledgehammer as a cane, the ten-pound steel head sinking into the dirt. Pistol in hand, Captain Gashes stood on the other side of the large stone. Due to his smudged makeup, it looked like his face was melting in Danny's unstable vision.

Danny said, "Bah... Bah... Bob?"

"My name ain't Bob," Captain Gashes growled.

"Finally," Boo-Boo said as she stopped her jumping jacks. Hands on her hips, she blew out an exhausted breath and said, "I thought he was never going to wake up."

"Fuckin' hell," Danny whimpered as he fidgeted. "No, no. This can't be real. N–No. You–You can't... Please don't do this, man. My–My mom is... Fuck, man, she's sick. My dad just–"

"Calm down," Captain Gashes said.

"–passed away last year. I–I'm all she has. She needs me. She–She needs her medicine. It's in my truck. I swear, you can see it for yourself. Please, don't kill me. I don't wanna die. I don't wanna die. Don't fucking kill me! Please, man!"

"Quiet!"

Danny screamed and cringed, then he started sobbing and mumbling incoherently. Tears fell from his jaw, plopping on the stone below him.

The song in the RV changed to *Stormy Weather* by Etta James. The music cut in and out for a few seconds, then the stereo turned off. Only Danny's whining echoed through the dark desert.

Captain Gashes said, "I don't want to drag this out all night. We've got places to be and I'm sure you've got things to do. Mom needs her medicine, right?"

Reduced to a sniveling mess, Danny nodded rapidly and stuttered, "Ye–Yes."

"We'll have you on your way in no time... as long as you cooperate. Now, I'm going to ask you a couple of questions. I want to hear the truth and nothing but, even if it hurts my feelings. If you lie to me or waste my time, I'm going to hurt you. Do you want to know what I'm going to do to you if you don't cooperate?"

"Don't kill me, don't kill me, don't kill me, don't kill me."

"It'll be far worse than death, boy," Captain Gashes said.

He pressed the muzzle of his handgun against Danny's left testicle, crushing it against the stone. Some of his pubic hair entered the pistol's barrel. Danny cried and thrashed about, the rope creaking and trunk groaning with his wild movements.

"*Ow!*" he screamed. "Ow, ow, ow! Stop! S–Stop!"

Captain Gashes adjusted the handgun slightly, reducing the pressure on Danny's testicle while keeping it pinned down. But Danny still felt like his scrotum was burning from within. He swung his hips, trying helplessly to free his balls. Splinters from the tree trunk pierced his ass.

"If you don't answer my questions, I'll put a bullet through this little 'bean' of yours," Captain Gashes said. "You'll lose a lot of blood, you'll lose consciousness—and that'll waste a lot of my time and make me angrier—but you won't die. When you regain consciousness, when you start to feel that numbness in your ball sac, I'll shoot the other one."

"They should call you the Nutcracker, Cap," Boo-Boo said, giggling. "No. No! The Nut-*capper!* You get it? 'Cause you're gonna bust a *cap* in his nuts! Isn't that right, Pips?"

Pipsqueak was half asleep. Danny sobbed and wheezed. Goops of foamy saliva fell from his mouth, joining the tears on the stone.

Captain Gashes said, "Tell me: Are we close to Goldbrush?"

The burning pain rolling through Danny's genitals had sent his mind into overdrive. Although Boo-Boo had threatened his town—his neighbors, *his family*—he could only think about cooperating in order to survive.

"Yes," he blurted, voice trembling with pain.

"How close?"

"One... One hour. Juh–Just an hour drive."

"That doesn't sound very close to me," Boo-Boo interjected. "You should shoot him for that, Cap."

"Don't, don't," Danny said. "Please, no. I–I meant

less than an hour. I just... I thought... It's dangerous, so you have to drive slow, okay? I was just trying to be helpful. Please don't shoot."

Captain Gashes asked, "How do we get there?"

Danny swung his head to the side, as if he were going to look over his shoulder, then said, "Keep... Keep going. Go north to... towards the mountains."

"You're going to have to be a little more specific than that."

"I–I don't know how else to explain. It hurts. I think it's... going to pop. Can you please take the gun off me?"

Captain Gashes said, "The only way I'm taking this gun off you right now is if I take one of your balls with it. Give me specifics."

"Okay, o–okay... Go north... mountains... Drive north for, like–like, forty-five minutes. Just go straight that way to the mountains. If–If you can't find Goldbrush... Shit... Wait until morning and you'll see hikers going to town. Follow them and they'll take you straight there. Or... Or I can take you there. If you let me go, if you promise not to hurt my mom, I can drive you to Goldbrush."

Danny's plan was simple: Drive the clowns to Goldbrush to win their trust and buy time, then drop them off at the police field office as soon as they arrived in town. He was convinced that his odds of survival would be better if he wasn't tied to that tree. And he could only save his mother by saving himself.

Captain Gashes took the gun off Danny's scrotum.

Echoes of pain lingered in his aching testicle. The clown swiped the muzzle against his abdomen twice, as if his dirty wifebeater could clean it.

He said, "That's good enough for me, and I'm a man of my word."

"Re–Really?" Danny asked with a glimmer of hope in his eyes.

"But *we*... are a team. For this 'circus' to succeed, we need to be on the same wavelength. A collective consciousness acting in perfect synchronicity... to incite total chaos. You feel me?"

"Wha–What? What are you talking about?"

Captain Gashes looked at Boo-Boo and asked, "What do you think? Was he honest enough for ya?"

"Hmm," the female clown hummed with her lips puckered. "I guess we won't really know the truth until morning, but I think..."

She paused to let the tension build up. She enjoyed watching Danny squirm and wail. Like an aphrodisiac, her victims' fear aroused her. She moaned with excitement, then tittered—one hand gripping the crotch of her dress and the other against her masked cheek.

"I believe him, Cap," she said. "Looks like we were going the right way after all. I'm sure we'll find Gold-brush before the night's over."

Captain Gashes said, "So far, so good, kid. But let's see what the last judge has to say. What do you think, big guy? You believe him?"

They all looked at Pipsqueak. The big clown stared

at the victim, his eyes blank. Danny noticed he hadn't said a word since he awoke tied to that tree. *Maybe he's a mute,* he told himself. *Maybe he doesn't care.* He stopped crying but continued panting and trembling.

But just as a spark of optimism started to flicker in his heart, Pipsqueak spoke up: "Nope."

And with only one word, Danny's world came crashing down around him. Images of his mother flashed before his very eyes. His stomach turned and cramped. His chest tightened and burned. He sobbed and gibbered, his voice like a baby's.

Captain Gashes said, "You heard the clown. Unfortunately for you, that means we can't let you go. Fortunately for us, we all have a thing for murder and showmanship. I speak for all of us when I say... it's time for the exciting finale of our show."

"Don't shoot me. Please, man, please. Don't kill me. Don't shoot."

"Settle down, boy. This thing isn't even loaded. Even if it was, I wouldn't use it on you. I'd beat you with it, but I wouldn't shoot ya. No, that would be too easy, too boring, too forgettable. We have something special planned for you."

"Oh fuck, please stop."

Captain Gashes tucked the pistol into his waistband, then began circling the tree and stone. Boo-Boo stomped her feet and made a drum roll noise with her mouth. Pipsqueak approached the stone. He raised the sledgehammer and leaned it against his shoulder.

"Do you know what a strongman is?" Captain Gashes asked. "These days, people confuse 'em for bodybuilders."

"Big guys with big guns," Boo-Boo chimed in before continuing her drum roll.

"Right. But believe it or not, strongmen actually originated in the circus. They'd tear license plates in two like paper, carry families—*entire* families—on their backs, lift dumbbells with their pinkies. I've seen strongmen *bend* crowbars and *wrestle* bears!"

The leader of the crew stopped on the other side of the stone behind Pipsqueak. Boo-Boo stopped her drum roll, caught her breath, then continued. Danny kept bawling his eyes out. He was out of words—out of strength, out of hope.

Captain Gashes said, "I don't have a talent like that. I can put on a show but not the type you see in the circus. No, my type of shows... You find them in snuff tapes and on the dark web." Danny cried louder and trembled harder. The clown resumed, "I know how to kill, how to cause suffering, how to whip up chaos. So, who better than me to teach these clowns how to put on a *bloody* good show, right?"

Short of breath, Boo-Boo said, "Can you... get on with it... Cap? I can't... keep this drum roll going forever, y'know. And Bob can't help... I cut off his lips and made him kiss his own ass, remember?"

"Yeah, yeah," Captain Gashes said before patting Pipsqueak's back and saying, "My friend Pips here is a real strongman. I've seen him tear a man's jaw off with his bare hands. You know something else? He gets the highest score on every high striker. You're familiar with the game, aren't you? It's that game where the player hits a lever with a hammer as *hard* as possible, launching a puck up a tower."

Holding its handle with both hands, Pipsqueak raised the sledgehammer overhead.

"No! Wait! Please stop! Please!" Danny begged.

He knew what was coming. He was grinding his ass against the tree trunk, trying to drag his genitals off the stone.

Captain Gashes said, "In this case, you're the tower... and your balls are the puck."

"Please! Please, I don't–"

Pipsqueak grunted as he swung the sledgehammer down, landing a direct hit on Danny's genitals. The stone cracked and the ground vibrated. Both of Danny's testicles burst with crunchy *pops*. His scrotum tore open down the middle vertically. The tube-shaped innards of his testicles poured out of his mangled ball sac like tiny worms.

The shaft of his penis was squashed, flattened into a rectangle of spongy flesh. It sank *into* his mutilated scrotum. Under the skin, blotches of blood spread across the shaft. Although the sledgehammer had missed the head, his glans was big, red, and swollen. It looked like he had an erection, except the shaft was flaccid.

Upon impact, a bolt of excruciating pain shot into Danny's abdomen. His mouth flew open in a soundless screech. He swung his head from side to side, but the rest of his body locked up. The color was drained from his face, leaving him with a cadaverous pallor. Blood was splattered on his crotch, the stone, and the ground. A single drop landed on his chin.

Boo-Boo scratched her head and said, "I thought a bell was supposed to ring if you win the game. Maybe you didn't hit him hard enough?"

"Maybe our big guy is getting soft," Captain Gashes suggested.

Snarling, Pipsqueak swung the sledgehammer overhead, stalled for three seconds, then brought it down with all of his strength. The glans of Danny's penis was flattened and gashed. Ropes of gooey blood sprayed out of his urethra as well as the new cuts. A ghoulish groan came out of his mouth, reverberating through the area, then a blast of projectile vomit followed.

The thick orange puke splashed on the stone, the sledgehammer, Pipsqueak's jumpsuit, and Captain Gashes' pants. Danny's head fell forward, his chin nestled down in the gap between his clavicles, while his eyes rolled up. Although he had lost consciousness, puke continued oozing past his lips.

"That's not really what a bell sounds like but it's good enough for this gal," Boo-Boo said. She ran up to

Pipsqueak, grabbed his hand and lifted it up in the air, and shouted, "Congrats, champ!"

"Thanks," Pipsqueak responded, chuckling. "Can I go to the bathroom now? I gotta take a shit."

"Oh. Well, you call me 'Boo-Boo' not 'Butt Plug,' so don't let me stop ya."

"We're not done here," Captain Gashes said.

Stomach rumbling and squeaking, Pipsqueak sighed in disappointment.

Boo-Boo asked, "What're you thinkin', Cap?"

"Get him down," Captain Gashes ordered. "We crushed his dick head already. Now let's crush his other one."

Danny's eyes fluttered open. He was already writhing and moaning in pain before he realized he had recovered consciousness. For a moment, his whimpers sounded like they were coming from someone else, somewhere else. Although parts of his crotch had gone numb, a ball of unbearable pain bobbled around in his lower abdomen.

The stench of cigarette smoke attacked his nostrils. His vision was dark and unfocused. He heard three loud *thuds* above him, like someone hitting a wall.

"I'm telling you, the dang thing is broken," Boo-Boo said.

"I can't drive without my music," Pipsqueak responded.

Danny retched a few times, but there was nothing left in his stomach to puke out. Although his vision was still a blurry mess, he could tell he was staring at the RV's undercarriage. Only his head was under the vehicle, resting under the camper door. The rest of his body was sprawled across the ground out in the open. The clowns' voices were coming from inside of the RV.

"I can sing you a song," Boo-Boo said. She coughed to clear her throat, then sang: ♪ *Da da dadada da–*

"No," Pipsqueak said, interrupting her rendition of *Thunder and Blazes: Entry March of the Gladiators.* "I need *my* music. I ain't driving without *my* music."

"Well, I don't know what to tell ya. It's broken."

"Hit it harder."

"What do I look like? A boxer? Why don't *you* hit it harder, big guy?"

The RV shook with a *bang.*

Something's Gotta Give by Sammy Davis Jr. started playing from the speakers.

"Wow, that actually worked," Boo-Boo said. "Hey, I should have got you to 'fix' my old man. He didn't work, either."

"That's my cue," Captain Gashes said.

His voice came from outside. He sucked in one last drag of his cigarette before letting it fall to the ground. He didn't bother stamping it out.

The leader continued, "I know you're awake, kid. If you can muster the energy to crawl out from under there, you're free to go. You won't last long without your balls, but... it's worth a shot, right?" He blew the smoke out of his lungs, then said, "It was fun, but we've gotta go. We have a show to start. We found those eyedrops for your mom in your truck. I'll make sure to say hello to old Mrs. Dakota Paddock for ya."

Danny cried. He tried to scream, but the pain—physical and emotional—tied his tongue. He could rock from side to side, but he didn't have enough energy to roll over. An unsettling numb sensation spread to his legs. Stepping over him, Captain Gashes climbed into the RV. He slammed the camper door shut behind him. The clowns' voices and laughter were muted. The engine sputtered to life.

The RV rolled forward.

Danny looked to his right. He saw the rear tire crawling towards him. His forehead hit the undercarriage as he attempted to sit up. He tried to slither out from under the RV, wiggling his hips and rocking his shoulders. But he was too late. The rear tire rolled over his face. The gash on his temple widened instantly. Blood flowed out of his nostrils in rivers of red as his nose broke. His maxilla—his upper jaw—started to crack under the weight as well.

Sitting in the driver's seat, Pipsqueak stomped on the gas and brake pedals. The RV shook wildly as the rear tires spun.

Danny's nose, which had been reduced to a nub, was torn off his face. It bounced across the soil like a pebble. Then his face was ripped off his skull, stuck in one of the tire's grooves. A mist of blood sprayed out from under the tire. Dislodged teeth flew from his lipless mouth. Blood came out of his ears next. A series of cracking sounds—like glass breaking under a thick towel—came from his head.

Then his skinless face collapsed *into* his skull. The top of his head opened like a lid and a slop of pulpy brain tissue spewed out. One of his eyes, partially crushed, was ejected from his crushed skull. The other one was ground into a gelatinous goop and blended into his jellified brain. Although he had been dead for over a minute, his legs shook violently.

Pipsqueak took his foot off the gas pedal. The RV moved forward. Two of the trailer's wheels ran over Danny's chest. He was left in the dark desert next to his truck—without functioning testicles, without a face.

The RV cruised off into the desolate desert as the clowns continued their search for Goldbrush.

6

REACQUAINTED

The door chime jingled.

"Good morning," Adeline Brown said in a chipper tone. "Have a seat wherever you'd like. I'll be with you in a second, hon."

Standing in the doorway, Angelina answered with a smile and nod. She settled into a booth near the entrance. The neighboring window offered a view of the village square. The first herds of hikers were just arriving at Goldbrush, finding places to rest and taking pictures of everything in their paths.

Angelina turned in her seat and ran her eyes over the restaurant's interior. She hadn't been to Goldbrush Eats since she was a young teenager. It didn't change a bit—same baby blue walls, same checkered floor, same employees. The place was owned by Adeline and her husband Felix. They were both on the cusp of retirement, but they shared every job.

Adeline brought two plates of breakfast to a pair of hikers at a table. They had ordered Felix's signature breakfast burrito—loaded with eggs, sausage, and potatoes—with sides of French fries and coffee. A scruffy man was eating pancakes at another table. He wasn't dressed like the regular hikers. He reminded Angelina of her father—a jack-of-all-trades.

So, she assumed he was a resident. She spotted a red-haired woman sitting at the bar at the other end of the restaurant. She didn't know her, either. She came to realize she didn't recognize most of the people at the diner. Yet, it all felt familiar and welcoming. Everyone seemed so nice and approachable.

It weirded her out a little. She couldn't help but feel like they were all hiding from the real world.

"I had a feeling I'd be seeing you soon, Angie," Adeline said as she approached the booth.

"Good morning, Mrs. Brown. I... didn't think you'd recognize me so fast."

"I didn't. I don't. Look at you, look at you. You've blossomed into a beautiful young lady. I would have taken you as just another out-of-towner if it weren't for Ben."

"So, *Ben's* been telling everyone I'm back in town."

"Oh, you know him. He's quite the blabbermouth."

Angelina nodded with a tiny smile. *The smallest towns have the biggest mouths,* she thought. She didn't mind, though. It wasn't like she was trying to hide her arrival from the townspeople.

"So, what can I get you?" Adeline asked, holding a server notepad and a pen in her hands.

Angelina hadn't even checked the menu, but she already knew what she wanted. She said, "How about... your famous waffles with a side of bacon and coffee. Black, no cream, no sugar."

"I'll whip that up for you right away, hon. Holler if you need anything else."

Angelina watched her make her way to the kitchen. The woman checked on the other patrons on her way there. Felix was taking a couple of plates of food to another table crowded with tourists. After delivering their meals, he took a moment to smile and wave at Angelina before getting back to work.

The elderly couple reunited in the kitchen. They were all smiles back there. They were wearing matching white aprons. Embroidered in red capital letters, the aprons read: *GOLDBRUSH EATS*. They were proud of the business and the home—they lived in an apartment upstairs—they had built together.

Angelina's smile grew. She looked at Adeline and Felix as the town's grandparents, especially since she rarely saw her extended family. Their happiness made her happy.

The door chime rang as a group of hikers entered the diner.

Adeline brought Angelina's order to her booth and said, "Enjoy. Made 'em just how you like. Crispy on the outside, fluffy on the inside."

"Thank you," Angelina said.

"Syrups on the table. If you need more, holler. Wish I had more time to catch up with you, sweetie, but you know how it gets in the morning."

"I understand."

"Let's have a chat later, you and me, yeah? Maybe over some tea?"

"Name the time and place, and I'll be there."

"I'll call your mom and set something up."

'Don't!' Angelina almost shouted. But before she could say a word, Adeline hurried off to welcome the other guests. Angelina sighed, looked out the window ruminatively for a few seconds, then ate her breakfast. During her meal, she overheard a conversation between Felix and the scruffy guy at the other table. The men discussed the historical village, and the Bunker family's involvement in the project.

The scruffy man believed it was taking up too much space, preferring to expand the community garden than to create a glitzy tourist attraction. Felix accused the Bunkers of attempting to buy their support. He understood their town—his business especially—needed tourism to survive, but he didn't agree with the Bunkers' methods. They hadn't even asked any of the life-long natives of Goldbrush for their input.

How can outsiders build a 'historical village' without understanding the history of Goldbrush? Angelina wondered.

Although she was only eavesdropping, she found herself agreeing with Felix. Upon finishing her meal, she paid her bill, said her goodbyes to the Browns, then headed out. She had considered asking Adeline to steer clear of her mother for a while, but she didn't want to drag her or anyone else into their family drama. She walked over to her old house at a leisurely pace, trying to delay her inevitable confrontation with her mother for as long as possible.

On her way, she saw Gilbert walking towards her with his head down and a backpack slung over his shoulder.

"Hey," she called out to him as they got closer to each other.

Gilbert lifted his head and looked her way. He looked like he had just snapped out of a daydream. He nodded at her, then waited for a group of hikers to walk past them before crossing the dirt path and joining her at the other side of the trail.

"What's up?" he asked.

"I'm going to go see Dad and... Mom."

"Dad's home, but if you want to see Mom, she's at the garden. She probably won't be back home until three or four."

Angelina's tight shoulders loosened as a feeling of relief washed over her. She still had time to mentally prepare herself for their next encounter.

"Okay, cool," she said. "And what's up with you?"

"What do you mean?"

"You look like you're getting shipped off to military school. I know your classes aren't *that* hard. What's with the glum face?"

Gilbert cast his eyes down at the ground. He kicked a pebble at the stone partition in front of the house to his left.

Angelina put her hand on his shoulder and, in an understanding tone, she asked, "What is it?"

"My teacher, Mr. Guzman," Gilbert said, avoiding eye contact. "He's cool and everything, but... his classes aren't easy. I'm passing, but Otto's grades aren't as good as mine."

"Otto? The Holts' son?"

"Yeah. He's been my best friend since forever. If his grades don't get better, we're not going to be able to go to the same boarding school. I don't wanna leave Gold-brush if I have to leave alone."

That wasn't what Angelina wanted to hear. She wanted to inspire him to explore the world beyond Goldbrush. She believed it was the only way for him to discover his true self and achieve his dreams.

She said, "I wouldn't worry about it too much. You still have a few months to, you know, study together and work it out." Gilbert's expression didn't change. Angelina said, "Okay, I'll tell you what: I'll talk to Alex about it next time I see him. We'll see if we can work something out."

"Alex? You know Mr. Guzman?"

Angelina could only blush.

7

HOME

"Ange," Kurt said as he opened the front door, eyes wide with delighted surprise. "I was just about to go see if you were at the lodge. Come in, come in."

"Thanks," Angelina replied.

As she walked into the home, her father gave her a tight one-armed hug. He shut the door behind her, then they went through the neighboring archway into the living room. Angelina sat on a three-seat sofa. Kurt took a seat on the recliner to her right. A glass coffee table stood in front of them. And on that table, there was a mug with a bit of leftover coffee in it.

"Sorry, your mom's not home," he said. "You just missed her, actually. She should be at the garden right now."

'*Thank God,*' Angelina wanted to say.

Instead, she said, "Yeah, Gilbert told me. I ran into

him on his way to school. Does Mom always leave so early?"

Kurt took a deep breath through his nose, then he shook his head. Angelina sighed and nodded. They both knew the truth and they didn't have to say it out loud. Heather had left early because she didn't want to be anywhere near her daughter. Kurt took a swig of his coffee, then sneered. It was cold and stale.

He cleared his throat, then asked, "How was your first night back? Anyone give you any trouble?"

"No, no, everyone was nice. It was, um... like old times, I guess. But there was that one woman. The new owner of the lodge. I'll be honest, she was kind of a bitch."

Kurt chuckled and said, "You're right about that. She give you that evil eye of hers?"

"Oh yeah. She wanted me to talk to mom about the historical village. When I told her I wasn't the right person for that job, she looked like she wanted to tear my head off."

They laughed together.

Kurt asked, "How was the room?"

"I wouldn't call it 'deluxe,' but it was actually pretty cozy. The bed was comfy, too. Better than the one I have at my place."

"That's good. You know, I helped renovate that lodge a few years ago after the Bunkers bought it."

"Really?" Angelina responded, smiling. She could

sense the pride in her father's voice. She was happy for him. She said, "It did feel like home."

"That's what I like to hear. And how about breakfast? Did you eat?"

"Yeah, I stopped by Mrs. Brown's place before coming here."

"Let me guess. Waffles with a side of bacon?"

"How did you know?" Angelina asked, giggling.

"I don't think you ever ordered anything else whenever we went out for breakfast. There was that one time you–"

Kurt's smartwatch emitted a series of beeps. He glanced at it, then tapped the small screen to stop the alarm.

He said, "Sorry, honey, but I have to get to work. Why don't you stick around here today? You can get settled in your old room. It's exactly how you left it."

"Oh, I don't know about that. I'm not trying to cause a big scene between us. I just want to talk to you guys. I want *her* to listen to me for once."

"We'll all sit and talk soon, I promise. I just want you to... to feel at home again. Maybe it'll make things easier for us—for you."

"But I left all of my stuff at the lodge."

"Don't worry about that for now. I can bring it over here later. Lindsay's not the nicest person in town, but she's not just going to throw your stuff out the window like an angry ex. Will you stay? Please?"

Angelina had a hard time saying no to good people,

and her father was the kindest of the kindest. She was out of good excuses, too.

She said, "Okay. I'll be here."

"Thank you, honey. Seriously, it means a lot to me. I'm sure it'll mean a lot to your mom and brother."

'*I doubt it.*' The words were on the tip of her tongue, but she stopped herself from blurting them out. She responded with a nod.

Kurt stood up, kissed her forehead, then said, "We should all be back before dinner. We can sit and talk then. Help yourself to anything in the kitchen. I love you. You know that, right?"

"I know," Angelina said. "I love you, too."

"I'll see you tonight."

Staying in her seat, she watched him walk through the archway. She listened to him as he dug through his pockets in the foyer, ensuring he had all of his belongings, then she heard the front door open and close before hearing the locks *click* and *clack*. A dead silence filled the house—no creaks, no groans.

Her eyes raked over the living room. Some pieces of furniture had been moved and others had been replaced. *New TV,* she thought. The photographs in the picture frames—hanging from the walls, sitting on the end tables, scattered across the entertainment center—depicted a happy family. She wasn't in any of them anymore.

She felt like she was visiting a long-lost friend—a friend who happened to live in a haunted house. She was afraid to go explore on her own despite knowing every inch of the home. She wanted to ask someone for permission first. Her chest started to ache and a bout of dizziness struck her. She realized she had been holding her breath for a minute. Her exhale broke the silence.

"It's only a house," Angelina whispered to herself.

Trying to stay busy and make some noise, she took her father's mug to the kitchen sink and washed it. She headed to her bedroom on the second floor. She noticed it had been cleaned recently—not a speck of dust in sight. All of the furniture was in its rightful place. She took a seat on her bed. It was smaller than she remembered.

As she glanced around the room, a tsunami of good memories surged through her mind. For the first time since she returned to Goldbrush, she felt truly comfortable. She felt at home.

She remembered doing homework at her desk and calling her friends, like Danny and Justin, for help with a walkie-talkie. She recalled Gilbert sneaking into her bedroom to snatch her Nintendo DS so he could play *Mario Kart DS*. Staring at the doorway, she thought about the many times her father had carried her to bed after she had fallen asleep in the living room.

She looked down at herself, a smile pulling up the corner of her mouth. She saw herself sitting in bed and listening to music with her mother. Starting in her chest, a pleasant warmth spread through her. Tears stood in her eyes—tears of happiness, of relief, of hope. She went over to her desk and opened the top drawer.

Amongst the old notebooks, pencils, and pens, she found her old iPod Touch inside. Her white headphones were wrapped around it. The charging cable—which was already connected to a wall plug—was rolled up and wedged in a corner. She took it out and started charging the device. To her surprise, it still worked.

While waiting for it to charge, she returned to her bed and checked under her pillow. Her childhood diary was under it. It looked like no one had touched it since she left home for boarding school. She knew this because she had always left it in the same position—horizontal at a slight angle with the cover down—to keep track of it.

If it was ever in a different position, she knew her brother or one of her parents had looked through it.

She leafed through its pages and skimmed through the handwritten entries. The diary brought more memories to mind. Most of them were good. A few of the entries were scribbled out of anger and sadness, but the bad times from her childhood couldn't compare to the challenges she faced as a young adult.

Slaving away to make ends meet and struggling with her self-esteem in the age of social media was worse than missing a birthday party or getting gum stuck in her hair.

She realized she didn't have many negative experiences in Goldbrush. She could see why her mother didn't understand her decision to leave. But as she read the diary entries about her goals and dreams, she knew she had made the right choice. Although her childhood was pleasant, she didn't see much of a future for herself in the isolated town.

"This is a place to retire, not a place to dream," she whispered as she closed the diary.

Out of habit, she put it back under her pillow in the same position as before. She grabbed her iPod Touch, plugged the earbuds into her ears, then lay down in bed and listened to music on shuffle. Her mother had filled it up with some of their favorites. *What's Up?* by 4 Non Blondes played first.

The music whisked her away. She felt like she was floating on a cloud, far above Goldbrush. Within minutes, she drifted off to sleep.

8

ABANDONED?

THE SILVER SUV ROLLED TO A STOP. IN BLUE LETTERS, the decals on the driver door and front passenger door read: *POLICE.*

Sitting in the driver's seat, Justin peered out the passenger window to his right. An RV was parked in the desert, just off a hiking trail. A lightweight trailer was attached to it. The vehicle was so filthy that it looked like it had come out of a junkyard. The cop's eyes went to his rearview mirror.

Goldbrush was a speck in the reflection. Beyond the town, the sun fell behind the mountains. The sky was a canvas of orange and violet.

Justin grabbed his radio and said, "Dispatch, this is Unit 42. I have a suspicious vehicle parked out here in the desert about a quarter mile south of Goldbrush."

"Ten-four," the female dispatcher answered. "Do you have a make and model?"

"It's a small RV with a trailer. White. Dirty. Can't see its license plates from here. Going to get a closer look. Standby for a possible code 8."

"Ten-four."

The cop turned on his emergency lights, then climbed out of the SUV. With one hand on his holster, he approached the RV. Standing on his tiptoes, he examined the cockpit. The passenger and driver door windows were caked in dust and streaked with hard water stains. An aluminum foil sunshade, frayed by age, blocked the windshield.

Although there was plenty of sunlight outside, Justin took a flashlight out of his utility belt. He flashed it at the windows, but it couldn't penetrate the grime. He circled the RV and trailer. Decrepit blinds covered the other windows. He caught glimpses of the RV's interior through the gaps between the broken blinds.

The camper was filthy, torn clothing sprawled on the dilapidated furniture and trash piled on the floor. Between pieces of garbage—food wrappers, crumpled plastic bags, crushed cans and water bottles—the brown carpet was flecked with dark stains. A stack of dirty dishes stood in the sink.

The trailer's windows were completely blocked from inside. The stench of decay seeped out of it. Justin was bothered by the scent. Although he had never smelled a dead body before, it reminded him of roadkill but stronger. It was the stench of death—

violent, *tragic* murder. He leaned in close to the trailer's door and listened.

Total silence.

As he walked back to the passenger side of the RV, he heard a faint *buzzing* noise. His eyebrows shot up as he glanced back at the trailer. His sweaty fingers touched the grip of his holstered handgun. He took a step towards the trailer, then stopped. The sound was coming from his right. He looked at the RV, then down at the ground.

A swarm of flies buzzed around the rear tire. The cop crouched down and, upon closer inspection, he saw something mashed into one of the tire's grooves.

It was Danny's skinned face.

Justin couldn't identify it off the bat. It was encrusted in a mix of blood and soil, so it was dark. *Has to be roadkill,* he thought.

He knocked on the camper door and said, "Police! Open up!" There was no answer. He knocked again, striking the door with his flashlight three times. He shouted, "Police!"

Yet again, no answer.

He tapped the cockpit's passenger window with his flashlight twice, then moseyed over to the driver door and knocked on it.

"Police!" he said. "C'mon, I just want to talk. You're not in any trouble."

There was no sound in the RV. As he took another look through the gaps between the blinds, the cop didn't notice any movement in the vehicle, either. He was tempted to force his way into the RV, but without probable cause, he was afraid of overstepping his authority, especially as a rookie.

On his way back to his SUV, he checked the ground for footprints. He found a few tracks, but they zigzagged through each other, traveling in every direction. Tourists liked to deviate from the main hiking trail to take pictures out there. He even spotted some wildlife tracks in the area. It was impossible for him to track the RV's occupants.

Speaking into the radio clinging to his chest, Justin said, "Dispatch, this is Unit 42. No license plates on that 11-54. Might be dealing with some tourists using the desert as their personal parking lot."

He focused on the RV's rear tire. He thought about reporting the possible roadkill and the stench from the trailer in order to request a cadaver dog. But he didn't want to be reprimanded for wasting police resources if he were wrong. Fifteen seconds ticked past on his wristwatch.

"Ten-four," the dispatcher said.

Justin waited for more, but the dispatcher stayed quiet. Puzzled, he looked down at his radio.

"Dispatch, please advise on how to proceed," he said.

Another fifteen seconds passed.

Then thirty.

Justin walked in circles while looking up at the sky,

wondering if there was some sort of interference disrupting their communication. Head on a swivel, he canvassed the desert. Standing in the open, he felt like someone was watching him through a rifle's scope.

As he stepped closer to his SUV, he said, "Dispatch, please advise on how to proceed. How do you copy?"

After another ten seconds of silence, the dispatcher said, "Ten-four. We have our hands full at the moment with a... situation. Officer Brewer is on his way to take your beat as scheduled. He'll handle the 11-54."

"What the hell is going on?" Justin asked aloud, although he wasn't pressing the push-to-talk button on his radio.

He had noticed his dispatcher sounded unusually stressed and preoccupied. He considered offering his assistance, but he felt useless. He believed he was being pushed aside because his superiors thought he wasn't capable of handling the job on his own.

He sighed, then said, "Ten-four."

He took one final glance around before getting back into his SUV. He turned off his emergency lights, then drove off.

9

GOLDBRUSH ESSENTIALS

THERE HADN'T BEEN A CUSTOMER FOR THIRTY MINUTES.

Ben Jones strolled through Goldbrush Essentials, preparing to close up shop for the night. He restocked and straightened up the shelves. He made sure the *House of the Dead 2* arcade cabinet and the slot machines were off. Then he mopped the aisles before turning off most of the lights. Only the light above the checkout counter stayed on.

Standing behind the counter, he counted the cash. The refrigerators and freezers hummed ceaselessly. After finishing the count, he took the cash register till into his office behind the counter and locked it in a safe. There was only enough space in the room for a desk with two monitors, some computer equipment, and a minifridge.

Another door in the office led to Goldbrush Sparks, Ben's defunct firework shop. Although it had been out of business for years, the shop was still filled with fire-works of all shapes and sizes.

As he turned off the light in the office, Ben heard a *bang* outside. It came from behind the convenience store. He reckoned it was either a wild animal who had gotten into the trash or a tourist trying to throw his garbage away in the dumpster before departing the town. They both annoyed him equally.

"What was the point of buying that sign if no one reads it?" he muttered. "It's a *private* dumpster, darn it."

He stepped out through the back door. It was dark, stars twinkling in the night sky. There were no animals or tourists in sight. He walked up to the dumpster next to the back door. Leaning his head back and pressing his index finger against his nostrils to minimize the effect of the stench, he lifted the lid and peeked inside.

Nothing but garbage.

He closed the dumpster, then glanced around the desert, searching for the source of the sound. *A car door slamming? One of the kids throwing a ball at my wall? My imagination?* he pondered. Weaving and bobbing his head, he squinted at the tiny rickety shed across the dirt path. The townsfolk used it to store maintenance tools and equipment.

He started to walk towards it when he heard the familiar *ding!* of his store's door chime. He raced back inside. The lights were still off, and the front door was closed. He leaned over the counter and checked behind the cash register, expecting to find a burglar attempting to steal the till. It was clear, though.

A refrigerator door popped open.

Ben turned his head so fast that he almost gave himself whiplash. Down the aisle to his left, he saw a man standing in front of a refrigerator. He was a tall, well-muscled guy in a wifebeater and white pants. Despite the lack of light, he was staring into a fridge full of milk and juices, cold air blowing on his bare arms.

Ben couldn't get a read on him. He could tell he wasn't a resident of Goldbrush, though. He knew everyone in town. He could identify them solely based off their hair, posture, and attire. His visitor didn't look like a tourist, either. Although they occasionally arrived ill-prepared, most of the tourists came to the area dressed for a hike.

"I'm sorry, mister, but it looks like you missed the sign," Ben said, pointing at the front door. "We're closed. It's time for you to go."

The visitor ignored him. He bent over and reached into the refrigerator. He took out a carton of milk, studied it for a moment, then shook his head and put it back. He walked away, allowing the refrigerator door to close behind him. He made his way to the front of the store. Ben kept his eye on him, matching his pace as he walked parallel to him.

"If you need directions out of town or to the lodge, I can give them to you," the store owner said. "But you can't stay and play your games here. I don't have time for your shenanigans."

The visitor stopped in front of the arcade cabinet. He took one of the light guns out of its holster. He pointed it at the game's dark screen, pretending to play for a few seconds, then he aimed it at Ben and squeezed the trigger. Despite knowing it wasn't a real gun, Ben flinched. The visitor snickered, holstered the light gun, then strolled down the aisle towards the owner.

The spatters of dried blood on his wifebeater and pants resembled drops of black paint in the moonlight. Then the silvery glow of the night illuminated his painted face.

It was Captain Gashes.

Ben took a startled step backward. Despite the clown makeup and the darkness, he could see the knobbly scars on the left side of his face. He was rendered speechless by his appearance.

Everyone was welcome in Goldbrush, but it was jarring to see a clown in the desert.

Captain Gashes grabbed a bottle of drain cleaner off a shelf. He read the label on the back of the product.

"Perfect," he said.

Drain cleaner in hand, he strode towards Ben. Ben walked backwards until he crashed into the checkout counter. The clown held the drain cleaner out in front of him. Ben looked at it, then back at Captain Gashes, then at the entrance. A sense of foreboding gripped him. His inner voice was telling him to run out.

The clown shook the bottle—the liquid sloshing inside—and asked, "Well? Aren't you going to ring me up?"

"We're closed," Ben said.

"The door was open."

"It was unlocked, not open."

"What's the difference?"

"An unlocked door isn't an invitation to make yourself at home in someone's property. That sign says we're closed, so we're closed. That's the end of it."

"Oh, don't be like that," Captain Gashes said. "This show isn't over until the fat lady sings... and *squeals*... and *shrieks*. Now, we need this drain cleaner for the next act of our show, so I ain't leaving without it. I *can't* leave without it. No way, no how. So, you can either sell it to me... or I'll make you part of the show. What do you say?"

Ben picked up on the threatening undertones of the clown's message. His fear turned to anger. He refused to be intimidated by a clown.

"Get. Out," he said angrily.

Captain Gashes moved his head forward a bit and scowled at him. His eyes burned with rage like the blue flame from a propane torch. His breathing grew louder —*angrier*—competing with the hum from the refrigerators. Then a devilish smile touched the sides of his mouth as he tilted his head back.

"I'll go, but not before I give you a sneak preview of tonight's main event," the clown said.

"That shotgun back there is *real* and *loaded*," Ben said as he swung his head back, referencing the double-barreled shotgun he kept mounted above the cigarette rack. "You go ahead and walk out with that drain cleaner—with whatever you want. I'll let the police deal with you in that case. But don't you dare lay a finger on me. I'm not afraid to defend myself from punks like you."

"Oh, looks like we've got a tough guy in the house. Tell me, mister, do you think you're some sort of cowboy out in this desert? You think you're a real gunslinger, hmm? You see yourself as a John Wayne or a Clint Eastwood? *Tell me,* 'tough guy,' do you really think you're fast enough to jump over that counter, draw your weapon, and shoot me? You think you're faster than me?"

"Make my day," Ben said, quoting Clint Eastwood's character Harry Callahan from the movie *Sudden Impact*.

Captain Gashes gave a belly laugh while wagging the drain cleaner at him. Ben leaned back against the counter, ready to roll over it at the first sign of trouble.

"Gladly" he said. "Why don't we start with some magic? For my first trick–"

"That was your last warning."

"–I'll make your shotgun disappear."

Before he could say another word, Ben froze up

with his mouth open. The clown pointed a finger gun at the cigarette rack.

As he pretended to shoot it, he said, "*Voila!*"

Scared to look, Ben turned his head slowly. He stopped moving as soon as the wall mount above the cigarette rack entered the periphery of his vision. His eyes grew with abject terror. He tensed up, shoulders rising to his earlobes and his teeth grinding against each other. The shotgun was missing.

Captain Gashes said, "You should really keep your guns in a safe. Now for my second trick, I'm going to make this drain cleaner... *disappear.*"

Without thinking twice, legs moving faster than his mind, Ben bolted towards the entrance. The clown gave chase. Ben pulled the door open an inch, activating the door chime. *Ding!* Captain Gashes yanked the old man's long hair back while simultaneously throwing his own body at the door to slam it shut. The door rattled and its glass panes cracked upon impact.

The clown pulled Ben back, spun around, and launched him into a shelf. It fell over and hit the shelf in the neighboring aisle, setting off a domino effect. One by one, the shelves tipped over and crashed into each other, products raining down in the aisles. Ben dropped to his knees *hard,* sending hot balls of pain bobbling up and down his legs. Cleaning products surrounded him.

Captain Gashes clutched a fistful of Ben's hair and helped him to his feet. He pushed his upper body over the freezer chest next to the entrance. With a tug of his hair, he pulled his head up towards his shoulder. Some locks of hair tore off his scalp with a *crinkling* sound. Then he thrust his head back down at the freezer, slamming his face against the glass sliding door.

Blood gushed out of Ben's busted nose, dying the white hairs on his mustache red. Captain Gashes pulled his head back up, waited for three seconds, then slammed his face on the freezer door again. The bridge of Ben's nose opened in a bloody crevice of cartilage and bone. Blood cascaded across the glass like rain on a windshield, blocking the view of the ice cream inside.

"Maybe I can make that honker disappear, too," the killer clown said. "The Cap's got your nose!"

He lifted his head up again. Now, every white hair on Ben's goatee was red. Blood lined his teeth, too. Before Captain Gashes could slam his face a third time, Ben elbowed his stomach and knocked him back. The clown lost his footing on a plunger on the floor. He lost his grip on the drain cleaner as he fell on his ass.

"You fucking rat," he snarled.

Ben reeled down the aisle, spritzes of blood spraying from his mouth as his lips fluttered. Captain Gashes scrambled to his feet and followed him. He made a grab for his victim's head but barely missed him by a hair. At the end of the aisle, Ben juked left. As he lurched to the back of the store, he opened a refrigerator door and then another without looking back.

Captain Gashes crashed into the first door face-first, his forehead bouncing off the glass with a *thud*. The impact dazed him. He wobbled into a shelf cluttered with bags of potato chips, then back against the door, inadvertently closing it. As he oriented himself, he rushed forward. He tackled the second door shut with his shoulder.

At the back of the store, Ben took another left down the last aisle. He was slowing down, stumbling with every step. He was out of breath due to the blood clogging his nose. His old age didn't help, and neither did the pain in his face and knees.

The door chime *dinged* again.

"Help!" Ben cried out. "Get help!"

Captain Gashes grabbed Ben's hair and yanked his head back. He thrust the side of his head at one of the neighboring slot machine's polycarbonate panels, fracturing his cheekbone. Ben's vision immediately blurred and his knees buckled. But the clown held him up by the hair. He slammed the old man's face on the slot machine once more, breaking his right eye socket.

Ben fell unconscious. When he reawakened seconds later, Captain Gashes was dragging him back towards the refrigerators. His vision darkened for a moment, but he still heard other footsteps in the store.

"Is he dead already?" a woman asked.

Ben's vision returned, half unfocused. He saw Boo-Boo standing in the aisle in front of him. She was holding his double-barreled shotgun. In the next aisle,

Pipsqueak was perusing the snacks. He helped himself to a bag of Flamin' Hot Cheetos.

Captain Gashes knelt in front of his victim and said, "He's still with us. The bastard made me chase him around this dump. Yeah, this one's a fighter. Get me something to restrain his hands."

"Sure thing, Cap," Boo-Boo said.

"Wha... Why?" Ben said weakly. "Wha–What do you... want from me? Muh–Money? The money's in the... the safe."

Captain Gashes said, "We don't need your money. Money's no good during an apocalypse. We want chaos. We want blood. And you've still got about a gallon and a half of that in you."

"Don't... Please, please... Take the money... Take anything..."

"Oh, we're going to take everything, all right."

"Found this, Cap," Boo-Boo said as she approached the men.

She handed him a roll of duct tape. While he removed the packaging, she held Ben's arms overhead with her free hand. The old man was too weak—too scared—to fight back. Captain Gashes taped Ben's hands to the refrigerator's handle above him five times over. Meanwhile, Pipsqueak crunched on his chips, the bag rustling after every bite.

"Perfect!" Boo-Boo exclaimed.

Captain Gashes said, "Give me that shotgun and go get the drain cleaner. I dropped it near the entrance."

"Can't Pips or Nikki do it? They're just standing there."

"I'm eating," Pipsqueak said.

"C'mon, I don't wanna be part of the 'stage crew.' I just wanna watch the show. There's something special about being part of the audience, y'know? Makes me feel like a kid again."

Despite his blurred vision, Ben could see there were only three clowns in front of him. But since he heard another woman's name come out of Boo-Boo's mouth, he wondered if there was another intruder lurking around in his store. He was only certain of one thing: He was surrounded by violent clowns. He felt like he was trapped in a nightmare.

"Who are you people?" he whimpered.

"If I send Pips, he's going to come back with the wrong thing three times in a row," Captain Gashes explained. "You can get the job done right the first time, and you're just standing there, too. Now go get the damn drain cleaner. It's the red bottle. You can't miss it."

"*Fine,*" Boo-Boo groaned like a teenager arguing with a parent.

She handed him the shotgun, then stomped away with her arms crossed over her chest. Captain Gashes spun the firearm around, muzzles pointing behind him, and held it by its barrels.

He said, "I told you I was going to make that drain cleaner disappear, didn't I?"

"You–You'll regret this," Ben stammered. "The police will–"

Mid-sentence, Captain Gashes jabbed the shotgun at Ben's face, striking his mouth with the butt of the weapon. From canine to canine, on top and on bottom, his teeth shattered. The broken pieces fell to the floor between his thighs, clattering like marbles. Some fragments rolled into his throat, causing him to retch.

Captain Gashes hit him with the shotgun again. The back of Ben's head hit the glass door behind him with enough force to crack it. Some of his teeth were completely ejected from his gums. He felt his teeth— whole and broken—floating in the blood flooding his mouth. His bottom lip was split in half down the middle vertically.

The killer clown struck him a third time. Ben's jaw broke with a *crunch*. Unable to close his mouth, threads of bloody drool hung from his busted, quivering lip. He groaned sluggishly, barely conscious.

Captain Gashes hit him a fourth time, then a fifth time, and then a sixth time.

Only Ben's molars remained in his gums. Slivers of enamel were trapped between his teeth. His tongue was coated in blood. His upper lip was partially detached, hanging from a strand of flesh. He was babbling incomprehensively. His eyesight cycled between blurry and dark while his ears rang endlessly.

"Here ya go," Boo-Boo said with a trace of annoyance in her voice as she approached them.

Captain Gashes gave her the shotgun, blood smeared on its butt, and took the drain cleaner from her. He beckoned to her as he unscrewed the cap.

"You wanna be this magician's assistant?" he asked.

"Really?" Boo-Boo answered, eyes sparkling.

"Yeah."

"Yippee!"

"All right, all right, calm down. Tilt his head back and hold him steady."

"With pleasure, Cap!"

She tossed the shotgun at Pipsqueak. He teetered as he caught it in his red Cheeto-dusted fingers. He started dumping the chips into his mouth directly from the bag. Boo-Boo knelt next to the victim. She grabbed his jaw in one hand. Her gentle touch triggered the fiercest pain in his face, making him sob hoarsely. His suffering only worsened as she pried his mouth open. She grasped his hair in her other hand, then tilted his head back, forcing him to look up at the ceiling.

"Don't blink," Captain Gashes said. "You don't wanna miss the magic."

He dumped the drain cleaner on Ben's face. The liquid made a *glugging* sound as it poured out. Ben's eyes slammed shut as drops of drain cleaner splashed on his eyeballs. He felt like his nasal cavity was set aflame as the liquid flowed into his nostrils and entered the gash on the bridge of his nose. And that agonizing heat radiated into the back of his throat. Most of the corrosive liquid entered his mouth.

A crop of blisters sprouted across his lacerated lips. The skin around the blisters started to peel off. His tongue and gums burned. He tried to scream, but the liquid quickly filled his mouth. Feeling like he was drowning, he swallowed, which turned up the heat in his aching throat. The burning sensation dropped into his stomach like a firebomb. A racking cough seized him, causing his entire body to spasm.

With the last *glug,* Captain Gashes said, "And it's gone."

"Ta-da!" Boo-Boo shouted.

Ben kept convulsing. He couldn't hear their words over the ringing in his ears. A debilitating headache laid waste to his mind. The pain warped his every thought.

"Pips!" Captain Gashes hollered. "Help me carry him to the register. I've got an idea."

Pipsqueak gave the shotgun back to Boo-Boo, then he crumpled up the bag of potato chips before sucking his gloved fingers clean. He helped Captain Gashes cut the tape around Ben's wrists, then they carried him to the checkout counter. They lay him down on the counter on his back like a product waiting to be scanned. His legs hung behind the counter while his head dangled over the opposite edge.

Ben floundered and clawed at his neck as he

breathed raggedly. Blisters swelled in his throat, shrinking it to a pinhole.

Captain Gashes took the shotgun from Boo-Boo and said, "Now, I'm going to make this gun disappear."

He thrust the shotgun at Ben's mouth. Some of the blisters on his lips popped. Since Ben was swinging his head crazily, Captain Gashes couldn't slide the barrels into his mouth. He angled the weapon so he was pointing it downward, adjusted his aim, then jabbed it at his face again—*bull's-eye*. The barrels entered Ben's mouth, hitting his hard palate with enough force to break his upper jaw. He tilted the shotgun so he was pointing it straight ahead, then he drove it forward.

Ben gagged as the barrels slid past his uvula and entered his throat, causing a hard lump to protrude from his neck. His body jerked, arms and legs flailing. Pipsqueak held his legs to stop him from rolling off the counter. Blood frothed out of Ben's mouth, bubbling around the shotgun's barrels. Captain Gashes met some resistance on account of the huge blisters in the owner's throat. Putting his back into it, the clown pushed the shotgun deeper and deeper—*and deeper*.

"You can do it, Cap!" Boo-Boo cheered, hopping with excitement.

With each thrust, the lump traveled farther down Ben's neck. It pushed his Adam's apple forward as the barrels slid past it. Muffled popping noises came from his throat as some of the blisters burst. The shotgun came to a stop at the base of his neck. Captain Gashes used all of his energy and weight to push the shotgun, but it wouldn't budge.

Ben had stopped resisting, convulsions weakening to some twitches. His breathing had slowed to a dangerous pace, only managing a snort of air every minute. The color was fading from his cheeks. His eyelids were cracked open, revealing his bloodshot sclerae. He was on the cusp of death.

Boo-Boo stopped jumping and said, "Looks like you still need some practice to pull this one off, huh? Maybe we should try the hat-trick again next time."

"I guess magic ain't my forte," Captain Gashes responded. "But at least I know how to end a show with a bang."

He squeezed the trigger. The shotgun went off with a *boom,* masked by Ben's insides but loud enough to escape the shop. Ben's chest exploded open. Like confetti, bits of his organs—his heart, his lungs, his liver, his esophagus—as well as shards of bone soared through a haze of blood in every direction. Threads of his torn shirt joined the gory rain.

The clowns staggered away. Most of the pellets from the shotgun blast were lodged in Ben's butchered organs, but a few escaped his body. One hit a cigarette pack next to Pipsqueak. Another ricocheted off the cash register. And two hit the ceiling. Nuggets of bloody human flesh splatted on Captain Gashes and Pipsqueak.

The clowns stood in awed silence for fifteen

seconds before Boo-Boo exclaimed, "Holy moly! That was frickin' amazing!"

She hopped in place, clapped, and giggled. Pipsqueak brushed the chunks of Ben's heart off his jumpsuit with the back of his hand. Captain Gashes leaned in close to his victim and examined the damage. The massive hole in Ben's chest was filled with blood. The force of the recoil had obliterated the old man's jaw and caused his cheeks to tear open in a wide Glasgow smile.

"Not bad," Captain Gashes murmured.

Boo-Boo ran up to him, grabbed his arm with both hands, and asked, "Can I do the next one? Can I? *Can I?*"

"We'll see."

"Oh, c'mon! I wanna shove it up someone's ass and watch their stomach explode! Or maybe I can stick it up a pussy! Or—*or*—if we find a pregnant lady, I can–"

"*We'll see,*" Captain Gashes repeated sharply. "Look, I fucked up and took things too far. We can't run around shooting everyone we see. We need to get back to the original plan. Do things like how we were taught. Prove them wrong. We take these people out one by one until we have the upper hand. Then, *if* we get our hands on more guns, you can have some fun with this one."

"Fine," Boo-Boo said while hanging her head in disappointment.

Captain Gashes gave the shotgun's stock a couple

of tugs. The gun came out with a goop of blood and a few more dislodged teeth. He wiped the barrels on his pants.

He said, "Turn off the lights and make sure the doors are locked. Start making some Molotovs. I'll look around for some more shotgun shells. Let's get this show on the road."

10

FAMILY DINNER

ANGELINA SAT UP IN BED, EARBUDS FALLING FROM HER ears. Through the darkness, she stared curiously at the window at the end of the bedroom to her left. A suppressed boom had awoken her from her sleep. Powered off, the iPod Touch lay next to her. Since she hadn't given it a full charge, the battery had died while she was napping.

Thunder? A car accident? A gunshot? she thought.

She turned the knob on the lamp on her nightstand. She was surprised it still worked. She slunk over to the window and peeked out from behind the curtain. The night was clear, starry with a bright moon. She didn't see or hear any cars on the dirt path in front of the home. Her intuition told her that the noise had come from a gun, although she had never heard a gunshot in person.

Soft voices downstairs captured her attention. She

couldn't make out any words, but she recognized them as her family's voices. She frowned at the floor while biting her fingernails. She knew she had slept through the day, and she assumed her parents and her brother were home now. She checked her cell phone's clock.

"Dinner time," she whispered.

She started pacing back and forth. She wondered if her mother knew that she was up in her room the whole time or if her father and brother had kept her presence a secret to keep her calm. She could tell Kurt and Gilbert had grown tired of the constant family drama. She was determined to end it.

"If she knew I was here, she would have woken me up, dragged me out of bed, and kicked me out," Angelina said to herself. "She doesn't know. She doesn't know."

Her mind spiraled into a whirlpool of uncertain thoughts. She started organizing the words in her head, writing mental speeches and even planning out counters to her mother's potential responses. Her thought process went like this: *'If she says this, I'll say that. If she says that, I'll say this. If she says... If she says... If she says...'*

"Stop it," she scolded herself. "Just go down there and do it, Angie. Go down there and tell them how you really feel."

She took a couple of deep breaths through her nose, put on a stern face, then marched out of her room. On her way down the stairs, the voices became clearer. She heard her father and mother in the kitchen.

"I'm not in the mood for this," Heather was saying. "Can we talk about it later?"

Kurt said, "You can't keep pushing this off."

In the living room across the hall, an episode of *Family Guy* was playing on the TV. Gilbert's laughter came out of the room. Angelina stopped at the bottom of the stairs. She swallowed another big gulp of air, then walked to the kitchen archway.

"Gilbert!" Heather yelled. "Dinner!"

She had just finished serving three plates of Tuscan chicken macaroni and cheese at the dining table. As she turned to take the pot back to the stove, she spotted her daughter in the archway. Her face turned to stone. The noise from the TV came to a sudden stop.

The house was unsettlingly quiet.

Gilbert stepped to his sister's side. He looked at Angelina, then at his mom, then back at Angelina.

"Are you gonna eat with us?" he asked.

Angelina shrugged at him, then looked at her mother and said, "I don't know. Can I join you?"

Heather's knuckles turned white as she held the pot and wooden spoon with a death grip. She wanted to yell at Angelina, but she didn't want her son to get caught in the crossfire. She knew an outburst was only going to push him closer to his sister.

"Kurt, can you grab another plate and something to drink for your daughter?" she said.

The kitchen was rife with tension. Angelina was seated across from her mother. The women eyeballed each other. Angelina's father sat to her left, her brother to her right. No one had said a word since Heather served the last plate. Kurt and Gilbert ate their food without haste, as if afraid they were eating poison.

Kurt grunted, then said, "So... How was school, Gilbert?"

The boy responded with a shrug as he stabbed a piece of chicken with his fork.

"Answer your father properly," Heather said without taking her eyes off her daughter.

Gilbert sighed, then said, "School is school. Same thing every day."

"I know we're not sending you to school to learn the same lesson every day," Kurt said. "C'mon, bud, what'd you learn today?"

"History. Math. English."

Heather broke eye contact with her daughter to smirk at her son. She said, "Gilbert, you can be more specific than that."

"We learned how to make ice cream in a bag for science class. That was pretty cool, I guess."

"And how did you do on your algebra test?"

Gilbert had passed his algebra test with a C minus. His parents had been pushing him to earn Bs and up, though. He didn't want to get in trouble, so he sought to change the subject.

He said, "Oh, yeah, um... Mr. Guzman didn't give 'em back yet. I guess he was busy meeting with Angie."

"Gilbert, what the hell?" Angelina said.

Her brother mouthed: '*Sorry.*' Then he shoved the chicken in his mouth and hung his head in shame.

"Typical," Heather said, shaking her head.

Angelina asked, "What's that supposed to mean?"

"You know what I mean."

"Say it."

"Excuse me? Watch your tone."

"Watch yours," Angelina said.

"Who are you to demand anything from me?"

"Who are you to... to... to *slut*-shame me?"

"Can we all calm down?" Kurt spoke up.

Heather said, "I did no such thing. You only think so because you subconsciously *feel* like a slut. And maybe you're right. Maybe that's what the world out there turned you into."

"That's bullshit and you know it," Angelina responded. "You always do this. You always try to flip everything and make it all my fault. And you're just too much of a two-faced coward to admit it."

"Coward?" Heather repeated, her face warped by spasms of anger. "You think I'm afraid of you? *You?*"

"You're afraid of losing control. You're afraid of ending up alone. You don't realize that the tighter you hold us, the more we want to leave. You're suffocating us with your grip."

"Us. You keep saying that word. You said you wanted Gilbert to make his own choice, but it sounds like you already made it for him. But he's not like you. He actually cares about his family and his town. He feels our love. He appreciates us. And you hate that. You hate to see us happy because *you* made some piss-poor decisions in your life."

Gilbert watched the argument in disbelief. *What have I done?* his face said. Kurt was tense, eyes filled with grave concern.

Angelina said, "Every time I hear your voice, I know I made the right choice. And you know what else? Every time you speak now, you show your true colors to Gilbert. I'm not making a choice for him. You are."

"Get out," Heather said.

"No. We're not done talking. You need to listen for once."

"Leave and never come back."

"I'm not going to let you–"

"Get out!"

Heather hurled her plate at her daughter. It missed Angelina's head by an inch, leaving a trail of macaroni and cheese on the table, her shirt, and the floor. It shattered against the wall behind her.

"You will not take my son from me!" Heather screamed.

She grabbed her glass of water. Before she could chuck it across the table, Kurt seized her wrist and pushed her arm down.

"Go to your rooms!" he shouted.

"Let go of me!" Heather yelled.

"Go!"

Kurt lifted her from her seat and wrapped his arms around her. The glass slipped out of Heather's hand, exploding at their feet. She continued yelling, face rosy and jugulars bulging. Shocked, Angelina and Gilbert became rooted to their seats. They had never seen their mother in such a feral state before.

"Now!" Kurt yelled.

Angelina felt like a kid again, compelled to follow her father's orders. She took Gilbert's hand and led him out of the kitchen. They went up to their rooms.

Heather screamed and grappled with her husband for another minute before dissolving into tears. She held onto his arms to stop herself from dropping to her knees.

"I'm sorry, I'm sorry," she cried.

"It's okay. Hey, everything's okay."

"God, I don't know what's wrong with me. I didn't mean to hurt her. I couldn't control myself."

"She's okay, Heather. You hear me? We're all okay."

Heather kept repeating the same sentence over and over: "I'm so sorry. I'm so sorry. I'm so sorry."

"Is something wrong with mom?" Gilbert asked, sitting at the foot of his sister's bed.

Angelina had been asking herself the same question. She stood in front of her desk with her back to her brother. She was charging her old iPod Touch again, hoping to find some comfort in nostalgia.

"Don't know," she answered.

"I've never seen her that angry. She was *super* pissed."

"At me. She was pissed at me. It has nothing to do with you, okay? So don't hold it against her."

Gilbert could tell his sister was trying to protect their mother's image despite the grudges they held against each other. He looked at the floor. The commotion in the kitchen had ceased.

He said, "I don't, y'know, have any hard feelings or whatever against you because you left. I know why you did it. I think it's cool. But Mom's right, too. I'm not like you."

"What do you mean?" Angelina asked as she turned around.

"I don't wanna leave Goldbrush. I don't wanna go to some boarding school all alone. I don't wanna start over without my friends."

"And by 'friends,' you mean Otto?"

Pouting, Gilbert gave a single nod. Angelina sat next to him and draped her arm over his shoulders.

"Do you want to know the truth about adulthood?" she asked.

"The truth?"

"The truth is, most friendships don't last very long. Even if you and Otto went to the same high school, chances are you'd most likely grow distant after graduation. You won't work in the same job. You'll meet different people—new friends, new lovers. You'll pick up new hobbies. You'll grow into the *real* you. Friends split ways, and I think it would be good for you if you accepted that fact now instead of later."

Gilbert said, "But we're different. We're best friends. Me and Otto have never abandoned each other. We see each other every day." He stood from the bed, then turned to face his sister and said, "I've spent more time with him than I've spent with you, Angie. We're like brothers, y'know? I don't... I, um... I lost a sister once. I don't want to lose a brother, too."

His words stung Angelina, but she knew he wasn't saying them to hurt her. He was only telling the truth. She had left him behind without saying goodbye. Although she wanted to convince him to explore the world, she was genuine when she said she wanted him to make his own decision.

She smiled and said, "You can always try to change his grades, so you guys can go to the same school." Gilbert narrowed his eyes and scratched the back of his head, as if thinking deeply. Angelina said, "I was joking."

"Yeah, I'll talk to you later."

"Gilbert. Gilbert!"

The boy left the room. Angelina thought about chasing after him, but she figured he needed some alone time. She didn't want to put more pressure on him.

Gilbert went to his bedroom across the hall and closed the door behind him. He took a walkie-talkie out from under his pillow.

He turned it on, then pressed the push-to-talk button and whispered, "Otto, you there? Over."

Fifteen seconds later, a boy answered, "Yeah, what's up, dude? Over."

"Can you sneak out and meet me at school? I've got a plan. Over."

"What kinda plan? Over."

"We're gonna do something about your grades, okay? We're gonna fix 'em. I can't tell you everything now 'cause someone might be listening, but... Just trust me, all right? I'm gonna make sure you graduate with me. I promise. Over."

Gilbert was lying. He had a goal—change Otto's grades—not a plan. He didn't know how he was going to do it, and he wasn't going to admit that to his best friend. He just needed his support. There was another fifteen seconds of silence.

The radio buzzed, then Otto said, "Yeah, dude, sure. My mom and dad are gonna watch a movie in their room. I'll sneak out after I smell their popcorn. See ya later. Over and out."

"Over and out," Gilbert said to himself as he lowered his walkie-talkie.

He tossed on a black hoodie, then crept out of his room and headed downstairs. He heard his parents cleaning up the mess in the kitchen. They were talking about something, but he couldn't make out their words. He snuck out of the house through the back door. Sticking to the darkness, hood over his head, he made his way through Goldbrush.

Although it wasn't his first time sneaking around town at night, he felt a pang of unease during his stroll. There was something in the air—apprehension, trouble, tragedy. It made his nose twitch and his arms goosebump. On his way to his school, he saw two of his neighbors standing outside of Goldbrush Essentials. One of the guys was trying to peek through a storefront window.

The man said, "Maybe something fell in there?"

"Was Ben going out tonight?" the other guy asked.

"No idea. I thought I saw his truck in front of..."

Hoping to get out of the public as swiftly as possible, Gilbert started jogging, so he missed the rest of the conversation.

11

GOLDBRUSH EATS

THE RATTLY KNOCKING ECHOED THROUGH THE HOME. Adeline was already in bed, propped up by a stack of pillows. A pair of reading glasses sat close to the tip of her nose. She held a tattered novel in her wrinkled hands. Felix sat at the other edge of the mattress, ready to slide into bed with his wife. He concentrated on the bedroom door. It was cracked open an inch.

More knocking came from the first floor.

Adeline said, "It's past nine. Who could that be?"

"At this hour?" Felix answered. "Might be an emergency. Maybe a lost hiker."

"Or a stranded one. Maybe they can't afford to stay at the lodge. You've seen the prices that Lindsay's been charging these days, haven't you? So greedy."

"Yup. Well, I'll go take a look-see. Be right back."

He slid his feet into his slippers and shuffled out of the room. On his way down the dark hallway, he heard another barrage of clattery *thuds* from the front door. He went down the stairs to the door at the bottom. He unfastened the security chain and turned the deadbolt, then opened the door. It led to Goldbrush Eats' dining area.

Straight ahead, past a wall of dining booths, Felix saw the front door. And through the glass panes on the door, he spotted the silhouette of a person. He squinted at the visitor from afar, but his poor eyesight couldn't pierce the darkness. He doddered across the dining area, then flicked a switch next to the door. Outside, the light above the door flickered on.

He cocked his head back in surprise. Boo-Boo stood there with her hands clasped behind her back. She had removed her mask, but she was still wearing her clown dress. The corners of her mouth jerked with an urge to smile. Despite his aging vision, Felix noticed the bloodstains on her clothing. He opened the door, activating the chime.

Only a locked screen door stood between them.

"May I help you, miss?" Felix asked.

Boo-Boo said, "Hello, mister. Sorry to bother you at this hour, but I'm kinda in a pickle. I've been walking all evening looking for help. You see, me and my friends were driving through the desert when this *ginormous* tree came out of nowhere and stopped our RV."

"A tree... came out of nowhere?"

"Yeah. They should really put some lights on 'em,

don't ya think? Anyway, it wasn't a pretty sight. Lots of cuts. Tons of blood. Some broken bones, too, I think, but I don't have x-ray vision, so what do I know? I got a nosebleed myself and I was just minding my own business in bed."

Felix was flabbergasted by her explanation. She didn't seem injured, shaken by the crash, or concerned for her friends. Her childlike essence, however, sparked his paternal protective instincts.

"I'll get the police," he said. He turned his head to the side while keeping an eye on his visitor, and he shouted, "Addy!"

"There's no time for that, sir."

"Adeline!"

"*Mister,*" Boo-Boo said sternly. "I already went to that police booth over there. It's empty. I'm only here 'cause I saw that snazzy pickup truck parked next to this building. It looks like it can carry all of my friends out of there."

"I wish I could help, miss, but I'm no paramedic. I'm a cook. I'm not trained to… to rescue people."

"You don't need training to be our hero. You only need a heart. You have a heart, don't you?"

Felix had a heart of gold. Once again, his protective instincts kicked in. A robe wrapped around her body, Adeline made her way down the stairs. She stopped in the doorway at the bottom of the steps. Her husband blocked her view of their visitor, but she could hear their conversation.

Boo-Boo continued, "Look, I'm trying to stay calm and not make a big scene, but this is kinda serious. My boyfriend's pinned to his seat by a branch. Becca, a hitchhiker we picked up on the road, she's got a young son. Like, one or two years old."

"Oh no, is he okay?" Felix asked.

"He was fine when we left him. His mom... she ended up with a broken leg. I heard it break like a twig. She wanted me to bring her boy with me, but I didn't want that kid to turn into a frickin' popsicle. It's freezing, and it's only getting colder. They're not going to last in that crappy RV. Time's a-wastin'."

"What's going on?" Adeline said as she approached them. She looked Boo-Boo up and down, then asked, "Is everything okay?"

Felix said, "This young woman and her friends were in a car accident. Crashed their RV head-on into a tree. Apparently, there's no one at that police booth. Get on the satellite phone and give Justin a call. Let him know the situation. I'm going to head out and see if I can bring these people back here safely."

"Why don't I just call Brewer or 911? It would be faster, wouldn't it? Justin left hours ago. He might be home already."

"Brewer's supposed to be at that police booth right now. I know for a fact he's on the night shift this week. If he's not there, then he's not going to answer. Justin's a local. He knows his way around and he actually cares about this town. Call him."

"Oh, I don't know about this, hon."

Felix went back up to their bedroom, put on a coat over his pajamas, and grabbed his key ring. Adeline followed him. She took the satellite phone off the base station on her husband's nightstand. She didn't agree with Felix's plan, so she hesitated.

"I'll be right back," Felix said as he hurried out of the room.

Downstairs, he found Boo-Boo waiting for him outside. He opened the screen door and stepped out. Boo-Boo stopped him from closing it.

"Wait," she said. She stuck her head into the restaurant and shouted, "Thanks, ma'am! We really appreciate the help! We'll be seeing you soon!"

Unbeknownst to Felix, she placed a small magnet in the door's strike plate hole, stopping it from locking. As she stepped aside, Felix attempted to lock the door, but to no avail.

Boo-Boo tugged on the old man's arm and said, "Please, sir, we're running out of time."

"Let me just–"

"Please! That boy needs us!"

Although he wanted to try to lock the other door, Felix gave in. He trusted his neighbors anyway. With the temperature dropping rapidly, clouds of vapor puffed out of his mouth with each exhale. He could only think about the toddler at the crash site.

He reluctantly led Boo-Boo to his truck. They drove

off and, following the clown's directions, they left Gold-brush in a hurry.

Sitting on the bed, Adeline used the satellite phone to call Goldbrush's police field office. Grasping the chest of her nightgown in one hand, she held the phone up to her ear and listened to the ringback tone. No one answered. She called the neighborhood snoop, Ben Jones, at his home. He didn't answer, so he called his convenience store. Again, the call didn't connect.

She was about to call Justin's cell phone when the door chime rang downstairs. Her eyes darted to the bedroom door. A disquieting silence befell the home. She stood from the bed cautiously to avoid making any noise. The frame squeaked anyway. She slunk forward, barely raising her feet with each step.

She pulled the door open, poked her head out, and inspected the hallway. It was dark and quiet. Her focus landed on the stairs to her left.

"Felix?" she called out. She heard a faint screeching noise, like a chair skidding across tile. She said, "Felix, you forget something?"

There was no response.

She closed the door and dialed Justin's number. The call connected as she sat on the bed.

"Hello?" Justin answered.

"Justin, it's Adeline. I'm sorry to bother you so late, but we have ourselves an emergency over here."

"Are you okay?"

"I'm fine. I–I'm spooked, but I'm fine."

"Spooked? Mrs. Brown, what's going on?"

Staring at the gap under the bedroom door, Adeline said, "We had a visitor. A young woman. She said she was in a car accident out in the desert. They crashed their RV into a tree. I don't know how many of them are there, but she said something about a woman and a baby. 'One or two years old,' she said."

"An RV," the cop whispered.

Adeline could hardly hear him. He had lowered his phone as he thought about the abandoned RV he had spotted outside of Goldbrush. The pieces were falling into place in his head.

"Felix went with the young lady to see if he could help," Adeline continued. "He's going to bring them back here. He asked me to call you."

"What about, um... Officer Brewer? What is he doing?"

"That young woman, she said there was no one in the police booth. I called just now and no one answered. I don't want to go check myself. I don't mean to sound like a child, but it's too dark right now and I'm scared. Please, hon, don't ask me to go out there."

"Mrs. Brown, I want you to stay in your home. I don't mean to alarm you, it's probably nothing more than an accident, but I want you to make sure all of your doors and windows are locked. I'll locate Officer Brewer and get to the bottom of this."

"Thank you, hon. Listen, I hate to bother you with this, but Felix wanted me to ask you if you could come back here and help us out. You know he trusts you like family. You're like a grandson, darling."

The line went silent for ten seconds. Adeline looked down at the floor upon hearing some creaks and clanks downstairs.

"I'll be there in a few hours," Justin said. "Don't hesitate to call me if you have any other concerns or questions, okay?"

"Yes, yes. Thank you, hon. Thank you so much."

"No problem. See you soon."

"I'll be here."

The call ended. Adeline put the satellite phone in its base station. She walked back to the door and cracked it open.

One foot in the hallway and the other in the bedroom, she yelled, "Felix, the police are coming. You don't have to go with her. Okay? Honey?"

Only a deafening silence answered.

She glanced back at the bed. She wanted to run back and hide under the covers, but the satellite phone reminded her of Justin's instructions: *'Make sure all of your doors and windows are locked.'* She felt like it was the smart thing to do. She pussyfooted down the hall, her shoulders high and tight with her hands balled up over her chest.

Halfway down the stairs, she heard a familiar *clink* —the sound of silverware. Someone was in the dining area. The door at the bottom of the stairs was closed but unlocked. She thought about locking it and running back up the stairs, but curiosity consumed her. She opened the door and stuck her head out.

She drew a short gasp. To her right, past the round tables in the middle of the room, a man sat at a booth. Light streamed through the kitchen's pass-through window. It was only enough to reveal his bare, burly arms and slick hair. He had a fork in one hand and a steak knife in the other. Moonlight from the storefront windows gleamed on the silverware.

Adeline couldn't identify the slab of food on the plate in front of the uninvited guest. She looked at the front door—it was closed—then back at the intruder.

"Ek–Excuse me," she stuttered. "What are you... doing here? We're closed."

"I'm eating," the man said.

"But... we're closed. You–You're trespassing. You should go. The police are on the way."

"You'd call the cops on the sick and starving?"

"What? No. Never. I'm not... We are good people, mister, but we don't know you."

"Then why don't you join me? Let's talk."

Adeline crossed the threshold, leaving the door open behind her for a quick escape. She sidestepped around the corner towards the kitchen door and flicked a switch on the wall. The light above the cash register turned on. Her face contorted with horror. She held her breath and ground her dentures.

Captain Gashes sat at the booth. In a puddle of blood, there was a piece of raw, carved up, fibrous meat on his plate.

Ben's heart.

Adeline didn't know he was eating her beloved friend. The mere sight of the blood and gore was enough to unnerve her, though. The clown shoveled a forkful of the mutilated organ into his mouth. He chewed it noisily, blood sprinkling out with each bite. From one cheek to the other, he swished it around in his mouth. He threw his head back and swallowed.

He let out a satisfied sigh, then said, "Well, what are you waiting for? Sit down, granny. There's plenty of food to go around."

Adeline began to pant and quiver, fear flooding her body with adrenaline. She glanced at the front door and thought about making a beeline for it. She didn't want to run past the clown, though. She looked at the wall behind her. She felt safe in her home upstairs, but she was afraid of cornering herself. A glance at the kitchen door made her think about the restaurant's rear exit.

"Don't make me tell you twice," the clown said.

Adeline lunged at the kitchen door. Captain Gashes jumped to his feet and rushed after her. As she ran around the kitchen island, Adeline noticed the open waffle maker and the bloody handprints stamped on the counter next to a sink. The waffle maker was heating up. Cannibalism was the first thing to pop into her mind. She staggered as her stomach contracted with dread.

She lurched towards the side door next to the fridge. Throwing her body against hers, Captain Gashes helped her reach it. He crushed her against the door with a strong tackle. She bellowed and crumpled to the floor. Her shoulder was dislocated, a few of her ribs were bruised, and her hip was fractured.

The killer clown grabbed a fistful of her hair and dragged her away from the door. Screaming, she clawed at his wrists and kicked the cabinets.

"I bet you didn't know clowns are great cooks," Captain Gashes said. "Who do you think makes all that popcorn and cotton candy and hot dogs and funnel cakes at the circus? We do. Jacks-of-all-trades... No, *jesters* of all trades, we do it all. You think I'm joking, but I really know one of the best cooks in the world. Wish I could introduce him to you. We call him Chef Cuckoo."

Keeping his fingers buried in her hair, he wrapped his other arm around her neck and heaved her up. The room was whirling, but she could see they were in front of the waffle maker. Standing behind her, the clown pressed his body against hers, pinning her against the counter. He grasped her hair in one hand and held the nape of her neck in the other.

"He likes to cook meat, I like to make waffles," Captain Gashes said.

As she sobbed, he slammed her face into the bulky waffle maker. She shrieked and thrashed as her skin sizzled. With her wild movements, the waffle maker moved an inch. Her face came off the waffle iron for a few seconds before the clown pushed her back down. He tightened his grip on her hair and neck.

After about thirty seconds, her screams turned to husky gasps. The hissing of her skin burning was louder than her breathing. Her mind was blank. The debilitating pain had limited her ability to think. Her survival instincts continued to control her body, though. She swung her arms around the counter, groping about for the waffle maker's power cord helplessly.

When her arms fell limp and her legs turned to jelly, Captain Gashes knew she had fallen unconscious. He pulled her head up. Pieces of burnt skin tore off her face. Some bits of skin were black and crispy, others were bloody and soft. Her face was a grid of deep burn wounds. Most of the gashes were on the right side of her face, but some reached her left cheek.

The remaining skin around the wounds was peeling. Her lower lip was burnt to a swollen, black crisp. Plumes of smoke rose from the burn marks.

Captain Gashes drew a paring knife from the knife block on the counter to his left. He turned her around, pushed her back against the counter, then let her slide down to the floor.

He crouched in front of her, tapped her forehead with the blade, and said, "Wakey, wakey."

Adeline's head jerked and a groan came out of her mouth. Her eyes appeared to be moving under her bloodshot eyelids.

"No?" Captain Gashes said. "Fine. But you better wake up for the grand finale. A clown without an audience is just an asshole in makeup after all. Don't you dare make me look like an asshole."

He pinched her flabby chin and pulled it towards him. He pierced the soft skin with the knife. As it scraped her jaw, he angled the blade upwards. Then he started sawing along the bone, moving up towards her left ear. As he reached the earlobe, he changed course and sawed up towards her hair. He followed her hairline.

With the blade halfway across her forehead, Adeline's eyes twitched open. She wasn't aware of the clown's plan to skin her face. She had no idea there was a knife *under* her skin. Her face was still burning from the waffle maker wounds, but now the left side was hotter than the other. The blood cascading across her face felt like it was boiling. She started to pant.

Captain Gashes said, "Don't start with your bullshit now. I'm almost–"

Adeline kicked him. He fell back against the kitchen island behind him. He kept a tight grip on the knife, so the blade cut through the woman's forehead vertically. Adeline wept and crawled away, leaving a trail of blood behind her. Half of her face hung from her skull. The flap of bloody skin blocked the left side of her vision.

As she reached the end of the kitchen island, Captain Gashes ran up to her and punted her stomach. She fell on her side, breathless with her arms crossed over her abdomen. The clown stomped on the side of her head. Although he was holding back, the kick was hard enough to put her to sleep.

"Sneaky bitch," he muttered as he rolled her onto her back. "Now, where was I? Oh, right, waffles."

He took a knee over her body. He slid the blade back into the gash on her forehead, then continued sawing towards the right side of her face.

Adeline awoke with a feeble, gasping breath. Parts of her face had gone numb, especially around her cheeks. She couldn't feel her lips whenever she closed her mouth. Other parts of her face were throbbing with pulses of white-hot pain. It radiated deep into her skull. She felt the burning sensation all the way back in her brainstem.

She was staring down at herself. She recognized the blue upholstery underneath her. She was sitting in one of her diner's booths. She was taped to her seat at the chest, waist, and thighs. The chest of her night-gown was spattered with blood.

"You're back," Captain Gashes said. "The timing couldn't have been any better. I *just* sat down and I was *just* about to eat. No, really. Look at my plate. Look at it."

As if hypnotized, Adeline lifted her head steadily to follow the sound of his voice. The clown sat across from her, smiling deviously while holding a knife and a fork. On the plate in front of him, there was a wedge of bloodied skin—*her flayed face*.

With his smile growing, Captain Gashes said, "Oh, how I wish you could see your face right now. Wait, you *are* seeing your face right now."

He laughed while Adeline whined and gagged. She realized why she couldn't feel her lips. They had been severed, leaving her bloodstained dentures on display. The grid of dark burn marks grooved her pulpy facial muscles. Parts of her skull were visible on her forehead and cheekbones. Only her eyelids remained.

The clown grabbed the glass syrup dispenser—filled with strawberry syrup—from the edge of the table. He drizzled it on his human waffle, blending it with the woman's blood.

"Let's have a taste test," he said as he stabbed the skin with his fork. "Don't worry. I'm an honest man. I'll let you know if it's better or worse than Chef Cuckoo's cooking."

He started sawing into the skin. As if she were

feeling the pain from her detached face, Adeline cried harder. Her tears stung her exposed cheek muscles. The knife screeched on the plate as the killer cut through the human waffle. It took him a minute to sever a big piece of her flayed cheek. With the skin impaled on its tines, he held the fork out in front of him and waggled it at his victim. Strawberry syrup and blood dripped from the skin.

"Looks delicious, don't it?" he said. "Yeah, yeah, I know. Don't worry, if it's as good as it looks, I'll save you a piece."

Adeline kept crying, her mouth moving in a voiceless plea for mercy. Snickering, Captain Gashes stuffed the forkful of flesh into his mouth. He chewed it loudly —*proudly*—with his mouth wide open. Fresh drops of blood dribbled down his bloodstained chin. But his smile began to fade as he struggled to tear through the skin. It was thin but gristly. He felt like it was growing with each bite.

He spat it out at his seat, then said, "Goddammit. You're too damn chewy. I should have served myself some milk or made some coffee before sitting down. Why didn't I think of that before, huh? I guess cooking's not my forte, either. Damn it. God-*fucking*-damn it. Well, no point in letting this go to waste. I've got another idea."

He scooted off his seat, sliding his plate along to the edge of the table with him. He unzipped his pants and pulled his flaccid penis out through the fly. He ogled his victim as he stroked his cock. The carnage aroused him. He became erect within seconds. He grabbed Adeline's detached face, wrapped it around his penis, and continued stroking himself.

He had turned her face into a real fleshlight.

Adeline tried to scream, but she could only muster some gasps. She watched her face ripple with each stroke. She looked up and saw the intruder's pleased grin. She fell into a state of total bewilderment. A killer clown was using her skinned face as a sex toy. Life didn't feel real to her anymore. She looked back down at his crotch.

The head of his penis—glazed with blood—slipped through one of her skinned face's eyeholes repeatedly, as if saying: *'Peek-a-boo!'* It made a wet squishy noise with each stroke.

"Here... it... comes," Captain Gashes said in a tight voice.

He leaned over Adeline's side of the booth and jerked his dick faster. His shoulders hitched up and his muscles went rigid. His teeth sank into his lower lip as he moaned. As his penis slipped through the eyehole once more, he ejaculated. Thick ropes of semen lashed her skinned face. Each drop felt like acid on her exposed muscles. A thread of semen hung from her earlobe like a stalactite.

She wept and wagged her head. Captain Gashes kept moaning and stroking his dick, squeezing every last drop out.

Breathing heavily, he said, "That was a big one, wasn't it? Your pretty face can make any clown go bonkers. Well, I'm finished here. But before I go... I promised to save you a piece, didn't I?"

He took her detached face off his blood-smeared penis. He rolled it up like a taquito, then he gripped Adelina's jaw—causing her to squeal—and pried her mouth open. Then he forced her skinned face into her mouth. He pushed it in until it entered her throat. Her eyes rolled up as she suffocated.

Captain Gashes looked down at his crotch. His dick was getting hard again. He was tempted to masturbate again, but time was of the essence. He shoved his penis back into his pants. After about a minute, Adeline's head slumped forward. The tape around her body stopped her from falling over the table.

The clown pulled his zipper up, then walked across the diner and turned off the light. He headed up into the Browns' home in search of weapons.

12

GOOD SAMARITAN, BAD LUCK

"I'M NOT SEEING THAT RV YOU WERE TALKING ABOUT," Felix said. "Are you sure we're going the right way?"

He was sitting in the driver's seat of his pickup truck, wrinkled hands clamped to the steering wheel at ten and two. He was cruising at a cautious fifteen miles per hour. Only the headlights illuminated the desert.

"What RV?" Boo-Boo responded from the passenger seat.

"From the accident."

"Accident?"

Felix furrowed his brow at her for a second before turning his attention back to the desert. Her casual indifference in the face of tragedy disturbed him.

He said, "The RV accident. You said your RV crashed into a tree."

"Oooooh, *that* RV. That was no accident."

"Huh? Now what is that supposed to mean, miss?

You said you crashed after a tree 'came out of nowhere,' remember?"

"I never said anything about a crash, gramps. If you remember correctly, I said a *ginormous* tree came out of nowhere and *stopped* us. Stopping doesn't mean crashing."

"I recall you saying there were cuts and broken bones. You said you had a nosebleed, and your boyfriend was pinned under a branch, and a woman and her baby were in trouble."

"Yeah, so? Think about it. What does any of that have to do with a car accident? I get nosebleeds all the time. All of my boyfriends have been pinned under a branch at some point in their lives. And women and their babies are always in trouble. That's life, man."

Felix gave her the side-eye. He suspected he had been played for a fool by a prankster. He turned the steering wheel slightly to the left, making a wide U-turn.

"What are you doing?" Boo-Boo asked. Felix stayed silent. The clown said, "What? Are you mad at lil' ol' me?"

Again, he didn't acknowledge her. She pivoted in her seat to face the passenger door. She took her clown mask out of the big pocket at the front of her dress and put it on, then turned around to face the driver.

"How can you be mad at a pretty clown like me?" she said.

Felix glanced at her, then did a wide-eyed double

take. He eased off the gas pedal, slowing the truck to about ten miles per hour. He looked back at the windshield, eyes slitted with suspicion.

"All right, what are you trying to pull, girl?" he asked.

"The knife out of your neck."

"The what?"

Boo-Boo drew a switchblade from another pocket. With a push of a button, a four-inch blade sprung out of the handle. She thrust it at Felix's neck. At the same moment, Felix leaned away from her. The blade grazed his Adam's apple. He turned the steering wheel hard to the left, causing them to sway, then he stomped on the gas pedal.

As she regained her balance, the clown thrust the knife at him again. Felix had raised his left hand over his neck, palm out, in a futile attempt at stopping the blade. Instead, it amputated his index finger at the base of it and partially severed his middle finger. The detached finger fell on his lap. Blood erupted from the wounds.

Felix held his mutilated hand out in front of his face, eyes huge and terrified. He stepped on the brake pedal, finally realizing speeding up wasn't going to help him escape from the clown in his truck. Boo-Boo plunged the blade into the side of his neck before being flung forward with the vehicle's sudden stop.

The blade had skewered his voice box, caught

between his Adam's apple and esophagus. Blood spilled down his windpipe.

Felix grasped at his neck with both hands. The moment he touched the knife's handle, he detonated a bomb of tremendous pain in his throat. His foot slipped off the gas pedal. The truck rolled through the desert. Blood squirted out from around the blade, splashing on Boo-Boo, the center console, and the dashboard.

"Oh lookie! It's raining! The drought is over!" the clown cheered, bouncing joyously in her seat.

Felix snorted as he struggled to breathe. He gripped his neck—careful to avoid the blade—as if strangling himself would slow the bleeding. With his other hand, he unbuckled his seat belt and opened the driver's door. As the truck trundled on, he leaned to his left and let himself fall out of the vehicle. Another geyser of blood shot out of his neck as he hit the ground.

"Hey!" Boo-Boo yelled. "That's my knife, you thief!"

The old man got unsteadily to his feet, swayed this way and that way, then lost his footing and dropped to his knees. Without taking his hand off his neck, he crawled away from the truck, dragging himself into the darkness of the night. He felt his energy draining with each passing second—with each drop of blood spilt.

Boo-Boo put the truck in Park before hopping out. Felix's blood had turned the soil reddish-brown. She followed his trail, skipping merrily over to him.

"There you are," she said.

He kept crawling away at a snail's pace, limbs trembling with exhaustion. His face was alarmingly pale and his head was bobbling as if it were attached to his body by a flimsy piece of string. Only gurgling noises and blood seeped past his lips.

"I knew you'd still be alive, y'know?" she said as she strolled behind him. "People are... strange. I saw someone slip on an ice cube once, smash his head on a tile floor, and never get up. A frickin' ice cube killed the guy! Terrible luck, huh? Oh, I know, I know. *You* have the worst luck, right? You think he got the easy way out, don't ya?"

Felix's hand slipped out from under him, causing him to faceplant on the soil. He squirmed and fought for air for a few seconds without success, then pushed himself up and continued crawling forward. Although her voice was high-pitched, he only caught a few of the clown's words. He felt like he was listening to her while submerged in a pool of his own blood.

She continued, "That might be true, but you should be proud of yourself. You're one of the strong ones. You're like this girl we killed a few days ago. We were almost done chopping her head off when we noticed her eyes were still moving. Crazy, right? We need more people like you. If everyone died by slipping on ice cubes, this whole night would be a bust."

Felix's arm gave out, lobbing him back to the ground. He tried to push himself up but promptly fell.

On his belly, he slithered forward—inch by inch, then centimeter by centimeter, then millimeter by millimeter. His eyes were open and fixed on the ground, but his vision had darkened. Near-death, he no longer knew what he was doing or how he had gotten there.

Boo-Boo strode ahead, then crouched in front of him. By then, her victim had stopped crawling. He was still trying to breathe, though.

She said, "Still kicking, huh? You really wanna go out with a bang, don't ya? Okay, let's see what we're working with... Let's see..." She scanned the area while humming in thought before continuing, "We already beat someone with a cactus, so that's out of the question. I'd run you over with your truck, but we kinda already did that, too. Oh, oh! I've got it!"

She crouched-walked over to a stone to her right. It was about the size of a gridiron football. It had sharp, jagged edges. She carried it back to the old man.

She said, "This bad boy should do the job. I'm gonna put you on your side, okay? Don't worry, I'll be done in a jiffy."

She rolled him onto his side, then straddled his upper body. Blood came out of the wound on his neck in a weak stream. Holding it in both hands, she raised the stone overhead, then swung it down. The stone hit the right side of the old man's jaw with a *crack*, leaving a deep indentation on his mandible.

Felix lost consciousness, but he continued writhing. Boo-Boo struck him with the hefty rock again. A large gash stretched across his jaw. The indentation on his mandible grew into a bloody crater. Some of his molar teeth crumbled, the fragments of enamel riding a wave of blood out of his mouth.

Boo-Boo hit him again and again—*and again*. She aimed exclusively for his jaw, smashing it into an unrecognizable mush of crushed tissue, minced muscles, broken teeth, and shredded skin. His tongue —lacerated by the stone's sharp edges—hung freely out of his mouth, licking the bloodsoaked soil under him.

After the tenth blow, she tossed the stone aside and caught her breath. She stared into his half-lidded eyes. His pupils had expanded, turning his irises into thin brown rings. A crackling noise came out of the wound on his neck, although he wasn't trying to breathe anymore. His body was motionless.

"I'm gonna need my knife back," Boo-Boo said. "It was a gift from the big boss."

She yanked the knife out of his neck. Some more blood fountained out of the gash. She wiped the blade on her dress, pushed a button to retract it, then returned it to her pocket.

She looked up and, as if she were speaking to someone, she said, "Thanks for listening, gramps. I'm not really good at the whole 'public speaking' thing, so I don't really get a chance to talk a lot when we're with the others. They think I'm loco. Wackadoo, y'know?

That's why I gotta work with Cap and Pips. They're not like the other clowns, either."

She nodded, as if listening to a response. Only a breeze whooshed through the area, though.

"Why do they think I'm crazy?" she said. "You already know the answer to that, don't you? It's 'cause of my special power. I'm a *real* magic clown. When I kill people, they become my dead friends. That scares even the scariest clowns. But hey, it's good news for you, isn't it, grandpa? That means you can live as long as I live. Friends 'till *we* die, right?"

Holding on to the corpse's shoulder to balance herself, she jumped up to her feet. She put her hands on her hips and looked around.

"All righty then, it's time for us to beat it," she said. "Now how do we get back to town?"

13

MISSING PEOPLE

ANGELINA WALKED QUIETLY TO THE TOP OF THE STAIRS, trying to eavesdrop. She had heard the doorbell ring twice, followed by someone knocking on the door with great urgency. Although she couldn't see them, she heard her mother's sniffling and her father's heavy footsteps in the foyer of the home. Kurt answered the door.

Samuel and Jenna Holt, friends of the family, stood on their porch. The couple lived on the other side of town. Like Kurt, Samuel worked as a handyman. He was a burly, bald, bearded guy. In addition to volunteering around town, Jenna was a tour guide. Her blonde hair was tied in a bun with a long hairpin sticking out of it. She was a tall woman, just two inches shorter than her husband.

Samuel said, "Kurt, hey, sorry to bother you so late. We probably should have called before–"

"Have you seen Otto and Flora?" Jenna blurted, hands clasped over her chest with her fingers wiggling out of control.

Otto and Flora were their children. Otto—Gilbert's best friend—was thirteen years old, and Flora was ten.

Eyebrows raised, Kurt glanced back at his wife. Looking equally confused, she shook her head. Even from upstairs, Angelina could feel the anxiety in Jenna's voice.

"No, they haven't dropped by tonight," Kurt said as he looked back at the Holts. "Did something happen?"

Just as Samuel opened his mouth to speak, Jenna said, "They're not home. They–They're not anywhere. We looked all over and all around the house. Every-where, I swear. We asked all of our neighbors, too, but no one has seen them. Gilbert's always talking to Otto. Can we talk to Gilbert? Maybe Otto told him something."

"Yeah. Yeah, of course."

On her tiptoes to avoid making noise, Angelina hurried back down the hall. She checked her brother's room.

Empty.

"Gilbert, honey, can you come down here for a second?!" Heather hollered from the bottom of the stairs.

Angelina rushed from room to room—the bath-room, the storage closet, the master bedroom, her own bedroom. Gilbert was nowhere to be found.

"Gil!" Heather shouted. "Gilbert, I know you're not..."

Her voice faded as her daughter made her way down the stairs. She clenched her jaw and lowered her head, ashamed of her own behavior.

Stopping halfway down the stairs, Angelina said, "He's not up there."

"What have they gotten themselves into?" Jenna said. "What if they went out into the desert? What if they're lost? Or hurt? The boulders, the snakes, the coyotes–"

"We'll find them," Samuel interrupted, forcing a smile. "They know better than to go into the desert at night. They're fine, I promise."

Kurt asked, "Did you call the police?"

"No answer."

"Did you go check if the guy's sleeping?"

"There's no one there. We asked around after seeing that deserted booth, but no one's seen Brewer all night. He's gone AWOL."

Kurt grabbed his coat from the rack hanging next to the door and said, "All right. If Gilbert's with Otto and Flora, then they're probably playing a game. Hide and seek or something. I'll help you find them."

Heather grabbed her tote bag and her coat as well.

"I'm coming, too." Angelina said as she raced down the stairs.

She avoided eye contact with her mother. Arms crossed, she marched out of the house. She walked with the Holts as her parents locked up behind her. Although they had known Angelina since she was a child, they didn't say a word to her. They were too busy thinking about their missing children.

Walking through town, they took turns calling the kids' names: "Gilbert! Otto! Flora!"

They visited their neighbors to ask about the children. No one had seen them. The village square was desolate. There were no streetlamps in Goldbrush. Some light came through the lodge's windows as well as a window from the Browns' home above the diner. Across the plaza, down the wide dirt road between the post office and helipad, they saw a group of people outside of Goldbrush Essentials.

Lindsay, wearing an overcoat on top of her pajamas, was watching the commotion from across the dirt path in front of the store. She was puffing on a cigarette.

As they approached her, Jenna asked, "Lindsay, have you seen Otto and Flora?"

"And Gilbert?" Angelina added.

"You mean the kids?" Lindsay responded.

Speaking quickly, Jenna said, "Yes, the kids. Our kids. Have you seen them?"

"Nope. They're probably running around here looking for Ben, though."

"Ben? What does Ben have to do with this?"

"You haven't heard? Well, I guess if Ben's not around to yap about it, how could you, right? They're saying he's gone missing. Someone heard a loud noise in his shop, and now it looks like it's locked up tight. He's not answering any of his phones, either. His old truck's still parked in front of his house, though. No way he left Goldbrush without it. It gets worse, though. No one can find our friendly neighborhood cop anywhere, and some people said they've been hearing screaming around town. Creepy, right?"

She had said that last sentence with a small, amused smile. Angelina looked at the convenience store and felt a chill creep down her spine. She knew something terrible had happened.

Kurt said, "Maybe Ben saw the kids sneaking around, playing loudly or causing trouble or whatnot, and he went after them."

Lindsay took a drag of her cigarette, blew the smoke over her shoulder so it wouldn't hit the others, then said, "You should also look into that teacher staying at my lodge. That Mr. Alexander Guzman. I don't trust him. He's an outsider and, honestly, he gives me 'serial killer' vibes. But those kids of yours trust him because he teaches them. And I don't go prying into my guests' private lives, but I've heard screams and groans coming from his room. Who knows what he could be doing to your kids?"

"Oh my goodness," Jenna cried as she slapped a hand over her mouth.

Heather hugged her and, while sneering at Lindsay, she said, "How could you even think about suggesting such a thing?"

"Serial killer vibes?" Angelina repeated as she glared at the lodge's owner. "*You're* the one with the evil eye."

Lindsay gasped. The group outside of the convenience store was watching the argument now, too.

Angelina continued, "And you're an outsider too, so don't try to pull that shit. You're just trying to make it look like you care about this town when all you care about is money. What you're saying about Alex, about my brother and his friends, it's... it's straight up baseless and fucking offensive. You should be ashamed of yourself."

"I'm an outsider? *I'm* an outsider? My husband and I have lived here for years. We've invested more in this town than anyone else. You... This is your first week here as an adult because you ran away and abandoned everyone. Oh, that's right, I've heard the stories. You haven't contributed anything to this town. You don't even pay taxes."

"Fuck you."

"Ha! Just like you're *fucking* that teacher, right? That's why you're trying to protect him, isn't it?"

The horde of spectators inched closer. Angelina's mouth hung open, but she couldn't find the words to respond. She clenched her fists, wrestling with a desire to take a swing at her.

Heather stepped between them and, jabbing her

index finger at Lindsay's chest, she said, "You stay out of my daughter's business. As a matter of fact, I don't *ever* want to hear you speak about my family again. You got that?"

Lindsay looked offended. Surprised, Angelina stared at her mother with a newfound sense of respect and appreciation.

"Hey, Lindsay," one of the men in the crowd said. "You really think that guy's a kiddie diddler?"

Another man asked, "You think he might have had something to do with Ben's disappearance?"

Lindsay had no reason to believe Alex was a sexual predator or serial killer—or both. Angelina had been right about her. She had only thrown those suggestions out there to sound helpful. Now, seeing red, she sought to use Alex to hurt Angelina.

She said, "I'm certain he's been up to *something* in his room. I don't think it's a coincidence that something like this happens on the same week he decides to stay at the lodge, either."

In the blink of an eye, Angelina witnessed the group of agitated residents turn into a vengeful mob. One of the men suggested hauling Alex out of his room to question him. A woman in the crowd recommended they arm themselves in case the teacher had a weapon of his own.

"Everyone, calm down!" Kurt yelled with his hands raised, his booming voice causing the chatter to soften. "We're talking about missing people here—about our kids. This drama is nothing more than a distraction and you all know it. We need to stop arguing with each other and start working with each other."

"But what if she's right about him?" one of the men asked. "Your kids could be in danger. We could all be in danger."

"That's right," a red-haired woman said. "And the police booth's been empty for hours. If that teacher already got to him, then who's going to protect us?"

Kurt said, "If we're all in danger, then let's all resolve this together. I say we split into groups and fan out. Some of us can go check on Alex at the lodge. I'm sure we've all met him before. He's good people. So, let's try talking to him before we try lynching him, all right?"

The crowd responded with murmurs. Some of them agreed with him, others were skeptical. Lindsay huffed and shook her head, then took a drag of her cigarette.

Kurt continued, "Some of us can go pay Ben's house a visit. We take care of his property when he's out of town, so we have a spare key. Under these circumstances, I'm sure he wouldn't mind if some of us dropped by for a... a wellness check."

"I'll get the key," Heather said before hurrying off to their home.

"The rest of us can walk through town and continue searching. If you have an ATV, maybe you can circle the town and see if you can spot anything unusual. If you can't or don't want to help, please go to your homes and stay near your phones in case there's an emergency."

Jenna said, "I'll meet up with Heather at Ben's place."

"Then I'll go check on Alex," Samuel responded.

He walked back down the dirt path behind him. Some of the men from the crowd followed his lead. Lindsay butted her cigarette out on a stone on the ground, then trailed behind the men heading towards her lodge. The red-haired woman walked briskly towards her home, ready to stay by her phone to keep everyone updated. Keys jingling in their hands, a pair of young guys ran off in the opposite direction to get to their ATVs. The townsfolk were more than willing to jump into action to help each other.

As the group dispersed, Kurt yelled, "Remember, we're looking for Gilbert! Otto! Flora! Ben! And Officer Brent Brewer!"

"Dad, wait," Angelina said. She pulled him aside before lowering her voice and saying, "I was talking to Gilbert earlier tonight. He was, um... worried about Otto's grades and school and stuff like that. I just remembered that I... Well, I *jokingly* told him that maybe he could change Otto's grades. If he took me seriously, then maybe he's at the school."

"When was the last time you saw him?"

"I'm not sure."

"Ange, when was the last time you saw your brother?"

"I don't know," Angelina said, voice rising with frustration. "I wish I could tell you the exact minute he left my room, but I don't know. It's not like I've always got my eye on the clock. I don't even know what time it is right now. I guess... I guess it could have been thirty minutes or maybe an hour by now."

Kurt said, "Then maybe we can still catch them if they're over there. Come with me."

14

—————

GOLDBRUSH EDUCATION CENTER

"WHAT'S SHE DOING HERE?" GILBERT ASKED.

He was referring to Otto's sister, Flora, who hadn't been invited to their rendezvous. Yet, the short-haired spectacled girl was standing behind her brother. She was wearing her pajamas under a fluffy puffer jacket. Otto's curly hair—styled in a bowl cut—stuck out from under his baseball cap. He was dressed like his sister, wearing pajamas under a jacket.

"Sorry, dude," Otto said. "She was spying on me when you called."

"I was not," Flora said meekly.

"She was gonna tell on us if I didn't let her come with me."

"Nuh-uh."

The truth was, she had been spying on him and she had threatened to tell their parents if he didn't bring her along.

"Whatever," Gilbert said. "But she can't tell *anyone* about this. *Ever*. Okay?"

Otto glanced at his sister, demanding an answer with his scowl.

"Okay," Flora answered.

"All right," Gilbert said. "Let's find a way inside."

They stood at the side of the Goldbrush Education Center, oblivious to the killer clowns committing simultaneous murders around town. At the back of the school, a nine-foot-tall fence surrounded a half-size basketball court and a jungle gym. Next to the school's back doors, there was a boys' restroom and a girls' restroom.

Staring at the top of the fence, Gilbert said, "Maybe one of us can climb over. The back door might be open."

"I can't climb that," Flora said.

"Then you can wait out here and keep a lookout."

"I don't wanna wait out here. What if a ghost gets me?"

"*Psst!*" Otto hissed from the front of the school. "Dude, check it out. The front door's open."

"Really?" Gilbert asked, scrunching up his eyes.

He walked to the front of the building. Flora scurried closely behind him, not wanting to be left behind.

Across the dirt path in front of the school, there was a large shed with a barn-red exterior. Above its doors, painted in capital white letters, a sign read: *GOLDBRUSH FIRE STATION*. The kids had never seen anyone enter or leave that shed. There had been a few kitchen fires in town, but they were nothing the residents couldn't handle with buckets of water and fire extinguishers.

Although he didn't see anyone else, Gilbert felt like someone was leering at them. The breeze felt like a man's moist breath hitting the back of his neck. He shivered with a case of the heebie-jeebies.

"You coming?" Otto asked.

Gilbert looked at him. Holding the door open, his friend stood in the doorway leading into the school. Flora was already inside, standing next to her brother.

"Aren't you, uh... like, suspicious or something?" Gilbert asked.

"What do you mean?" Otto responded.

"They never leave the door unlocked. Why is it open this time?"

"Maybe Guzman forgot to lock it. Who cares anyway? C'mon, man. You're going to get us busted standing out in the open."

"Yeah, c'mon" Flora chimed in.

Gilbert said, "Okay, okay."

He entered the school. Otto took another peek outside, making sure the coast was clear, then he closed the door behind him.

The wall to their right was covered with lockers, most of which were empty. Shafts of moonlight fell into the corridor through the rectangular windows above the lockers. There were four doors on the wall to the left. The first one led to the main office. The other three opened up to classrooms. The double doors at the other end of the hall led to the playground.

"Where should we start?" Otto asked.

Gilbert said, "I'm not sure."

"But you said you had a plan."

"I do. I did. I mean, I *thought* I did. I just don't know where to start, okay?"

"If you're gonna fix Otto's grades, why don't you start with Mr. Guzman's computer?" Flora suggested.

"I told you she was spying," Otto said.

"I was not."

"Yeah, you were."

"I was not!"

Gilbert said, "Chill out, guys, or someone's going to hear us."

"All right, all right," Otto responded, raising his hands in a peaceful gesture. "So, what are we gonna do?"

"Well, um... I guess Flora's right. Let's check Guzman's room first. Maybe he has our grades on his computer or in a notebook or something."

The kids entered the first classroom to their left. It was a tiny room with nine desks—each with an attached chair—for students organized in three columns and three rows. There were never more than nine students enrolled at the school every year. The teacher's desk was in front of the classroom, and a whiteboard covered the wall behind it.

The boys went straight to their teacher's desk. Gilbert turned on the computer on top of it while Otto rummaged through the drawers.

"Cool," Flora said as she inspected the room from the doorway with a smile. "I've never been to school at night."

She flicked the light switch next to the door. White light washed the classroom and streamed through the windows.

"Don't!" Gilbert yelled.

"Turn it off, stupid!" Otto shouted.

Shocked by their reaction, Flora hit the light switch again. The darkness returned. They stood in silence for a long moment, as if expecting someone to barge in and catch them.

"Do you want them to know we're in here?" her brother asked.

Gilbert said, "Flora, you have to be careful. If we get caught... I don't know what'll happen, but it won't be good. Please, just... just don't touch anything else, okay?"

Red-faced, the girl pouted and nodded. The boys went back to their search. Otto sifted through the folders in the drawers, leafing through graded work and blank worksheets for future assignments. Gilbert tried to log in to Alex's computer. He needed a PIN code, though. His first guess was: *1234*. It didn't work. His second guess was: *4321*. Again, it was incorrect.

He whispered, "Do you know Guzman's birthday?"

"How would I know that?" Otto answered.

"I don't know. I'm just asking. I need a PIN code."

"You try 1-2-3-4?"

"Yeah."

"How about 0-0-0-0?"

Gilbert entered the suggestion.

Incorrect.

"It didn't work," he said.

"What about that badge thing he usually wears around his neck? It probably has his birthday or some numbers on it, right?"

Gilbert started searching the parallel column of drawers. Over the murmuring and rustling at the desk, Flora heard a soft *thud* behind her. She peeked back at the doorway and listened. She didn't hear anything else, so she shrugged it off. She took a stroll around the classroom.

Short bookcases—filled with encyclopedias, textbooks, and novels—hugged the wall to her right. Across the room, a wall of awning windows offered a view of the desert. At night, the mountain skyline was hardly discernible in the distance.

"Can we go to my class, too?" the girl asked from the back of the room.

Otto said, "Shut up."

"Hey, don't tell me to shut up."

Gilbert asked, "Why do you wanna go to your class? It's pretty much the same as ours."

"Nuh-uh. We have a snack drawer."

"*Flora,*" Otto said angrily. "If you don't shut up, I'm gonna..."

His voice petered out upon hearing a *thud* in the hallway, then another—and another. It was a set of approaching footsteps. In perfect synchronicity, the kids turned their heads slowly to look at the door. The stench of cigarette smoke wafted into the room. As the footsteps closed in on them, Flora ran to the desk and cowered behind the boys.

Alex emerged in the doorway, peering into the room with immediate disapproval. He turned on the light and stepped inside.

"What are you doing here?" the teacher asked.

Otto said, "Um... What are *you* doing here?"

Alex laughed, amused by his gall, then said, "If you must know, there was an incident at Ben's shop. I don't know what happened, but it looked serious. I went for a little walk and–"

"You were smoking," Flora interrupted while staying behind the boys.

"I was. And I know I–"

"You said smoking is bad for us. You said it causes cancer."

Smirking, Alex said, "And I know I said it's bad for you. It is, so don't start, okay? 'Do as I say, not as I do,' yadda, yadda." He walked to the middle of the white-board before continuing, "As I was saying, I went for a little walk and, lo and behold, I saw one of you on the basketball court. I thought I was going to catch you playing a game. That would have still been trespassing, but maybe I could have let it slide. This? This is a *serious* crime."

Gilbert said, "Mr. Guzman, we... we didn't go to the playground. We were standing outside next to the fence earlier, but we weren't on the basketball court."

"Yeah? Then how'd you get in here?"

"The front door, um... It–It was open."

"No, it wasn't. Don't lie to me, Gilbert."

Otto said, "He's telling the truth. I didn't lock the door when we came in here, either, 'cause I didn't want to get stuck in here."

"Now I know you're lying," Alex said. "The front door was locked when I got here. I know that for a fact because I unlocked it a few minutes ago. Now, if you want to stay out of *serious* trouble, I need you to start telling me the truth. What are you doing here?"

The kids looked at each other, hesitant. Flora was close to breaking down. Otto shook his head at Gilbert, communicating without uttering a sound: *'Don't say anything.'* Gilbert's face, screwed up as if in pain, was flushed.

He said, "Mr. Guzman, we... It's not... This was all my idea. Don't punish Otto and Flora."

"*What* was your idea?"

Gilbert was about to confess when the melody of *Pop Goes the Weasel* started playing in the hallway. It played at a reduced speed. Alex glanced back at the doorway, then at the kids.

He asked, "Is someone else here?"

Gilbert shrugged while the Holt siblings shook their heads. Flora was holding Otto's hand now. Trembling and mewling like frightened kittens, they were all creeped out by the music.

Alex walked back into the hallway. He looked right, then left. The light pouring out of the classroom helped him investigate the dark corridor. His gaze landed on a beat-up Jack-in-the-Box toy on the floor in front of the school's back doors. He didn't see it when he first arrived. The distorted tune made the hairs on his arms stand at attention.

He told himself it was part of a prank, though, so he refused to show fear in front of the kids. He convinced himself that the toy had been there all along and he had only missed it because of the darkness.

Eyes stuck on the Jack-in-the-Box, he asked, "What are you trying to do here? Hmm? You making something for YouTube?"

The kids looked befuddled.

"It–It's not us," Gilbert stuttered.

The teacher said, "Yeah, right. I warned you about lying, didn't I? Well, now you're in serious trouble. We'll see what your parents say when they see this."

As Alex walked towards the toy, Flora ran after him and cried, "Don't leave us! I'm scared! Mr. Guzman, please! I'm scared!"

Otto reluctantly followed her. He argued with his sister every day, but that didn't mean he didn't love her.

As if he were standing in cement shoes, Gilbert couldn't take a step. A mix of fear and stress had paralyzed him.

Alex stopped in front of the Jack-in-the-Box. Flora caught up to him first. She grabbed the bottom of his shirt, nearly pulling it out of his pants. Despite the darkness, he noticed the primal fear in their eyes—the fear of the boogeyman, the fear of the unknown. He started second-guessing his original theory. Otto stood next to them, confusion scrawled on his face.

The door to the classroom to their left was open now, but they were too preoccupied by the music to notice. The room was pitch black. As the tune neared its famous climax, Alex took a knee in front of the toy.

Pop!

The upper body of a toy clown jumped out of the musical box, startling the young siblings.

And a second later, there was a thunderous *bang* and a brief yellowish flash of light.

Alex's head exploded in a storm of blood, chunks of scalp with short dark hair still attached, shards of skull, and shredded bits of wormlike brain. The human head cheese splattered on the kids, the surrounding walls, and the adjacent lockers. Jellified brain tissue entered Otto's mouth and his nostrils. Like shrapnel from a grenade, sharp fragments of Alex's skull riddled Flora's face. Some shards pierced her eyes, damaging her vision and sending bloody tears down her cheeks.

Accompanied by severe headaches, the kids' ears rang harshly, making them sob and hobble in all directions. Alex's body toppled over in front of them, sprawled atop the Jack-in-the-Box. More than half of his head was gone—*Poof! Goes the brainpan!* Like liquid from an active blender without a lid, blood continued to spray out of what remained of his head. His body moved as if he were trying to wiggle away.

Retching and gasping, Otto looked to his left. Through the doorway, he saw Pipsqueak take a step forward in the classroom. He was still pointing a double-barreled shotgun at them.

Otto grabbed his sister's arm and pulled her away from the dead teacher. He ran away from the clown, covering the back of his head with his free arm as if that would stop a shotgun blast. He ducked into the classroom and slammed the door behind him. Flora fell to her knees, weeping hysterically. Her eyes hurt so much that she refused to open them. Gilbert was a bundle of nerves, frozen in place but shaking all over.

"What was that?" he squeaked out. "Wa–Why is there... blood on you?"

"Fuck, dude, the door doesn't have a lock!" Otto shouted in a nasally voice.

"A–Are you guys okay?"

"We need to block it!"

"Where's Mr. Guzman?"

Otto slid a desk in front of the door, then pushed another one in front of it. He tasted blood in his mouth with each swallow and each breath through his nose stung, so he pressed his finger against his right nostril, then blew forcefully. A nugget of brain shot out of his nose like a snot rocket. He didn't care, though. He hooked his arms under Flora's armpits and forced her to her feet.

Dry-heaving with each pause, Flora cried, "I can't... see. It... hurts! My face... hurts!"

Otto shushed his sister as he escorted her to the windows. Gilbert stared at the piece of brain on the floor, awed. It was slathered in blood and mucus. From the corner of his eye, he caught a glimpse of Pipsqueak peeking through the window on the door. The double-barreled shotgun was slung across his back. He moved away from the window. Gilbert's jaw dropped and his eyes widened.

Otto opened one of the awning windows, then put his hands on Flora's shoulders and said, "You have to run, okay? Get Dad. Get everyone."

"I don't wanna go!" Flora yelled, eyes clenched shut. "I can't see! My eyes hurt too much!"

"You have to–"

"And I'm scared! I'm so scared! I–I'm going to throw up!"

"Flora, please! You're the only one that can fit through the window!"

Pipsqueak kicked the door open, breaking the makeshift barricade with his first try. Flora screamed upon hearing the noise. Her legs quit on her, but before she could drop to her knees, her brother wrapped his arms around her and picked her up. He pushed her against the window to stop her from falling again. Pipsqueak stepped to the side, disappearing behind the wall.

"It's a clown," Gilbert whispered, his bottom lip quivering.

Footsteps and groaning came from the hallway. Then Alex's limp arm swung out from around the corner, as if waving hello. Gilbert could see the clown's gloved fingers on the corpse's shoulder.

"Heya, kids," Pipsqueak said, speaking in a deep but goofy voice. "Are you ready for the... best? Greatest? Bestest?"

He sounded like he had forgotten his lines, murmuring indistinctly to himself. In a panic, Otto forced his sister's head through the open window. He had a hard time catching her flailing arms, though.

"What's happening?" Gilbert said, eyes wet with tears.

"Oh, right," Pipsqueak said. "Are you ready for the most amazing puppet show in the whole wide world? Everyone, say hello to, uh... the Headless Puppet!"

He stepped out from behind the wall. He was holding Alex's corpse out in front of him, an arm wrapped tightly around the dead man's waist. Alex's slack, droopy legs slid across the floor as the clown plodded into the classroom. He kept his head low, as if he were trying to hide behind the dead body. His presence was obvious due to his enormous figure, though.

Gilbert's eyes expanded even more and the gore made his stomach churn. He crossed his arms over his abdomen, clenched his jaw, and swallowed his saliva, but he couldn't fight it. A mere five seconds after spotting the corpse, his mother's macaroni and cheese erupted from his mouth. The chunky yellow puke splattered on the floor in front of him.

"Go!" Otto sobbed. "Flora, please! Hurry!"

Both of Flora's arms were out of the window now, chest against the windowsill and feet off the floor, but she was still thrashing about. Her cries for help had been reduced to gibberish.

Pipsqueak flung the corpse's arm around and, raising the pitch of his voice almost imperceptibly, he said, "Oh, c'mon, kids, the show hasn't even started yet. Let me tell you–"

"He's gonna kill us!" Otto interrupted, ropes of bloody mucus hanging from his nose.

"Hey, you're ruining the show."

"Dad! Mom! Dad! Help! Help!"

"Don't hurt me, don't hurt me, don't hurt me," Gilbert said rapidly, his voice drowned out by the Holt siblings' screaming.

Returning to his regular voice, Pipsqueak said, "You're not playing right. You're supposed to watch me before I kill you."

The kids were watching him, but they weren't

interested in his show. Pipsqueak threw Alex's body forward. The corpse landed jaw-first in the mushy puke. Gilbert staggered back until he crashed into Alex's desk. He pissed himself as the clown marched towards him, a dark spot spreading across his crotch and his left pants leg. His sock soaked up the warm liquid like a sponge.

Pipsqueak ignored him and went straight for the Holts. He elbowed Otto's shoulder, knocking him down, then he grabbed Flora's legs and pulled her back into the classroom. Her face bounced off the floor, teeth flying out of her mouth. He dragged her unconscious body to the center of the room. Her slippers fell from her feet. His ass hit the desks, pushing them away effortlessly.

"Let her go!" Otto yelled.

He tackled Pipsqueak, but the clown didn't move an inch. Pipsqueak slapped the boy, swatting him away like a pesky fly. Otto fell onto one of the nearby desks. As if he were blind to the clown's larger size, he jumped at him and hit him with the bottom of his fists. Again, Pipsqueak pushed him away with a slap. Blood dripped from a gash on his lower lip.

Otto dashed to the teacher's desk. He took a No. 2 pencil from a pen holder next to the computer monitor.

He gave Gilbert a little shove and cried, "Do something!"

Gilbert couldn't move, though. He just stood there,

leaning against the desk with his palms glued to the table. Pipsqueak rolled Flora onto her back. Otto rushed back to his sister, holding the pencil over his shoulder like a knife in the icepick grip. He swung it at the clown, but before he could make contact, Pipsqueak hit him in the chest with his elbow.

Otto dropped the pencil as he plummeted to the floor. He propped himself up on one arm and grasped at his chest with his other hand. Each wheezing breath kindled a flare of pain and made his ribs crackle. His young, naïve mind harked back to the first time he watched Ridley Scott's *Alien*. He believed his chest was going to explode and an alien was going to burst out.

Pipsqueak picked up the pencil and looked it over as if he had never seen one before. He knew what a sharp point could do, though. Otto rose unsteadily to his feet. He teetered back while looking for a weapon. He saw the open door to his right, but he didn't consider running. He only cared about protecting his sister. His eyes stopped on a textbook in one of the bookcases.

As the boy took a step towards the shelves, Pipsqueak lunged at him and drove the pencil into his neck, making him reel back to the whiteboard. The pencil speared his Adam's apple and voice box before stopping in his esophagus. His hands moved to his neck, fingers splayed around the writing utensil.

Back against the whiteboard, he leaned forward.

Blood ran down the body of the pencil before dripping from the eraser.

Gilbert gasped as Otto looked in his direction. Face knotted—eyes squinched, mouth gaping, forehead creased—Otto looked like he was trying to scream, but his damaged vocal cords struggled to generate a sound. He took one hand off his neck and reached for his friend in a wordless plea for help, then he dropped to his knees.

Gilbert only had control of his head, though. He looked to his left upon hearing a set of footsteps. Pipsqueak was walking towards him. Gilbert shrank back.

The clown raised his hands at the boy, palms out, and said, "Thanks for sticking around, kid. Show's not over yet. I, uh... I got a good trick coming. Wait there, okay? Yeah, wait there."

He walked out of the room and turned right, heading towards the entrance. A door opened down the hall and the clown's footsteps softened. Gilbert stared at the open door.

Run! he screamed at himself. *Run, you fucking idiot! What are you doing?! Run!*

He glanced at Flora. Returning from the realm of unconsciousness, she was whining and squirming on the floor. He looked at Otto. The kid's legs were now folded under him, so he was sitting on his heels under the whiteboard. He stared at the floor, drained of energy and fighting for air.

"I–I'm sorry," Gilbert croaked out. "I can't... moo–move. I can't... I can't... Please don't die. Otto, don't go. I need you."

Pipsqueak returned to the classroom, a duffel bag slung over his shoulder. He gave an oafish smile as he walked past the boys, totally unperturbed by his actions. Towering over Flora, he put his bag down on the desk next to him and dug through his supplies, glass *clinking* and steel *clanging*. His right hand came out of the bag with a cleaver.

He said, "Gimme a sec, kid. I need more toys for this next part."

He stepped on Flora's left leg, his shoe planted firmly in the back of her knee, then he swung the cleaver at her ankle. The girl shrieked and convulsed as her Achilles tendon was severed. The scream echoed through the town. She felt her heel cord jumping *in* her leg like a downed electrical wire, sparking a blaze of ceaseless pain.

Pipsqueak yanked the cleaver out. Blood sprayed out of the gash and flew off the blade. Some of the blood sprinkled on Gilbert's hoodie and neck like cologne. The clown chopped Flora's ankle again, the blade clanging against her bones. Howling, she grabbed the leg of a desk and tried to pull herself forward, but she couldn't overpower the man.

With the third chop, he lopped off her foot. A torn piece of her pink sock rimmed the stump at the end of her leg. The girl gasped, then her eyes rolled back and her face hit the floor. She was conscious but fading. Pipsqueak turned his attention to her other leg. He repeated the process: stepped on her knee pit and swung the cleaver at her ankle.

It took him five chops to amputate her right foot. By then, she had fainted from the shock and loss of blood. Once he was done with her feet, he stomped on her right elbow and started cleaving her wrist. It took him another seven swings to break her bones, tear through the cartilage, and shred her ligaments and tendons. Her hand was severed with her fingers outstretched.

Cycling between crying and gagging, Gilbert watched as the clown hacked off her other hand. Flora stopped moving after the amputation. She lay on her back in a spreading pool of blood—footless, handless, lifeless. Pipsqueak set the cleaver down on the desk next to his bag, then collected the severed extremities.

Cradling the amputated body parts in his arms, he said, "Watch this, kid."

He juggled the girl's hands and feet. He only lasted five seconds before he dropped one of the hands. And when he leaned over to pick it up, he dropped another hand and a foot. He gathered the pieces, then started juggling again. Five seconds later, a hand fell to the floor and a foot landed on Flora's unmoving back.

"Oh my God," a woman's voice came from the hallway.

Great relief and hope swept through Gilbert as he

spotted his sister and father standing in the doorway. They looked beyond appalled, mentally wrecked by the carnage. Dumbstruck, Pipsqueak dropped all of the extremities. The clowns had made contingency plans in case their shows were interrupted, but he was drawing a blank.

He drew his double-barreled shotgun and aimed it at the doorway. Kurt and Angelina closed their eyes and recoiled.

"No!" Gilbert yelled.

There was a loud *clicking* noise.

Then silence.

At the same time, Kurt and Angelina cracked their eyes open. Pipsqueak was still aiming the shotgun at them, but he was staring wonderingly at the weapon. It wasn't loaded.

Kurt shouted, "Get them out of here!"

He charged towards the clown, unwilling to give him the opportunity to reload. Pipsqueak pulled the trigger again and again, as if he were expecting it to shoot without any shells. Kurt tackled him into a cluster of desks. He pushed the shotgun away so that it was aimed at the back of the classroom, then grabbed it in both hands and rammed it against the clown's chest.

Pipsqueak copied him, holding the weapon with one hand on its stock and the other on its barrels. They wrestled for the weapon, crashing from desk to desk. Meanwhile, Angelina ran to Gilbert's aid. She slapped her hand over her mouth and teetered to her right upon noticing Otto's grisly injury. Then she staggered to her left as she spotted Flora's dead body.

"Oh my God, oh my God," Angelina cried. She grabbed Gilbert's arms and asked, "Are you okay? Huh? Don't look at them. Look at me, Gilbert. Are you hurt?"

"I–I don't... I'm... He hurt them. I'm okay, but he hurt them. They need our help. We need to save them."

Angelina pulled him away from the teacher's desk and said, "We're leaving. Don't let go of me."

"No! Wait!" Gilbert shouted. "Otto! We can't leave him! He's still alive! I know it! Ange, stop!"

"We can't do this right now! We can't–"

"And Flora!"

"–carry him! We have to go!"

"We can't leave them!"

Angelina ushered her brother towards the door, but he broke free from her grip halfway there. He ran to Otto's side. The boy was clinging to life.

"I'm sorry," Gilbert said. "This is all my fault. It's all my fault, man."

Angelina tugged on his shoulder and said, "Gilbert, stop!"

"Let me go! They need us!"

"We need to get help, damn it!"

"I'm not leaving them!"

In the middle of the classroom, Kurt launched a

knee towards the clown's crotch, hoping to debilitate him with a hit to his testicles. But he missed his genitals and hit his belly instead. Although it still hurt, his fat absorbed the blow. Growling, Pipsqueak lunged forward and went for a headbutt. But he slipped on one of Flora's dismembered feet and tumbled to the floor, losing his grip on the weapon on his way down.

Shotgun in hand, Kurt caught himself on the desk behind him. He spun the gun around and held it by its barrels like a baseball bat. As Pipsqueak wobbled to his feet, Kurt smashed the shotgun's stock against the back of his head, ripping his scalp open. The clown dropped to a knee, his head and eyes spinning uncontrollably. Kurt swung the shotgun at him again, but Pipsqueak protected his head with his arm at the last second.

The clown scrambled to his feet, snatching the cleaver and duffel bag off the desk in one swift movement. Dazed by the blow to the head, he jostled past Kurt and lurched away. Using her body to protect her little brother, Angelina wrapped her arms around Gilbert and screamed as the clown rushed towards them. Pipsqueak stumbled past them and exited the room. He ran to the rear exit, sliding on Alex's blood before making his escape.

Kurt gave chase but his children's crying stopped him before he could reach the door. Rage and sorrow had fueled a primitive need for vengeance within him. He didn't want to risk his kids' safety, though. He slung the shotgun across his back and returned to his children. He was unnerved by Otto's condition. He glanced back at Flora. He could tell she was dead. He had never seen such a level of barbaric violence against children before.

"He's still alive, Dad," Gilbert said, his voice shaking. "We can't leave him. Don't make me leave him. Please, Dad, please."

Kurt said, "You two, go outside through the front door. *Run* as fast as you can. Go straight to the village square and don't look back."

"Dad, I don't wanna–"

"I'll carry Otto, Gilbert. We'll be right behind you. Okay?"

"O–Okay."

Voice quavering like her brother's, Angelina said, "What about..."

Her voice died away. She wanted to ask: '*What about Flora?*' But she saw the answer to her question on her father's grim face before she could finish asking it. She nodded at him. One arm around her brother, she helped him stand, then led him out of the classroom. Kurt carried Otto in his arms, careful to support his neck to avoid aggravating his wound. He took one last peek at Flora before departing the room, heartbroken.

15

THE CLOWNS ARE IN TOWN

WITH THEIR VOICES OCCASIONALLY OVERLAPPING, Angelina and Gilbert took turns yelling one word: "Help!"

They ran around the fire station and down another dirt path. Lights came on in the isolated homes, flashing through the windows. Most of the residents, however, were already out and about, roaming the town in search of their missing neighbors. Down another path, the siblings saw a group of people gathering in the village square. Beams of light shot out of their flashlights.

"He's not in his room," Lindsay was saying, standing on the lodge's porch. "He must have heard us coming. If he jumped off the balcony, then he's probably hiding in the community garden or the historical village, or he's making a run for the mountains. He could even be trying to break into one of our homes right now."

The crowd responded with a garble of anger. Standing next to Lindsay, Samuel was trying—and failing—to keep the group focused on finding his kids and the other missing people instead of pursuing a suspect of a crime that hadn't been confirmed.

Along with a few other concerned residents, Randy Holloway stood in front of Goldbrush Eats. He was an older man, his white hair a tangle of bedhead and a short white beard covering his face.

Staring up at the second floor of the diner, he cupped his hands around his mouth and shouted, "Felix! Adeline! Y'all in there?"

"I don't think they're here," a woman said as she peeked through one of the storefront windows. "Felix's truck is gone. They must have gone out."

"They wouldn't have left their lights on if they went out. You heard that noise earlier, didn't you? It sounded like gunfire."

"I don't think it came from here, though. It would have been a lot louder. Maybe someone's hunting."

"That's what I'm worried about. Felix! Addy!"

A pair of hikers—a young man named Adin Byrne and a younger woman named Gabriela Rojas—stood a few meters away from the group, recording the commotion on a cell phone and an action camera. One man's tragedy was another's ticket to internet fame.

As they approached the village square, Angelina

yelled, "Help! There's a–a... a fucking killer after us! Help!"

"It was a clown!" Gilbert cried.

They made their way to the center of the plaza. The residents looked at them, baffled. They chattered amongst themselves, questioning the kids' claims. Heather and Jenna came out of the lodge. Samuel followed them as they pushed through the crowd.

"Gilbert?" Heather called out. "Where have you–"

"Did you say there was a killer after you?" Jenna interrupted, words tumbling out of her mouth in a rush. "Where are Otto and Flora? Please tell me you were with them. Tell me they're okay."

"Mrs. Holt," Angelina said with grave reluctance.

"Where are they?!"

The siblings flinched, caught off guard by her aggressiveness. Samuel held Jenna back, stopping her from lunging at them.

"It–It was the clown," Gilbert said softly.

"Where are my babies?" Jenna asked, zany-eyed.

"We... were at the school and... and..."

His words crumbled to whimpers. The crowd had fallen quiet. A ghastly sense of apprehension befell the town.

"Call a medevac!" Kurt's voice broke the silence.

He jogged towards the group, carrying Otto in his arms. Samuel and Jenna ran to him. The crowd started to spread out. The reality of the situation began to sink in. They were all in danger.

"Oh God, no!" Jenna screamed.

"Otto, Jesus Christ," Samuel said in a pained voice.

They helped Kurt lower the injured boy to the ground. Down on her knees, Jenna cradled Otto's head on her lap. Crouched down, Samuel's unsteady hands hovered around the pencil sticking out of the kid's neck.

"I wouldn't touch it if I were you," Randy said, standing on his tiptoes to sneak a look at the kid. "It could be the only thing keeping him alive."

"I don't know how to fix this," Samuel whispered. "What do I do? I–I don't know what to do."

Rubbing the boy's pale cheeks, Jenna said, "Otto, baby, it's okay. Everything's okay now. Mom's here. Ma– Mommy's here. Oh God, you're cold. You're so cold." She looked at the crowd and yelled, "Get an ambulance! Don't just stand there! Call a damn ambulance! Get help!"

A man ran to a hut next to the helipad to call for an air ambulance. Adin crept closer to the family. He was shooting a video with his phone's front-facing camera. In the video, his mouth was agape with excitement.

He mouthed: '*This kid's dead.*'

Jenna stroked Otto's forehead and said, "Be strong, baby, be strong. We're going to get you to the hospital, okay? You can... You'll ride in a helicopter. Yeah, you can ride the helicopter now. You and your sister... your sister..." She looked up at Kurt and asked, "Where's Flora?"

Kurt's silence and sad, regretful eyes spoke volumes about the situation.

"No," Jenna whined.

Face stamped with devastation, Samuel said, "Kurt?"

"Oh God, it can't be. You can't do this to us. She's okay. She has to be okay. Sam. Samuel! We have to get Flora. She... She can ride with Otto to–to the hospital and they'll be fine. They always wanted to... to fly in a helicopter, remember?"

"Kurt... What happened?"

Lindsay stepped off the lodge's porch and said, "I'll tell you what's happening. *She...*" She pointed at Angelina and waited a moment to make sure all eyes were on her before continuing, "brought *hell* to our town."

"Excuse me?" Angelina responded, taken aback by the accusation.

"You heard me. We were perfectly fine—*perfectly safe*—before she came back to town. And I bet she didn't come back alone. You all heard them, didn't you? She brought a *killer* to Goldbrush. She brought *death* to our home."

"They're not dead!" Jenna screamed from the ground. "Don't you ever say that, you bitch!"

The gathering devolved into a mix of shouting matches and finger-pointing. Heather stood in front of her children to protect them from the mob. The Holts continued screaming for help while the chaos left Kurt at a complete loss.

"Look out!" Randy shouted.

But he was too late. Headlights broken and engine roaring, a black pickup truck plowed through the group, tossing the residents around like bowling pins. A series of thuds, cracks, clinks, clanks, and groans and shrieks exploded through the town.

Upon impact, the vehicle's front bumper pulverized every bone in Adin's pelvis. The hiker was thrown *over* the truck's cabin, his face hitting the windshield on the way. He ended up in the cargo bed, knocked out. With a woman trapped under it—her mangled arm stuck in the wheel arch—the truck moved like a mechanical bull, swinging and tipping every which way.

The vehicle swerved to a stop just past Goldbrush Eats, leaving a trail of bodies, blood, broken glass, and shoes and slippers behind it. The crash victims floundered on the ground. Some had difficulties breathing due to broken ribs. Others had trouble standing because of their broken hips and legs. Bleeding profusely from his head, a man had a seizure in front of the lodge.

Randy found himself lying on his back on the dirt path. He had been struck by the vehicle. He felt like the ground was shaking under him. In his blurred vision, it looked like the stars were falling towards the earth. Every part of his body hurt, but the worst pain lanced his right leg. He rolled onto his stomach, then pushed himself up to his feet.

He immediately howled and clutched at his right knee as the pain intensified. He limped forward, though, determined to check on the other victims.

After a few steps, his right heel cord split with an audible *snap*. He spun around while tumbling forward. He landed on his back and curled into a ball, holding his leg up in the air with both hands. He rocked to and fro, screaming at the top of his lungs. His right foot was barely attached to his leg.

The truck's driver window slid down.

Boo-Boo, wearing her clown mask, popped her head out and said, "Oopsies. I think I hit something. Let me give you a hand... or *a tire!*"

Pedal to the metal, she reversed towards the downed victims while laughing maniacally. One of the tires rolled over an unconscious man's stomach, flattening his abdomen. As she attempted to crawl away, another woman's leg was run over. Her ankle was twisted so badly that her foot had turned 180-degrees, toes pointing behind her.

Like a deer in headlights, Samuel froze as the truck came barreling towards him. Kurt scrambled into action and pulled him away at the last moment. They watched the truck hit another fleeing woman. Over the chorus of cries and screams, they heard her spine crackle like glass as one of the tires rolled across her back.

Jenna approached the men in a hurry, carrying Otto in her arms. She held the boy out in front of Samuel and said, "Get him to the ambulance when it gets here. I'll get Flora and meet you there."

Samuel's body was working on autopilot while his mind was running on overdrive. Although he disagreed with her plan, he took the boy in his arms on impulse.

"You can't go," he said. "No, we have to stay together. We have to–"

"We'll be together soon, but you have to protect him. Take care of our boy. I'll take care of our baby girl."

"But Flora is... She..."

"She's alive. I know it."

"Jenna," Kurt said pleadingly.

As she ran off, Jenna yelled, "She's alive!"

Samuel was about to run after her when Kurt grabbed his shoulder and pulled him back.

"What are you doing, damn it?!" Samuel shouted. "Let me go!"

Kurt turned him towards the wide path between the post office and the helipad. Captain Gashes strolled towards them from Goldbrush Essentials. He was armed with a hunting rifle, which he had stolen from the Browns' home after murdering Adeline. The crowd of residents began to scatter, abandoning their neighbors. Only a few people stayed to help their loved ones.

A group of survivors stampeded into The Gold Star. In the rush, Lindsay was pushed to the ground outside of the lodge. When she tried to get up, she was knocked back down. By the time she got to her feet, the survivors were already barricading the front doors and windows. She had been locked out of her own building. So, she ran off to her home.

Heather shouted, "Kurt!"

"Dad!" Angelina and Gilbert blurted out simultaneously.

Kurt saw his family running off with the rest of the survivors. Boo-Boo stopped the truck, put the vehicle in Drive, then put her foot on the gas. One of the bodies stuck under the truck came loose. Rolling behind the vehicle, the corpse flopped and twisted as if boneless. Kurt and Samuel followed the others.

They heard the whirring of the truck's engine behind them. On a straight path—lined with homes on each side—Boo-Boo had the perfect opportunity to run them over, but she toyed with them instead. She sped up, tapped Kurt with the front bumper, slowed down, then sped up again. She honked the horn to startle them, cycling between short beeps and long, obnoxious blasts.

They could hear the clown's childish laughter as well as doors slamming in the surrounding homes and survivors screaming.

"There!" Kurt yelled.

He pushed Samuel towards a tall brick partition to their right. The truck rolled right past them, continuing to chase the other stragglers. The men hustled through an open gate in the wall.

A flagstone walkway—fringed with artificial shrubs —led to a two-story house up a short, gentle hill. Motion-sensing lights illuminated the fake lime-green lawns, which were enclosed by wrought-iron fences. Surveillance cameras were installed around the house as well as on the brick border surrounding the property, recording 24/7. Security bars covered the windows on the first floor of the home.

The house, built like a fortress, was owned by Lindsay and her husband Brett Bunker. It was the most secure building in all of Goldbrush.

A group of survivors had already made it inside. Lindsay was trying to shut the front door while Angelina and Heather were fighting to keep it open.

"You're going to get me killed!" Lindsay yelled.

Kurt and Samuel pushed their way into the home, unintentionally knocking the women back. Heather slammed the door shut and pressed her palms against it, as if expecting one of the clowns to try to ram it open. Although she wasn't eager to share her home with her neighbors, Lindsay fastened all of the locks.

With a thousand-yard stare, Samuel trudged through the archway to the left of the front door and carried his son into the dining room. Dakota Paddock—a 47-year-old woman with short black hair—was standing in front of a window overlooking the front yard, peeking out from behind a curtain. Shivering and sniveling, Gilbert was sitting on the floor in the corner, knees up to his face and arms wrapped around his shins.

Samuel set Otto's unconscious body down gingerly on the long, rectangular dining table. He kissed the boy's forehead, kissed him again, then wept brokenly as he went in for a third kiss.

"Oh my," Dakota said upon noticing the pencil in Otto's neck and the lack of color on his face.

As he walked into the dining room, Kurt said, "Make sure all of the doors and windows are locked. All of them, you hear me?"

He went to the window and looked out at the front lawn. There were no clowns in view, but he could hear faint shrieking and the truck's horn blaring in the distance. Checking every lock, Angelina ran through the first floor while Lindsay checked upstairs. Heather ran to Samuel's side. She rubbed his back delicately and grabbed his arm with her other hand.

In a calm, understanding tone, she said, "I need to check on him. We can't help him if we can't see him."

"My boy... God, how could they do this to him? How? Why?" Samuel said, his voice on the verge of breaking.

"Is he gonna be okay?" Gilbert whined from the corner of the room.

Heather said, "Sam, please."

Samuel knew she was right and he sensed the urgency in her voice. He stroked Otto's hair, then kissed his forehead again before leaning away from him.

Heather took his place. She tilted Otto's head back and, with two fingers on his chin, she pried his lips apart. She put her ear over his mouth and listened. His breathing was weak, sporadic, and hoarse. She pressed on his inner wrist and checked his heart rate. The kid's pulse had slowed to a crawl, nearly imperceptible.

"Is he gonna be okay?" Gilbert repeated.

Heather said, "I need a... a bowl of warm water... a big bowl... towels... pillows." Samuel paced behind her, but no one else moved. Raising her voice, Heather said, "*Please.*"

"I can do that," Dakota said.

She had been in the house before—for teatime and dinner parties with the Bunkers—so she knew her way around. She rushed through the archway on the parallel wall.

Breathing hard, Angelina stumbled into the other archway leading to the foyer and said, "First floor's all locked, I think." None of the survivors looked her way. Angelina's gaze fell on Otto. She asked, "How... How is he?"

"Mom, is he gonna be okay?" Gilbert cried out.

Heather heard them. She knew the answer to their question, but she didn't want to answer it in front of Samuel. She wanted to be wrong so badly. Dakota returned to the dining room with a large stainless steel mixing bowl filled with warm water and two towels. She placed the supplies on the table before running off again.

Heather soaked the towels in the warm water. She wiped the cold sweat off Otto's brow with one, then slipped it under his head. She used the other towel to apply gentle pressure *around* the pencil in his neck, which she was too scared to remove. Dakota returned once again with two throw pillows from the living room.

Dakota said, "Do you..." Her voice trailed off as she caught another glimpse of Otto's injury. She looked away, swallowed loudly, then asked, "Do you need more?"

"This should be just fine, thank you," Heather replied.

She put the pillows under Otto's legs to elevate them. From outside, the sound of the gate crashing into the brick partition reverberated into the home.

"They know we're here," Kurt said.

Angelina, Heather, and Dakota gathered around him to look out the window. Captain Gashes stood towards the middle of the walkway, megaphone in hand. Parked on the dirt path in front of the house, the black pickup truck could be seen through the open gate behind him. The last body trapped under the vehicle had been freed somewhere in Goldbrush— *human roadkill.*

Captain Gashes held the megaphone in front of his mouth, pressed the push-to-talk button, and—in a droning voice—he said, "Ladies and gentlemen, boys and girls, the living and the dying. Come one, come all. The traveling circus is in town with a thrilling presentation you do not want to miss. Hurry, hurry, hurry. Gather 'round, gather 'round."

"What in heaven's name is going on out there?" Dakota murmured. "Who are these people?"

Heather said, "Angelina, you and your brother... you said something about a killer and a clown at the school. Is that... Christ, is that a killer clown?"

"No," her daughter responded. "I mean, I think he's a killer clown, but that's not the same guy from the school."

"Then this is premeditated. It's like a... a terrorist attack."

Captain Gashes resumed his speech: "We are here to entertain you, the world, and—most importantly— ourselves. Step right up and meet the magic clown with more dead friends than a school shooter. That's right, this girl kills in the name of friendship... and you'll be *dying* to befriend her. Please give a warm welcome to... Boo-Boo!"

Leaving it running, Boo-Boo climbed out of the

truck and frolicked over to her boss. She dropped a curtsy, then waved at the house with both hands.

Captain Gashes said, "If I'm correct, I believe some of you have already encountered the other member of our troupe. Unfortunately, he's not around to introduce himself right now. He's taking a moment to catch his breath and prepare for our next act, but I'll tell you about him anyway. He's a strongman gone mad or maybe a madman gone strong. Give a round of applause for Pipsqueak!"

The clown lowered the megaphone and waited, as if he were actually expecting the survivors to cheer. Only moans from the victims scattered at the village square and on the dirt paths blew through the town like gusts of wind.

"Kurt, what are we going to do?" Heather asked.

Sounding defeated, Kurt said, "I don't know."

Captain Gashes brought the megaphone back to his mouth and said, "And then you've got me. I'm sure some of you will recognize me when I get close to you —and believe me, I like to get *real* close to my audience when I perform. For now, you can call me Captain Gashes. You can think of me as the ringleader of this crazy sideshow of ours."

"I don't hear any clapping!" Boo-Boo shouted. "What?! You ain't got any hands or something?"

"Now listen, you don't have to applaud us, but you will respect us. I have a feeling you know why we're here. That was no robbery at that convenience store. No home invasion at that diner. No 'corporal punishment' at that school. No car accident in your little town square. We're here for *you*, and we ain't leaving until we get what we want. But we don't have to do this the hard way—the *painful* way. No, we can work something out. You see, we were sent here by Deadface. If I'm the ringleader of our little crew, he's the ring*master* of this circus. We call him the 'catalyst of chaos.' He wants to see you all bound and gagged and lined up in this desert in front of some cameras."

"Kinda like one of those terrorist videos!" Boo-Boo piped up.

"He wants you to watch our show and accept his message. Simple, huh? If you don't come out... You're a close-knit community, aren't you? Well, if you don't cooperate, we're going to start by executing all of the stragglers. Right here. Right in front of you. Pipsqueak is bringing someone to us as we speak. Could be a life-long friend. Could be a family member. You better hope it's not someone you love. You have until Pipsqueak gets here to decide the fate of your neighbors. And once we get tired of them... we're going to force our way into that house of yours and drag you out, kicking and screaming and bleeding. Clock's ticking."

"Tick! Tock! Tick! Tock! Tick! Tock!" Boo-Boo said as she skipped circles around her boss.

In the dining room, Heather gripped her husband's arm tightly and asked, "What do we do?"

"Kurt, Danny didn't come home with my medicine tonight," Dakota said with a tremor in her voice. "I–I was on my way to ask you all about him before that… that 'incident' at the village square. Did you see him? Can you help me find him? Kurt?"

Angelina noticed the spasms of acute stress rippling across her father's face. The pressure was getting to him. She looked over at Samuel. The man was sobbing over his son's unconscious body. Racked with guilt, Gilbert was still in the corner of the room.

"We need to stay here and get ready to hold them off," Angelina said. "They'll kill us if we go out there. You saw what they did. We can't just give up. We can't."

"But if we don't cooperate, they'll kill everyone else," Heather countered. "I know it's risky, but if we all go outside together, maybe we can… I don't know, outrun them or overpower them."

"That one has a rifle, Mom. The other guy had a shotgun. Dad was able to take it away from him, but who knows what else they have? There could be more of them, too."

"I understand what you're saying, but we can't just sit here and wait for–"

"You have to see this!" Lindsay shouted.

Through the archway leading to the foyer of the home, they saw her come down a flight of stairs to the right of the front door. She was holding a satellite phone in her hand.

She beckoned to them and said, "Quick! Before it ends!"

Kurt touched Dakota's shoulder and said, "We'll talk about Danny soon. I need you to keep an eye on those... psychos for a while, okay? Scream if they do anything suspicious. Anything at all." As he hurried off to follow Lindsay, he shouted, "Gilbert, help Mrs. Paddock!"

Gilbert stayed put on the floor, shaken to the core. Lindsay kept a keen eye on the clowns. Boo-Boo continued capering about while Captain Gashes appeared to be studying the house. Angelina and Heather followed Kurt. Down the main hall and through another archway, they joined Lindsay in the living room.

Lindsay turned on the massive television in the entertainment center and flipped through the channels until she stumbled upon a news program. Under a red BREAKING NEWS banner, a headline read: *LVMPD issue emergency shelter-in-place order.* Under it, the subheadline read: *Las Vegas under siege, hundreds dead in simultaneous shootings and bombings.*

In the footage, the cameraman was taking cover behind a bullet-riddled news van. He caught footage of a shooting in progress. From several broken windows on different floors at a nearby hotel, gunmen shot down at the surrounding streets with modified rifles. Staying low, cops moved from cover to cover—from one abandoned car to another—inching closer to the building.

Although they were armed with rifles as well, the police hesitated to return fire due to the possibility of collateral damage since the hotel hadn't been evacuated yet. The relentless hail of bullets stopped them from rescuing the incapacitated pedestrians on the road and drivers trapped in their vehicles.

As the bullets stopped striking the news van, the cameraman made a run for it, figuring he was safer close to the police than on his own. He screamed and his camera shook with great force as bullets hit the pavement around him. He crashed into a wrecked minivan. The camera recorded the cameraman's shoes, glass crackling under his feet.

"You need to get off the fucking street!" a commanding voice barked off camera.

The cameraman yelled, "They killed my–"

Off-screen, an explosion rocked the street. The camera soared towards the minivan. Then the broadcast came to an abrupt end. The footage cut back to two news anchors sitting behind a desk at the news studio. Upset, unsettled, and unsure of what to do next, they sat still in total silence.

Standing in front of a three-seat sofa in the living room, Lindsay started flicking through the other channels. All of the other news networks covered similar terrorist attacks in different cities. The other survivors stood behind the sofa, their big, shocked eyes fixed on the TV.

"They're saying it's happening all over the world," Lindsay said. "They're talking about clowns. They're everywhere. It's like a–a... a doomsday cult or something."

One hand over her mouth, Heather whispered, "This can't be happening."

Kurt said, "If they're everywhere, then everyone has to know about it already. The government, the police, the national guard, they have to be... mobilizing. We only have to get a call out to them and let them know it's happening *here* before it's too late."

Wagging the satellite phone at him, Lindsay said, "I already tried calling the police. I couldn't connect."

"Shit... Brett's out of town, isn't he?"

He was referring to Lindsay's husband. The man was in Phuket, Thailand on a business trip.

"I tried calling him, too," Lindsay responded. "He's not answering his damn phone."

Heather said, "Your car. We can drive out of here in your car."

"Brett took the truck. And even if he didn't, there's no way I would try to drive out of here with them out there. You saw how dangerously that maniac was driving that truck. They'd ram us before we even got out of Goldbrush. If not, they'd gun us down."

"Then... what if we cooperate? If we do what they say–"

"Mom, *no*," Angelina interrupted.

"–if we surrender, maybe they'll just tie us up and force us to watch a stupid show like they said. Maybe we can buy time for the others—for our children."

"If you go outside, they're going to kill you. You can't trust them. They're evil. They're going to kill us all as soon as they get the chance."

"For once, your girl is right," Lindsay said. "These people are pure evil. You can't 'cooperate' with them. And there's no way I'm letting any one of you open any of the doors in *my* house again. You already jeopardized my safety enough by leading them here."

"We can't just sit here and watch our friends die," Heather responded. "We have to do something."

Dakota called out to them from the dining room, but they couldn't make out her words.

Kurt asked, "Do you have any guns? A shotgun? A rifle? A peashooter?"

"No, no, and no," Lindsay answered. "We came here to get away from the violence, not contribute to it."

"There's another one!" Dakota shouted, standing in the foyer now.

The survivors hurried back to the dining room. Except for Gilbert and Samuel, they huddled in front of the window and looked outside. Pipsqueak had joined his fellow clowns. Bellowing and writhing, Randy was sprawled across the walkway in front of them. Blood from his butchered ankle left a trail behind them.

Holding the megaphone up to his mouth, Captain Gashes said, "And here's our first participant of the night. Looks like he could be someone's grandpappy. If you know him, come and claim him. Save this poor man's life. If you don't recognize him or if you hate the guy... Well, take your seats, get your popcorn ready, and enjoy the show 'cause we're starting in ten seconds. Ten. Nine."

"That's Randy!" Heather exclaimed, jabbing a finger at the window. "We can't just let this happen! This is wrong!"

"Eight. Seven."

Moping, Dakota said, "He's a good man. He was there for me when my Melvin passed."

Melvin was her deceased husband.

Captain Gashes continued the slow countdown: "Six. Five."

Lindsay said, "No matter what we do, they're not going to spare him."

"Anything's better than standing here doing nothing," Heather said. "I'm going out there."

Kurt grabbed one of her arms and Angelina seized the other, stopping her in her tracks. Her daughter's big, wet puppy eyes said something along the lines of: *'Please don't go.'* On her husband's face, Heather saw utter hopelessness. Although she couldn't see him through the dining table, she heard her son's cries, too. She knew she wasn't going to be doing them any favors by marching into danger. She nodded at Angelina, then stepped back towards the window.

"Help!" Randy was screaming. "God, help me!"

Captain Gashes said, "Four. Three. Two."

"Jeez, I don't think they like you very much," Boo-Boo said to the victim.

"One. Guess he's part of the circus now."

"Yes! More friends for me!"

Captain Gashes handed Boo-Boo the megaphone, then he stomped on Randy's right foot. Blood spouted from the victim's torn ankle as the wound grew. Randy fell into the throes of agony, bawling and shaking violently. Captain Gashes placed more pressure on his partially amputated foot. His ligaments snapped like strained guitar strings.

"I can't watch," Dakota whined, turning away from the window and lowering her head.

"I'm sorry," Kurt whispered to himself.

Outside, Boo-Boo shouted, "Oh, oh, I wanna help!"

She jumped on Randy's right leg, landing with one foot on the side of his knee and the other on his shin. Something *crunched* in the limb, and a column of blood shot out of his ankle. She stayed on his leg with her arms outstretched, rotating them as if trying to keep her balance on a skateboard. She jumped on his leg again.

Another *crunch*.

Another spurt of blood.

Randy released a tortured bellow before passing

out. While Captain Gashes continued to apply pressure to his foot, Boo-Boo jumped again—higher than ever before—and landed with both feet on his shin. Randy's foot was amputated with a clear *pop*. It was so loud that the survivors could hear it in the dining room.

Randy was screaming before his eyes even fluttered open. Sickening stabs of pain ripped through his leg. He stared down at himself in utter disbelief. He saw his severed foot under Captain Gashes' shoe. But still, he felt a throbbing burning sensation *in* his amputated foot. The idea of 'phantom pain' was difficult for him to comprehend, especially for his pain-wracked mind.

Unable to stop himself from screaming and incapable of handling the torment, his body shut down entirely. He was breathing but unresponsive.

Captain Gashes picked up the severed foot, tossed it up in the air, caught it, then pitched it at the dining room window. It bounced off the security bars, making the survivors flinch. Lindsay yelped, covered her head with her arms, and squatted behind the others. A few drops of blood pattered on the glass. The foot landed in the flowerbed under the window.

While Boo-Boo giggled and jumped in the blood on the walkway like a kid splashing in a puddle, the male clowns lifted Randy from the ground and dragged him to the wrought-iron fence to their left. Pipsqueak hoisted him up. Making sure the victim was facing the dining room window, Captain Gashes swung Randy's head down at a spear-shaped finial at the top of the fence.

The finial penetrated Randy's chin, the floor of his mouth, his tongue, and his palate. It came to a stop in his nasal cavity. Blood gushed from his nose like water from a spigot. It spilled from the drooping corners of his mouth, too. His sclerae turned ruby-red. There wasn't a hint of white in his eyes.

As Pipsqueak released him, Randy's body sank and the finial rose deeper into his skull. The tip rubbed up against his olfactory bulb—located at the front of the brain. The finial was between his eyes *in* his skull. Yet, the man continued breathing and twitching. He was ready to die—he *wanted* to die—but his body refused to quit.

The will to live came naturally to people, stronger in some than others.

Captain Gashes took the megaphone from Boo-Boo and spoke into it: "You can still save this man. Okay, I won't lie to you, he isn't going to make it. But at very least, we can put him out of his misery... *if* you cooperate. I hope you're thinking about what he's going through. He might not be speaking, but I'm sure he's still hurting and I'm sure he's still thinking about something."

"You better hurry!" Boo-Boo yelled. "Or your friend's going to be *my* friend soon!"

Hands over her mouth, Angelina staggered away from the window. The violence made her ill, and although she had never met him, Randy's suffering made her heart ache. Heather lowered her head and cried, afflicted with a mixture of shame and regret. Dakota refused to look, but she heard the guttural croaking and gurgling sounds outside.

Kurt pressed his fist against the window and stared at the front lawn—jaw clenched, lips shaking, eyes angry but teary. He felt scared and frustrated and useless.

Captain Gashes sighed into the megaphone, making his disappointment clear, then he said, "You're some cold-hearted sons of bitches. Maybe we need to warm this town up a little."

"I can do that, Cap," Boo-Boo said excitedly. "I know a couple of fire tricks, too, y'know?"

"Then go show this town what you're made of."

As she walked back down the hill, Boo-Boo took the duffel bag from Pipsqueak. It was filled with Molotov cocktails. She climbed back into the truck and drove off to the neighbor's house.

Captain Gashes said, "Remember, I can still call her off. You have a few minutes before every building —*everybody!*—is burning. Don't make us do this the hard way."

"What's the hard way?" Pipsqueak asked.

"You don't remember? It's when we break their doors down and skull-fuck every single one of them. Kids and elders included."

With a big, goofy smile, Pipsqueak said, "I like the hard way."

"Me too, fella, me too. Now go find me the next participant. Preferably a woman or a child. This show needs some variety."

"Okay, boss."

Pipsqueak waddled off. Captain Gashes stayed behind, scowling at the dining room window. Despite the blinds, he was making direct eye contact with Kurt. The orange glow from a fire flickered over the brick partition. Boo-Boo had set the neighbor's home ablaze. A woman's strangled shriek reached the Bunker house. Moments later, orange light emerged from another house.

More screams.

More anguish.

More death.

16

CHOICES

Eyes glazed in a deathlike trance, Angelina stared out the dining room window. She couldn't see Captain Gashes or Randy over her father's shoulder. Although she was focused on the columns of black smoke rising from the burning houses, she could still see Randy's head impaled on the fence. The afterimage of the gore was burned into her retinas. Trauma had a way of leaving scars on the mind. Tears rolled down her face, but she didn't blink or move.

"What are we going to do?" Dakota asked.

She stood with her back to the dining room window, twiddling her fingers while staring at the floor. She didn't want to see Randy or Otto. A bout of repulsion left Lindsay dizzy and queasy. She leaned against the archway leading to the foyer and took some deep breaths. Frustrated by her own lack of action, Heather wanted to stay busy—stay helpful—so she went to check on Gilbert. The kid continued apologizing to Samuel and Otto inaudibly, unaware of the bloodbath outside.

Dakota glanced around, searching for a leader. The second she caught a glimpse of Otto, she looked back down at the floor.

She said, "I need to find Danny. I need to find him before they do. He was supposed to–"

"No one is leaving this house," Lindsay interrupted. "We have to wait until the police get here."

"Whe–When will that be?"

"They're not coming anytime soon," Kurt said, keeping his eyes on Captain Gashes. "We saw that news report. These people are attacking major cities across the country. You think the police or national guard are going to rush out to Goldbrush before they secure Vegas? We're at the bottom of their list."

Lindsay said, "It doesn't matter if we're at the bottom, the middle, or the top. The police *are* coming. They *will* come. We just have to wait it out."

Heather placed her hands over Gilbert's ears, looked over her shoulder, and asked, "You want us to wait and watch our friends die?"

"What don't you understand?" Lindsay snapped. "They're going to die either way. They're going to kill us all. Didn't you see what they did to him? Hmm? Why do you want to make it easy for them?"

"I want to protect the people I care about. You can't

understand that because you're a selfish, self-serving bitch."

"I'm selfish? I was just locked out of my own lodge by the 'people you care about.' They didn't have any issue leaving me—and all of you in case you forgot—out with those killers. This isn't about being selfish. It's about being smart."

"And we're smart enough to think of a way to save ourselves and everyone else. I know it. Right? Kurt? Angie?"

Kurt wasn't ready to commit to a decision. He believed he could handle Captain Gashes in a one-on-one fight, but the clown's rifle created an uneven playing field.

"We need to find weapons," Angelina said as she wiped the tears off her cheeks. "We have to be ready to defend ourselves. We can't surrender."

"*Angelina,*" Heather said in a stern voice, as if her daughter had said something offensive.

"Lindsay's right, Mom. We need to buy time. We– We can't talk it out with these people. You saw how they... they... Fuck, you saw what happened. They're monsters. They're fucking monsters. And that's what they want to do to us. If they didn't, they would have burned this house to the ground like the others. They probably know how many of us are in here. They want us alive so they can hurt us. You heard what they said. They're going to line us up in front of a camera like a 'terrorist' video. I've seen what happens in those videos and *that*—what they did to him—was worse than most of them."

"Then... Then let's go out there and fight. We outnumber them, right? Let's fight back."

"They have a gun," Kurt said matter-of-factly.

Angelina asked, "Do you think Gilbert can fight back? Do you want what happened outside just now to happen to him? Or... Or to me?"

Heather stood with her mouth ajar. She was always going to pick her family over her neighbors, but it pained her to know she couldn't save everyone. She shook her head at her daughter, and Angelina nodded at her. They didn't have to say another word to understand each other. Despite all of their differences, the years they spent without communicating, and their recent arguments, they shared a deep love for one another. Adversity revealed their true emotions.

Angelina said, "We need weapons. Sooner or later, they're going to try to force their way in or smoke us out of here or... burn us alive. We need to be ready to fight back."

"She's right," Kurt said. "But someone needs to keep an eye on that clown while we get ready. We can't lose track of him. They outgun us, but we technically have the higher ground. We can't lose our only advantage."

Angelina looked at Dakota. Heather and Lindsay did, too.

"Me?" Dakota asked. "No, no, I can't. Not like that.

Not with... with Randy like *that*. I can't bring myself to look at him again. Please don't make me."

"You have the worst eyesight out of all of us," Lindsay said. "You can probably barely make him out from over here anyway."

"I–I can see everything."

"And you won't be able to help us find any weapons in here. I'm not going to act like I know what I'm doing, but I know my home better than anyone. I can help."

"I can help, too," Dakota cried.

"For crying out loud, we're wasting time."

Lindsay crossed the archway and headed upstairs. Heather went through the other archway and started searching the kitchen for weapons. Kurt refused to take his eyes off the clown until he was certain someone else was watching him.

Angelina held Dakota's hands with a gentle, reassuring grip and said, "Mrs. Paddock, I know it's hard. It's... fucked up. These people... They're depraved. But we need you to do this. We need to move fast and—I hate to say this—you'll only slow us down."

"But... I'm scared, sweetheart. I'm so scared."

"I know. Me too, me too. But you don't have to look directly at him. Look at the stars. Just keep that monster in the corner of your eye. If he moves, scream. Gilbert... I think he's going to stay here. Mr. Holt, too. You won't be alone, and the rest of us will be right back. I promise."

Dakota sensed the sincerity in Angelina's voice.

Deep down, she knew she was right about everything. She reluctantly turned towards the window and looked up at the sky. At the bottom of her vision, she could see the clown's head.

Kurt moved away from the window. He made sure Dakota was watching the clown, then he ran out of the dining room through the archway leading to the foyer. He went down the hall. Angelina was going to join her mother in the kitchen, but she stopped next to her brother.

She crouched in front of him, put a hand on his shoulder, then—speaking in a hushed voice so Samuel wouldn't hear her—she said, "Gilbert, you have to listen to me, okay? Hey, are you listening?"

"I'm sorry," the boy kept saying. "I'm sorry."

"It wasn't your fault, okay?"

"I'm sorry."

Angelina shook him gently and repeated, "It wasn't your fault."

Gilbert looked her in the eye. *'It wasn't your fault.'* He had been dying to hear those words since the attack at the school, but he wanted to hear them come from Samuel's mouth. He sought forgiveness. Survivor's guilt was festering within him, eating him alive.

"I'm sorry," he said for the umpteenth time.

"Don't do this to yourself. Those bastards did that to Otto and Flora, not you."

"But I told them to–"

Angelina shushed him. She didn't want Samuel to

overhear them. She glanced over at the dining table. Otto looked dead. Samuel grieved for his son tearlessly, each dry cry shredding his throat like sandpaper.

Angelina looked back at Gilbert, stroked his hair, and said, "You did nothing wrong. You don't deserve to be in this situation. None of us do. But we're here, Gilbert, and we're going to need each other if we're going to get out of this."

"I can't... do anything."

"You want to get Otto out of here on that helicopter when it gets here, right?"

Gilbert nodded at her. Saving Otto was the only thing he wanted.

Angelina said, "Keep an eye on Mrs. Paddock until I get back. You don't have to look outside. Actually, whatever you do, *don't* look outside, okay? Just... If she moves, you call me or Dad or Mom or anyone. If she says something's going on outside, you scream. Can you do that?"

"I'll try," Gilbert whispered.

"Good. I'll be right back."

On her way to the kitchen, Angelina heard Samuel say: "We'll leave soon. We–We'll find your mother and your sister. We'll leave this place together. We'll leave... We have to leave..."

Angelina feared he was going to do something rash. She wanted to comfort him, too, but she didn't know how to alleviate his severe sorrow. One wrong word could have triggered a nervous breakdown. She frowned and continued walking.

In the kitchen, water was boiling in a stockpot on the stove. A drawer was left wide open. The room was empty, though.

Angelina searched the counters, cabinets, and drawers for some sharp cutlery. She found plates and bowls and cups, but no knives or forks. She stumbled upon a two-liter fire extinguisher in one of the cabinets, though. It had some heft to it, weighing nearly eight pounds. She took it, then followed a quiet voice down the hall to the living room where she found her parents.

Heather had brought a wooden knife block, a silverware tray, and a roll of duct tape from the kitchen, and Kurt had disassembled a pair of standing lamps. They were building homemade spears, using the duct tape to attach knives to the ends of the lamps' aluminum tubes. They planned on using the spears to engage the clowns from a safe distance, and the knives if the clowns managed to get close.

Kurt still had Ben's double-barreled shotgun, too. He remembered hurting Pipsqueak with it at the school, so he was prepared to use it as a blunt instrument.

Angelina entered the bathroom down the hall. She set the fire extinguisher down and rummaged through the medicine cabinet in search of another weapon. Bottles of medicine, tweezers, floss, Q-tips, cotton balls, it all seemed useless in a fight for survival. She pulled a bottle of hairspray out of the cabinet.

On the back of the bottle, at the bottom of the label, a message read: *Safety Warning: Highly flammable contents. Pressurized container. Do not use near open flames, near heat, or while smoking.*

Angelina took a lighter out of her pocket and whispered, "This can work."

A muffled voice came from down the hall. Then there was a rush of footsteps upstairs.

"Dad!" Gilbert shouted from the dining room. "Angie!"

The fire extinguisher in one hand and the hairspray in the other, Angelina hurried back to her brother. Except for Samuel and Gilbert, the other survivors had already gathered at the dining room window with their weapons. Kurt and Heather held their makeshift spears and knives. Heather had given a paring knife to Dakota. And Lindsay had armed herself with a hairbrush and a pair of sewing scissors.

Angelina heard feminine screaming outside as she approached the window.

17

HUMAN BAIT

"And here's participant number two!" Captain Gashes blared into the megaphone.

Arms hooked under the victim's armpits, Boo-Boo lugged Gabriela between her legs towards her boss. She let the hiker fall to the ground towards the center of the walkway. Curled into the fetal position with her eyes squeezed shut, Gabriela grasped at her left knee and wailed. The white, bloodied, sharp end of a broken bone stuck out from the side of her knee.

Next to them, Randy had passed away. The fence's finial had skewered his brain, coming to a stop against the crown of his skull.

"I know her," Lindsay said, pointing at the hiker. "She was staying at my lodge. She's not from around here. We don't... We don't have to watch this."

"She's only a girl," Heather said.

"She's twenty. I remember seeing her driver's license."

"That's a *girl*, Lindsay."

'*Like me*,' Angelina wanted to say. Although they hadn't met, she felt an instant connection to Gabriela due to their age. A twinge rocketed up her leg from her left knee in a case of vicarious pain. She felt like she was watching a preview of her own inevitable execution.

Leaning close to Captain Gashes so the megaphone could pick up her voice, Boo-Boo said, "This one tried to run after I set that lodge on fire. I guess she didn't like my fire trick. Luckily for us, Pips stopped her with a sledgehammer to the knee."

"And where is the big guy?" Captain Gashes asked.

"He's in the truck taking care of the other two participants."

"You heard that, didn't you, folks? We have not one, not two, but *three* participants for the next act of our show. You know what that means, right? There's a good chance we have one of your loved ones with us. Like this dog here. Does this stray bitch belong to anyone?"

"I'm not watching this," Dakota said as she turned her back to the dining room window.

Heather asked, "What do we do?"

Eyes on the sky, Lindsay said, "We wait. The police will be here soon. They have to be."

"That girl has a family."

"We all have families."

Looking directly at the survivors through the window, Captain Gashes smiled and said, "I knew it. You *are* some cold-hearted bastards. I like that. I can tell you don't give two shits about this whore. I don't either. No need for a countdown then, huh? Enjoy the show, you sick cunts. I know I will. Boo-Boo, do your thing."

"Yay!" the female clown cheered. "I'll be back in a jiffy!"

She dashed back to the pickup truck parked in front of the house. Another woman was screaming beyond the partition.

"Stop! Please stop!" Gabriela cried. "Please... Mom... Dad... Mah–Mommy, help me..."

Keeping one hand on her knee, she clawed at the walkway and tried to drag herself forward. Randy's blood helped her glide across the flagstones. She inched towards the house. She could see the survivors watching her from the window.

"Please!" she yelled at them. "Help me! Help! I don't wanna die! Please!"

Angelina lowered her head and let out a shuddery breath. She felt her throat closing up and her chest tightening. Then her mother wrapped her arm around her and, although it lingered, her anxiety abated. She buried her face in her mother's chest and cried. Heather held her tighter—*closer*. She was afraid that if she let her go for even a second, she would end up like the hiker.

Boo-Boo returned to the walkway with a bottle of overproof rum and a torch. The torch had a padded grip and an aluminum shaft. The wick on the tip was already burning. She unscrewed the rum bottle's cap with one thumb. Like a stone skipping on water, the cap bounced across the puddle of blood under her shoes. She stopped over Gabriela.

"No! No! God, I'm begging you!" the hiker screamed. She looked at the dining room window and yelled, "Why aren't you helping me?!

The clown said, "Relax, cupcake, I'm a professional. I'm going to make sure you go out in a blaze of glory."

She poured the rum on Gabriela's head. It drenched her short black hair and cascaded across her face, stinging her eyes and burning her nose. Due to her frantic panting, she unintentionally inhaled some of the alcohol, setting off a violent coughing fit. The rum ran down her neck and soaked the shoulders of her shirt, too.

"Why don't we clean that leg of yours while we're at it?" Boo-Boo said.

She dumped some alcohol on Gabriela's injured knee. Through the open fracture, the liquid streamed *into* the fleshy cave in her leg. The excruciating pain jolted her into unconsciousness. Every muscle on her body stiffened. Her teeth popped and squeaked as she ground them. She awoke only ten seconds later, eyes on a fake shrub to her left.

Boo-Boo said, "Now let's see what you think of this fire trick."

She lifted her mask to her forehead. The survivors were surprised to see she looked like a regular person. She could have been one of their neighbors—and that disturbed them. Monsters weren't supposed to look like them.

Boo-Boo took a deep breath, then she poured some rum into her mouth. She passed the bottle to her boss. Captain Gashes took it and took a few steps back. Boo-Boo held the torch out in front of her face, she swung her head back, then flung it forward and sprayed the alcohol out in a fine mist at the open flame, igniting a massive ball of blue fire.

The flames lapped at the surrounding shrubs, but they didn't burn. Gasping and screaming, the survivors cowered away from the window. Captain Gashes buried his face in the crook of his elbow and drew back. Boo-Boo released an ear-splitting yelp as the flames lashed her lower lip and chin. The heat cooked the tip of her tongue as well.

Gabriela was squirming and shrieking. A coat of blue fire had swaddled her head. It spread across her neck, turning it into a pillar of flames. The blue fire danced on her shoulders, too. Her face swelled and reddened, layers of skin peeling away. Clusters of blisters sprung up across her forehead, cheeks, and chin. Her hair crinkled and her scalp sizzled.

She rubbed her face on the walkway, but she

couldn't extinguish the fire. The heat boiled her eyeballs, blinding her. Discombobulated, she crawled forward, then right, then left. As the flames entered her mouth—roasting her tongue, gums, and the back of her throat—her screams were reduced to horrific croaks.

Sticking her burnt tongue out, Boo-Boo said, "I can't believe that worked."

In the dining room, Angelina stared down at the fire extinguisher in her hand. *Do something,* she told herself. *You can save her. Don't just stand there. Move. Move!* But she stayed still. Noticing her daughter's internal conflict, Heather grabbed her hand—both to stop her from running out and to comfort her. And it worked.

The fire ate away at the skin on Gabriela's ears, exposing the yellowish cartilage underneath. Then the heat ruptured her eardrums. Disoriented and nauseated, her arms slipped out from under her and she plummeted to the ground. Her eyeballs were liquefied, the gooey remains dripping from their sockets like mucus from a sick kid's nose.

The hiker's head and neck became charred, black and scaly. Most of her hair was burnt off, wisps of white smoke rising from the remaining patches. Her lips had melted into her face, fusing with her baked gums. She stopped moving.

Boo-Boo said, "Well, that went a lot better than expected."

"You almost blew yourself up," Captain Gashes responded as he approached her. "Now put that out before you blow me up with you."

"Oh, c'mon, you know I had everything under control."

Boo-Boo blew the torch out. The exhalation irritated her burnt tongue and lip. Grimacing, she slid her mask down over her face. She tossed the bottle of rum and the torch onto the lawn to her left.

Speaking into the megaphone, Captain Gashes said, "Looks like she's still burning. That's a fire hazard if I've ever seen one. Don't worry, folks, we pride ourselves in running a safe, inclusive circus. We'll put that right out for you before someone gets seriously hurt."

"Wouldn't want that," Boo-Boo said, snickering.

Captain Gashes approached Gabriela. She was barely breathing. He started stomping on the side of her head. Boo-Boo joined in with a kick to the back of the skull. They took turns stomping on her. Her skull cracked several times—here, there, *everywhere*. They stamped the fire out and turned her brain off in the process. Although her body was still kicking, she had no chance of surviving her injuries.

But Captain Gashes wasn't done with her. He wanted to send a message with her death. He gripped the back of her burnt shirt, then dragged her towards the house. In front of the porch, he took hold of her head with both hands. Her jaw dangling, he pushed her mouth towards the edge of the first stair, forcing her to bite down on it. He glanced over at the survivors, making sure they were still watching.

Kurt was glaring at the clowns, keeping track of all of their movements. The others were glancing out the window every now and then, traumatized but curious.

Captain Gashes raised his knee up to his stomach, then stomped on the back of Gabriela's head. Her jaw broke and four of her teeth spilled out of her mouth. A pink liquid leaked out of her ear canals. The curb stomp killed her.

The clown held the megaphone up to his mouth, looked at the survivors, and said, "I'll give you a few minutes to soak this all in. Think of it as... an intermission. But I won't beat around the bush. My patience is wearing thin. If you don't come out... this big bad wolf is going to huff and puff... and blow this fucking house to kingdom come."

The megaphone caught Boo-Boo saying, "We can't do that. Deadface wants..."

Captain Gashes took his finger off the megaphone's push-to-talk button. The survivors couldn't hear the rest of their conversation. After exchanging a few words with her boss, Boo-Boo headed back to the truck. Captain Gashes returned to the center of the walkway, spun around, then stood perfectly still and stared at the dining room window.

Like dew, beads of blood clung to the artificial bushes and grass. The stench of smoke with a hint of rotten eggs tainted the front lawn and seeped into the house. A gust of wind carried flakes of charred skin past the dining room window. An atmosphere of unease smothered the room. The survivors were keyed up.

Kurt kept his eyes on the clown outside. Gilbert was now sitting at the end of the dining table with his head down. Dakota stood in the corner, wiping her nose with a handkerchief. Lindsay paced between the window and the archway leading to the foyer, muttering to herself.

Knuckles planted on the table, Samuel leaned over his son's body. The boy had passed away during Gabriela's execution. He didn't have to check his vitals to know it. He just did. The cramp in his stomach—the tug on his heart—told him that he was gone.

Angelina and Heather stood next to each other behind Kurt. They looked defeated but comfortable around each other.

I could have done something, Angelina thought as she stared at the fire extinguisher. *I should have done something.*

"Dad," she said. He didn't acknowledge her, so she spoke louder. "Dad, I want to go outside. Alone."

Brow wrinkled, Kurt tore his gaze away from the clown to glance at his daughter for a second. He looked back at Captain Gashes and asked, "What are you talking about?"

Heather said, "Angie, you don't know what you're saying."

"I do," Angelina said. "They're not going to stop until we're all dead. We have weapons, but... we don't stand a chance. Maybe Dad can fight them, but if they double-team him, if they shoot him... we're not going to make it. But I can sneak out through the back door, climb over the wall and–"

"We're not opening a single door or window," Lindsay interrupted.

"*And* I can go to Ben's shop. You'll have plenty of time to lock the door right after I leave. It's not like they're standing right next to any of the exits, right?"

"They could be," Heather said. "You saw the news. This is a–an attack. There could be dozens of them in Goldbrush. Someone could be waiting in the backyard for one of us to walk out. It's too risky."

"If that's true, then we're fucked anyway, right? I'd rather take this risk than wait for them to blow this place up."

"They're not going to do that," Kurt said.

"How do you know?" Angelina responded. "You guys wanna talk about the news? There were explosions in Vegas, remember? What makes you think they won't set one off here?"

Dakota whispered, "God, don't say that, don't say that."

The talk of bombs made Gilbert's blood curdle. He had seen glimpses of the massacre outside, but he hadn't heard about the coordinated terrorist attacks occurring across the globe.

Kurt said, "That woman, she said they can't blow us up. She said something about... 'Deadface.' It's not the first time they've mentioned him, either. He's their leader. This guy, this 'Captain Gashes,' he can't call a shot like that. I'm not saying they won't try to barge in here, but they're not going to bomb us."

"Either way, we have to do something," Angelina said.

"And what are you going to do at Ben's shop? He was missing, too. No one's seen him for hours, Ange. They probably got him earlier tonight, those goddamn bastards."

"That shotgun. It's Ben's. I've seen it a hundred times before. Maybe I can find some... some ammo or another gun that they didn't see. His firework shop is right next door, too. Maybe he still has some old fireworks in there. I can shoot one of those mortars at them. They're threatening to blow us up, right? Well, let's turn the tables on these fuckers and blow *them* up first."

Kurt glanced back at her. He felt a blend of fear and pride. He could see she was determined to fight back. He admired her courage, he liked her plan, but he was worried about her.

Heather said, "Kurt, you can't seriously be thinking about letting her go."

"I can do this," Angelina responded. "You have to believe in me."

"Angie... we just got you back. We... *I* can't lose you again. There has to–"

"Please welcome participant number three!" Captain Gashes said through the megaphone. "And looky-looky, we've got participant number four, too."

Slack-jawed, the survivors gazed out the window. The clowns had gathered on the blood-streaked walkway in front of the home. Captain Gashes was standing in front of the pack. Boo-Boo stood behind him to his left. Flora's dead body lay on the ground face down between her feet. Pipsqueak was leaning against a bush to their right. Jenna's unconscious body was slung over his shoulder.

Captain Gashes held the megaphone up to his mouth and said, "Looks like these two got separated from their family. It happens often in the circus. Too many people. Too much to see. Too much to do. But the circus is supposed to be a family experience. You *come* together, you *laugh* together, you *wonder* together... you *die* together. So, why don't we *work* together and reunite these two with their loved ones? Hmm? Do any of you recognize them?"

All of the survivors at the window heard the same answer in their heads: '*Yes.*' They had to fight the temptation to look over at Samuel and tell him the truth. They were worried he would react recklessly and endanger them all. The man was trapped in a stupor of grief—ruminative, unstable, *broken*. The survivors came to a wordless, reluctant agreement: they had to keep him in the dark to keep the clowns out.

"No? Nobody?" Captain Gashes asked. "Unfortunately, these ladies weren't carrying any identification. Where'd you say you found 'em, Pips?"

Pipsqueak cleared his throat, then said, "Outside the, uh... red place. She was too loud, so I bopped her good on the head."

"The red place, huh? That sound familiar to any of you?"

"He's talking about the fire station," Boo-Boo explained. "I saw it while I was cruising around town. I don't think anyone works there, though. I mean, look at all the fires around here."

Captain Gashes said, "You heard all that? Two whores found outside of a fire station. They belong to any of you? If not, we might have a case of 'finders keepers' on our hands. Anyone? No? Really? If you don't claim 'em, we will. I'll tell you what: I'll give you ten seconds to decide if you love them or not. Ten. Nine."

Kurt's breathing sped up. He continued scowling at the clowns, his mask of confidence beginning to slip. The other survivors tensed up as they looked at each other. They all wanted someone else to take charge.

Kurt felt all of their eyes gravitating towards him. The clown was halfway through his countdown, stalling for a few seconds between each number.

Angelina said, "We need to do something. I'm going to Ben's. One of you has to lock the back door behind me."

As she turned to leave, Lindsay jumped out in front of her with her arms out like a basketball player on defense. She said, "You're not going anywhere. We are not opening those doors for anyone except the police."

"We've been through this before, damn it. What are you expecting? Huh? You think they're going to send an army of cops or a fleet of helicopters? To fucking *Goldbrush*? They're not coming while Vegas is burning. We are on our own."

"You're wrong, Angie," Heather said as she grabbed her daughter's hand from behind. "We have each other. We'd only be alone if we started splitting up. I know you want to help, but... please give us some time to think of another plan."

"We're out of time, Mom."

A second later, Captain Gashes said, "One."

The survivors looked out the window, fearing the consequences of their inaction. The room seemed to turn frigid with an air of collective shame and guilt.

Captain Gashes said, "Guess they belong to us now. Pips, start with the girl."

A malicious grin broke across Pipsqueak's face. He tossed Jenna down on the ground in front of his boss carelessly, slamming her face on the walkway. Then he grabbed Flora's arm and dragged her out from under Boo-Boo. He threw the girl onto the fence, her upper body hanging over one side and her legs dangling over the other. Three spear-headed finials pushed into her lower abdomen. Blood dripped from the stumps at the ends of her limbs.

Captain Gashes said, "Now *marvel...* at the *behemoth* of the carnival of chaos... as he makes his *hog...* disappear in this *piglet.*"

"I like 'em young, cold, and quiet," Pipsqueak chortled.

He unzipped his fly, then stuffed his hand through the opening and fished around. He took his semi-erect penis out, dripped a string of drool onto it, then started stroking it. With his free hand, he pulled Flora's pants and underwear down to her knees.

With the first glimpse at Flora's bare bottom, Kurt's poker face melted away. He looked down and let out a thick sob. The severe agitation and disgust were obvious on the other survivors' grimacing faces as well.

With a mischievous twinkle in his eye, Captain Gashes said, "So, you do know them. Great. Now let's see if you love them."

He handed the megaphone to Boo-Boo and stepped over Jenna's body. Behind him, Pipsqueak unleashed an obnoxious moan of pleasure. The fence rattled as he penetrated the corpse. Captain Gashes bent down and pulled the long hairpin out of Jenna's bun. He took a handful of her hair and lifted her head from the ground. Two wavy strips of blood ran down from her broken nose.

He thrust the hairpin into her right eye. The sharp tip slipped past her eyelids, which were partly open, and penetrated her eyeball. It came to a stop in the center of her eye. A mix of blood, tears, and vitreous fluid cascaded down her cheek. She groaned and twitched for three seconds before the intense pain—pulsing across her face and shooting through her brain—awoke her.

Then her groans turned into horrifying shrieks and her twitching harshened to thrashing. A shadow covered most of the right side of her vision, allowing only some blotches of light to shine through. She reached up and raked her fingernails across the clown's arm, leaving his wrist crisscrossed with thin cuts.

Captain Gashes pushed the hairpin deeper, making her howl louder and thrash harder. Bloody vitreous fluid spurted out of her eye, and more blood slicked her entire eyeball.

In the dining room, Samuel looked up from his son's corpse. He heard a note of familiarity in the shrieking voice outside. It reminded him of his wife's screeching when she gave birth to Otto. Then a disturbing realization gripped him: It *was* Jenna's voice outside. He rushed to the window, bulldozing through the others.

An expression of horror dawned on his face as he

watched his wife's torture and his dead daughter's abuse. His legs felt rubbery as revulsion crawled in the pit of his stomach.

"No... No... No! No! No!" he said, getting louder and louder with each word. He made a run for the front door, but Kurt stopped him in the archway by wrapping his arms around him tightly and pushing him back. Fighting to break free, Samuel shouted, "Get the fuck off me! Goddamn it, let me go!"

Kurt yelled, "Stop it! Not like this, Sam! Not like this! You open that door–"

"Get off me!"

"–and we're all dead! You'll kill us!"

"They're killing them!"

Dakota was whimpering in the corner of the dining room. Gilbert had moved to Otto's side. He put one hand on his friend's motionless chest and the other over his mouth as he cried. Keeping their distance, Heather and Lindsay tried to defuse the situation, but the men didn't hear a word out of their mouths.

Angelina stared out the window. Captain Gashes turned the hairpin in Jenna's eye, as if he were using a manual pencil sharpener. Then he pulled it back towards him like a lever. The hole in her eye expanded while the muscles attached to it tore. Her eyeball jutted out, perched on her cheekbone. Her screams turned gravelly.

"Nothing?! Really?!" Captain Gashes yelled. "Maybe I was wrong! Maybe you hate this bitch!"

Although he wasn't using the megaphone, his voice echoed through the house. Boo-Boo strutted in front of them and held the megaphone up to her mouth.

"Testing, testing, one, two, three," she said. The megaphone caught one of Pipsqueak's moans in the background, too. Boo-Boo said, "Hey, Cap, maybe they want to see another magic trick. Why don't you show 'em that one you've been practicing?"

"The rabbit in the hat?" Captain Gashes asked.

"No, no, not that one. The balloon one."

"Hmm. I suppose I can give it a try. Get my hunting knife, will ya?"

In the house, Kurt slammed Samuel against a wall in the foyer and yelled, "There's nothing we can do! Nothing! They'll kill you! They'll kill us!"

"I'll kill you if you don't get out of my fucking way!" Samuel growled.

"Sam, please. Think about Angie. Think about Gilbert."

"What about my kids?!"

Samuel got an arm loose and decked Kurt in the face, knocking him back. Keeping his arms wrapped around him, Kurt slammed him against the wall again. Samuel pounded the left side of Kurt's head with three more punches, then he freed his other arm. He hit him with a barrage of lefts and rights.

Kurt's cheeks reddened and swelled. Burying his face in Samuel's chest and holding onto him with one arm, he started punching his ribs. He didn't want to hurt his long-time friend, but he was out of options.

Angelina watched as Boo-Boo handed her boss a hunting knife. It had a sharp five-inch blade with a partially serrated edge. The hairpin was left sticking out of Jenna's eyeball.

Captain Gashes leaned back and lifted Jenna's head higher. Pulling on the victim's shirt, Boo-Boo helped him prop her up. Next to them, Pipsqueak accelerated his thrusting. The fence sounded like it was about to fall apart.

Captain Gashes raised the hunting knife overhead, rotated it so that the blade was horizontal, then swung it down and stabbed Jenna above her right hip. The woman gasped. Unadulterated agony put an end to her screaming. Captain Gashes sawed towards her other hip while wiggling the blade to separate her muscles.

Jenna's mouth gaped open, but no sound came out. Urine darkened the crotch of her pants and feces filled her underwear as she unintentionally soiled herself.

Captain Gashes stopped sawing as the blade reached her other hip. Boo-Boo squeezed Jenna's stomach, securing a firm grip on her soft flesh, then she pulled her hand up towards the victim's chest, causing the long gash across her lower abdomen to widen with a shredding sound. Coils of intestines, mutilated and steaming, hung out of the cavernous wound. Jenna fell unconscious.

The clowns released her, letting her body hit the

ground. As she went into spasms, they pulled her guts out. They cut segments of her small intestine with the hunting knife.

"We're out of time," Angelina repeated to herself, tears dripping from her eyes with each blink.

She looked to her right. Over her mother and Lindsay, she could see her dad and Samuel trading blows in the foyer of the home. The men were getting closer to the front door. Angelina glanced over at Dakota. Overcome with horror and physically unfit for a fight, the woman was more of a burden than a help.

"You did it!" Boo-Boo yelled, jumping and clapping.

Angelina looked outside, her face deforming with anguish. Like a balloon animal, Captain Gashes had twisted, folded, and tied a severed tube of Jenna's small intestine into the shape of a dog. If he wasn't holding it up, though, it would have looked like another droopy, bloody chunk of meat. Regardless, he wore a proud expression, beaming from ear to ear.

Speaking into the megaphone, Boo-Boo said, "Did you see that, folks? Our beloved captain has finally found his true talent as a clown. He made a special balloon animal just for *you*. Think you can make them anything else, Cap?"

"Well, let's see what else we've got."

He threw the pretzeled organ into a bush to his right, then dug his hands into Jenna's abdominal cavity. He pulled on her guts, lifting her body slightly off the ground with each tug. Boo-Boo helped him with her free hand. Jenna was already dead. Like eels, her intestines snaked across the pool of blood on the walkway.

Angelina ran over to Gilbert's side and put the fire extinguisher on the table in front of him. She said, "Those clowns are going to break in here soon. When they do, you *have* to fight."

"Wha–Wha–What?" the boy stammered.

"Use this fire extinguisher. For the guys, you aim for their balls. You hear me? You smash them as hard as you can. That woman, you break her mask, then you break her fucking face."

"An–Angie, no, I–I don't wanna do this."

"You have to. You fucking have to. Promise me you'll fight. Promise me, Gilbert."

Although he saw desperation in her eyes, Gilbert could hear the love laced into her words. She was only trying to protect him.

"Okay," he squeaked out.

"Then take the fire extinguisher. Show me that you mean it."

Gilbert took the fire extinguisher off the table. Heavier than he expected, he nearly dropped it. In the foyer, Samuel and Kurt were fighting over the locks on the front door. The door chain was broken and the deadbolt was turned halfway.

Angelina said, "I'm going out through the back. I'll bring help or weapons or... or something. But I *will* be back for you, okay? I just need you to lock the door behind me. Come on."

She took him by the arm and led him to the back door. They went through the kitchen to avoid the others.

In the foyer, Samuel headbutted Kurt, knocking him down to the ground with a busted lip. Heather ran to her husband's side and helped him up. Dazed by his own headbutt, Samuel stumbled out of the house. He caught himself on the porch railing. As if on cue, Pipsqueak shuddered and moaned monstrously as he ejaculated into the corpse.

"No!" Samuel cried as he lurched forward.

Kurt made a grab for him but missed. He took one step down the porch steps before stopping. He was unarmed and unprepared to face the clowns.

Samuel tackled Captain Gashes and slammed him on the ground. The hunting rifle slung across the clown's back absorbed some of the impact from the slam. Soaking up the blood, the back of his wifebeater turned red. The hunting knife fell out of his hand. Samuel squeezed the clown's neck to choke him and pin him down, then he punched down at his face repeatedly.

The left side of Captain Gashes' face began to swell and welt. Blood flowed out of a gash on his cheekbone, leaving a red streak across his painted face. He bled from his gums, too.

It took the other clowns twenty-some seconds to

react to the attack. They expected the survivors to defend themselves. They weren't expecting them to go on the offensive.

Boo-Boo snatched up the hunting knife, then drove it into the side of Samuel's rib cage. The blade penetrated the intercostal muscles between a pair of ribs. The tip punctured his lung. Samuel slapped Boo-Boo's arm away and fell off of Captain Gashes. The knife remained in his rib cage. Pumped full of adrenaline, he got to his feet and attacked Pipsqueak.

The big clown's cock—now semi-erect—still hung out of his zipper, a glob of semen dangling from his urethra. Samuel took a swing at his head but struck his chest instead. Pipsqueak stepped back, but the punch didn't hurt him. He threw Samuel against the fence. Flora's body fell onto the lawn on the other side.

Winded, Samuel threw a weak punch. Pipsqueak could have easily beaten him to death with his bare hands, but he tried to restrain him instead. During the commotion, they didn't notice Captain Gashes had gotten up. The leader hobbled over to them, then fired his rifle at Samuel's knee at point-blank range.

Samuel's leg crumpled under him, bringing him down to his good knee. He uttered a stifled, gurgling scream.

Captain Gashes hocked a bloody loogie at Samuel's face, then looked at the porch. He saw Kurt standing there, frozen. The front door was wide open behind him.

"Boo-Boo, take care of this bastard and his woman," the leader said. "Pips and I are going to put an end to this shitshow."

"What about Deadface?" Boo-Boo asked. "We're supposed to make a video for him, 'member?"

"We'll try to keep them alive, but if they fight back... we'll bite back. You got a problem with that?"

Boo-Boo stared blankly at him for a moment, then shrugged and said, "It's no skin off my ass. More friends for me, right?"

"Whatever you say. Now get to work."

"Sure thing, bossman," Boo-Boo responded with a salute. She looked down at Samuel and said, "I'm gonna get some rope. I'll be right back, okay?"

Samuel ignored her. Bawling, he dragged himself to Jenna's corpse. He caressed her face and whispered unintelligibly to her, then he attempted to push her butchered intestines back into her body.

Captain Gashes sprinted towards the house. Pipsqueak followed his lead while shoving his penis into his jumpsuit. Kurt staggered back into the home. Heather and Lindsay shut and locked the door behind him. The door shook violently as Captain Gashes and Pipsqueak took turns ramming it with their shoulders.

"They're coming in," Kurt said. "This is it. Everyone, get ready!"

Lindsay barricaded the door with the console table and bench in the foyer. Realizing no amount of furniture was going to stop them, she got her weapons ready: Her sewing scissors and her hair-brush. Kurt hurried into the dining room with his wife. They grabbed their kitchen knives and home-made spears.

"Gilbert? Angie?" Heather called out. She crouched and checked under the dining table, as if expecting to find them cowering under it. She ran to Dakota and, speaking loudly but not quite screaming, she asked, "Where are my kids?"

Dakota said, "I'm sorry."

"What happened? Where are they?"

"They went to the back. I think Angelina left..."

"You let them leave?"

"What was I supposed to do? I–I... I don't want to be here! I want to go home! I want my Danny! Whe–Where's Danny?"

The door roared with each violent blow. The clowns were using Gabriela's body as a battering ram, slamming her burnt head against the door. Kurt and Heather joined Lindsay in the foyer. Gilbert approached them from behind, fire extinguisher in hand.

Heather asked, "Where's your sister?"

"She... left," Gilbert responded reluctantly.

"*Where?*"

"To Ben's."

Eyes on the front door, Kurt asked, "Were there more of them back there?"

"I don't think so. I didn't see anyone else. She

jumped over the wall, then she... she just disappeared."

Heather said, "I should go after her. I have to–"

"Don't," Kurt interrupted. "She's long gone. You have to trust her. She knows what she's doing."

Heather looked down the hall behind her. When she thought about Angelina now, she saw her daughter as a moody teenager. She had to remind herself that Angelina had been on her own for years. Although some doubt clung to the back of her mind, she had faith in her daughter's survival skills.

She said, "Gilbert, go with Mrs. Paddock and wait upstairs. Lock yourself in a room and don't open the door for anyone except us."

"But what about you guys?" Gilbert responded.

There was a moment of silence.

Then the door rumbled and groaned again.

"We'll see you soon," Heather said, fighting back tears. "Dakota, take Gilbert upstairs please!"

"But Mom, I–I can help. Angie, she said I can–"

"Dakota, please!"

Holding her paring knife, Dakota came into the foyer of the home. She took the opportunity to leave the frontlines. She grabbed Gilbert's hand and led him to the stairs while mumbling an apology. Teary-eyed, Gilbert kept glancing back at his parents as he went upstairs. The sadness and regret flowing through his body made him feel like he was never going to see them again.

"I'm going, too," Lindsay blurted before hurrying up the stairs.

"Hey, no!" Heather yelled. "You can fight! What are you…"

She stopped as Lindsay disappeared at the top of the stairs. She heard footsteps, suppressed cries, and the sound of doors slamming on the second floor. She knew words weren't going to convince Lindsay to help them, so she saved her breath and concentrated on the imminent fight.

Kurt and Heather tucked their knives in their waistbands, careful not to nick themselves, then held their homemade spears with both hands. They looked at each other. Their eyes—wet, sad, scared—said the same thing: '*I love you.*' They shared a weepy kiss, tasting each other's tears.

Then the front door burst open.

18

ASSAULT ON THE BUNKER HOUSE

GABRIELA'S CORPSE FLEW THROUGH THE DOORWAY. THE top half of her crispy head had been mashed down into her skull. Lumps of fried brain tissue were strewn across the porch and foyer. The body landed between Kurt and Heather, causing them to stagger away from each other. They didn't have a chance to react to the desecrated corpse.

Captain Gashes and Pipsqueak rushed into the home. Kurt thrust his homemade spear at Pipsqueak. The blade poked a hole in his lower abdomen. Although it was still painful, layers of thick fat protected his organs. The spear's handle bent under the clown's weight as he ran forward. Pipsqueak tackled Kurt into the dining room.

He threw him against the table, its legs screeching against the hardwood floor. Otto's head swayed. Then Pipsqueak slammed Kurt against a cabinet. The windows on its doors shattered. A shard dug into his scalp. As his head swung back and forth, dribbles of blood ran down the nape of his neck and his brow.

Pipsqueak pulled him away from the cabinet, then pushed him against the neighboring wall. A picture frame fell to the floor. The photo inside depicted Lindsay and her husband Brett—a fortysomething man with graying hair and salt-and-pepper stubble—standing at a beach with their arms around each other.

Kurt hit Pipsqueak's stomach, amplifying the pain from his stab wound. He drew the knife from his waistband, but before he could use it, the clown tackled him, using his weight to easily overwhelm him. The knife fell out of Kurt's hand as they stumbled into the kitchen.

Meanwhile, Heather thrust her spear at Captain Gashes. The knife sliced his right bicep open. He screamed—more out of anger than pain—and crashed into the wall next to the staircase. His arm went limp for a few seconds, blood jetting from the muscle. Heather thrust the spear at him again, but he jumped back and dodged the blade.

While stepping back towards the front door, he swung his bloodstained rifle out from behind him. He crashed into the sidelight. Holding it with one hand, he aimed the gun in Heather's direction and squeezed the trigger. She gasped and winced as the gun made a loud *clicking* noise. To their surprise, the rifle was empty.

Throughout his career as a serial killer, Captain Gashes had enjoyed using blunt and sharp instruments to torture and kill his victims. Firearms tended to steal the thrill of the kill, although he wasn't opposed to using them if he were cornered. His knowledge was limited to the basics: Point and shoot. So, he didn't know he was using a single-shot rifle.

Heather made her move and drove the spear towards Captain Gashes. He slid to the side. The blade cut his shirt and nicked his abdomen before colliding with the sidelight. The spear's fragile handle wobbled upon impact. Captain Gashes struck it with the rifle. The spear slid out of her sweaty hands, plummeting down to the porch.

Captain Gashes turned the rifle, then rammed the butt of the gun against Heather's breasts—once, twice, *thrice*. She crossed her arms in an X over her chest, hunched forward, and tottered back. Daggers of pain pricked her breasts. She felt the pain worsen with each quick breath. The clown smashed the butt of the rifle against her face, breaking her nose and two of her upper incisor teeth.

Bleeding, groaning, and spinning, she took a tumble near the bottom of the stairs. For a second, she considered running up to the second floor. But she remembered her son was hiding up there. She could only think about buying him some time. She scrambled to her feet and made a run for the back door.

Captain Gashes ran up behind her and swung the

rifle at the back of her knee like a hockey stick, sweeping her leg out from under her. Heather fell backwards. The wind was knocked out of her as she hit the floor. The clown swung the butt of the rifle at her head, but she rolled out of the way.

Lightheaded from the lack of air, she used a chest of drawers in the hall to help her jump to her feet. She drew the knife from her waistband and lunged at Captain Gashes. He dropped the rifle and grabbed her forearm to stop her from plunging the blade into his chest. They pushed each other down the hall, fighting for their lives.

In the kitchen, Pipsqueak had gained the upper hand against his victim. Pressing his large body against Kurt's to limit his movements, he gripped the man's neck in one hand and held his right arm in the other while pushing him back over a counter. Kurt swung his other arm around, reaching for a weapon but finding nothing but air—air he couldn't breathe.

His throat and lungs burned. The burning sensation spread into his skull. He felt it behind his watery eyes, then *in* his eyeballs. His fingertips and toes tingled. The strength left his limbs. His blurred vision darkened, as if someone were turning down the brightness on a smart bulb in the room.

Mind infected with terror and body reacting with panic, Kurt felt like he was floating away, watching his own strangulation from a corner in the ceiling like a surveillance camera. He only thought about his family.

Over the sound of the boiling water bubbling on the stove, he heard his hand hit something hard. He grabbed it without looking and, with his last bit of energy, he swung it at Pipsqueak's head. It was a blender's glass jar. It exploded against the clown's face. The shards slashed his cheek, temple, ear, and bald scalp. Some fragments flew into Kurt's eyes, too.

But it was the glass particles that had entered Pipsqueak's ear canal and dusted his eardrum that hurt him the most. His ear rang incessantly. Whining, he slapped his hand over his ear and fell to his knees. Kurt collapsed next to him, gasping for breath while grasping at his own neck with both of his hands as if trying to strangle himself.

Back in the hallway, Captain Gashes pushed Heather into the living room. The TV displayed a 'No Signal' message. He swung Heather to the right, then to the left, throwing her against the TV. A web of cracks spread across the screen. She dropped the knife and fell to the floor. She reached for her weapon, but the clown kicked it towards the entertainment center.

"I've had enough of your shit, bitch," he snarled as he picked up the kitchen knife.

Heather crawled to the other side of the living room, searching desperately for another weapon. She felt the killer clown lurking behind her.

As he closed in on her, Captain Gashes said, "You don't want to go outside? Fine. We'll bring the show straight to your living room."

Heather spotted the silverware tray and the knife block on the floor between a sofa and a coffee table. Only a butter knife remained in the knife block, so she took a fork out of the silverware tray. Just as the clown crouched down to stab her, she flipped over and swung the fork at his face. The tines pierced his cheek. One punctured his gums and another slid between two of his molar teeth.

While he screamed, she kicked his chest. He fell on his ass, but he held onto the knife. Scooting away from him, Heather opened her tote bag and took out a bottle of saline solution. She unscrewed the cap, then splashed the liquid on Captain Gashes' right arm. Horrible pain bolted up to his shoulder and down to his elbow as the saline solution entered his mutilated bicep.

Holding onto the sofa and coffee table, Heather pushed herself up to her feet. She saw an opportunity to attack him, but there were no other weapons around and she knew—even in his current condition—she couldn't kill him with her bare hands. She focused on her family, hoping to help them.

Despite his suffering, Captain Gashes swung the knife at her leg as she ran past him. The blade cut a ligament at the back of her knee, causing her to yelp and lurch forward. Gritting her teeth through the pain, she limped out of the living room. Behind her, she heard the clown cycling between growls of anger and howls of pain.

As she made her way to the foyer, she saw Pipsqueak swaying on his feet in the kitchen, a palm pressed against his ear.

He said, "It's too loud. It's too loud. My music... I need my music!"

He charged towards her. Heather stopped dead in her tracks. She felt like she was watching him run in slow motion, feeling every vibration from each heavy step. Her fight-or-flight response told her to give up. Before the clown could cross the archway, Kurt put him in a rear naked choke and pulled him back into the kitchen.

"Get the kids," he rasped.

Heather hesitated, startled by her husband's hoarse voice. She wanted to help him, but she could tell it was too late. She cried as she limped up to the second floor.

Pipsqueak ran backwards and slammed Kurt against the refrigerator. Liquids sloshed and glass clinked inside. Kurt continued choking the clown. Pipsqueak lumbered to the archway, then he ran backwards again until he rammed Kurt against a counter. Kurt felt a painful *pop* in his lower back. His grip on the clown's thick neck wavered.

Leaning back against his victim, Pipsqueak drew some wheezing breaths and rubbed his injured ear with his palm. He seemed unworried about the guy stuck behind him. Kurt's legs were like noodles, but the clown's body stopped him from falling. After catching his breath, Pipsqueak turned around to face his victim.

He grabbed the chest of his shirt with both hands and carried him to the stove. The water was still boiling in the stockpot. Heather had prepared the boiling water as a weapon against the clowns. Now, it was going to be used against her own husband.

Holding him by the back of his neck and his hair, Pipsqueak dunked Kurt's head into the boiling water. He felt the heat through his gloves. The water splashed as Kurt unintentionally screamed. Close to tipping over, the stockpot jiggled with his thrashing. His face reddened and puffed. Within seconds, his skin started to peel away and blister.

Like his skin, his tongue swelled and blistered. From his nostrils, feathers of blood spiraled through the water. Some of his blisters bled as well. His eyes inflated, growing too large for their sockets. His sclerae turned red while his corneas became cloudy. He lost his eyesight, but he was in too much pain to realize it. The boiling water was cooking his brain and eyes.

Kurt had a violent convulsion. The stockpot fell to the floor. Boiling water rippled across the tiles. Pipsqueak stopped Kurt from dropping to his knees. His face was a mass of yellow and red blisters. A cloud of steam billowed up from his head. While keeping his grip on his hair, Pipsqueak moved his other hand from the nape of Kurt's neck to the victim's chest to support his body.

Then he thrust his face at the burner. The stove rattled upon impact. The blue flame burned his forehead, cheek, and eye. The searing cast-iron burner grate branded the side of his face with a diagonal burn mark, popping another blister on his cheek. One of the grate's prongs cut his eye open vertically.

Pipsqueak continued slamming Kurt's face on the burner—over and over and over again. His bones cracked. His skin sizzled. More of his blisters popped. The flame burned some of his hair, too, producing a foul smell akin to rotting food. He was dead after the fifth blow, but the clown didn't stop until the tenth.

He let Kurt fall into the puddle of boiling water at his feet. The man's face had been beaten to an unrecognizable mush of blood, bone, and blisters.

Pipsqueak walked out of the kitchen, grimacing as he rubbed his injured ear with his palm. He could barely hear his squeaky footsteps over the ringing. He made his way to the front door.

"Hey you!" Captain Gashes called out.

Pipsqueak turned around. He saw his boss leaning against the wall next to the archway leading into the living room. Sweat glistened on his arms, chest, and shoulders. The sweat—as well as the blood from the cut on his cheek—ruined his makeup. His right arm was shaking, blood dripping from his fingertips. He limped over to the foyer.

"Where do you think you're going?" he asked.

"My ear... It hurts... I need my music. I can't hear my music."

"Calm down."

Pacing while smacking the side of his head, Pipsqueak said, "I can't hear it! I need it! Where's my music? I need my–"

"Calm. Down," Captain Gashes repeated, this time pausing between each word. Pipsqueak kept slapping his head, as if a good whack would turn off the high-pitched buzzing in his ear. Captain Gashes said, "Remember what I told you last time? The music's still playing in your head. You just gotta make it heard. Sing it, Pips."

Pipsqueak smacked his head a few more times, then muttered indistinctly to himself, then he started humming Bill Haley & His Comets' *(We're Gonna) Rock Around the Clock*. He slapped himself once more, then stopped pacing and stared at his boss while continuing to hum the tune.

Captain Gashes said, "That's it. Now, listen. I like what you did in that kitchen. I need you to do the same thing upstairs. The woman—that sneaky *cunt!*—ran up there. There are others, too. I can hear 'em moving like rats. You know what you do to rats, don't you? You exterminate 'em. But these rats, these *fucking* rats... They're resilient, right? You know what we do to tough pests?"

Pipsqueak stopped humming to say, "I–I need my sledgehammer."

Then he continued singing with his lips sealed.

Captain Gashes said, "That's right. We squash 'em. We're gonna go out and 'resupply,' then I'm going to let you loose. I'll send something hot up to 'em from outside, then I'll join you. You get all that, big fella?" Still humming, Pipsqueak nodded. The leader said, "Good. Keep singing. You'll be killing in no time. Follow me."

They went outside through the front door. Boo-Boo, Samuel, Jenna, and the pickup truck were all gone. Boo-Boo had left the clowns' duffel bag—as well as Captain Gashes' trusty hunting knife and Pipsqueak's handy sledgehammer—on the walkway, though. The men gathered their supplies and prepared for their second attack on the Bunker house.

Pipsqueak hummed along to the song playing in his head: *Take Good Care of My Baby* by Bobby Vee. The poor rendition of the tune haunted the house. He lugged his sledgehammer up the staircase, its metal head slamming against each step. At the top of the stairs, he found himself in a hallway. The second floor was silent.

He opened the first door to his left. It was a guest bedroom—quiet, clean, undisturbed. He walked to the bed and, too tired to get down on his knees, he tossed the mattress off the frame with one hand. No one was hiding under it. He checked behind the curtains. There was no one there. Then he opened the closet—no clothes, no people.

He exited the bedroom. A creak down the hall caught his attention. Instead of following the noise, he opened the first door to the right. It was a bathroom. The light was off, but he could see it was vacant. He zigzagged down the hall. The second door to the left opened up to a storage closet. He pushed the coats aside with his sledgehammer—*empty*.

The second door to his right led to Brett's home office. At the other side of the room, there was a desk and a filing cabinet under a window overlooking the front yard. Slits of orange light from the burning houses throughout Goldbrush seeped through the closed blinds. On the desk, there were two monitors, a laptop, a notepad, and a pen holder.

The wall to the left of the desk was covered with shelves, decorated with picture frames and books. The books—fiction and nonfiction—had fresh, uncreased spines. A printer sat on one shelf. There was a couch, a television, and a closet in the home office, too. Although there weren't many great hiding places, Pipsqueak was drawn to the room. He smelled fear in the air.

And he was right.

Lindsay stood in the cramped closet, eyes swimming with tears. Fingers curled around the hairbrush's handle, she was pressing the back of her hand against her mouth to silence herself. Through the blinds on the door in front of her, she watched as the clown walked into the room. The sledgehammer's head scraped the hardwood floor.

Pipsqueak pulled the office chair away from the desk and checked under the table. He found a computer and a jumble of tangled cords. He pushed the curtains aside and looked out the window. Standing on the walkway, Captain Gashes hurled a Molotov cocktail at the house. It exploded in a wave of fire on the porch roof. The flames lit up the room with a dull red glow.

Pipsqueak squinted at the bright fire. The explosion didn't scare him. He seemed unconcerned about the approaching flames.

Lindsay knew she wasn't safe in the office. She needed a new hiding place. While Pipsqueak watched his boss prepare another Molotov cocktail, she eased the closet door open. The door hinges squeaked, but the clown didn't notice it over the crackling fire. Holding her breath, she slunk out of the closet. Taking wide, quiet lunges, she sidestepped towards the exit.

She froze as Pipsqueak turned to face the shelves. He appeared to be reading—or *trying* to read—the spines of the books. She stayed as still as a mannequin. In her head, she was screaming: '*Don't turn around! Don't turn around! Don't turn around!*' Tight, hot, and heavy, she felt like her lungs were about to burst. Like paper, her legs were close to folding under her weight.

Pipsqueak turned around. Lindsay drew a horrified gasp. The clown squinched up his face and cocked his head back, as if asking himself: '*Was she standing there earlier?*' They stared at each other for what seemed like forever. Then Pipsqueak raised his sledgehammer overhead and ran towards her.

Lindsay screamed and swung the hairbrush at his face. She raked the bristles against his eye and the lacerations on the right side of his face. Some of the cuts opened up like small mouths, ejecting fresh streams of blood. He dropped the sledgehammer behind him and slapped a hand over his stinging eye. The hammer's heavy head snapped a floorboard.

"Die!" Lindsay shouted as she swung the sewing scissors at the clown's neck.

To her dismay, the scissors got stuck in Pipsqueak's ruff collar. He only felt the tip of the blades poke his neck. He grabbed a fistful of her hair, then turned around and threw her onto the desk. One of the monitors fell off the table, the pen holder tipped over, and the office chair rolled away and crashed into the shelves.

As she struggled to find her bearings, Pipsqueak pulled Lindsay off the table. While holding her head by a fistful of hair, he ripped the window's curtains and blinds down. He took another handful of hair, then thrust her face at the window, shattering it. Shards of glass tinkled on the lower-level roof before sliding down to the gutter.

Lindsay's face was split open diagonally. The gash stretched from the left side of her forehead, through an eyebrow, across the bridge of her nose, and ended on her right cheek.

Pipsqueak pushed her head downward at the serrated, sawtooth glass protruding from the windowsill. The shards penetrated the junction between her chin and neck. Some of the glass broke upon colliding with her jaw. A large shard entered her mouth. Her tongue was barely attached by a thread of tissue.

The glass severed an artery running along her chin. The cut bled badly. Blood poured out of her mouth and dripped from the windowsill. It ran down the lower-level roof, lining the shingles.

"Bitch," Pipsqueak muttered before starting to hum along to *Good Golly Miss Molly* by Little Richard.

He grabbed his sledgehammer and exited the room. But Lindsay wasn't dead. She was stuck, legs hanging loosely under her. She felt the heat from the growing fire on the porch roof, sweat beading her face. She was forced to look out at the front lawn and the neighboring homes. It looked like a battlefield down there.

Goldbrush had turned into a war zone.

From the walkway, Captain Gashes saw her glaring at him. He smiled half-heartedly as he lit the Molotov cocktail in his hand.

He said, "Y'know, with evil eyes like those, you could have been one of us. I probably would have let you join us if you only played nice. You should have taken the easy way out, you bitch!"

He threw the Molotov cocktail. Lindsay watched it soar over her head into the office through the broken window. It exploded in the middle of the room. The fire spread quickly—to the couch, to the shelves, to the desk. Smoke blanketed the ceiling. Lindsay felt the heat approaching from behind and from outside, flames licking her heels.

She was close to nodding off due to the loss of blood. She only hoped she would fall unconscious before the fire could start cooking her alive.

Pipsqueak approached the door at the end of the hall. He turned the doorknob—*locked*. He knocked on the door and waited for a couple of seconds, as if expecting one of the survivors to open up for him. The smoke came out of the office behind him, crawling across the hallway ceiling in plumes.

Holding the tool like a battering ram, he slammed the sledgehammer's head against the door next to the knob. With the second hit, the door flew open.

The master bedroom was spacious. Windows to the left and right overlooked the back and front yards. Through one of the windows, the dull red light from the fires on the roof flickered into the room. Across from the king-sized bed, there was an entertainment center with a wall-mounted TV, a record player, a Blu-ray player, and a sound system. The door next to the bed led to the en suite bathroom.

Pipsqueak limped over to the bed. Every once in a while, he stopped humming to hiss in pain. He had trouble keeping his injured eye open.

Heather emerged from behind the bedroom door, fire extinguisher in hand. She crept towards the clown. She raised the fire extinguisher over her shoulder and, as Pipsqueak lifted the mattress, she slammed it against the back of his head. His humming turned into a slow, ragged groan. He leaned against the bed's footboard, his head whirling.

As Heather thrust the fire extinguisher at him again, Pipsqueak spun around and swung the sledgehammer. The fire extinguisher struck his funny bone —a direct hit on his ulnar nerve. A hot, tingling sensation shot across his arm. At the same time, the sledgehammer hit her knee, pulverizing her kneecap and snapping her leg.

Her knee was bent backwards like a less-than sign, extending far beyond her back. Her tibia and femur bones had splintered into sharp shards, piercing the skin at the pit of her knee and cutting through her pants. She crashed to the floor, shrieking with blinding pain. The fire extinguisher rolled towards the door.

Meanwhile, Pipsqueak—still stunned by the blow to the head—fell face-first onto the bed. Below him, Heather screamed and screamed and screamed. The sight of her snapped leg made her sick. She felt her stomach knotting up and her heart rate accelerating.

"Dakota, kill him!" she cried in a raspy, unsteady

voice. "Kill... Kill him! S–S–Stab him! Do it before... before he gets up! God, kill him! Kill... Dah..."

Breathless, her words dissolved into incoherency. She felt like her head was floating away as the strength left the muscles on her neck. The smoke flowing into the room from the hall didn't help.

After a minute, the bathroom door cracked open. Dakota walked warily out of the bathroom. She held the paring knife out in front of her, swinging it around unintentionally like a magician using a wand. Her face—eyes puffy, nose red, corners of her mouth drawn down—gleamed with tears. She coughed into her elbow as the smoke irritated her throat and lungs.

Upon spotting her, Heather said, "Do it. Stab him... in the neck. Kill him before he gets up. He'll kill you... us... if you don't kill him."

Keeping her elbow over her mouth, Dakota took a step towards the clown. The man was snoring. She pushed his ruff collar aside with the knife, then poked the fold of fat at the nape of his neck with the blade. She couldn't even pierce his skin.

"Harder, damn it," Heather cried.

Dakota sniffled quietly. She poked him again, pricking the back of his neck. A droplet of blood oozed out of the tiny cut. It was enough to make her queasy. Even though he didn't feel a thing, the violence made her sick. A wave of self-disgust hit her. She was a real pacifist—the gentlest of souls.

She turned her back to the clown and said, "I can't do this."

"No... No! You have to. He–He'll kill..."

Heather couldn't finish the sentence. She hesitated to say her son's name out of fear of manifesting his death.

Pouting, Dakota said, "I'm not a killer."

"Please. It's us or them. Save us."

Dakota stood in silence for ten seconds before another coughing fit gripped her. She glanced back at Heather but gasped and looked away a second later. The condition of her leg unnerved her.

"I'll bring help," she said as she hurried to the bedroom door, hanging her head in shame. "I'll come back for you, I promise."

"No, no, don't go! The knife!"

"I'm coming back!"

"Give me the knife!"

Dakota went into the hallway.

Heather yelled, "You bitch!"

Sobbing, she crawled towards the door, dragging her legs behind her. She only moved about a foot before the pain in her ravaged knee stopped her.

"Angie, hurry," she whimpered.

The crackling of the spreading fires grew louder. Yet, she could still hear the thuds and creaks in the hall. She lifted her head and looked at the door. Walking backwards, Dakota returned to the bedroom. She was holding her paring knife with both hands, but it didn't make it any steadier. Then Captain Gashes crossed the threshold.

He wagged his hunting knife at Dakota and said, "My knife's bigger than yours."

Dakota continued walking backwards, mouth wide but tongue-tied. Following her, Captain Gashes looked at his incapacitated partner, then down at Heather. A twisted smile warped his face.

He said, "And look at you. Got yourself a little scratch there, huh? Well, you 'cleaned' the cut on my arm. It's only right–"

"Fuck you!" Heather shouted.

"–I return the favor. I'll find some rubbing alcohol and we'll clean that right out. You'll be as good as new in no time. Let me just take care of your friend here first."

Dakota screamed and ran into the bathroom. Captain Gashes chased after her. She closed the door, but before she could turn the lock, he rammed it open with his shoulder. The edge of the door crashed into her face, breaking her nose and cutting her lips. Her feet tangled as she stumbled back. She dropped the knife and landed on her ass between the toilet and the bathtub.

Heather started to crawl around the bed, but again, the agonizing pain in her knee stopped her. She wanted to call out to her son, but she was afraid of jeopardizing his safety.

In the bathroom, Captain Gashes ran forward and

punted Dakota's face. Her jaw broke with a *crunch*. Her eyes rolled up as her upper body fell back. The back of her head *thudded* against the wall behind her. Upon impact, she moaned and clenched her fists tightly. Her mouth ajar, blood dripped from the edges of her lips.

Captain Gashes took her by the hair, pulled her away from the wall, then slammed the side of her head against the toilet bowl's rim. He thrust her head at the toilet a second time—a third time, *a fourth time*. She bled from somewhere on her scalp, the blood outlining her ear. Her eyes appeared to be swiveling under her closed eyelids. He pushed her back against the wall.

As he unbuckled his pants, he said, "I've got a game for ya. It's a classic. Even I played it at the county fair back when I was a youngster." He pulled his pants down and sat on the toilet. Voice tightening as he exerted himself, he said, "Don't worry... this'll only take a minute. I've been... holding it in all day."

In the bedroom, Heather had managed to pull her upper body around the bed. She couldn't get her injured leg around the bedpost without hurting herself, though. From her position, she could see the clown sitting on the toilet. Over her own crying and Pipsqueak's snoring, she heard Captain Gashes' flatulence as well as the sound of feces *plopping* in the toilet water.

And Captain Gashes was right. It only took him a minute to empty his bowels. He pulled his pants up without wiping, then lifted Dakota slightly from the floor.

He said, "You heard of bobbing for apples? I call this 'bobbing for turds.' I'll let you eat what you catch."

He dunked her head in the toilet. The rim hit her throat on the way down. Chunks of vomit spewed from her mouth, joining the logs of shit floating in the bubbling water. Her limbs twitched erratically. Her hands hit the neighboring wall and the cabinet under the sink while her feet kicked the bathtub.

After twenty seconds, Captain Gashes pulled her head out of the bowl. She coughed up some bloody, shitty, pissy water.

"Anything?" he asked. "No? Then let's go for round two."

He dipped her head back in the water and started counting in his head. After fifteen seconds, her resistance weakened. The water continued sloshing, though. He waited thirty seconds before pulling her head out of the toilet. She looked half-dead—pale, unmoving, barely breathing. He guffawed as he spotted the small piece of shit lodged in one of her nostrils.

"You're supposed to catch it in your mouth, woman," he said, snickering. "Let's give it another try. Open wide."

He pushed her head back into the dirty water. Although the water churned, she didn't put up a fight. She passed out after about thirty seconds, but he kept her head submerged. He had plenty of experience strangling people. He knew asphyxiation took time.

Hidden by the shower curtain, Gilbert had been sitting in the bathtub with both of his hands over his mouth—doing exactly what his mother had told him to do. He hadn't seen the murder, but he had heard enough to picture every detail. Dakota's suffering broke his heart.

He felt an odd mixture of relief and dread as he listened to his mom's cries. He was happy she was alive but saddened by her pain. He had never heard her wail like that. The room was getting hot because of the fire, but he felt the cold hand of death caressing his neck.

He had no choice but to wait and pray for rescue.

19

FIREWORKS

ANGELINA SQUATTED BEHIND THE HUT NEXT TO THE helipad, drenched in sweat. She stifled a cough with her sleeve at the crook of her elbow as she glanced around. Smoke rolled through the village square and the surrounding roads. The burning houses turned the town into an outdoor oven, suffocating the remaining survivors with an inescapable heat. Faint screams plagued the town, but there was no one in sight.

Angelina heard the purr of an engine, but she couldn't pinpoint its location. It sounded like it was traveling in circles—closing in on her, cruising away, then swooping back in—buzzing around her like a mosquito. Through the smoke blowing across the road, she could see Goldbrush Essentials directly ahead of her thanks to the light from the fires. She leaned forward and planted her palms on the ground, preparing to make a dash for the convenience store.

She took five quick steps before the sound of the approaching engine made her drop to the ground. She lay flat on her stomach and looked around. The pickup truck barreled through the bank of smoke. Boo-Boo was sitting in the driver's seat. Samuel and Jenna were tied to the back of the truck at the ankles with durable rope. Dragged for several minutes, their jackets had been torn off and the back of their shirts ripped to shreds.

The truck cruised past the hut, giving Angelina a better glimpse of her neighbors. Her eyes bulged with disgust and shock.

Jenna's abdominal cavity had been hollowed out, her mangled intestines strewn across town. Samuel was alive, gasping and groaning. Most of the skin on their backs and outer arms had been scraped off. As the truck turned at the village square, their bodies were thrown into a stone partition. Samuel took the brunt of the collision. Even from afar, Angelina heard his rib cage *explode* like a fallen chandelier.

Then the bodies followed the truck around the corner. The sound of the engine softened. Boo-Boo honked the horn a few times.

Traumatized and terrified, Angelina lay still for another minute. She knew the world was a dark place —her morbid curiosity often led her down the darkest rabbit holes on the internet—but it was different witnessing a heinous crime firsthand than reading about it through an article or seeing it in a grainy video. Tragedies hit harder when they were close to home.

After recomposing herself, Angelina got up to her hands and feet, like a sprinter waiting for the sound of a starting pistol. She looked around nervously. The truck was long gone. She took a deep breath, then launched herself forward. She ran straight to Goldbrush Sparks. The firework shop was more like a kiosk attached to the convenience store.

Security shutters covered the kiosk's window. Taped to the shutters, a sign read: *CLOSED. Out of business.*

Frustrated, Angelina swung the bottom of her fist at the shutters but stopped herself before she could hit them. She didn't want to attract Boo-Boo with the noise. She ran to the entrance of Goldbrush Essentials. The door was locked. She peered inside through one of the storefront windows. She saw the fallen shelves and a dark liquid on the floor, but the store looked empty.

She ran to the back of the convenience store. The door next to the dumpster was locked, too. She looked around for another way in. Her eyes were drawn to the awning window above the dumpster. She didn't have time to search for a blunt object to help her break in. She climbed onto the dumpster, then struck the window with her elbow.

"*Shit,*" she hissed.

She was expecting the glass to shatter. Instead, she

felt like her elbow had been fractured. She elbowed the window again—and she cried out loud again. She nearly staggered off the dumpster. Movies made trespassing look easy. She had to hit the window with her elbow three more times before the glass broke.

She climbed through the opening. On the other side, there was a tower of crates under the window. She carefully lowered herself onto it, then hopped off. She found herself in the storage room. It was dark, but she could make out the maze of cardboard boxes and crates sprawled across the room. Shelves—filled with more cardboard boxes—hugged the walls.

The door at the end of the room to her left led to the freezer. She opened the door to her right and entered the shopping area.

"What the fuck?" she whispered.

The liquid on the floor and checkout counter was clear to her now: *Blood*. She seized up, memories of her visits to Goldbrush Essentials and her chats with Ben flashing through her mind. Tears welled in her eyes and her throat tightened. She knew the truth already —and she knew she couldn't avoid it. She approached the cash register.

From the periphery of her vision, she saw Ben's mutilated body on the floor behind the counter. He was left face up, leaving the enormous hole in his chest exposed to the world.

She gasped and turned away, tears coming out of her eyes in a flood. Legs wobbling, she put her hand on the counter to stop herself from spilling to the floor. She wept while apologizing to him in an indecipherable mumble. She didn't know why she was apologizing, but it felt like the right thing to do.

Keeping her back to him, she walked to the other side of the counter. She yelped as she accidentally kicked his foot. Before she could reach the office door, she saw the pickup truck cruising towards the convenience store. She ducked down behind the counter. When she noticed Ben's blood around her shoe, she shut her eyes and pouted.

She heard the truck's engine thrumming louder as it sped towards the convenience store. She was certain the clown had seen her. She believed the psychotic killer was going to crash the truck through the storefront windows. But she heard the vehicle make a sharp turn at the last second. A bone-crunching *thud* accompanied the sound of glass rattling and cracking.

With the truck's sudden turn, Samuel had been thrown at the window. His head had collided with the glass. The impact was so hard that he was instantly decapitated. His head bounced away into the desert like a tumbleweed. Boo-Boo didn't notice it, though. She just kept driving recklessly through the town.

Angelina stood up. She opened the door behind the counter and slipped into the office. She felt like she was close to vomiting. It took her longer to get a grip on herself. She had always thought frequent exposure to violence was supposed to be desensitizing, but it wasn't getting any easier. Every act of savage cruelty she witnessed left a mental scar.

There was only one other door in the room, so she went straight to it. She was relieved to find it was unlocked. The door led to Goldbrush Sparks' storage room. There were shelves on every wall and cardboard boxes stacked in the middle, all filled with unused fireworks. She wiped the tears from her eyes, then scoured the shelves for the perfect explosive.

She recalled her parents warning her about the mortars. She had heard horror stories of the shells detonating inside of the tubes, causing users to lose fingers, entire hands, eyes, and their lives. She found a product called *Sky Inferno*. The warning at the bottom of the box read: *CAUTION: Shoots explosive projectiles. Carefully read all instructions before use.*

"Perfect," Angelina said as she tore the packaging open.

She took the mortar tube and three of the shells, then returned to the office. She stopped in front of the door leading back to the convenience store. She didn't want to see Ben's corpse again. With her eyes on the ceiling, she exited the room. She blinked back the fresh tears in her eyes as she sidestepped around the dead body.

After passing the corpse, she ran to the entrance, unlocked it, then exited the store. She hurried back towards the Bunker house, oblivious to the massacre waiting for her.

Mortar tube in hand, Angelina snuck through town—moving in a crouch, hiding behind partitions, sticking to the shadows. She listened for the truck's engine, changing paths to avoid it. The smoke forced her to cough, so she covered her mouth with the crook of her elbow and hid in a ditch. As she caught her breath, she recognized the house across the dirt road.

It was Dakota's home. A fire had caused the roof to collapse. The house was decorated with Christmas lights, which no longer worked. Her husband Erik had put them up years ago and, after he passed away unexpectedly during that holiday season, she never bothered to take them down or replace the bulbs.

Angelina ran ahead. She could see the tall partition surrounding the Bunker house. As she approached the front gate, she heard the sound of an engine revving, falling silent, then revving again. Straight ahead, off in the distance, she saw the pickup truck on the road. It was facing her direction.

Since she was closer to the house than Boo-Boo, Angelina had the perfect opportunity to run through the gate to avoid the truck. But she didn't want to retreat. She had left her family and neighbors in the house to find weapons so they could *fight*. She was done hiding. *If we're going to get out of here, I need to stop that damn truck,* she told herself.

She dropped one of the artillery shells into the

mortar tube. The arrow on the shell pointed upward. Then she took her lighter out of her pocket and flicked its spark wheel, her thumb shaking uncontrollably. It wouldn't ignite. The engine roared as the truck raced towards her. She flicked the spark wheel a few more times before a flame shot out of the lighter.

She lit the fuse, then aimed the mortar at the speeding vehicle. She stretched her arms out in front of her and turned her head to protect her face. *Hurry! Hurry! Hurry!* she was screaming in her head. Then, as if she had suddenly realized what she was doing, her inner voice was saying: *Please don't blow up in my hands. Please don't blow up in my hands. Please don't blow up!*

The shell shot out of the mortar tube. It flew over the truck, then exploded behind it in a shower of red sparks.

Angelina leapt off the road, narrowly avoiding the truck. As if their bones had been ground to dust, the dead bodies tied to the back of the vehicle rolled and flopped like rag dolls. Boo-Boo made a U-turn at an intersection down the road. She revved the engine again to toy with her victim. Having the time of her life, she *wanted* Angelina to try to stop her.

It was all a game to her. And this game made her feel like a raging bull in a running of the bulls, ready to gore anyone in her path.

Angelina scrambled back to the road and loaded another shell into the mortar. Boo-Boo stepped on the gas. Angelina ignited the fuse. She lowered her arms a little and adjusted her aim. The fuse finished burning, but the shell didn't shoot out. It was a dud. She saw the truck racing towards her. Fear put her under a spell of paralysis.

As Boo-Boo passed Dakota's home, a police SUV came out of the desert from the side and T-boned the truck. The deafening *bang* of the crash sent shock waves through the town, making the surrounding smoke ripple. A discordant symphony of screeching metal and shattering glass followed.

The truck spun out, then flipped as it rolled into a ditch. It landed upside down on the side of the road. The SUV careened into a stone partition.

Angelina was awed by the crash. She glanced over at the Bunker house, then at the crash site. She heard some weak groaning coming from the wrecked vehicles. Although she wanted to help her family, she had to make sure the clown was neutralized before turning her back on her. She loaded her last shell into the mortar tube and walked towards the wreckage.

From afar, she could see Justin in the patrol car. He was out cold. Boo-Boo was crawling out of the truck through the broken driver door window, glass crunching under her elbows. The bottom half of her mask was broken. Her bottom lip was cut down the middle, mirroring her cleft lip. On her right arm, her wrist as well as her ulna and radius bones—her forearm bones—were broken.

She leaned against the truck, then slid up to her

feet. A sense of giddiness brought her back down to her knees. She laughed weakly.

Justin suffered from some broken ribs and a cracked sternum. The airbag also burned the skin off his nose and around his left eye. That eye was swollen shut, blood lining his eyelids. Fragments of glass cut his face, sparkling like red glitter in the cuts. He awoke to his ears ringing. His chest burned with each shallow breath.

Although it was steady, he felt his SUV moving like a boat on turbulent water. He popped the door open, struggled with his seat belt for a moment, then fell out of the car after taking his first step out. He crawled around on his hands and knees, aching all over. He leaned against a rear tire and drew his handgun.

He saw the overturned truck across the narrow dirt path, but he couldn't see the driver. He was seeing double—sometimes triple—through his only good eye. He hadn't encountered the killers, so he wasn't expecting to find a clown behind the truck. While circling the town and reporting the fires to his dispatcher, he had witnessed the attempted vehicular homicide.

"Hands... Show me... Show me your hands," he said brokenly as he aimed the gun at the truck.

Angelina shouted, "Shoot her! Please! Kill her! You have to kill her!"

Justin could barely hear her voice over the ringing in his ears. Taking cover on the other side of the truck,

Boo-Boo took her switchblade out of her pocket and drew the blade. Catching a glimpse of her movements, the cop shot at the truck three times. The bullets hit the side of the vehicle. He got to his feet, then started teetering across the road.

Angelina could tell Boo-Boo was going to wait for the cop to get closer before pouncing on him. She was a patient killer. Angelina recoiled as Justin shot at the truck three more times. She was worried he was going to run out of ammunition by the time he reached the truck. She had to buy him some time.

"I'm over here!" she yelled at the clown. "You want me? Come and get me! Come on, bitch!"

Boo-Boo ignored her. Angelina took the faulty shell out of the mortar tube. In a last-ditch effort to save the cop, she loaded her final explosive and lit the fuse. She aimed the mortar at the overturned truck and, after a few seconds, the shell shot out of the tube. Upon spotting the flaming ball, Boo-Boo threw herself onto the ground and shielded her head with her good arm.

"No!" Angelina screamed as the shell traveled past the truck.

It detonated against Justin's chest, shaking the ground and breaking the remaining windows on the wrecked vehicles. His ballistic vest couldn't save him. The blast blew his chest out, pecs peeled off his ribcage. His broken bones crumbled. Some of his ribs were ejected from his chest entirely. Joining the metals from the shell, sharp chips of bone pierced his lungs and heart.

Leaking blood, his organs were visible through the gaps between his remaining ribs and patches of burnt flesh. His heart was beating. Like water balloons, his lungs jiggled in his chest cavity. His neck was skinned and a chunk of his jaw was blown off. Half of his tongue was missing. He collapsed in the middle of the road.

Angelina dropped the mortar tube as she stared at the cop—her old friend. His injuries reminded her of Ben's. *I'm just as bad as them,* she thought. Her mouth moved but nothing came out. Guilt and shock stole her voice.

Boo-Boo stood up and patted the dirt off her knees and dress. She walked around the truck. She looked at Angelina, then at the cop, then back at Angelina.

She cupped one hand over her bloodied mouth and shouted, "Nice shot! Hey, have you ever tried a dunk tank? I bet you'd be great at it! We use acid in ours, y'know! Makes it more suspenseful!"

"Fuck you!" Angelina screamed.

Out of fireworks, she lurched to the Bunker house. The truck was disabled—no thanks to her—but she failed to kill the clown. Instead, she had murdered her friend, the only cop in the area. And now, she only had a bottle of hairspray and a lighter in her possession.

She was back to square one.

Smoke curled over the front door's head jamb, billowing up towards the porch's ceiling before drifting into the air in front of the house. Stamped with blood, bits of skin and brain clinging to the slivers of wood, the front door was splintered and chipped towards the middle. It was wide open.

Angelina stumbled through the doorway. She buried her mouth and nose in the crook of her elbow. The smoke had spread through the first floor while the fires remained upstairs. Wood creaked and groaned and snapped all around her. She heard a hollow *thudding* noise, too.

"Mom!" she yelled, voice muffled by her elbow. "Dad! Gil–"

She coughed. The smoke and heat irritated her throat and stung her eyes. On her way to the dining room, she tripped over Gabriela's legs. She caught herself on a dining chair. She looked back at the brutalized corpse. Her gasp of terror was cut short by another unexpected cough.

"Gilbert!" she shouted. "Dad! Mom! Suh–Suh– Somebody please! Plee–"

Another cough stopped her. Holding the back of the chair, she lowered herself closer to the floor, pulled the collar of her shirt over her nose, and tried to breathe. It didn't help much. She cried as she glanced around.

Although it had been her decision to leave the house in search of weapons prior to the clowns' raid, she felt abandoned, choked by the smoke and an atmosphere of loneliness. She had no idea her father was lying dead in the kitchen next door. The *thudding* upstairs called to her.

Staying crouched down, she returned to the foyer, stepped around Gabriela's corpse, then clambered up the stairs. The heat intensified with each step up. She had to take off her sweater. She reached the top of the stairs on her hands and knees. Smoke covered the ceiling. The fires in the rooms illuminated the hallway with a red glow.

Hell, she thought. *This is hell.*

She heard the thudding coming from the master bedroom at the end of the hall. The door was left ajar. She crawled towards the room, holding in another cough. The thudding became clearer—metallic, squishy. Outside of the bedroom door, she pushed herself up to her feet. She took the bottle of hairspray out of her pocket and removed the cap, then prepared her lighter.

She pushed the door open. Pipsqueak was kneeling next to the foot of the bed. He swung the fire extinguisher down at Heather's face—what was left of it, at least. He had pulped her face into a stew of flesh, the back of her skull like a bowl. Her eyes, nose, lips, and teeth blended with her crushed brain.

Yet, Angelina recognized her right away. Her heart

hammered away at her sternum. Like twigs, she felt like her legs could snap at any moment. Memories of her mother flipped through her mind like the cards of a Rolodex. But in every image, she saw her mother with her mashed face.

"Mom!" Angelina cried as she lit her lighter.

She shot the hairspray at the flame, creating a ball of fire. Pipsqueak dropped the fire extinguisher and toppled over as the flames licked his face. His ruff collar was set ablaze, a ring of fire surrounding his neck. Angelina sprayed the fire at him again, setting his sleeve aflame. The comforter and footboard burned, too.

Swinging his arms frantically, Pipsqueak climbed onto the bed and rolled across it. The fire on his arm was extinguished while his collar continued burning. The skin on his neck peeled.

Hellbent on exacting revenge, Angelina kept shooting the hairspray. She was ready to burn the house down with her improvised flamethrower.

"Stop!" Captain Gashes barked.

She turned towards his voice. Her scowl softened instantly. She took her finger off the nozzle but kept the lighter on.

Captain Gashes stood in the bathroom doorway. Holding his hunting knife up to the kid's neck, he was forcing Gilbert to stand in front of him. The clown dragged the boy to the window overlooking the backyard. It was cooler on that side of the room.

Eyes locked with Angelina's, he said, "Calm your ass down, Pips."

"It's hot!" Pipsqueak shouted.

"You act like you're burning alive. Use one of those pillows to put that fire out. Or use that fire extinguisher right there. The one with all the *dents* and all that *blood* and all those *brains* from–"

"Let him go," Angelina interrupted.

"Or what? You think you can 'cook' us with that? I can slit this boy's neck—practically cut his head off—before your little fire even warms my skin."

Gilbert let out a frightened sob and he wet himself for the second time that night. Although he could only see his mother's legs, something inside of him told him that she was dead. Pipsqueak sat up in bed and tilted his head back. He grabbed one of the pillows and swung it at his neck, swatting the fire out. The back of his collar continued to smolder, burning the nape of his neck, so he lay down and rocked from side to side.

Angelina said, "If you hurt him, I'll burn this room down. You won't get out of here alive."

"This boy won't, either. If that's your mom down there—that's what you called her, right?—then this must be your brother. Your sweet, innocent little brother. I found him hiding in that bathroom back there. Oh, you should have seen his face when he saw me. So scared. So hopeless. So alone. I could tell he was waiting for someone. He was waiting... for you."

"Shut the fuck up and get your hands off him."

Captain Gashes coughed, then said, "You're a spunky one, huh? You think your tough talk will change anything? Hmm? I can tell the difference between bravery and desperation, girl, and you're as desperate as all of the others I've killed. But I can see this kid's important to you and I can appreciate that—family is everything after all—so I'll let you decide how he dies."

"Damn it, shut up!"

"Death by decapitation... or immolation? You want me to kill him or–"

"Let him go!"

"–would you like to do the honors?"

Angelina felt the scorching heat creeping up on her from behind. The fire was eating through the walls, spreading into the bathroom down the hall. The floor in the office collapsed with loud cracking and snapping noises, falling into the living room. The fire spilled into the first floor, too. Outside, flames rose from every shingle on the roof at the front side of the house. Time was running out.

Angelina knew she couldn't beat the clowns. She wasn't even sure if she had enough hairspray to burn the rest of the bedroom. She was prepared to sacrifice herself, but she wasn't willing to put her brother in harm's way. The kid was mumbling now. His words were unclear. But Captain Gashes and Angelina understood what he was saying. The clown had heard it all before, and Angelina shared the same thoughts as her brother.

Gilbert was crying for his parents and begging for mercy.

"Let him go and take me," Angelina said.

Captain Gashes gazed thoughtfully at her, as if seriously considering her offer. Then he smiled thinly and huffed.

"Let him go and take me!" Angelina repeated sternly. As Pipsqueak stood from the bed, she pointed the can of hairspray at him and yelled, "Don't fucking move!"

Captain Gashes spat a loogie at the floor, then said, "You're not in the position to call the shots, girl. I'll tell you what. Throw that can and your lighter over to my associate here. If you behave yourself, we can all walk out of here together. If you keep wasting time... we'll make sure this 'wood oven' cooks you and your brother. Me and Pips, we'll be fine."

He's right, Angelina told herself. She took a peek over her shoulder before looking back at her brother. Knowing her mother was dead and suspecting her father had suffered the same fate, she only had two viable options: Cooperate with the clowns to stall them, or run away and save herself. She refused to abandon her brother, though. She tossed the can and the lighter at the bed.

"Let him go," she pleaded.

Captain Gashes said, "I'll let him fly."

He threw the boy at the window. Some of the panes cracked, but the window held up. Gilbert landed at the clown's feet, screaming while clutching at his busted shoulder.

"No!" Angelina yelled as she ran towards them.

Captain Gashes lifted the boy from the floor and hurled him at the window again. The window burst. At the same time, in a knee-jerk reaction, Angelina lunged at her brother. They both flew out of the window. Their screams lasted a second. Angelina fell on her back in an artificial flower bed while Gilbert landed on a walkway headfirst.

Captain Gashes leaned out the window and looked down at them. Angelina was squirming with her eyes shut. Bleeding from his head, Gilbert didn't move a muscle.

"Are they dead?" Pipsqueak asked as he waved the smoke away from his face.

"Let's go find out."

Captain Gashes and Pipsqueak headed down to the first floor. The fire in the living room had spread to the main hallway, blocking their path to the back door. So, they exited the home through the front door and took in big gulps of air. They found Boo-Boo limping up the walkway. She was holding Justin's pistol in her right hand.

She asked, "You guys see a girl run past here?"

"No," Pipsqueak answered.

"*Yes,*" Captain Gashes corrected him, sounding

annoyed by his stupidity. "You talking about the short-haired girl with the nose ring?"

Boo-Boo said, "I think that's the one. She still alive?"

"She fell out a window. Why are you asking?"

"That crazy bitch was shooting fireworks at me. But I think she was just playing with me 'cause she missed each time. She blew up a cop that was trying to kill me! You believe that? She saved lil' ol' me! I think we owe her one. How about we give her a front-row seat to the main event? Y'know, the grand finale? I know you still got one more trick up your sleeve, Cap."

Captain Gashes smirked and said, "I suppose I do. But it's pointless if she isn't alive to see it—to *feel* it."

Boo-Boo said, "I'd cross my fingers, but my good hand is full and I can't feel the other one."

The clowns hobbled around the side of the house and made their way to the backyard. Pipsqueak stood over Gilbert's body and prodded him with his foot. The boy didn't wake up. Captain Gashes and Boo-Boo stopped in front of Angelina. She was alive.

"At least we caught one," Boo-Boo said. "Not bad for a couple of 'rejects,' huh?"

"Better than nothing," Captain Gashes responded. He beckoned to Pipsqueak and said, "My arm's fucked up. I need you to carry this one back to the RV."

Pipsqueak pointed at Gilbert and asked, "Can I take him, too?"

"For what?"

Grinning, Pipsqueak said, "He's young, cold, and quiet."

Boo-Boo snorted with amusement.

"If you can carry both of 'em, go for it," Captain Gashes said. "But if she wakes up, you better not lose control of her."

The female clown pointed her gun at Angelina's head and said, "Don't worry, Cap, I'll make sure she doesn't try any funny business."

Pipsqueak threw Angelina's body over his shoulder. Then he grabbed Gilbert's arm at the wrist and pulled him along like a toddler dragging a stuffed animal. Boo-Boo walked behind him, keeping the gun aimed at Angelina's head at point-blank range. Captain Gashes led them away from the Bunker house. They headed out into the desert, the town burning behind them.

20

THE GRAND FINALE

ANGELINA REGAINED CONSCIOUSNESS. HER EYES CRACKED open to a blur of white while darkness invaded her peripheral vision. She noticed she was lying down. She tried to turn onto her side, but she was strapped down at the legs, the abdomen, the chest, and the arms. She could wave her hands, but she couldn't lift her feet. She heard the hum of an engine and felt the sway of a speeding vehicle.

She couldn't remember the moments before she blacked out. She believed she was strapped to a gurney in an ambulance.

"Is it on?" a familiar male voice asked.

"N–No," Angelina whimpered.

A woman said, "Yup."

As her vision focused, Angelina saw herself in the filthy mirror installed on the ceiling. Nude, she was bound to an examination table. As she swung her head around, she saw the grimy, cracked mirrors on the surrounding walls and the shelves filled with instruments of torture underneath them.

She spotted Marshmallow, the white rabbit, in the cage in the corner, sitting on his hind legs while gazing at the prisoner. She was trapped in the clowns' mobile torture chamber. In the opposite corner, she saw a heap of severed heads. Some were covered in blood, others were pale, a few were rotting.

Captain Gashes was sitting on a stool in front of her. Boo-Boo stood in the corner behind him, aiming a camcorder at Angelina.

"Smile for the camera, girl," Captain Gashes said. "You want them to see your good side, don't you? This one's going to go out to the whole world soon."

"Whe–Whe–Where's Gilbert?" she stammered.

From behind the camera, Boo-Boo asked, "Did she say '*Dilbert?*' What kinda name is that?"

"Gilbert! Where's my brother?"

"Oh, *Gilbert*. Hmm... Never heard of him—or it. Is that like a spin-off comic?"

Rocking her shoulders and shaking her hips, Angelina shouted, "You bitch! You fucking monsters! What did you do?! Where is he?!"

Captain Gashes glanced at Boo-Boo and said, "She's talking about the boy." He looked back at Angelina and asked, "You wanna know the truth?"

"Where is he? Tell me. Plee–Please tell me," Angelina said, words flying out of her mouth.

"He's in the RV with Pips."

"R–RV?"

"That's what I said. He's driving right now. Hauling us away from that inferno in that shithole of a town."

"Is he… Is he alive?"

Captain Gashes responded, "We're clowns, not paramedics. I've seen junkies OD on heroin, only to get revived hours later. I'm talking as pale and still as a corpse in the morning, and back to walking and talking and shooting up by night. So, I can't give you a 'yes' or a 'no.' Anything's possible. But I can tell you that, if he is alive…" He paused and let a smug grin cross his face before continuing, "he won't be for long once Pipsqueak's done impaling him with his hog."

The clowns laughed, as if tickled by the idea of someone being raped to death. Angelina's cries of horror seeped out of the trailer. No one was around to hear her in the desert, though.

"All right, all right, that's enough chitchat," Captain Gashes said. "We've got a show to finish and you, girl, are part of the headlining act. Just follow my lead and you'll be a star by the end of the night."

Angelina continued sobbing while fighting with the straps around her body. Captain Gashes took a metal speculum—the same type doctors used for pelvic exams—off a shelf. Boo-Boo got a closeup of the medical instrument with the camcorder. Its blades were crusted over with blood.

"I'm going to need some lube," Captain Gashes said.

"Oh! I've got an idea!" Boo-Boo said.

She handed him the camcorder, then teetered over to the shelves to her left. She ran her eyes over the tools. She took a pair of pliers from one of the shelves, then walked between Captain Gashes and Angelina.

"Why are you doing this to me?" Angelina asked in a shrill voice. "I only wanted to–"

Boo-Boo closed the pliers over her nose ring and tugged at it with all of her might. It tore off, tearing her nasal septum and splitting the tissue between her nostrils. Angelina let loose a series of sneezes, spraying fine mists of blood and mucus at the clowns. Blood came pouring out of her nose, too.

Boo-Boo held the pliers up for the camcorder. A piece of tissue—the columella—clung to the nose ring. Captain Gashes gave the camcorder back to her. He didn't need his partner to tell him what to do. He held the speculum under Angelina's disfigured nose, lubricating its blades with her blood.

"Now, open wide," he said.

With the blades closed, he forced the speculum into her anus sideways. Angelina gasped, then gritted her teeth. She felt painful pressure in her rectum, as if the organ were about to explode. The pain worsened as Captain Gashes turned the speculum so the handles were pointing up. Then he squeezed the handles to separate the blades.

Angelina's anus stretched slowly. Captain Gashes met some resistance as her sphincter tightened around the tool. He squeezed harder and wiggled the speculum around. He heard something *crinkling* in her ass. The blades were wide open, so he locked them in place by sliding the long handle upward and the short one downward.

He let go of the speculum. Unable to control the muscle, her sore sphincter helped it stay in place. She was whimpering and writhing with extreme discomfort and intolerable pain. He leaned forward, closed an eye, and peered into her ass. He saw the smooth, red walls of her rectum. It was too dark to see the curve of her colon, though.

As if she were about to perform a colonoscopy, Boo-Boo pointed the camcorder at Angelina's expanded anus. She leaned in close and moved the camcorder around, getting a shot from every angle.

The trailer vibrated as a low-flying helicopter flew overhead. It was heading to Goldbrush.

The crackling of flatulence came out of Angelina's ass. Boo-Boo giggled and leaned away from her. Captain Gashes waved his hand in front of his face, as if to say: '*Pee-ew.*' Then a sludge of shit spewed from her ass. It splattered on the floor between them.

"Ew," Boo-Boo said, laughing louder.

Captain Gashes said, "At least you have some extra space now, girl. But you're not ready yet. We need to open you up a little more."

"Kill me," Angelina cried.

Violated, brutalized, and left without a family, she had lost her desire to live. She just wanted the pain and humiliation to end because she knew it was only going to get worse if she stayed alive.

Captain Gashes took a rusty pipe off a shelf and said, "This should do the trick. Ready, Boo-Boo?"

"Ready, Cap!" Boo-Boo said enthusiastically.

Although it hurt her broken arm, she grabbed the speculum clenched in Angelina's ass with her free hand. She unlocked it and pulled it out. The blades were smeared with blood—old and new, nasal and anal—as well as feces. Before her sphincter could close up, Captain Gashes forced the pipe into Angelina's asshole. Her sphincter snapped like a rubber band under too much pressure.

The tube came to a stop about an inch inside of her. He jiggled it around, pulled it out a little, then pushed it harder. Now, it was about an inch and a quarter inside of her. He repeated the process each time the pipe became jammed in her ass: jiggle, pull, push. As it moved a quarter of an inch at a time— sometimes half an inch—the rust on the pipe scraped her rectal walls.

He encountered more resistance as the pipe reached the end of her rectum and the organ curved into her colon. He tilted the pipe to match the curve, then kept pushing. He twisted it like a screw, too, grating her rectum. Blood outlined the pipe and dripped from her ass, plopping on the floor around the pile of feces. Boo-Boo looked through the tube with the camcorder.

Angelina held her breath, acting as if she could suffocate the pain. It only made it worse, though. She was convulsing, saliva foaming out of her mouth.

The pipe stopped in her colon, seven inches deep.

Captain Gashes grabbed the captive's thigh and tugged on the tube. Angelina felt the cuts in her rectum widening. A terrifying warmth spread through her pelvis. Her eyes rolled back and her neck arched. Then she fainted as the pipe exited her ass. Her anus stayed open.

"Let's see where you're at now," the leader said.

One eye closed, he peeked into her ass. He pulled Boo-Boo closer to him and pointed at Angelina's crotch, gesturing for her to record it. Boo-Boo made sure to zoom in to the victim's intestine.

"See that, folks? Empty," Captain Gashes said. "But this 'hat-trick' isn't over yet. We've got a surprise for you."

Boo-Boo stopped the recording and said, "I've been waiting for this part all week."

Angelina awoke several minutes later, moaning. A dull ache radiated from her lower back. Her pelvis felt tight with pressure. A throb of pain bounced between her hips like a Ping-Pong ball. She felt nauseated, too. Then she felt something move *in* her pelvis. She couldn't tell if it was more shit, if her intestines had somehow gotten tangled, or if her captors had forced their hands into her.

But she saw the clowns in front of her. Boo-Boo was filming her with the camcorder again. Captain Gashes sat on the stool. She could see their hands clearly. Her mind was sent into a tailspin as she cycled through the awful possibilities. *They put a sharp rock inside me*, she thought. *They put a bomb inside me. My organs are falling out.*

"Wha–What... did you... did you do?" she asked haltingly, her head spinning.

Speaking to the camera, Captain Gashes said, "And now for the moment you've all been waiting for."

Angelina squealed as she felt his hand slide into her rectum. The examination table sounded like it was going to collapse as she twisted and turned. She stopped fighting as her eyes landed on the cage in the corner of the room.

Marshmallow was gone.

Captain Gashes said, "Watch me pull a rabbit out of thin air."

Angelina screamed as he pulled his arm out of her. His hand came out with a dead rabbit. Marshmallow's fur was smeared with blood and flecked with feces. The stiff rabbit was moving involuntarily in his hand with cadaveric spasms. He held Marshmallow up for the camera, looking like a hunter posing with his trophy.

"You did it! You frickin' did it!" Boo-Boo exclaimed, jumping with joy.

She turned the camcorder to Angelina. She had passed out again. Part of her rectum ballooned out of her asshole in a bloody prolapse. She got a closeup of it, then ended the recording. She closed the camcorder's viewfinder, put the device on a shelf, then leapt forward and hugged Captain Gashes. They almost fell over as the trailer swayed.

"How'd it look?" Captain Gashes asked.

"Amazing! I thought the lil' guy was going to get stuck in there like the last one we tried, but you pulled it off."

"It looked believable? Like real magic?"

"Oh yeah, definitely. I'll edit it before we upload it, so it looks like it was all one take. You're going to be a star, Cap. There's no way the others can call us rejects or outcasts or losers or anything like that after this. We're going to headline this whole circus. You, me, Pips, Bob, Patty, Becca, Richie, Simon–"

"Okay, okay, I get it," Captain Gashes interrupted. He took a walkie-talkie out of his pocket, pressed the push-to-talk button, and said, "Pips, can you hear me?"

After a brief period of silence, Pipsqueak answered, "Uh-huh."

"Are we back on the main road yet?"

"Nope."

"Good. Find somewhere to park. We're done back here."

"Okay, Cap."

Captain Gashes put the walkie-talkie back in his pocket. He took a hatchet and a machete off a shelf. He gave the machete to Boo-Boo.

"You know what to do," he said.

Captain Gashes chopped Angelina's neck with the hatchet. Her face tightened but she didn't awaken. Blood squirted from her pierced jugular as he tore the hatchet out of her. Holding it in her good hand, Boo-Boo swung the machete at the other side of Angelina's neck, cutting her other jugular.

The clowns took turns chopping at her neck. Geysers of blood sprayed out of her in swirls like water from a garden sprinkler. It cascaded down the mirrors on the walls and drenched the killers.

Captain Gashes and Pipsqueak dropped Angelina's decapitated body between a bunch of cacti. Sitting at the top of the mound, her severed head joined the others in the trailer. Boo-Boo waited in the driver's seat of the RV, eager to continue their journey. *Sea of Love* by Phil Phillips & The Twilights played on the stereo.

Pipsqueak lumbered back to the RV, humming along to the music. Captain Gashes put his hands on his hips and surveyed the area. They were in the middle of the desert. Orange beams from the sunrise came over the mountain range far in the distance in front of him. He sighed, then returned to the RV. Pipsqueak was sitting on the sofa, taking up a seat and a half.

"Where to?" Boo-Boo asked as she heard the camper door close.

Captain Gashes sat sideways at the dinette and said, "We can't pick a destination until we know where we are. We need to regroup. Catch our breath. *Think.* Take us back to the main road. You remember the way?"

"'Course I do. And if my memory gets a little foggy, Danny will help us get back. Isn't that right, bud?"

She nodded at the vacant passenger seat, as if the dead Goldbrush resident were her copilot. She started driving with only one hand on the steering wheel due to her broken arm. Captain Gashes interlocked his fingers over his abdomen and leaned back. Exhausted and sore, he shut his eyes and drifted to sleep. Pipsqueak was already snoring, one hand over the cut on his stomach.

Captain Gashes awoke as the RV hopped. Pipsqueak was staring dumbly at him. They were back on the road. Early morning sunshine poured into the vehicle through the windows. *Cry Me a River* by Dinah Washington played through the speakers.

"Turn that off and slow down," Captain Gashes demanded.

Boo-Boo took her hand off the steering wheel for two seconds to turn off the stereo, then put it back and asked, "Why? The coast is clear, Cap. We're home free."

"We're driving away from the scene of a crime—a fucking *mass* murder. We're cut up and covered in blood. You're hauling *my* trailer with a *decade* worth of DNA samples from dozens of dead people. We'll never be home free. You don't speed unless you want to get caught."

"I was listening to that," Pipsqueak chimed in.

"You *never* speed."

Boo-Boo eased off the gas pedal and said, "Okay, okay, relax."

"I was listening to that," Pipsqueak repeated.

Captain Gashes said, "Now you're listening to me. You can get your music back when we have a plan. Boo-Boo, where are you taking us?"

"I'm just driving," she answered with a shrug. "I saw some signs that said Vegas is this way."

"We should go back to Deadface's compound. See who else is there. Maybe we can find out what happened to the others."

"Well, Danny's never been to the compound, so he's not gonna be able to tell me which way to go."

"I can drive. Pull over and we can switch."

Boo-Boo started to pull to the side of the road, but then she swerved back into the lane. She said, "Shit. Cap, come here."

"What do you think you're doing?" Captain Gashes asked. "What'd I tell you about being reckless?"

"Hurry!"

Captain Gashes growled as he stumbled over to the cockpit. He sat in the passenger seat and gazed out the window. The scowl was wiped off his face.

They approached a place called '*Motel Ace.*' It stood between a diner called '*Gold Diner 80*' and a convenience store named '*Hassan's Market.*' The parking lot was swarming with cops and emergency vehicles. There was broken glass and blood all over the pavement. Some of the hotel room doors were open. A police cruiser had been driven *into* one of the hotel rooms.

Captain Gashes took Boo-Boo's mask off, looked down to hide his face, and said, "Don't slow down, don't speed up, don't look their way, don't make any sudden movements."

"Jeez, that's a lot of instructions," Boo-Boo said. "You trying to make me nervous or something? You could have just told me to act natural."

"That's exactly what I don't want you to do. Be anyone but yourself."

"Can I be... Pips?" Boo-Boo asked playfully.

"Be a law-abiding citizen for five minutes."

"Fine. You're no fun."

They coasted past the motel. None of the cops noticed them. The killers sat in silence as they drove for another three minutes.

Boo-Boo whispered, "Cap, look."

Captain Gashes lifted his head a bit to peek out the

windshield. There was an overturned campervan on the side of the road. He recognized the decal of a Pierrot on the rear door. There was a crashed patrol car close by. Police had cordoned off the crash site. They didn't spare a glance for the RV as it cruised past.

Boo-Boo said, "Holy shit, that was Pumpkin's van. Puddin' was with him. You think they're okay?"

"Focus on the road. We're not out of the woods yet," Captain Gashes said.

Boo-Boo saw a patrol car speeding down the oncoming lane, sirens wailing and emergency lights flashing.

"Shit," she muttered. "The cop that blew up in town, I have his pistol in the glove compartment. It's still loaded."

Captain Gashes retrieved the handgun. Finger on the trigger, he held it close to his hip and pointed it at the driver's door.

Boo-Boo said, "Try not to shoot me."

"Try not to get us pulled over."

The patrol car quickly approached. Captain Gashes kept his head down to hide his swollen face and clown makeup. From outside, he could have been mistaken for someone staring down at his phone. Boo-Boo sucked her lower lip into her mouth and tilted her head to the side to hide her injuries. Pipsqueak stayed on the sofa, sneering while drumming his fingers. He was bored out of his mind.

They heard the patrol car speed past them.

Captain Gashes and Boo-Boo kept their eyes on it through the sideview mirrors. They were expecting it to make a U-turn. They didn't breathe until the car disappeared from their sight. Yet, Captain Gashes continued gazing into the sideview mirror, brooding over the situation. He suspected Pumpkin and his crew —another group of killer clowns operating under Deadface's command—had failed their mission at Motel Ace.

Boo-Boo asked, "So, what's the plan, bossman?"

Captain Gashes put the gun back in the glove compartment, then said, "Looks like we succeeded where the others couldn't. We should check up on Deadface. Let's go to Vegas." He turned on the stereo, then turned a knob to change it to a radio station. There was no signal. He said, "Keep your ears open for any news. We should be hearing about our friends any minute now."

"This should be fun."

"Remember what I said: No speeding. We can switch after I take this makeup off and patch myself up."

"I got this, Cap. Trust me."

Captain Gashes walked over to the sink in the kitchen. He washed his hands, then started scrubbing the makeup and blood off his face.

Pipsqueak said, "My music. Can we play my music now?"

"Not now," Captain Gashes responded.

"But you said I can listen after we made a plan. We got a plan, but I don't have my music."

"We need the radio, Pips. Go clean yourself and find something else to do."

"But my music! I need my–"

"Clean yourself off," Captain Gashes said, raising his voice while casting a murderous glare over his shoulder.

Pipsqueak grumbled inaudibly as he stormed off. Captain Gashes watched him walk into the tiny bedroom next to the bathroom at the back of the RV. Gilbert's motionless body was on the bed. Used as a makeshift bandage, a dirty shirt was tied around the boy's head. Pipsqueak pulled his zipper down, then turned around. He snarled at his boss before slamming the door.

Captain Gashes huffed, then muttered, "These psychos better not get me killed."

JOIN THE MAILING LIST

Did you enjoy that night of killer clowns and bloodshed? Hoping for another sequel? Maybe a whole new trilogy? Are you a fan of extreme horror? Good news: I've published over 50 extreme horror novels, and I continue to push boundaries with new books every year. I write more than slashers, too. I've dabbled in many, many subgenres—revenge thrillers, coming-of-age, dystopian, post-apocalyptic, cannibals, snuff, supernatural, political, psychological. I have something for everyone.

If you like what you read and you want to stay in the loop, I highly recommend signing up for my mailing list. By signing up, you'll stay up to date with my latest releases and you'll ensure you won't miss any of my *huge* book sales. I usually send one email a month. I *might* send two if it's a busy month. And I might not send anything if I have nothing going on.

And this newsletter is only about my writing. You won't be getting any opinion pieces, political preaching, or even updates on my personal life (unless I'm in serious need of help). Best of all, it's completely free to sign up.

Visit this link to register: *http://eepurl.com/bNlɪCP*.

DEAR READER

I never expected this series to reach so many readers and grow to this point. This is my *first* omnibus after all. It's a special thing, I think. I even went all out and commissioned a snazzy new cover as well as an exclusive illustration. (You'll see the latter right after this letter, so stick around!)

I've been writing slashers since the beginning of my career as a novelist. *Butcher Road*—my first slasher —came out in 2016, just a few months after I made my debut with *The Harbinger of Vengeance*. (Which was re-released in 2023 as an Author's Enhanced Edition, so don't forget to check that out!) The next year, I published *Camp Blaze*, *The Social Media Murders*, and *Spit and Die*. You might be able to argue that Cannibal Creek—also published in 2017—counts as a slasher as well.

I ended up taking a break from the subgenre

because I felt like I wasn't adding anything original to it. *Butcher Road* was obviously inspired by The Texas Chainsaw Massacre and The Hitcher. *Camp Blaze* was heavily inspired by Friday the 13th. *The Social Media Murders* was 'my take' on Scream. I just started drifting away from that, and I became more confident in my *original* stories.

The first *Do Not Disturb* book was both strongly inspired by the 2016 clown sightings—which I believed was the perfect backdrop for a slasher—and my need to take a breather from the heavier subjects I usually explore. I was working on this book while I was finishing up my controversial novel *The Groomer* and my disturbing character study *Lovelorn*. If you've read those books, then you can probably tell why I needed a break.

And after *Do Not Disturb* came out, readers asked for more. People were contacting me on its *release date* to request a sequel. Before I even published that first book, though, I had already started outlining potential sequels with one idea in mind: make each story take place in a unique location. I wanted each setting to be character—to stand out just like the clowns and the survivors. That gave each book a new unique vibe: from secluded terror to balls-to-the-wall action-horror.

With this first trilogy completed, I'll be taking a break from this series. However, I already have a new trilogy of *Do Not Disturb* books planned out. New crews of killers clowns are going to be heading out to very unique locations. I'm sure I've teased some of these before, but I'll keep them a secret for now. In the meantime, I may take the opportunity to write a whole new slasher. Now I'm not promising anything—and you might not see anything come from this comment until 2026 or 2027—but I have recently been infatuated by Dario Argento's giallo movies...

On a more personal note, my writing speed has decreased significantly recently. I haven't been online much, either, so I'm sorry if I've missed your comments or messages. You see, my daughter started attending a nursery school in late 2023. This was supposed to give us—my wife and I—more time to focus on our jobs. Unfortunately, since starting nursery school, it seems like my daughter gets sick every week—fevers, diarrhea, and so on. And since I'm self-employed, I'm the one who takes time off work to take care of her when she can't go to the nursery. So, there are weeks where I only get to write for three or four days.

I'm not really complaining. I'm obviously going to put my daughter's health over everything else. But I felt like you deserve an explanation—especially people who've contacted me and feel like they've been given the cold shoulder.

On top of all that, one of my current projects fell apart. I'm still planning on finishing it, but it'll be a while before you see it. I think the writing was good, but I couldn't get into the 'flow'—for lack of a better term. So, the wait for my next book will be a little longer than usual. And yes—although I hate to admit —that also means the long-anticipated sequel to *Our Dead Girlfriend* might not release this year. The wait will be worth it, though!

Whether you read one or all of these books before or if this is your first time experiencing the Night of the Killer Clowns, thank you for reading my first omnibus. And a big thank you to all of the readers who have been supporting this series since 2020. I've had a blast writing this series. And it's because of you that I've rediscovered my passion for slashers over the past few years. I can't wait to share what's coming next. Just give me a little more time.

Until our next venture into the dark and disturbing,
Jon Athan

P.S. Check out that exclusive illustration! The killer clowns will return!

THE
KILLER
CLOWNS
WILL RETURN...
SUMMER 202?

www.ingramcontent.com/pod-product-compliance
Lightning Source LLC
Chambersburg PA
CBHW031227310726
48971CB00004B/911